THE WARLORD

MALCOLM BOSSE resides in New York
City with his wife and son. He has
lived in India and has travelled
extensively throughout south-eastern
Asia, in Japan and Taiwan, and in
China.

The cranes overhead go in silence.
Below them the wolves are quarrelling.
The war has saddened me so I can't sleep.
Who has the strength to bring order to heaven and earth?

TU FU

And you wait, are awaiting the one thing
that will infinitely enhance your life:
the powerful, the uncommon,
the awakening of stones,
depths turning toward you.

RILKE

Malcolm Bosse

The Warlord

Fontana Paperbacks

First published in the USA by Simon & Schuster 1983
First published in Great Britain by Hutchinson & Co.
(Publishers) Ltd 1983
This continental edition first issued in Fontana Paperbacks 1984

Made and printed in Great Britain by
William Collins Sons & Co. Ltd, Glasgow

NOTE

Pinyin is the generally accepted phonetic script for
modern Mandarin, but because so many transliterations of
Chinese are familiar to us through other systems (at least
four), I have often used those alternative spellings for the
sake of recognition at the sacrifice of consistency:
Soochow, for example, instead of Suzhou.

For Marie-Claude and Malcolm-Scott,
intrepid, with love . . .

PRINCIPAL CHARACTERS

PHILIP EMBREE — Graduate of Yale Divinity School
VLADIMIR KOVALIK — Comintern agent
ERICH LUCKNER — Weapons and electric fan salesman
VERA ROGACHEVA — White Russian living in Shanghai

TANG SHAN-TEH — General Defence Commissioner, Southern Shantung Province

BRIGHT LOTUS — A Kong daughter
CHIA JU-MING — Major in Tang's army. Chief negotiator, Peking
CHIN — One-eared bandit leader
CHU JUI — Former Chekiang general. Aide to Chiang Kai-shek
FAN CHEN-WU — Captain in Tang's army
FU CHANG-SO — Sergeant in Tang's Big Sword Cavalry
JEN CHING-I — Hopei general. At Thousand Buddha Mountain and battle of Hengshui
KU — Kovalik's friend in Shanghai
LI CHUNG-LIN — Kovalik's interpreter
NI FENG-LIN — Embree's 'servant'
OLGA — White Russian prostitute
TANG PING-TI — General Tang's nephew
WEN-YUN — Red organizer, Shantung Province
YANG — Aide to General Tang

Historical Personages

BORODIN, MIKHAIL — Comintern adviser to Chinese revolutionaries

CHANG HSUEH-LIANG — Son of Marshal Chang Tso-lin

CHANG TSO-LIN — The Old Marshal. 'Protector of Peking' and the 'Old Manchurian Tiger'

CHANG TSUNG-CH'ANG — Governor General of Shantung Province, 'old Dog Meat'

CH'EN CHIUNG-MING — Warlord of eastern Kwangtung Province, in control of Swatow

CHIANG KAI-SHEK — Generalissimo, Kuomintang Army

CHU TEH — Red commander, Kiangsi-Hunan area

DOU YU-SENG — Grand High Dragon of the Green Circle Gang

FENG YU-HSIANG — Warlord, Northwest provinces. Enemy of Marshal Chang Tso-lin

HO CHIEN — Hunan warlord

HO LUNG — Red commander, Kiangsi-Hunan area; former bandit

KONG PATRIARCH — Holy Duke of Extended Sagehood. Seventy-sixth descendant of Confucius

LOMINADZE, BESSO — Comintern agent, Wuhan

MAO TSE-TUNG — Red commander in Hunan

SUN CH'UAN-FANG — Kiangsu warlord

WANG CHING-WEI — Kuomintang politician

WHITE WOLF — Shensi bandit chieftain

YEH TING — Red commander, Kiangsi-Hunan area

YUAN SHIH-K'AI — Early president of the Republic

PART ONE

1

'*Bitte*.' The elderly, bearded passenger offers a pack of Capstan cigarettes to a blond young man sitting opposite him in train compartment.

'No, thank you, I don't smoke.' But the young man hesitates, as if he'd like to try it.

'Forgave, forgive? Forgive Englisch. I learn that from Schwedisch woman one time. Forget most.' The old man, leaning forward, smiles. 'You are American?'

The young man has rather hoped to be taken for French or at least British on his first trip abroad, but everyone, including Chinese porters who speak a little English, calls him American. He wonders if it's the seersucker coat, the white suede shoes. 'Yes,' he admits glumly. 'I'm American.'

'Where in America?' persists the bearded German, who has watery eyes.

'Connecticut.' Father once told him men with watery eyes are usually drunkards.

'Con-nect-ti-cut,' the old German repeats with difficulty. 'Is east of America?'

Philip Embree nods but turns deliberately to the window. The old man wants to practice English, so he's trying to keep the conversation going. But Embree has no interest in describing his unexciting life in Connecticut when just beyond the train window, in the Year of the Hare, 1927, the landscape of China is passing.

Their departure from Shanghai last night had been delayed by rumors of wayward troops, detached from a local warlord's army, causing trouble on the line to Kunshan. It was after midnight before the train left the Chapai Station; it is now shortly after dawn. For the last half-hour, awakened by first light, Embree and the old German have watched in silence the alluvial green plain of Central China jiggle past the window. Hearing the old man sigh in prelude to more conversation, Embree stares hard at the country-side, not wanting to break the mood of discovery.

7

A Chinese waiter enters the compartment. He wears a white jacket, white gloves, and carries a tray loaded with eggs, wheat buns, jam, tumblers, and a large teapot. Embree's father had warned him that travel in China is difficult, without amenities, but so far the Blue Express has been comfortable: a hearty breakfast in a compartment featuring leather seats and a lace doily under the table lamp. These are details he will keep from father.

'Do you have milk for the tea?' he asks the waiter in Chinese.

The young waiter shakes his head sullenly and leaves.

A few minutes later, with his mouth full of eggs, the old German says, 'You learn the Chinese in Con-nect-ti-cut?'

Again the young American is disappointed. He has hoped that people would assume his command of Chinese has been acquired here. There's no way to disguise inexperience. 'I learned in college,' he admits.

'In college for Missionhaus?'

'Pardon me?'

'Is right? Missionhaus? I think you be Missionar,' the old man declares with a triumphant smile.

'Yes, I'm a missionary.' Embree drops a large piece of egg from his awkwardly wielded chopsticks. He knows the language but can't eat the food yet; there hadn't been Chinese restaurants in New Haven.

'Is good Chinese to know,' says the old man with expansiveness, now his guess has proved correct. 'Seven years long ago I come, was good place. *Ausländer* live good. But this *Frühling – Frühling*?'

Embree supplies the word. 'Spring.' He can read German.

'In spring in Shanghai was this army, that army. Bomb. Killing. Green *Bande*.' He makes the motion of a knife crossing his throat. '*Einem den Hals abschneiden*. To Shanghai come General Sun Ch'uan-fang – *Mord* there. Come General Chiang Kai-shek – *Mord* there. Everywhere *Soldat*, bandit. Run from *Soldat* in bandit, run from bandit in *Soldat*.' Sighing, the German rolls his eyes. 'In Shanghai I saw on post – post? On post is *Korb* –' He waits for Embree to translate.

'Basket.'

'Basket with heads in.'

'Human heads?'

The old man grins at having impressed Embree. 'On post on street. Heads in basket. *Ja*. I saw nothing this way *vorbei*.' Putting

8

down his chopsticks, the German belches softly and wipes his mouth.

Feeling the train slow down, Embree leans from the window to watch the station approach. It is crowded with peasants bowed under huge bundles. Beggars extend their hands at the windows when the train halts. Police in billed caps briskly shove people in and out of streams of traffic. Noise is deafening; there is a smell of fried fish, burlap, and other things that Embree can't identify. He strains to look closely at Soochow, the city of gardens, but too many people get in the way.

'Is Soochow here,' the German says. He points with a newly lit cigarette at buildings with upturned corners rising in the distance above the ramshackle station. 'Is there Wang Shih Yuan. You know?'

Garden of the Master of the Fishing Nets. Embree knows about it from his reading, and about the Garden of Stupid Officials and the Garden of Harmony and the Garden to Linger In and the others. Not even the garrulous German can diminish his excitement. In the sleeping-car passageway there's a sudden commotion. The compartment door flings open and a tall, ruddy man enters, wearing a pith helmet. Coolies at his heels lug in two large wicker traveling bags. He orders them in English to put the bags on a top bunk. Removing the helmet and mopping his forehead with a handkerchief, he sits down heavily next to the German.

On the train track a Beyer-Garratt articulated locomotive is emitting torrents of white steam; beyond the track lie the grim brick hovels of Soochow in front of Victorian government buildings and a nine-story pagoda rising above everything else on the skyline, leading the eye toward a distant ring of baldheaded granite hills. The elderly German, leaning from the window, buys peaches from a one-eyed hawker. The newcomer, staring briefly at the breakfast plates, whips out a newspaper from his safari jacket. Immediately he isolates himself behind the London *Times*, which must have taken days to reach him by packet mail from Hong Kong.

Chugging heavily out of the station, the Blue Express leaves in its tumultuous wake a thick cluster of peasants who haven't been able to board. They clutch baskets of live ducks and packets of sweetmeats, hunkering down to await the next train, due the next day.

Munching on fresh peaches – he has bought a whole dozen–the

9

the old German begins a rambling monologue, intended for his mature traveling companion behind the newspaper. Sucking noisily on a pit, he condemns the high price of silk in Shanghai. Not that he deals in silk. He has a very successful import business, he tells the raised newspaper, with a quick glance at Embree, whose eyes are fixed on the passing landscape. Of all European sundries sold in China these days – so he tells his indifferent audience – the best-selling item is the Thermos bottle. To buy a Thermos the Chinese peasant will sell his daughter, the old German claims with a guffaw. Pausing long enough to take another peach from his lap, the bearded importer turns next to the political scene. It's an international disgrace the way Peking allows these warlords to run wild through the country; he gets it said in a muddle of German and English, but somehow sustains a certain rhetoric of logic and passion. China has been a republic for fifteen years. It has rid itself of spendthrift emperors and a corrupt Manchu court which has been dominated by eunuchs who wore diapers. Yet what has the country done with its freedom? It has let warlords set up little kingdoms everywhere – military adventurers who pay no more than lip service to the president and parliament. Worse is the way these Japanese take anything they want.

Embree turns with mild interest to the little man munching a peach. What the German has just said about the Japanese is an exaggeration, but there's some truth in it: the sort of statement father makes. In 1914, at the start of the Great War (Embree had been ten), the Japanese took over the German Concession in Tsingtao. At the time father had been enraged at the audacity of their illegal action and at their duplicity as well, for they sent their troops into the Chinese city under the guise of protecting 'Asian interests' from the Germans. Since then, of course, they haven't been pried loose from Chinese soil. Indeed, soon afterward they presented to the Peking government their 'Twenty-one Demands,' which assumed their right to control large areas of the country. Had they all been accepted, China would have become a Japanese protectorate. That a few had been accepted – leaving Japan secure in some parts of Manchuria and in Tsingtao – infuriated Embree's father. And now the pinched look of fury on the old German's face reminds him of father at the dinner table, ranting against foreign opportunism in China. Father has always felt the only foreigners allowed in China should be missionaries.

Throughout the German's harangue against Chinese

10

incompetence and Japanese aggression, the florid newcomer has remained behind the London *Times*, coming out briefly to light a pipe. Embree wonders if he's a former military man. The years have softened the flesh on his large frame, but his erect bearing suggests past discipline.

Embree's attention shifts once again to the countryside as it bobbles past the window: wheat fields lined with thorny pepper bushes and apricot trees; small lakes with causeways lined with willows; mud villages marked by crumbling walls. Philip Embree is in China; twenty-three years old and in China. He no longer has to listen to father recount tales of India, when missionaries were God-fearing men of courage and pluck – not like the timid youth of today. Out there, beyond the window, lies the future.

'Fountain pen. Called fountain pen?'

Reluctantly Embree turns to the old man. 'Yes, fountain pen's right.'

'*Verkauf* – sell – sell good in China.' He winks at Embree. 'I speak *besser*?'

'Yes, much better.'

'I practice *Englisch*. I remember it.' He glances at the man beside him, who is puffing on a dark-grained pipe. Ruddy and perspiring, the newcomer looks straight ahead. With a sigh of exasperation the German turns again to Embree. 'So, Missionar.' He waits until Embree gives him attention. 'So you go now in Missionhaus?'

'Yes, I'm on my way to the mission.' Embree doesn't volunteer that it's his first assignment.

'Where is mission?' The old German is going to presist in his practice. His beard glistens from peach juice.

'In Harbin.'

The German chortles. 'Harbin!' He begins peeling another peach. '*Kalt* there. Too much *Japaner* and *Russe* there.' He turns to the smoker, as if for confirmation, but that traveling companion is contemplating the baggage rack with light-blue eyes. '*Russe*. They *stehlen* the shoe is on your foot, *Junge*.' He wrinkles up his nose and leans forward. 'They smell *Zwiebel* – what is *Zwiebel*?'

'Onion,' Embree translates. 'They smell of onion.'

'They smell of onion. Drink too many vodka.' Finished peeling the fruit, the German begins eating it with quick little bites. Turning to the smoker beside him, he says, 'You are Britisher?'

The man nods, but with such coldness that nothing more is said in the compartment for a long time. The train passes through the town of Chen-chiang on the south bank of the Yangtze. Gazing at the jumble of boats tied along the quay, Embree is tempted to say, 'I think Marco Polo stopped in this place,' but the German is too busy with his peaches, the smoker with his *Times*.

Then the train is coming into the northern suburbs of Nanking. While it stands in the station north of the old ramparts, the German speaks again, after a loud introductory sigh. 'In Nanking now is Nationalist *Regierung*.'

'What did he say?' asks the newcomer, looking at Embree.

'He said the Nationalist government's here in Nanking.'

'Yes, I mean government,' says the old man.

'Nationalist?' The newcomer puffs fiercely on his pipe. 'Those bloody bastards aren't nationalists.' He speaks a clipped English.

'*Ich bitte um Entschuldigung*,' says the old German with the formality of someone unfairly corrected. 'I practice English. *Ubung macht den Meister*.'

'Don't call them nationalists. Don't tell the lad here that. Kuomintang or KMT or National People's Party or anything you want – they're still a bloody lot of murderers. Out for what they can get, just like all the slopeheads.' The Englishman, now fully engaged in conversation, waves his pipe for emphasis. 'In Shanghai Chiang Kai-shek and his Nationalists massacred three or four thousand people.'

'Green *Bande* did.'

'Chiang hired the Green Gang. They did the dirty work, that's all.' The Englishman looks at Embree. 'Lad, don't let anyone fool you. Chiang's just another warlord.'

'Killed Bolsheviks in Shanghai,' says the German.

'Anyone he wants out of the way he calls a Bolshevik. One slope-head's as bloody as the next is what I say.'

'I said to Missionar same way. I said heads in basket. I said *Soldat*, bandit same way. I told Missionar.' He is clearly glad to agree with the Englishman, to have a conversation for his practice. With a sigh, forgetting which language their talk is in, he adds, '*So kann es nicht bleiben, Es muss anders werden*.'

'What's he saying?' the Englishman asks Embree.

'It can't go on this way. Things must change.'

'Damn true,' says the Englishman.

'Where I go' – the German takes up yet another peach – 'they call me dog to the face. Face? Call me *aüslandisch* dog. Call me turtle. Dog, turtle – Gott damn them!' Leaning back, he concentrates on the peach, peeling it with a pocket knife. He finishes with a single curled ribbon of yellow skin. Of the dozen peaches in his lap, only three are left. The peelings and pits lie in a neat pile on his handkerchief beside him. Embree studies him briefly: shoes cracked from the accumulated polish of many years; white socks gathered around his skinny ankles; trousers threadbare and shrunken from countless cleanings; stained shirt and frayed collar; linen jacket with elbow patches; and a tiny metal pin, perhaps military, fixed in a buttonhole. The man is shabby. Shabby and alone. Shabby, alone, peddling Thermos bottles and fountain pens to people who call him foreign dog and a turtle, terms of extreme contempt in Chinese. Embree has expected to meet unusual people, but none so shabby and forlorn.

And none so pessimistic as the old salesman and the Englishman. It is not so much their perception of China's turmoil as the intensity of that perception which surprises him. Embree studied the language and religions of China at Yale, but his knowledge of its politics has mostly come from articles in New Haven and New York papers. He's tried to keep up in a general way, but with general results. He knows this much: In fifteen years, ever since the overthrow of the Manchu Dynasty and the establishment of a republic, the government hasn't worked. Parliament has often been dissolved and when in session has never been effective against presidents and cabinets equally ineffective. Provisional constitutions have focused power for short periods in the hands of men who didn't know how to use it. Confusion has led to interminable squabbling among the political factions – Embree can't keep them straight. They seem to choose sides along geographical lines, north and south. And then into the vacuum created by this political mess have rushed the military men, the warlords with their semiprivate armies. They've been fighting a civil war among themselves for a decade. In spite of the shifting alliances and the endless battles, no warlord has put himself high enough above the others to take charge. A young mission worker in Shanghai told him that China's nothing but a loosely allied group of principalities that establish whatever law there is through force of arms. And Embree knows the Great Powers of Europe continue to enjoy the best of China: economic privileges, cheap labor, urban gaiety. And Japan openly covets the unused potential of the countryside.

So *kann es nicht bleiben*, says the old drummer. *Es muss anders werden*. And the Englishman agrees it *must* change. So the situation is apparently worse than Embree expected.

Good.

Embree didn't want a safe mission; that's why he chose an assignment in China. He wants people back home, especially father, to realize how dangerous the posting is. Onward Christian Soldiers. As his father did in India, he'll prove that Philip Embree is one of them.

The day brightens across the countryside and he looks at it from the window. But what he sees is not fields and villages – he sees himself, a soldier, marching through this tremendous land.

By midafternoon the compartment is sweltering, as the China sun beats down on the metal roof. They rattle deeper into the interior, heading north through Suxian and Xuzhou and beyond toward the province of Shantung. When the overhead fan breaks down, the Britisher calls angrily for the porter. Coming into the compartment to work on the fan (he fails to fix it), the porter gives Embree a sudden glance of pure hatred. Embree is shocked at the naked emotion. The young porter makes no attempt to modulate it but stands feet apart, looking down at him.

The moment passes. The young porter leaves, yet the intensity of his look remains with the American, who has never seen such hatred on a human face. Uncommon malevolence. Uncommon. Or are such looks common in China? What he knows is from reading and hearsay, unattached to his own experience. He hasn't learned to judge the reality of China, so how can he hope to judge the expression of a train porter? Even so, there was enough loathing and fury for a murder in that young face.

Embree shrugs off the fancy, because that's what it is: fancy. Both here and at home he has been warned about his youth, his inexperience, about the tendency of the inexperienced young to fall into traps set by rumor and ignorance. Now he warns himself to be sensible. Taking up his knapsack from the leather seat (getting warm as the heat of day increases), Embree pulls out a book.

Both onlookers in the compartment stare at it briefly, with apparent indifference, and return to their isolation.

The book is the Scofield Reference Bible, given to Philip

Embree by his father two months ago, when he graduated from the Yale Divinity School. The flyleaf inscription, quoting lines from Luke, is signed with a huge scrawled FATHER.

> *And the Lord said, Simon, Simon, behold, Satan hath*
> *desired to have you, that he may sift you as wheat;*
> *But I have prayed for thee, that thy faith fail not.*

How like father to admonish him before he has done anything wrong. And how like father to remind him that this new phase of his life must be viewed as a test. Once again, as he has done under father's guidance since childhood, he must think of himself as a moral battleground where the forces of good and evil engage daily.

Idly opening the book, Embree glances at it, then stares at the unreeling landscape: immense flat areas of earth broken at intervals by patches of woodland or granite outcroppings around which the long train slips like a lazy stream around a boulder. As his eyes return to the page, the word 'breasts' looms out at him. Breasts. The single word is suffcient to conjure in him a recollection of Shanghai, his few days there: singsong girls in their tight silk dresses slit to mid-thigh, inviting him to bed in pidgin English as they mince along the street in a broken-kneed gait. Two fellow missionaries had not given the girls a second look. How can other men resist temptation with such equanimity? Desire had burned in his heart, smoldered long after he returned to his quarters. He rereads the passage:

> *Let thy fountain be blessed, and rejoice with the wife of thy*
> *youth. Let you be as the loving hind and pleasant roe; let her*
> *breasts satisfy thee at all times, and be thou ravished always*
> *with her love. And why wilt thou, my son, be ravished with a*
> *strange woman, and embrace the bosom of a foreigner?*

Embree is engaged to the daughter of his father's best friend, also a missionary. The fathers worked together in India many years ago for the love of God Almighty. Ursula is a fine girl, Embree surely acknowledges that, but she does not have breasts. Or she doesn't seem to have them – he has never had the chance to find out. A persevering girl, Ursula wore out a Bible before her fifteenth year. She is fully capable of matching Embree stride for stride on a hike, although he was captain of the Yale rowing team and a superb athlete. A strong, persevering girl committed to high moral standards, as befits the daughter of a Servant of God.

'Be thou ravished always with her love.' It is difficult for Embree to envision such a love with Ursula. They have kissed dryly a few times, and the frustration shining in her eyes must have been shining in his too.

'The ways of men are before the eyes of the Lord –' Embree is reading this passage when abruptly, from the seat opposite, comes a grunting sound, like air expelled by someone who's struck hard. Over the edge of his Bible Embree sees the gray head of the old German blossom into a crimson flower, a corona of deep red, as blood jets rhythmically from a wound above one ear. Driven by the impact of the blow, the German's head lies now against the shoulder of the Englishman, who, stunned momentarily, looks sideways in surprise, as if believing the old man has chosen to use him for a pillow.

A loud series of crackling reports is now coming from the track. Leaning toward the window, craning his head through it, Embree sees a large number of horsemen firing rifles as they ride alongside the train. They keep pace easily, because the locomotive is slowing down. One rider, dressed in cotton pants but without a shirt covering his muscled body, grins at Embree before pulling the trigger of a rifle held by one hand. Embree hears something go past him, a thudding sound against the wall.

'Get down, damn you!' he hears.

Dropping to the floor, Embree stares at the Englishman, still clenching his pipe between his teeth, the side of his safari jacket soaked with the German's blood. The old man lies among peach skins, slack mouth full of fruit.

'Bandits,' mutters the Englishman.

The train is lurching to a halt.

'They probably threw a log across the damn tracks. Now we're for it.'

'What will they do?' Embree asks and points to the dead man. 'That was an accident. Do they murder foreigners?'

The sound of riflefire intensifies. Alongside the train men are yelling above the pounding of horses' hooves. Embree hears someone scream, perhaps from inside the train.

16

'What will they do?' Embree repeats his question.

With the pipe still in his mouth, the Englishman shrugs.

'Can we fight?'

Embree's question amuses him; he grins broadly and steadies his pipe to keep it from falling out of his mouth. 'Wouldn't try it, lad. When they come in here, do what they say. Don't tell them you're a missionary.' He studies Embree a moment for signs of panic; reassured, he says, 'They might damn well skewer you on the spot. In Nanking a bunch of Hunanese regulars shot a Yankee missionary – soldiers, lad, not like these. These rotters here, who knows what they'll do.' He takes the pipe in one hand and holds it out like a schoolmarm's pointer. 'Don't resist or you give them an open invitation.'

Angry yells in the corridor, a burst of gunfire, a cry.

The compartment door slides open and the young porter stands framed in the empty space, panting and wild-eyed, a big-barreled Mauser in his white-gloved hand.

'So the boy was one of them,' murmurs the Englishman, but smiles placatively when the young porter strides in to kneel at the German's side. Still holding the pistol, the boy searches the dead man's pockets, turning them out deftly with one hand. He yanks loose the gold chain of a vest-pocket watch, and, after a wary glance at the two foreigners, holds the watch to his ear, grinning when the tick-tock assures him it works. Taking money from the wallet, he flings it, scattering papers across the dead man's paunch. On his feet he looks hard at Embree, who for an instant is sure the boy means to school him. In those dark eyes is the same hatred that had shocked him earlier.

'Get up and go outside,' the boy commands in Chinese.

'What does he say?' the Englishman asks. 'I don't speak it.'

'He wants us to leave the train.'

'If he wants it, let's do it. I don't think he knows how to handle that Mauser.'

With the porter waving the big pistol behind them, they move into the passageway. Ahead are four men in pin-striped business suits, each carrying a briefcase, whispering among themselves.

'They got on with me at Soochow,' explains the Englishman, looking down at Embree, who is a head shorter. 'Japs.'

Just beyond the Japanese are two Chinese in the brown uniforms, billed caps, and epaulettes of officers. They are being pushed roughly by rifles toward the far end of the sleeping car.

Joined by a couple of bandits, the young porter, growing bold and enthusiastic, rams the Mauser hard into the small of Embree's back, making him stumble. 'No foreign dog gets away with anything when I'm around!' the boy yells gleefully. The porter's boast seems to challenge one of the bandits to do better, because he whacks the Englishman across the shoulders with a rifle barrel and buckles the big man to his knees.

'Oh, Christ,' murmurs the Englishman, head hanging down between his legs.

'Get up, you fucking turtle,' the bandit screams and kicks him.

Embree helps the Englishman to his feet. 'Thanks, lad. That took the wind out of me.' He glances at the porter and the bandits, who are giggling at him. 'See what I mean? One wrong move –'

Ahead in the corridor is the exit. Outside, waiting, stand at least ten bandits, grinning. 'Jump,' whispers the Englishman, 'before you get bloody pushed.'

Embree jumps onto the gravel of the track bed. Immediately bandits surround him and the Englishman, both of whom shield their eyes from the blinding light. Each bandit, sweating from the hard ride, holds either a pistol or a rifle. Some wear crossed bandoliers over naked torsos. A few wear broad-brimmed straw hats; only a few have shoes or sandals. 'Stay here,' one quietly orders.

Embree translates for the Englishman, who grunts in acknowledgment. 'Never thought of going anywhere.' He rubs his shoulder, wincing.

All along the length of the train is pandemonium. Bandits climb into the cars, routing out passengers, hauling down suitcases and bundles. They rip open packages and strew the contents on the ground. Peasants are ignored, but anyone looking prosperous – merchants, landlords – is stripped, searched, pummeled, and left whimpering in the dirt.

Near the two Westerners stand the four Japanese, but a bandit with one ear, brandishing a riding crop, soon approaches to talk to them. After a quick exchange of bows, the Japanese are allowed to reembark. They return to the sleeping car without a glance at Embree and the Englishman.

'Didn't search the Japanese,' Embree observes.

'The slopeheads aren't stupid, lad. If they roust those Tokyo businessmen, a bloody lot of Jap troops from Tsingtao will hunt them down. That's the way Japs are.'

'Shut up,' the porter snaps in English and waves his pistol under the Englishman's nose.

Now the leader with one ear approaches; a floppy cotton hat doesn't hide the puckered hold on the left side of his head. He slaps his thigh rhythmically with the riding crop. 'I speak English,' he announces proudly, but with considerable effort. 'Speak good.' Then, swaggering away, he shouts his orders at the milling bandits who continue unloading their plunder from the train.

The busy looters must number at least a hundred. It suddenly occurs to Embree that he left his bags inside the train. He won't get them back either, not with those hundred men at work. He has nothing now but the clothes he wears. Nothing else – not even the Bible. Not even the Scofield Reference Bible presented to him by father with a dire admonition on the flyleaf.

Good.

Embree is swept by the wind of freedom. I am free, he tells himself, while men are pillaging a train and passengers are whimpering with fear. Free, but of what? he asks. The question is big and terrible, and anyway there isn't time to think of it. Things are happening as he squints into the hot sunlight.

The leader blows a whistle – three, four times, like a rowing coach.

In a surging motion the bandits gather around him. The one-eared leader stands back from the train, arms akimbo, his baggy pants blowing in gusts of wind coming across the plain. Horses pawing restlessly cause the dust to rise in clouds above the train. A half-dozen bandits part the crowd, pushing ahead of them the two Chinese in military uniform, whose hands have been tied behind their backs. Neither wears his billed cap any more. The younger man has a puffed, bleeding eye. A shoulder epaulette has been ripped from the older man's tunic.

'Looks to me like they've got a couple of important army officers,' the Englishman observes in a whisper. 'One a commander. Ask who they are.'

Turning, Embree looks at the young porter. 'Pardon me,' he says with Chinese formality. 'Forgive a fool for bothering you with a foolish question, but if you answer it, I will be profoundly grateful. Excuse me, but who are those two men? Pardon me for asking. I am unworthy.'

After a long pause, during which he assesses the proper response to such a respectful question, the porter raises his chin slightly and says, 'On the train you stuffed yourself on eggs.'

'I beg your pardon.'

'You and the dead one eating like pigs. It made me sick.'

'I profoundly beg your pardon.'

The porter waves his hand impatiently as a roar comes up from the crowd. 'They are men of Tang Shan-teh.'

'I thank you humbly.' Then Embree tells the Englishman, who breathes out a whistle of surprise.

The one-eared bandit walks slowly around the two officers, swatting his thigh with the riding crop, studying them. A hush descends; the locomotive can be heard steaming. The bandit stops abruptly in front of the younger officer and mutters something. A few men nearby are chuckling. Did he tell a joke? Embree wonders. The one-eared leader backs off a few steps in mock-serious appraisal of the young officer. 'Where is his hat?' the leader calls into the crowd. Someone comes rushing up with it.

'Fine, beautiful,' the leader coos while putting the billed hat on the young officer's head. 'What are you, a captain? A general?'

The crowd roars as the leader swaggers around the young officer, who is staring at the ground. 'An example of Tang's invincible army,' the leader yells, and the crowd summons up more laughter.

'What will they do?' Embree whispers, but the Englishman, face tense with anticipation, waves him off.

Abruptly the leader stops his circling inspection of the officer and turns toward the ring of bandits. 'You.' He points with his crop to the front row. 'Yes, you.' Impatiently he beckons with the crop. 'Come here and shoot this pile of shit.'

A young bandit steps forward hesitantly.

'That's right. You.'

The hush descends again. Inside the train a baby cries, and the hissing of locomotive steam can still be heard, but a hundred bandits and twice that many peasants leaning from the train windows are silent.

'Shoot him,' the leader says.

Walking up to the bound officer, the youthful bandit stares at him.

'In the guts,' orders the leader.

The bandit lifts his rifle, an old straight-pull repeater, and fires.

The impact bends the officer double. He writhes in the dust; his hat, sailing clear, lies ten feet away.

'Go on,' the leader says impatiently. 'Finish it.'

Stepping forward, the young bandit puts the muzzle close to the fallen man's head and fires again. He stares a moment, then straightens up and starts to walk away.

The leader detains him by putting the crop in his path. 'You look like a damn fool,' the leader tells him. The young bandit is shirtless. A piece of orange silk has been stuck hastily under the rope holding up his pants. A Western felt hat, too large for him, sits on his head – or rather on his ears, bending them forward. 'Take off the stupid hat.'

The crowd belly-laughs as the chastened young executioner pushes past them, holding his hat; he goes off to brood near some open crates.

'Are you praying?' the Englishman whispers to Embree.

'I'm trying to.'

'For God's sake, do it in silence. They may hate Christians.'

Embree knows that. In Shanghai he'd been told of a strong anti-Christian feeling that had accompanied the Nationalist troops on their sweep northward from Canton. Of course it had always been a problem for missionaries. But the Nationalists with their new phrases, learned from their erstwhile Russian friends, have intensified the resentment against foreigners preaching about a god who isn't Chinese. Missionaries are being called 'imperialists' and their converts 'running dogs of the imperialists.' It's the kind of situation father would welcome – God against politics. Embree continues his prayer in a low voice, but not silently as the Englishman has warned him to do.

Then he forgets the prayer altogether when the one-earned leader hauls the second officer into the center of the crowd. 'Have a good look at this one.' The leader jabs the riding crop into the man's stomach. 'He's next in command to Tang Shan-teh. Can you believe this turd is next to a general? That shows you what a turd the General is too.'

'What's he saying?' the Englishman asks Embree. They have moved into the crowd, becoming part of it; no one seems to notice.

'This is a chief of staff,' the leader continues, moving around the bound officer. 'I wouldn't let him clean my shithouse.'

'I asked you, what's he saying?'

Embree translates.

'So they got Tang's chief of staff. Bloody fools.'

'Get me a big bag,' the leader calls out. 'Where is Li Shun?' A tall man with a stringy mustache pushes through the crowd. 'This is going to be your job, Li Shun,' the leader says, pointing with the crop at the officer. Someone clutching a burlap bag rushes up and gives it to the leader, who takes it over to the bound officer and holds it in front of his face. 'Look at this bag,' he says, but when the officer stares straight ahead, avoiding the bag, the leader slashes his nose with the riding crop. 'You're a turtle. You fucked your mother. You opened your sister's second road, you sonofabitch. You got this stuff' – he flicks the crop at the remaining epaulette – 'by sucking off Tang.'

The officer doesn't blink, although a welling cut has opened up across his nose and left cheek. He has taken a wide stance after the blow, as if bracing himself for more.

'I know who you are,' says the leader, moving around him. 'You're Wu Sheng-chi. He's a colonel, men. He has people like us polish his boots and light his cigarettes. I want to ask you, Colonel Wu, do you know what this bag's for?' The leader turns to the men who are jostling closer; the ring has squeezed to a small size. From where he stands, the leader can see each face distinctly. 'We *could* hold him for ransom.'

Some of the bandits cheer. Others regard the officer curiously.

'Kill him!' someone shouts. A few others join in and make a chorus.

Holding up his arms, the leader yells for silence. 'I'd hold him for ransom if I thought Tang would pay. I heard of a warlord around Kaifeng, I think it was, who paid some fellows like us more than ten thousand taels just to get a concubine back.'

The men smile.

'And believe me, she wasn't worth one tale after those fellows got through with her. I'm telling you I'd hold this sonofabitch for ransom and I know his Excellency would want me to, if we could get Tang to pay for it.'

'Who's his Excellency?' Embree whispers to the Englishman, while the leader continues to circle the bound officer.

'I don't know.'

'But, men,' the leader says after a while, 'let me tell you – Tang won't He's too *honorable* to pay ransom. He's a fucking Confucian!' the leader yells, stepping in front of the bound officer. 'Did you know that? Tang wouldn't pay a single *cash* for your goddamn head! You stupid fool.' After a moment of tense hesitation, he adds in a low, brooding voice, 'Colonel Wu, on your knees.'

The bound man does as he is told, accomplishing the motion, hands tied behind him, with slow grace.

Circling him, the leader appraises Colonel Wu as if he were a horse at auction. 'I promise you this, Colonel. Your head is going to roll into Tang's camp like a ball. I mean it. I promise it.' He motions with the crop at the tall man, Li Shun, who has been waiting quietly to one side. Now Li Shun strides forward and stands directly behind the kneeling officer.

'Do it,' One-ear says.

Li Shun removes a long, curved sword from the scabbard he wears. Raising the blade in a fluid motion, he brings it down in a wide arc, as if cropping wheat with a sickle, and strikes off the head of Colonel Wu Sheng-chi.

Embree has been craning his neck in the crowd to get an unobstructed view of the execution. He has not been praying for the man's soul, as he should have been, but the fascination of violent death has gripped him with such urgency that he would have traveled miles, countless miles, through this hot alien country just to see it happen – this, a man's head cut cleanly off his torso. As a small fountain of blood pulses in quick but diminishing jets from the neck, Embree feels that something of immense importance has just happened to himself. He can't say exactly what it is, but Philip Embree knows that he will divide his life at this moment, before and after this moment. What he feels is not compassion for the dead man – a surprise for someone raised in Christ – but involvement in the execution itself, making him as close emotionally to the swordsman Li Shun as to the victim Colonel Wu. It is very strange. He feels as though he never knew himself until this moment, now, being jostled in a crowd of Chinese bandits. Just as the dead man's life force is pouring from his headless trunk, so Embree's life force seems also to be pouring from him, out into the world, flowing beyond the confines of his missionary body into a strange new universe where such things as decapitation occur. Never before has he felt so completely alive, so filled with a zest for experience, so inherently powerful. Appalled by this sudden discovery of his secret nature, changed forever, Philip Embree staggers out of the crowd and turns away from it toward the blue hills in the distance, hearing the locomotive hiss, a baby cry.

The bandit leader reaches down and catches up the severed head by its hair, not waiting for the blood to empty from it. He holds it up, triumphantly. 'Think of Tang's face when this thing rolls into his camp!' Tying the end of the bag into a knot, he tosses it to a man in the front rank of the crowd. 'Take this to Qufu.'

The stocky man with broad Mongolian cheekbones stares thoughfully at the blood soaking through the burlap.

'Get this to General Tang,' says the leader, 'and you'll be rewarded. Can you do that?'

'I want a saddle.'

'You'll get a saddle.' One-ear adds, 'Slip into camp and put this bag somewhere where they'll find it. When we hear Tang has it, you'll get a saddle.'

The man, brightening, gives One-ear a little bow. Soon mounted, he gallops bareback across the plain with a bloodstained bag knocking against his horse's flank.

'Bloody fools,' mutters the Englishman, who has joined Embree beyond the bandits' circle. Together they watch the men scatter and return to their looting – almost completed now, save for the mail car from which letters are being scattered into the wind.

The one-eared leader of the *tufei* band strides buoyantly toward the Westerners, plainly satisfied with himself. His riding crop beats a faint but steady tattoo against his leg. He stares up at the tall Englishman, whose puffy face, its capillaries broken by whisky, is now reddened further by the sun. 'You sell?' One-ear asks him in English.

'Me?' The Englishman, grimacing, looks around. 'You're talking to me, general?'

'Sell gun?'

The Englishman shakes his head. 'Beg your pardon, general, but I'm a construction engineer.'

The bandit can't handle that much English, so he scratches his nose and frowns. 'You sell gun?'

'I build bridges.' With this big hands he tries to demonstrate what a bridge is.

After a few moments of this the bandit interrupts impatiently. 'You sell gun!'

'I build – I don't sell guns – I build bridges. Bridge. Like this.' Beginning the gestures again, he throws up his hands in despair. Turning frightened eyes to Embree, he says, 'Explain to him, lad, for God's sake.'

Embree tells the *tufei* chief in Chinese that the Englishman builds bridges and does nothing else.

One-ear grins skeptically. 'You' – ne addresses Embree – 'give me papers.'

Embree turns to the Englishman. 'He wants our papers.'

'He means our passports.'

Embree has left his on the train, and tells the bandit so. Taking the Englishman's passport and flipping through its pages without looking at them, the bandit hands it back, then turns to Embree. 'What do you sell? Airplanes?'

'I am traveling through China.'

'Selling guns?'

The Englishman's warning fresh in his mind, Embree says nothing about the mission. 'I'm a student.'

'Why do you speak my language?' asks the bandit, frowning.

'It is a beautiful language; my poor study is unworthy of it. It is honored, it is old, it is very beautiful.'

Regarding him closely, the bandit begins to smile. 'Did you know him?' He points with the crop at the decapitated body.

'No, I did not know him.'

'He was riding with you.'

'I ask your forgiveness, sir, but he was not riding with me. On the same train, maybe in the same compartment, but not with me.'

Placidly the bandit nods, yet his mouth is set in a skeptical grin. 'That sonofabitch lying over there, I knew him. He and Tang kidnaped my brother, put him in their stinking army, and forced him to charge the machine guns. Know why they killed him? They fear me, Chin Yu-wen!' He taps his chest proudly with the crop. 'My ancestors will sleep better tonight.' Pointing at the Englishman, who is mopping his sweaty brow with a handkerchief, the bandit grins broadly. 'Now tell me the fucking truth. Does he sell guns?'

'No, he does not sell guns,' Embree maintains, forcing himself to meet the bandit's eyes. 'He builds bridges.'

'Do you build bridges with him?'

'I am a student visiting your great country.'

'I think he sells guns. I think I saw him once in Shanghai. He was with other English sonofabitches on the pier, unloading crates of ammunition for Tang's army. Or someone's army.'

'What's being said?' the Englishman asks nervously.

'He still believes you sell guns. He insists on it.'

'These people think every foreigner sells guns.'

'Do you?'

25

The Englishman studies Embree a moment. 'You're a quick study, aren't you.'

'What does that mean?'

'Well, you seem at home with these people. On their side.'

'I'm on your side.' Embree adds with curious emphasis, 'Of course.'

'Tell him I'm building a bridge on the Wei River some four hundred kilometers north of here.'

Embree tells him.

When the bandit grins in response, the Englishman says tensely, 'For God's sake, lad, tell him again. Make him believe it!'

'I'm trying.' Turning to the bandit, Embree repeats what he has said. 'This man builds bridges. He doesn't sell guns.'

'Sure he sells them.'

'In his country and mine, a bridge builder never sells guns.' Embree pauses to think. 'In China would a scholar sell guns?'

'No,' the bandit says without hesitation.

'You see then? In our countries it's the same with a bridge builder. Because there a bridge builder is a kind of scholar.'

Pursing his lips, the *tufei* examines this logic. He looks down at his dusty cotton shoes, tapping his thigh slowly with the crop.

'Goddamnit, lad,' frets the Englishman, 'tell him again.'

But Embree says nothing, not even when the Englishman grips his arm. He waits for Chin Yu-wen to arrive at his own decision; no more talk is going to sway the man.

Finally the one-eared bandit spins on his heel and strides away.

'Well, goddamnit,' says the Englishman, softly this time. He watches the man walk toward the train. 'I think the rotter believes you.' He lets go of Embree's arm. 'Thanks, lad.' Mopping his forehead again, he says, 'If they think I sell guns to warlords, they'll do me harm.' He chuckles at the understatement. 'You just saved my bloody life.'

Embree stares at the shaken man. 'Your life? Would they go that far with a foreigner?'

'Lad, lad –' Sighing, he kneels in the dust, his eyes never leaving Chin Yu-wen, who is giving orders to some of the men. 'A gun sold to a warlord is a gun turned against them. They shoot gunrunners.' The Englishman spits, as if the idea is a bad taste in his mouth. 'You saved my bloody life. Maybe your own, too.'

Since boyhood Embree has wondered how he would react to danger. Sometimes in college he and his roommate, instead of studying theology, would discuss this matter of courage under fire. As missionaries in turbulent countries, would they be brave if the occasion demanded? Where in a man do you find the source of his strength? In prayer? In faith? In neither? Then where?

Embree hasn't prayed for strength, yet now he feels the relief of someone who has been tested for the first time and come through well. He has behaved the way he and his roommate had hoped – rather wistfully – they would under such circumstances. Embree feels good.

'Look at the bloody fools,' murmurs the Englishman in disgust.

Embree follows the man's gaze: Bandits are loading their plunder on the rumps of their ponies, on pack mules. All along the track suitcases have been flung open, cheap unwanted articles of clothing scattered around, and pages of letters left to blow across the plain in hot rushes of wind from the Gobi, hundreds of miles to the northwest.

'Bloody fools?' Embree repeats. He is squatting now beside the Englishman in the lee of the train; a babble of voices comes from the cars where passengers, herded back in, are baking from the intense heat. The bandits work as hard as coolies.

'Sure they're bloody fools,' the Englishman declares, shaking his head. 'They could loot the train without killing those officers.'

'Who are they?'

'They could be some of White Wolf's gang. That's who "his Excellency" might be – White Wolf. These bandit chiefs like fancy titles. I read in a Shanghai paper White Wolf's men had come out of the hills for a bit of looting and kidnaping. All in a day's work, lad. But I can't see them killing Tang's chief of staff. That's trouble.'

'Their leader told me he did it for revenge. His brother died in Tang's army.'

The Englishman winks. 'And revenge is what Tang's going to want too.'

'Is he powerful?'

'In this province he is. In at least part of it. In China a general's power goes as far as his troops can march in a few days. But from what I know of General Tang, he won't let this insult pass. Oh, Christ.' He takes out his pipe and points with its stem. 'Look at them, will you. Bloody slopes.'

Two men, bent over the corpses, are searching through the pockets. One bandit pries open the mouth of the younger officer.

'Not like your Sunday school, hey, lad?'

With his pistol butt, the bandit hammers at the mouth; then, thrusting his fingers into the gaping hole, he flicks out a few broken teeth. Both men examine them carefully, then argue. Finally, the one who knocked the teeth out puts them into his pocket.

'For the gold fillings,' says the Englishman, spitting in the dust. 'God forgive them.'

Grunting, the Englishman tamps new tobacco into his pipe. 'Better ask the Almighty what's going to happen to us'. Lighting the pipe, he draws thoughtfully a few times. 'They might let us reboard. Or they might hold us for ransom. Second's likely.' He adds after a pause, 'But I don't know. With all the loot they won't need money for the short run. And they tend to think for the short run. So I wouldn't worry.'

'I'm not worrying,' Embree says defensively.

'That's a good lad. Because I think they might let us go.'

By midafternoon the bandits are ready to leave. They put the two foreigners on powerful Mongolian ponies behind bandit horsemen. The tall Englishman looks awkward, his long legs nearly trailing in the dust. Embree hopes he looks less foolish. Over his shoulder the Englishman calls back to Embree. 'See what I mean, lad? They let us go. Nothing more predictable than the yellows!'

The caravan sets out at a slow pace alongside the motionless train. About noon a few bandits had tied ropes to three logs lying across the tracks in front of the engine. Straining ponies had pulled off each log. Now the locomotive waits for the file of ponies and mules to cross the tracks before continuing the interrupted journey to Peking. Bandits wave at the engineer, who waves back as if nothing has happened during this four-hour stop, as if a dozen peasants hadn't died in the initial attack, as if a foreign passenger hadn't been shot through an open window, and as if the execution of two military officers hadn't taken place in full view of everyone.

The file of mounted men crosses the track and circles an outcropping of granite, behind which, earlier in the day, they had waited for the train to come chugging down the endless miles toward ambush. Seated behind his bandit on the pony, Embree glances back at the train: The black Skoda locomotive, two coal tenders, some flatcars, carriages overflowing with peasants who thrust their heads from the open windows to get a breath of air, the dining car, the first-class sleeper in which Embree had spent last night and in which a garrulous old German with a lonely heart now lies dead among peach peelings, two ransacked mail cars, a baggage car now empty, more flats and boxcars, more third-class wooden carriages, and finally a caboose to whose railing a mob of peasants cling, incredibly capable of hanging on for hours with the grip of a single hand.

The caravan picks its way among rocks at the foot of a steep cliff, then descends to the plain, much of it planted in wheat, the golden tassels rippling like waves. As far as Embree can see, the fields stretch across the Chinese world to a cloudless horizon. He can't judge where the earth ends and the sky begins, both wrapped in the haze of distance. Lightly he clasps the waist of the bandit riding in front of him. He can feel the body heat, the man's muscles tensing in conformation to the animal's gait, even as beneath his own thighs Embree feels the warm pistonlike motion of the horse, as it sends them through a countryside simmering with heat.

He is Philip Embree. He tells himself this more than once. He is the same Philip Embree who boarded a train yesterday in Shanghai. He wore a seersucker suit, a white shirt neatly open at the neck, and white suede shoes. Two bags accompanied him, along with a knapsack containing his passport and Bible. Seated in the compartment and watching the train puff out of the Chapai Station, he took satisfaction in the constant knowledge that people back home would care what happened to him: Yale classmates promised to write when they could; his fiancée studying at a Boston mission school promised to write weekly; and without needing to promise, his father would pray daily for his immortal soul.

That was Philip Embree last night.

Today's Philip Embree has seen men casually murdered, their bodies rifled, the teeth hammered out of their dead mouths. His own fate hangs in the balance, as the bandits take him toward an unknown destination. He is not the Philip Embree who boarded the train in Shanghai. For one thing, he doesn't know what to expect of himself. Instead of feeling outraged by the murders or afraid for his own life, amazingly he feels only excitement, that neutral emotion, quite detached from personal safety and moral judgment. He is simply going forward, being carried through unpredictable moments into more excitement.

As the caravan moves deeper into the interior of China, he thinks of his older sister and wishes she could see him riding behind a bandit on a Mongolian pony. She would approve. Mary might even say, 'This is what I meant by freedom.'

A few months ago, in a New York speakeasy, they had discussed freedom. He was in the city to visit the mission headquarters before leaving America. Recently divorced – her second time – Mary worked for a publisher and continued to live 'the fast life,' as father called it. Sitting across the table from her, Embree glanced shyly at her mid-thirties attractiveness in the candlelight. He noticed a man nearby doing the same. Mary drank wine and smiled when Embree refused a glass.

'So you're bound for adventure.' She reached out to touch his hand, as if making sure this blond young man was her brother.

'We aren't supposed to call it adventure,' he told her with a smile. 'It's an assignment.'

'Call it whatever you want, it's freedom. Maybe not for some, for men like father, but it will be for you.'

'Why do you think so?'

'Because you need freedom. I never thought we were alike as children. But then I left home when you were still young. I remember this little boy reciting Scripture.' Mary laughed. The man at the nearby table was staring openly at her bobbed hair, her large, expressive gray eyes. 'What a memory you had! That's all I remember – that memory attached to a solemn little boy. Won't you have some wine?'

'No thanks.'

'I knew we were alike when you ran away. How old were you? Fifteen?'

'Thirteen and a half.'

'You were gone more than a day, weren't you?'

'Two days.'

'Two days,' she repeated, recapturing her surprise at his audacity. 'The minister's little boy ran away for two days.'

'The police picked me up in Bridgeport.'

'When I heard, I couldn't believe it. Model boy runs away because he says he wants to see the world. Until then I thought you'd grow up in father's shadow. Suddenly I was sure you wouldn't be like him. I mean, *in the end* you wouldn't. Of course, after that escapade, you faked it again. You did what you were told, you showed the right face, but I knew who you *really* were. Mother would have known too had she lived.'

30

'Well? Tell me. Who am I?'

Mary's eyes were shining. 'You're someone who wants to find out what the world is. Exactly what you said when you ran away, only you didn't know how true it was then. You'll do whatever's necessary to find out.'

Embree laughed. 'That sounds a little sinister.'

'Of course it is. But that's you – you're one of *us*. And finally you've got the freedom that'll let you prove it.'

'I'll have that glass of wine.' He stared hostilely at the man nearby, who turned away.

For the first time in his life Philip Embree got drunk. Before his sister sent him off to his hotel in a cab, she told him he was sweet and embraced him. Swaying, she whispered against his ear, 'Don't be ashamed, never be ashamed.'

'Of what?' He pulled back and looked at her.

'Of what you do, of what you feel.' She stared at him a moment, then smiled, breaking the mood. 'Hell, what would father say if he saw you now?' Lowering her voice, she mimicked their father: 'Philip, you will end like Al Capone. You will end your days in speakeasies and gambling dens, defying the Lord.'

Embree joined her in laughter. 'Exactly what he'd say.'

Learning forward, he kissed her on the lips. The kiss lasted until she pulled back. 'Go on, go on with you. Go to your adventure!'

'Assignment!'

'Adventure!'

Driving away in the cab, Embree marveled at that kiss; he couldn't remembering having kissed Mary before.

Now, riding a Mongolian pony, he recalls their talk and that kiss. The memory is fresh. To find out what the world really is. Excitement surges through him, as wheat fields pass on either side of the trotting pony. He looks around eagerly. Few peasants can be seen in the countryside, attesting to its great size, for this is a densely populated area. When Embree does see them in the distance, they are wearing conical hats and carrying hoes that might have been carried here a millennium ago. The hundred *tufei* riders move slowly across the sweltering land toward a mountain range in the west, passing a few lakes of sparkling brilliance along the way, with herons poised at the shore or flocks of wild ducks sitting on the blue surface like bits of tattered paper. Hour after hour the file leans into a wind that brings in its vortex clean yellow dust from Central Asia.

The band does not halt for food, although on horseback the men eat pieces of wheat cake and sweetmeats taken from train passengers. The *tufei* are a motley column, many wearing battered straw hats or felt Western hats taken today from Shanghai people. Most riders have bagfuls of loot dangling from the flanks of their horses. It is an engorged, sluggish caravan that traverses the warning afternoon into a burning sunset. Embree thinks he has never seen such a twilight: red becoming violet, the dark sky submerging the land with a marine liquidity, drowning it, as if the ocean had broken loose to cover the earth.

During the journey Embree and the Englishman have been separated, but that evening when the band halts and makes camp on a barren stretch of plain, they are allowed to stay together. They are not bound or fettered; after all, where can they go, two foreign dogs in the midst of rural China? Sitting on the ground, still warm from the day's sun, they watch the fires spring into the darkness. Embree notices that many bandits have Thermos bottles – three or more – hanging from their rope belts, and perhaps a dozen fountain pens clipped to their shirts, pants, and even their straw hats. The old German must have had crates of these items stacked in the baggage car. Embree takes a deep breath, hauling in the smells of burning wood, sweat, and summer earth. Then the deeply pungent odor of pumpkins.

'Christ.' The Englishman grimaces. 'It's pumpkin, lad. I can't abide the stuff, never could. It's a filthy thing. But this lot here will eat pumpkin morning, noon, and night. Pumpkin's cheap, see. That's why they eat it. That's why they eat anything – because it's cheap. Blast them, the slopeheads.' Clearing his throat, he spits before getting his pipe out for a smoke.

Soon the fetid smell of pumpkin frying in rancid lard drifts into the night air. It becomes an overwhelming stench, and although Embree likes pumpkin pie, this is no church social, no artfully cooked pie. He starts to feel nauseated, a feeling intensified when someone roughly thrusts a wooden bowl of fried pumpkin into his hands. In the firelight it has the gruesome look of decomposing flesh – and smells as putrid. Yet hunger overcomes revulsion, and with his fingers Embree picks up a gob of steaming pumpkin and stuffs it into his mouth. He glances at the Englishman puffing on the pipe. 'You'd better eat,' Embree says, licking the lard-soaked pumpkin from his fingers. 'To keep up your strength.'

The Englishman eyes him sulkily. 'Christ, lad, you're a bit of a survivor now, aren't you. I think you're growing fond of the slopeheads.'

Embree laughs but at the same time wonders if his companion may be right. He surely does not feel unhappy among these men who, like him, are lapping the sticky fat from their fingers.

Later, when the fires shrink to embers and let the darkness engulf the camp, he feels positively good.

In the last firelight the Englishman can see the contentment on Embree's face; he says wryly, 'You look like you've been to tea at Buckingham Palace.' After a pause he adds, 'Have you any idea what you've got yourself into, lad?'

'You mean, besides being captured?'

The Englishman shakes his head. 'It's lovely you speak their language, but what do you really know about the slopes?'

'Not much,' Embree admits. 'I've read books.'

'About religion?'

'And some history.'

'School subjects. That's what I thought. Let me tell you something. People who come to China think of it as the land of tradition – of religion and history and art. When Europe was in flames centuries ago, these Chinese had their kites and good food, their silks and fans. People think China's solid, it never changes.' The Englishman digs with his hand into the dirt. 'But this is the real China. It's not rock, lad. It's nothing but earth.' He lets the dirt run through his fingers. 'The slopes can be as violent as the next man. Never forget it. They've got revolt and insurrection in them. You're giving me a look. Don't you believe it's possible?'

Embree knows from history that it is but, wanting to hear what the Englishman has to say, remains silent.

'Let me tell you something, lad. The slopes believe in the Mandate of Heaven. When things go right, it means Heaven is pleased. When things go wrong, it means things go wrong because Heaven is not pleased. The leaders have lost Heaven's approval, so Heaven punishes them by making things go wrong. Get it?'

'Yes.'

'Then the people think, well, if the gods are angry, what we've got to do is throw out our leaders and make the gods happy again. Revolution, lad. The slopes have been overthrowing governments and rioting and raising hell for centuries – just like us Europeans.' He lets the rest of the dirt slip between his fingers. 'Don't sell them short on guts either. Or recklessness. Look around at these bandits. You won't find a more reckless lot.'

'I believe that,' Embree says with a short laugh.

'Plenty of them have been soldiers. They know what they're doing.'

Embree remembers the little German salesman: Run from soldier into bandit, bandit into soldier. It seems as if they are all the same. 'Is there a difference between them?' he asks.

The Englishman wipes his hand on his jacket. 'Soldiers get paid sometimes. Bandits have to fend for themselves. But when the warlords don't have the money, their soldiers become bandits. Clear?' He stretches out on the ground, hands behind his neck.

'No.'

'I don't think it is to them either. Peking's supposed to pay the warlords. I mean, they're official generals, servants of the government, right? Most of them is bandits is what I say.'

'This General Tang too?'

'He's another story. Maybe, maybe not. Scratch a slopehead you find a mystery. I've been here two years now, but I don't know any more about them than I do about their crazy language. You're going to teach them the Bible?'

'That's my mission.'

'I wish you luck.' He turns on his side, cradling his head on his arm. 'Well, tomorrow's another day. At least let's hope so.'

Embree doesn't think the attempt at a joke is funny. Somehow the Englishman annoys him just by being here. Lying down too and studying the pattern of stars overhead, he feels privileged to be among these people whom the Englishman calls slopeheads. Smug in his understanding, Philip Embree listens to the men coughing and snoring, until finally, like a wornout child, he falls asleep.

Next morning, first consuming more pumpkin (this tme the Englishman gloomily eats a bowlful too), many of the bandits open their plunder bags to find better clothing for the journey. Breaking camp, they split into two groups and set out on different paths. Embree feels a tug of regret as he waves at the beefy Englishman disappearing down a rutted lane. I am truly alone, Embree thinks. The idea holds a certain satisfaction. There is no one in the world for him to count on now. Of course, father would say no man is alone – God is here, ever vigilant, studying human behavior for signs of iniquity. Aside from God, however, Embree is now free of authority, of rules that have governed his twenty-three years. All he possesses of the past is on his back. For the first time he can recall, there's no Bible at hand, no prayer book nearby. Even the photographs of his dead mother and his fiancée Ursula were left on the train, where the history of Philip Embree ended.

'Where are we going?' he asks the bandit riding in front of him. Getting no reply, he says, 'We're going westward. Is that into Shansi?' Still no reply. All right, Embree tells himself, let it come. Whatever it is, let it just come.

All morning the column proceeds at a languorous gait along paths scarcely wide enough for a single wagon. But there are no wagons. No wagons, carts, people, oxen, mules. Nothing moves on the road except the *tufei* column. Save for herons and flying insects the landscape seems empty. Embree wonders if the sight of fifty mounted and armed men, leading pack mules staggering under loads of plunder, has discouraged the farmers from tending their fields, from driving their flocks. Toward noon he sees rising from the tawny plain a flat-topped hill with paths running at gradual angles up its sides. Clusters of mud-and-thatch huts are visible along the terraced ascent. In half an hour the column is near the village, but preceding the riders for a long time has been a steady clanging sound from the hill.

Embree, leaning forward, puts his mouth close to the bandit's ear. 'What's all the noise?'

'They're sounding the alarm. Until we leave, not even chickens will move.' The rider chuckles. 'A peasant thinks you want what he has, even when he has nothing. Now that village there – they haven't anything we want. No money, no opium, no broken shoes.'

'Broken shoes?'

'Whores. Their own women are old by twenty, and you can be sure with that gong going like that they've hidden the younger girls already. But they're lucky.' The rider spits into the dust; he seems less nervous than earlier about a foreigner riding behind him. 'If it was late in the day, we'd stop and take what they have.'

'Does the time of day matter?' Embree thinks the man is joking.

'Sure it matters,' the man says in a tone of annoyance. They ride awhile before he explains. 'At the end of a long day, you want something. Even if you don't know what it is.' He spits again; Embree wonders if he suffers from tuberculosis. Mission people

35

told him the disease is widespread in rural areas. 'You ride all day,' the man continues after a brief fit of coughing, 'you want something.'

'I think I understand.'

'No, you don't,' the man tells him with a laugh. 'But you will.'

Slowly the column skirts the village, a silent clump of mud huts, and then passes outlying cabbage-and-bean plots. They plod along-side millet fields that are lined with cassia trees; they pass irrigation wheels and weeding poles fixed with protruding nails and straw hats left behind by fleeing farmers. Embree has often wondered what it must feel like to be feared. He has never been feared, although certainly he has feared his father. His mother feared only God, but feared Him terribly, until hospital work during a flu epidemic took her to Him. Embree realizes with a shameful thrill that he is riding with men capable of eliciting a fear powerful enough to be just short of divine.

They are heading into the path of gathering cloudbanks, which pass overhead in lumpy procession, promising rain. At a fork in the road they halt and Chin, the one-eared leader, gives orders, gesticulating with his riding crop. Once again the bandits split into groups, each numbering about twenty-five. Embree suspects that the idea is to confuse any pursuers; it is like a movie. The last he saw was *Flesh and the Devil*, with John Gilbert and Greta Garbo, in a dark, comfortable, safe theater. Is he where he seems to be?

'You must ride alone.' Chin has come alongside Embree and holds the reins of a pony. 'You'll slow us down otherwise.'

'I want to ride alone,' Embree claims, but until yesterday he has never been on a horse, except once in a New York armory, where his rich cousin exercised jumpers in the winter season.

Embree tries to be nonchalant as he slides off the rump of one pony and grips the reins of another. Taking a deep breath he swings one leg up and clutches the horse's mane, as he has watched the other riders do. His eager mounting nearly propels him across the animal to the ground; what saves him is his white-knuckled grip on the mane. A few of the bandits chuckle.

'Listen to me,' Chin says when Embree has regained his balance.

'I am listening, forgive me.'

'Disobey, you die. The pony doesn't mean you can ride off.'

'Yes, sir, I understand.'

'Stay close to me, me alone.'

36

'I will.'

'You must.'

'I will, I must. I will obey. I'm a poor man who begs your forgiveness for my stupidity.'

Chin strokes his cheek in thoughtful regard of the young foreigner. 'The way you speak surprises me. You almost sound Chinese.'

'I speak badly. I've tried to learn your beautiful language. Five years I practiced every day, but my shortcomings are too many and I've not gone far.'

Chin smiles in approval. 'You certainly do speak well. For a foreigner.'

'I speak worse than a child. And I know only Guoyu. I can't speak one word of Wu and Yue.'

'Forget about them,' Chin says angrily.

Embree realizes he has made a mistake: he must not admit to this speaker of northern Mandarin that the southern dialects are worth learning. Even so, when the group sets out he receives a quick but unmistakable smile from the *tufei* leader.

The storm breaks. Rain slants horizontally across wheat tassels, castoroil bushes, across the rumps of ponies, needling into the riders, blinding them while filling their nostrils with the earthy scent of wet fields. Then the storm passes as rapidly as it came, leaving a huge rainbow shimmering on the horizon. It is beautiful, Embree thinks, as he grips the pony's flanks desperately when the animal lurches in the mud. Soaked to the skin, Embree looks down at his white shoes, sticking out from the round belly of his mount: white shoes, ridiculous shoes. They mark him as different from the others. He wishes to wear straw sandals or nothing at all. He would have flung away his own shoes that very moment but for fear of looking wasteful or crazy.

2

It is late afternoon, the road dry, for it hasn't rained here. Ahead, smoke rises from the adobe hovels of a village set in the midst of wheat fields. Silently the riders move through the grain as if fording a sluggish golden stream. Chin turns in his saddle – only a few have them – and yells at Embree. 'Remember now – obey!'

Embree nods, but hasn't time to draw another breath before

Chin, striking with the crop, gallops toward the small village. Embree digs his heels into the pony's flanks, then holds on as the powerful little animal surges through grain standing belly-high. Behind Embree the other men prod their mounts too, until all are leaping like dolphins. Two peasants, carrying manure buckets on long poles, must have been too busy with their loads to notice the approaching horsemen until it's too late. Throwing down the poles, they attempt to flee. One zigzags out of the way, but the other stumbles, falls. Embree sees him rise out of the wheat, mouth open in a great O of terror, arms spread to the sky, announcing his defenselessness. A rider, leaning from his pony as if to pluck a rose, slashes at the farmer with a sword. There is a blunt agonized cry. From the storm-tossed deck of his pony, Embree turns to watch him go down: the oblique ribbon of blood from shoulder to waist, the convulsed face disappearing beneath hooves. Why? Embree wonders. For no reason! But he cares really for only one thing: to stay on the pony. Forgetting the dead peasant, he clutches the mane with both hands, feeling the powerful neck move under his fists at each bound forward, like the slithering coils of a huge snake. Stay on. If I fall now, the shame – the shame! Stay on! Embree tells himself breathlessly.

Chin reaches the main road into the village and here reins in, yanking out his pistol. He shouts at three peasants running into a mud-brick house. 'Stop! Come back!' When they keep going, he shoots and cuts down the trailing man. Leaping off his pony, Chin starts along the street, glancing to either side of the low-slung houses, a few kiln-dried brick, most of them crumbling adobe, and all of them closed, either boarded up or without windows on the street. Behind him limps Embree, who reined in too quickly and for this error was thrown into a ditch. He go up in muddy seersuckers, chagrined beyond imagining yet obliged to set aside his shame in the need to follow Chin closely. Mangy brown dogs cross the path of the advancing dismounted men who are leading their ponies. With scruffy tails slipped under their haunches, the dogs lead the way; they look bedraggled but cunning, alert to anything that may happen from which they can profit.

Riding crop in one hand and gun in the other, one-eared Chin strolls along. Finally he turns when they come to a threshing area, a flat clay surface in the middle of the village. He tells the men to split up and bring back anything of value. He mutters 'Follow me' to Embree.

Two others accompany them down a narrow ochre-colored lane, its muddy ditch smelling of urine and rotted vegetation. At the first door on the lane, Chin glances into the small courtyard of a village house. Embree looks inside too. The door is open – perhaps the owner left in haste. A ray of sunshine coming through a roof hole illuminates one room of the house: bed of straw, sickle leaning against a wall, a few cooking pots on top of a huge pottery barrel.

'What are we looking for?' Embree asks.

One of the men looks at him with a smile, and Embree recalls the rider on the pony: 'You ride all day, you want something.' So they are looking for something; from the man's smile, it's something terrible. In the village there are the echoing reports of gunshots: three, four, five.

They've killed someone, a villager. What did the man do? Probably nothing, probably he just tried to run away, and for his unreasonableness got killed. Perhaps the bandits killed him to show they can do it. That way the farmers won't be tempted to defend their village by coming in from the fields wielding sickles. It's like a war; the bandits kill for their own survival. Looking at it that way, Embree can't feel the indignation he knows he should. And he's with them at the moment, so in a sense he's one of them. It's a concept the old Philip Embree of twenty-four hours ago would not have understood.

Chin stops to appraise an enormous pink sow lying against a brick wall. A chain around its neck is attached to an iron ring and rod plunged deep into the ground. Running his tongue along his lips, as if already tasting roast pig, Chin turns with a smile to his men. 'Not a bad village. We'll get this sow later.'

We're not done looking for something, Embree thinks. They are going to loot, commit more murder.

They halt frequently along the lane to inspect houses. 'Wait,' Chin whispers abruptly, cocking his head at the entrance to a courtyard. 'Hear that?' He enters a brick gateway in the wall and brushes past a line of hanging laundry. Facing the little courtyard is a low building, a hut really, with a thatched roof. From within comes the sound of crashing. Something has dropped. A jar? Finger to his lips, commanding silence, Chin motions for his men to go forward, which they do, dashing across the yard to the wooden door. It is shut, perhaps bolted. One of the men fires three times into the frame, shattering it; both bandits leap into the darkness. A cry – thin, feminine.

Chin looks at Embree with a smile. 'We're in luck.'

Inside the small house, Embree blinks in the faint light coming through the shattered doorway. Three people are standing next to a big iron stove: two children and a young woman, all wide-eyed. One child, sobbing, clings to the woman's arm.

'Out!' Chin yells at the children and makes a motion as if shooing chickens from the house. 'Out! Out!'

They scott away, slip under the laundry, and vanish through the gate.

'Not you.' Chin catches the girl's arm as she too tries to leave.

It occurs to Embree that in his week in China he has never been this close to a peasant girl; on the train they were segregated, and during the looting he had only a glimpse of them being herded here and there. Now, a few feet away, he sees a girl in a blue jacket fastened high at the throat; it reaches down to her hips, their shape hidden by voluminous gray trousers. Her large eyes watch Chin as he touches her thick hair, which is drawn back from her forehead in a large coil at the nape of her neck. She doesn't move, although her lips tremble. With a quick motion Chin undoes the coil by pulling out a bamboo pin that holds it. Black hair cascades to her shoulders. The sudden loosening of her bound hair changes something for Embree: the act transforms a frightened girl into a frightened but desirable woman. Apparently Chin feels the change too, because he clucks his tongue in appreciation. Reaching out he touches her round cheek with the pad of one finger. 'Nice girl,' he coos. 'Sweet little girl.' He grips the high collar of her shirt and for a moment does nothing more, as if in deep contemplation; then he yanks so hard that the cotton, giving way, rips like paper. The girl staggers against the wall, holding the torn shirt across her breasts.

'I won't hurt you,' Chin says. 'Neither will they.' He points his riding crop at the two bandits squatting on the earthen floor.

Embree tries to pray for her. Think of God, ask His mercy. Think of God. God – breasts swelling within the torn shirt. He has never seen a naked woman, except in the art books he took from the library and hid in a drawer. Twenty-three, Philip Embree is going to see a naked woman for the first time. His mouth feels dry, gritty from dust.

Chin starts untying the rope that holds up his trousers. 'Take off yours,' he tells the girl quietly.

She remains motionless, as if pinned against the wall.

'Go on, take them off. It's going to happen anyway,' he

explains patiently. 'So why not be nice.' Approaching her – one hand holding up his trousers, the other his riding crop which comes at her shoulder-high – Chin keeps saying, 'Be nice, be a nice girl,' as if coaxing a panicky child away from an open window. 'Be a good girl,' he says. 'Make it easy for yourself.'

The girl is rigid. Embree is certain she can't move even if she tries.

Coming closer, the one-eared bandit says harshly, 'You are not nice,' before striking her across the face with the riding crop. After a shriek of pain, the girl slumps to the floor, face down. Chin stares a moment, then steps out of his trousers and kneels beside her. For the first time Embree can remember, the bandit leader has let go of the riding crop.

'You're all right now?' Chin asks the girl gently.

The girl nods and moves her head to one side. Embree can see her bleeding cheek.

Pushing the girl firmly, but without undue roughness, over on her back, Chin then falls upon her, abruptly savage as he rips away her trousers and invests himself of her body. Embree is standing where he can see the side of Chin's head that lacks an ear. This physical flaw claims the young American's attention. Rape has always conjured in him a fantasy involving two perfect creatures: the man darkly handsome, the woman pale but lovely. Whereas here in this room smelling of earth and garlic, the man covering the woman has only a withered flap of flesh where an ear has once been, and the woman has a three-inch slash on her cheek. Moreover, the man did not bother to remove his shirt, and the bleeding woman beneath him does not resist at all, but allows him to adjust her legs impatiently as he wishes.

Weak in the knees, Embree leans against the cold stove and watches as the other two bandits follow Chin.

'God,' he murmurs under his breath, 'God in Heaven.' but can't think of more supplication for mercy or deliverance, because as Philip Embree watches the girl lying inert under the onslaught of three men, each obscenely ridiculous with buttocks wagging goatishly and in one instance with trousers gathered about the ankles, as the young American gawks in disbelief at this unspeakable outrage against which generations of his family have set themselves, he feels in his own loins a terrible kindling of lust.

'Go on,' he hears at his shoulder. Turning, he faces Chin, who points the riding crop at the girl. 'It's your turn. It costs nothing.'

41

Embree stares at the girl – at last free, she is curled up fetally, whimpering. The words 'Take heed to yourself' rush at him like an avenging wind from some half-remembered passage of the Book.

'Go on.' Chin goads him with the crop.

'No, I must not,' Embree replies in English.

'What's that?' Chin gives a snort of exasperation. 'I told you, it costs –'

But something blocks the light in the shattered doorway, something hurtles through the air and flashes down in a long swift arc. To avoid it, Chin steps backward and falls. The thing – a large ax – is raised in a man's hand again, and starts downward over the fallen bandit; Embree lunges out and grabs the descending haft. For a few moments he grapples with the intruder, until, wrestling the ax away, Embree throws him down. The man starts to rise, but with an arm made powerful by collegiate rowing, Embree pushes him down again.

One of the bandits has time enough to unholster his pistol and fire. A deafening noise fills the room. The intruder jerks, lies motionless.

Chin yells at Embree, 'Get out of the way!' while unholstering his own pistol and firing from where he lies on the ground – three times, until the room swims in the acrid smoke of gunpowder.

Scrambling across the floor, the girl flings herself across the body.

Embree feels his own body trembling uncontrollably. This is melodrama, a cheap movie, the kind he saw in New Haven. It can't be real life. God in Heaven have mercy – Embree coughs in the smoke.

Sprawled over the dead man as if protecting him, the girl, who hasn't spoken a word since the intruders' arrival, begins to scream. Her shrieks pile into a crescendo of anguish and horror.

'Let's get out of here,' Chin mutters and gloomily leads the way into the lane. Turning to Embree, he shrugs his shoulders, as if in apology. 'Peasants can fool you. They give in like sheep. They run away and hide. They offer their daughters if you'll let them alone. But suddenly one of them does a thing like this,' he declares bitterly.

'The man must have been her husband,' Embree says, hearing as they walk the sound rising from the house like a column of fire.

'To do that, he had to be someone in her own family. Brother, cousin. Would a husband kill himself for a mere wife?'

The other bandits giggle.

'Well, do you want to keep that?' Chin asks.

Embree looks down at his hand, which still holds the ax. The wooden haft is set in a grooved hollow of the metal. The weapon's driving weight is obtained by a long heavy knob of wood projecting past the blade.

Embree stares at the thing he grips so hard. Does he want it? Perhaps he has never wanted anything as much. 'Yes, I do,' he tells Chin.

'Then keep it. A gift for saving my life.'

Embree shoves the ax handle between belt and seersucker trousers, then strides forward at the bandit's side. He thinks of the girl back there. He tells himself he *must* think of her. *Think* of her. 'God have mercy,' he intones in his mind. 'I am like a green olive tree in the house of God; I trust in the mercy of God forever and ever.' Think of her, ask mercy. But his attention shifts to the huge pink sow they're now approaching. When one of the bandits shoots the iron ring off, all of them, including Embree, grip the taut chain and grapple the big animal to a standstill. Staring at it and panting, Chin exclaims, 'Not a bad village at all!'

That night the *tufei* band remains in the village and cooks over bonfires in the threshing square. They eat stores found in the houses – sweet potatoes, cabbage, eggs – and roast whatever chickens they find, but keep the big sow aside for the journey next day. From earthenware bowls they drink yellow wine supplied from jugs carried by old women who have nothing to lose in returning to the village. A few of them, along with a feeble old man, collect bowls that have been flung aside and now sit together outside the ring of fire, against clay walls, gorging themselves on leftovers.

'That was a very good train,' says a bandit sitting near Embree at a bonfire.

'White Wolf is going to be happy,' says another. 'And about the head too.'

'Did you see how Li Shun did it?' A man, draining his wine bowl, makes a sweeping motion through the air. 'Took off the head with one blow. Where did he learn that?'

'I hear he was an executioner for the *Ching pang*. When opium merchants wouldn't pay their dues, the *Ching pang* sent him out with his sword. Then they paid.'

'White Wolf will be happy about the head, but General Tang won't,' says an older man, pouring more wine.

A young bandit, eyes red from dust and wine, grins at the older one. 'Don't you understand, grandfather? That's the idea: Tang won't be. And someday White Wolf is going to have Tang's head too.'

'Don't call me grandfather. What do you know about anything?' he says to the young man, who is gesturing at an old woman to bring another wine jar.

'As much as you do.' But he doesn't add 'grandfather' – the older man is broad-shouldered, with ham-hock hands.

'None of you know anything. I served with Tang once.'

'What is that like?' someone asks.

'If you fight over women, you are shot.' The older man has a harelip that slurs his speech. 'If your company retreats in battle without orders, Tang shoots your captain. Once a company ran, all of them, and he had every tenth man shot.'

The young bandit laughs. 'Stories.'

'This is no story. My own cousin was a tenth man in that company.' The harelipped man sips from his bowl and glares triumphantly around the campfire. 'Think you know it all? Let me tell you something. Tang will come for White Wolf. It was a mistake to kill that colonel.'

The listeners glance at the next fire, where Chin is drinking heavily. Their eyes narrow at the memory of Chin's command, 'Do it,' and Li Shun's flashing sword.

'It wasn't our fault,' one of the men mutters sullenly.

'Before Tang attacks, do you think he'll ask whether it was or not?' The harelip grunts. 'Tang is the best soldier in China.'

Grinning over the rim of his wine bowl, the young bandit says, 'Then why didn't you stay in his army?'

'I do better with White Wolf. When I collect enough money, I can beat it. But when you're in Tang's army, you belong to him. If you want to quit, you can't. Or you have to escape and that's dangerous. The difference between him and White Wolf is discipline.'

'Then I'll take White Wolf.'

'At last we agree on something,' the old harelip says with a smile and touches wine bowls with the younger man.

Embree has been listening with interest, not so much for the significance of what is said but for the language the bandits use. He's gratified by his ability to understand their colloquial Chinese. In college he had not been a good divinity student;

44

theological questions either bored or confused him, and the history of religion seemed tiresomely complex. His strength had been languages. he possessed a good command of Latin, understood German and Italian pretty well, and had mastered French. His last professor of Chinese had urged him to give up divinity school and concentrate on Asian languages.

Lying that night alongside drunken bandits in the open air, Embree wonders if he might take that advice some day – quit missionary work, pursue knowledge. He has a prodigious memory. It has not always been admired by father, however, who used to say, 'It is one thing to memorize the Bible, it is quite another to understand it.' Mother thought better of his talent. Even under the worst of circumstances she took pride in Embree's ability to remember things. Even that day when he was twelve and she came to his room.

Sitting on his bed, she said after a long, thoughtful pause, ' "To be carnally minded is death." Where is that found, son?'

'In Romans. But I forget the exact chapter. Ten?' Then he quoted the verse fully: ' "For to be carnally minded is death, but to be spiritually minded is life and peace." '

'Chapter eight, verse six. But very good, son.' Her pride was obvious, yet her face became cloudy and pinched. ' "To be carnally minded is death," ' she repeatedly slowly, looking first at the floor, then at time. 'It is death, Philip. We have noticed, I mean, your father has –' She seemed under pressure; Embree had rarely seen her so tense. 'Well, you spend a lot of time in the bathroom. Your father thinks too much time.' Her face reddened. 'He asked me to speak to you about it.'

'About what, mother?' But he knew what she meant; the anguish, the embarrassment, the horror of it have remained with him until this night under the China stars.

'About self-abuse, Philip. Son.' Then she spoke rapidly, not wanting him to interrupt with confession or denial. She quoted the Bible, verses that spoke in general praise of fortitude and restraint, in general condemnation of license and lack of control. Without pausing to hear his own comment, having done her duty, she left, and the subject was never mentioned again. Embree sat in his room that afternoon until darkness fell; mortified, ashamed beyond belief, he hated his father for having sent her to discuss his sin.

Today he has seen a woman raped.

But he forgave mother. After all, she had come to him at father's command. What he did not forgive her was a betrayal of trust at an earlier time. He hadn't believed she would do such a thing, but she did; she told father what she promised to keep secret – that Philip had a slingshot. He had bought it from a schoolmate with his allowance and kept it in the garage, stashed under some canvas. During dinner one night father roared at him – 'A boy who shoots birds will someday shoot his fellow man' – and for punishment sent him down to the cellar for the night. The whole night in the cellar. Nothing could have been worse. Mice were down there, and they terrified him. Moreover, father turned off the light and warned him to keep it off. He sat all night in darkness against the damp cellar wall and listened for scurrying feet. He strained to hear them rustling. Most of that sleepless night he held one hand clamped over his mouth to keep from crying out. Next morning, when the cellar door opened, his mother stood on the landing and told him in a trembling voice to come up. When he reached her, Embree saw that she was crying.

'Don't be too hard on your father,' she sobbed. 'He does what he thinks is right.'

'Father? I'm not hard on father,' Embree said coldly and walked past her into the kitchen. She had cooked his favorite breakfast, a stack of pancakes swimming in maple syrup. Embree sat down, pushed the plate away, and drank his orange juice. Finished with that, he got up to leave.

Mother stood at the sink, clenching a dishrag. 'I don't know what possessed me, son. I just couldn't keep it from him, he hates violence so. I prayed to God to tell me what was right. I thought your father would only tell you to get rid of it.'

'Don't worry,' Embree said. 'I didn't cry, not once.'

'Forgive me, son.'

Embree looked at her tear-streaked face a moment, then left the kitchen. The words trailed him like dark smoke – forgive me, forgive me – but he never turned back.

And today he has seen a woman raped. He didn't try to stop it, and though appalled by the brute violence, by her helplessness, there was a moment when horror became desire. Forgive me, Lord, forgive me.

Long after his companions have fallen into a drunken slumber, Philip Embree considers the prurient nature of his sin. The memory drills into his consciousness like a toothache.

Forgive me, mother. Forgive me, Lord.

Next day the bandits ignore the passing villages and ride quietly, drowsily under the hot sun. In midafternoon Chin veers off the main road onto a rut-filled lane and leads his band across a grassy knoll to a plot of ground near a stream lined with maples. 'Now we feast!' he announces grandly. He calls by name a half-dozen men who, so Embree judges, have done this sort of thing before: They make roasting tripods and a spit from saplings, kill and gut the sow. Other men build a large fire. Within an hour of making camp, the pink sow of yesterday is a spitted carcass turning over flame. Embree has stood out of the way, watching. He hears someone say, 'That's Chin. He wouldn't take the pig to camp. That's why I like riding with him. If we find anything special to eat, we eat it, we don't haul it back to camp like fools.'

Men begin strolling down to the stream for a bath. They strip and toss sparkling handfuls of water over their grimy bodies. Like children released from the rigors of school, they jostle one another and laugh, until, encouraged by their infectious good humor, Embree ventures down the bank to bathe too. A little to one side of them, timidly, he removes all his clothes except his shorts, and wades into the stream. Like the others he squats in the rapid current and scoops up water, luxuriating in the sensation of cool liquid against hot skin. Philip Embree loves the water: limpid Connecticut lakes; breakers on the Sound. He always liked the beach, but every time he urged Ursula to go with him, she had other plans. Perhaps she didn't want him to see her in a bathing costume.

Embree holds water in his cupped hands and studies the trembling dappled surface. Today he's in the dusty foothills of China, whereas his best hours, at least until now, have been spent on the water, most of them as stroke oarsman for eights in regattas along the East Coast – battling Harvard, Princeton, and Cornell for tall silver cups. He preferred sweep rowing to sculling; he liked the catch, pull through, and recovery in tandem; the smooth blade-work of eight long oars. When did he last row?

Summoned from this reflection by a vague uneasiness, he glances toward the bank and sees half a dozen Chinese bandits eying him. Embree stands up and stares, as they are doing, at his dripping body. Are they looking at his shorts, curious about his genitals? Or are they studying his torso? Is something wrong? Embree fingers the whorls of blond hair that mat his body from chest to groin. Is that it, the hair? Are they astonished – their taut faces and open mouths suggest astonishment – by so much hair? The Chinese lining the bank are as hairless as boys. In college Embree's dormitory nickname had been 'the Hirsute Priest.'

Embarrassed by their solemn appraisal, he wades quickly ashore and dresses without drying himself. Sitting in the weeds, he finally stretches out as others have done, and naps while the fragrant smoke of a cooking fire drifts over him. Roughly awakened – someone digs a heel into his ribs – Embree looks up at a sullen face. 'Chin wants you.' When Embree reaches the campfire, most of the men are already seated around it, holding bowls brought from the village. Several cooks have prepared vegetables to complement the pig; its fat, dripping into the fire, sizzles musically.

Chin beckons Embree on. 'Sit beside me! Here! The guest of honor!'

Embree regards the welcome as some kind of joke but sits beside Chin as he is told. Men stare at the pig, across whose split roasted skin the late sunlight is slanting.

Chin hands Embree a cup of wine. 'All the way!' the bandit leader demands, emptying his own. Embree drinks until tears fill his eyes. '*Gan bei*!' Men grin around the campfire when Embree finishes. A bandit scrambles forward and fills Embree's cup – on Chin's order. 'All the way!' Again the young American drinks, sputters, drinks. Chin points the riding crop at a cook near the fire. 'Give my guest the best piece!' Slicing off a hunk of flank meat, the cook brings it on knife point to Embree's bowl and slides it in.

'Why give the foreigner the first piece?' someone grumbles, peevish from hunger. 'It's not funny.'

'Funny?' Chin glares, his wine cup halfway to his mouth. 'Did the foreigner save my life? Is *that* important? You bastard, he did more than you'll ever do!' Turning to Embree with a grim smile, he says, 'Eat. You are my honored guest.'

Embree lifts the slice off the knife point with his fingers, jiggles it a moment, then bites off a smoking portion.

'Good?' Chin asks with a frown, watching him chew.

'Best pork I ever tasted.'

'It is unworthy of my honored guest.' Chin throws a look of

challenge at the men awaiting their own meat. When they avert their yes, he yells out, 'Everyone! At the pig!' Men leap up, gather around the spitted animal, and slice off great slabs of steaming pork.

Embree gorges himself and drinks many cups of wine, until aware that for the second time in his life a young American missionary, Philip Embree by name, son of the Reverend Marshall Embree and betrothed of Ursula Davidson, is drunk. Apparently so is Chin, because he keeps poking Embree's arm playfully and acting the gracious host with an ostentatious display of solicitude – even feeding his honored guest piece of cabbage with his own chopsticks. 'What do you want? Tell me. Tell me anything, I'll get it for you,' the bandit leader maintains eagerly. 'Any fucking thing you want, you get. Hear that? Anything!' He frowns across the dying campfire at the other bandits. He stares long at the man who objected to the foreigner's having the first piece. 'Want that bastard's nose? I'll give it to you. I'll cut if off myself.' Chin slaps Embree hard on the back. 'You saved my life. Anybody calls you a foreign dog is going to be dog meat.' He laughs at the witticism. 'Is it understood? Is it?' Scrambling to his feet, Chin surveys the feasting men, most of them drunk, belching, reclining in the weeds, holding bowls of meat and vegetables. Turning again to Embree, he shouts, 'Tell me! What do you want? Guest of honor! Tell me! Anything is yours! Anything!'

Slipping wine, Embree grins at the one-eared leader. 'I'd like some other clothes.'

Bending down to get a better look at him, Chin says, 'Other clothes? What other clothes?

'Clothes like your men wear.'

Blinking rapidly, Chin waves toward the feasting men. '*Their* clothes?'

'Yes, sir, theirs.'

'Then you will have them. Nothing's too much for my honored guest. You –' He points at the first man who catches his eye. 'Stand up.' When the man does, Chin circles him slowly. 'About your size, honored guest.' He yells at the man to take off his clothes. Pausing to make sure his leader means it, the man starts unbuttoning his tunic.

Rising unsteadily to his feet, Embree takes off his own clothes.

'I'll see they aren't stolen,' Chin says, picking up the seersucker trousers.

'No, this is an exchange,' Embree tells him. 'His clothes for mine.'

Chin looks at the young American standing there, then laughs. So do the other men. They watch the hairy blond foreigner remove an expensive suit from the fashionable shop of J. Press, New Haven, Connecticut, and disappear into ill-fitting cotton pants, blue tunic, and conical straw hat. The man laugh even louder at their embarrassed comrade, who looks more awkward in double-breasted seersucker than the foreigner does in the frayed outfit of a renegade. Although the man's cotton shoes are too small for Embree, he insists on giving up his own white suedes. 'Deal is a deal,' he slurs thickly. Then he shoves his ax between tattered blouse and the leather thong that serves now as his belt.

'What else do you want?' Chin asks in the throes of hospitality. 'Come on, what else? Honored guest, tell me!'

Embree grins drunkenly. 'There's one thing –'

'Yes, go on. Tell me!'

'But you won't allow it.'

Flushed and red-eyed, Chin walks up close. 'I said anything.'

'Well, I'd like to shoot.'

Chin stiffens. 'All right. Who? You want to shoot someone? Point him out.'

'No, no, no.' Embree shakes his head. 'I don't mean shoot anyone. I just mean *shoot*. I never fired a gun in my life.'

Chin, staring thoughtfully at him a moment, says, 'All right, as guest of honor you can shoot.' Unholstering his gun, he motions at Embree. 'Follow me.'

They leave the campfire and walk down to the stream. It is dusk but still light enough for them to see a tall maple on the opposite bank.

'You can shoot that.' Chin thrusts the weapon out – a Colt 38-caliber double-action revolver.

Embree does not take it. 'Show me first what to do.'

With a sigh of exasperation Chin breaks open the cylinder and displays the bored chambers holding the cartridges. 'See it's loaded first.' Closing the cylinder and flicking off the safety, he hands the gun to Embree. 'Keep it pointed away from me.'

Embree holds a gun for the first time. It is heavier than he expected and cold to the touch, but immediately he likes the way its stock fits into the hollow of his palm, the way his finger curls around the trigger.

'What now?' Gingerly he points the gun toward the tree.

'Line it up.'

Embree attempts to keep the gun steady as the sight meanders off target. 'Now what?'

'Squeeze the trigger. Slowly.'

Embree does. The following blast, though expected, still manages to surprise him, and so does the recoil that jerks his hand skyward. He's so fascinated by the tingling imparted to his arm that he fails to see if the bullet hit the tree. 'Did I hit it?'

'No,' Chin says with a laugh. 'Try again.'

Embree squeezes off four more shots in rapid succession. The heavy black object jumps in his hand as if possessing a life of its own. 'Did I hit it?'

'No.'

'Not even once?'

'No.'

It's all right for the first time, Embree decides triumphantly. Handing the gun back to Chin, he bows low.

The bandit leader ejects the spent shells, holsters the gun, and regards Embree with abrupt sobriety. 'White Wolf is going to wonder where I got you.' He purses his lips and looks the young American over:. barefoot, pants too short, blouse too tight, the conical hat hiding a wealth of blond hair. 'Guest of honor, you are a strange thing. Wearing peasant clothes, carrying an ax, shooting five times at a tree without hitting it.'

'I'd like to shoot more.'

'That's enough,' Chin says firmly. 'Even a guest of honor can't waste ammunition. This is China, my friend.'

Watching the one-eared bandit head back to the campfire in gathering shadows, Embree savors 'my friend.' He wants to have Chin as a friend. Outlaw, but also a man of spirit. Not to different, perhaps, from the strong, willful men of the Hebrew tales on which Embree had been raised.

He can still feel the shape of the gun. Looking toward a mountain range on the horizon, like gray islands on a twilight sea, Embree knows the camp of White Wolf lies in that direction. He overheard some men say earlier that they will reach it tomorrow. Embree flexes his hand.

The camp is in a mountain fastness between Lin Fen and Ping

Yao, near the Fen River, which bisects the province of Shansi. A winding road leads up the mountainside, pockmarked by little caves from which people emerge to watch the column of horsemen. What strikes Embree is the primitiveness of the shelter. But as the caravan moves higher and passes more of these small caves, he understands that for these people this is home; they have never lived otherwise.

'Who are these people?' Embree asks a man riding beside him. 'They don't look like the Han.'

'No, they're not Chinese. They're some kind of mountain people. We don't bother them, they don't bother us.'

The scantily clad men, women, and children who stand at the mouths of their smoky caves regard the horsemen with passionless eyes, as if watching some clouds drift by.

At the top of the small mountain is a rugged plateau on which tents have been pitched: simple ridgepoles covered with faded blue cloth and animal pelts. Women come out of the tents as the band arrives. Riders, dismounting, lead their ponies and mules toward the tents and are greeted with hunks of wheat bread, jars of wine. The conscripted farmers pull their carts father on toward a central tent. The lattice framework, roof and sides, is covered by pelts and anchored to the ground by ropes secured to boulders. Smoke curls out of a hole in the tent top. Chin dismounts in front of it and calls out to Embree, 'You! Foreigner!' Embree is surprised by the impersonal, peremptory tone after yesterday's friendliness.

Dismounting too, he approaches Chin, who waits impatiently, holding the crop as if to strike with it.

'Wait here, foreigner. He'll want to see you. Call him Excellency and don't be a fool.'

'I don't understand.'

'Don't tell lies.' Chin turns and, pulling back the tent flap, enters.

A hot wind swirls around the treeless mountaintop, blinding Embree as he squats in the dust outside the tent. Through the blowing wind he hears a familiar voice: 'Lad, is that you? First I thought you were a slopehead in that hat and pants.' Coming toward Embree between two rows of tents is the Englishman, pipe unlit in his mouth.

Looking down at Embree, he says, 'We got here yesterday after butchering a dozen poor devils here and there. Have any trouble?'

'No, none,' Embree replies, although his mind carries an image of the spread-eagled girl.

The Englishman turns his beefy face toward the tents where the arriving *tufei* are unloading plunder. There's a babble of voices, a short cry. 'Listen to them,' he mutters, wiping his neck with a handkerchief. 'Christ, it's hot. They'll be tearing one another to pieces tonight. Over bits of cloth. That's what my bloody lot did last night after they drank enough.' He studies Embree frankly. 'What in hell has happened to you? Did they take your clothes?'

'I made an exchange.'

'You made an exchange.' Squatting beside Embree, the Englishman shakes his head in disapproval. 'Don't take up with them. I've seen men do it to their regret. China's not for us, lad. Do what you came for, then get out. That's advice you'll be glad you took.'

Embree smiles in bland response. He doesn't care about the Englishman's advice. They don't inhabit the same planet any more. He has traveled a long way, not only from Shanghai but from Connecticut as well, from Connecticut and America and from the church itself and from his fiancée and his father; he is not the Philip Embree who shared a sleeping car with a talkative old German and this British engineer he no longer understands.

'White Wolf is trouble.' The man is staring at the tent, drawing hard on his unlit pipe. 'A Buriat Mongol out of Ningsia. One of them that speaks English told me. Look at that yurt.' He points with the pipe stem at the tent. 'White Wolf had it brought all the way from the goddamn Gobi, just to make himself at home in the land of the Chinese. Scratch a half-breed Buriat like White Wolf, you find a dirty Mongol with his damn sheep and his fermented mare's milk. Let me tell you, their liquor is the world's worst. Bad enough to make you swear off drinking.' He spits on the ground. 'Mongols.'

Embree says nothing.

'Wish I had tobacco. I ran out this morning.' The Englishman glances hopefully at Embree, then shrugs. 'Bloody fool bastards. Take a train, kill a warlord's mate, butcher the countryside. Now they sit around drinking, playing with women. You'd think the fools hadn't a care in the world. I hope we get clear of this place before Tang comes looking for them.'

Scarcely hearing the Englishman, Embree watches the tent flap of the yurt. Finally he sees Chin peer out, beckoning to him. Without a parting word, Embree leaves the Englishman and bends to enter the tent, but no sooner has he put one foot inside than two men grab him. A third yanks the ax from his belt. Then they let him go.

Smoke fills the tent, and within seconds his eyes are watering. About a dozen men are standing or sitting; and at the far end, on a raised platform covered with tiger pelts, hunches a thin little man with the pronounced epicanthic eye folds of a Mongolian. His smooth face is the color of pale ivory – hence White Wolf? He wears a silk robe of Manchu style with long sleeves and high collar. On each finger is a ring; one slippered foot rests on a cushion with a golden dragon covering its surface. On a beaten-bronze stand beside the platform lies a long-stemmed pipe with a tiny bowl, and an open glass lamp.

Opium.

In Shanghai he heard the young missionaries describing the way it is smoked. Opium.

'Kowtow,' Chin whispers as they advance a few steps.

Embree was told in Shanghai how it's done – casually and elaborately. He'll do it elaborately for White Wolf. Falling to his knees, Embree stretches full length on the rug-covered earth, taps his forehead three times against it, three times more, then three times more. There is silence, the only sound a ceaseless rippling of the thick hides that line the walls. He remains supine, vulnerable, wondering if he should rise or wait. Embree waits; at last a reedy voice orders him to rise.

When Embree gets to his feet, the little man sitting on the platform is staring hard at him. 'You are a missionary man.'

There's no sense contradicting the bandit chief. He remembers Chin warning him not to lie. 'Yes,' Embree admits. 'I am a missionary man.'

'That is why you know Chinese. So you can tell us about the Jesus.' he grins at a clump of listeners who stand at the left side of the tent.

'Yes, your Excellency.'

A firebrand attached to a post throws light on the man's unwrinkled face. He seems neither cruel nor fierce, unlike the bandits Embree has seen in movies. He might be a neighborhood laundryman dressed up for the New Year festival.

'I know the Jesus,' White Wolf affirms with another glance, this one triumphant, at his retainers. 'Had a woman once who talked about the Jesus. She had gone to mission school –' He pauses, stares into the empty distance. 'No, not her.' He coughs, a hard, racking sound. Clearing his throat, he continues. 'That one died of a fever. It was another one. When was it?' He is asking no one. 'Two, three years ago. She was from Turfan.' He seems momentarily lost in the recollection. 'She learned about the Jesus from Russians there. I scolded her for talking about him. How could this man be a god when he had no land, no army, and couldn't do magic?' He lifts a ring finger like a teacher. 'That's when she argued. She said the Jesus man *did* do magic. Did he, missionary man?'

After a pause, Embree says, 'Yes, in a way.'

'In a way?' White Wolf laughs scornfully. 'You don't do magic in a way. You do it or you don't. Did he?'

'He did, Excellency. He walked on water. He cleansed lepers and gave blind men back their sight, he fed four thousand people with seven loaves of bread and a few little fishes.' Embree feels for the first time since arriving in China that he's doing what he has been sent to do.

The urge to preach seizes him, but the little man on the platform is waving his hand listlessly. 'Enough, enough of that,' White Wolf says. 'Maybe the Jesus is better than most Taoist priests, but he still never won a foot of land in battle.' Sighing, the little man seems to feel he has spoken the final word on that subject. He leans forward to study Embree. Through the tent haze, Embree can see dilated pupils, a tremor around the mouth, a sluggish movement of the hands. Opium.

'You saved Chin's life?' White Wolf asks abruptly.

'It was all I could do to repay him, Excellency.'

'Repay him?' White Wolf laughs and displays a gap-toothed mouth. 'You repay him for taking you prisoner?'

'To repay him for treating me well, Excellency.'

'I notice he lets you carry an ax too. Right into my tent. Yes, that's wonderful treatment of a prisoner. Isn't it, Chin?' But there is no real bite to the sarcasm. Yawning, White Wolf shows his gums again. Then he squints at Embree. 'Let me see your arms.'

'Excellency?'

'Your arms, missionary man. Roll up your sleeves.'

Embree does.

The little man purses his lips judgmentally. Turning to the retainers, he says in a voice of awe, 'Ever see so much hair?' With a grimace he turns back to Embree. 'Roll them down, roll them down.' He seems repelled by the sight of body hair – curiosity

55

conquered his aversion only for a moment. 'Well, you're welcome to stay with us.'

'I am honored to stay. I am happy.'

'Are you?' White Wolf laughs soundlessly. 'You're right, Chin. He isn't like foreigners. Tell me something, missionary man, did you see the beheading of Tang's dog?'

'Yes, Excellency.'

'And what did you think?' A light of interest gleams in the little man's eyes. 'Did you find it amusing? Did you like it?'

Had he like it? The strange question unsettles Embree, who has only a moment to wonder what he felt during those terrible moments. He almost says, 'Somehow it changed my life,' but instead he says, 'It was done quickly,' adding, 'with skill.'

White Wolf sits back, apparently satisfied with the answer. 'You are right, chin. He's not like any foreigner I ever met. You have please me in three ways, Chin. By taking the train, by bringing this strange missionary man here, and by executing Tang's dog. Tang is a fool, a bastard, a fool, and *I've* brought him dishonor!' The ivory hue of White Wolf's face shines like a carving in light fluttering at the tent post. 'Tang won't like it that you had the dog killed in front of everyone on the train. The sonofabitch. I am White Wolf. I can make a fool of these army bastards with their uniforms and motor cars and Shanghai women and their saluting. . . .' For a moment his voice trails away. He leans one cheek meditatively against his ringed hand, then seems to remember what he is saying. 'Yes,' he says, clearing his throat. 'Someday I'll cut his belly open with my own hand and pull his guts out with a peeled stick and feed them to chickens in front of his eyes, as I've seen done on the border.' He glances at his retainers. 'When I was a child I saw it, near Ulan Goom. Believe me, you see it done, you don't forget. Now, what was it? What was I saying?' He looks around as if looking for something of indifferent importance. Then his glazed eyes come again to Embree. 'Yes, you,' he says. 'You are our honored guest, so accept our poor hospitality. Your humble servants. Now go.' He waves his hand. 'You too, Chin.'

Following Chin's example, Embree bows very low and backs out of the yurt. A man at the entrance gives him his ax, which Embree jams under the leather thong serving for a belt. He takes a deep breath of air, feeling good.

'White Wolf is pleased with you,' Chin observes simply and walks away.

56

To Embree's annoyance, the Englishman has waited for him, squatting in the dust. 'Well, lad, how much time did you get?'

'How much time did I get?'

'Before the ransom's due.'

'Nothing was said about ransom.'

The Englishman smiles indulgently. 'There has got to be ransom. I don't know in the name of God who will raise mine – the Shanghai manager is on leave.'

'What do you mean, ransom?'

'Ransom is why we're here, lad, rather than dead on the rail tracks or safe now in Peking. They'll dispatch someone to a town with a wireless and send a message to your consul in Shanghai. All quite businesslike. Amount of money. When it must get here. Consequences if it's late. Of course a ransom.'

'I don't believe it. They said nothing about it in there.'

'Lad, you speak Chinese but you don't know China. Just be glad you're not a slopehead yourself. A man hereabouts, a Chinese, is being held like us. Only being one of them, he's treated differently. They already cut off a finger and sent it to his family, big landlords in Shantung. If they don't pay quickly, White Wolf will send them another finger or maybe an ear and will keep sending things until there isn't enough left of him to send home at all. With foreigners they're a bit more understanding, so be grateful.' The Englishman regards Embree a moment, then adds, 'I must say, you don't seem unduly concerned.'

'I'm not,' Embree replies coolly and goes to find Chin. He finds him sitting outside a tent, smoking a cigarette in the gathering dusk. Beside him sits a round-faced girl with large, impudent eyes, her arm draped across Chin's shoulder. Embree gives her a long, interested look – those eyes, those large hard eyes! – before speaking to Chin.

'What is White Wolf goint to do with me?' he asks.

'You'll stay with us awhile.'

'Am I being held for ransom?'

Chin takes a puff on the cigarette before replying. 'Yes, my friend, you are.'

'You didn't tell me. You could have told me,' Embree says reproachfully. The girl smiles.

'I would have told you tomorrow,' Chin says. 'After you slept. Does it matter so much?'

'At least you could have told me.'

'Are you afraid?'

'I just think you might have told me.' As an afterthought Embree says, 'I would have told you.'

'Don't worry. Tomorrow a man goes to the wireless station at Lin Fen.'

'I'm not worried.'

'Good, because your government will pay or your missionary people will. You'll be saved.'

'Saved from what?'

The girl, her eyes widening, smiles again.

'Saved from what?' Embree asks, forgetting all propriety.

The girl, after whispering in Chin's ear, smiles more broadly; it is a mean smile. 'No,' Chin tells her after a glance at Embree. 'He is different.'

'Saved from what?' Embree continues. 'From being shot?'

'Only if the money doesn't come in a month. But it will. You foreigners never worry about money.' The girl is stroking Chin's hair back from his forehead. 'Don't worry. White Wolf likes you, he thinks you're different.'

'Yet he'll have me shot?'

'If the money doesn't come. But it will. Anyway, that's business. We Chinese learn about business from you foreigners.'

The girl guffaws; taking the cigarette from Chin, she drags deeply on it, allowing the smoke to escape slowly from her mouth.

Embree's eyes meet hers.

'And you're luckier than the Englishman,' Chin says.

'I don't understand.' Embree finds it difficult to look at the man instead of the girl; her eyes are watching him all the time – Embree knows this without looking at her. His mind is divided between her and Chin, between an insolent girl and his own survival. 'How am I luckier?' he asks Chin.

'Tomorrow he will be shot.'

Embree isn't sure he has understood. 'Did you say shot?'

'Executed.'

'But isn't his ransom being raised?'

'It has nothing to do with money,' Chin replies coldly. 'He's a gunrunner.'

'Are you sure? Do you have proof?'

Although Chin speaks with conviction, his eyes carry uncertainty. 'The man's a liar; anyone can see that.'

'But tomorrow – you'll shoot him without proof?'

'If the man sells guns to a general, they'll be used to kill us. Of course we'll shoot him. Yes, he must be shot; this bridge builder sells guns.'

Whispering again, the girl laughs against Chin's ear. Chin smiles at Embree. 'She says you are very afraid.'

'No,' Embree says, 'I am not. But shooting that man –'

'She says foreigners are all alike. Look alike, think alike. The Englishman and you. She says you're both afraid.'

'Tell her she's wrong.' Embree stares at the girl, whose face although sullen is attractive. 'Tell her, Chin, if I am shot she must come and see how I die.'

Chin laughs. 'Tell her yourself. You speak the language. She's listening.'

The girl looks away, pouting.

Chin eyes Embree with amusement. 'Would you like to have her? Maybe someday I'll give her to you. What do you say to that?'

Bewildered, Embree looks at the ground.

'Well? Would you like her, my friend?' Chin pokes the girl's arm; she faces the tent, avoiding the eyes of the two men. 'I think she'd like to be with you. What do you say?' he whispers in her ear, giggling. 'I think you'd like the foreigner.'

'Tell her,' Embree says, feeling a warmth in his face, 'I'm not afraid of dying.'

'But are you afraid of her?'

Chin's laughter follows Embree as he turns and strides briskly away. He won't look back for fear of meeting the girl's dark eyes. Once out of her presence, his mind focuses on one fact: Tomorrow, on nothing more than suspicion, they are going to kill the Englishman.

The horror of it dispels his enthusiasm, which has been mounting the past few days, for the bandits and their way of life. One of his own, a Christian man of his race, will be cold-bloodedly murdered; the idea is not real.

This entire country is not real, Embree thinks, as he wanders among the tents searching for the Englishman. Everywhere he goes the young American asks for the other foreigner. People regard him curiously, as if they have never heard of the Englishman. Through the smoky camp Embree wanders, unable to confirm the man's existence, much less learn his whereabouts. Under the circumstances Embree finds it difficult to hold on to reality. He tries to anchor himself in a world beyond this mountain-top with its yurts and bandits and smoking fires. In the rose Bowl last year Alabama and Stanford tied seven all. The great football players Oosterbaan, Nagurski, Grange, and Nevers. He holds on to these facts. He tries to recall the population of the United States, the name of every teacher he had in divinity school, the color of Ursula's eyes.

Later, when he has eaten the evening meal surrounded by curious faces at a campfire, Embree sits near a yurt in desperate solitude. He smells the leather, smoke, and excrement. He listens to laughter, the impatient shuffling of hooves as the ponies ready themselves for sleep. It is all real. And God is real. What has the Almighty thought of him since his capture? Has God been disgraced by the ease with which His servant donned the clothes and manner of these heathen who defile women and slaughter the innocent? His father would hide his face in shame to think that an Embree, bearer of the Lord's word for generations, would have so quickly forgotten his heritage, his faith.

'The Lord testeth the righteous; but the wicked and him who loveth violence his soul hateth.'

Promptly the young missionary gets on his knees and puts his hands together in the attitude of prayer. It doesn't matter that people nearby are giggling. Embree prays for the soul of the doomed Englishman, then prays for his own; he moves from these prayers to a supplication for courage in the event that he too is executed.

He will show the girl how he can die.

Embree's hands lower to his sides as he contemplates the scene: He standing in front of the executioner or executioners (how many will they use?), and she watching him with those dark disturbing eyes. And the thought of it braces him more than prayer. If the Shanghai Mission raises the ransom in time, he will live. If not, he will die like a man. The resolve is so overpowering that Embree feels the payment of that ransom might deprive him of the greatest moment in his life.

3

Qufu at dawn. It is the Hour of the Hare. Objects begin detaching themselves from the blackness of night to assume crepuscular outline: tree, gateway, roof. A thin brassy light is easing across the eastern sky, uncovering a town, its clay roads radiating from an old drum tower with roofing of tubular green tiles. Set off by a high brick wall, a huge enclosure rises from the early light, revealing wooden pavilions with scarlet columns and orange roofs. At one roof's curving end a fierce creature takes shape in the spreading glow: Winged and fanged, a dragon of glazed ceramic is glaring down at a park of evergreens. Pines and cypresses, many of them centuries old, stand alongside upright slabs of granite on which inscriptions have been chiseled to commemorate events and visits that took place here long before the trees were planted. The stone messages swirl out of the mist. Early sunlight begins to gather and slide across shaggy greens and white parapets, to enwrap in gold the pillars of the main gateway, its tall posts mounted with two stone warriors who have stood guard here a thousand years. Between marble railings, within the third gateway, runs a sluggish thread of water, dotted with summer lotuses and spanned by three halfmoon marble bridges. From here the pavilions and halls, more than six hundred of them, emerge from the mist, along with nine courtyards and many steles, a few from the Han Dynasty – two thousand years old – some carried into eternity on the backs of stone tortoises. The ancient greenery, the elegant halls, the potted trees and sculpture, all attest to the sacredness of this spot, holiest in China, for this is the temple of Kong Fusi, the sage known in the West as Confucius.

East of the temple lies another large complex of buildings. This is the home of his descendants, called by imperial decree 'the Dukes of Extended Sagehood.' Seventy-six generations of Kongs have acted as custodians of his exalted memory. In turn they have been spared by succeeding governments and dynasties the ordinary fate of mandarins: looting during war, taxes during peace. Their present mansion was restored during the last century; many of the buildings are now in need of repair, but in the present chaos the Kong family cannot obtain a government allotment to do the renovation.

Even so, within the temple grounds a timeless calm is palpable, is deepened too by the early hour and soft light. Confucius walked here five hundred years before the birth of Christ; and on this lovely morning he might well be walking here again – a tall man in a simple gown, listening to birdsong in the pines or sitting on a stone bench to compose poetry or merely watching another man who at the moment is playing Tai Chi Chuan in a courtyard.

Dressed in loose cotton trousers and tunic, the Tai Chi player is moving across the flagstones at a snail's pace: left foot, right foot, each raised and lowered with the composure of a heron striding through a pond.

This man is General Tang Shan-teh, Defense Commissioner of Southern Shantung Province.

Having started before dawn, he is now halfway through the final section of an exercise as old as the courtyard in which he practices. He has passed beyond the usual admonitions a player gives himself: Breathe as if the breath is silk drawn slowly from a cocoon; make each motion continue into the next, so none is complete in itself; stay alert but feel empty in the round world. He tells himself nothing. He has no expectations, not even the wish to find whatever mystery the great masters discovered at the heart of Tai Chi Chuan. He simply moves. His body begins to feel limitless; the rounded motion of arm and leg draws to him the world outside, and the outside world merges into the spaces encompassed by the motion: pine tree, finch darting in azalea leaves, flagstones struck by sunlight. This is the core of paradox: he is here but not here; both here and there; neither there nor here. But that familiar idea will occur to him later, not now, not while his body moves through Needle at Sea Bottom, Raise Arms Like Fan, White Snake Puts Out Tongue – intricately balanced patterns of motion that follow the rhythm of breath. His mind remains uninvolved, motionless, as blank as the wall.

Toward the end of the exercise, however, his breath loses its mastery of the motion; mind collapses back into body. The General discovers his arms and legs are moving correctly toward the final patterns. Then, in the completed calm, he feels his breath go out as it pleases, releasing him from the tension of what he realizes has been ecstasy.

Standing with head lowered, absorbing the last of that pleasure, he stares at the pebble mosaic underfoot in the courtyard. It was a good decision to play Yang this morning. The sequence is shorter and he'd have been too restless for the more demanding Chen style of Tai Chi.

One hand fisted at the small of his back, he leaves the courtyard and heads for his quarters in the West Wing of the Kong Residence. He passes through a labyrinth of covered galleries that lead to halls for study, unused guesthouses, and abandoned libraries. Although roofing tiles have fallen from some of the small buildings and vermilion paint has peeled off many of the wooden columns, the look of disrepair is compensated for by flowers. Gardeners are already out this morning, carrying porcelain pots and trowels. Who in the world loves flowers as we Chinese do? the General asks himself with satisfaction. Beyond a trellis overgrown with wisteria, he comes abruptly to a portico fronting a long, plain wooden barracks. It houses members of his staff – a cheaply constructed military building in the midst of roses and oleander.

The present Kong Duke insisted last year that the General put it up for the staff. The Duke wants the army here in Qufu and will make any concessions necessary to keep it. Nevertheless, General Tang restricts his officers to the immediate area and won't allow them to wander into either the central yamen or the East Wing, both used by the Kong family and their secretaries and servants. Tang wants to spare the Kongs any discomfort because of the military presence – which, in fact, they so welcome. During these troubled times it's a safeguard for the Kongs to have such an army in their midst. Royalty for two thousand years, they have never understood what has happened to China since 1911 when the trouble began. They heard from afar about the strikes and rioting against the Imperial Manchu Government, then about the Manchu defeat. They heard with satisfaction that the southern revolutionary, Doctor Sun Yat-sen, had performed a solemn rite of respect in front of the Nanking tomb of the founder of the Ming, the last native dynasty in China. They heard with indifference, however, that he'd been made provisional president of the new Republic and had chosen a cabinet. Later, they heard that the Boy Emperor, after the actual fact of dethronement, had abdicated formally and with his court had retired to Jehol behind the Great Wall.

At Qufu they received a new president, Yuan Shih-k'ai, who dissolved the parliament that elected him, then promulgated a new constitution by which he assumed for a short time the power of a dictator. In conversation with the General the Kong Patriarch still mentions Yuan today: a gruff, rotund old man with a white plumed hat and a chestful of medals, who had to be helped up after kowtowing to the statue of the Great Sage in the main temple. From a distance the Kongs heard with vague displeasure of Yuan's desire to establish a constitutional monarchy – the very name seemed even more threatening than a republic. The Kongs were told that he got the parliamentary votes through intimidation, then dissolved the assembly again and made plans to create a new dynasty to replace the Manchu. He had even chosen his reign title – *Hung Hsien* (Glorious Constitutionalism) – but died before climbing to the Dragon Chariot. And then, safely ensconced in the Qufu of their ancestors, the Kongs heard of the terrible bickering among Yuan's successors, who couldn't seem to solve the questions of government: civilian or military rule, central power or provincial autonomy, a strong president or a strong parliament. In consequence, the Kongs watched with growing dismay how order began to break down everywhere; they came to realize that their own tradition might be a victim of the chaos.

It was then that General Tang acted. He had recently been appointed Defense Commissioner of the southern half of the province by Marshal Chang Tso-lin (ostensibly by the Premier and the Minister of War, neither of whom had any say in the matter). The move, Tang well knew, had been taken by Chang Tso-lin to keep his vassal, Chang Tsung-ch'ang, in line. The vassal controlled the rest of the province. When Tang accepted his new post, the main elements of his army had been billeted in Jining, on the Grand Canal southwest of Qufu. The town controlled the canal traffic and had rail facilities as well. But after a meeting with the Kong Duke of Extended Sagehood, who had heard rumors of both bandits in the countryside and warlords in nearby provinces speaking covetously of temple wealth in Qufu, the General moved an army corps to the town. The troops are garrisoned on the outskirts, the officers and himself and their headquarters right in the Residence.

Approaching the staff barracks now, he hears loud talk and laughter, which stop when he strolls past the first window of the line. Voices rise again once he's in the next courtyard. Here comes his old servant Yao, carrying a hooded exercise cage for one of the General's canaries. Tang halts a moment to lift the back cloth cover and peer inside. Then Yao is off again, swinging the cage to simulate for the imprisoned songbird the motion of a tree branch in brisk wind. To keep its balance the bird must flex its muscles, thereby getting the exercise that makes for good singing. Yao will walk each of the three male singers in turn; he has been walking birds for half a century. The General never fails to look back and watch the old fellow shuffling through the courtyard, swinging the bamboo cage, bowed legs traveling rapidly across the flagstone past the dwarf trees in their shallow pots. Tang watches him for the sake of humility. It is unlikely that anyone in the present generation will match such a stride in old age. Often Tang sees the man in the evening, sitting on a porcelain taboret to view the moon.

Suddenly Tang sees Su-su rounding a corner of the Hall of Inner Peace. She must have just left his quarters. She had been with him last night. A few months ago she had been given to him as a testament of good will by the mayor of Lin Yi, who in turn had obtained her from a landlord seeking favors. At first Tang had accepted her out of courtesy without the intention of making her his mistress – a strictly celibate life of some months had appealed to him. But it had not been long before she appealed to him more than a Taoist concept he was merely experimenting with.

Su-su doesn't see him and disappears behind the green-and-gold building.

Remaining on his retina is the image of her back hair, plaited in braids that reach to the swell of her buttocks. While he has been exercising, Su-su has been nimbly working those strands of hair into thick black swinging ropes. The sight of them recalls the previous evening, when he clutched that jasmine-scented hair in his spasmodic fingers at the moment of greatest pleasure.

Finished with a simple breakfast of millet gruel and persimmons (the same fare eaten by his troops encamped on the outskirts of town), General Tang sits at a rosewood desk (compliments of the Kong family) under a scroll of mountains in a mist. A punkah hangs motionless from the ceiling, although the morning has begun to heat up. Yang, his aide-de-camp, stands at the General's shoulder and hands him one document after another.

This one is a blue-tinted engraved invitation from the Shanghai Rowing Club. Tang is pleased by it, although he has no intention of standing alongside intoxicated Britishers while rich yachtsmen founder in Soochow Creek. The invitation means he continues to be regarded with respect by those who study the political scene.

'Refuse with polite regrets,' the General tells his aide and studies the next letter. He glances up at the aide, realizing that Yang has held this one back – the young man has a gift for drama. Behind the airy compliments and profound regrets is a refusal by the provincial government to pay the monthly defense appropriation. There's no real explanation for withholding funds that the General needs to maintain his army. It is doubly regrettable because yesterday the Peking central government declared its own inability to pay him his stipend. Inability? Deliberate refusal. It has happened before in recent times. Withholding a stipend is one way of keeping military officers in line. Chang Tso-lin in Peking and Chang Tsung-ch'ang in Jinan have held up the General's stipend to bring him under control. He knows what they want – his public agreement to give more provincial concessions to the Japanese. In Manchuria, with Chang Tso-lin's help, the Japanese government has built railroads and taken over vast timber lands. Now Chang Tso-lin and his vassal want to help their Japanese friends push beyond Tsingtao into the western and southern parts of Shantung – and perhaps farther.

The General won't aid them in the scheme. Never. It is a betrayal of his country and his clan.

Even so, his refusal to cooperate may bring him down. Where can he find the money to pay troops and buy arms? He controls his features under Yang's steady gaze.

There's faint but persistent knock at the door. At the General's command a thin old man enters the room. Dressed in rags he shuffles forward, mottled lips working. He's a camp beggar who claims to be a Taoist monk. Actually he's a former soldier who long ago served in a regiment commanded by General Tang's father. Every few days he comes to consult the Yarrow Stalk Oracle for the General; in this way he gets enough money to buy a few pipes of opium.

The General has little time to spare and because of the bad news little inclination to have his fortune told, yet he won't offend someone who served his father loyally; controlling his impatience, he tells the old fellow to proceed. Counting out fifty dried stalks of the yarrow plant onto the desk, the beggar discards one and divides the remaining stalks into two random heaps. He then places a few stalks between his dirty fingers, counts in a high but commanding voice, then discards them and gathers up more. 'A nine plus an eight plus an eight,' he says. 'Each with a value of two makes six. The old *yin*.' With a nub of pencil taken from the same worn bag that held the yarrow stalks, he draws two shaky lines on a crumpled piece of paper, also taken from the bag. He picks up more stalks, resumes the complicated counting, and repeats the procedure five more times, until he has drawn the following pattern:

Bending over to study it, the old man shivers into life, his eyes gleam, his pointing finger steadies. 'Not one line that is still. See that? Not one,' he exclaims, a puff of spittle on his lips. 'Old *yin* and *yang*, all moving. All six moving. Look.' His dirty finger jabs at the top three lines. 'See that, Excellency? Heaven.' Then he jabs at the bottom three. 'Water.' He strokes his chin like a physician making a grim diagnosis. 'General, your Excellency, this is the hexagram of Conflict. See how the trigrams move away from each other? Heaven is upward, but Water goes down. They move in opposite ways, definitely. Now, with your permission –' Without awaiting it, he draws a thumb-worn Book of Changes from his rags and flips pages until he stops to read aloud: ' "Conflict. Although sincere, you are being obstructed. A cautious halt halfway brings good fortune. Going through to the end brings misfortune. It furthers one to see the great man. It does not further one to cross the great water." '

The old man parts his lips in anticipation. 'Excellency, have you been obstructed today?'

Glancing at the letter on his desk, the General guffaws ruefully. 'Yes, I think I have been obstructed today.' The old man smiles in triumph. 'I gather from the oracle some people are blocking my way, but I must be patient.'

'Yes, Excellency, it's what the oracle says.'

'But who is the great man?'

'the oracle will not say, General. But crossing the water, if I may be permitted, means there is danger in starting anything new.'

'Perhaps that's always true,' the General says with a smile.

The old man squints hard at his worn book. 'It says conflict within can destroy the power to conquer danger without, Excellency.'

Tang feels no inner conflict, so he tells himself that's an insight wasted on him. He knows what he is doing, why, and where he wants to go.

'We must consult the interpretation of the Duke of Chou,' the old man continues, 'because of so many moving lines in the hexagram.' From another section of the book he reads again, then points at the split bottom line, 'The Duke of Chou says if old *yin*, the six, comes at the beginning of the Sung hexagram, the thing to do is drop the issue, especially when the adversary is stronger. Don't push for a decision, Excellency. In the end all goes well.' When the old man, pausing for breath, looks down to read farther, Tang halts him.

'No more today, thank you.' He nods at his aide, who comes forward.

'But, Excellency,' persists the old man, 'if I may be permitted, all six lines are moving. It is a difficult hexagram – strength above, danger below. We must consult the ancient commentaries as well.'

'Tomorrow,' Tang tells him with a smile.

The aide Yang thrusts a tael into his hand. With a low bow, still muttering, 'A difficult hexagram,' the old man shuffles out of the room.

The General rereads the letter from Jinan about the stipend. It comes from the Shantung Province Ministry of Finance, under the signature of someone named Chao Heng-t'i. A minor functionary has just informed him that an army of forty thousand men won't be given funds to feed and arm them. Neither Peking nor Jinan wants the army to disintegrate; it would leave a vacuum that rival warlords would rush to fill. Chang Tso-lin in Peking and Chang Tsung-ch'ang in Jinan simply want to pressure the General into accepting the idea of expanded Japanese concessions in the province. They must have considered relieving him of command, but at present he's very popular in Shantung, having repelled the invasion of a southern warlord at the border last year and thereby prevented wholesale plunder of towns and villages. The two Changs are going to make life very unpleasant for him and his troops, but he will not give in. He will not let the Japanese crawl through his own countryside. He will not.

'Yang,' he says, 'have you any more surprises for me this morning?'

'Excellency?'

Tang looks at the smooth young cheeks, the bushy eyebrows, the complaisant expression – a steady young man and resourceful. The General pushes aside the papers with a sigh. Then he puts on a full uniform (but without insignia), a Sam Browne belt, a visored cap, and black riding boots. He holsters a Webley-Fosbery

.455-caliber semiautomatic. He hates the British yet has chosen one of their weapons for his own. Paradox and contradiction shape his world, a thought that follows him into the sunlight of midmorning. Perhaps he's more beset by conflict than he knows. Sometimes the reading of the oracle upsets him. At the outset he never believes the old beggar and the book; later he frequently does. His father always believed in the oracle, but perhaps a man of today, aware of Western science, can't give himself entirely to the ancient Book of Changes. Yet the General often ends by believing it. Twenty-five centuries ago the Great Sage counted the yarrow stalks here in this same town of Qufu. And only this morning perhaps the authority of the old book has been demonstrated once again. It is true, as the Sung hexagram claims, that the General is beset by enemies and surely is in danger of losing everything if he pushes too hard, too fast. The old man with the wretched little bag of yarrow stalks must not be discounted. Confucius taught humility for good reason.

The General rides out of town with an escort of young officers. His chestnut mare seems exhilarated by the brilliant light, the gusty wind. Cucumber patches and onion fields dominate the plain, except toward the north, where a division of his army is now billeted. Row on row of brown tents usurp the ground there, with long flimsy shacks housing the stored machine guns, howitzers, and ammunition. The smoke of cooking fires and camp dust mingle overhead in a low cloud that is visible for miles in this flat country. The General leads his retinue down a rutted lane toward the camp. He gallops the last hundred yards toward the smells of horse and leather, the sounds of thudding feet and brisk command. Officers button their tunics and straighten their caps when they see him approaching, and sweepers pause over their brooms to stare at the riders.

Colonel Pi takes the General on the daily inspection tour. The Colonel, a small dapper man who wears epaulettes, has selected a route that has been recently policed, a fact known to the General without asking. He does not expect to see leggings or shirts hanging on poles to dry or fruit peelings in the swept paths. The Colonel behaves as if he has total control of the camp, a foolish pose in the General's opinion. No one truly controls the camp of a Chinese army, whose members are peasants, an obstinate and deceptive crew if ever there was one. Tang wishes for a little more humility from Pi, a little more good-natured acknowledgment of the facts of military life in field tents. He has yet to place his trust in the Colonel, although the fellow is now acting as his new chief of staff. Wu Sheng-chi would never have selected the neatest route for inspection. Not Wu, a man capable of calling his men 'my flea-bitten mongrels' while sending them home to visit ailing parents on his own money.

The General halts the tour near a field where infantry platoons are raising dust at calisthenics. 'Nothing yet?' he asks the Colonel.

Pi shakes his head. He has a round face, the high color of a heated boy in his cheeks. 'This is the third day, Excellency. It should come today.'

'It should, but will it?' the General comments dryly.

Nearby is a wooden shed with a tin trough in front of it and behind it a deep ditch filled with quicklime – a latrine. Next to the latrine sits a cage of bamboo, about waist high. Wedged inside is a naked man, feet and legs bound to a stool, hands tied behind his back. Between his knees a bamboo stake has been driven into the ground, with its sharp point positioned so it just touches his throat. If his head drops forward, the stake will impale him.

The General kneels beside the bamboo ribbing and studies the man inside. Midday heat, beating on the cage, turns it into a caldron. A mustache of sweat beads the prisoner's upper lip; rivulets roll down his forehead and fall into his eyes. Blinking away the moisture, he keeps his gaze fixed straight ahead, signaling the intensity of his concentration on the need to remain motionless.

General Tang appreciates the man's difficulty. After two days in the cage, he must be giddy from lack of sleep and prey to moments of panic when it becomes cruelly apparent that he can't fight off sleep forever. But will he give in soon? The Colonel maintained confidently that the prisoner should give in today, but in twenty years of military life the General has learned never to judge the courage or stamina of any man. Never. He leaves such judgments to others, like the young colonel whose battle experience has been limited so far to several skirmishes and one major encounter last year. Through the narrow spaces between the bamboo, Tang notices a smear of dried blood zigzagging down the prisoner's throat. So he must have nodded off for a moment and let his head jerk forward. Two days already, the third begun. Time is the master, always. Time is going to win. Time will break anyone. But how long will it take with this fellow?

Long ago Tang saw a man caged in this fashion, which is why he is using the procedure now. At that time the prisoner had decided to die rather than confess to whatever the charge was – Tang has forgotten. But he has never forgotten what the man did: arched his head backward as far as possible, then, with his remaining strength, drove his throat down hard upon the stake. At least that had been the plan. But at the last instant the man had drawn back, so the stake had not penetrated deeply enough; as a consequence the man took a long time strangling on his own blood.

His mouth close to the bamboo slats, Tang demands quickly, 'Who sent you? Where do you come from?' Receiving no answer, he adds, 'Tell me and you'll get out of there. I promise you on my father's grave.'

Blinking rapidly, the man continues to look at the bamboo a handsbreadth away. His mind is steady on his fear and determination.

'Who sent you?' With a gloved hand the General flicks away a fly buzzing near his nose. Long ago the flies have discovered that the caged creature can't defend itself, so they stride the naked flesh like a conquered land, busy at every orifice.

'Who sent you with the head?'

General Tang waits, flicking at more flies. He asks again, 'Who sent you? Believe me, it's a matter of importance. Do you think Tang Shan-teh will do nothing about it? The man was my friend. Who sent you?'

Shouting from the exercise field briefly draws away the General's attention. Staring gloomily in that direction, he mops his forehead with a handkerchief. To the cage he says again, 'Who sent you? White Wolf? I think so. This looks like the work of his men. Nobody else would be that stupid.'

The prisoner swallows. Carefully. But the movement brings his throat down on the point, making an indentation at the contact. Muscled tension ripples along his jawline.

Tang remains kneeling. Apparently the prisoner will be very difficult. A week ago this man walked an exhausted horse into Qufu. He had a burlap bag slung over his back. Guards had not stopped the dusty traveler, who might have had a pumpkin in the bag. But a young soldier – since then promoted to corporal – had grown suspicious of a bag the wine color of dried blood. In the ensuing capture of the man, he had knifed a recruit. Beaten in prison, he remained silent. During the interrogation one testicle was smashed, an arm broken. More beatings and there would have been no one left to interrogate. That was why the General had decided the cage would be more effective.

'Tell me who sent you,' he persists, 'and I'll give you a reward. You'll get medical attention and your horse back. Is it White Wolf? Where is he?' The General stares between the slats at the naked, sweaty man with Mongolian features. A strong odor of urine drifts from the cage. So he can still urinate. Tang is impressed, but such stamina is also irritating. Inside the cage is his country's hope and despair. Submitting to torture is a peasant whose family has tilled the soil for centuries and extracted from it, with help from no one but with the relentless hindrance of tax collectors and landlords and bandits, enough grain to stay alive just long enough to produce yet another generation to suffer on that selfsame earth. Tang looks at the man who seems content to die for a brute like White Wolf. Because his brain, shaped by millenniums of acceptance of authority, has formed the idea that by obeying an order, any order given by someone in authority, he can save his own life, or perhaps more important, somehow protect his ancestors' land.

Getting to his feet, the General puts one fist at his back and watches the men exercising in the field. Some are climbing ropes hanging from a large frame; it was an exercise admired by Tang's father, and therefore Tang features it in the training of his own troops. The sky is the color of Shantung silk. And there is plenty of time, he thinks. Wherever the bandit White Wolf is, he will probably stay awhile. Opium and age have settled him down from the days when he roamed Central China like a *wonk*, a homeless dog.

Tang glances at the caged man. 'All right,' he says calmly, 'I can wait '

He continues the inspection with Colonel Pi: artillery sheds, field kitchens, the ammunition dump. But his mind holds fast to the loss he has sustained: Wu Sheng-chi, gifted officer, close friend. Wu had studied artillery three years at the famous Shikan Gakko Military Academy in Japan. And on the night the General's second and favorite wife died of fever, Wu sat with him until dawn, one hand on his shoulder. Tang has never forgotten that hand on his shoulder, and now a Mongolian barbarian has dared to execute Wu Sheng-chi.

72

'I want a company of horse ready to leave at a moment's notice,' he tells the Colonel when they sit at a table under the shady gallery of an adobe battalion headquarters. 'Horses saddled, men fully equipped. Give me the Big Swords. I want them ready if I snap my fingers.'

'Now, Excellency?'

'Of course now. When the man talks, we leave.'

'You will command?'

Tang looks at him disdainfully. Is it necessary to explain his need for revenge? Tang pours himself tea from a pot on the table. He stares at a nearby shed in which foundrymen are repairing old machine guns that will probably jam anyway after firing a few hundred rounds. The two letters denying him funds – they are like pronouncements of incurable illness in a family. 'Yes, of course I will command,' he tells the Colonel.

'This morning we caught two deserters.'

Tang glances at the cherubic face of his chief of staff. 'How many this week?'

'Eight.'

Men restless for their pay or farmers who want to go home for the harvest.

'We caught them in a village about fifteen kilometers south of here. They raped a girl.'

'Shoot them. Are they recruits?'

'I'm afraid not, General. One has been with you a long time.'

The General shakes his head. 'A pity. Have their company fall out in uniform to witness it. Have them dig their graves in front of the company. And give the company a bonus for watching. We are soldiers, not rapists.' In the shed a heavily muscled foundryman is hammering on the leg of a machine-gun tripod. What I need, Tang thinks, is a hundred Madsen or Hotchkiss or Vickers machine guns or the Revelli .50-caliber with heavy barrels, let alone pack howitzers and trench mortars, but in the Department of Finance of the Shantung Provincial Government a minor bureaucrat by the name of Chao Heng-t'i has decreed otherwise. If Confucius lived today, what would he do?

Tang sips his tea and watches the men in the exercise field strain at the climbing ropes.

Late afternoon finds him at his desk again. The three male

canaries are singing in the bedroom. It cheers Tang to think that the small bright creatures, even caged, can find sufficient beauty in themselves and the world to sing so joyously. When Su-su comes tonight, she will stop at each cage as always and put one finger against the slats.

The afternoon has been difficult. Huddling with his staff in the courtyard – cooler there than in the Conference Room – he discussed money, not tactics, ethics, not strategy. Like a recurrent nightmare, insolvency has plagued his military career – but then it plagues the whole country. Anywhere he turns, anyone he meets, the problem is always the same: money. Lack of it distorts judgment, leads to corruption, theft, violence. Provincial officials fail to report the activity of bandits for fear of not being compensated for the wireless message. Farmers sell their daughters to pay the rent. How can the precepts of Confucius apply to such a land? Tang is still shaken by the afternoon meeting at which the further taxation of an overtaxed population was discussed. Land taxes have already been collected three years in advance in his districts. The *likin*, the tax levied on goods in transit, might be increased and perhaps also include the transport of beancake, shoes, and opium lamps, which have not been taxed before, but the income thus raised would not be enough. The General has already floated military bonds in the cities of the province without much success. The staff went over each item of standard taxation for possible increases: grain, tea, cotton yarn, wheat vermicelli, paper. They advocated a higher surtax on foreign cigarettes, stiffer fees on the slaughtering of pigs, brothel and gambling-house licenses in the towns, and a few other items, but in sum the army needs a more comprehensive means of raising funds, now that Peking and Jinan have withheld the rightful stipends.

A staff officer at last suggested a desperate measure: The General could issue *zhun-yong-piao* – military notes, unsupported by any bank (they are all controlled by the Jinan government) but good enough to issue to the troops and purchase supplies from local merchants.

'Print our own currency?' Tang had said, looking hard at the young officer. 'Worthless paper!'

'It will give us time, Excellency, to make other financial arrangements.'

Another put in, 'It has been done in Honan.'

'In Anhwei too,' said another.

Expectantly they looked at the General, who understood the consequences of such an action: Within a short time the peasants will discover the money has no value, but until then they will accept it from troops for goods and services. In a few months they will realize that their military protector, a man of their own province and a leader of reputation, has cheated them as viciously as any landlord.

That afternoon General Tang agreed to the scheme; with a single act he sacrificed his hard-earned honor to expediency.

How sweetly the canaries sing, he thinks, rising from the desk and going to the lattice window. Through it, in the waning light, he sees across the courtyard the weathered patina of an old wall. How sweetly they sing. His favorite died of old age last year, but a young male of purest flaxen yellow is bringing new melody to the cage, leading the other two into extended periods of chorusing. He wishes for Su-su to hear them now. Love of songbirds is one thing he shares with the girl.

On a table the General examines the titles of a few books. He selects a volume – ragged from use – and turns the pages until he comes to a passage he has read often. It is from *The Three Kingdoms*, a novel about civil war in the third century. An adviser speaks to the beleaguered hero, Liu Pei, who wishes to restore good government to the country: 'If you cling to established principle, you will not be able to proceed at all. Rather, you should choose flexibility.'

How sweetly they sing, he thinks, pausing over the book before continuing the passage: 'When things are settled, if you make amends sensibly while enriching the land and bringing it new strength, what trust will you have betrayed? Remember, if you don't take power, another will.'

Of course. Another will, he thinks. Another has already taken more than his share: the young southerner, Chiang Kai-shek, has overrun a half-dozen provinces and taken Shanghai. The Bolsheviks control the central interior through the tricities of Wuhan. And Generals Chang and Feng dominate the North. Positioned between the North and the South, he himself holds the balance of power.

Nothing can be accomplished without an army. A third of his infantry carry old-fashioned gingalls and no grenades. He has opted for flexibility by deciding to issue military notes. And as *The Three Kingdoms* suggests, someday he will surely make amends, when he drives a wedge between existing alliances – when he reunites China under his own leadership.

Yet even a quotation from *The Three Kingdoms* is not enough authority to assuage his conscience. He can't match his perception of ancient virtue with the shabby compromises of today. Would the old Confucian scholars condone the issuance of worthless currency? It is a bitter question the General asks himself, even though he realizes that these wisemen are immortal precisely because their ideas have conformed to the shifting demands of each age.

He picks up another book, for it is his hour of study, set aside each day. The General is reading the work of Hsun Tzu, a philosopher who insisted that Man, though basically evil, by mastering his destiny can behave as though he is good. Before Tang has read a page, his aide enters the room.

A foreigner waits outside, accompanied by a Chinese translator. They have come to Qufu by pack horse.

A foreigner? By pack horse? Tang decides it must be a missionary or a scientist looking for old bones – no other foreigners take pack horses through this rugged country. 'If he's a missionary, tell him I send my deepest apologies.' He has encountered them before – men who insinuate themselves into camp by offering to treat the sick, then slink around talking of their God.

'This man is a Russian.' After a pause Yang adds, 'A Bolshevik.'

'Well, let him in.' Sitting back, the General looks across the room at a framed photograph of his father in uniform. From the wall the old man glares sternly at the room. He was a true Confucian, whose moral code, exquisitely precise, restricted his rise within a military system gone bad. From the wall he judges the world with steady eyes, his thin mouth set in commitment to principles no longer practiced. Tang feels the shock of his own betrayal of principles and is in a glum mood when the door opens.

Coming into the room is a towering fellow in the gray cotton of a peasant. His face is uncommonly white, however, even for a foreigner, below a bulbous nose is a thick black mustache. It amuses the General to see the Russian wearing the garb of a Chinese peasant. It puts him into a better mood, this foreigner's blatant attempt to hide self-interest behind some cotton yarn.

Alongside the brawny Russian stands a small, rather youthful

Chinese, who at least looks comfortable in the peasant clothes. He sports a wispy goatee. 'Your Excellency, may I present Comrade Kovalik, who has been sent by the government of the Soviet Socialist Republics to give you assistance in the struggle against reactionary forces in your province.'

Nodding blandly, Tang appraises the young Russian. Blue eyes, heavy lidded, reptilian. An expression either placid or stupid. Broad shoulders, broad. A little paunch already – perhaps the fellow is self-indulgent. Big feet in soft cotton slippers which have been specially made, because no Chinese could keep them on. Someone has tried, unsuccessful, to give this mountainous Russian the look of a Chinese coolie. It is indeed amusing. Tang approaches the interview with a certain zest.

The goateed interpreter is fulsomely expressing Comrade Kovalik's gratitude.

Gratitude for what? They're a tiresome pair!

'I ask your permission,' the interpreter continues, 'to state the purpose of Comrade Kovalik's visit.'

'I thought you already did,' Tang says bluntly. 'He wants to help me with reactionary forces.'

'He will consider it a privilege, Excellency.'

Tang claps his hands twice. Yao appears in the doorway and takes the order for tea.

'Is your Russian asking for asylum?' Tang says to the interpreter.

'No, of course not, Excellency.'

'Because Russian Bolsheviks are not very welcome in China any more.'

While the interpreter translates, the big Russian crosses his legs awkwardly and stares at his huge slippered feet.

He is stupid, Tang thinks.

Finally the Russian speaks, in a deep bass voice, and the interpreter translates: With all due respect to his Excellency, General Tang, it is not accurate to say that the Russian people are no longer welcomed by the Chinese people. It is of course true that the renegade warlord Chang Tso-lin engineered a raid on the Soviet Embassy in Peking, which resulted in preposterous charges that the Russian diplomatic corps was engaging in espionage and other clandestine activities, but otherwise Russia has always worked diligently to foster good relations with Peking.

Tang knows this much: Marshal Chang did in fact plan the raid, but the documents seized there pointed to Russian involvement in Chinese affairs. He knows this too: The evidence linked the Russians with his own archenemy to the north, General Feng Yu-hsiang.

With huge hands balled in his lap as if to help him concentrate, the Soviet agent continues to speak through his interpreter. It is also true, he says, that the southern outlaw, Chiang Kai-shek, has turned ignominiously against his Russian friends and advisers, who in the past gave him arms and helped him in many ways. It is common knowledge, for example, that they helped him found the Whampoa Military Academy in which he was able to train young officers loyal to his own personal command.

It is indeed common knowledge, the General thinks; he has envied the southerner the chance to train a loyal cadre of young officers.

Furthermore (the Soviet agent continues through his interpreter) it is regrettably true that when Chiang Kai-shek undertook the Northern Expedition in an effort to conquer all of China for himself, *whatever was required for the push had been supplied by Soviet aides*: logistic plans, field tactics, propaganda strategies, everything. The Russian agent leans forward to claim, however, that Mikhail Borodin was convinced this military adventure would only further divide the nation and lead to more bloodshed without solving the problem of national unity. As a consequence of upholding principles of harmony and good faith, Mikhail Borodin and other Soviet advisers fared badly at the hands of Chiang Kai-shek and his Kuomintang henchmen.

Tang notices that the Russian is sweating profusely. Is it the heat or the effort of putting together this little speech?

The interpreter translates the final words. 'Comrade Kovalik, as a representative of the Union of Soviet Socialist Republics, wishes to express his government's sustained desire to help true Chinese patriots such as yourself. Comrade Kovalik is not discouraged by the behavior of Chaing Kai-shek and the other running dogs of imperialism. He is here to serve you and through you China.'

The Russian's not stupid, Tang thinks, but suffers from the garrulity of the idealistic young. For a moment the General remembers a speech he gave once in a town to a crowd of bedazzled villagers who understood not a word of his patriotic fervor. He had been a new lieutenant then, bedazzled himself by his own words. Tang smiles at the recollection even as he turns to the goateed interpreter. 'This huge Russian you brought here – what do you know about him?'

Before the interpreter can reply, Yao comes with tea. The General, a hospitable host, waits until his guests have sipped their tea before sipping his own. 'It's a poor brew,' Tang murmurs.

'We are deeply grateful for your consideration, Excellency.'

Tang stares at the young interpreter, who is not stupid either. 'What's your name?'

'Li Chung-lin, Excellency. You asked me about Comrade Kovalik –'

'Wait.' The General glances at the big Russian, who is staring at his hands, resting again, palms placidly up, in his lap. 'First tell the comrade I'm asking you about *your* background.'

Li speaks to the Russian, who nods solemnly.

'You told him,' the General declares, 'I was asking about him.'

Li blinks rapidly. 'Do you understand Russian then, Excellency?'

'No, but it's only natural you tell your comrade what I'm really asking. Have you been a Communist long?'

'Yes, Excellency.'

'Tell me about your Russian.'

'There's not much I know. Some months ago he arrived in Wuhan.'

'How does he intend helping me?'

'Well, Excellency, he's a military expert.'

Tang glances at the big fellow, who still looks down at his hands in an attitude which can suggest either calm assurance or embarrassed indecisiveness. Which is it? Tang wonders. 'So your boy is a soldier.'

'He isn't a boy, Excellency. He's more than thirty.'

There's an impertinence in Li's voice that the General dislikes. Perhaps communism strips a man of good manners.

'Comrade Kovalik fought in the Russian Revolution and the Civil War,' Li says. 'He has a saber scar on his left arm.'

'Was he an artilleryman?'

'A cavalryman. An officer.'

The General needs an artillery expert now that Wu, his chief of staff, is dead. His cavalry officers are the best in his army, so if he lets the Russian stay, he won't be getting the advice his troops could use from a foreigner, he will only be getting a foreigner. 'So

79

you both came from Wuhan,' he says to the interpreter.

'Yes, Excellency.'

He is interested in their coming from Wuhan, a city that at the beginning of the year became the ideological battleground of China. Communists, joined by their Soviet advisers, and radical followers of the late Sun Yat-sen arrived there to form an alliance with right-wing politicians from the Kuomintang Party. It was a shaky alliance which Chiang Kai-shek made untenable when he broke with the Communists and began a purge of other left-wingers from the KMT ranks. In his Qufu headquarters Tang has received reports of Wuhan politicians choosing sides: Chiang Kai-shek or the radicals. He has heard that the Chinese Bolsheviks have been unable to maintain an alliance with either side, and their mentors, the Russians, have been helpless in fostering the Bolshevik cause during this political turmoil. Tang expects all these warring factions ultimately to collapse, leaving the northern militarists, himself among them, in the ascendancy. For the moment he forgets the Soviet adviser. 'What's happening now in Wuhan?' he asks Li.

'Chiang Kai-shek is losing ground.'

'Really?'

'Defectors from the Kuomintang are coming to the city every day, hundreds of them. They are joining the radical movement.'

'I understand one of the radical generals, General Hsia, has defected to Chiang Kai-shek. Is my information incorrect?'

'Permit me, Excellency, but I think his defection is a rumor.'

'Is it also a rumor that Changsha has fallen?' A few days ago the General received a wireless message to that effect: a combined force of Bolsheviks and other radicals had lost a pitched battle to KMT troops.

The interpreter is silent.

'I have another question,' Tang says, already knowing what the answer will be. 'Does your Russian comrade still believe in Mikhail Borodin?'

'He does, Excellency. So do I,' Li adds boldly.

'Will you explain then how Borodin can maintain control of Wuhan – torn apart, we both know, by factions?'

'Permit me, Excellency, but control isn't the correct word to describe what Comrade Borodin wants in Wuhan. He wants only to give us advice.'

'Your comrade here' – Tang smiles in the Russian's

direction – 'Seems to think his country has a great deal of influence on ours.'

Li hesitates before replying. It is clear to the General that Li is fearful of saying too much in defense of Russia. At last the interpreter says, 'I think, Excellency, foreigners sometimes overestimate their influence.'

'I'm relieved you understand that. Why then are you here?' When he sees the interpreter turn toward the Russian, Tang adds quickly, 'Don't ask him. You tell me.'

'We came here because you're the best of the northern generals.'

'Who told you that?'

'Borodin himself.'

'I've never met Borodin.'

'But he knows of you, General. He said –' Li pauses thoughtfully. 'He said, no matter what happens to the Comintern in China, we must support the best men, even those who are unsympathetic to communism. Borodin sent us here.'

Although the interpreter has spoken those words with a show of sincerity, Tang is cautious about believing them. In fact, he doesn't have to be told the real reason for the two Bolsheviks appearing in his camp. Having lost the South and being in the process of losing Central China, the Communists want some kind of foothold in the North. Well, not a foothold, maybe a toehold. Or maybe not even that. The General glances at the two men; neither can count for much in Moscow. Nor can they count for much here in Qufu. For a moment he pities them. Should he let them stay? If he does, they will surely try to indoctrinate his troops, although to what ultimate purpose he can't imagine, given the sorry state of communism in China today. They can do him no harm; the question is, can they do him any good?

'I know what happens when Bolsheviks get into an army camp,' he says gruffly to the little goateed interpreter. 'I want my men left alone. No Communist speeches.'

Li nods, plainly disappointed. 'We had hoped to speak informally, in small groups. Not about communism but about matters in general.' Li opens his hands out and smiles. 'As a kind of diversion. To stimulate thinking in general. That could be a way of helping you. A small way, but a way, Excellency.'

Should he let them remain in camp? Confucius said, Keep your enemy near enough to touch, your friend at a distance. And perhaps he might benefit from having a Soviet agent here.

'Very well.' Tang claps his hands on his knees decisively. 'You can stay. I'm not yet sure how you can serve – certainly not by making speeches on matters in general.' He looks at the Russian, who sits there like a big sulky boy, yet the impression may well be a wrong one. 'I need arms,' Tang says. 'Perhaps your Russian can persuade Moscow to send me some.'

'He will do what he can. Believe me,' Li says earnestly, 'Comrade Kovalik will try.'

Tang begins to describe weapons he needs with the growing enthusiasm of someone daydreaming about a long-treasured hope. '– and armored cars. Two, three.' Outrageous – only a few warlords in all of China can afford them. But when Li translates the request, Kovalik nods confidently. So Tang continues, allowing his hope to rise beyond reason. 'I need hand grenades – the potato masher. I need ammo for Moisin-Nagant rifles. I have five hundred in storage, but no ammo.'

When Li translates, the Russian's eyes grow wide. 'Comrade Kovalik is surprised you have Russian rifles.'

Tang smiles. He won't explain they were purchased from an arms dealer who tricked him – and others as well. The man was Swedish. Tang understands the Swede escaped from China much richer than when he came. For almost two years the rifles, oiled and wrapped, have lain in their shipping boxes. 'I also need ammo for a few thousand Austrian Mannlicher 8-millimeter and German Mauser 7.92-millimeter rifles. Translate that carefully.'

While Li translates, the Russian listens and nods, flicking at mites that dance in swirls around his fleshy nose.

'As for machine guns, a few dozen Revellis. General Ma Chien has them. I understand they're practically jam free. Or the light Danish Madsens for assault. And I like your long Russian triangular bayonets. Are you getting it all?' The General waits for the translation to end before shifting to artillery. Then it occurs to him that desperation has blinded him to the truth: This big fellow will get nothing from Moscow. For a delicious moment the General has deluded himself; aware it is all a farce, he relaxes and pours another cup of tea.

Thoughtfully pulling on one ear, Kovalik has apparently put each request to memory.

Translating for him, Li says to the General, 'Your request will be put into writing and sent immediately through channels to

Moscow. He feels certain it will be honored.'

Tang smiles. 'How will the arms come through?'

After a short exchange, Li says, 'Across the Gobi by truck and pack camel. They can unload at Changchiakou near the Mongolian border and come by train from there.'

Intelligent, the General thinks; he smiles at the Russian: earnest, ambitious, more spirited than his bearish appearance would suggest. Even so, his superiors will view his recommendation with disdain or skepticism and, considering the present status of Russia in China, reject it.

Rising, the General ends the interview. 'Yes, we will talk more,' he says, accepting the proffered hand of the Russian and shaking it vigorously. Tang is surprised by the flaccid grip; perhaps the big fellow is afraid of his own strength. Tang watches him stride out of the room. Intelligent, but naïve. Something of a fool, even with that translator to set him right. He has come here anxious to promise the world for a chance to prove himself, although Moscow has probably given up hope of holding on here. Or if Trotsky and Stalin expected to alter the situation by helping generals uncommitted to either Chiang or the radicals – someone like himself – they would send more and better advisers. Kovalik is clearly expendable; therefore they can gamble and let his instinct carry him anywhere. Perhaps, Tang thinks, in a few days the Russian and the interpreter had better go. Or perhaps stay; it matters little.

What matters is the decision this afternoon, forcing him into a moral position beyond his imagining. Still, by paying the troops in military notes, he can save the Mex dollars in the coffer; since the Mexican silver is good on any Shanghai bank, he can use it to purchase weapons from the German arms dealer arriving tomorrow. If the fellow proves more honest than the Swede. The General understands that in Shanghai this man Luckner has a reputation for honesty. So be it. This time, if he is cheated, Tang will see to it that the man doesn't flee China as the Swede did.

The birds have stopped singing, the General realizes with a sigh. He's tired, but there is time before the evening meal, so he uses it by riding his horse over to the Kong Temple, as he often does at twilight. Tying the reins to a post near the main gate, he strolls into the temple. The calm of it instantly envelops him: tall pines, still ponds, arched bridges, pavilions drawing back into the shadows.

Tang hears the pine needles shifting in the wind; like the birdsong earlier, the sound refreshes him. Passing slowly through each successive courtyard, he comes finally to the Apricot Terrace, where Confucius once held classes for his disciples under an apricot tree. Tang looks with deep pleasure at the pavilion, whose roofing shimmers in twilight, the tiles like old coals. Beyond the pavilion is the Hall of Great Achievement.

Going into the pavilion, Tang sits on a stone bench; behind him is a wooden balustrade that faces the cobbled yard. Looking up at the intricate fretwork of the pavilion ceiling, he feels enclosed, as if safe within the confines of an umbrella during the rain. He lingers in the feeling awhile: the comfort, the safety, the calm. For a thousand years a pavilion has stood on this spot to commemorate the exchange of Truth that took place where the General is now sitting. He tries to imagine it: the bearded old scholar facing his students; a bird peering down from a branch; ground mist rising; perhaps a flute wailing faintly in the distance; an apricot blossom falling through the twilight air.

The pavilion surrounds Tang and holds him tremulously, like softly beating wings, within the imagined scence. He knows it is a moment to be cherished. He cannot hear the Master's words, but the vision of uplifted faces, those of the seated disciples, tell him the Truth is here. Right here. He feels it around him, surging in tides back from twenty-five centuries. The Yarrow Stalk Oracle this morning was wrong. He feels utterly at ease, as if playing Tai Chi especially well, and there's no conflict in his heart. It is going to be all right. He will save his beloved country, or die in the attempt; either way is the Great Way, the one destined for him. Father and he would agree about that. And for these blessed moments under the pavilion roof, he thinks of himself flowing into the twilight, into the dusk now settling in soft blue waves across the temple enclosure, submerging the dragon ornaments, drowning the green world in a welcoming darkness.

4

Fortunately the Duesenberg has a double cowl, so there's a windshield for the rear seat that protects her from some of the dust blowing in, which has been blowing in for nearly three days, ever since they passed the outskirts of Shanghai and like great adventuring fools made contact with the terrible rut-filled roads of interior China.

A big floppy hat has kept the sun from her white skin. Because it's her white skin, she tells herself, that Erich wants this Chinese worlord to see. She wears gloves; she can't extend a hand for kissing that's been chapped by the winds of three provinces. Why has Erich insisted on this marathon drive through a country notorious for bad roads, when the trains are better? Another of his grandiose ideas – arriving in Qufu in this enormous car. This rented-at-a-step-price Duesenberg. She glances at him; smoking a cigarette, wearing a touring cap, Erich looks pleased with himself. But then he usually does, whatever he's feeling. Perhaps his Teutonic blood has given him this gift of deceptive stoicism. She, on the other hand, possesses a mobile Russian face that provides her no protection from her feelings; it can betray her any time – a grimace at the wrong moment, a tremor along the mouth, a small tic at the edge of her left eye. But Erich? Nothing. His smooth boyish face gleams with good health. Yet she fears him. Although she can't say why, she feels the signs are there for her to read. They must be there, signaling his indifference and dissatisfaction, twin horrors for a woman trying to hold a man.

The car jolts (driver swerving to miss an oxcart) and throws her up hard against Erich. What does he do? He hardly glances at her, but rights himself and continues to puff on his cigarette, his blue eyes squinting in the late sunlight.

Vera sighs; she watches the light dancing on the Duesenberg hood. Three days ago the hood had been polished like a watch doctor's skull – Erich has used that image. Now the metal is encrusted with dust and grime, the dark skin of China. Again she glances at him. She does not want to lose Erich; this man has been good to her. It took flair for him to take a Russian woman out of a Shanghai jail and make of this former whore a respectable mistress. Not every man is capable of such daring. But every man is capable of changing. And when things seem fixed, circumstances have a nasty but familiar way of changing for the worse. Her own life is a brilliant illustration of that: one day the pampered child of Russian aristocrats, the next day a shivering refugee plodding across the tundra of Siberia. Sometimes she thinks of herself as a thing made up from a cheap imagination.

Why has Erich brought her along? A sensible question, considering his penchant for planning everything. Does he want to exchange her for something the warlord has? For money? Of course, Erich has never forced her on another man, but there often comes a time between lovers when romance takes a strange turn into avarice and worse. She has not arrived at this conclusion theoretically; no, she has come to it through experience. Whatever Erich's reason for bringing her, she has no desire to flirt with a Chinese warlord, much less sleep with one, not from what she has heard of their boorish, sadistic ways. Idly Vera wonders how many concubines the warlord has gathered to himself. Not that she begrudges a man sexual variety. But she has no real interest in learning about the ways of Chinese men in bed. She has learned quite enough about men, Chinese or otherwise, to satisfy her, but she is not sure about women. After all, the great love affair of her life had been in the brothel – an opium addict, a Chinese girl, dead now or probably dead.

'Vera? Did you hear me?'

It's not like her to be lost in her own thought around men. She blinks at him.

'You are Vera, aren't you?' Luckner asks testily. 'Or have I brought someone else along by mistake.'

He speaks good Russian, acquired during prisoner-of-war days after his 1916 capture on the Eastern Front.

Vera apologizes, taking a proffered flask of rum.

'I repeat,' he says. 'I think you'll find the General interesting.'

'I'm sure of it.' Her eyes meet his. This is a man who asks for more than compliance; he demands enthusiasm, which makes him difficult. 'Tell me about the General,' she asks, although it's hard to muster enthusiasm for his business deals. Guns no longer hold a fascination for Vera Rogacheva. There had been a time when little else mattered. Across the frozen landscape of war-torn Russia she had lived intimately with guns, observing what they could accomplish, fearing them, wanting them to protect her, hating their power, worshiping their power. But that's behind her, and so Erich's business of selling guns and the people he sells them to hold as much interest for her as last week's *North China Daily*.

'Come on,' she urges, 'tell me *everything* about your general.'

She tries to listen intelligently, but keeps wondering if she has heard it all before. Erich says this general is a leading warlord in Shantung. Rumor has him losing ground to Dog Meat. The name is sufficiently arresting for her to respond to it. 'Who or what is Dog Meat?' she asks, glad to have a question. Luckner, assuming a rather professional air, explains that General Chang Tsung-ch'ang, another leading warlord in the province, earned his nickname by consuming large portions of fried dog garnished with seasonal vegetables. Apparently the Japanese, whose influence in the province has been increasing recently, prefer Dog Meat to Tang, because they can more easily control Dog Meat, a stupid, avaricious fellow.

'Yes,' Vera remarks intermittently, 'I see.' She tries to follow the convolutions of Erich's lecture – it includes references to Peking, Jinan, Shanghai, Sian, and a host of warlords – but Chinese politics always seem to her a confusion dreamed up by little boys playing at war.

'So I think some of the northern warlords want Tang out of the way,' Erich concludes, lighting a new cigarette and handing it to her. The little display of consideration heartens her. 'This is sure,' Erich says. 'If Tang goes under, Japanese influence in the North will increase enormously.'

Vera searches for an intelligent question. 'Doesn't he like the Japanese?'

'No, Tang doesn't like foreigners, any of them. He's a hard-bitten patriot.'

This conversation seems unusually dry to her. Why doesn't he say what is really on his mind? If he wants to leave her, she must make other plans. When men were going to leave them, she has seen girls fail to make other arrangements, from laziness or stupidity or even infatuation, and suddenly vanish in the quagmire of degradation that awaits women without protection in Shanghai, the City of Sorrows. Vera pulls back from such thinking. She mustn't lose him through fear of losing him. Erich is always interested in his clients, especially the new ones, so Vera tries to establish her own interest in General Tang. 'If Tang's on the way out, why come here to see him?'

'He wants to buy guns. What he does with them – win or lose – is his business.'

There's a sudden familiar note of callousness in his voice that

87

she hates. Vera looks at the man: sharp features, blue eyes, slicked-down blond hair. There's a boyish quality to him, yet frequently his eyes have a flat, depthless cast that makes her wonder about his sanity, if he goes in and out of it like so many men who have been in the war. Sometimes she imagines Erich Luckner as the citizen he might have been in a Germany that never fought the Great War: pleasant, efficient, a family man who tends his garden.

He is speaking of his new client again. Vera listens intently, forcing herself. 'The General won a large battle last year. Saved the province. They say he's brilliant on the battlefield, but lacks imagination politically. By that they mean he lacks guile. But I don't know – he may win. It's possible in the current situation.'

'In the current situation anything is possible.' Vera is pleased with herself. She has just sounded intelligent, informed, and in the last few minutes Erich has responded to her; at least he gave her a cigarette, lit.

'They say he's a Confucian.'

'Really?' Vera says. 'I thought all the Chinese claim to be Confucians.'

'They say he works at it.'

'A man of honor?' she asks with a smile.

Shrugging, Erich takes the flask from her, drinks, and, again showing consideration, gives it back. Vera drinks too. She likes rum because it doesn't hold bad memories. Vodka brings to mind the young Cossacks she watched die on the icy steppes; wine means the French who betrayed the White Army when the Reds could still have been beaten; and beer reminds her of the loutish British tars who mauled her in the brothel. But rum comes from a warm place, carries no unpleasant connotations. With zest she drinks again.

'He makes his headquarters in Qufu to be near the bones of Confusions.' Luckner guffaws at the idea.

'Can it be ture?'

'There are stranger things in this country. Anyway, the Kong family is happy to have him. Believe me, they'd rather have him in their back yard than Dog Meat. Still, I think it the end he will lose.'

'Who will lose?'

'Tang will, in the end. He's badly situated.'

Vera feels a little tug of interest; it is refreshing not to take it.

Erich explains that the country Tang controls is in the corridor between North and South. To go from Canton to Peking you go through his territory, so he's dead center in the middle of bad traffic. The region has been war-torn for years; in China everything is geography. 'Look at Chiang Kai-shek,' Luckner says. 'When things would get hot around Canton, he'd run for the mountains and stay clear of trouble for a while. The flat terrain here is against Tang. Eventually they'll squeeze him out.'

'That's too bad.'

Luckner turns those cold blue eyes toward her. 'What's too bad?'

'Well, for an honorable man to lose.'

'Who said he was honorable?'

An honorable man losing: it's a sad thing to contemplate. She thinks of her brother Alex. The last she had seen of him Alex was joining the White Army in the West, on his sleeve the blue coat of arms of General Kornilov, and his hand a *nagaika*, the Cossack whip he was barely old enough to carry. Fourteen years old and determined to save the Motherland. Is amy Alex still alive? Somewhere in Europe perhaps?

'Vera?'

'Yes?'

'Where are you?'

She touches Luckner's hand. 'Sorry.'

'I was saying, who knows what honor means to the Chinese? All they believe in, as far as I can see, is rice and power. They tell me Tang can be as ruthless as any warlord. He's just ruthless about different things. A murderous idealist.' The phrase, appealing to him, brings a smile to Luckner's face. He has perfect teeth, which often hold her attention like an odd work of art. 'Does my general interest you?'

Knowing the answer he wants, Vera says, 'Of course he does.'

'Good.' Luckner sighs contentedly. 'That is helpful.'

They do not meet General Tang that evening on their arrival at the Residence in Qufu. He has gone to a performance of an acting troop come to entertain his soldiers.

'The Chinese love it when their leaders act democratically, as long as it's not done too often,' Luckner observes during dinner in their guesthouse. Afterward they stroll in the courtyard, which is glowing in moonlight. The moon looks icy to Vera, although she is sweating in the humid courtyard. The moon is a cold thing; she has seen it rise over the central steppes of Russia, its ghostly white rays slanting across the unheated train compartment while the temperature outside plummeted to sixty below zero. And finally, when her little sister could go no further, she watched a frigid silver of moon hang above the small gasping mouth as it whispered, 'Mother,' although there had been no mother for weeks. Moonlight on a child's gasping mouth – it is the stuff of cheap melodrama, yet for Vera the moon continues to be a sign of wintry death. Except tonight, because now it shines magically on the upswept tiles, pours like milk down the glazed plates of the roofs, dripping upon flagstones, outlining the shaggy conformation of potted camellias.

Tomorrow she will see Qufu. During her years in China, almost eight now, she has rarely left Shanghai. One thing or another prevented her: lack of money, the Civil War, the whim of a man who was keeping her. But tomorrow she is going to see the legendary town of Qufu. And she is going to meet the warlord who chooses to live in such a place of beauty. She has met only one other warlord: in Shanghai, at a party given by a Japanese businessman (she was at the time his son's mistress). The warlord of some province or other had waddled in like a heavy-laden river scow – fat, rumpled, with a chestful of medals probably bought from a Hong Kong company whose chief profit (a Britisher once told her this at the race track) comes from supplying Chinese militarists with phony medals. The warlord refused to remove his shoes, although the house was furnished with tatamis. Eating too much, drinking far too much, he vomited at last into a silk pillow. Assisted to his feet, he pulled a gun, waved it crazily in the air, and threatened to kill all the foreign devils in Shanghai.

As they stroll, Luckner repeats a Shanghai rumor: the Kong family maintains a fantastic bank account abroad, just in case the country falls apart.

'If they were waiting for that, why haven't they already left?'

Back in the guesthouse, claiming exhaustion, Luckner goes promptly to bed. There is plenty of reason for exhaustion, Vera admits. Even in the big Duesenberg they were tossed and buffeted for hundreds of kilometers on roads choked with goat herds, mule carts, and coolies. A tough, exhausting ride, and yet last year Erich would have stayed awake until she got into bed. And he would have kissed her. Now he snores.

She is losing him.

Slipping into a cotton nightgown, Vera stares at his parted mouth in the moonlight that now looks icy and funereal again. Does she feel anger or sorrow at the thought of losing this man? She lies beside him and listens to the rhythmic male breathing. Women never sleep as soundly as men: a woman is always near the edge of wakefulness, Vera thinks, like a small animal awaiting attack. Will she find another man easily? Gently she runs her hand across each ample breast. She has good legs, only a hint of plumpness at the hips. She is still desirable at twenty-seven – an achievement, considering the life she's led. Perhaps she can find another German, or a Dane – that would be nice – or a Spaniard or a Britisher. No Frenchman, of course. Her first language, spoken in childhood, was French, not Russian – typical of aristocratic circles in Petrograd – but ever since the president of the French Senate betrayed the White Russian government-in-exile in 1920, Vera has refused to speak a word of French. In the brothel she never accepted a Frenchman. British sailors half mad from months at sea and Italian exporters with breaths of garlic and all the rest of them, men desperate or furious because of wasted lives, tramped in and out of her sultry little room, but never a Frenchman. On one occasion, pressed hard by her madam to accept a visiting French diplomat, Vera threatened to slash her own face with a razor and thus deprive the establishment of steady revenue. Result: no Frenchman.

Her hand moves down the soft rise of her belly to rest upon The Triangle That Drives Men Wild, a euphemism learned from Yu-ying, who also taught her to shave the public hair into a delectable triangle. Sometimes the two of them wove little silk ribbons into it until neither could stop laughing.

Vera feels her body stiffen, as if it senses the onset of fear or grief, two emotions never far away. Often she wonders if Yu-ying still lives. If the small frail girl with skin the color of tea-stained ivory is out there in the teeming Shanghai alleys. Of course, it's not possible for Yu-ying to be alive. And every day Vera prays to God in Heaven that He did not allow the girl to suffer, but let her go swiftly, say, in a fall from the Soochow Creek Bridge or by a quick merciful knife-thrust during an argument over a thumbnail amount of opium. It is now almost five years since Yu-ying disappeared. If still alive, doubtless she'd be reduced to a bag of bones; she'd work in a den, summoning each day enough courage, strength, and stamina to sweep the floor of vomit and cigarette butts before another group of ghosts shuffled in for their daily pipes.

Yu-ying, Yu-ying. Feckless girl. She had taught Vera how to handle drunks, to help the impotent regain their sexual confidence, to wheedle tips from stingy clients. Yu-ying had learned those things for herself as an orphan who began her brothel apprenticeship by cleaning douche pans, emptying ashtrays, running errands. Once she taught Vera the most important thing of all: how to abort by using chopsticks as if lifting a single peanut from a plate. The tiny Chinese girl, younger than herself, had steered Vera among the rocks and shoals of brothel life. After rough handling by clients, Vera often went to Yu-ying's room to lie down quietly and spend the morning beside someone she could trust. Above the chronic noise of Shanghai lanes, their bodies streaked by sunlight flickering between window slats, they smoothed each other's skin, which had been roughened by hairy men with sandpaper hands. And then, leaving the house, they strolled daily through the Native City, bought each other flowers for their hair, munched cakes in the Willow Pattern Teahouse, watching beneath the footbridge huge goldfish squirm and flash in vortexes of agitated water. They wore identical dresses, like twins, and kissed in the cinema and held hands climbing stairs and disregarded those girls in the brothel who resented their happiness. Slowly, savoring each step of the process, they became passionate lovers, unattainable for other women or men, shored up against the miseries of Shanghai life by their tenderness in bed.

Then one morning Yu-ying was not in her room when Vera, rattled by an especially difficult night, came to it. The Chinese girl did not return to the brothel until the following night: moon-eyed, placid, silent. With grinning satisfaction a spiteful Korean girl explained to Vera Yu-ying's sudden disappearance and peculiar contentment upon her return: Yu-ying had gone back to opium. Vera refused to believe it. Why would Yu-ying do such a thing after giving up the habit for their love? Girls came to Vera's room, where she lay facing the wall, and told her to forget Yu-ying. Denial, they explained, had bottled up in the little Chinese girl a backlog of desire, so when she had allowed herself a small taste of opium for old time's sake, the floodgates burst and irresistible longing rushed out, carrying off hope, pride, everything, and emptying her of love.

Vera cried, swore, pleaded with the girl. She accompanied Yu-ying to the wretched den a few times and smoked too, hoping for an addiction to match her beloved's. But she only got sick, while Yu-ying drifted on a tide of consuming desire, until Madam Lotus threatened to throw her out, in spite of her skill. Madam Lotus, a middle-aged Eurasian who ran the brothel, had taken in the orphaned girl years ago and raised her like a daughter. But to maintain discipline in the house, she demanded that Yu-ying keep steady hours and be dependable, just like the others. Vera contributed her own money on the girl's behalf, but the bribe did not placate Madam Lotus for long. As she explained, Yu-ying's behavior was bad for morale. And then the frequency of her absences increased, until Yu-ying disappeared for a week at a time, returning only to borrow money from Vera – no one else would lend her a single *cash*. And then one day led to the next, and she was gone forever. Or so the girls told Vera. Three days led to four, four to five, and then ten, twelve, and Yu-ying did not return. Vera went to the girl's favorite den, but they turned her away at the door. They told her never to come back. On the sixteenth day of Yu-ying's disappearance, Vera vowed to search all of Shanghai. Held down on her bed by two Russian whores and Madam Lotus, while next door a shabby French merchant groaned loudly over his Burmese purchase, Vera struggled to get free and go find her lost, beloved girl. Then at last, in full understanding, she lay back and quietly sobbed. For three days she did not work, but lit joss sticks in a sand-filled porcelain bowl for Christ in Heaven to accept into His Kingdom a little Chinese girl whose only sin had been to grow up orphaned in Shanghai.

So love came to an end. And with the end of love, Vera felt for a long time that her life had ended as well. But in some ways her life had only begun. At the end of a dark tunnel of hot nights there had been a prison cell and Erich.

Vera turns on the pillow to regard his handsome features in cold, annihilating moonlight. Erich has been good to her in his way. She will hate losing him.

She wants to move back into sleep or forward into full waking, but not to remain here trapped by nightmare. It begins, as always, with snow. Only a landscape of whiteness until a breeze starts to ruffle the drifts. Once the wind gains force, rising to the velocity of a gale, it blows the snow off a large mound until something inside begins to appear – the fleshy haunch of an animal, the bloated corpse of a saddled horse, its gut split open, its crupper half eaten. Like the edge of a toothed saw the blown snow cuts into a serpentine column of staggering figures. Someone is shouting through the wind for everyone to stay awake and keep moving. Men are running in circles, grunting and laughing and whimpering. Blue faces swim out of the whiteness, then vanish in a fresh maelstrom of snow. A girl lies on her stomach against the slick frozen surface of a lake, looking down into the crystalline depths. the girl is herself, always. And then she feels the insatiable thirst that follows the drinking of melted snow. Implacably the nightmare follows its own rules. Always when she feels the thirst come on, the scene shifts. Hot sunlight glints against troika wheels, gun carriages. Swarms of blackbirds rise and fall from bundles of tattered clothing on the plain. Inside the clothing are bodies. Her eyes roam among the images of death, searching for mother and father and two sisters and a younger brother and nieces and nephews and uncles and aunts, a whole army of relatives. She is thorough, she investigates carefully in the nightmare. It won't allow her a superficial examination of the decomposing corpses. She may or may not find someone familiar among the rotting bodies – this is where the nightmare proves flexible. Today it seems to take longer than necessary before it releases her from the task. Then comes the watering trough. Always the watering trough. After all these years it is as familiar to her as her own body. The same emaciated cow halts to drink from it and in doing so nudges aside the severed head of a child. The dead girl's hair fans out like filaments of weed in the brackish water. Her eyes staring up in astonishment meet Vera's, which study each detail of the girl's face: nose, lips, cheeks, forehead. It is not at first (as always) a face familiar, but the more Vera examines it, the more the face changes, altering at last into the features of her sister Natasha.

Sitting bolt upright, Vera tries to hold back the sobs. Bathed in sweat, she is trembling. It is always the same: a sudden wakefulness, sweat, trembling. Glancing at Erich, she is relieved to see that he sleeps. He knows of the nightmare, but she wants to spare him its consequences. Now the headache, the terrible thirst. As always.

Getting quietly out of bed, she groups through the faint light of dawn toward a decanter on the table. Tilting it back, she drinks greedily. In a while, however, the thirst will return. As always. If the nightmare pays more than one visit in a day, the thirst will remain unslaked for hours.

The nightmare is what she calls it, although it isn't really that. It is a memory transformed by time, guilt, and sorrow into punishment for her surviving the Siberian March. So she understands, but the understanding never brings comfort.

Her whole body shaking, Vera holds her forearms in a protective gesture across her breasts and goes to the latticed window. The headache, as always, begins to throb terrifically at her temples. Sometimes in the aftermath of the nightmare little lights start to flicker – as they do this morning – as if pieces of foil are turning at great speed near a candle. Vera stares at the courtyard, prepared with patience to wait for the lights to go away. They do and leave her a clear view of what is there in the courtyard: A Chinese man moving in slow ritual postures through the sea-blue air.

In shapeless cotton trousers and tunic, his half-crouched figure seems to be emerging from the mist of a Sung painting. Vera knows what he is doing. On the shady lawn of the Bund she has often paused to watch men playing Tai Chi Chuan along the Whangpoo waterfront. The exercise has never seemed profound to her, for all its slow heraldic movement. Her childhood had been filled with livelier images, of more meaning to her: *Pavillon d'Armide* at the Imperial Theatre, for example, with Pavlova and Nijinsky dancing the principal roles.

Even so, the sight of this lone man playing Tai Chi at dawn here in Qufu has its appeal, maybe comfort; he moves with a purity and calm that seem to drain off the nightmare's terror. He appears to be carving hunks from the soft air like a sculptor carving wood. She envies him his concentration. Her fascination turns to awe. One foot raised, slowly put forward; the other raised, gracefully kicking –

'What's out there?'

Vera turns to see Erich regarding her from the rumpled bed. He seems watchful, concerned, as she replies, 'Nothing.' Approaching the bed, Vera bends down to kiss him. She runs her fingers gently along his jawline, down his throat, but Erich catches her hand and holds it away.

'What's wrong, darling?' she murmurs.

Dropping her hand, Luckner asks for a cigarette. When she gets him one, bringing it lit, he puffs vigorously a few times. 'Nothing's wrong. I'm just thinking about Karlsruhe. I woke up with it.'

Vera nods; Karlsruhe is his obsession. After they make love sometimes, in a soft mood Erich will reminisce about his homeland, especially Karlsruhe, which glows in his memory like something cherished by a child, a fabled treasure in a fairy tale.

'I was thinking I may never see it again.'

'Of course you will,' she reassures him.

'You mean, the same way you'll see Petrograd?'

A spiteful remark. Erich has a gift for dragging her into his depressions – the pampered boy in him overwhelms the complaisant veteran. Vera waits, knowing him well enough to expect some kind of confession. Like most men he is vulnerable in the morning, before he has marshaled his defenses for the daily battle. It is the hour when Erich confides.

Cigarette poised in air like chalk held thoughtfully at a blackboard, Luckner stares into the distance. 'I am goddamn worried,' he declares.

Vera waits. Sitting on the bed next to him, she lays one hand gently against his cheek. With Erich her best moments are when she treats him like a child.

'It's the Japanese,' he continues. 'The bastards will ruin me.'

Her thirst returns in an agonizing rush. Vera can't help getting up and going to the water decanter, although Erich wants her full attention. She pours a glass to the brim.

'Are you listening?' Luckner watches her drink fiercely, water trickling down the edge of her mouth. 'I said the Japs are wrecking my business.'

Vera pours another glass, sipping this time, and returns with it to the bed. 'How can they do that?'

He launches one of his little lectures. Wanting to extend their influence in China, he tells her, the Japs are supplying arms almost free of charge to certain bootlicking warlords. They are shipping over a lot of 1907 Arisakas – a long, unwieldy rifle, but the Chinese will take anything they can get, especially if it's cheap. 'I need a smoke,' he says, crushing out in the ashtray the cigarette that has burned down to his fingers. Watching her drink again, he says rather impatiently, 'Can you *please* get me one?'

She does, lighting it first. 'Sorry, darling.'

'In this province they're supplying arms to Dog Meat.'

'Whom they can control.'

Luckner smiles faintly. 'You were listening yesterday. Well, Dog Meat was an old customer, so now I've lost him.'

'Meaning you really need Tang.'

'Yes, I need him. I need a good sale at a good price. Otherwise, Karlsruhe goodbye.'

Whenever things go wrong for Erich, he feels it's a threat to his eventual return to Germany. We all have our obsessions, Vera thinks sadly.

'I'mn willing to help,' she says.

'What do you mean?'

'It's why you brought me, isn't it – to be nice to the General?' She is thinking that after all, it isn't the first time a man has wanted this particular favor from her.

But Luckner doesn't admit his real intention, as she perceives it. He protests that he merely wanted her along for the best of reasons: they belong together. It is a sweet little remark, but Vera goes past it. 'Don't worry, darling. I'll be as nice as necessary.'

Leaning forward, Luckner kisses her forehead, chastely but with feeling. 'Maybe you care for me more than I deserve.' Throwing back the sheet, he gets naked out of bed. Vera watches him stride briskly toward the bathroom. Tight buttocks, dimpled. No hip fat, no paunch. She doesn't want to lose him, this attractive man, even though his lovemaking is often glacial and his conversation, aside from Shanghai gossip, unimaginative.

Vera picks up the decanter again and pours. It is always like this after the nightmare has paid a visit.

After breakfast (brought to their room by a boy in the cottons of a soldier), Luckner leaves for a morning appointment with the General; Vera remains in the guesthouse. Most of her adult life has been spent waiting for men, none of whom have encouraged her to do more with the time than waste it. In the brothel she played cards with bored girls like herself until clients came knocking. This was after Yu-ying's disappearance. Then about six months later she accepted the proposal of a Swedish exporter to live with him. She was lucky in her choice, as he proved to be a good man, but she found herself isolated for long stretches of time. At first she worried that so much solitude would give the nightmare greater access to her. Soon she learned, however, that the nightmare had nothing to do with anything outside the rhythms of her own mind.

So she started to enjoy her solitude. Perhaps the vastness of Siberia had prepared her for it. She had been too frightened, too cold, too sick to appreciate the enormous solitude of Central Asia when by train, wagon, horse, and foot she had traveled across windswept miles where time was like space itself, just as the earth and sky seemed to merge into one indistinguishable reality at the distant horizon. Kept by one man in a large house, faced with long periods of waiting, she had the leisure to recall the beauty of vastness, and of solitude, the concomitant of vastness. Eventually, of course, she realized that she must somehow fill her solitude or come to hate it.

So she took up calligraphy.

At first it was a mere pastime, like playing cards. In a Nanking Road beauty parlor she overheard an elegant Chinese lady discussing the benefits of doing calligraphy. Well, why not? Vera told herself. She already knew enough characters to read a newspaper and her spoken Mandarin was becoming fluent. But until the day she applied for lessons with a master calligrapher, she had never written a single character of Chinese. For three years now she has been practicing the art. Every day she begins with the eight basic strokes found in the character 'Yung' – Eternity. The greatest of all masters, Wang Hsi-chih of the ancient Jin, had spent fifteen years, according to legend, perfecting this single character. Vera knows she will never become an accomplished calligrapher, yet already she has developed a feeling for the art that gives her deep pleasure. She has experienced the difficulty of holding the brush properly, so the hollow space in the palm of her hand can hold a small egg. She has felt the joy of imitating the brush strokes of the masters, for in itself imitation is an Eastern art, not despised as in the West. In her Russian childhood she had been taught music, painting, and literature as a matter of course, but here in China she has learned through calligraphy a great truth: Art can be crucial to survival.

From her luggage Vera takes the following: a coarse linen cloth, three fox-hair brushes, a purplish ovoid stone, a few rectangular ink sticks, and a thin roll of mulberry-bark paper. The latter she partly unfolds on the table, holding it down with an ashtray and a glass. After pouring some water into a groove at one end of the stone, Vera grinds an ink stick slowly against the flat plum-colored surface, then mixes the ground powder of pine soot and glue with water until the resultant ink has the sluggish viscosity of oil.

Lifting some of it on the point of her brush, Vera lets it drop, testing its denseness. She will get a new stone someday; this one has become slippery from use and doesn't grip the ink; moreover, it has always been too absorbent, allowing the ink to dry up quickly.

Vera is ready to begin. First she will practice the traditional eight strokes, the way an athlete warms up. Then she will copy a poem by Kao Ch'i, a poet of the Ming. It's a poem about exile, containing images of winter that touch her profoundly. If she can stroke out a few characters with verve and confidence during the next hour, she'll be happy. Happy with a few. Vera will be happy with only three or four swiftly flowing, spirited characters. Or with even one.

Luckner returns shortly before noon. He is smiling. 'We're going to lunch with the General,' he announces.

Vera understands that the interview has gone well. Erich looks Teutonically handsome: tall, blond, lean, blue-eyed.

While she's dressing, Luckner sits with the flask of rum in the bedroom. 'Tang wants more than I can get him. And I think he can pay.'

In the bathroom Vera runs a comb through her dark hair, cut short for the summer. Crow's-feet at the edge of her eyes. Five good years left. Maybe six if she stays out of the sun.

'We close the deal tonight.'

'And then a banquet,' Vera comments.

Luckner laughs. 'Of course a banquet.'

She can see him in the mirror, lounging on the bed. What has always impressed her is Erich's ability to go all day without mussing a single hair on his blond head. 'I hope the General doesn't serve sea slugs. They're a Shantung specialty,' Vera says. 'Each time I've eaten them, I've been sick.'

'Maybe you could eat one. All right? To please him.'

Vera moves toward the bathroom door and looks out at him. 'Is that how I'm supposed to be nice?'

Waving the flask, Luckner gives her a sheepish grimace. 'You know, laugh at his jokes. Smile.'

'And eat sea slugs.'

'Forget them. Just be, you know –'

'Nice. I told you, darling, whatever is necessary.' Vera applies kohl to the lids of her green-flecked eyes. 'Whatever is necessary,' she repeats. She looks at him through the mirror; their eyes meet, his turn away. Vera blinks rapidly at the mirror, letting his image go to concentrate on her own. Not large eyes, but she has a way of widening them to achieve 'an effect of limpid intensity' – an English phrase she got from a clever British naval officer one evening at the Shanghai Boating Club.

From the bedroom, in a droning voice, Erich is reviewing his talk with the General. It is filled with details, a description of weapons, so Vera stops listening. She puts on a knee-length tube dress of orange silk, purchased in a good Shanghai shop. She leaves the top buttons of her sleeveless blouse unbuttoned to focus attention on her voluptuousness. Vera has learned to calculate her impression carefully. She learned before twenty what the requirements for survival are, if you're a White Russian refugee. Her future depends quite simply on her continued ability to attract and hold men. Erich or others. Simple as that, difficult as that. Close scrutiny: she looks quite fresh and animated today. Is she really animated? Well, the calligraphy went well. She is not animated by the prospect of meeting a warlord. Glancing down, she turns one leg, inspecting the calf, which has a nice curve to it without unseemly muscles. Today her legs will flash in the sun. Vera hums a snatch of folk tune remembered from childhood. She has long since forgotten the words.

When she walks into the bedroom, Luckner has changed a white shirt for a blue silk one. He looks like a yachtsman on his way to the pier, and Vera tells him so. Usually this pleases him, for he's attracted to great luxury and would have made a cheerful duke.

Instead of looking pleased at the compliment, however, he is staring at her. 'One thing,' he says.

It occurs to Vera that he might have been brooding about this 'one thing' while she dressed.

'There's a Soviet adviser in camp.'

Vera stiffens. 'I won't meet him.'

Luckner, rising from the bed, puts his arm around her. 'I understand you, darling.'

'I won't, I can't.'

'It's unlikely Tang would invite a Bolshevik to lunch with us, but if the fellow's there –'

'I won't stay.'

'If by any chance –'

'I won't stay.' Vera shrugs off his arm. 'Forgive me, but I won't.'

Luckner shakes his head. 'If I asked, you would sleep with this warlord. You'd be as nice as necessary. But you won't have lunch with another man.'

'With a Bolshevik? No. I won't. I can't.'

Someone is knocking.

'I won't,' Vera repeats.

'Come in,' Luckner says, and the door opens. A somber-looking officer with thick eyebrows informs them coolly that if they are ready, it will be his great privilege to escort them to the dining room.

'This is Captain Yang, the General's aide-de-camp,' Luckner says.

Vera nods curtly. 'I won't stay,' she murmurs.

'Captain Yang, will the Soviet adviser be at lunch?'

'He is not invited, sir.'

'You see?' Luckner takes her arm. 'The General understands perfectly.'

Understands? How can he possibly understand, Vera thinks, as they walk through the sunlit courtyards and shady galleries. Not even Erich understands, and he had been a prisoner of war in Russia, chased by the Reds across Siberia too. But he had not been raped, had not lost an entire family there, had not lost everything except memories. She will not meet the Red, she will not stay. If necessary she will sleep with this damn warlord and his entire General Staff, but she will not stay one minute in the same room with a Bolshevik.

The dining room is in a lovely hall, built, according to Captain Yang, in the sixteenth century. Vera regards the aide coldly: he's the sort of Chinese who annoys her with an excessively polite manner coupled to a blatant air of superiority. She knows him. His mind is filled with an intricate set of behavioral formulas, as precise as the roll on a player piano.

When they enter a hall, someone rises in the dim light from an overstuffed chair at the back of the reception room.

She recognizes the Tai Chi Chuan player.

When they are introduced, Vera says with a smile, 'I saw you playing Tai Chi this morning.'

'You know Tai Chi?' But it is not really a question; it is a compliment designed to flatter her knowledge of things Chinese.

His hair, clipped short in military style, and his brown skin, tight against the skull, give an impression of vigor, of tension under control. He has the look of a general, but Vera searches his eyes for a clue to his character. Long ago she learned not to look for mood or response in the Chinese mouth, not often in gesture either. Expression is found in the eyes, where sometimes it dances remarkably, suggesting a turbulence of spirit Vera had been taught to believe the Almighty kept in reserve for Russians. His eyes? Well, what about them? They don't belong somehow to the leather belt, the holster. Gentle? Possibly. Curious? Yes. Discriminating? Yes.

'I heard that you speak Chinese,' he tells Vera, escorting her into the dining room, 'but I hadn't expected such perfection.'

Vera smiles in acknowledgment of the compliment, but in truth she has always detected something quaint and archaic in Chinese courtesy. When she asks the General if he speaks English or German, he laughs and displays a gold tooth. It is something modern in a picture of himself otherwise traditional. It is the one blemish in a face she finds attractive.

At the round table another officer joins them and sits opposite her. She is on the General's right. She is glad not to have this Colonel Pi as her luncheon partner; his gaiety is forced, even for a Chinese. The luncheon menu is more sensible than she had expected: stewed pork with radishes, bean-curd soup, and cold spinach laced with dried shrimp. Vera has attended more than enough banquets with their emphasis on the exotic rather than tasteful. No self-respecting Shanghai tailor will measure her for a dress without inviting her to a ten-course *chiu-hsi*.

The food is well prepared, the host attentive. He himself keeps her wine cup filled with warm Shao-hsing wine. He drinks sparingly, and Vera suspects that at heart he is ascetic. Erich and Colonel Pi are having an animated discussion of weapons – the words 'caliber' and 'millimeter' are repeated interminably. The General, however, gives her his full attention. His table talk is inconsequential, typical of a proper host, but in his manner there is also something of indefinable interest, perhaps a shy warmth or even sexual power. Earlier she saw gentleness, curiosity, intelligence in his eyes. Now she sees intensity. Why? Is it her silk blouse with three buttons unbuttoned? Vera feels the excitement of attracting him, of drawing him out of an ancient world of stylized manners. She drinks more wine and asks herself if it's only the alcohol that has kindled within her the desire to charm, to entice. Perhaps it's merely the bright tablecloth or the light laying a golden path across the little forest of bowls and plates. Or is it really the man who gives her this sense of well-being? She attempts to pull him from the edge of conversation into something involving. For a Chinese the subject of food is irresistible, so Vera is mildly surprised by his lack of interest in Foochow sliced snails and shark's fin in silver netting. All right, he is ascetic, she thinks, and falls silent.

Finally the General locates a subject of mutual interest: the town of Qufu. He explains that there are three important areas – the Kong Residence, the Temple of the Sage, and the Burial Ground. It strikes Vera that without knowing his occupation she might have taken him for a scholar.

'I've wanted to see Qufu for a long time,' she says and notices the quizzical look in his eyes. 'Erich?' She waits for Luckner to finish an exchange with the Colonel. 'Erich, I think the General has doubts about my interest in Qufu.'

'I can assure your Excellency of one thing: Miss Rogacheva would not have come this distance from Shanghai had Qufu not been at the end of all those bumpy roads.'

A nice little speech, Vera thinks. Erich has a gift for rising to occasions, especially when they involve clients.

'She is also a calligrapher,' Luckner adds.

'Practices calligraphy.' She corrects him instantly. Her eyes meet Tang's. 'I practice it amateurishly. I've studied only three years.'

Her honesty seems to appeal to him; the smile he gives her is genuinely warm. 'To practice it at all is enough.'

'But she really is a calligrapher,' Luckner insists, giving her a quick frown. 'She's at it every day, General.'

'I'm sure she is.'

His bland reply disheartens her. The man is difficult, someone who resists enticement, who pulls back warily at the slightest disturbance of his own intentions. Yet she feels powerfully that he is not always reserved, that he is a man of the heart. Vera wants deeply to impress him. In her life it has been a familiar emotion, first experienced as a child: Her tall father, dressed in a velvet frock coat and redolent of strong tobacco, dallied her on his knee and chuckled at her solemn recitation of nursery rhymes. Vera knows from experience, not all of it pleasant, that the desire to impress is a prologue to infatuation.

'Allow me to show you Qufu,' the General says abruptly.

Luckner, hearing, leans forward. 'Vera, there's the guide you wanted. Obviously there's none better.'

She thanks General Tang, giving a smile to both men.

Luckner claims that the General has been gallant enough to release him so he can accompany Colonel Pi to the drill field that afternoon.

Another pretty speech, Vera thinks. If Erich doesn't watch out, he'll become too Chinese for a return to Karlsruhe.

Outside the dining hall, with an expansive wave Luckner guides the Colonel away by the elbow. As Vera walks beside the General, she wonders if he will take her directly to bed. Perhaps it is an event Erich both expects and wants – to seal the arms deal and commit Tang to future deals. Or perhaps he no longer cares. It is even possible that he is foisting her off on the General as a new concubine, just to rid himself of her presence in Shanghai. He has never given her reason for such suspicion, but Vera always guards against the profound error of naïveté.

Through a labyrinth of courtyards, she accompanies the General to the front gate of the Residence. So they are actually going somewhere other than his bed. She feels a certain neutrality about this decision. Saddled horses and grooms are standing on the flagstones. They can tour by horseback, Tang explains, or the car can be brought around.

'I prefer horseback.' Vera strides briskly toward the waiting animals. Glancing over her shoulder, she notices him staring at her bare legs. Deciding that the bigger horse must be his, Vera puts her hand on the pommel of the other's saddle. 'Too bad I didn't bring a riding habit, but I can manage sidesaddle.' It will be better, she thinks – the breeze ruffling her dress. She feels wonderfully desirable and the need to impress this man seems to be growing in her.

Coming up, Tang says, 'You enjoy riding?' His voice betrays his doubt.

'All my life.' All my life, she thinks, nearly adding that her childhood had been full of horses, that she had jumped a beautiful roan named Ivan when she was ten. But this would only confuse the Chinese general, who thinks of her as the concubine of a foreign gunrunner. Even so, she wants desperately to impress him. She would like to impress him with stories of Ivan, who came from Tomsk, the home of Russia's finest horses. She would not mention, however, the Tomsk horses that she had seen in her eighteenth year, on the road to Irkutsk. Accompanied by grooms in red-and-gold livery, they were wearing crown-embroidered blankets. Their sires and dams had been world-famous trotters, pampered in marble stalls with warm straw up to their bellies. But on the brutal Siberian steppes this limping herd, escaping from Bolshevik plows that would come in the spring, scratched beneath the snow for withered grasses and huddled dumbly together against the cutting wind. From the bumping cart in which she was riding, Vera had called out a faint greeting to the proud, nervous animals. She wished them Godspeed in full knowledge that a month later not one of those Tomsk horses would be alive on the wintry plains.

The memory is in Vera's mind as she mounts with a groom's help that she doesn't need and reins up alongside the General. The Tomsk horses, for a moment, bring into her vision a familiar white landscape, swirling snow, the wind blowing it away from a large mound.

Not that. Not that now, she tells herself furiously, and spurs her mount into a trot.

When the General moves up beside her, Vera gives him a bright smile, made especially intense by her memory of the Tomsk horses. 'Wonderful day,' she says enthusiastically. 'Where do we start?'

'With your permission, the Burial Ground.'

Vera doesn't question his choice. It's clear already that the man has created for himself a special relationship with the Confucian past of Qufu. They ride under the Drum Tower, go by a small market, and soon leave the town behind. She has a whiff of night soil drifting from outlying vegetable gardens. A fresh, pungent smell that she associates with China. Then they pass under a stone gateway with a chiseled inscription that she can read: Eternal Spring. The General explains they are now entering the Forest of the Great Sage. Another gate is opened by an old attendant in a faded blue coat, who bows repeatedly to the General. Vera finds herself in a vast walled enclosure. Tall pines and cypresses, rising from thick undergrowth, stand in towering grandeur above the chunky sculptures of countless stone dogs and horses. As they ride down a narrow path, the trees emit a cool breath of scented wood and leaf; and in the distance, among weathered trunks, Vera can see hieratic stone figures, discolored by centuries of rain, with their hands clasping granite scrolls, the bearded faces and hunched shoulders expressive of immense energy focused on a beadlike zone of contemplation.

Dismounting, the General approaches Vera to help her from the horse, but before he can reach her, she has jumped down lightly. 'Tell me, General, do you think foreign women are too weak to ride horses?' She laughs, knowing many Chinese would consider her impudent.

Tang's laugh matches hers. 'We can never accuse foreigners of weakness as long as Chinese women are crippled by footbinding. This is called the Avenue of Honor.' He points down a tree-lined path. 'It leads to the Tomb of Confucius.'

'I thought there was less footbinding today.' It is to this remark of his, not the Avenue of Honor, that she pays attention.

'In the back country it's still done. After all, women have been following the disgraceful custom for a thousand years. These are tomb guardians.' He is pointing now at stone carvings of panthers and griffins on either side of the path.

'Disgraceful?'

'We must give it up entirely.'

They are almost at the end of the path. 'Guardian scholars,' he observes, pointing at two huge stone figures. They come to a small building roofed with green tiles, supported by crimson pillars. 'The Temple of Offering. Behind it is the Tomb.'

Thoughtfully she strolls beside him around the side of the temple. A difficult man, she thinks, who evades an easy understanding. At the lunch table he often seemed quaintly traditional; here in this most ancient of places he appears suddenly progressive, a man who might be at home in the foreign salons of Shanghai. Perhaps he's too formidable, Vera thinks, sensing in him something of danger to herself. As they walk along, cicadas sing above them in the pines. He keeps a fist at the small of his back; does he know that Napoleon affected the same mannerism? She wants very much to impress him, to have him look at her, to gain his attention.

Rounding the corner of the temple, she looks for the Tomb of Confucius, but sees only a grassy mound enclosed by a small brick wall. Tang halts. 'Is this the Tomb?' she asks in surprise.

'I think you expected something grander.' He looks at a tall stele nearby. 'Can you read that?'

Chiseled vertically on the stone column are characters; they are not in modern script. With difficulty she attempts a translation.

'Tomb of the Prince Wen xuan. Very . . . accomplished. Very – is it holy?'

'Good!'

'But who is Wen xuan?'

'An emperor gave Confucius the title in 739. Centuries after his death, of course. In this country a man can still accumulate titles and honors after he dies.'

It's a practice with which Vera is familiar. Why does he treat me like a foreign visitor? It crosses her mind that he's resisting the idea of her. Perhaps he senses in her something of danger to himself. What better way to keep her at arm's length than to consider everything about her foreign? Vera feels strengthened by this possibility. She has impressed him.

Continuing to act like a guide to a foreign visitor, Tang points past the Tomb toward a small weathered pavilion. 'Buried under there is his most loyal disciple. For six years the man meditated at the Sage's grave site.' He extends his arms to include the whole immense park. 'More than seventy generations lie here. Is there anything like it in the world?'

'Not to my knowledge.' His enthusiasm rather subdues her.

'Shall we see more?' His hand, reaching out, impulsively grazes her bare arm.

Vera feels the contact enormously; from the startled look in his eyes, so does the General.

'I'd like to see all of Qufu,' she tells him. As they retrace their steps down the Avenue of Honor, she asks abruptly, 'Do you ever come to Shanghai?'

'Rarely.'

'That's too bad.' She gives him a smile of calculated allure.

'I stay close to Qufu. That way I protect the Kongs from bandits and my own command from other generals.'

Is he playful or serious? Vera has long realized that a perception of irony is the last thing learned about a culture. Ahead, at the end of the paved lane, their horses are tethered to a stone railing. Perhaps he takes lightly her question about Shanghai. Perhaps he has no desire to see her again. Vera feels within herself the irritable sensitivity that goes with infatuation. The idea of revealing her own desire to see him again is displeasing, yet here's a chance to establish something on which they can build in the future. 'I know a calligraphy shop that may interest you,' she says. 'If you come to Shanghai.'

Tang halts – to emphasize his awareness of her attempt at maintaining contact. 'If I come to Shanghai, I know a shop that may interest you as well. Perhaps Mister Luckner will permit me to take you there.'

'I'm sure he will.' In spite of the outrageously formal quality of their exchange, Vera is enchanted by it. The very formality makes her feel young, shy, tentative. She wants to touch him again, subtly – perhaps brush against his sleeve. How many wives and concubines does he have? Is he gentle with them? Her Japanese lover was gentle until drunk; then he was sadistically cruel. If she knows anything, Vera tells herself, the General is gentle in bed. If she knows anything, Vera tells herself a second time, there is no way to tell whether a man is gentle in bed unless you're in it with him. Half-recollected feelings of adolescent infatuation crowd in. She has never forgotten through the years a short passage from a romantic novel kept hidden under her pillow in girlhood: 'Anatole's dark eyes seemed to burn deeply into Eugenia's very soul!' Perhaps she has always remembered it to balance her tendency to foster silly hopes in such matters. Right now, this moment, she wants to laugh at herself outright. She also wants to grip the General's hand and run with him as if they were children through the piny woods among ancient tombstones, transforming militarist and concubine into the shyest of young lovers.

Fool, she tells herself, coming to the end of the path.

'Have you ever cast the Yarrow Stalks?' General Tang asks just at the moment two horsemen appear in the lane ahead. They are galloping.

A few minutes later, Vera is sitting alone on a stone bench near the Avenue of Honor. Two horses are still tethered to a railing, but neither of them is the General's. The other one belongs to a young officer who waits to escort Vera back to the Residence.

The General had galloped off with the other officer, after a brief conference, stopping long enough to bow curtly in Vera's direction.

So he is gone. Vera glances up at the waning light in the spiny branches of evergreens. The spell is broken, and she is glad of it. All the telltale signs of infatuation had been with her this afternoon: the desire for touch, escape, and laughter; the extravagant sensitivity; even the childish giddiness. Damn fool. Of course, she has an excuse. Her present vulnerability comes from fear that Erich will leave her. Any reasonably charming luncheon partner would have done as well as the General. With the tip of her shoe Vera kicks at a pebble.

No explanation, he just galloped away to review his troops or whatever these Chinese warlords do to earn themselves headlines. She is angry – no, furious – no, outraged. That goes, of course, with infatuation. But it is finished now, the momentary spell broken. She is getting thirsty, damn it, and they came out here without anything to drink. What's wrong with her? If anybody knows it, she certainly knows it is no good acting like a girl from a Petrograd finishing school who adores any boy she dances once with at a ball.

The young officer, waiting to take her back to the Residence, glances nervously her way. What is he thinking? Vera wonders. That he can have me if he half tries? Testing him, she smiles alluringly, and as she expects, the young man looks down awkwardly at his feet. At the moment he seems timid, but given the right circumstances what might he do? Vera has never trusted a man since that night in a cold train station on the way to Omsk.

The stationmaster's room, January 1919. In its filthy confines, with the wind howling outside, she had given herself to three Czech legionnaires in exchange for their promise to let her sick uncle stay in the only heated compartment on the train. Until that night she had been a virgin. They propped her up like a doll upon a table that shook with each laughing assault. She can remember even today the smell on them of salt beef that made her gag as they kissed her. She can recall too the lamplight flickering crazily above her head, the feel of her petticoat gathered about her lifted thighs, the cool air on them and the rough cloth of the legionnaires' shirts. Later the men turned her family out of the compartment. In two days her uncle died, his breach a slowly diminishing plume of frost in a crowded freight car. Vera had sworn never to hope for anything good from men again, yet many times thereafter she had dared to hope. Sometimes she considered herself in love with a man, but this always proved to be nothing more than the folly of a moment. All she hopes for now is comfortable survival, the rest is for cheap novels and people who have the leisure for illusion.

As Vera perceives it, the trouble lies in her own heart. For at the core she believes her heart is as frozen as Lake Baikal had been that winter when her dying mother and youngest brother set out across it in a wagon that never reached the other side.

The light is softening, climbing higher in the pines, leaving their trunks in murky blue depths. How long has she sat in this Burial Ground from which the General takes his strength? Because he really does take it from this place, from the roots of trees nourished by the bones of thousands who have had their own source in a single individual, the sage Confucius. This land, she feels strongly, has also taken sustenance from the dead who lie in it. Once in her life Vera had seen a similar bond between the earth and the human spirit: Her grandmother had walked five miles every day through the grounds of the *dacha*, rain or shine, in heat or winter storm, five miles, singing to herself, mixing the veins of the earth with her own. Such things happen rarely, but they happen. Often on the Siberian trail Vera had remembered her grandmother and sometimes the memory assumed sacredness, as if she had witnessed a saint in action. Such things do happen. And although surely she does not regard the General as saintly, she considers him uncommon, one of the rare ones who see into the heart of things. And so? So nothing. It doesn't matter.

Rising with a sigh, Vera motions to the young officer. 'Take me back.' He rushes forward and gives her a stiff bow. Timid, she thinks, nothing more.

At the guesthouse, she is surprised to find Erich gone. How long will they stay in Qufu? She feels restless, eager to begin the long dusty trip back to Shanghai, a real place unhampered by the past. Leave Qufu to generals who should have been ancient scholars. Well, the truth is she is still angry. Finding the flask of rum, she upends it and drinks until she coughs. Her hands tremble. Either the rum or a sign of the nightmare returning. Sometimes it happens that way before the nightmare pays a dreadful visit: a tremor in her hands. No, none of that. Once today is enough. She will fight the return, and eventually she must refuse the visits altogether. She will be brave like the Rogachevas who died on the march, crazy with fever, disfigured by the running sores of typhus, coughing their lungs out, shaking like rattled dice – No, she will not think of them, their bravery or their suffering or their deaths. Enough, no more today. No more memory, no more disgusting guilt.

Disgusting. She takes a long swallow of rum, pours a glass of water to assuage her thirst, and sits down. She will think only about the rum, the hot heavy ball it makes in her stomach. She drinks more rum, enlarging the ball, and downs two glasses of water. She will not let the nightmare in. She will not.

The door swings open. 'Pack up!' Luckner shouts.

His hair is mussed; Vera notices this immediately. It seems funny to her. Perhaps he ran his hand nervously through the slicked-down hair. Amazing. She pours another drink, after which Luckner, coming up, takes the flask from her.

'Pack up,' he repeats tensely. 'We're getting out of here.'

'Pack up?'

'Are you drunk?' Luckner throws himself into a chair, holding the flask chest-high in preparation for using it. 'General Tang has left. He's gone. Without closing the deal.'

'What happened?'

'Wasn't he with you this afternoon? Didn't he say anything?'

'We were in the Kong cemetery and some officers came and he left.'

'Yes, that's all I know.' Luckner blows out his breath in exasperation. 'Except he tortured a man in a cage.'

Vera blinks dully at him; the rum is working.

'So all of a sudden he's gone. They won't tell me why. You know the Chinese and their goddamn secrecy. He's just gone. I heard he's already left with a company of horse.'

'Already?'

'Are you drunk? Didn't you say he left you in the cemetery? Do you understand *anything*?' Luckner is shouting. 'Must be on the road by now. I can imagine the dust rising. They must be galloping.' He grimaces at Vera. 'Can you imagine it? Can't wait long enough to close a deal that will save his stupid army, but he has got to be galloping in the darkness with a company of horse. I just can't believe it.'

She is thinking of the man playing. Tai Chi at dawn. 'Neither can I.' Torturing a man in a cage? 'No, I can't believe it either.'

Luckner, jumping to his feet, begins pacing. He runs both hands through his hair – that is wonderfully odd to Vera – making strands of it stick out wildly, like wire. Here is a man, Vera thinks, who can make love without mussing his hair. Today he treats it like a bundle of straw to be rummaged through for a solution. Funny. And a little scary. Or why is she frightened? Or is what she feels really fright?

'I will never understand these people,' Luckner declares softly. 'Didn't stop long enough to settle his business with me. Can you fathom it? He has us come all the way here. I drive up in a big car hired at *great* expense just to give him a nice ride afterward, maybe to Jinan or Tai Shan, whatever he wanted, and the dumb sonofabitch gets on a horse and leaves me high and dry. Can you believe it?' Luckner halts his pacing and turns to her. 'I have a reputation to protect. The last ten years I've been the most reliable dealer in China – maybe not the one who made the largest profit, but the most reliable. Now this bastard treats me like a coolie. It's an insult, it won't help me in Shanghai.' Luckner slumps into a chair; his face looks haggard below the disheveled blond hair. 'I will *never* understand these people. Only had to sit down together an draw up the bill of lading. Take an hour, two at the most. He could have delayed until morning whatever goddamn wild goose chase his Chinese mind has set him on.' Luckner shakes his head in disbelief. 'I'm finished with the bastard. Pack up, Vera. We'll drive all night, I don't care. I just want to get back to Shanghai.'

'To civilization.'

'The Japanese cutting into my business. Now this fucking warlord humiliating me. Karlsruhe? See it again? What a laugh!' Luckner drinks from the flask, grimacing. 'So goodbye, Karlsruhe. I'll end my days in this mad country.' Luckner huddles in shadow, miserable, his hair tousled boyishly.

Vera rises unsteadily and searches for her suitcase by the light of a single lamp. They won't get away until nightfall, but she agrees with Erich that it's necessary to start back now. Right now. Throwing the suitcase on the bed, she begins packing. For the last few hours I have been in danger, Vera tells herself. But it's finished now; I will never see the man again. I'm glad, glad he's gone. I'm glad he's a brute who can torture someone in a cage, because it puts him beyond my understanding, because this way he's no threat to me, because he's the kind of man who can hurt me.

So my departure from Qufu will be an escape.

'Hand me the flask, please?' She looks up from the suitcase.

But lost in his own worries, Luckner does not hear her.

5

Philip Embree can't sleep.

It has nothing to do with his lying on the ground; after all, tonight most of the camp is sleeping outside their tents, which stink terribly in the heat.

Embree has been made restless by anticipating tomorrow, when they execute the Englishman. His anticipation is unfortunately complex. Naturally he is appalled by the idea of a Christian – an innocent one, too – being murdered by heathen renegades; but, on the other hand, Embree is aware that part of his anticipation stems from nothing nobler than curiosity about the ritual of execution itself. Will they shoot the Englishman with his hands tied behind his back, the way they executed the army officers at the train? Will they blindfold him because he's a foreigner? What will they do? Embree sits up, glancing around at the people sleeping nearby. Tomorrow a man dies without trial. Pray to God, Embree tells himself, but although he did pray earlier in the evening, he's unable to do it now. Caught in the unseemly opposition of proper compassion for the Englishman and improper curiosity about the manner of the impending death, Embree has struggled for hours with his own impulses. None but those trained religiously like himself could be as keenly aware of the battle taking place between right sentiment and perverted desire; on such matters rests the final disposition of the soul. What surprises, let alone frightens, him is his lack of preparation for the spiritual contest. He feels vulnerable, without resources to fight the good fight. At the same time, in the dark silence, he finds in himself uncommon logic and clarity of thought. Back home there were always things to do, places to go, classes and prayer meetings to attend, which provided escape from his doubts about himself and his calling. In spite of those doubts, he had always respected the principles of a religious life, had trusted its ultimate value, and apparently had at last convinced everyone, including himself (but perhaps not father), that he was capable of serving the Lord.

Clearly in the past few days he has lost not only his copy of the Good Book but some of his faith in it as well. This is true; he can't deny it in the midst of these sleeping bandits and their women. Words that he labored to set by heart through childhood and adolescence now seem to his ear empty, platitudinous, unreal, whereas reality lies in tomorrow, when they kill the Englishman.

'Once in, always in. Remember that, Philip,' his father said on the day Embree left home. Perhaps father had divined in him a tendency to surrender his convictions when he stepped on foreign soil – almost immediately, without decent struggle.

Embree feels weak, ashamed. China has taken him by surprise. Perhaps there had been more truth than he realized in a speech he heard in Shanghai. At the time he had judged it to be harsh, unfeeling. It had been delivered at the Baptist University there. Lying now beneath the stars of Shansi on a mountaintop, he remembers the lovely Shanghai campus with its promenades, shade trees, and brick buildings reminiscent of the ivy cloisters at Yale. Yale: how far away it seems, both in time and distance. For that matter, how far away Shanghai seems too. But on the evening of that speech, not more than two weeks ago, Shanghai had seemed intensely immediate. The speaker was an old man, big and gruff, in physique reminding him of father. At the little podium, under a slowly revolving fan, the old minister told the assembly that having spent two decades in this troubled country, he owed newcomers a word of truth. 'What a mess of evil the missionary in China must contend with,' the old man declared in a ringing voice. 'The Bible says no liar or idolater can reach Heaven. Well, these people are all idolaters and liars. China is a nation of liars, mark my word. You have read your guidebooks, but mark my word, they won't help you in this land of scoundrels and liars. Among the lost and forsaken – those going to eternal death – I reckon there must be more Chinese than any other people on earth. So watch out, godly, earnest, and faithful young people: You have come to the land of Satan.'

Those opinions had sounded woefully simplistic that evening to Embree, although his own faith was conservative too. Now, under the stars in a bandit camp, he wonders if there wasn't some truth in the old man's words, at least the warning to guard one's faith while living in such a country. That makes sense now to Embree, as he wonders what is happening to him. China is real, more real than anything he has encountered. It has the power to uproot in him the beliefs of generations of Embrees, of that he is already sure; and he is aware that when day breaks, his ancestors and father and school and the entire tradition will have lost. Curiosity has won. He wants to see the execution more than he wants to kneel here and pray for a man's departing soul.

Yet when people begin moving about the camp, he remains

fetally curled up on the ground, and he remains that way, feigning sleep throughout the morning, until gunfire tells him the execution has taken place. Sweating and breathing heavily, he sits up.

He is still sitting there, gazing with empty relief at the earth between his outstretched legs, when a pair of shoes – not Chinese cotton but Western leather – come into his view. Looking up, he meets the grinning face of Chin, who points with the riding crop at the shoes.

'Like them? They don't fit, though. Englishmen have big feet.'

Glancing at the shoes, Embree stares at the bandit. 'Is he really dead?'

'I thought you'd be there, praying for him. I heard you were praying on your knees last night. What happened this morning?'

'I slept,' Embree lies. At least, he thinks, I did not surrender to the wicked desire to watch a Christian die.

'You needed the sleep. You foreigners need more sleep than we do. Still, they aren't so big I can't wear them.' Chin turns one foot, regarding it critically like a grand lady in a boutique. 'Among peasants you find this belief: Before executing a man you must take his shoes; otherwise he'll give their spirit to a ghost who will follow you around.' Chin bends down to flick some dust from the toe of the left brown-leather brogue.

'So he's dead.'

'Don't feel sorry for him. He was lucky.' Chin squats beside him, bringing his eyes level with Embree's. 'We put four bullets in him. Not that he deserved to go fast that way. Fucking coward. He sat on the ground and cried.' Chin spits near the right brogue. 'Said we should wait and make a deal with him. But did he offer guns? No, some damn bridge spans or something. Right to the end he was afraid of admitting he sold guns to warlords. Don't blame him for it, though. I remember when White Wolf caught one of those English gunrunners and had him strangled.' Chin searches Embree's face for a reaction, then smiles. 'It took an hour.'

'An *hour*?' Embree repeats in horror.

'Li Shun did it. Remember Li Shun?'

Embree does: The execution site near the halted train; a tall man with drooping mustache; the curved Manchurian sword.

'Li Shun can strangle someone for as long as you want. He judges the man's ability to stay alive – does it by the skin color and look of the eyes. That's what Li Shun claims, and I believe him, because I saw him work that time. Took a whole hour.' Chin

115

shakes his head in appreciation. 'If you think it's easy to strangle a man that slowly, try it. The windpipe is a delicate thing.'

Embree senses that Chin is telling him these details to make him squirm. Horror and disbelief must be showing on his face, so Embree tries to compose his features.

Studying the young foreigner, Chin rises and slaps his thigh once, decisively, with the crop. 'Remember,' he says, 'life goes on.'

Watching the one-eared man stroll away, Embree feels hungry. In the back of his consciousness for a long time has been the pungent odor of fried pumpkin. Now the smell moves to the center of awareness. Pumpkin cooking. Wonderful. Rising, Embree looks in the direction of smoke from a cooking fire.

At midmorning, when Embree sits beside a tent while camp life sweeps past – women with pots, untethered mules, bandits already drunk or heading for dice – two men come along and stop in front of him. One wears a derby, soiled and battered, of ancient vintage; baggy pants, cinched by rope and rolled at the bottoms above skinny legs; and cotton shoes with toes peeking through frayed holes. This man, doffing his derby, falls to his knees and kowtows.

At the sight of this strange obeisance, Embree gets to his feet and stares down at the fellow, whose shaven head remains bowed, forehead pushed firmly into the dust.

'What's this?' Embree asks the other man nervously.

The man says, 'Chin sent it.'

'Sent what?'

The man points contemptuously at the fellow in the dust. 'It.' Turning, he goes away.

It is clear to Embree that the kowtowing fellow will stay eternally in that position unless something is done. Sitting down again, Embree leans forward and roughly shakes the man's shoulder. 'Get up.'

The man slowly raises his head, then, grinning, does as he has been told. He is middle-aged, with a missing front tooth and a broad flat nose. 'I am pleased to meet your Holiness. I am your low, miserable, and unworthy Ni Feng-lin.'

It takes Embree a long time to unravel this mystery; it doesn't help that the man is both linguistically circumspect and too eager

116

to please. At last, however, Embree sorts it out. From whatever motive it is impossible to say, Chin has sent this man, Ni Feng-lin, to act as Embree's servant, Ni was a coolie until the bandit gang pressed him into service a few months ago. He is also a Christian, which may account for his assignment to a foreigner. He is also a Catholic, it appears, but serving a Protestant makes no difference to him. For that matter, in the next hour Embree tries in vain to make the distinction in Ni's mind between Catholic and Protestant. After the long explanation, the small coolie nods politely. 'Yes, we love the Blessed Jesus.'

Embree decides to leave it at that – no great theological error – but finally succeeds in persuading Ni to forgo the 'Holiness,' substituting for it the less controversial 'Master.' Has Chin sent the fellow for a joke? The one-eared bandit is capable of it. Even so, as the day wears on Embree begins to appreciate a servant, for it is clear that he has been abandoned to his own resources. It is through Ni that he wheedles dinner out of a hostile camp woman and gets himself the pony.

Getting the pony, even with help, is difficult. Although there are more ponies than men in camp, at first the guards are reluctant to let Embree touch one.

'I can't go anywhere, I can't escape,' he explains to the guards, who regard him in silence. 'Where can I go? A foreigner? In the middle of nowhere?' He raises his arms to encompass the whole mountaintop and surrounding plains in the darkness beyond the torch-lit camp. But the men don't reply.

'I only want to sit on a pony,' he argues. 'Not to ride it, but to sleep on it.'

'Sleep on it?' One of the guards gives a little snort of disbelief.

'Wait, Master,' says the coolie Ni. 'Let me talk to them.'

Ni huddles with the guards, while Embree stays at a discreet distance from the gesticulating and whispering, and at last approaches him to say. 'It's settled. If you bless them, Master, you will get your horse. I told them you would –' Ni gives the sign of the cross – 'Father, Son, and Holy Ghost. That's what they want, Master.'

'But I can't do that. I'm no Catholic priest. And why will they give me a pony for doing that anyway? They aren't Christians, are they?'

'I told them it's magic and will keep them from harm. It is magic, the sign of God, isn't it, Master?'

Embree can't determine how ingenuous his servant is, but if the scheme works, then he will try it. So in front of the two guards Philip Embree of the New Protestant Mission crosses himself in the name of the Father the Son, and the Holy Ghost. For good measure, since the guards seem genuinely humbled by the mystery, he adds, 'Hail Mary, full of Grace, hallowed be thy womb.'

So the pony is his for the night. Curious, the guards and his servant watch him mount the animal, which is tethered along with a dozen others to a long rope. After a while the guards begin to smile. Later they giggle, while Ni Feng-lin squats nearby and watches solemnly as his master sits on the pony, which is trying to find a comfortable stance for sleep. Later, when the camp torches are extinguished, Ni Feng-lin curls up and goes to sleep too, using his derby for a pillow.

Embree adjusts himself often on the pony's back and tries to figure out what to do with his hands. Shall he fold them or place them on the pony's neck and shall he lean forward or attempt to sleep with his body rigid, upright? What had the Mongols done eight hundred years ago when they conquered most of the known world and slept every night just as he is trying to do now, on their horses, far from home? One hour leads slowly to the next; Embree is unable to shut his eyes for long, much less to sleep. How did the Mongols do it? There must be a way, he tells himself, to find the body's balance in this position, enabling a man to stay mounted, yet sleep as well. To his relief, he finds that the pony doesn't seem to mind the experiment.

Perhaps the expectation that a warrior might try such a thing has been bred into the pony's blood through generations on the Mongolian steppes. But the animal doesn't remain completely motionless; each time it shifts weight in an effort to find comfort, Embree starts violently, as if the pony has bucked. At such a moment one of the guards sleepily eyes the mounted foreigner, then drowses until yet another tremor of movement occurs among the tethered ponies. Finally, some time near dawn, Embree succeeds in drifting off to sleep, unaware of the position of his hands – and falls off the pony with a thud that awakens all three guards. They titter, seeing the blond American lying beneath the hooves and sagging bellies of a dozen nervous ponies. Without a word, he rolls out of their way, gets up, dusts off his pants, and remounts. He is seen this way – back hunched and hands folded on the animal's neck – by early risers passing with water buckets.

'Can I help you down now, Master?' Ni asks anxiously, staring up at the haggard, red-eyed face.

Embree shakes his head, dismounts, and walks stiffly away from the tethered herd, while the guards regard him with a mixture of amusement and confusion.

That day is spent mostly in begging. Neither master nor servant has any money, and few women in the camp are willing to feed a foreigner and a coolie for nothing.

While they scrounge for millet gruel or a steamed bun, Embree learns about Ni, who is not reluctant to speak of his life. Indeed, Embree is his first audience ever, and he takes full advantage, giggling at his own history, which has little in it of amusement. He had been raised in a Shansi village south of here, near Changchih, where Franciscans built a church in the last century. A peasant with a few *mou* of land then, Ni Feng-lin went to the orphanage there to purchase a wife, having heard it was cheaper to buy one from the Christians than from neighboring farmers. The rumor proved true; there were many choices because the orphanage was filled with girls.

'Why so many girls?' Embree asks, while they prowl the mountaintop begging food.

'Nobody else wanted them. If you feed a girl for twelve or thirteen years, what do you get for it? You can sell her for grain or give her in marriage, but either way you get back less money than it took to feed her all those years. That's the way people think, so they give girl babies away. The church in Changchih was very nice. They took in girls who might be left out to die and they raised them. I bought a nice plump one.' Ni laughs at the memory. 'I couldn't have her, though, until they put water on me and said the words.'

So first baptized, then married, he had returned to his village. The conversion had occurred in more than name, because soon in defense of his new religion Ni came into conflict with family and neighbors over matters of ritual in conducting weddings and funerals. He no longer accepted the worship of ancestors, therefore refused to make contributions to the local Buddhist association. He recalls perfectly what a Chinese Catholic priest had warned him of during his stay in Changchih: 'No more worship of ancestors, Ni Feng-lin. Your revered ancestors, being heathen, are in the lake that burns with fire and brimstone, and as even Confucius and Buddha did, they have perished everlastingly.' Ni laughs at his splendid recall of words that must have seared him to the bone at the time. 'I remember what the priest said, exactly. I did what he told me.' In succeeding years he matched his wife in loyalty to the Church, even after villagers started muttering that he practiced witchcraft and was responsible for a calf dying, for water tasting like clay in a landlord's well.

'I remember this too.' But he says something in English that Embree can't decipher. A few 'the's' become clear after a few repetitions and the word 'church' and perhaps 'blood,' but the phrase remains resistant to Embree's American ear.

'Say it in Chinese.'

The little coolie scratches his head, after removing the derby, and stares a long time into the distance. Finally he nods in good-natured acknowledgment of his ignorance. 'I think I only heard it in English. It's supposed to be important to Christians, so Father had learned it in English, and I learned it from him, but he never told me what it meant, if *he* knew what it meant. He taught it to me, though. I know it,' Ni concludes proudly.

Life in the village having become intolerable because of their Christianity, Ni and his wife moved to a village nearer to Changchih. Here there was a larger Catholic population, and the Bishop often came to give his blessing. At his arrival they fired the village cannon and held an umbrella over his head. Ni joined the local Society for Progress; this membership gained him merit in the eyes of God, so he would get to Heaven faster than Catholics who failed to join. The society was managed by a layman, a local merchant named Fan Ching-ho.

'Fan Ching-ho,' the coolie repeats with slow, special emphasis as if pronouncing the name can make something happen.

It was this Fan Ching-ho who persuaded Ni to take out a loan to rent some land from the society. The loan, of course, came from the society as well, and when the interest on it proved too much for him to pay, even after a satisfactory harvest, Ni's trouble began. Having defaulted on the debt, he was charged additional interest, which was compounded each month.

It takes Embree half the afternoon to piece out these complications, which seem to have a comic quality in Ni's own view, the result perhaps of his ignorance of exactly what had happened to him.

After three more months had passed in default, a collector arrived from Changchih, demanding payment and also an additional fee for his own travel. Although Ni promptly sold his two pigs, he couldn't pay the entire debt, so the Society for Progress threw him off the land. Meanwhile, his wife, who did housework for a local landlord, was cheated of her wages and, when she complained, was summarily dismissed. Fan Ching-ho offered to make them another loan, this one from him personally rather than from the society. A stipulation, however, awarded him three months' interest before the principal was handed over – interest so compounded that Ni received less than half the loan agreed upon. Explaining this transaction, Ni giggles. At the end of three months he failed to make his payments again, so Fan confiscated all his belongings, everything, down to an old pot for cooking rice. Ni and his wife drifted through the village, begging food, until she starved to death and he almost did. At last, pressed by a few citizens in the village, the Society for Progress took him in and fed him until he was strong enough to work again. To pay this debt for his room and board with the society – a corner in the stable and millet gruel each morning – he did hard labor without pay for Fan Ching-ho.

Ni has laughed his way through this terrible history. 'Then when the bandits of White Wolf came through the village, they took me because I had a strong back. Very good men.' He waves his hand to encompass the mountaintop. 'But they killed Fan.' He doesn't seem glad of it; in fact, it is the only time a note of sadness has crept into his voice. 'So I've been with them. Look at this beautiful hat.' He takes the derby off, turning its dented surface lovingly. 'They gave it to me after a raid. They say it belonged to a Kaifeng banker.' Putting it back on his head, Ni grins. 'Imagine someone like me wearing the hat of a great man from Kaifeng.'

'And you still have faith?' Embree asks in wonder.

'It is not God's fault men are bad.'

Embree studies the benign expression, the gentle eyes, the languid mouth, and finds in this coolie what he has read about in books and what he has been exhorted to discover for himself during prayer meetings: the pure acceptance of God's will. It humbles, chastens him. Embree looks at the coolie in a new light.

That evening the young American returns to the herd, mounts the same pony, and attempts to sleep, while his servant lies nearby, derby under his head, and the guards chuckle nervously at the odd sight.

This time Embree succeeds in falling asleep twice – and falling off the animal each time.

The next day is much like the previous one – a monotonous search for something to eat. He and Ni wander through the hot, smelly camp, where people sleep when they are tired from too much dice or muzzy from drink; they sit in clusters for long aimless conversations, munching on fruit like ruminative cows, or go inside their tents for a smoke of opium.

That night Embree again mounts his pony. Within an hour he feels the thrill of discovery: Somehow his body is conforming to the animal, molding against it; his back, humping forward, seems to lock into position, as if he can't be knocked off. Moreover, his hands (right crossed over left) form on the pony's neck the apex of a triangle with the base of his shoulders; this pose seems capable of sustaining him for hours, even while his conscious mind sleeps. This time he knows he will succeed. When he falls off the horse again, Embree remounts without a sense of discouragement; when finally he opens his eyes the next morning, it is clear that he has slept an appreciable amount of time on the pony's back.

About noon, while he sits near a ring of men gambling with wooden dice, Ni at his feet like a faithful dog, Embree watches the one-eared Chin coming along, beating the crop against his thigh at each step.

'What is this,' Chin asks instantly in a harsh voice, 'about you sitting on a horse all night?'

Embree, sensing trouble, gets to his feet. 'Yes, sir. It is true.'

'What are you doing on the damn horse anyway?'

'Sleeping.'

Chin stands with arms akimbo, glowering. 'Are you a madman?'

'During the trip someone said the Mongols used to sleep on their horses. I want to prove I can do it too.'

'You want to prove you can sleep on a horse.' After a long, searching appraisal of Embree, the bandit leader taps him on the shoulder with the riding crop. 'Wait till White Wolf hears this. He's a Mongol to his toes, yet I doubt if he ever slept on a horse.' Chin shakes his head in disbelief. Then, leaning forward, he says, 'You call yourself a Christian, but you lie. You're not one of *them*.' Pointing with the crop at Ni, who has assumed the position of kowtowing, Chin says, 'That cringing thing there is a Christian. But you? You are –' He searches vainly for a word; then, striking himself on the chest with the riding crop: 'You are like *me*!'

With a parting chuckle, another disbelieving shake of his head, Chin swaggers off.

That night Philip Embree, formerly of Yale, now officially attached to the New Protestant Mission of China, sleeps with considerable success on the back of a Mongolian pony.

The following day, like the others, begins with Embree and his servant begging pumpkin and millet gruel from women at the morning fires. Finally, when they have a bowl of watery gruel to share, Ni pushes it away. 'I'm not hungry.'

'I demand you eat too.'

Ni slurps up a little, then pushes the bowl away again. His manner is surprisingly decisive. 'No more, Master. A priest of God like yourself should not beg food. In Changchih the priests rode in chairs and ate three times a day.'

Embree doesn't try to force him but leaves a little gruel in the bowl. Setting it down, he waits.

'There is still some left, Master. Don't waste it.'

'I don't want any more.'

'In China, Master, the first thing a child learns is never to leave anything in a bowl.'

'Then finish it for me.'

'Master,' Ni murmurs disapprovingly, but he complies. For a while they sit and watch two women picking lice from each other's hair. At last Ni turns and dips his head apologetically. 'Forgive me, Master, but I have a request. This morning, may I have permission to go hear the spirits talking?'

Embree looks at the small coolie in the battered hat. 'You want to do what?'

'A man in camp here can talk to the dead. This morning he's going to do it for people. I'd like him to speak to my departed wife and find out if she's doing well, but I haven't any money, so I'd just like to listen to him speak for others who do have the price.'

'I thought you no longer believed in spirit worship,' Embree notes with a smile.

'I don't believe in worshiping them. That is not Christian. But they're out there –' He glances around as if expecting to see one dancing through dust motes in the hazy sunlight. 'Do I have your permission, Master?'

'Of course. Go listen to your spirits talk.'

'No, they don't talk to us, you see. Only to this one man.'

'And he tells you what they say. I understand. Now go on and enjoy it.'

Ni looks solemnly at him. 'Jesus will bless you, Master. You are a good man.'

Minutes after the coolie in his oversized pants and dented hat has left him, Embree still feels the bitter irony of those words. Good? He is nothing of the sort. He is enjoying a vagabond life alongside cutthroats and scoundrels. And yet he can't help it; the freedom of this mountaintop is exhilarating. He is thinking about it when the Englishman's brogues appear between the row of tents.

Chin is smiling. 'Get up, my friend. You're coming with me today.'

Rising to his feet, Embree notices two young women a few paces behind the one-eared bandit. He recognizes one of them – the sullen but pretty girl who accused him of being afraid. The girls are leading four ponies.

'Mount,' Chin tells him. 'You know your own pony by now, don't you.'

When they are all mounted, the sullen girl gives Embree a faint smile of recognition; she wears a peasant tunic and a baggy pair of trousers, but her braided hair, long for a Chinese, is tied with a fetching piece of blue ribbon. He remembers her eyes from their first meeting – intensely black, brilliant, steady.

They set out between the tents, people moving out of their way as they take a narrow path that curves through camp to the road leading down the mountain. 'You still carry that?' Chin is staring at the ax stuck in Embree's rope belt.

'Always.'

'Always,' Chin repeats, clucking his tongue in amusement.

Embree doesn't ask where they are going or why the women are following behind them single file down the mountainside. He has already learned that the Chinese enjoy surprise, that from a sense of fun or a need to keep others off balance, they resist the predictable act. Embree has come a long way from his propensity to ask questions when anything strange happens. Understanding this accomplishment, he values it and therefore keeps his mouth shut.

Once past the caves and their silent, primitive inhabitants, Chin leads the way toward the surrounding plain, fiercely hot under a hazy sun. He summons Embree to his side and they ride along in silence, the girls trailing. Small mountains rise everywhere, like the backs of whales in a golden sea – grain is ripening for the harvest. It is beautiful, Embree thinks: the tilled land, distant trees, the dirt path on which they ride; everything seems open and generous, a China to love.

Abruptly Chin turns and squints at him. 'How do you like your servant?'

'Very much.'

'Good then. Otherwise I'd send him away.'

'Please let him stay with me.'

'To pray together?' Chin asks sarcastically.

It occurs to Embree that Chin resents the easy relationship between foreigner and coolie, so he says, 'I like him because he does what I tell him.'

Chin raises his eyebrows expectantly.

'When he's slow. I kick him.'

'Good.' The bandit nods in approval.

Again they ride in silence, with the women a respectful distance behind. But Embree is constantly aware of the sullen one's presence; he can feel her dark eyes watching him.

'Can you believe,' Chin says after a long while, 'I came from a village much like your servant's? Do you see anything similar about us?' His tone is faintly threatening.

Embree knows what his answer must be. 'Nothing at all.'

'Sometimes I look at creatures like him,' Chin says with a triumphant laugh, 'and I wonder how I raised myself so high.'

Sensing that Chin wishes to talk about it, Embree says, 'Well? How did you?'

'I started by getting into debt,' Chin says. But unlike Ni Fenglin, he did not sell land or livestock to pay the mounting interest. Chin had grown opium on a nearby mountain, harvested the small patch, and sold it on the sly to local gentry. He was starting to recoup his finances when the gentry abandoned him after discovering a grower whose price was lower than his. Chin went to his rival's field and slit the man's throat. Furious at the loss of their cheaper source of opium, the gentry were going to prosecute him for the lesser crime of growing opium, because they lacked evidence to get him for the murder. What saved Chin from legal action altogether was his agreement to give his pretty sister to a local landlord for a house servant; most of her housework was done on her back in the great man's bed.

Chin shrugs. 'You must live. I learned that a long time ago on the day I lost this –' He taps the flap of skin where his left ear had been. 'I stole a chicken. The local magistrate, whose chicken it was, had two constables hold me down and they sliced off my ear with a kitchen knife. I was eight years old.'

Having made peace with the gentry after the opium episode, Chin became a collection agent for the *Chu*, an association of district landlords. He collected rent from peasants, a task that often entailed beating them. 'That made the difference,' he says. 'I was a peasant looking at peasants from the other side of the wall. I saw myself in them. What I saw was weakness, fear, stupidity. I told myself I wouldn't be any of those things.' Ruthless diligence made him a success as the local enforcer, but his good fortune ended when the *Chu* discovered he had been collecting more than he turned in to the association. For days he was one step ahead of the local militia. He joined a northern warlord's army as an ammo carrier, then a soldier. He nearly froze to death in a harsh Manchurian winter, and nearly lost his life during a pitched battle near Peking, when a shell landed in the midst of his company; another man, standing in front of him, took the full impact of shrapnel meant for Chin. 'In another life I must have been a good fellow.' When the army fled in defeat, Chin removed his blue armband – which identified him with that particular warlord – and along with a few other men roamed the countryside, trying to survive.

'In China we say, "Bandit one day, soldier the next, bandit the next, until you die." ' His small band had looted, raped, set fires, and generally despoiled an entire valley in southern Shansi before they were captured by a larger group of bandits, those under the command of White Wolf. 'It took me only a short time to get White Wolf's trust,' Chin claims proudly. 'But I won't stay with this work forever.'

'What will you do?' Embree asks, as they ride along.

'I want to live in Shanghai. I want to become a Big Teapot.'

'What is that?'

'A man who owns many women.' He glances over his shoulder. 'Like those two, only better. I'd like to run a brothel on Nanking Road.'

Again they ride in silence, passing wattle huts set haphazardly alongside the lanes. Four or five crowd together, as if there were no room on a plain that seems to stretch endlessly. The flat vista is

126

broken infrequently by the round hump of a grave or a solitary bullock cart or a ruined stucco building standing incongruously in a field like the residence of a great official long dead.

Embree feels the eyes on him, boring through his back. He would like to turn and meet her dark look, but he doesn't want to give her the satisfaction of knowing he's aware of her. Embree decides the girl is unlikable. He won't think about her any more.

'I am surprised, my friend, you haven't asked me.'

'About the women?'

Chin laughs scornfully. 'No, not about them. About yourself. You haven't asked me if we heard from Shanghai.'

'Well, have you?' Embree feels curiously detached from the question of his ransom.

'The wireless at Lin Fen doesn't work.' Chin waits a long time before continuing, as if to build suspense. 'So we can't send for your ransom until it's fixed. That will take time.'

'Then I'll be with you longer than a month,' Embree says with a smile.

'Aren't you impatient to leave us?'

'No.'

'No,' Chin repeats, shaking his head slowly. 'I will tell White Wolf what you said. Now look over there. That's where we go today.'

A low mountain floats in the far distance, its base visually lifted from the earth by refracted light; in front of it is a solid line of fringed greenery.

'We go to that mountain?'

'No, to the river in front of it you can't see yet. The Fen.' Chin kicks his pony to improve the pace.

Within an hour they come through the line of poplars to the bank of a meandering river, sunken and thin in its channel.

Gazing at it, Chin observes, 'Within the week there'll be a torrent here. You won't be able to get a boat to the other side.'

Embree stares. The Fen River is hardly deep enough to come to his waist and sluggish enough for a child to cross.

'In a week,' Chin says, following Embree's dubious look. 'You'll hear the sound of it a mile away. Trees breaking up in it. People too, carried from upstream.' He dismounts. 'Good thing too the monsoon's coming. General Tang won't think of attacking in those rains.'

Embree squints up at the cloudless sky.

'Don't worry about clouds. They'll be here soon. The monsoon's overdue.' He motions for the women to dismount. 'That's why we came here today. For a picnic. For a celebration before the rains come.'

A picnic!

It hasn't occurred to Embree that the long trek has had as its purpose something so innocent, so – American. Embree has rather expected a search for someone in a nearby village, an interrogation of a farmer, or even food gathering, which would explain the two girls – picking berries for White Wolf's table while Chin requisitions a pig for a bandquet in the great yurt.

Anything but a picnic.

And yet soon enough they are eating steamed buns and dried thorn dates taken from bags carried on the girls' ponies; and in a shady glade on the banks of the Fen, they are washing the food down with drafts of *paikar*, a heady liquor distilled from kaoliang. Cicadas build a wall of sound behind poplars fronting the river, and from inside the cool shade Embree squints at the bright sky, at the insects swooping down on the sluggish brown water. He remembers a painting seen somewhere – he has little memory for such things – but this one featured a couple of gentlemen of a bygone day feasting in a sylvan glade with naked beauties. He tells himself, I am Philip Embree, held for ransom by bandits, having a picnic on the bank of a Chinese river. He pours more of the liquor, and as he drinks it, Embree becomes increasingly aware of the girls, who on their part virtually ignore him in their efforts to flirt with Chin. The bandit leader, Embree notices, pays more attention to the other girl than to Wu Fu-fang – Embree caught her name during the ride. Of course, the other girl is somewhat prettier, but isn't it obvious to Chin that Fu-fang is the more interesting of the two, in spite of her impudent manner?

Taking a big swallow of *paikar*, Chin belches and gets to his feet. Looking down at the girls, he smiles.

Embree understands. The bandit is going to choose which girl is his. Embree can tell because the girls part their lips and meet the bandit's smile with solemn faces.

Chin, reaching down, grips the other girl's hand at last and helps her to her feet.

Embree glances at Fu-fang, whose expression doesn't change when Chin and the other girl move without a word deeper into the glade, trailing behind them a little laughter.

Embree stares at a half-eaten bun; ants are crawling single file across it like a marauding army. *Fa-zai*: loot, that's what the insects are looking for, just like the *fa-zai* taken from the train and from villages along the way, making the men in White Wolf's mountain fastness so placid and gentle. Why is he thinking such things? Embree doesn't look up, but watches the ants at their plunder.

'They say you sleep on a horse.'

Embree forces himself to look up and meet her dark, steady eyes. Her face is too round, he decides, and her lips pout too much. But the blue ribbon in her braided hair is pretty enough. And her eyes are really – they are really –

'Well, do you?'

'Yes,' he replies with a little shrug. 'I sleep on a horse.'

'To prove you aren't afraid?'

Embree picks up the bun, brushes the ants off, and takes a savage bite from it.

'Why do you carry that ax?'

'I always carry it.'

'They call it the White Ax, meaning it's yours. They say you saved Chin's life with it. Did you?'

'Where are you from?'

'Soochow.'

'Why are you here?'

'Chin told me to come along.'

'I mean, why are you in White Wolf's camp?'

Now it is her turn to shrug. Giving him a reproachful glance, Fu-fang says, 'Why all these questions?'

Embree offers her another drink of *paikar*, but she refuses it. Taking one himself, emboldened by it, Embree says, 'I ask questions for the same reason you do. So we can get to know each other.'

The girl gives him a cautious smile. 'Do you want to know me?'

'Of course.'

'Of course? Why of course? You don't want to know me. You're a foreigner. And anyway, what is there to know? I was married to an old man but he died. In Kaifeng I stayed with an aunt who was going to marry me off to a man even older, so I left. And so I'm here,' she concludes rapidly. 'Is that what you want to know?'

'Thank you.'

The simple politeness apparently disarms her, because her face relaxes. Fu-fang leans back on one elbow, playing with the sunlight's patterns on the grass. Embree watches her become increasingly agitated, however, now that they have nothing more to say. She plays with her hair, moving one hand behind her head to whirl the braid like a rope. Sitting up, she fakes a yawn, throws him a quick glance of impatience, yawns again, flings the rope of hair.

'Where have they gone?' Embree asks nervously.

'You mean those two? I guess they're off fucking somewhere.'

Embree looks at her in astonishment. Does he understand the Chinese? This casual use of a gross obscenity is exciting to him. He has never heard a girl use it in English, much less Chinese.

'Why are you thinking about them?' the girl asks, cocking her head, the rope of hair hanging straight down, away from her shoulder.

'Why didn't Chin choose you?' Embree asks in a trembling voice.

'Because I'm for you.'

Embree looks down at the earthenware jug of *paikar*, and when he speaks, he speaks to it. 'If I were Chin, I'd have chosen you.'

'I'm a small thing for a man to give to someone who saved his life.'

Embree, with considerable difficulty, raises his head and looks at her.

She is smiling. It is a rare smile, as compelling as the look she carries in her eyes. 'You would have chosen me?'

'I would have.'

'Then you have. Haven't we talked enough? Come over here if you want to.'

He must have dozed off from the heat, the excitement, the aftermath of ecstasy, because opening his eyes abruptly Embree sees the bushes part and the brogues step out of them, then Chin grinning, and the other girl.

Aware instantly of his nakedness, Embree grabs the trousers that lie crumpled nearby, and in this moment catches a glimpse of Fu-fang smiling at him, whether in tenderness or amusement he can't pause to wonder as he struggles to get clothed. Only after he has his trousers on can he judge the extent of Fu-fang's own modesty: Her pert breasts disappear inside the cotton tunic with leisurely grace and just as unhurriedly she pulls on her baggy trousers under the placid gaze of Chin and the other girl.

Wordlessly, seated in a circle, they pass the jug of *paikar* around while sunlight moves beyond the glade, leaving it cavernous, dank, but still cosy. Embree can scarcely hear the others, although they are talking lazily of the coming rain (the sky still cloudless). He can think of nothing but this afternoon with Fu-fang; he glances often at the round-faced girl who sits next to him with the matronly indifference of a long-married wife. Nor is the spell broken for him when finally they mount their ponies and start back to camp. As they had done on the way out, he and Chin ride ahead of the women. The intimacies of the afternoon have not affected the hierarchy of travel, although Embree wishes he could ride with Fu-fang. What is she telling her companion as they ride along? Embree wonders. That he made her thrash about in ecstasy? At the recollection he feels pride.

He glances now at the one-eared bandit riding next to him. Embree has made few friends in life – most of them crew members on the rowing team. Perhaps in some way father prevented him from making friendships, he doesn't know. But he knows this: Chin is his friend, and so is Ni Feng-lin, and behind him rides the girl who has changed his life. He can't suppress a smile at the thought of her being there, a few feet behind him, her dark eyes watching his back.

Dusk is upon them before they reach the mountain, and the homey smoke of fires in farm huts curls out of the flat land like a soft blue fog. They ride along a path lined with white-barked pine, its green needles losing their outline in the twilight, flowing toward the coming dark. It is quiet, it is beautiful. All that Embree hears is the steady clomp of hooves on the dry path. He could go on this way forever, and while they ascend the mountain, passing the cave dwellers ghostlike beside their cooking fires, Philip Embree tells himself with mingled wonder and determination that he will not leave the camp of White Wolf, even if the ransom is paid and he is told to go. Not for the mission, not for his father, not for Ursula, not for the church of his childhood, not for the investment in memory and hard study, not for anything that he has known or thought or felt will he leave this camp. Incredibly, but with rising conviction, he understands that his home and destiny are here, on a mountaintop in China, among cutthroats and whores.

131

Ni Feng-lin waits anxiously for Embree to dismount. Twisting the rim of his derby in both hands, the coolie explains that he has worried all day about Master. His face taut with resolve, Ni ignores the presence of the girl, and declares that he must lay down his life for Master because that is what God has told him to do.

'God has spoken to you?' Embree asks with interest, his attention only partially deflected by the girl dismounting behind him.

'Spoke to Him. Spoke to God,' Ni says with a vigorous nod. 'When I came back this morning from the man who talks to spirits, I found you gone and a terrible coldness went through me and I got down to pray and then He came out of the air. Looked just like the priests told us He would look: a big man with a white beard like Kuan Yu. I saw Him as plainly as I see you now, Master, and He told me, he said, 'Ni Feing-lin, you must protect the Master always because he is a Priest of Jesus Christ.' Then He went away.' Ni grins in self-approval.

The girl laughs scornfully.

'What is it, Master?' Ni looks from him to the girl and back. 'What is happening?'

The girl stops laughing and looks hard at Embree. 'Tell your Christian I am yours.' Glowering at the coolie, she says, 'You better watch out!' Then, turning to Embree, she says, 'Do you have any money?' Hesitating only a moment, she mutters, 'I thought not. So how do we live? I'll take care of things, but only for now. Come on.' Fu-fang turns and walks away without looking back to see if Embree is following. But he is, along with a puzzled and fearful Ni, both of them trailing her through the camp, lit by torches casting shadows against tents, against people strolling and ponies being led.

'Stay here,' the girl tells Embree, stopping in front of a tent; then she pulls back the flap and enters. Voices rise quickly in argument. Finally a head appears in the tent entrance – a girl glaring at him angrily. Again loud voices, and finally the girl emerges with a bundle in her arms to give Embree a withering glance of scorn.

'Come here,' Fu-fang calls from within.

Embree enters the hot dark tent that smells powerfully of garlic. He can't see Fu-fang, but when her hand touches his face, he gathers her into his arms.

'This is now ours,' she says, pulling free. 'It cost me two dollars

Mex to get her out of here. That's money you owe,' she adds harshly, but then starts giggling. 'The great Christian priest owes two dollars Mex to a Soochow whore.'

Later, as they lie together in the stifling heat, their bodies drenched in the sweat of love, Fu-fang murmurs sleepily, 'In Soochow there are canals and many bridges. In the markets you see fish flopping in baskets. No one buys a still fish. There's no food like the food of Soochow. No ham tastes quite like Soochow ham. It's the way pigs are fed. Rice slop does it. I remember pigs eating rice slop in our back yard. Did you have pigs?'

'No.' Embree kisses her. 'No pigs.'

'I remember so much. I remember my mother balancing water buckets on a shoulder pole, two full buckets, water to the brim, without ever spilling a drop. I never saw her spill a drop, not ever. Only Soochow women can do that.'

He kisses her again, but she pulls away with a chuckle of impatience. She wants to talk more. 'There's nothing like the language of Soochow either. It has a wonderful sound. Do you know the dialect? They say it's better to hear Soochow people quarrel than the Cantonese talk of love.'

'Love,' Embree repeats, kissing her again. 'Let's do it again.'

'What, again? Not tonight! Are you always so greedy?'

'Yes,' Embree lies, proud of the lie. 'Always.'

'How many children do you have?'

Children? He's never thought of having them. It's like asking him how many battles he's fought. 'I don't know how many,' he tells her with yet another kiss.

'Wait now – enough. I'm tired. Tomorrow.'

'Early tomorrow.'

She giggles. 'Are all the men in your country so eager?'

'No, I don't think so.'

'Lucky for the women. If you need so many women, why didn't your mother buy you a house girl or two? Wasn't your family rich enough to afford a girl? A good mother would see to it her son was happy.'

'My mother died when I was thirteen.'

Fu-fang says nothing, but moves restlessly in his arms, finding a position for sleep.

The idea of mother buying him a girl is something to ponder! At father's command, mother had once given him a lecture about sex – a vague, sentimental description of intercourse and childbirth – but he had learned more of the truth from books and some interesting fantasy from schoolmates. Aside from that single dutiful lecture, mother had never discussed love, much less girls, with him. Girls didn't seem to exist in the world she wished him to occupy. In her view, God and family were quite enough for him.

So it had come as a terrible shock that day when she entered his room and lectured him on self-abuse. There had been only one other shock comparable to it in his life. That had occurred the night after mother's funeral, when father came to his room. Father sat down on the bed, head bowed, clasping his big hands. Embree was ready to kneel, seeing in father's clasped hands a preparation for prayer; but then it occurred to him that the hands were clasped not for prayer but in grief. In hermetic silence father sat there a long time, as helpless as a child. Embree had never seen him like this. There were tears in his eyes, his lips trembled, and when he spoke, his deep basso that boomed each Sunday over the heads of his congregation was reduced to a low, tremulous whisper that Embree had to lean forward to hear.

'She was a good, good woman,' father said. Embree was surprised that father didn't say 'a good Christian woman,' which is how he always described the women of his congregation who died. 'She was so good to me,' he said. He never once mentioned God. 'She was everything, she was everything I loved.'

Those words were a revelation to Philip Embree. They explained what had often puzzled him: Father's anger whenever he caught mother giving Embree a caress. If she stroked Embree's hair or kissed his cheek, 'Enough of that,' father would growl, and turn her attention elsewhere, as if the sight of such affection led to thoughts of human frailty and sin.

But father hadn't been thinking of sin; he had been thinking of love, of making love to this woman who was his. The sight of her hand on another shoulder, her mouth against another cheek – even a child's – had been too much for him. He had not only loved her soul, as he professed to love the souls of the other women in the congregation, but he had loved her body as well, just as today Philip Embree, his son, the fruit of that love, loves the body of a Chinese girl. It is amazing, mysterious; all of it.

And yet what would father say if he knew about Fu-fang? Embree has no trouble choosing an appropriate quotation: 'For the lips of a strange woman drop as an honeycomb, and her mouth is smoother than oil, But her end is bitter as wormwood, sharp as a two-edged sword.'

Father had sat a while longer in the room that night, then with a sigh had risen and left without another word. Nothing intimate was ever said between them again. And six months later Embree had run away to Bridgeport on his first adventure.

He listens now to Fu-fang's rhythmic breathing. When he used to daydream about sex, he never included among the images what is happening now: A woman is breathing trustfully in his arms; the expelled air against his cheek is warm. Very gentle and warm.

'I am in love,' Embree says aloud in awe; the miracle guides him into sleep.

Next morning, when he parts the tent flap, Embree sees two things: a cloudy sky overhead; and beneath, curled up on the ground like a faithful dog, his servant Ni.

Breakfast causes trouble, because the girl and the servant both wish to provide it. Fu-fang wins because she has money. It is with great difficulty that Embree persuades her to give a bowl of gruel to Ni as well.

'For this much food,' she announces grimly, 'he must work very hard.' Fu-fang sends him down the mountain to gather fagots. Then, under her supervision, he piles the fagots in the tent, layering the earth that will soon be soaked by monsoon rains. When the job is finished, the girl shoos him out of the tent and spreads a few camel hides over the foot-thick brush.

Our home, Embree thinks. He sits down, hearing the twigs crackle under his weight.

Fu-fang, watching him, says briskly, 'We'll make a lot of noise tonight, if I know you.'

Lying on the uneven bed, Embree looks at her face framed in the gray light of the entrance. 'Fu-fang, you are the woman I love.'

Acting as if she hasn't heard him, the girl sticks her head out of the tent and yells at Ni, squatting nearby. 'Here's money, you! Go buy some *paikar* for us.' Then, turning to Embree, she says, 'We'll celebrate before the rains come. When the rains come and make a mess of everything, then see if I'm the woman you love.'

'You will be.'

'When the rains come and we stay in this wet tent for days, we'll see.' She laughs briefly. 'The monsoon's a test.'

'It won't make a difference.'

'Yes? Do you know monsoon rains?'

He says with a smile, 'In my country we have tornadoes.'

'How many die?'

'Well, maybe fifty, a hundred people.'

'That's not much of a country.'

'When the rains begin, where will Ni sleep?' Embree is struck by the idea of his servant being outside in the downpour.

'How should I know?' the girl mutters indifferently. She picks up one of her frayed cotton shoes. 'I need new ones.'

'Where will he sleep?' Embree persists.

'I need shoes. In a few days, when my money's gone, how will we get food? You better find some money.'

'He can't stay out in the rain.'

'What's so different about this monsoon? I bet he's stayed out in them before.' The girl shrugs. 'Perhaps someone will let him inside a tent.' Peering at the shoe, as she turns it in both hands, Fu-fang says, 'Don't worry about him. People like him manage.'

'We will let him in here.'

'No.'

'We will let him in here.'

Their eyes meet, then the girl with an ironic smile looks away. When she looks at him again, her eyes are softer. 'But when we make love, out he goes. Maybe it's different in your country, but here a woman wants privacy. I don't care how hard it's raining. Ax Man, *I'm* with you now. I want respect. I've been with a lot of men, but I'm not a whore who fucks in public.'

'He'll go outside even if it's raining hard.'

'Good. That way the women around here will respect me. And the men you. Otherwise everyone will think you come from a soft country.'

'Where only a hundred die in a tornado,' Embree says.

'That's what I mean.' She pretends to a renewed interest in the frayed shoe.' 'And you better get money.'

Later, drinking *paikar* outside the tent – Fu-fang has shooed the coolie out of listening range – the girl repeats the warning. 'You better get money soon.'

'How can I? Everything I had was taken on the train.'

'Get money the way they all do.'

'You mean, from looting?'

'Oh, I forgot.' She laughs derisively. 'You're a Christian priest. Your god says the coolie there will protect you.'

Embree goes past her sarcasm into a contemplation of her outrageous proposal: He, a missionary come to this land a month ago to do God's work, must turn to banditry so he can keep a Soochow whore on top of a mountain during the monsoon! Outrageous, yet he might do it; yes, he might do it to survive, because here it is all survival, because survival here is the only religion, because he simply must, and because he loves this woman.

'I'll ask Chin,' he says quietly. 'When they go out next time, I'll go too.'

Studying him a moment, Fu-fang takes his hand and turns it tenderly in her own, like an object of worth. 'Forgive me.'

'Why?' He's surprised at her tone.

'I'm ashamed of my life. There has never been a whore in my family until now. I got into this thing willfully. I chose to ruin myself out of spite, and now my ancestors will never forgive me and you won't either.'

Embree is stunned into humility of his own by the intensity of her emotion. He is betraying the faith of his people too, with no forgiveness possible either. They belong together, two sinners in the eyes of East and West. 'We must forgive each other,' he says, but the idea goes past her.

'Shame makes me stupid and mean,' Fu-fang murmurs, looking at the ground. 'And I'm getting old.'

'You're not old!'

'I am thirty.'

'Thirty the way you Chinese count. In my country you are twenty-nine. I am thirty,' Embree lies.

'You?' The frown vanishes, replaced by her familiar ironic smile. 'Maybe after you carry that ax another five years.'

He grips her wrist, she pinches him and whispers, 'Let's go inside.' Soon they are tumbling on the bed of crackling twigs, in the full blush of sudden passion, and he has pushed down her trousers when someone shouts at the entrance of their tent.

Embree, scrambling to the tent flap, peers out.

Chin, standing there, frowns and taps his thigh with the riding crop. 'Come here.'

'Is anything wrong?' Embree gets to his feet. 'Is there word from Shanghai?' he asks in fear.

Abruptly Chin smiles and delivers another surprise: White Wolf has invited Embree to the main yurt this evening for a feast to celebrate the coming monsoon. Glancing at the clouds overhead, Chin adds, 'All day two Taoist priests have been working magic to start the rain, but I don't believe in them. The rain had better come soon or we'll have to pack up and leave.'

'Why?'

'Foreign friend, have you forgotten General Tang?'

'Then you believe he'll come?'

'If it doesn't rain in the next few days.'

Embree has never seen the bandit so darkly thoughtful. 'With your permission I'll bring Fu-fang tonight.'

'No, not if you live with her,' Chin tells him sternly. 'Come alone like the rest of us. There'll be plenty of women to choose from.'

Embree watches the man walk away, then reenters the tent, aware that Fu-fang has heard the conversation.

She is turning the cotton shoe in her hand, her mouth sullenly small.

'I won't go,' Embree says.'

She looks at him in genuine horror. 'You can't refuse.' Turning the shoe, Fu-fang gives him a sidelong glance. 'It's all right with me. Do as he says, and when you're through, come back if you want to.'

Touching the shoe so they both hold it, Embree says, 'I will come back.'

6

The central yurt is full of smoke, noise, commotion. White Wolf's favorite comrades and some young women are feasting on delicacies unknown to the rest of camp: fried duck liver and tongue, eggs steamed in duck fat, salted fish, yams, and beans simmered in Shansi vinegar. White Wolf himself remains aloof on his dais, smiling down woozily on the celebration. Beside him a girl awaits his order to prepare another pipe.

Sitting cross-legged on the rug among the other men, Embree eats heartily and drinks quantities of *huang chiu*. The women who refill his bowl look good to him, all of them – women with flat Mongolian faces, women with the longer faces of the Han Chinese. All look good to him, his for the asking. Already, along the yurt walls, men are groping in the tunics of giggling women.

He had seen a movie like this. Who was in it, Douglas Fairbanks, Rudolph Valentino? If he has one of these women tonight, no one, not even Fu-fang, will care. She told him only to come back later. Freedom: heady stuff like the yellow wine. Someone is pounding a drum; three horns with flared bells are screaming. And he is in the midst of all this, Philip Embree of New Haven. Of New Haven? Of the world. He is contemplating his freedom when a blow across his back doubles him over. Looking up he sees Chin, drunk, hovering above him.

'Get up!' Chin says, waving his arm brusquely. 'I see you looking at the women. You'd fuck a goat if it stands still long enough. Just like a Mongol. Come on.' Helping him to his feet, Chin encircles his waist with an arm. 'Come on, Christian Priest, his Excellency's asking for you.'

Emboldened by the wine, Embree doesn't kowtow in front of the platform or even hesitate, but steps up on it beside the chieftain's chair and says, with a curt bow, 'Here I am, Magnificent Highness.'

The little man regards him coolly for a moment, assessing whether the foreigner has gone too far. Presently a thin smile crosses White Wolf's face. 'Do you still carry the ax?'

'Yes, Excellency, but not in your yurt.'

'So you've learned that. Is it true you sleep on a horse?' A bubble of spit forms on his lower lip.

'Yes, it's true. Yes, yes.' With difficulty Embree keeps from laughing. The *huang chiu* has made him reckless, but he doesn't care. 'Know why I sleep on a horse? To be like a Mongol.'

'I never did it,' White Wolf says dryly. 'I never saw anybody else do it either.' He studies the yound American: blond hair, getting long; pale skin reddened by sun and by shaving with a knife and cold water; thick-set torso; broad shoulders. 'Do you like my camp, missionary man?'

'I love your camp,' Embree replies. 'I think your camp's the best place I've ever been.'

White Wolf stares at Chin, standing below the platform. 'What is this foreigner, a crazy bastard?' Turning again to Embree: 'Let's see the hair on your arms.'

Embree, swaying slightly, rolls up one sleeve and displays the forearm, turning it slowly, like something spitted over a fire.

Leaning forward, peering myopically a few moments, the old chief smiles through his wet lips. 'Never saw so much hair. Is there a lot below?'

Full of wine, Embree feels anything is possible tonight. Untying the rope securing his pants, he drops them.

The bandit chieftain stares at Embree's groin a long time before a frown turns into a smile and his tinny chuckle signals up general laughter in the yurt. 'Turn around' – White Wolf motions with a ringed hand – 'so they can have a good look.'

Embree, grinning, obeys. He stands there accepting the laughter until Chin tells him good-naturedly to pull up his pants again.

'Missionary man, you are one crazy bastard,' White Wolf says. 'What do you want from me? I'll give it to you. Want one of them?' He sweeps his hand toward a group of girls serving themselves at the long table now that the men have all eaten. 'Or this one, my new one?' He points at the girl beside his chair, next to the opium works on the bronze stand.

'I want to stay here, Great Highness.'

White Wolf stops smiling, his expression changing to bewilderment.

'I want to join you,' Embree continues, feeling there's nothing he can't tell the bandit chieftain tonight. 'I like it here, I belong here, this is my home.'

The little old man glances at Chin, standing below the platform. 'What in hell is he talking about?'

'I want to stay,' Embree goes on. 'Even if I'm ransomed, I want to stay right here.'

In a voice heavy with astonishment, White Wolf repeats the words. 'Stay right here?'

'With Chin and the others. With my friends.'

White Wolf cocks his head, as if listening to a strange boy unfold a wild fantasy. 'Chin? What is this? Can you believe it?'

'Yes, Excellency, I can,' says Chin solemnly.

'Then by the Queen Mother in the West, let him stay.' White Wolf slaps the chair arm. 'Let him stay then. I like the crazy bastard. Sleeps on a horse,' he murmurs. Abruptly, almost while saying those words, White Wolf loses interest in the strange foreigner and calls out for the girl to fix a pipe.

When Embree steps down from the platform, Chin says to him, 'I told you you're like me. Now you know it. You're with us and I'm glad. Now go drink.'

Taken in hand by a couple of laughing men, Embree drinks another bowl of yellow wine. They applaud him as he reels toward the yurt entrance, suddenly aware of his stomach turning. Can't get sick in front of them, Embree tells himself desperately. Lurching into the night, he kneels beside the entrance and vomits until tears fill his eyes. Two hands on his shoulders steady him as he continues to retch. When the dizzines and nausea subside, Embree turns to see who's been supporting him.

It's Ni Feng-lin.

'Good friend,' Embree murmurs thickly, and with the coolie's help struggles to his feet. 'Drunk, Ni, that's what I am. Dead drunk,' he says airily, as they sway toward the tents, lit by poled torches. 'Drunk, damn happy. Wish father could see me.' He giggles and clutches Ni's shoulder for balance. 'Tell him a thing or two, old goat. Tell him, 'Father, I am seriously considering new career – looting for White Wolf.' Serve him right.' Embree, laughing, nearly falls. He leans down and puts his face close to the coolie's. 'You, Ni. Best man I *ever* knew. More Christian in your little finger than me in my whole body. Than father in his. Real meaning of word 'Christian' is you, old friend. I love you, you crazy little saint. Love Chin too. Don't care what he does, we're alike. Love Fu-fang the most. Love her, *love* her. Crazy in love, you know that? Never thought I – but I'm in love. Go anywhere, do anything for her. Love her more'n life. Love her more'n Christ.' Sobered an instant by this last declaration, Embree halts. 'Don't know why, but she's just – what I want. Tell you something else.' But instead he staggers forward and they go in silence until reaching the tent. 'Drunk, dead drunk, but who gives a damn!' Embree allows the coolie to ease him inside the tent, where other hands take him.

'Good night, old friend!' Embree calls from the tent, but Ni doesn't answer, having no idea what Master says, because all the way from the central yurt, Philip Embree has spoken English.

When he awakes headachy the next morning, on his dry lips are familiar words, learned before he could read or write: 'Take heed to yourself!' A thread of light defines the tent flap; it is becoming day. Fu-fang sleeps beside him; snuggling close to her, Embree feels the veins throbbing in his forehead even as one hand traces the curve of her hip. Moving lower, his fingers touch the light down of her groin, sending through his body, sluggish from alcohol, a little thrill of desire. 'I saw a woman.' Words that open his way into the hectic world of the Bible, with its declamations

141

and wars and jealousies and threats and suffering, just as he experienced it during childhood when, at dawn, he knelt until his knees ached, while father boomed out prayers with the windows open, even in wintertime, to make sure that everyone stayed alert to the word of God. ' "I saw a woman sit upon a scarlet-colored beast, full of names of blasphemy, having seven heads and ten horns." ' The only thing father has ever really liked about him is the prodigious memory that enables him to absorb languages like a sponge and quote the Good Book for as long as anyone will listen. ' "And the woman was arrayed in purple and scarlet color and bedecked with gold," ' Embree recites soundlessly, his hand lightly touching the soft pubic hair, ' "and precious stones and pearls, having a golden cup in her hand, full of abominations and filthiness of her fornication; And upon her forehead was a name written, 'Mystery, Babylon the Great, mother of harlots and abominations of the earth.' " ' Mystery indeed. Embree feels the corners of his mouth lifting into a smile. Once those words would have sobered him into wrenching fear of a woman like the one now lying beside him on a bed of twigs in a smelly yurt on a Chinese mountaintop. Now they are nothing but words, just words, just as father's words would be if he could witness this scene and rail at his son the way Jeremiah railed at the Hebrews.

Embree is still contemplating the amazing change in his life when there comes from the distance, then quickly nearer, the sound of riflefire, then the thunderous clamor of hoofbeats, then wild cries; almost before he can sit up, Fu-fang is up too, fully awake like a small animal caught in the light of a flare. 'Quick,' she mutters, scrambling for pants and tunic. The sound of rapid gunfire is closer, almost upon them, before Fu-fang has pushed back the tent flap to peer out. Embree, on his knees, is looking frantically for the ax.

Fu-fang has her head outside the tent for no more than ten or fifteen seconds, but it is enough time for destiny: Back into the tent's darkness her body comes hurtling like a bundle of flung clothes. Ax in one hand, Embree crawls over to her and touches her face, but it isn't there. With tenderness his hand explores for a terrible moment, as if searching for the pain of a child who can't describe it, and then slowly he withdraws his fingers from a matrix of blood, skull, and brains. He is not thinking, not at all. Turning, he staggers out of the tent, seeing on the ground his servant Ni Feng-lin, curled up in the attitude of sleep, the derby lying bowl up nearby. A few people, screaming, run past. Embree glances dully at them. He doesn't bend down to see if Ni is dead; something in the angle of one leg, a certain heavy look to it, tells him as surely as if he felt for a pulse. Water glistens on the sallow cheek, the closed eye.

It is raining.

Embree looks from the sky to a galloping horse, just turning into this row of tents. A man, leaning forward close to the animal's neck, fires a rifle with one hand. More surprised than he has ever been in his life, Embrees sees the blast come from the barrel through the murky light and knows it is for him, then feels a searing blow and falls.

Has he lost consciousness for long? No sound of hooves or guns or screaming. There is something new to be heard: a kind of sighing, like the wind playing across tassels in a cornfield. It is the rain. Opening one eye wide, he sees from the mud in which he's lying plumes of smoke above the tents. Then his vision blurs. At first he thinks it's from the rain, but, rubbing his eyes, he brings away fingers soaked in blood. Embree tries to sit up, but a profound weakness holds him to the ground. Rubbing his eyes again, he focuses on an object some feet away: It is Ni, mouth parted slightly as if in sleep. For a few moments Embree tries to remember something. What is it, what is it? Something about the dead coolie, his friend. Words, an incomprehensible English learned from a priest. Words, garbled in Ni Feng-lin's Chinese mouth, but somehow important. Why important? Important to Ni.

He is running all this rapidly through his mind when from nearby someone says, 'That one.'

Turning slightly – the motion makes his head throb – Embree sees three men on horseback.

'You,' says the middle rider. 'Are you badly hurt?'

'I don't know,' Embree replies weakly.

One of the riders dismounts and approaches. Embree has every expectation of being helped; even as he lies there, awaiting the help, he remembers a time in boyhood when he fell hard and a woman, either mother or his aunt, cradled his head in her arms, murmuring sweet words. But now he feels only the toe of a boot pushed roughly in his side, moving him cautiously, like a rock under which a snake might be coiled. Through a blur of blood he sees a face bending down to his, peering at him dispassionately.

Then the face goes away, and Embree hears, 'Flesh wound in the head.'

'Who are you?' the middle rider asks harshly. He repeats the question twice before Embree, stunned into a kind of lazy acceptance of things, is aware that the question is his to answer.

'American,' he says thickly, trying to move. In spite of his throbbing head, Embree brings himself up on his elbows to stare at the middle rider, a powerfully built man, erect and square on the horse.

'What are you doing here?' the rider demands.

In control of his faculties, Embree might have told the truth – that he's a missionary – but all he can think of is the reply he gave at the train. 'Student,' he mutters. 'I'm a student.' Later he will often wonder if those few words changed the course of his life.

'Were you taken at the train?'

Nodding, Embree sits up with difficulty. Holding his wrist against his forehead a few seconds and coming away with blood, he locates where he has been grazed.

'Bring him,' the middle rider tells the other two men; clucking to his horse, he rides away.

At this moment Embree faints.

When he regains consciousness, someone helps him sit up, then stand up. Someone has wrapped a few lengths of gauze bandage around his wound, stanching the blood, and someone else shoves a wheat pancake into his hand. Someone helps him walk a few steps before he has to sit down again. Someone helps him rise and put on a shirt too small for his broad chest. He wears it open, like a jacket, above trousers soaked in bloody rain. Stuck in the rope that holds the pants up is his ax; somehow he has summoned enough energy to demand it and someone has given it to him. He is helped onto the back of a tall horse with a saddle. Numbly he glances around, blinking rapidly to make sure he maintains consciousness. Most of the yurts are burning or have already burned down. In the gray rain corpses lie in attitudes of defense or escape; few hold weapons, because the attack, brutally swift, came at first light in a soft drizzle and caught everyone unaware after the night of celebration.

Trying to maintain his seat on the horse, feeling giddy and nauseated, Embree watches some of the attackers – they must be troops of that general whose name for some reason he can't remember – come along with wicker baskets. They halt near the central yurt, or rather the remains of it, for the frame and hides have been reduced to embers. They bend over something, and it takes the groggy American, whose horse has been led forward, a few seconds to understand what they are doing, what it is they are bending over.

Heads.

They are packing heads.

As long as he lives Embree will never forget it: the look of heads detached from bodies, set in a neat row like melons in a market. Silently, quickly, the men lift each head and stow it in a wicker basket. Leaning forward, abruptly alert, Embree begins to recognize individual faces, although each wears a distorting expression of pain or terror unfamiliar to it in life. There are more than a dozen of them, the heads of men with whom he drank last night. He sees White Wolf's dissipated face, now whitish like a fish belly, lifted grinning from the ground into its basket.

Then he sees Chin's head. It lies askew, not upright like the others. A bullet piercing one eye has hideously mutilated the face. When the head is lifted, a chunk slips loose from the skull, dangles a moment, falls. The man holding it laughs nervously and mumbles an obscenity to his companions.

Embree retches, then almost immediately a peal of thunder rends the cloudy sky and lightning shivers across a section of it to the west, then another thunderclap causes his horse to buck and almost throw him. 'Give me the reins,' he says to the man holding them. 'I can ride.' The man shrugs and hands them over. Thunder and lightning and the heads in a row have cleared Embree's mind; although weak throughout his body, he feels in control of it, and when the horsemen set out (once the trophies have been secured to pack mules) he moves with them through the smoking camp, where vultures with great flapping wings have already begun to settle. Embree looks in the direction of his own yurt, his home, and realizes that along with its neighbors it has been torched; a faceless girl lies inside, being consumed by fire. He puts both hands on the saddle and leans on it for support. Don't think, he tells himself, ride. He follows the tail and wet round flanks of the horse ahead, that's all. Where he is led, he will go, that's all. The rain comes down harder as the mountainside descent begins. Embree doesn't look back at the smoldering camp under the patter of rain. Women from the camp straggle down the path, unmolested but moaning and crying, pushing back their soaked hair, limping from wounds, clutching little bundles of clothing and train loot in their arms.

On the way down Embree notices that the cave dwellers have vanished. Perhaps they huddle in their caves, secure as their ancestors had been through the centuries while the rest of China played at war.

The first days on the eastward march, Philip Embree fully occupies himself with the task of staying mounted, no small achievement considering his fatigue and periods of dizziness. His wound is not dressed again, and he has too little experience of Chinese soldiery to understand that the bloody gauze bandage wrapped around his head is in fact a generous gift, representing the solicitude of host for guest. He will live to see men with greater wounds travel for days with no dressing. On this march, however, he believes the medieval neglect is deliberate, the sort of treatment reserved for prisoners of war. Perhaps it's appropriate, Embree thinks; after all, he feels like a prisoner of war. Except to his church and rowing crew, his only allegiance in life has been to those bandits who captured him. From his position now in the column of plodding horsemen, he has glimpses of a man sitting erect on a chestnut mare, the rider who ordered him brought along. From inquiry he has learned that the man is General Tang Shan-teh. The Englishman had been right: Tang would not let the murder of a high-ranking officer go unavenged. The General's revenge has cost Embree a great deal: two friends and the woman he loved. All because the rain was slow in coming. To consider nature the enemy hasn't been part of his training. Calamity issues from sin, bad motive, disrespect, and rebellion, not from the sluggish movement of clouds from west to east. Hanging on tenuously when his horse lurches in the thick mud, Embree asks the same questions again and again. Why had the monsoon come late? Why had White Wolf failed to move camp earlier? Why had the bandits been such bloody fools, to use the dead Englishman's phrase?

Mosquitoes add to his frustration. Since the very first hours of the ride through monsoon weather, the column has contended with them. At the summons of rain they begin to appear, hovering in small clouds above each horse: probing, relentless, mean. They

146

vanish only in a downpour, then reappear in drizzle and descend hordelike in the mist. At night, when the horsemen stop in a field for a few hours of rest, the mosquitoes attack with fierce spirit. Embree's skin doesn't merely itch – it seems on fire. The first night he removes his cotton shoes to feel more comfortable out of the wet fabric, but the next morning, when he lifts one of them, a torrent of mosquitoes pours out of it, sluggish, elephantine in flight, heavy with his blood. In retrospect he will wonder if they kept him alive on the march (Embree never doubts that a failure to keep up with the column would mean execution) by harassing him into a state of vexed alertness.

Throughout the ordeal he never asks for better treatment. This is a matter of honor – 'I never begged, father' – and common sense, because there is, in fact, no better treatment, not even for the General, as far as he can judge. Huddling at campfires (when they can be made), he accepts what food is given to him. With the men he displays a calm fortitude calculated to gain their respect. On the march he devises a way of passing the time. It gets him through rainstorms and mosquito attacks, and it shores up his mind against the loss of Fu-fang.

What he does is attempt to decipher the meaning of Ni Feng-lin's holy formula, given in a language the little Chinese never understood.

To a few known words – 'blood' and 'dear' and 'see' – Embree appends endless combinations of words and syllables to release the sense of the formula. He rifles his memory of the Bible and other doctrine for the Christian mantra that Ni clung to with the ardor of the devout.

On the afternoon of the third day, while the column is slogging through a dripping stand of birch trees, the phrase suddenly comes to Embree entire: 'The blood of martyrs is the seed of the Church.'

Of course, it's nothing more than Roman propaganda.

Even so, it had been the truth for Ni Feng-lin. It gave him succor and courage even though its meaning lay embedded like a mysterious jewel in the strange syllables. For Ni the words had the force of revelation, an utterance contained in them of the order that changes the common into the visionary. Embree knew well enough. He had read all about such experiences, and in college he had often sifted through religious doctrines in search of a message that would inspire him too. Because he had been serious. He had wished to transform his mechanical prayers into celebrations and devotions, into the real thing, signaling the kind of commitment to God that he had noticed in a few of his classmates. In this desire for conversion he had read widely, even in alien religions, absorbing more facts about them than his divinity school classmates and teachers felt necessary, surely more than his father felt proper, for as the white-haired clergyman used to tell his son, 'You'll be out there converting, not being converted. If you spend your time studying idolatry, what time will you have for Christ?'

Yet he had persisted. He occupied himself for nearly a semester with the Roman Catholic saints (but he never told father), because their lives were often filled with the sort of dramatic conversion and passionate commitment that he desired for himself. His heroic model those days had secretly been Saint Augustine – like himself impure in heart and indecisive – who one day in a garden had heard a child innocently chanting, '*Tolle lege, tolle lege*' – 'Take up and read, take up and read' – and thereupon Augustine, interpreting this as a sign from Heaven, hastened to find as quickly as possible an oracular statement and in consequence did take up and read from the Gospel of Matthew and later his friend Alypius read to him from Paul's Epistles, 'Him that is weak in the faith, receive ye,' words that set them both on the great path. But it won't happen to Embree, he is sure; and unlocking the mystery of Ni's talisman merely adds to his misery on this long, wet march.

On the evening of the fourth day they halt in a village. People scatter, while the exhausted troops consume what they can find and lie down on the dry floors of the huts. They leave the women alone, apparently on the General's orders, and Embree sees this as the chief difference between bandits and soldiers, at least the soldiers under Tang's command. He remembers Chin saying, 'Bandit one day, soldier the next, bandit the next, until you die.' Such thoughts occupy Embree while he sits in a dark room with men equally hungry, who are gnawing on carrots, waiting impatiently for a pot of millet to cook.

A soldier enters and beckons to him. Embree follows the man into a hard rain that soaks him thoroughly before they reach a building somewhat larger than the rest. At the soldier's gesture Embree enters and parts a curtain that leads into a candle-lit room with a series of wooden altars at the far end, each crowded with dolls – on closer inspection ceramic replicas of fierce-looking gods.

Seated to one side of the altars, behind a makeshift desk, is the General.

Must I kowtow? Embree decides against it, for there's a vast difference between this shoddy little temple and the proud yurt of White Wolf, just as there is between the two men: one muzzy from opium but robed in silk, the other cool-eyed but shabby in a drenched field uniform. Suddenly Embree remembers the ax in his belt. Remove it? But, misinterpreting the move, Tang might shoot him.

'I forgot to leave the ax outside.'

Tang shrugs to indicate its unimportance. 'How is your wound?'

At least the question establishes the General's civility, so Embree relaxes a little. 'Better, sir.' He has a moment to study the man's smooth features, broad cheekbones, wide-set watchful eyes. He notices on the General's rather thick neck a prominent vein – the pulse of authority?

'You are traveling in China?'

'I'm a student,' Embree replies. He hasn't forgotten the Englishman's warning. Moreover, curiously, he feels it would be dishonest to call himself a missionary now. Recently he's been nothing of the sort. He's been a student, a student of life.

'You speak Chinese better than most foreigners ever do,' Tang comments thoughtfully. 'What are you studying?'

'Everything I can.'

'Everything you can.' The General repeats the declaration without sarcasm, as if considering it. Lighting a cigarette, he shoves the pack across the desk toward Embree, who remains where he is, arms loose at his side, respectful but not rigid.

Feeling the need to be more specific and therefore more convincing, Embree adds, almost without thinking, 'I'm interested in the religions of China.'

The General raises his eyebrows. He points with the cigarette at the altars. 'Do you know what sort of temple this is?'

'Taoist?'

'Yes. Buddhist as well. Over there on that altar is a Kuan Yin and a Maitreya. In villages it's all the same – Buddhism, Taoism, mixed in with ancestors. Are you a Christian?'

'Of course, General.'

'Of course?' Tang smiles faintly. 'If you stay in China long enough you may see religion in a new light.' Holding out the cigarette, he watches the smoke rising into the dark upper air of the dank room. 'Perhaps one reason for your coming here is to see things in a different light.'

Embree nods uncertainly. Nothing the General says is clear, or rather it is clear but also suggests something more – another, if ambiguous meaning. Or perhaps fatigue is what confuses me, Embree tells himself. Fatigue, the candles flickering in front of the idols, the rain beating hard on the temple roof.

'I once met a man from your country – you are English?'

'American.'

'Well, he was English. He came here to study ancient temples. Before he finished, he became a monk in one of them. I am curious – it's not every day I talk with a foreigner and a student. What do you think of Confucius?'

'He was a great thinker, sir.'

'Just so.' Tang smiles. 'He was a thinker. But people made him a god. I think it's strange, because what is divine in what he tells us? Do good to people. Work at your given task. Words of a sensible man, no more.'

'They are simple but not simple,' Embree offers.

'Exactly. Which is why people made him a god. Of course, *you* did a similar thing.'

'Sir?'

'You in the West. You made the man Jesus a god. Or so the missionaries tell me.'

Embree hasn't the stomach for a theological discussion, although perhaps Tang wants one. So Embree shifts the subject a little. 'May I ask, sir, what you think of missionaries?'

'Brave men. But intolerant.'

Embree would have argued had this been a discussion in divinity school. He'd have pointed out that thousands of Buddhist monasteries were leveled in the ninth century at the instigation of intolerant Confucians and Taoists.

As if divining Embree's line of thought, the General tells him the Chinese are also intolerant. 'Usually about things other than religion,' he adds. 'Often under the guise of religion.'

'The same's been true in the West.'

Tang nods as if already knowing it. 'But here we have one advantage. Whatever comes into our country is changed by it. Nothing remains pure in China, not even religion. It will be the fate of Christianity to change too, if it stays long enough.'

Embree senses that the General is waiting for him to react. There has been too much talk about religion. Does the General suspect him of being a missionary? Perhaps the Chinese suspect all foreigners of coming to their country for this reason. Clearly this general won't be converted to Christianity by anything he might say. So Embree says nothing.

'You claim you're interested in everything,' Tang says after an extended silence. 'Are you interested in art?'

'Less than in other things.'   .

'Art might tell you more about us than religion.'

'Then I'll pay attention to it.' He wants to say more, but stops. Embree fears the General might lead him into some kind of trap. What kind? He doesn't know. This is his first encounter with a Chinese of education and subtlety.

'Go on,' says Tang. 'What is it you want to say?'

'Well, I'd like to study the people.'

'The people? How?'

'By living with them. As I've been doing lately.'

'You've been living with bandits,' Tang observes coolly. 'Well, thank you for coming tonight. It has been interesting for someone as ignorant as myself.'

Embree bows low, trying to think of an equally self-deprecating remark to complete the circle of polite humility. But all he says is, 'Thank you, Excellency, for talking to me. It has been my pleasure.' Turning, after another deep bow, he walks to the front of the temple. As he approaches the entrance curtain, he realizes suddenly why it hangs there: it is placed there to prevent evil spirits from getting into the temple. Because they travel only in straight lines, they can't turn the corner.

So much for evil spirits in this land of practical solutions. Yet most of his conversation with this Chinese general has been about spiritual matters. His hand is on the curtain to draw it aside, when the General calls him: 'Student.'

Turning, Embree waits.

'Your name?'

'Philip Embree, sir.'

'Philip Embree, we don't hate the teachings of that good man Jesus Christ. But sometimes we hate the teachers of it.'

Next morning the monsoon intensifies. Thunder squalls alternate with steady downpours that either lash the countryside brutally or monotonously hammer water into every depression of the land. Gray silt spreads like mush across the leachy soil and oozes into every hollow of it, making eroded meadows as smooth as butter. Tang drives the men without rest and for good reason: another few days of such flooding will mire the horses belly-deep in the muck of Shansi, like flies caught in amber.

In spite of bad weather and the hard ride, Embree begins to regain his strength, drawing on youth and a lifetime of exercise. Exhilarated by a sense of physical renewal, he rips off the bloody bandage and tosses it into the sluch under his mount's hooves. He studies with interest the awesome way that nature is transforming the land into featureless bogs and ponds. A mist descends each morning like the slow smoke of a diminishing forest fire and envelops the column in a strange light. Hunched over his horse, Embree watches his companions ahead vanish into the haze, then reappear farther on. It is a world unlike any other: liquid, silent, endless. And yet the men are moving like a single individual toward the attainment of solidity; nothing can stop them, not even nature. He starts again to feel the sense of brotherhood that had meant so much to him in the *tufei* camp. When the column halts in a clump of woods, too exhausted to find better shelter, he huddles back to back with other men, propping themselves out of the water in which they sit almost to the waist; and in this manner passes the night with them, jerking in and out of consciousness, his back and shoulders touching theirs, a single plant with four leaves.

Next morning, awaking upright, his legs aching and cold while his forehead perspires and his lips feel hot, Embree notices through the overhead branches of an elm the clouds rolling by in thick ugly convulsions. The sight transfixes him: clouds like intestines flung across the sky. Perhaps he feels disoriented from having slept in such a position. Although he wants to rise and break the spell of this dismal morning, Embree waits until other men stir too before getting to his feet. Before the column sets out again, someone hands him a corn dumpling, some salt turnips. Embree mounts his weary horse with enthusiasm.

That morning a biblical exhortation begins to plague him: 'Take heed to yourself, that your heart be not deceived, and ye turn aside, and serve other gods, and worship them.' He gets rid of it by questioning the rider behind him: 'Where are we?' 'Honan.' 'Where in Honan?' 'The north.' 'Near what city?' 'Anyang.'

Anyang. He remembers it from his reading: capital of China three thousand years ago.

In the afternoon they cross a tributary of the Chang. As the horses are driven one after another into the brown torrent, Embree remembers Chin describing what would happen to the Fen River. When they picnicked along its insignificant bank, Embree hadn't imagined how such a thing might happen, but now he's in the middle of a similar happening: His snorting horse surges through the roiling water, neck pumping like a piston, until finally, flexing its withers in triumph, it staggers from the flood. Embree looks back at the eddying water that carries the flotsam of humanity with it: pots, bits of clothing, a weeding pole, entire sections of wood-framed dwellings. It strikes him that the monsoon has already wiped out many villages. Passing swiftly in front of his eyes is the existence of enough people to populate a city in Connecticut. 'You come from a small country,' Fu-fang had told him scornfully.

Turning to the nearest soldier, Embree says, 'Are the rains always this bad?'

The man shrugs. 'I think so.'

'How many people drown?'

'I never heard of them being counted. But don't worry so much. They're the lucky ones. If they live in flooded country, it's better to go quickly, like him – '. Embree follows the man's gaze. In the rapid swell of water a bloated corpse turns slowly, gracefully. 'The ones left behind take a lot longer to die from starvation and disease. Believe me, this way is better.'

Late that afternoon the column comes to the verge of an endless marsh lying between Honan and Shantung. Clumps of bush and grass are strangled by the silt as far as Embree can see; in another day this whole area will be a single heaving lake of rust-colored water.

That night they enter another village. The rain has dwindled to a cool, vaporous atmosphere, charged now and then by wind gusts and drizzle. Hooves splash heavily through the flooded lanes as the column passes what is left here. Carts stand sunken in mud to the axles. A crow clutches the tile of an upturned roof and caws defiantly at the slow-moving horses. Crumbling walls, sagging doors, the caved-in roof of a clan temple. Not one human. When the dismounted men go into the houses for shelter, it is obvious that the villagers have all slogged into their drowned fields to spend the night.

Sitting in a hut that smells of damp clay, Embree eats some corn dumplings. The half-dozen soldiers who share the room with him eat greedily too, although the dumplings are hard and stale, probably left by anxious villagers to appease the troops, to discourage them from firing the houses.

After their meal, the men sit on the *kang*, a raised platform serving as bench and bed. The fire beneath it has long since gone out. They breathe slowly in shallow gusts of exhaustion.

Embree has said very little during the march, yet curiosity now compels him to speak. 'Tell me,' he says in the twilight, 'what sort of man is General Tang?'

A soldier remarks, 'Listen to the foreigner. I've heard foreigners before. They never spoke that good.'

'What do you mean, what sort of man?' another trooper, somewhat older, asks Embree belligerently.

'I mean, do you like him?'

The older one answers. 'It isn't our business to *like* generals. We just do what they tell us.'

'Tang's a good general,' another offers.

'Why?' Embree asks.

'Why?' The man looks around at his comrades, as if expecting one of them to supply an answer. 'We sleep in tents back in Qufu. He pays us most of the time. You want to join up, foreigner?'

His question brings a peal of laughter.

Embree waits until it subsides. 'Why did General Tang cut off those heads?'

'That's a stupid question. How can he prove White Wolf's finished without the heads? Haven't you foreigners got any sense?'

Embree says nothing. The men settle against the *kang* and the walls. The final gray light of dusk lingers in the doorway; thick clouds lumber overhead, threatening more rain. A man peers in the doorway and calls for Embree. The General wants him again.

Embree finds the General in a candlelit hut, munching a corn dumpling just like those devoured by the troops.

After finishing, the General says, 'Your wound's better, but it'll leave a scar.' He is sitting on the *kang*, his prominent cheekbones shining in the light. He sets the bowl, a few dumplings left in it, on the brick beside him. 'Having a scar doesn't seem to bother the Ax Man.'

Fuzi nanren: Ax Man. Is the General making fun of me? Embree wonders. Probably, in a way. Yet there's something attractive about the name. Ax Man. Am I the Ax Man? Good. 'A

154

scar,' he replies, 'doesn't mean anything, sir. I take what comes.'

'You take what comes. We Chinese say it's difficult to be poor without complaint; it's easy to be rich without arrogance. Perhaps it's also easy to take what comes when it's easy to bear. But if what comes is the loss of an arm, a leg, an eye?' Tang regards Embree with open curiosity. 'When we last talked, I suggested Christianity might change if it stays in China. You said nothing. I'm interested in your view.'

'I don't think Christianity would ever change,' Embree says frankly. Then he stops.

'Please go on. I told you, it isn't often I talk with Westerners.'

'Well, the Bible says there's only one method of finding salvation, and that's through Christ.'

'Your Bible – wasn't it written by men?'

'Inspired men. Men who reported the truth.'

'Go on.'

'It's reported in the Bible that Jesus said, "I am the way, the truth, and the life; no man comes to the Father but by me."'

'You believe that?'

'I'm a Christian.'

'Chinese have also been Christians. In the last years of the Manchu, people joined the Christians to escape arrest as revolutionaries.'

'They were not real Christians.'

'And others have coveted the wealth of your priests.'

'Rice Christians, yes. I've heard of them. They're not real Christians either.'

'We Chinese are a practical people,' the General says with a smile. 'As a real Christian, Ax Man, what do you believe in?'

'I believe in the everlasting truth of Jesus Christ.'

Tang rises from the *kang* and begins pacing, hands fisted at his back. Stopping after a while, he turns to Embree. 'Does that mean you believe in ultimate truth?'

'Yes, the ultimate truth of Christ.'

'Confucius rejected the idea of finding ultimate truth – assuming it exists at all. Thinking about it is a waste of time.' The General continues pacing; the room smells of clay and garlic.

After another long silence, Embree says, 'Is it impertinent of me, sir, to ask what you believe in?'

Tang stops pacing. Slowly his hands drop to his sides. 'I believe in China.'

The two men stare at each other. Then, pacing again, the General says with his back to Embree, 'Thank you again for coming. You are kind to explain such matters to an ignorant man.'

In his boyhood Philip Embree used to walk to and from school through an Italian district of New Haven. Potbellied bowlers smoked cigars while studying their boccie game; women yelled at one another in their mother tongue from open windows; pungent smells, rarely encountered in the bland New England kitchen of his own home, drifted from the doorways of little restaurants along the way. Finding himself isolated in Italy for a dozen blocks each day, Philip Embree began holding conversations with an imaginary boy called Wilbur. Wilbur was not Italian either, but like Philip Embree was a boy obsessed by the thought of travel and adventure. Together they talked of the future, when they would see the real Italy and other places as well. Sometimes they traveled during these sessions to ancient Rome, which Philip was studying in school, and to Africa and Egypt. Sometimes they discussed Philip's classmates or a hated teacher. Philip Embree became adept at holding such conversations with his imaginary friend, but when he entered high school he forgot about Wilbur.

Now, riding through the pelting rain in an alien land, he feels once again the need to hold such conversations. But he's too old to resurrect his boyhood friend. He wants to speak with someone real, someone from home. Certainly not his father, but someone he can trust.

Finally Embree chooses his sister. In imagination that day he talks to Mary.

'And in the bandit camp,' he tells her, 'I fell in love with a girl.'

'Good for you.' It's what Mary would say; he's sure of it.

'I also got drunk.'

'I've done that too, dear brother.'

'And I swore to stay with the bandits.'

'That's a bit strange.'

'Yes, isn't it. But I meant it, and if the General hadn't interfered, I'd still be there with them.'

'You liked their freedom. Tell me about the General.'

'He's a curious man. He asked me about Christianity. I think he likes power. I think he's strong.'

'Does he remind you of father?'

'Yes and no. He's strong like father, but he wanted to know my opinion.'

'That's certainly not like father. Do you want to stay with this General too?' The question Embree devises for his sister is a difficult one to answer.

'I don't know,' he says.

'Think about it, Philip.'

He thinks a long time. Finally he says to Mary, 'Maybe I should stay with the General. I can learn more in his army than I can in the Harbin Mission.'

'Learn about what?'

'The Chinese.'

'You can learn about them at the mission,' she argues.

'In his army I'd learn more about myself.'

'Is that more important than doing what you're trained for, what father wants you to do?'

'Yes.'

'Then do it. It's what I would do if I were you, dear brother. Just do it.'

Here the imaginary conversation ends. He rehearses it again, however; the words, his and hers, are said again and again in his mind.

That evening, when the column stops in another village, Embree is again brought to General Tang, who is sitting in a straight-backed chair in a cobbled courtyard. A tall magnolia droops in one corner, its wet leaves fired by the last sunlight coming through the clouds. The General has opened his tunic; the holster belt has been removed. Embree has never seen him so relaxed.

'In a few days,' Tang begins, 'we'll be in Qufu. I'll send you by escort to Jinan, where you get the train to Peking.' After a pause he adds, 'Where you can pursue your studies. I envy you the chance to spend your time in study.'

'Excellency.' Embree hesitates. 'Today on the march I thought a lot about it, and I don't want to go to Peking.'

'Oh?' The General crosses his legs and cocks his head a little. 'Where do you want to go? Shanghai? Do you want a steamer home?'

'I want to stay in Qufu. With your army.' Embree takes a deep breath. 'I want to join your army.' He braces for ridicule, at least for surprise. Neither comes.

General Tang sits impassively, staring at the shiny magnolia leaves. After a long silence he says, 'What would you do in my army?'

'I'd learn to be a soldier.' Searching for a further explanation, Embree says, 'I'd learn about your people. I'd learn, sir, I'd learn to appreciate . . .' His voice trails away like sunlight from the magnolia. He has become lost in an explanation he himself doesn't really understand. He should be going on to Harbin, to the sanctified work of the Lord.

'In my experience,' Tang begins slowly, 'the foreigner who speaks good Chinese always wants something. Either he wants to take the wealth of my country or he wants to change its people. Now I don't think you're a businessman. So do you want to tell my soldiers about your Jesus and change their minds?'

'I won't speak of Jesus.'

'Because I already have a man in camp who's eager to speak of Marx.'

'I don't want to teach anything,' Embree declares with conviction. 'I want to be taught.'

'Do you expect me to believe that?'

'I hope you believe it, sir.'

'Have you eaten?'

'Yes, Excellency.'

'Good. Thank you for coming.'

Embree bows and leaves the courtyard. The General's response is tantamount to a refusal, and Embree realizes he should be relieved that the outrageous request was not granted. But by the time he joins his companions in the hut, he hopes with all his heart that the General will change his mind.

Next day they come to the Yellow River. He has seen photographs and read about it. Rising in the Tibetan plateau, China's Sorrow meanders three thousand miles through the central plain, watering on its way a basin as big as France. Generally it's a sluggish river, choked with silt that raises the river bed dangerously until, in the monsoon season, it often sloshes over its banks and flows across the countryside, inundating immense areas of land and causing untold devastation. No bridges span its shifting channel; the only way of crossing it is by native craft: junk, flat barge, sampan.

158

Embree has read about it, but nothing has prepared him for his first look at the Yellow River. Its great brown ruffled surface reminds him of a powerful beast flexing its muscles. The sun-baked banks, under the hammering of rain, have become a rank-smelling treacle sliding away from the river's swell. People of the district are at work, shoring up the banks, when Tang's column reaches there. Already the water is lapping at woven mats placed against the tamped soil, held down by rocks and boulders. As the column moves upstream along the bank, thousands of people – men, women, and children – are toiling with baskets, hauling mud, building up the retaining wall. All morning and half the afternoon, in a fresh downpour, Tang leads his troops upriver. Feverishly active, sensing a defeat that will bring certain death, the workers struggle doggedly in the mud, hauling mats and baskets of earth in a last effort to contain the beast. Threat of flood is imminent by the time Tang's column reaches a small flotilla of boats huddling near the shore, their anchor lines taut in the current. A dozen soldiers, cradling rifles, stand watch over the boat owners, who will be shot if they try to get away. Tang has sent this advance party to corral enough boats for a crossing.

On Tang's signal the boats row for shore. They come alongside, their large sweep oars at rapid work like the fins of fish trying to stabilize themselves in a swift current. Boats begin loading. It is slow, difficult, becuase the boats swing in and out, fighting the beast under them. Horses, tethered to railing and stern, are forced to swim across. One is lost. Its reins, poorly tied to a railing, pull free, and the river carries the horse into midchannel, where it turns and rolls, unable with its earthbound hooves to get a purchase on empty air or raging water; the great round rump glistens; the mouth opens in a rictus of terror; and the bulky brown shape is pulled into the distant mists above the flood.

By the time most of the boats have crossed, light has faded; men and horses can't be seen on the opposite bank. Tang, who has directed the operation from the shore, turns and gestures impatiently at the group of remaining horsemen.

At first Embree doesn't realize the gesture is meant for him; then, slipping in his haste to reach the General, he falls into the mind. Embree hears laughter from men nearby when he struggles to his feet and wipes the mud from pants and tunic. Approaching the General, he's in a fury of embarrassment.

Tang's attention is on the loading. Three boats, one of them a sampan, are left. Turning abruptly, as if remembering something, he stares at Embree. With a certain impatience – they might have been arguing for a long time – he says, 'Very well, this is my decision. If it amuses you to join my army, perhaps I'll be amused too – as long as you behave like a soldier.' Turning to avoid an expression of thanks, he walks briskly down the bank to the waiting sampan. Here he says with a quick backward glance, 'You'll join a training unit.'

'Cavalry?'

Waving his hand in assent, the General boards the sampan.

Accomplishment, not gratitude, is what Embree feels. In his perception he has won a battle of wills. But what really has he won? The chance to serve in a Chinese army, while people back home await word that he has survived and continued on his way to Harbin.

Embree watches a half-dozen coolies, aboard the sampan, battling tons of water with their long oars. The prow disappears in the lowering mist; General Tang at midships vanishes within a veil of cloudy dusk; the entire boat fades from sight. When his own boat touches shore, Embree climbs aboard. He is going to cross the Yellow River, as dark as death.

'Take heed to yourself.'

The biblical words follow him across, but they are only words. Whereas his pounding heart tells him anything is now possible.

7

Long before crossing the Yellow River into his own province, even before reaching and destroying the camp of White Wolf, almost before leaving the beautiful Russian dumfounded in the Kong Burial Ground and galloping out of Qufu with his cavalry detachment, General Tang understood the profound error of seeking vengeance while the rest of China – mercurial, seething – carried out stratagems that might well dismantle his future. He has no idea what news awaits him at headquarters. Surely much has happened during his journey four hundred miles away from camp into the hinterlands of Shansi, leading his company of horse like a warrior in an old Ming romance, out of contact with the great world and therefore vulnerable – either schemed against or contemptuously ignored.

But he would do it all again. He couldn't have done otherwise and held the loyalty of his troops. They expect of him what he demands of them: commitment to something else than personal gain. A steady display of virtue – meting out justice and shunning decadence – has set him apart from many warlords. His idealism, nevertheless, has always been tempered by a resolve to act forcefully, if need be savagely. He has taken heads. He is glad of it.

The General discovers that he has not overestimated the velocity of events. When the ragged column plods into Qufu at twilight, he is met by his chief of staff, Colonel Pi, with plenty of news, most of it bad.

First, in a swift march from his Northwest stronghold, General Feng Yu-hsiang took the strategic city of Chengchow. Then, in a meeting there with Wuhan radicals, Feng sided with them against Chaing Kai-shek. A week later he reversed his position and made statements of cautious support for the Kuomintang. This naturally leaves in doubt Feng's allegiance, if he has any.

Next, while Feng was marching westward, Marshal Chang Tso-lin was declaring himself Protector of Peking. The old Manchurian Tiger has controlled Peking for years through a series of puppet officials, cabinet members, and presidents, but with this formal statement (public ritual having the force of truth in China) he has declared his intention to resist any alignment between Feng and Chiang Kai-shek that might threaten his autonomy in the Far North.

General Tang leans back in a chair and sips tea. The last shreds of sunlight cling to the opposite wall of his living room, cling and vanish. His old servant Yao lights a kerosene lamp, and in the light General Tang can see the round bland face of his chief of staff. At such a time, with crisis hovering near, he wishes for his old friend, Wu Sheng-chi, who now lies headless somewhere beside a railroad track, picked clean by scavengers. Tang feels exhaustion setting in, so he sits bolt erect and sips more tea. It is time to test Colonel Pi's acuity. 'What do you think of Feng's strategy?'

The Colonel puts down his own cup and composes his features with difficulty. He seems aware that the question is a test. When slowly he replies, the words come out with a measured tread. 'I think from his public statements General Feng has definitely chosen to support the Generalissimo.'

Tang looks sharply at his chief of staff who has used the

grandiose term that Chiang Kai-shek has assumed without earning it. Has the Colonel picked it out of a recent Shanghai newspaper or has the entire staff fallen prey to Kuomintang propaganda? Notwithstanding his annoyance, Tang doesn't comment on 'Generalissimo,' but instead pursues his line of inquiry. 'Colonel,' he says, 'why would General Feng support a man who's lost so much support – his Russian advisers, the Bolsheviks, the radicals in Wuhan, and some of his own right-wing Kuomintang Party members in Nanking? Or at least that's how it was before I went into Shansi. Have matters changed?'

'No, Excellency. Except now people know where Chiang Kai-shek stands. He's lost allies, but maybe that's in his favor. At least now he doesn't seem like a tool of the Russians.' Pi seems abruptly aware that his words may be construed as defending Chaing, so he adds, 'I think it's how General Feng has looked at the situation. For the moment he's chosen Chiang because Chiang is stronger for having broken with the Russians and the Chiness Communists.'

'He's really chosen the southerner over Marshal Chang Tso-lin?'

'I think he really has. Chiang has control of the entire South, Shanghai, and Nanking. He'll have Wuhan too now that the radicals have collapsed. For the moment Chaing's strong.'

The General nods. It's a good analysis – too good for Pi to have arrived at without help. Doubtless the staff, during his long absence, has discussed these matters endlessly. What the General doesn't agree with is the analysis of Feng's choice between Chang Tso-lin and Chiang Kai-shek. Like most northerners, Feng has contempt for southern armies. Surely he looks on Chaing as a bothersome upstart dragged into prominence by why Russians and reckless Cantonese politicians, among them Sun Yat-sen, who luckily died before surrendering China to the Russians or to any other nation that flattered him sufficiently. Feng doesn't care about the squabbles between Wuhan radicals and Nanking conservatives. His latest move, typically ambiguous, has simply thrown both sides off balance while he considers new ways of dealing with his ultimate rival in the North, the Marshal. That's Feng and his strategy. Pi and other staff members are too young to realize that Feng has been following a similar policy for years. There's an advantage to age, the General thinks. 'Any other news?' he asks the Colonel.

Pi seems to be holding back.

'Well? What's happened?'

'Excellency, when the Marshal proclaimed himself Protector of

Peking, he made another decision. For this province.'

Tang holds a newly filled cup at his lips. 'Go on, tell me.'

'He created a new post: Governor General of Shantung. The Marshal sent you a wireless four days ago. The province is no longer under the supervision of the Inspector General of the Ministry of the Interior.'

'In other words, the Marshal is letting go of personal control.' Tang likes that, even if it's a formality. It means that for the first time since the formation of the Republic this province will have a degree of autonomy; other provinces have managed it, but only by force of arms and great distance from the capital. Tang sees himself in the post; attempting to hide his anticipation from the Colonel, he asks crisply when the new post will be filled.

'It already has been Excellency. Chang Tsung-ch'ang is the Governor General.'

Leaning forward, Tang slams down the cup. 'I want to see that wireless.' Chang Tsung-ch'ang selected over him? Old Dog Meat? That drunken illiterate's most recent military accomplishment was to lose a pitched battle to the Nationalists outside Nanking.

Pi takes the message from his briefcase. The Marshal's promulgation is curt, formal, offering no explanation for the move. But upon brief reflection the General needs none. It is obvious that Chang Tsung-ch'ang is the choice of the Japanese. Perhaps by appeasing the Japanese the Marshal is trying to enlist their aid if the Nationalists push farther north. They'd be crucial allies for him against Chaing Kai-shek – worth sacrificing Tang for.

A convoluted plan but logical. The General attempts to assimilate it. The Japanese will try to rob the province at will, sending troops, engineers, and businessmen in flotillas from Japan. The area he controls will be vital to their economic plans and therefore, increasingly, the two Changs will attempt to force his cooperation by legal means. Very well, let them. China, tragic republic that it is, is ultimately not controlled by laws but by force of arms. He won't let the Japanese inside the borders of his jurisdiction, and if the two Changs try to remove him, he won't leave, he'll fight. Like warlords elsewhere, he will simply do as much as his army gives him freedom to do.

'The banknotes have been printed, Excellency. They're ready for distribution.' He starts to open the briefcase. 'Do you wish to see one?'

'Tomorrow. That can wait for tomorrow.' Facing the fraudulent banknotes is too much after such a hard journey. In the rain and mud of the Shansi march he had often asked himself how a man could follow an honorable path of conduct by issuing worthless money to his own troops. Yet with the future of China in jeopardy, he'd not be fulfilling his duty unless every measure for protecting his country was taken – even if it meant dishonoring himself. Here's an irony he appreciates: Belief in his patriotic duty is forcing him to swindle the men who fight for him.

He tells Colonel Pi good night. After the chief of staff has left, he calls in Yao to discuss dinner. It's what the old servant demands – an appreciation of his planning of the menu, which the General dare not change. While they're talking, someone knocks at the door. It's loud, peremptory.

Yao opens the door and a servant from the Kong family enters. He wears a dark gown, an orange girdle at his waist – the color of the clan. He has come, he announces, from the Holy Duke, who would appreciate seeing the General at any time convenient.

'Any time convenient' means 'now' to the General. Immediately he accompanies the servant across the courtyards of the West Wing to the central yamen, where the clan offices are – most of them no longer operative. They pass the buildings that house the various departments – the Departments of Seals, of Rites, of Temple Ceremonies (still very active), of Documents, of Music, of Civil Administration (long defunct), and of Estates. They go around the Great Hall, which is fitted with the dais and desk of a magistrate, with brushes, seals, and a gong that used to summon petitioners forward in the days when the Kong family governed the whole countryside. A covered way leads the servant and General Tang into a courtyard lined by other halls, some of them used in ancient times for examinations in music and rites. Pomegranate trees and lilac bushes are visible along the way in the torchlight flickering from poles. Behind this area are the quarters for women; the two men veer eastward here and enter that part of the Residence reserved exclusively for the Duke. This eastern section has fallen into disrepair over the centuries. The Pavilion of Imperial Writings is nothing more than ruins. But nearby are a few guesthouses now used for libraries. The archives and books had been kept in the West Wing, but with the General and his staff living there, everything has been removed here – far away from the military presence. The servant takes him to a small building, still well kept, which might long ago have been an apartment for minor relatives of the clan.

It is hot; the door is open for a breeze, so Tang can see inside. There are hundreds of manuscripts lying flat in tall shelves, musical instruments and scrolls hanging on the wall, camphor-wood trunks and rosewood furniture. In the center of the study is a low, narrow table on a raised platform. Stretched alongside the table, his elbow on it, is the Duke Patriarch, who reads a book by lamplight. He is near the General's age, a stout, plumpfaced man who has the long fingernails of a scholar. He wears a mauve gown, a skullcap. The white soles of his black cotton shoes are visible from the doorway, where General Tang drops to his knees and kowtows three times, his head touching the polished floor.

'Please, please,' the Holy Duke murmurs, as if embarrassed by the General's show of respect, but he doesn't offer his visitor a chair. 'I trust you had a comfortable journey home. You were in Shansi on business, I hear.'

'Yes, your Highness. On business. I had a comfortable journey, thank you.'

The Duke nods with satisfaction. He sits up, drawing his feet under the mauve gown. The center of it, across his chest, is embroidered with an orange phoenix. 'I've been much too busy myself.'

'Regrettable, your Highness.' Tang smells cloves; the room is filled with the scent of them.

'Yes, thank you. There are always the two monthly ceremonies, of course, and now the Master's birthday approaching. I'm afraid the Master will be disappointed with me this year.'

The Duke speaks of a man dead twenty-five centuries as if he were still living. It is wonderful, Tang thinks.

'Ah, these ceremonies,' the Duke says with a sigh. 'Nobody remembers the rites, let alone their sequence, any more. Nobody knows the little things that mean something. For example, in 1371 the Board of Rites made changes in the number of *pien* and *tou* vessels used in the ceremony. The number was changed then from eight to ten. Today nobody knows that or that there were sixty musicians during that period and in the ritual pantomime there were forty-eight performers.' The Duke shakes his head in a show of annoyance. 'That makes a hundred and eight in all, not including temple acolytes. Ask an attendant – someone I'm counting on during the ceremony – ask him any of these things and he won't know them. But in my opinion you have to know the history of ritual or what is it? The Master knew everything. So did the Great Seventy-two Disciples. All of them knew everything and today nobody knows anything. It's all very well to abolish the old examination system – I'm for a certain amount of judicious progress – but the men who passed the Third and the Final Degrees used to know something. Even those passing the First Degree of Flourishing Talent did. Please sit down, General.'

Tang sits in a straight chair placed rather far from the dais; he feels close to the corner, but it's the chair Duke Kong has pointed to. And the smell of cloves envelops him.

'Have you seen the garden?' the Duke asks. 'It's blooming now. Ah, the last bloom of summer, I'm afraid.'

The General has had only a glimpse of the garden – its ponds and Tai Hu rocks and flowers – and has never set foot in it. He won't go unless granted explicit permission. The Duke hasn't yet granted it.

'Yes,' the Duke says, as if struggling for conversation. 'So, General, you concluded your business in Shansi.'

'I did, your Holiness.'

'To your satisfaction?'

'To my satisfaction, thank you.'

'Ah.'

Looking at the soft, distant eyes, Tang isn't sure if the Holy Duke knows what happened in Shansi. This is a man who has lived only the scholarly life; there's no way of knowing what he understands of the world around him.

A servant enters with tea. When they have their cups – Tang waits until the Duke sips first, although Tang is the guest – their conversation turns to philosophy. Knowing of the General's interest in the work of Hsun Tzu, Duke Kong quotes a section from it: 'If a man asscioates with men who are not good, then he will hear only deceit and lies; he will see only conduct that is marked by evil, wantonness, and greed.' The Duke smiles. 'He said – I quote – "Environment is the important thing, environment is the important thing" !'

The General fidgets, looks down at his feet. So environment is the important thing, so the character of men around you determines your own. The Duke has obviously used the words of Hsun Tzu to imply that military men should be shunned if possible. Surely that's the traditional view of scholars, and although accepting his protection, the Kong Patriarch can't like him: he has even been seated tonight far from the noble presence. Even so, Tang will submit to the insult meekly, for in the ideal scheme of things a military man should indeed be inferior, should be shunned as men 'not good.' Father would agree with this assessment; father's spirit would be shamed if the General replied with even the slightest annoyance to the lines quoted by the Duke. Tang steadies himself as the Duke stares expectantly at him.

'Yes,' the Duke says finally, 'environment is the important thing. We must not associate with men of evil and violence.' After another long pause, he says, 'Do you believe with Hsun Tzu that men are evil, General?'

'I do, your Highness.'

'All men?'

'Yes. That's my reading of Hsun Tzu, and I agree with it.'

'Mencius is more to my liking. *There* was an optimist. He felt that men were pure in nature and would know it for themselves, if only they looked within.'

'Hsun Tzu has his own kind of optimism, if I may suggest it, your Holiness.'

'By all means. Let me hear your argument.'

'Hsun Tzu said, 'Because wood is crooked, we use carpenter's tools to straighten it.' The same applies to men. Because our nature is evil, we must acquire moral virtue through conscious effort. Hsun Tzu believes we can master ourselves, we can change our destiny.'

'I'm writing an easy on Han Yu.'

'Admirable, your Holiness.' The General has always considered Han Yu narrow-minded and illogical. He was a zealous Confucian of the Tang Dynasty, strongly influenced by Mencius. He wrote unflagging criticism of Buddhism. In an essay entitled 'The Bone of Buddha' (the General has read it in modern script), Han Yu petitioned the emperor to suppress the Buddhist religion on the ground that Buddha was a barbarian who wore different clothes and spoke a different language from the Chinese. For his impertinence – the emperor was a Buddhist – Han Yu was banished. He is still known for the perfection of his literary style, but the General can't read him with any seriousness.

'Han Yu accused Hsun Tzu of holding impure views,' says the Duke, putting down his teacup and fingering the base of a water pipe set near him on the table. 'Han Yu died in 824, nearly a thousand years after your Hsun Tzu. Did you know the date of Han Yu's death, General?'

'No, your Highness.'

'Time is the strangest thing in my life,' says the Duke with a long sigh. ' "To live till seventy has been rare since time began." '

The General knows the quotation is from a poem by Tu Fu. He can recite the next line – 'Deep among the flowers the butterflies go their way' – but doesn't.

'There's something, General, I wish to – ' But the Duke is interrupted by the appearance in a rear doorway of two boys. One is almost full grown, the other five or six. They have come to say good night to their father. Clapping his hands once, the Duke calls them forward to kowtow to the General, then asks them if they're well. 'Yes, Illustrious Father,' they murmur in unison. He asks them if their sisters are well, and they reply in like manner. He tells them they may go.

To the General he says with a smile, 'Mencius said: "The great man is he who hasn't lost his child's heart." We must enjoy our children, General.'

Tang isn't sure whether the Duke knows he has no children. He nods politely.

'General, there's something I wish to discuss. I've petitioned the Peking government for an appropriation. My secretary worked very hard on the wording of it. I wrote it out with my finest brush in the Slender Gold Style. Permit me this immodesty, but I have a fine hand for the Slender Gold.' Spreading both arms out to encompass as much space as possible, the Duke drags his long mandarin sleeves across the table. 'You've seen the state of ruin here, the need for repair.'

'I have, your Highness. If it will help, perhaps you can move back to the West Wing. It's in better condition. I can move myself and my staff –'

'No, no, no. That's not the point. We need you where you are. We welcome you. Ten thousand blessings, General. What I'm saying is I have the upkeep on the Residence and on the Burial Ground to deal with. And the ceremonies. Now the Master's birthday coming up. My secretaries tell me the cost is too high for our revenues. What I get from the government and the estates and a little elsewhere – private donations, you understand – simply isn't enough. Oh, the cost!' His face goes slack at the thought of it. 'No money for anything – and no time either. I've so wanted to visit Tai Shan. Especially the Master's great temple at the summit. Surely he wants me to see it again before I die. Do you know I haven't been there in almost three years?'

'Regrettable, your Holiness.'

'Regrettable, yes, thank you. But it's only the essential repairs I petitioned for. Then a few days ago I received an answer from the Ministry of Finance.'

'They turned you down.'

'In such language I felt the letter bordered on insolence. I can't believe it. Our clan has weathered the centuries. Governments have treated us with courtesy in the worst of times, during wars and plagues and famines. But someone in the Ministry of Finance has been allowed to write a letter of discourtesy. It's impossible to believe! The Master said: "Grieve not that men don't know you; grieve that you don't know men." '

'If I can help in any way, your Highness –'

'I appreciate that. What I'd like is for someone to write a letter in my behalf.'

'Will you grant me the privilege of writing a letter?'

'That's an interesting idea, General.' The Duke flicks his plump cheek with the end of a long fingernail, as if deep in thought. 'Well, yes.'

'I'm grateful for the opportunity. But you must understand, there's little hope of success.'

'I know, I know –'

'The Ministry of Finance is overburdened with requests. These days, your Holiness, what funds are available go for defense.'

'For armies. For *your* army.'

'What money I get goes for food and arms.'

'I know, I know. I wrote the president and every member of the cabinet. Nothing but refusals.' He adds after a thoughtful pause, 'But at least they were polite refusals. This letter from the Ministry of Finance –'

'A minor functionary must have written it.' Tang thinks of the clerk who informed him that his own stipend from the province would not be forthcoming. 'Your Highness, I doubt if he's aware of his disrespect.'

'Really?'

'These days in the bureaus they have young men who aren't well trained.'

'That's the result of giving up the examination system. But the

Master said: "I don't murmur against Heaven." So I'll just have to bear my troubles and not complain about it.'

'I'll write the letter tomorrow, your Holiness.'

'Good, good. Why not.' The Duke looks away, as if imagining a time when his clan entertained emperors and the Residence warehouses, falling apart now a few yards from here, were bursting with grain.

Rising to leave, Tang bows low. The Duke gives him a long look, then says wistfully, 'To know Tao is not as good as loving it; to love it is not as good as practicing it. But nobody cares about the Master's words any more.' When Tang bows again, the Duke says, 'Look there.' He points to a moon guitar hanging on the wall. 'One of the struts is broken. Who's to pay for it?'

With a final bow, Tang leaves the room by walking backward in traditional style. Strolling through the sultry night, the General feels uplifted by having spent time with a direct descendant of a very wise man who walked here, right here where his own feet step through the courtyards, twenty-five hundred years ago. Another irony he appreciates is involved in his relationship with the Duke. Though he believes the intricate family system has often crippled his country, encouraging people to be corrupt and selfish in gaining the ends of their families, each time he meets the Duke it seems all of history surges forward and meets them there, all the traditions, the glory of courtesy and respect and filial piety – no matter what sort of man the Duke himself really is. The irony? The General loves a system of life that he blames for much of China's troubles.

Back in his own quarters, Tang eats a good dinner – with his servant Yao's smiling approval. Near the end of his meal he's interrupted by a junior officer, who stands hesitantly in the doorway, obviously afraid to bother the General.

'Well, young man? What is it?'

'Excellency, a man came back with the Big Swords –'

'Yes, they were all men who came back.'

'The foreigner, General. We don't know what to do with him.'

'Begin by feeding him.' Tang pours a small cup of wine.

'Where should he stay tonight, Excellency? In the Residence here?'

'In a tent, like the other troops. Where he can learn about God.'

'Excellency?'

'Feed him, give him a uniform, assign him to a tent.' The General waves his hand with a smile.

170

Quickly the young officer shuts the door, but it has hardly closed before there's another knock. Tang knows by the soft, tentative sound who is knocking.

He calls out, 'Come in!'

Su-su, wearing a purple gown embroidered with red cranes flying, hobbles slowly in.

Awakening from an obscure nightmare, by reflex he reaches out for the girl. Lightly grasping her wrist – the girl snuffles in her sleep – he turns to regard her moonlit body. The edge of a flung sheet covers one leg to the knee; otherwise she is naked; to his gaze, more vulnerable sleeping than awake. He is always startled by the delicate smallness of her after watching her move about in voluminous swathes of cotton and silk. Innocent in her sleep, Su-su looks more child than woman tonight, and reminds him of his own sister when she was curled up on the *kang*. But his sister had been full of laughter and tricks, whereas Su-su is a solemn girl who rarely smiles, even in response to a smile.

She's like many girls he has known: They fear displeasing their masters because such fear has been rooted in them since childhood. Moreover, Su-su is not a legal concubine, merely a gift from the mayor of Lin Yi, therefore discardable without notice. Tang's assurance that he will provide for her welfare, whatever happens – a promise often given and meant – she accepts with downcast eyes. In her view obviously it is nothing more than another of the formalities that bind her life, even as cotton cloth tightly binds her feet.

Her feet. In brief moments of somber coquettishness, Su-su parades through the bedroom, displaying her pigeon-toed gait that nearly pitches her forward into a fall. She does it in the hope that her tiny feet, her 'golden lilies,' will give the General pleasure. Unlike most men, he does not find such misshapen feet exciting; for him they have other connotations, social and political, and signal the worst elements of China. When Su-su thrusts them from under her gown as a sexual temptation, Tang thinks of pain, the girl's pain on her fifth year, when her mother wrapped them in thick cloth, forcing the toes down, under the arch. Through childhood and adolescence her toes had remained curled in hard casings like the retracted beaks of dying birds. Su-su walked the first year with the aid of canes, feeling herself lucky to escape gangrene. Her

171

parents, like those of many village girls, had sacrificed the labor their daughter might have contributed to the family – let alone her own well-being – had tortured and ultimately crippled her in the hope of making her beautiful, therefore marriageable, or at least salable.

Tang stares in the moonlight at one exposed foot; it has the look of a small mangled carcass, a dead mouse. Often he has heard men say of women, 'If a pretty face is worth fifteen percent of beauty and plump breasts another fifteen, then lily feet must be worth the other seventy.' A thousand years of pain for nothing but vanity and the appearance of wealth. He can't look at such feet without anger, even now, when he has no wish to be 'modern.' As a young army officer Tang had belonged to *T'ien-tsu hui*, the Society for the Liberation of Feet. Once, with two other men, he draped some footbinding cloths on a pole outside a government building. The act of defiance nearly cost him his commission, horrified his mother, whose feet had also been golden lilies since she was five, and resulted in the only quarrel he ever had with his father. He can remember to this day his father pacing, hands clenched behind him, tensely muttering about the damage such impudent mischief might do to the clan. In those days, soon after establishment of the Republic, like other young intellectuals Tang had shifted toward the radical end of the political spectrum, but now in middle age he has lost that innocent ardor for quick solutions, and views more cautiously the effect of change upon a land as traditionbound as China. Even so, he can't look at the crippled feet of young women without a sense of fury and frustration. Publicly he has sworn to outlaw footbinding someday, sometimes in the near or distant future. Which will it be? Will such a future ever come? Will he rule this country? It seems that any deep-night thinking, however it begins, always comes round to this question.

The girl stirs in her sleep, flicking with a thumb at her cheek, moistening her lips, turning away. Tang regards her tapered back and firm buttocks dispassionately. Even the glistening sweat – it is a very hot night – on her young skin fails to arouse him. Perhaps age makes a difference. Age, fatigue, worry. At nineteen, when he married his first wife, Tang had mounted the fourteen-year-old with the fierce lust of a rooster, and their encounters – quick, violent – had been more like military skirmishes than love. Yet in their weeks together they were happy. Often they spent the Hour of the Hare, just before dawn, giggling like children as they explored each other with joyous curiosity.

Now he can't remember her face.

On marches, when the recall of happiness can help to make miles go by, his failure of memory used to bother him. Perhaps if he had known her longer than a few months or had been the companion of her dying moments, the face of his first wife might have remained in his memory, but she was gone quickly. While he was on military assignment in Peking, she vanished without a trace along with everyone else in the Shantung village of two thousand, when a flood destroyed everything, blowing away scores of villages with such thorough savagery that returning survivors could not locate the sites where they had been born. Whenever Tang thinks of her manner of dying, he thinks too of the land – such disasters its heritage. Nature here simply lets go, acting out its brute passions on a colossal scale. The result: rivers where there were roads, plains where there were hills, gullies where there were fields, and a few tons of mud where there were human settlements and young girls living in them. The fate of his bride in a context of such upheaval measures as much as a drop of water. So someone told him, but Tang can't remember who did, any more than he can remember the girl's face.

He has an easier time remembering his second wife, but after all, they had years, not weeks, together. She gave him two fine sons. And it is difficult to forget the features of someone you have seen die slowly, in agony. He had been home on leave – they were living in Jinan – when her first symptoms appeared: headache, sore throat, nausea, chills and fever. When she developed severe abdominal pain, the local doctor diagnosed it as a mild case of typhoid. But in spite of herbal drinks the condition worsened. Tang sat beside her bed day after day while her temperature remained steadily high, draining her strength.

He hears a faint thud in the dark bedroom. One of the canaries, having awakened, has hopped down to the floor of its cage. Tang thinks of Su-su's love for birds. Perhaps they're the only thing that has never threatened her. This evening, before undressing, she had paused at the bamboo bars, whistled softly, and brought a canary hopping toward her, until her lips and its beak nearly touched.

His second wife never had time for pets. She had been too busy raising the boys. A strong woman, she was also a hearty wife who took as much pleasure as she gave. At the last there had been florid diarrhea, labored breathing, a sudden fall of temperature (affording an illusion of hope), and a final curious outpouring of sweat before she died of convulsive strangulation.

Wu Sheng-chi had been there with him. Wu had pried his fingers from the cold wrist and led him away. Wu had sat with him in silence that night and all the next day in a freezing room.

And the next month, when both fine sons also succumbed to the disease, Wu had been there too.

I did well to avenge him, the General thinks.

For the past five years, since her death, Tang has refused to take another wife. Offended by this decision in a land mastered by family life, people have often tried to interest him in remarrying. Perhaps if his clan were still flourishing, he might welcome this responsibility, but his clan, aside from one brother and one nephew, no longer exists. Parents, uncles, aunts, nieces, nephews – all dead, executed.

It had happened in 1916, the Year of the Dragon, when Yuan Shih-k'ai, then president of the Republic, wanted to ascend the Dragon Throne as emperor and create a new dynasty. Factions rose against him, hoping to maintain the Republic, at least until a man of honor could take the throne. There was much plotting in those days, and among the conspirators was Tang's father. Finally caught by Yuan's men, he was beheaded. However, by a practice sanctioned since the ancient days of the Chin, not only the conspirator but his entire clan must also die. Tang, then a young officer in Sian, went into hiding, and Tang's brother, a Shanghai businessman, fled with his family to Hong Kong. Further slaughter of political opponents ended soon after that, when the wildly insane Yuan (he once massacred a favorite concubine and their newborn child with a ceremonial sword) fortuitously died of a stroke. But it was too late for the Clan of Tang. One hundred thirty-two of them, including infants, were executed, burned, their ashes scattered to the winds; their ancestral tablets were removed from the family altar in Weifang, broken into pieces, and thrown into the river.

Without the clan to persuade him otherwise, Tang has substituted a philosophical concept for ancestral piety: He argues that China is best served today by the development of a national spirit beyond the confines of family interest. It may well be that the country won't flower again until the old familial rules are given up. In this opinion too he is 'modern,' almost against his will. Sometimes he wonders if his refusal to marry is a form of self-punishment for having survived the clan. He will die without a son to perform his funeral rites, as such rites had been denied to all one hundred thirty-two.

Moving close to Su-su, he gently places his hand on her breast, assaying its soft weight in cupped fingers. He once read somewhere that our flesh is a little miracle created by Tien Ti to help us savor the mysteries of another and better life beyond the Yellow Springs where eventually we go. Our departure leaves to the next generation the contemplation of the same miracle. Gently, gently, his fingers trace the curved flesh. His fingers halt a moment, when her breathing falters in its rhythm, then continue.

Tonight old Dog Meat must be in bed with two or three women. Fat, drunk, he's probably watching them perform together at his command – it is rumored that alcohol and opium have unmanned him. Newly appointed Governor General of Shantung.

Tang withdraws his hand, pulls it into a fist at the thought of Chang Tsung-ch'ang in his mansion of fifteen halls. Chang Tsung-ch'ang, seated lumpily on horseback, reviewing his troops while White Russian bodyguards, their bannered lances and gold braid and plumed helmets glittering in sunlight, surround his August Person, his Majestic Presence –

Drawing his legs up, shutting his eyes in an attempt to sleep, the General lets images drift through his consciousness until it begins to dim: canaries in their cages; Su-su's lips nearing a yellow beak; old Dog Meat leaning closer to observe his naked girls at love; those White Russian bodyguards in their finery; the White Russian woman beside him at the Tomb.

Opening his eyes, Tang blinks in the moonlight. That Russian woman, their ride to the cemetery. He had never seen such white skin, such limpid eyes, such a way of being.

Other images drift along, fade, and accompany him into sleep.

Finished with Tai Chi Chuan and breakfast, the General has moved his work desk into a courtyard to take advantage of breezes on this hot day. He sits beneath a *Sophora japonica*, the dragon-claw pagoda tree, with stiffly drooping branches that give him shade and almost enclose him, like one of the covered galleries that connect one hall of the Residence to another.

He has just received a wireless message sent by Chang Tsung-ch'ang from the provincial capital at Jinan. It invites him to a conference at Thousand Buddha Mountain in two weeks 'to discuss current affairs.' Sometimes the General wonders if China's problems might all be quickly solved if its leaders stopped using ambiguous phrases, such as 'current affairs,' in a foolish effort to mask their intentions. Obviously old Dog Meat wants to impress people with his new position. But which people? The old scoundrel says nothing about that. It is, however, a meeting the General must attend, for to remain isolated longer will invite disaster. It is time for him to get out and see what his rivals and allies are doing.

Yet it is peaceful here in the Kong Residence; while checking reports and documents, he has often glanced up this last hour to watch the light shifting on the far wall, drawing shadows from it and transforming one section into a rusty pink square; his eye moves slowly past a wisteria trellis, a pot of camellias, a grillwork window, before grudgingly returning to the print on a document handed to him by Yang.

'Excellency.' The young man leans toward him. 'The Russian wishes to speak to you.'

Russian? The woman, is she back? That startling possibility lasts but a moment; then Tang realizes his aide means the Bolshevik, who has been in camp a month now. Perhaps it's time to let the fellow know where he stands. 'Bring him here,' Tang says and sits back, glad to interrupt the paper work.

A minute later Yang leads the big Russian and his small interpreter through a fan-shaped gate into the courtyard. They halt at the edge of the shade, their sunlit faces looking in on the General at his shadowed table.

The Russian is still affecting the common dress of a peasant. Half rising, the General extends his hand and the Russian hastens forward to take it. The same flaccid grip that the General remembers from their first meeting. Even so, the Russian may not be as weak as his handshake suggests; perhaps he merely conveys the appearance of weakness while entertaining the hope of subverting an entire army!

Formalities are exchanged through the interpreter. Tang will address his remarks to this fellow Li during the interview, not only because they speak the same language but because he suspects of the two men it is Li who makes the decisions, although perhaps the Russian doesn't realize it. The big fellow's heavy-lidded eyes seem indifferent, yet he pulls nervously at the ends of his long black mustache. For the Russian this is an important meeting.

Tang doesn't wait for him to speak, however; bluntly the General asks if the Soviet government has granted his arms request.

He fully expects the answer he gets: There has been no reply from Moscow yet. Accompanying this obvious news is an explanation, long-winded in the need for it to be translated. The request, having been sent to Mikhail Borodin in Wuhan, was then relayed through proper channels to the Politburo; this took time, of course, and the ensuing reply must follow the same routing.

'We will soon have it,' Li says. 'Comrade Kovalik is certain it will be affirmative.'

'Certain,' Tang repeats. He tells Yang to bring tea; and motions to the Russian and interpreter to take chairs placed on the pebble mosaic of the courtyard.

Smiling at Li, the General says, 'How has your *sovetnik* liked his stay in my camp?'

'He is most pleased with his accommodations,' Li replies without questioning Kovalik. 'But if I may be permitted, Excellency, he'd welcome more freedom of movement.'

'I don't understand,' Tang tells him, understanding perfectly.

This time, before replying, Li consults the Russian, who speaks while twirling one end of the thick mustache.

'Comrade Kovalik feels he has spent too much time in the compound and not enough with the troops. He does wish to serve you, Excellency, as well as possible.'

Tang waits.

'For example.' Li speaks with frequent pauses to make sure he doesn't overstep the bounds of propriety. 'When he leaves his quarters, half a dozen escorts go with him. To ride out of town to the camp, he must request a horse days in advance. He eats alone, never with your staff. He has never attended a staff meeting, although he asked written permission of Colonel Pi.' Now Li waits, small and deferential, in command of his features.

Again Tang chooses not to comment.

So in a low, respectful voice, Li says, 'Comrade Kovalik wishes to ask a very small favor, Excellency.'

'By all means let him ask.'

'He wishes to form a little study group, perhaps among the junior officers. It would be designed only for general discussion.'

'For general discussion,' Tang repeats. 'I am interested in

knowing where a general discussion might lead, if not to politics?'

At the corner of Li's mouth there's a slight tremor. He doesn't translate for Kovalik but chooses to reply on his own. 'Excellency, the comrade won't make political speeches. After all, you've forbidden it. He's not here to promote Soviet ideas but to help in any way he can. He won't work against you.'

'I am sure he won't.'

'He merely wishes to meet young officers and talk with them.'

'I see, talk. Talk about art, philosophy, Sung history, or the poetry of Tu Fu?' Although the remark is sarcastic, it's made in the same calm, serious tone the General assumed at the outset. He continues without requiring a reply. 'Is the food acceptable to the *sovetnik*?'

'Completely. We are humbly grateful.'

'And you say the accommodations are satisfactory?'

'For both of us. We are deeply grateful for your illustrious concern; such generosity is beyond our modest expectations and even more modest deserts, Excellency, but –

'Then I haven't failed to treat you with the distinction you deserve. Thank you. I am humbly grateful.'

Tea comes. While cups are poured and handed out by old Yao, the General hears from his quarters, beyond the gray wall separating this courtyard from the next, the trio of male canaries bursting into song.

'Excellency? The study group?' Li asks softly, after they have sipped the tea.

'Plenty of time to consider that,' says Tang, opening both hands out. 'As long as you and your *sovetnik* are satisfied in other ways.' He watches the goateed interpreter convey this news to the Russian, whose broad, pale face indicates his understanding: Permission denied.

Now is the time, the General thinks, for a general discussion of my own. 'I have a favor to ask of the *sovetnik*,' he says to Li. 'Will he tell me who's in charge these days in Moscow? Trotsky or Stalin?'

The abrupt shift in the conversation has the big rumpled Russian leaning forward. His blue eyes glance around as if trying to anchor on something visually. Li gives him time to collect his thoughts by saying to the General, 'Are you a student, Excellency, of Russian affairs?'

'Not at all. I know nothing and won't know anything unless your *sovetnik* tells me.'

Li seems to relax as he and Kovalik talk between themselves. Hereafter their replies to the General require careful structuring. In answer to his Excellency's question, Li explains in hesitant, measured phrases that at such a far remove from Moscow it is difficult to assess the current situation, but in the Comrade's opinion there are no irreconcilable differences between the two leaders. In Soviet Russia free exchange of opinion is encouraged; foreign observers might see it as a quarrel or even a divisive conflict, when in reality such expression merely aids in the formation of policy beneficial to the people.

'This Soviet adviser in Wuhan – tell me about him. This fellow Borodin.'

The reply takes a long time in coming. 'Mikhail Borodin is definitely committed to the independence of China,' Li finally declares. He adds, searching carefully for words, that Comrade Kovalik wishes to point out the following: In 1924 the Russian government renounced all previous treaties made with China that infringed on Chinese sovereignty. No other foreign power has done the same – not one. Moreover, Russian has abandoned all claims to Boxer indemnities and has demonstrated its willingness to treat with China on terms of full equality. No other foreign power has done the same – not one.

'Thank you. But I'd like to know something else about Borodin. Whose man is he? Does he represent Trotsky or Stalin?'

A long exchange takes place between Li and Kovalik, but the eventual reply is short: Borodin represents the will of the entire government.

'Is it true the Wuhan clique wants him out of China? That when he goes, so goes the last of Soviet influence?'

The reply comes more quickly: The Soviet government wants only to help where it can and make China safe against renegade imperialists like Chiang Kai-shek.

'I thought Borodin and Chiang used to be on good terms.'

'Borodin is still on very good, very close terms with the government at Wuhan.'

'No dissension?'

'None at all.' Li is no longer consulting the Russian, whose big hand awkwardly holds the delicate teacup. 'Wuhan and Borodin have only one enemy, and that is Chiang Kai-shek.'

'Tell me about the man Roy.'

'Manabendra Nath Roy is a member of the Presidium of the

179

Comintern. He's here as part of the China Commission.'

'Thank you, but I wish to know about Roy.'

The Russian is questioning his interpreter. Clearly he feels left out of a conversation that is picking up speed.

'The Comrade doesn't understand,' Li continues after a long exchange with the Russian, 'what it is you want to know about Manabendra Nath Roy.'

'You might begin with the message from Stalin.'

'Excellency?'

'I'm talking about the instructions from Stalin.'

'Perhaps someone in Wuhan is relating incorrect information to you, Excellency.'

'Tell your *sovetnik* this: China is a land of secrets where everything is known.'

Kovalik's reaction to the aphorism is a faint, bitter smile.

'The Comrade says there was a certain communication – perhaps you're referring to it. The message was read at a meeting of the Politburo of the Central Committee of the Chinese Communist Party.'

'And what does the Comrade think of it?'

After consultation, Li replies, 'The message was somewhat ambiguous.'

'It was a set of instructions from Stalin. Am I right?'

'Some people say that.' Li shrugs.

'Perhaps your *sovetnik* says that too.' When Li doesn't reply, after translating Tang's words to the Russian, there is a long silence. The General hears the birds singing in his room; somehow the sound brings him comfort even in the midst of this tense conversation. Tang looks at the two men, both sweating under the fierce sun. He has a choice. He can tell them what he knows: that Stalin's instructions were deliberately contradictory, designed to cover every eventuality in China and therefore to save his skin back home, where Trotsky's followers await the chance to blame him for a China failure; that Roy, by revealing the full extent of the instructions, unwittingly turned the Chinese Bolsheviks against Moscow, as they recognized that their own fate was being tied to internal Russian politics; that there would be no arms shipment from Russia; that a Soviet agent like Kovalik can do nothing in behalf of his government, because it has in fact deserted him; that the Comrade might as well go home – he and Russia are finished in China.

But the General has another choice: He can leave his own preception of the situation ambiguous. He can play along with the Russian. But to what purpose? There's no political advantage in such a deception. But there is the personal satisfaction of deluding and therefore humiliating the representative of a government bent upon dominating his own country.

Tang claps both hands on his knees with an air of decision. 'Well, so much is rumor these days.' He has made his choice. 'By the time facts get to Qufu, they are often fantasies. Tell the Comrade I regret having bored him with so much misinformation. My apologies.'

Li relays the General's words to the big Russian, who forces a smile, then wipes his sweaty forehead by drawing his sleeve across it.

'Our talk has been most instructive,' the General continues, rising. 'As for your study group, perhaps we can manage something. We have time, haven't we? In the meantime, my humble facilities are at your disposal. Comrade Kovalik is my honored guest.'

Again the weak handshake. For an instant Tang meets the light-blue eyes of the Russian. Is there rage in them or despair or possibly hope? It is difficult to read the expressions of a foreigner.

When his visitors have left by the fan-shaped gate, Tang calls his aide. 'Yang, remove the guards. They're no longer necessary.' After a pause, he adds, 'The Russian is harmless.'

'Will you let him stay here, Excellency?'

'He can stay as long as he wishes. He can stay forever for all I care,' Tang says with a smile.

Yang's bushy eyebrows rise slowly, as he begins to appreciate the General's little triumph over a foreign power: a representative of the Russian government left here without function, wholly isolated, like a cork bobbing on a vast sea.

'And what about the other foreigner, Excellency?'

'He stays too.'

Yang smiles faintly. 'They say he slept last night on a horse.'

'I believe it.' Tang sits down at the desk under the shade tree. Beyond its blue circle the light is intense – the white of death against the opposite wall. For a moment he thinks of the bandits' heads, fastened with spikes to the town gates; they will whiten into the look of a garden wall at noon: harmless, silent witnesses to his revenge. Breaking free of the thought, he says to his aide, 'Put the American into a uniform.'

'That's been done, Excellency.'

'Have you assigned him to a training unit?'

Yang pauses before replying. 'I wanted to make sure, Excellency –'

'Yes, I meant it. We'll see how this American student studies war.'

Yang places a sheaf of papers on the desk. 'The old beggar is waiting to cast the Yarrow Stalks.'

'Bring him here.' Tang feels in need of the oracle today. Last time the old diviner cast the stalks, their message was most interesting – and correct: 'You are sincere and are being obstructed.' There had also been something about 'going through to the end means misfortune; and a cautious halt brings success.' He had been obstructed by White Wolf, and by going through to the end and avenging himself on the bandit, he had allowed political events to take place without his presence on the scene. 'A cautious halt brings success.' Could that possibly refer to the conference on Thousand Buddha Mountain? If so, he shouldn't attend.

Or he should attend in defiance of the oracle?

His father's spirit would be appalled at that – defying the oracle. But it may well be what he must do. It's necessary for him to feel the pulse of things; all of China is trembling with change. Perched in the north above him are two archrivals, Feng Yu-hsiang and Marshal Chang Tso-lin. Nearby is old Dog Meat, ensconced with the Marshal's blessing in Jinan. The Japanese prowl along the Shantung coast, wolflike, awaiting their chance to make use of Chinese resources inland. And holding Nanking and Shanghai, as well as the South, is Chiang Kai-shek, like himself a newcomer to power but unlike himself in command of urban wealth. At least there is no longer a need to worry about the Blosheviks. The interview with the hesitant Russian has confirmed his understanding of that situation: bad policies in Moscow have pushed an irreparable wedge between the Chinese Bolsheviks and their Russian advisers; and to compound their trouble, both have lost the good will of other radicals in Wuhan. Not that the radicals themselves have retained their power. Their association with the Bolsheviks has hurt them badly, and Wuhan, the political capital of leftist organizations, must be as quiet these days as a city smoldering in the aftermath of a fire. Corrupted by their own squabbling and now scattered by Moscow's stupid interference, the leftists – all of them, the trade unionists, the Bolsheviks, the socialists – are no longer formidable. He needn't cast an anxious eye in the direction of Wuhan. His adversaries are as follows: Feng, the Marshal, Dog Meat, and Chiang Kai-shek.

A new burst of song captures his attention. Such lively birds filled with such natural art. His mind drifts. Images appear and vanish: Bent-backed old scholars drinking wine in a glen; a waterfall in the high mist of a mountain; a shady grove of bamboo glimpsed perhaps in a painting he has forgotten; and the lips of a girl against the slats of a bird cage.

Adrift, he doesn't notice the old diviner shuffling into the courtyard. The General starts. He smells, clinging to the old man's clothes, the sweet pungent smoke of opium.

The old diviner, after a deep bow, throws a fistful of dried yarrow stalks on the desk. 'Six, Excellency. The old *yin*. Plus a seven, the young *yang*.'

Tang sits back, hearing the birds warble mightily, and awaits his future.

8

What was all that about Stalin and Trotsky? He will never understand the Chinese.

Entering a guesthouse in the West Wing, glancing moodily at the elegant room, Kovalik flings himself on the bed. Four men trailed him here, two of them peeling off to follow Li. For the past month they've always been watched. Sometimes, waking in the night and rushing to the window, Kovalik has seen someone in the moonlight, leaning against a pillar or a wall. Often he is given a little bow of respect.

These Chinese.

He must say they have imprisoned him discreetly. Little has been denied that he didn't want; almost everything has been delayed that he did. With Li's help he has tried to extricate himself from this spider web, but nothing works. He has learned to appreciate the Chinese genius for isolating people, for incarcerating them without uttering a rude word.

To pass the time he tried initially to study Chinese, but it's a fearsome language. He has gone little further than 'thank you' and 'sorry.' So Kovalik has come to rely on a pastime learned in the army: wood carving. His only possession of value is a jackknife he has carried with him – mounted or on foot, in boxcar or on battlefield. With it he models any piece of wood he can find. Here in Qufu he works with yellow pine, a soft wood that requires a sharp blade. He likes to make dolls and give them to children. Perhaps today in the villages of Siberia there are men and women – children then – who have kept the little carvings, the dancing bears and girls wearing babushkas, and Red Army soldiers carrying guns. Sometimes at leisure – and he has plenty of it these days – he recalls a special village his unit went through. Log cabins immersed in snow, and from them came blocky people immersed in clothes; the great fur hats, hiding faces, made everyone look alike. Except the face of a small boy. Kovalik, reining in his mount, had looked down at the woebegone expression, the enormous haunted eyes, and had taken from his pocket a dancing bear carved from oak; leaning over, he had thrust it into the boy's hand. Slowly the expression changed; Kovalik will never forget the smile that spread across the small pale face like a glow of warm coals. There were crows everywhere in that village. On the outskirts lay a pile of corpses which the birds fed on. The populace was too weak from starvation to break through the drifts and bury their dead.

As a good Bolshevik, he never carved religious icons, although he had seen comrades do it on the march, quite unconscious of the irony.

Taking out the large clasp knife, Kovalik studies the blade with an expert eye. He'd like to have a piece of oak now, to carve into its hand, close texture.

What was that about Stalin and Trotsky? The General wanted to know about Borodin and Roy as well. Or perhaps he was just laughing at the Russian failure in his country.

Fidgeting, Kovalik gets to his feet and paces. Standing near the grillwork window, he looks at the courtyard. Camphor and oleander trees, a drooping willow over there. All very pretty, he thinks in disgust. The fruits of idle wealth, reminding him of the aristocratic life of his own land's oppressors.

He has the knife in his hand, holds it to the light. What he needs is a carborundum stick to sharpen the blade. That's what Li went to get for him. Where is Li? he wonders impatiently. Li will know what the General was doing; after all, they are both Chinese. Does the General know that Stalin miscalculated, that Borodin, once the most powerful man in China, can no longer hold together various factions in Wuhan? Does the General know that the great

184

Trotsky, true heir of Lenin, is now in political limbo, the mere director of an electric power committee? What really does Tang know? And the study group? Where in hell is Li?

Through a round window in a wall across the courtyard Kovalik can see a huge monolithic rock in the next courtyard. Because there is a similar rock in his own courtyard, it appears as if the window is actually a mirror and the distant rock is a reflection of the nearer one. Visual tricks, designed to amuse the spiritless rich. It is all so pretty that the courtyard sickens him, makes him feel guilty. Beyond the wall is a fish pond with bullfrogs croaking in the water weeds, and beyond this pond are gazebos set strategically to create perfect vistas among gardens and pavilions, with zigzagging galleries leading to covered bridges leading to piles of fantastic rocks, water-modeled, hauled here perhaps centuries ago by groaning thousands of coolies.

And in Wuhan, because of Stalin's stupidity, the Chinese are giving up faith in Bolshevism and defecting to the Nationalists, to the treacherous Chiang Kai-shek and his capitalist cutthroats.

And I stay here, whittling soft wood.

From the table Kovalik picks up a block of pine as big as his hand. Already shaped in the round, it will be a dancing bear. He sits on the edge of the bed and holds the knife above the grainy wood.

Where is Li? He should be here, explaining the devious mind of that Chinese general.

It seems to Kovalik that nothing has made sense or gone right since he left Vladivostok months ago. He had arrived there, an agent of the Soviet government, full of optimism as he envisioned fighting on Chinese soil for international communism. He consumed hot Russian tea in tall glasses while the landlocked harbor thawed slowly in the spring air. He took long solitary walks on rough cobblestone, dreaming of self-sacrifice and a new world. How naïve it seems now!

He slashes at the wood, cutting deep into its soft grain.

And later, when he arrived on Wuhan, city of revolutionary fervor, his hopes had soared in the midst of posters and marches and daily strikes. He was gratified by the closing of foreign banks; he felt the end of resistance was at hand when foreign businessmen moved aboard their national ships in the Yangtze, afraid of the city at night. And he had faith in the Russian overseer of this Chinese revolution, Mikhail Mikhailovich Borodin, who had already masterminded the emergence of a strong Chinese army in the South. In spite of Borodin's split with that southern bastard Chiang Kai-shek, the great man still commanded the loyalty of both Russians and Chinese when Kovalik arrived in Wuhan.

It had taken a few weeks for Kovalik to sort out the truth that lay behind the street demonstrations and bold speeches: Borodin was not really in charge here; someone halfway across the globe was, and that was Stalin, who had been ousting Trotsky – Kovalik's hero – even as Kovalik was leaving Vladivostok by steamer for China.

Since then, nothing had made sense or gone right. Stalin's manipulation of Russian agents in Wuhan for his own purposes had led to Chinese suspicion of Russia. In such a climate of deception and fear, many Chinese Bolsheviks left the Communist Party and slipped out of Wuhan to join Chiang Kai-shek while there was still a chance. Weary Russians, watching Borodin's grip on the situation grow weaker each day, simply wanted to go home. To bolster his own spirits Kovalik drank beer with Chinese still loyal to the idea of communism. In their company one night he met a tall, delicate-looking young man from Hunan. They sat up late in a tea shop, arguing through a translator. The young Hunanese insisted that revolution in China must be different from Russia's; in Russia the city workers led, because they were the source of power; here in China the power was in the countryside, among the peasants. Kovalik was not at all convinced; for one thing the thesis was contrary to Leninist doctrine, and for another, his own experience had taught him the peasant was usually a cunning opportunist – he had seen too many of them scavenge the dead bodies of both Red and White in the Russian Civil War. Moreover, Kovalik was suspicious of such a bold, unprecedented opinion coming from someone with the smooth, boyish cheeks and intellectual approach of this young man, who was obviously more political dilettante than committed revolutionary. They argued passionately and parted unreconciled.

The next day at headquarters Kovalik learned that this young man, Mao Tse-tung, was known as a troublemaker. He also wrote Chinese poetry in classical meters, which substantiated Kovalik's skeptical opinion of him.

Where is Li? What is the General's game? Aware that he has hacked amateurishly into the pine, Kovalik tosses it aside. Where is Li? Kovalik has known for a long time how much he depends on the slim young Chinese. Li is a remarkable fellow. Few men his age, only twenty-seven, have done so much. During the Great War, at fifteen, Li had served in a Chinese labor battalion in France. Back home he went to military school at Whampoa under the tutelage of Chiang Kai-shek, who was then the commandant. There he had met a quiet radical named Chou En-lai, who introduced him to socialist thought. Coming from Peking originally, Li spoke Mandarin; in the South he had learned Yue. He had acquired his Russian during a stay in Moscow at Sun Yat-sen University.

Having held similar views to those of the troublemaker Mao – that revolution should begin with the peasantry – Li Chung-lin had been punished by the Party. His punishment: to accompany Kovalik as interpreter on this assignment. His punishment was, of course, the Russian's reward, as Kovalik keeps telling him. 'My only good fortune since coming to China,' Kovalik says often, 'has been to meet you, my friend.'

But where is Li now? Picking up the block of wood again, Kovalik begins whittling impatiently. Time passes. Shavings litter the floor. Finally lost in the work, he is startled when Li opens the door and walks in.

'I can't find anything to sharpen your knife with,' Li says, grimacing. 'Here they use big grindstones, that's all.'

Kovalik tosses the wood aside and puts the knife away as he says anxiously, 'Well, what about today?' When Li looks puzzled, he adds, 'I mean the General. What's happened? Has he denied us permission?'

'I think we'd better forget the study group, at least for a while.'

So he confirms Kovalik's own opinion. The Russian looks at the wood carving he has thrown on the floor. Two crude haunches, the round belly of a bear. Perhaps I should do nothing but carve wood, he thinks ruefully.

'At the end,' Kovalik says after a silence, 'the General said something about the study group. Did he mean we can make a deal?'

'No.'

Getting up, Kovalik shambles to the table and pours himself a drink of *mao tai*; it is the closest thing to vodka he can get in China. 'Want one?' He is mildly surprised when Li nods yes. The little Chinese rarely drinks. 'What does the General want with us?'

'I can guess,' Li says, taking the proffered *mao tai*. 'Have you ever seen a cat play with a mouse?'

187

'Do you think I'm so stupid as to live like this without knowing why? He wants to humiliate me.'

'Yes,' Li says quietly.

'Does he hate Bolsheviks so much?'

'It's not Bolsheviks. The General hates foreigners.'

'But I hear he's got another one here. An American.'

'That's cat and mouse too. Or maybe he's just curious.' Li shrugs.

'What else is he, Li? Who's got hold of us?'

Li purses his lips. 'A fine general in the field. Last year he kept a warlord from overrunning the province, although he was outnumbered. A fine, very good general. Yes, he's that.'

Kovalik, who's been pacing, sits down at the table with Li. They face each other across a streak of sunlight. 'That's what they said in Wuhan before we left. Borodin himself told me. He said: Watch Tang closely, learn about him. Did Borodin think he'd become powerful?'

'I'm sure Borodin thought so.'

'But you don't?'

Li considers awhile, sipping the *mao tai*. 'He's new – in China where the old keep the power. Ten years ago he was a division commander. Some people look at him as an upstart. He has few connections in Peking.'

This is ground they have gone over before, yet Kovalik continues the conversation because it seems that everything they talk about they've talked about before. 'His prospects?'

'Tang will be crushed without allies.'

'And meanwhile we sit here, slowly dying.' Kovalik goes to the window and stares at the rocks. They haven't moved since last he looked at them. They won't move for centuries, yet frequently he stands here and checks to make sure. Gloomily he studies the rest of the courtyard: *Fu* dogs in bronze, a huge porcelain pot on the cobblestones, a solitary lime tree rising in spindly profusion above the orange tiles of the adjoining roof. And the camphor trees. And the oleander trees. Everything in place, as always. Everything positioned for eternity, while his own time runs out.

'We will die here,' he announces quietly and turns to Li. 'Is that what Tang has in mind?'

'It's possible.'

'And Borodin? Did he send us here for the same reason?'

Li shrugs and drinks off the *mao tai*.

Kovalik begins pacing, talking half to himself. 'Borodin never had faith in a Chinese revolution. He was just carrying out Stalin's orders. He doesn't want people like me to go back to Russia.' He halts a moment and looks at Li. 'Did you know Osetrov and Tikhvinsky? Trotskyists like me. They've been sent to outlying places like this too. Clear, isn't it. Borodin doesn't want me to go back home and tell the truth about China.'

'Take comfort in one thing.'

Again halting, Kovalik turns to the little Chinese.

'Borodin won't return to Moscow in triumph.'

'Yes,' Kovalik says. 'There's comfort in that.' Again he sits down, resting his chin on his hand, fingering a drink of *mao tai*. The silence lengthens. Yes, he thinks, there's comfort in knowing that Borodin, by carrying out Stalin's orders, has failed here in China. But everyone left here will die to hide the fact. Good revolutionaries will end up in the hands of Chinese generals like Tang, without orders ever being cut to release them. A strange thought: Stalin and Borodin conspiring with a Chinese general to get rid of a representative of the Soviet government. A strange fate for a revolutionary who was there at the beginning. Who was in Petrograd during the initial strikes. Who had seen the battlefields of civil war. Who had seen the great leaders, rubbed elbows with them. Who had been there in August 1918 when Trotsky gave the order to execute every twelfth man in a regiment that had retreated without permission from Kazan. Who had been bayoneted in the arm by a Don Cossack in December 1918. That was at Perm. Who had been with the Red Army when it broke through the Irtysh lines in November 1919 and put all of White Siberia on the move. Who had seen the thousands of imperialists in the distance, struggling by horse, wagon, and foot through the snow, running from a Russia they had bled dry under the Czar. Who had seen all that and more. Who had survived imprisonment and a massacre. Who had fought across ten thousand versts for the Revolution.

And who is now going to die here, in this backwater town. Die, forgotten by his own people, despised by the people here.

So this is the fate of a revolutionary?

Shaking his head, Kovalik rises and goes to the window again, where he checks on the rocks. They haven't moved one inch. And the trees and the pots and the bronze *Fu* dogs are still there. Nothing has changed. Yet a sense of change stirs in him. He feels something actually has changed.

Where are the guards?

At least two always stand or squat in the shaded gallery. If he leaves the guesthouse, they follow like faithful dogs; at the first corner two or more join in.

But now they aren't lounging in the portico. Kovalik cranes his neck for a better look. No one against the wall or sitting on the gallery bench, arms draped over the balustrade. Going to the door, he looks again, steps into the courtyard and, shading his eyes, slowly examines every nook and cranny of it.

No one. It is empty. His heart leaps.

'Li, come here.'

Joining him at the doorway, Li squints into the sunlight.

'What do you see?' Kovalik asks.

'The courtyard.'

'Yes, but what else?'

'Nothing.'

'That's it. Nothing. Where are the guards, the watchdogs?' Kovalik grins. The courtyard has changed marvelously; time has loosened within it, flows again. 'The General called off the watchdogs.'

Striding briskly into the courtyard, Li turns in a slow circle at midpoint. He inspects the end of each gallery leading from the court; and then he stands in a vase-shaped gateway through which they pass to other sections of the Residence. Coming back to Kovalik, he says in a flat voice, 'They're gone.'

'Let's have a drink on it!' Kovalik is ecstatic. Inside the room he pours two *mao tais*. 'Our talk this morning had its effect.'

'No drink for me, please.'

Sitting on the bed, Kovalik swallows the searing liquor and grimaces happily. 'He took off the watchdogs. Next he'll give us our study group. You'll see! It won't be much, but we'll have work.' He is looking at the window ablaze with light. The study group won't be much, but at least they'll be part of something again, part of something greater than Tang, Borodin, Stalin: the community of men, communism, the world socialist order. At this moment he recaptures the intense enthusiasm of the early days when people marched together, holding flowers along with their guns, sharing bread, smiling, making of improbable speeches a reality keen enough to sustain them in memory later on, fighting and dying for a repeat of such moments. He has been penned up so long that the possibility of walking free in this Chinese town

190

extends itself to other possibilities – including the realization of his mission here.

'We got somewhere this morning, my friend,' he declares, turning to Li.

The goateed Chinese is frowning, his hands balled in his lap.

'What's wrong? He listened to us. We got somewhere.'

'We got nowhere.'

'But we did,' Kovalik insists, almost angrily. 'Otherwise he wouldn't have taken off the guards.'

'He took them off, but for what reason?'

'Good will.' Kovalik struggles for a more viable explanation.

'It could have been good will if we'd offered something in return. But we offered nothing.'

Reaching down, Kovalik picks up the wood carving and stares at it. One haunch is good, the belly is good; it will be a good carving, and he doesn't want to think of anything else.

'He took the guards off,' Li declares slowly, 'because he no longer needs them. We can't do harm. He can't learn anything from us. Chinese are practical, my friend. Why assign good men to us when he can use them better elsewhere?'

After a long silence Kovalik murmurs, 'I see.' Lying down on the bed, he turns toward the wall and closes his eyes. He knew the truth, of course, before Li put it into words. He has known from the beginning that this mission was hopeless – as hopeless as the whole Russian presence in China. Even so, he'd a good Bolshevik, trained to take orders. Borodin sent him here, and here he will stay until Borodin orders him home or until he rots under the foot of this Chinese general.

Kovalik hears the door open and close. So his friend Li has gone out. So the rocks in the garden don't move, and the trees and pots and bronze dogs remain where they are. Nothing breathes in the courtyard; nothing has changed. Boredom's going to be the worst of it. Maybe he'll concentrate on it to pass the time: the idea of perpetual boredom, extending to the end of his life, a life spent here in this forsaken Chinese town. But he's a good Bolshevik; he'll do as he's told.

Kovalik hears the door open and close. Without turning from the wall, he says, 'How long have you been gone?'

'Perhaps an hour.'

'That long?' A man learns how to deal with lost time, he thinks. I am learning. An hour? It went like a few minutes.

'Get up, my friend. We have things to do,' Li says.

Kovalik turns and looks at the smiling Chinese. Then he looks at the ceiling. When Li says, 'Look at me,' Kovalik looks.

'Get up. It's time we had some pleasure. Come with me.'

Kovalik looks away from him, stares again at the ceiling.

'At least we can move around freely now. Let's enjoy ourselves.'

'I believed in the Revolution. I fought for it,' Kovalik says. 'Now I'm going to die here for nothing.'

'Come, my friend. Get up.' Li sits on the edge of the bed. 'Come on. I just talked to someone. We're going out and find pleasure. We're going to bite clouds.'

The phrase intrigues Kovalik. 'What was that?'

'Come on, get up. You'll see.'

Minutes later, having traversed the maze of courtyards and walked under the main arch, they are heading down the broad dusty streets of Qufu. The Drum Tower has already been left behind. Kovalik glances frequently over his shoulder. Coolies, trudging under the weight of baskets strapped to their backs, give him curious stares, but no one is following. The General has definitely called off the guards.

'We turn here, I think.' Li veers into a street so narrow that his big companion could touch both sides of it with outstretched arms.

'Can you tell me now where we're going?'

'I told you.'

Kovalik returns the bold gaze of curious shopkeepers who gather at the dark entrances of their tiny stores, hands hidden in their long sleeves; they line up to see the *waiguo-ren* pass by.

'You said we're going to bite clouds.' Kovalik glances down at Li, who doesn't come to his shoulder. 'Is there pleasure in that?'

'There's definite pleasure in biting clouds.'

Puzzled, Kovalik says, 'Women?'

Without replying, Li stops to check the directions he'd been given. Finally, at the end of the crowded lane, they come to a weathered door leading into a small courtyard. Chickens puff by; an old sow, tied up, snoozes in the mud next to a dilapidated two-story house.

When Li reaches out to knock on the door, Kovalik grips his

arm. 'Wait,' he says. 'Before we go in there and do whatever this is, this biting clouds, I want to say something. I want to apologize. What I said back there about fighting for the Revolution was selfish. I wasn't thinking about this assignment from your point of view. After all, this is your country. You must be suffering more than I can know.'

'My country's poor, it has no plan. I suffer for it. But you suffer because you're far from home.' Li shrugs as if none of it matters. 'Today we bite clouds.' He knocks hard. Slowly the door opens a crack, and a withered tawny face appears in the gap.

'We've come for *Ta-yen*,' Li says.

Watery eyes appraise the tall foreigner, shift to Li, and then the door swings wide. A little woman bows to them; she has a cloth tied around her head like the sweat rags worn by dock coolies.

'There, go there.' She points to a narrow staircase, dimly visible beyond her.

Li goes up with Kovalik following. By the time Kovalik reaches the second-floor landing, he detects a sweet odor, like burned cinnamon. Turning sharply, Li enters a small room lit by a spirit lamp. Kovalik can see, as he too enters, a few men lying on wall benches; half asleep, they blink at him.

Seated near the lamp, a tiny old fellow beckons for the newcomers to sit beside him on the floor. Exchanging words with Li, he glances sullenly at the Russian.

'That smell,' Kovalik says.

'Yes, it's opium. We call it *Ta-yen*, the Big Smoke,' Li explains and then continues talking to the old proprietor. Finally, Li smiles. 'We're in luck. He has a supply of *Ta-yen* from Yunnan Province. That's the best in China.'

Kovalik watches the man open a small porcelain box and with a chopstick lift out a thumbnail-sized gob of dark substance. He slides the stuff – thickly mobile, like ointment or glue – into the tiny bowl of a long-stemmed pipe and hands it to Li.

The young Chinese gazes thoughtfully at the pipe, as if at the face of a lovely but puzzling woman. Holding the bowl over the flame of the spirit lamp, he waits until the opium bubbles and starts to melt; then, puffing swiftly, he finishes the pipe in two deep drags.

Kovalik studies his friend, who sets the pipe down. Li doesn't seem to have changed. 'Is that all?' the Russian asks.

'That's all.' Li smiles. 'We'll bite more than one cloud today.'

Kovalik watches the owner prepare another pipe and offer it to him. When the pipe is in his hands, the Russian stares at the bead of opium in the bowl. 'It looks like soft cow shit.'

Li chuckles softly. 'Go on. Bite clouds.'

For a moment Kovalik hesitates, unsure if he wants to go on with it. He never drank heavily, not even in the harsh Russian winter, and events throughout his life have demanded a discipline that has kept him ascetic. Yet why not a little pleasure? Otherwise he has a long, boring afternoon to live through, going to the window to see if the rocks have moved.

Copying Li's procedure, he heats the *Ta-yen* and puffs rapidly, pulling as much smoke into his lungs as possible, merely three times before the substance in the bowl is consumed. He feels nothing but the effort of sucking in and the sensation of raw smoke going down his throat; that's all. Finished, he gives the pipe back to the proprietor with a shrug.

'Next-time,' Li tells him softly, 'draw deeper.'

Kovalik watches his friend take another pipe, this time from a supine position, resting his neck on a small wooden pillow next to the spirit lamp. 'Is it better lying down?'

Li grins contentedly. 'Do as you please.'

Kovalik glances around the smoky room; the other half-dozen clients, stretched out on benches, their eyes half shut, are as motionless as men sleeping. They seem far away in the large room. Is it a large room? Kovalik sits erect, fighting the narcotic. It is a small room. They are not far away, but close. Then he watches Li suck in the second pipeful.

When the proprietor fixes another pipe for him, Kovalik mutters in Russian, 'Well, why not.' He takes the pipe and stares at the dark wood of the bowl. The constant smoke has given it a rich color; he'd like to carve a piece of wood this beautiful. Sensing the austere old man is watching him, Kovalik gets at the task of melting the opium. When he inhales this time, he feels the smoke invading his body, getting into the tissues. He tries to draw deeply; if he doesn't get all the smoke, he can have another pipe. And even another. Time expands in the small room, opening like a door upon infinite possibilities. He thinks of the courtyard back at the Residence. If he thinks hard enough, perhaps the rocks will move slightly out of phase, destroying the mirror image they have made all these days, these maddening days, when he looked at them from the grillwork window. Infinite possibilities. Infinite.

He wants to lie down. Seeming to divine his wish, the owner slides one of the wooden pillows toward him across the bare floor. Oh, he feels the *Ta-yen*, he really does. He feels it wonderfully as he arranges himself lengthwise and places the wooden block under his neck. The smoke has curled through his body and brought the life of him leadward, depositing total sensation between his eyes in a small throbbing ball. He hears a voice, soft and remote.

'Is it good?'

Kovalik is staring at the bead of light in the spirit lamp; the wavering gold is a fragile thing that might burst apart, explode; the flame holds together tenuously; he is fascinated by the way so many parts of it keep entwining.

'Is it good?'

The voice is speaking to him. He realizes then that the voice belongs to Li.

'Yes, very good,' he murmurs, watching the light. His mind is going somewhere, and for an instant he resists its going, then lets it go. It moves toward the light and through it into a sea of images drifting, drifting. He fixes suddenly with a most satisfying clarity on a bead of water gleaming in the sun. A lake? It's a lake. There were lakes north of Wuhan. He had gone rowing on one of them with someone – it doesn't matter with whom – but the lake matters, all right, and the oar. He dipped the oar – was it then or now? – into a sheet of bluest water, shattering it like a mirror. It broke into shards of brilliant crystal. Dipped the oar again. A globule of water clung to the wooden blade, tremulous as an insect wing, then elongated into a cone, an erotic shape, pulled free of the oar and dropped with a heavy thud into the lake. He saw the oar dip again, come up with clinging drops of thick water.

It didn't happen in Wuhan. It is happening now.

'Do you feel better?'

Maybe the flame has pulled apart and come together again; the threads of it entwine and wiggle in lovely golden spirals, twirls. Just like something else. What else? Something, anything else.

'You are feeling better, aren't you.'

Glancing beyond the lamp, he sees Li taking another pipe from the shop owner.

'Better,' he murmurs, smiling. Everything is better now. He wants to see golden streams of light; and the thought itself is enough for him to see them, or think he sees them. Is he seeing the thought? Never mind, there's all the time in the world to consider both possibilities. New smoke balloons up in the room: it must be from Li's pipe. Good old Li, wonderful Li.

'So now you are biting clouds,' Li says lazily.

Kovalik reaches out for the new pipe offered by the grim-faced proprietor. Biting clouds. Exactly what it is.

9

She knows the facts: Built on mudflats between two rivers, fifth port of the world, largest manufacturing center in Asia, Shanghai is the prey of a dozen foreign powers, the victim of gangs, a city where every morning squads from the *Dong Jen Fu An Tong*, a benevolent society, collect the hundred or more corpses left in Hongkew alleyways or under piers on the Whangpoo. But none of these facts tell of her Shanghai.

Vera Rogacheva leaves a hairdressing salon on the Avenue of Two Republics at the edge of the Chinese or Native City. She comes out of a world redolent of perfume and powder puffs into a world of harsh yells and pungent odors. She has had her dark hair bobbed in the latest fashion, hoping Erich will like it, and under an electric fan has endured the idle chatter of rich matrons and arrogant mistresses, who listen to the shop's radio playing Rio Rita songs. Outside, within five steps of the entrance, stand a dozen pullers, their rickshaw handles thrust into the air, giving the shape of these vehicles the sad look of sinking boats. Seeing her emerge, the men rush forward to bang the handles down at her feet. Quickly she draws back, having once broken a toe because of a puller's eagerness to get her business. For a few moments she haggles over the price of a ride to the International Settlement, knowing full well that when she arrives there, the puller will claim a higher fare. That's the Shanghai she knows.

Getting into the rickshaw, she notices a column of mounted policemen maneuvering through the crowd. A little man in a Panama hat, possibly a Filipino, halts on his way and stares at her boldly; then, touching the Panama's brim, he bows low, elegantly enough for Vera to give him a quick smile. Why not? It costs nothing. A few streets farther, while her puller strains to weave through a pack of rickshaws and wheelbarrows and sweating coolies, from the upper window of a ramshackle shop comes a woman's scream, piercing and horrible. Few heads turn in that direction, but Vera searches the open shutters for its source. In the old days she herself might have been in that house, among the *piao-tzu*, vulnerable to any whims of her drunken customer. Has a girl up there been slashed? There's a sort of man who likes carving the female breast; she has known girls with such scars, crude designs harbored in fantasy suddenly become real.

Vera is heading northeast through the French Concession, which has little river frontage, less than a mile. The street signs here are in French. She glares hostilely at the new Cercle Sportif Français on Rue Cardinal Mercier. Small, dark Annamese policemen eye her impassively, their hands resting upon their brown belts, the right hand always near the holster. They have a reputation for violence not always related to events. The court protects them if they shoot someone innocent; there is less crime in French-town than elsewhere in the city.

Her rickshaw comes upon the Quai de France, then moves along the boulevard of the Bund, to the right of which lies the harbor; it is choked with vessels of every description, from cabbage sampans to great ocean liners. Shading her eyes from the glare, Vera absorbs the look of the Whangpoo: brown trapezoid sails of junks; the shiny metal funnels of huge steamers; the low-slung godowns across the river at Pootung. It is a dazzling, vertiginous sight. On the other side of the boulevard stand the massive Edwardian buildings of the Great Powers: the Asian Petroleum Building on the corner of Avenue Edward VII; the Shanghai Club, a stodgy pile of stone housing the longest bar in the world, where the taipan British discuss tobacco and silk over a peg of gin; the Nisshin Kisen Kaisha Bank of Japan; the British P & O Banking Corporation; and the Hong Kong & Shanghai Banking Corporation with its colossal white dome and two ponderous bronze lions flanking the entrance, their paws shiny from Chinese stroking them for good luck. Vera has never come upon the Bund without a deep sense of excitement; there is nothing like it in the world – the boisterous, swaggering, convulsive river fronted by stolid façades of power. She glances now at the riverside park with its leafy sycamores and shady benches. Chinese are allowed in the park these days; they pay a slight fee and that keeps the rabble out. Elderly men are playing Tai Chi Chuan in the garden, and it reminds her of the Chinese general she met a month ago. Lately she is often reminded of him – by events or people incongruous to the memory. Here, however, the men playing Tai Chi bring logically to mind that early morning when, at the window, she watched him move about the courtyard like an apparition, like one of those ancient sages in Sung painting.

Vera shrugs off the memory as her rickshaw turns past the old Palace Hotel onto Nanking Road. She has a final glimpse of the Bund's last buildings before Soochow Creek leads into the Japanese section: the old business house of Jardine and Matheson's; the Canadian Pacific Steamship Line; the Banque de l'Indochine; and the palace-sized British Consulate. She feels young today, pretty and vivacious as the rickshaw moves through a stream of traffic toward department stores and their French perfumes, German cameras, English leather goods, Chinese silks. Behind her, coming from the waterfront, is the sound of coolie stevedores chanting '*Hai-yo, hai-yo, hai-yo,*' which helps regulate their breathing during a hot afternoon of work.

Another rickshaw comes alongside. It is a private vehicle, well polished, with pneumatic instead of iron tires. The puller wears an exquisite emerald-green Cantonese silk jacket. Years ago, when she first arrived in Shanghai, Vera had naïvely assumed that such lovely jackets worn by pullers were an emblem of their success. This type of silk, however – she was later to learn – feels gentler on the skin after it has been soaked in human sweat, then washed. Because the owners of such rickshaws make it their business never to perspire, they lend their new jackets to the pullers for conditioning. Now in the rickshaw beside Vera's sits an elderly Chinese wearing glasses and a tight-fitting black mandarin cap. He turns to look directly at her. In the riotous manswarm, with tram whistles shrilling and pullers yelling and horns honking, Vera abruptly feels a single presence – that of the rich old Chinese in the next rickshaw. What is he thinking behind his yellowish mask of composed features, narrow eyes, thin mouth? Does he want her? Can he be thinkinf of a foreign woman instead of a Chinese beauty, one of his own, with a stalklike neck holding a porcelain face? The moment passes; Vera's attention is directed to a column of men marching down the tram tracks: Americans. An army or marine detachment; she doesn't know the difference. But she does know that Shanghai, in recent months, has exchanged its own warlords and British colonial troops for the Nationalists of Chiang Kai-shek and his allies among the other Great Powers, including the Americans.

The tall, pink-cheeked Americans are singing lustily as they march along; coolies scatter in front of them like chickens, dexterously swinging away from the ranked soldiers, somehow managing to ease throught the crowd with their shoulder poles weighed by thick casks and burlap-wound boxes.

A few soldiers wave at her, whistle. One boy, winking, obscenely shoves a finger in and out of the trigger guard of his rifle. She returns this wink with a stare of such contempt that he looks away, sings louder than before.

This too is her Shanghai.

Near the Wing On Department Store she notices a Wanted poster with a picture of Mikhail Borodin. It is the third such poster she has seen today, and the sight gratifies her. Vera cares nothing for Chinese politics, the convolutions, outrages, and surprises. But one recent development has delighted her: The Nationalists have broken with the Russian Bolsheviks and, it is rumored, will soon throw them out of the country. It is the sole politics that has any interest for her, but when she tries to discuss the subject with Erich, he seems indifferent. Erich. Where is he now, this minute? In his small office on Iron Street, importing electric fans to cover up the gunrunning? Or somewhere in Chapei with a Chinese girl? Or at the Race Course with a Russian younger than herself or with a new arrival from the Philippines or an almond-eyed whore from Burma discovered in a dance hall?

Sincere Emporium goes by, and the Da Kiang Book Store. A turbaned, bearded Sikh directs traffic from a steel tower. He waves on a horde of rickshaws, Vera's among them, all jiggling past the Tiene Film Company and gold-lettered clothing shops. At her command the rickshaw turns into an unmarked side street. Immediately she is plunged into deepest Asia. A Chinese band is blaring, heralding a funeral procession in one of the twisting lanes. Noisy workshops, open to the street, display brassware, silver vases, and carved ivory pieces for mahjong. She smells fish frying in portable street kitchens. She hears the raucous clang of gongs from a radio set, the click of abacus counters, the staccato cry of a vendor selling crickets in tiny bamboo cages. She has a whiff of incense from a religious store where paper money is sold for gifts for the honored dead. She looks with interest at a row of drugstores, featuring roots shaped like fetuses, dried frogs and fish bladders, jars of ox penises and duck eyes. Old women, huddling against the wall, eat rice from a communal bowl and scratch their bare feet beneath ankle-tied trousers. The broad back of the rickshaw puller gleams from sweat as he weaves down the narrow lane, his heel-and-toe gait imparting to the carriage a rapid rolling motion, not unlike a boat's in a choppy swell. And this too is her Shanghai.

Vera shouts at him to stop when they approach a shop somewhat larger than the others. Two men lounge outside, arms crossed, watching the passing throng. They are watchmen; both carry knives and pistols under the blue cotton jackets. Vera, getting out of the rickshaw, exchanges a few sharp words with the puller, who withdraws his demand for more money when the two watchmen glare. Paying him, Vera enters the windowless shop through double doors. But it's not a shop, only the façade of one, leading back to a courtyard with rosebushes, artfully placed rocks, and a single willow tree. At another door she knocks and waits, beating an impatient tattoo with her forefinger on the bag she carries. It takes a long time before the door swings open a tentative inch, then all the way.

Mister Ho, the store owner, extends his arm in a gesture of welcome that has something about it of indifference or contempt; Vera can't be sure which. He amuses her. The old man doesn't know how to judge her worth or station. In the early days, when Erich was uncommonly generous, Vera bought a crackle-glaze bowl (copy of a Northern Sung masterwork and valuable in its own right) and later a first-rate Ching handscroll from this old merchant. Recently, although continuing to visit the store, Vera has bought nothing. She has spent frugally, because Erich claims to have financial troubles. Or flagging ardor may account for his reluctance to encourage extravagance in her as he used to do. Of course, Mister Ho, who must discard concubines as easily as frayed gowns, would have little comprehension of a European male's tendency to send out economic signals as a prelude to discarding a woman. Vera feels the old eyes on her, appraising her ability to buy. Surely he must be wondering what sort of man keeps her. Has the foreign woman recently changed men? Does that explain her failure to buy? Even as he offers her a chair in the cluttered shop, Vera knows he's busy at his analysis. A boy brings tea. Lifting her cup, Vera smiles at Mister Ho. The old scoundrel must be weighing the chance of selling her something against the urgency of other work in his back rooms.

Apparently he makes the choice in her favor. 'I have some interesting new things,' he tells her, then adds with a mirthless laugh, covering his mouth with a mandarin sleeve, 'Of course, not really *new*.'

Lifting one hand, he extends a finger. From behind a counter rushes a young man who wears a blue grown, like his employer. Vera has watched him on other occasions give her a thoughtful look – he's not judging her ability to buy. If he owned the shop, she might bring off some wonderful purchases at a bargain price merely by flirting with him; or so it pleases her to imagine.

'Bring the jade buffalo,' Mister Ho tells the young man sharply. Turning to Vera he says in a softer tone, 'This is a superb piece. Thirteenth century. I can definitely authenticate it.'

The young man returns with a piece of jade small enough to fit in his palm. Vera always marvels at the quick efficiency of Chinese in their shops – and their lack of it outside. The assistant gives the piece to Mister Ho, who in turn, with extravagant care, hands it to Vera.

What is submitted for her inspection, Vera sees instantly, is a lovely bit of work: a jade buffalo seated with tail close to its round haunch, legs neatly folded under its great belly. The sculpture wastes nothing of the stone's natural shape and grain.

'Very fine,' purrs Mister Ho, leaning forward as if to look at it for the first time. 'Most steel points won't scratch jade. It's so difficult to carve.' He points a long, trembling finger at the gray-green figure Vera gently holds. 'This jade comes from the river beds of Sinkiang. Notice the special sheen. Bring that lamp closer,' he orders the young man, who, leaping forward, grabs an old lamp from the counter and thrusts it at the piece. Mister Ho speaks in the low, measured cadences of a scholar, telling Vera what she already knows. 'In early times, Madam, a nobleman's rank was measured in jade. To signify a new position at court, he was given a jade token by the emperor and by it his new situation was known.' Vera smiles politely, moving the piece in her fingers to experience its smooth surface. She might well add to his explanation that the *pi* disc had been the badge of office for viscounts and barons; the *kuei* for dukes and marquises. But pedantry annoys her.

'Surely it's clear, Madam, why jade is called the Stone of Heaven.'

'Yes, it's clear.' She is thinking the old merchant now expects her to ask the price.

'Do you like the piece?'

'Yes, it's rather good.'

'Thirteenth century.'

'Yes,' she says noncommittally.

After studying her a few moments, Mister Ho waves his hand slightly. He has made a new decision: The foreign woman will not buy. His voice struggles not to show irritation when he tells her that pressing business requires his attention; his assistant will be most honored to help her in any way. 'If you will kindly permit your humble servant –'

Vera watches him move down the narrow aisle and vanish behind a curtain. She's glad to be rid of the old fellow, although he's too cautious to treat her rudely. Perhaps he thinks she might become a customer later on, when she's found someone more generous to keep her. Vera feels her spirits lift: It means Mister Ho considers her still attractive enough to do well. Faded, she'd receive worse treatment from him.

Rising and placing the jade on the counter, Vera strolls down the aisles, the watchful assistant a few discreet steps behind her. She looks at some Ching porcelain; her attention is held for minutes by a copy of a Shang wine vessel of the *kuang* style, combining the features of three different animals in a single mythological beast. Vera enjoys the atmosphere of such a tiny, crowded, dimly lit shop, its cosy ambience enhanced by the presence of old art. Behind the curtain and the closed doors of inner rooms to which Mister Ho escaped is without a doubt a world of incomparable beauty: Ming landscapes, Yuan flower paintings, tea tables, the scent of incense drifting across the rich calligraphy of scrolls.

She catches the assistant staring hard at her. Vera's hand goes to the top button of her blouse, fingering it to hide, for a moment, the cleft between her breasts. Abruptly she wants to leave. There are times when the hungry look of a man repels her; something in the taut expression, the fixed eyes, the slightly parted mouth reminds her of the Czech legionnaires in the cold train station, bending her over the table, awaiting their turns with the solemn watchfulness of dogs.

Brushing past the young man – he draws quickly back with scrupulous regard for her person – Vera returns to the counter for a last inspection of the jade buffalo. It is an exceptional piece of carving, although the claim of its being from the thirteenth century is undoubtedly false. She knows how difficult it is to date Chinese art accurately, and therefore how easy it is to misrepresent its age. Even so, nothing in this shop is of poor quality; and the jade buffalo is immensely appealing. But Vera doesn't ask the price. She wants the piece – desperately – which is why she must not ask. Next time, perhaps, she'll make a show of trying to remember a piece of jade she has seen and, after a cursory look at it, ask for the price without enthusiasm. On a third or fourth visit the haggling might begin. Within weeks, maybe months, the piece will be hers at half the asking price, unless by chance someone takes it beforehand. She's lost more than one good piece that way. The risk goes with collecting antiques in Shanghai. Thus far she's lucky that Mister Ho treats her as an amateur, not as someone who has acquired the skills of a professional collector – for so she views herself. His confusion about her ability to pay, mixed with a native scorn of foreigners, may work to her advantage.

'Very lovely,' the young assistant remarks, bending close as Vera continues to turn the jade in her hand.

Their eyes meet; his look away. There are premature bags under them, suggesting he may suffer from insomnia. Lying there, thrashing on his bed, thinking of women. When Vera regards him steadily, his hands disappear into the long sleeves of his gown.

Leaving the monastic calm of the shop, freeing herself of its carved and painted ancient presences, Vera wonders about the young assistant. After work does he find a plump girl fresh from the country in the hot back alleys of Chapai? She can imagine him forcing a girl against the wall and for a few dragon coppers taking her roughly in recompense for his own servitude. Or does he merely lie tumescent in his bed, dreaming of such adventure? She's done well to stay clear of Chinese men. At times there's a pent-up fierceness, a withdrawn power about them that frightens her.

Vera hails a rickshaw and heads out of the Settlement, unsure of her destination. She tells the puller to go forward, that's all. Something has upset her. Perhaps it's the look of that young man, his face tense from sexual need. Swaying along, abruptly she thinks of the painting. Like the nightmare this painting has the ability to return at will, haunting her. Vera first saw it a year ago in a local museum. Called *The White Hawk*, it was done by an Italian in the eighteenth century. Coming to China as a Jesuit missionary, he remained at the Manchu court and took the 'painting' name Lang Shih-ning. Long after other work has faded from her memory, this one stays with uncommon vividness. In the painting a huge white hawk dominates the foreground. In the indeterminate distance a gentle waterfall splashes down an outcropping of rock. An amber monochrome, pervading the background, suggests tranquillity and silence. Perched on a tree trunk, which is tilted at a precarious angle, the great hawk thrusts its predator beak forward. It is muscular, rigid, alert. Its hard eyes are gazing at something beyond the viewer's vision. She has always asked herself what the painting means.

Strange, but less than an hour ago she heard a woman screaming from the second floor of a building. She had forgotten it. Perhaps something seen by the Italian churchman here in China encouraged him to paint the moment of beauty that precedes violence. The waterfall, the calm brown distance, the perched hawk. And then the dark flapping of wings across the world, a final moment, the swooping down. How could she have forgotten the screaming woman? She ought to have found a policeman and taken him there. But he wouldn't have gone. He'd have smiled at her indulgently and gone about his business of collecting protection money from the neighborhood. This too is her Shanghai.

On impulse Vera tells the pullar to head for the Native City. She knows now where she's going, where she often goes, especially in a mood of restlessness bordering on dread. Now that her direction is set, Vera is impatient to get there, but she won't yell at the puller to go faster. 'My dear lady, almost a decade in China and you still think of rickshaw coolies as human?' Someone made that remark at a consulate lawn party. It was meant to be a joking appraisal of her naïveté (all women were naïve to the man who said it), but it was also a commentary on the plight of rickshaw coolies. She has seen taipans screaming like madmen at pullers for more speed, although the Shanghai sun was too hot for them to let their race horses leave the stable. At that same party an Italian – she recalls he spoke wonderful Russian – maintained that we mustn't make fun of Shanghai coolies; if properly armed, they could overrun Europe.

Opening her purse, Vera takes out a linen handkerchief and mops her brow. It is that hot or is she just nervous – is the nightmare approaching the edge of her mind? She looks to both sides of the rickshaw at the swarming people, at the incredible motion and color they lend to the street. Perhaps the Italian wasn't joking at all, but meant what he said: Harness these people to a purpose and they might conquer the world. It is almost noon before Vera reaches her destination in a long bustling street deep within the Chinese City.

204

Halting across from a five-story building, Vera sits in the rickshaw and stares at it. A faded sign hangs above the entrance: HOTEL – in English. It's the only foreign word along the entire street. The building itself looks strange among the low-lying shops of wood and tin. Made of brick, fitted with ornate but chipped cornices over each window, the hotel has a decrepit European look, as if shoved together with discarded bits and pieces from hotels a century ago. Vera knows its dark interior, its sweltering little lobby, the narrow staircase, without needing to go inside. She can smell in memory the upstairs corridors doused with disinfectant, and the odor of onions drifting from open doorways where the foreigners, most of them Russian refugees, cooked their meals over small braziers. She had come to this hotel in late 1919 at the age of nineteen with a Russian sailor. His name was Leonid Safarov, and he'd been good to her. In Vladivostok, where she'd arrived from Harbin by train, Vera had met him. She was begging on the street, nearly starved and half frozen, having been abandoned by an old merchant who didn't want to pay her steamer fare to Shanghai. Leonid Safarov had fed her, bought her a warm coat. He had been a poor lover: quick, efficient, getting it over with in the same brisk manner he ate a meal. They went by ship to Shanghai and stayed in this hotel for a few weeks. Leonid was a good man whom she remembers with gratitude, yet he never told her about leaving until the day he left. Looking up from the rickshaw, Vera stares at the third-floor window, right. It was in there, while he lay on the bed, that Leonid told her.

'Dear girl, I'm leaving today. I've got a ship.'

'What am I to do?.

He scratched his head. 'Well, there's plenty to do in Shanghai.'

'But I don't know what to do. I've got no money, I don't know where to go.'

'As for money –' He put some taels on the bed, then got up. 'Sweetheart,' he said with a patient smile, 'you worry too much. A girl like you won't starve in a city like this. Today you ask Maxim. He knows everything about Shanghai.'

Maxim did. He's probably in there now, Vera thinks – sitting behind the front desk, a colored fan in his pudgy hand, his shirt unbuttoned across his vast belly, a little spit curl dark with sweat on his forehead, his face bloated and pink. Maxim told her what she already knew: A Russian aristocrat, nineteen and without skills, had to earn money with her body, just as she had made her way across Siberian tundra by the same method. Maxim gave her the name and address of a house.

She would go there now too, for a look at her past, only it burned down six months ago in a flash fire that destroyed a whole block of tinderbox houses. Madam Lotus burned with it. She won't forget Madam Lotus. The name itself is enough to bring a smile to Vera's lips, even as she sits in a rickshaw, parked across the street from the HOTEL in English.

It's hard to say what Madam Lotus's nationality was. She spoke a number of languages – had probably forgotten others. She was small, dumpy, heavily rouged, with a tawny skin that suggested she might have had some Malay blood. But her hair was red – dyed to keep out the gray. She might have been sixty. She liked jewelry; you could hear her coming long before she arrived: the chains and beads clanking like an army in full gear.

Studying Vera for the first time, Madam Lotus walked around her and then, coming close, ran her hands slowly across the nineteen-year-old's breasts.

Startled, Vera stood with hands rigid against her sides.

'Stop trembling. I'm not interested in women myself. What were you, a countess? Well, you're built good. Do you read Gogol?'

'Yes.'

'I read him too, in French though. I think he's funny. Are you good in bed? Never mind. We'll find that out, won't we. I have a nice clientele here. Sometimes the young sailors get out of line, but we've got two boys who can handle anything. One's from your people. We call him Ivan. Ivan's a fine Russian name, isn't it. But Ivan doesn't help my Russian, because he hardly says a word. He's about ten feet high. And we've got this Filipino kid. We call him Jimmy. I don't know where he got that name – from the Americans, I suppose. Comes no higher than your shoulder, Missy, but he's a mean little sonofabitch with a knife. I've seen him use it.' Madam Lotus blew her breath out in remembered awe. 'We have this house and also the cabaret next door. What you do you meet your man there and bring him over here. Room at the end to the right on the second floor. That's your own room. None of our girls have to double up. You start tonight. You'll like the girls. I'll have Yu-ying show you around – she's my jewel. The girls are clean and we keep them clean. We have this French doctor who comes every week. Where else do you find that in Shanghai?'

And so Vera had entered the house of pleasure.

Looking at the HOTEL, she remembers the day she returned to it – long after working for Madam Lotus, long after the disappearance of poor Yu-ying, long after a stint in a cabaret. Taken from the cabaret by a Swede who kept her half a year, Vera had been passed from one man to another for varying intervals, until one day she told herself no more – no more of their whims and her constant fear of losing their protection. So she went back to see Maxim, bless his heart, a sweaty pink mountain behind the front desk. She told him she was tired of being a whore and a mistress; she wanted to make money on her own, enough to protect herself and to hell with men. Maxim sat under the pigeonholed mail rack – most of it empty – and mused awhile, popping sugar cakes into his mouth the way other people eat peanuts. Then Maxim told her there were some Russians upstairs who had a plan.

That's when she met Alexei Voitinksy, a tall, dyspeptic former cavalryman in the Imperial Guard. He told her all she had to do was guide them through the maze of streets; they'd do the work and everyone would get rich. Where is Alexei now? Still rotting in a crowded cell? The horror of that possibility makes her shudder. If she's grateful to Leonid Safarov for getting her out of Vladivostok, she's doubly grateful to Erich Luckner for getting her out of a Chinese jail.

'Take me to Wayside Park,' she tells the rickshaw coolie. She wants to feel good, she wants to feel secure. She wants to curl up somewhere with a comforting hand on her cheek. She needs caresses, soft music, curtains asway in a breeze, a cool drink nearby, a voice murmuring at her ear. Damn the young man in the antique shop with his sad little need for a woman, with his suppressed desire and fury. Sweat pours from her brow in the noisy chaos of a Shanghai afternoon. Getting free of the streets may help. Yet as the puller-weaves through traffic, Vera isn't sorry for having come to look at the HOTEL, where she first stayed in this city. It's a kind of home, a terrible rundown stinking hole, but a home. It anchors her in the wild currents of Shanghai.

Vera sits erect in the rickshaw, gripping the handkerchief. Frequently she stems the tide of sweat with it. The Jesuit from Italy, who took a Chinese name and painted a terrible bird, knew something about the world. The hawk poised to strike. Perhaps it's always there, poised to strike. At me, she thinks; at everyone. She can't stop sweating.

Sitting in a flagstoned garden bordered with neat squares of boxwood that give a sweet scent, Vera begins to feel calmer. It was good sense to get away from the Shanghai multitudes. This garden is open only to Europeans and amahs with their charges. Nearby some children, yelling their demands in English, are playing in sandpiles, on swings. Vera doesn't turn to watch them. Children depress her. They make her think of the abortions, one of which nearly killed her. They make her think of lost opportunities, of time pulling her toward oblivion. The little voices behind a ranked mass of sycamores seem to be calling out, 'Vera! There's yet a chance for your own! But who will be their father?' A dispiriting idea, one to turn away from. She fixes her attention on a nearby lily pond; it is filled with pink and creamy flowers, floating in waxlike fragility on the motionless water.

An old man, wearing a straw hat and a seersucker jacket, hobbles by with the aid of a cane. He has the splotched face of a drinker, an air of independence. What is he? Tall enough for an old Norwegian gentleman. Erich often deals with Norwegian ship captains who bring in munitions and anchor south of the city, near Yangtzepoo, scooting up the river after midnight to have the launches unload before patrols come along. Dangerous business at which the Norwegians excel. Is the old fellow an exgunrunning skipper?

Age transforms you out of your profession. Vera touches her cheek appraisingly. It still has the soft yielding texture that nameless men have found compelling, that others have sought to possess for sustained periods of time. But how long will such skin last? Five more years, that's all. *Perhaps* five before age dries it up, along with the possibilities of her life.

'Hello! Hello! Imagine meeting here!'

Vera, startled, looks around from the stone bench to see a pretty girl in peacock-green gauze lined with white silk – a Chinese tailor's concept of a European concept of a Chinese dress. The girl, honey-blond, quite young but already voluptuous in a Russian way, leads a Pekingese dog with a blood-red bow in its hair.

'Look at the nice lady, Nastasya,' exclaims the girl in a lisping voice reserved for dogs and children. 'Do you remember me?' she asks Vera with a smile.

Nodding politely, but unsure where they have met – the girl is familiar, however – Vera says, 'Won't you sit down?' Her frantic afternoon in the streets of Shanghai has given her a desire for company, for a frame of reference beyond her own obsessions.

With a gloved hand the girl brushes the stone bench, then cautiously sits on the edge of it. 'It was at the Race Course on Trophy Day.'

Now Vera remembers. Through someone influential on the Racing Board, Erich had managed to get Trophy Day seats near the Municipal Council Box. Vera had met this girl with her father, a police commissioner, like so many of the Czarist officers who reached China. Even the name comes to her: Sudilovskaia; and she says it, 'You are Miss Sudilovskaia.'

The pleased girl adds, 'Eugenia,' to promote a touch of intimacy; in her self-satisfaction, however, she fails to ask Vera's name. 'I often come here with Nastasya, *ma petite.*' The girl smiles down at the little dog. 'With Chinese in the parks now, it's hard to find any peace. My father says in another year there won't be a nice park left. What I can't stand is the spitting. Do you know what I mean?' The girl frowns. 'Everywhere you go, they are hacking and spitting terribly. My father says they have weak lungs. It's in them to have weak lungs. Have you had tea? Shall we have tea together? Oh, let's do!'

Vera finds the creature very pretty. Moreover, she's amused by the girl's eagerness to make of her an afternoon's companion. What would the innocent girl think if she knew she was chatting with a former whore in a Nantao brothel? Wonderful!

So Vera agrees to have tea with Eugenia Sudilovskaia, who chatters breathlessly as they leave the park together, with the little dog possessively close to the girl's heels. 'In your part of the city,' Eugenia goes on, 'are you affected by the water workers' strike? Father says we won't have a drop by Tuesday. I mean, our house won't. Ah, well, *etes vous allé á l'Odéon derniérement? Maintenant qu'ils laissent entrer les Chinois, mon pére dit qu'á peu prés la moitié des spectateurs sont Chinois. La nuit derniére j'ai vu Norma Talmadge dans quelque chose, j'ai oublié le nom. Ah, sans les movies Shanghai serait insupportable!*'

Vera nods pleasantly. 'I agree without movies Shanghai would be unbearable. Norma Talmadge starred in *Smiling Through.* In spite of the Chinese, I still find the Odéon enjoyable. I do not speak French.'

Eugenia, halting, gives her companion a perplexed smile. 'A Russian lady who doesn't speak French?' The girl laughs uncertainly. 'How do you manage in Frenchtown?'

'I use Chinese or Russian or a little English. I do not speak French.'

'You mean, you *will* not speak it. Because you certainly understood me.'

They have reached the park limits. Across the street is a small teahouse. In November of 1920, Vera explains patiently, the president of the French Senate no longer recognized the White government; that was because Baron Wrangel's army had just been defeated, and the Reds had the upper hand. 'The French chose the expedient way of dealing with a temporary Red victory.'

'Temporary?' the confused girl asks.

'Temporary. The Reds won't last, Eugenia.'

'No, of course not.'

'In November of 1920 the French ceased to be friends of the Russian people. I do not speak French.'

'Yes, yes, I see the point. Father would agree.' But her voice trails off doubtfully. 'So you actually speak Chinese. I find there simply isn't time to learn it. I haven't time to catch my breath. Graham, he's my English fiancé,' Eugenia says, her voice lifting with pride on the word 'English,' her face breaking into a dazzling girlish smile, 'he claims Shanghai is nothing more than a huge party that never ends.'

They cross the street and enter the dimly lit teahouse. Eugenia leads the way to a secluded table, where old Chinese gentlemen, seated at other tables, can't observe them. When they sit down, Engenia orders the waiter to draw the curtain. 'I won't have people staring at me,' the girl says in a low voice. 'Father says the Chinese are the most curious people in the world. Aren't they terribly, terribly curious, *ma petite*?' Reaching down, she pets the dog and touches the red bow on its head.

Vera watches enthralled as the girl removes her gloves from long, slim, white fingers. Beautiful hands. Often in 1919, when Reds stopped the trains, everyone had to get out in subzero weather and take off their gloves. People whose hands lacked calluses were shot. This girl would have been shot, this beautiful girl. In those days the Reds, mad with fury, would not even have raped her first – just stared at the lovely hands and shot her where she stood.

The girl is saying something about the latest dance craze, the Yanko, a Chinese folk dance sweeping Shanghai. Beautiful arms too. They will soon grow plump, then fat from inactivity and overeating, but right now they must be delicious to the touch. Vera envies the Englishman who has access to such flesh.

'Are you from Petrograd?' the girl asks suddenly. 'Father was a captain in the First Petrograd Guards.' She has thus established the family reputation. Doubtless her family fled Russia early, before the slaughter began, and arrived here financially intact. The lucky ones. They hadn't holed up in Harbin for months among Koreans and Japanese, begged on the corners and watched Russian youth, awaiting immigrant papers, become drug addicts along the main street of Kitaiska. They hadn't slept in parks, on jetties or tugboats or doorsteps upon their arrival in Shanghai, nor had they, like so many Whites, later crowded a dozen together in six square yards of living space, working sixteen hours a day as watchmen or houseboys or dishwashers, or hiring out as strike-breakers to keep from starving. Nor had they endured the peculiar fate of latecomers in ships from Vladivostok, who proudly flew the Czarist blue-and-white when entering port. Denied entry because of the Red Consulate – at the time Borodin was in favor – the poor devils had stayed at anchor for *years* far down the Whangpoo, dying of dysentery and boredom. Vera watches the beautiful girl sip her tea daintily.

Eugenia looks up with a sigh. 'Do you miss your tea the Russian way? From glasses? I used to sweeten my tea with a spoonful of jam,' the girl observes wistfully, her eyes wide at the recollection.

She's only a child, Vera thinks.

'Are you from Petrograd?' Eugenia asks again.

'I'd rather not talk about Russia.'

'Oh, of course. I understand,' the girl acknowledges with a clumsy note of sympathy in her voice. 'I was a child when we left. You see, I have few memories of Russia.'

How old does she think I am? Vera wonders gloomily. The specter of age intervenes between her and the little cakes set on the table. She pulls her hand back empty.

Eugenia talks happily while feeding cake to Nastasya, who now sits on her mistress's lap. The dog glowers at Vera, whom she probably takes for a rival; Vera, amused, glowers back now and then, and for her impertinence receives a low, tremulous growl.

'As I said, without movies Shanghai would be completely impossible. Have you seen Douglas Fairbanks in *The Thief of Baghdad*? Graham is jealous of him.' The girl giggles, showing an

211

even row of white teeth. 'I tell him I'm jealous of Mary Pickford for the same reason. Aren't the American movies the best? Don't you agree?' With hardly a pause, Eugenia says, 'What really makes Shanghai impossible is the water.'

'You mean the water workers' strike?'

'That too. Of course.' The girl waves her hand – those slim white fingers without calluses. 'But what I mean is boiling the water. Father becomes livid when the servants don't do it properly. We tell them it's for our health, but they only smile and bow and never do it. Father says he thinks sometimes they want us to get ill. Yesterday he kicked one of them out of the house bodily. With his boot. Father's such a big man and this boy was so small. Sent him flying like a ball.' Eugenia titters, petting the dog in her lap. 'That's the third servant this month we've lost because of boiled water. Do you like the greyhounds?'

'Yes.'

'Graham says the greyhounds won't last. I think the popularity is a good thing. So does father, he loves racing. Graham just loves cricket, and that's all. But then you can't blame him, he's British. He's very handsome.' Another dazzling smile that takes Vera's breath away. 'A foot taller than I am and so handsome.'

Is the girl really in love or is she flattered by the attention of a grown man or does she merely wish to become a British citizen? The girl's in love, Vera decides. Her judgment brings with it contempt for the pretty empty-headed Russian with her arrogant father who served in the First Petrograd Guards. The Rogachevas of Petrograd would not have allowed those military philistines in the house. The girl is definitely in love, Vera thinks sadly.

Eugenia is relating more dull anecdotes about Graham. Vera learns that he's a silk exporter who complains of Chinese filatures because in spite of using first-class Italian machines they can't keep hair out of the silk. Graham sounds like a bore to Vera; the possibility is a comfort.

'Have you seen the Fordor Sedan?' Eugenia continues, finishing her tea and wiping her full red lips with a napkin. With the same napkin she wipes Nastasya's runny nose. 'It has lounge seats upholstered in leather. Electric windshield wipers. Graham says it can travel a hundred kilometers an hour. Not on Chinese roads, of course. He knows cars.' Eugenia slips the gloves back on those long white slim hands. 'He drove a Talbot, but now he has an Austin. I tell him because of patriotism; no one can possibly like an Austin. It's our joke.'

Vera realizes she could fall in love with the girl's white skin and naïve brown eyes. Yet could any amount of sexual excitement compensate for spending a full day with Eugenia Sudilovskaia and the horrible dog with a runny nose? Vera has always wondered at the ability of men to sacrifice everything for the feel of a soft body. She wonders about it until she remembers Yu-ying, her dearest . . .

A few minutes later, outside the teahouse, they stand on the street corner to hail rickshaws. Nastasya, secure in the girl's arms, pants lazily and gives Vera a last hard look of disapproval.

'Oh,' the girl exclaims while climbing into her rickshaw, 'you never told me where you live!'

'Oh Bubbling Well Road.' Vera doesn't give the full address, assuring herself that this is the last time they will meet.

'Do you like it out there? I hear the mosquitoes are perfectly terrible.' Settling into the rickshaw carriage, Eugenia briefly shows a smooth expanse of white thigh – made for kisses, Vera thinks. 'I understand the new apartment houses in Jessfield Park are marvelous. We're thinking about them. Graham says Hung Jao District looks good too, but only if you want an estate. He has a friend –' The rickshaw puller has moved into a flatfooted jog, but the girl is still talking. 'Do you like the opera? We didn't discuss it! Tonight I'm seeing Mai Lan-fang. The female impersonator from Peking? At Wing On Gardens. They says he's *sensational*. Graham got tickets, though I don't know how he managed! Shall we meet there?' Glancing over her shoulder, defeated at last by the increasing distance between them, she waves at Vera and calls out with youthful zest, 'I loved our tea! Wonderful! I want you to meet Graham! You simply *must*!'

Vera stands there, waving back, suffused with good humor and affection for the pretty girl who forgot to ask her name.

That night she meets Luckner in a Nantao restaurant. Seeing his tall figure rise from a table, his groomed blond hair and craggy handsome face, Vera feels a twinge of pleasure, as if only recently she has become his mistress. In spite of her awareness that loyalty can be dangerous, even fatal, in Shanghai, she always finds it difficult to let go of a lover. Perhaps because it marks an aging – like finding a wrinkle at the edge of an eye.

Kissing her cheek, Luckner compliments her on the bobbed hair. He's sensitive to whatever makes her more attractive, Vera thinks – or less attractive. Does he really like the bobbed hair? She looks searchingly at the light-blue eyes and finds nothing there to judge by.

Luckner is sitting with a bull-necked Japanese, who leaps to his feet and bows enthusiastically during the introduction, then appraises her with calculating eyes, as if wondering how much she costs his host to keep. Vera doesn't mind a frank estimate of her worth; it's been done countless times. And Erich's business associates probably study her for a clue to his financial status and emotional stability. But the man's presence is unwelcome, for she has rather hoped to go alone with Erich tonight to, say, the Roof Garden Ballroom. The smiling Japanese will change things, of course; he looks ready for other entertainment. After so much whisky, he won't need Strauss waltzes; he'll want Ladow's or Delmonte's, where the pretty hostesses insist on real champagne before going to a hotel. Or he'll want rough sex. Looking at him, Vera can't tell. Perhaps it's too early for that sort of judgment. Erich is attentive to the squarely built man, which means he's either wealthy or has connections. From the look of him, connections. What has made him venture south of Soochow Creek? Few Japanese do for an evening out, but remain in Hongkew, their own district, for their entertainment. He has come along, as much as Erich, for benefit.

Having lived with a Japanese four months, Vera knows some of the language and tries it on Erich's guest – to the man's delight. Erich, watching them talk together, fairly beams. Vera wonders if she'd have been invited this evening had she not spoken some Japanese. Dear Erich, practical.

While they are eating cold Nanking salt-water duck – Erich declares this restaurant has the best Nanking duck in Shanghai – Vera listens with indifference to their talk of parimutuels and greyhounds. In her presence the men are studiously noncommittal, perhaps using her as a welcome excuse to be rid of business awhile. They both seem relaxed and appear to like each other. Of course they like each other – mutual benefit of some kind. Erich makes sure his guest is liberally supplied with Scotch from a quart bottle on the table. When the Japanese waves off a refill, Luckner pours anyway and exclaims, 'If a man is seen drunk in Shanghai, he's a tourist. If he carries his liquor well, he's a resident. You, Nakamura, are a resident!'

The bull-necked Japanese seems to enjoy the rough-hewn flattery; his head bobs like a bird drinking. In Vera's opinion, Erich is a rather shrewd judge of what people want; he has a sense of their desires – true to his own hedonistic spirit. On the other hand, she saw Erich fail with the Chinese general at Qufu. The man absolutely befuddled Erich, and in doing so hurt his pride in a way she has never seen before or since. For a moment her mind wanders back to the pines of the Kong cemetery, her magical stroll among them with the General.

'Vera? Vera, we're going to this place I heard of in Frenchtown. For a bit of gambling. It's a new place. Will you come along?'

Erich's invitation is actually a command; Vera recognizes it as such. Turning with a smile to Nakamura, she tells him in his own language the invitation to accompany them delights her. A slight nod of respect adds to the good impression. Seeing Nakamura smile, Luckner smiles too. Vera is certain now that he needs her help with the Japanese, who for some reason is important to him. So her eyes never leave Nakamura; and when he speaks his clumsy Chinese, Vera leans forward intently to catch every word. By the time they leave the restaurant Vera is satisfied that the man finds her appealing. She touches his coat sleeve when they stand outside, waiting for the chauffeured limousine (Erich has hired it for the evening). She is careful, however, not to give the Japanese any definite hope. They sit in the back seat. To maintain his interest in her, Vera allows her thigh to contact his; nothing more. Erich, by design, sits next to the driver. It's definitely by design, although he might deny it. He's counting on her having the good sense to rub up against Nakamura, yet with discretion. She and Erich make a good team, Vera thinks; pity to break it up.

A little drunk now, Nakamura tries out his German – probably learned in a Tokyo high school – on poor Erich, who attempts in vain to understand any of it. Vera can scarcely keep from laughing; to divert her attention from this pair, who are bent upon impressing each other, she gazes steadfastly from the car window at the passing lights of Shanghai.

The casino on Avenue Joffre is large, expensive, and new. Three iron gates at the entrance, guarded by two armed men, lead into a courtyard and a well-furnished Edwardian house. The featured games are roulette, dice, and *shih-men-tan*, which is played with marble stones – Vera doesn't understand it. Waiters in red jackets bear interminable trays of drinks and free cigarettes. There's a supper club attached and a garden outside with an Italian fountain. Luckner, typically, goes out of his way to meet the new manager, a potbellied Cantonese who speaks French with a thick accent. Vera answers him in Chinese. She listens patiently while Luckner tells the manager one of his favorite stories. Earlier in the century, it seems a Peking army commander once lost the entire monthly pay for his troops on one turn of the wheel. It changed the course of Chinese politics for a decade. The manager, although chuckling, does not seem amused. He escorts them to the gaming tables and leaves.

While Nakamura is betting on roulette, Luckner beckons Vera aside. 'I think he's getting bored.'

Vera watches the bull-necked man deliberate before placing a bet. Perhaps the whisky has slowed him down; but Erich is right: Nakamura looks bored. 'Why didn't you bring along a woman for him?' Vera knows that Erich has two or three pimps who supply him with girls for important people.

'He said he didn't want one.'

Again Vera looks at the Japanese. He's betting small amounts – a token observance of the game. Either he doesn't have the money for gambling or he prefers to spend it on something else. He's a short but powerful man, his movements quick and decisive, although lacking grace. She suspects at one time he did hard manual work. Nakamura is not the man to lose his money on something abstract like gambling. 'I think he'd like a woman now,' Vera observes. 'I think he'd like one any time. Maybe bringing me was the problem. You know Japanese decorum.' Asserting this makes her in part responsible for the dilemma; her presence has soured the Japanese on the evening. But she wants Erich to recognize his miscalculation of Nakamura. 'If he's important to you,' Vera says, 'I suggest you get him a woman now.'

Luckner touches his hair without mussing it. Only once has Vera ever seen him disarrange that blond hair: at Qufu, when the General left him with a rented Duesenberg and no sale.

'It's too late to make that sort of arrangement,' Luckner decides. 'I mean, I have to be sure of the girl. I'm not going out in the street and call one over. Not in Shanghai.'

'I know someone at the Red Dragon. I'll get him someone good, if you wish.'

216

Luckner, boyish in his relief, gives her hand a squeeze.

She watches him sail through the crowded casino toward Nakamura, who is idly thumbing chips in a gnarled hand.

They leave Frenchtown for a place in Chapai, driving by limousine down tiny streets much like those Vera traveled by rickshaw that afternoon. It is past midnight, but the noise and motion contain the energy of midday commerce. The car can't traverse the final lane, so the driver parks on a wider thoroughfare and waits while the trio stroll the last few yards, past a street juggler and some children begging. Nakamura has been silently expectant since learning of their destination. Perhaps, Vera decides, he has a dumpy wife in Hongkew, and even when he goes whoring, chances are he seeks out girls of his own race, in chauvinistic fashion. This will be a treat for him, and his tense anticipation is a good sign for his continuing relationship with Erich. If she can put the Japanese in Erich's debt tonight, a step has been made toward holding the team together. Erich and Vera: maybe not Eugenia and Graham with their cars and wealth and innocence and youth, but a team nevertheless.

The Red Dragon is a small but lively cabaret with a loud Filipino band and varicolored lights festooned from the ceiling, a perpetual Christmas, like most cabarets in Shanghai. On a small dance floor girls in long evening dresses are swaying in the arms of their clients. Not a Chinese man among them. Vera has chosen the Red Dragon for two reasons, one being that Chinese aren't welcome here. Their Japanese guest wouldn't appreciate a dance floor full of Chinese; he'd think Erich was treating him like one of them.

Luckner selects a table back from the dance floor, away from the blast of music. The Japanese nods silently when Erich suggests champagne. Vera searches the tables, many of them occupied solely by girls. They eye her curiously, for it's uncommon to have women accompany men to this place. There was a time when she sat at such tables, gazing jealously at women who had somehow escaped her fate. Vera can't help basking now in their admiration and envy.

'Excuse me,' she tells the men and leaves the table, heading for the lavatory. On the way she beckons to a buxom blonde at a table. This is the second reason Vera has chosen the Red Dragon.

Waiting for the girl in the hall near the lavatory, Vera lights a cigarette and thinks back a few years. Yes, life is very strange. After Yu-ying disappeared into the opium world of Shanghai, Vera left the house of Madam Lotus and worked as a cabaret girl. It was in a place much like the Red Dragon that she met her first protector, a tall Swede who liked women with very white complexions and very black hair.

'Good to see you, Vera,' says the buxom blonde, coming into the hallway. She leans against the wall. 'Give me a smoke, will you.'

Anticipating the request, Vera holds out the newly lit cigarette.

'You had it ready for me?' The girl seems delighted. They are speaking Russian. 'I thought I saw you come in. With the European and the Jap? One of them's yours, I suppose.'

'Yes.'

'For your sake I hope it's the European.'

'You think something's wrong with the Japanese?'

'I never said that, darling.' Both women scrutinize the bull-necked man from the hallway; he's brooding over a glass of champagne, while Luckner talks at him. Nakamura, hunched over, is a picture of intensity: a man gathering his forces. 'Am I for him?'

'That depends.' Vera studies the girl, who in her mid-twenties has probably been a whore for ten years. In a couple of previous meetings with the girl at one cabaret or another, Vera listened patiently to claims that were ridiculous. The big-breasted girl swore that she was a count's daughter from Kiev. From her accent, she's probably the offspring of peasants who migrated to Siberia and got caught in the war. Of more interest to Vera is the girl's reputation for being good in bed.

'You want me for him or not?' the girl asks Vera petulantly. 'Otherwise I'm going back out. I'm in demand.'

Vera judges her. It may well be the truth. She watches two sloe-eyed girls, Thai or Burmese, sidle by; although much prettier than the Russian girl, they are probably phlegmatic as well. 'He's for you if you promise to make him happy. I want him satisfied.'

'Is he important to you?'

Odd that the girl uses that phrase, Vera thinks, recalling her own similar questioning of Erich. 'He's important to the man I'm with.'

The girl shrugs indifferently.

Vera steps closer to the girl, inhaling the cheap perfume, the Chinese vodka – half the White Russians in Shanghai are killing themselves with it. 'Listen,' Vera says tensely. 'Whatever he gives you will be over and above this.' She takes enough money from her purse to match a week's earnings for a cabaret girl. 'But if you don't satisfy him, you'll hear from me.' Vera shoves the money into the hand of the girl, who instantly and methodically counts it.

'What is he, trouble?' the girl asks with a frown; but folding the money, she slips it into the bodice of her tight-fitting dress. 'Because otherwise why give me so much?'

Vera glances at Nakamura; she recognizes in him the same signs as the girl does: the moody silence in anticipation of being with a woman. 'I don't know him.' She turns to the girl leaning against the wall. 'Just be good to him, that's all.'

'Or your boy friend will give me trouble, right?'

Vera stares at her. 'He won't be happy.'

'Look, darling, I've had enough trouble in my sweet young life.' She puts her hand to her breast, as if ready to take out the money and give it back.

'It's your decision,' Vera says coldly.

The girl frowns in the throes of conflict. 'Look, darling, I'll fuck him and suck him and he can have me in the ass, but I won't let him tie me up.'

'You'll let him do what he wants or you can give the money back now.' Loyalty to Erich has fashioned her callousness. It has been done to her in the past; now she is doing it to someone else: forcing a choice between freedom of action and a lot of money. I am not your sister, Vera thinks; none of us who live this way are sisters. 'Well? Make up your mind.'

Hand held at the cleft between her breasts, the girl looks into the cabaret from the hallway. 'Goddamnit,' she mutters hopelessly.

'Give me the money back. I can't wait all night.'

'Wait a moment, darling, will you? It's just – I don't like his looks. Six months ago one of them tied me up and I've got five cigarette burns on my thighs to prove it.'

'One of them? A Japanese?'

'No, he was a Britisher. Looked just like the one sitting out there – brooding about things. Vera, I'm the daughter of a count. Can you imagine it?'

'I have to get back to the table.'

The girl's hand remains at her breasts. 'Well, all right then.'

Vera gives a little sigh. 'The man I'm with, he wants him satisfied. It's important.'

'Sure, you told me.'

'If it goes wrong, you'll be responsible,' Vera warns. She is making sure the girl will do well. Russians – she being one herself and aware of it – are notorious for independence and moodiness in bed.

'Oh, hell,' the girl says with a broad smile, relaxing against the wall. 'I'll do it.'

'Good, sweetheart.'

'Don't worry about a thing, Vera. I'll take care of him. How about another smoke?' When Vera gives it to her, lit, the girl smiles. 'He'll never forget it.'

'That's a good girl. Now after I go back in, you go sit at your table, and I'll send my boy friend over to get you.'

'So he gets the credit.'

Vera can't restrain a smile at the girl's shrewdness – an acquired trait, learned the hard way. 'Sorry, I forgot your name.'

'Olga. Here they call me Plum Blossom.' She says 'Plum Blossom' in English with difficulty.

'Don't fail me, Olga.'

'When I make my mind up, darling, I make it up.'

Studying the girl one last moment, Vera believes her. Returning to the table, where the Japanese continues to sip champagne silently, Vera smiles at Erich. In Russian she tells him where the girl is sitting and what her name is.

'Is she good?' Erich says with a smile, as if they are discussing something inconsequential, like the quality of table champagne. 'Because I want him to think I can get him what's good – in this, in business.'

'Of course. I fully understand. The girl's very aware of it.'

A few minutes later, while the band blares, Luckner whispers in the bull-necked man's ear, then laughs and declares loudly, 'Did you think I forgot? I was just being choosy. You're going to be pleased!'

Nakamura watches expectantly as the tall German crosses the room and returns with a voluptuous blonde. The look in his eye is familiar enough to Vera. She doesn't envy Olga. All men are the same, from the Chinese assistant in the antique shop to this heavy-set Japanese businessman. Hawks, all of them hawks, poised to strike.

220

The addition of Olga to the table brings it to life. Erich, a master of false gaiety, rummages through his bagful of Shanghai jokes; to match him Vera laughs in a strident manner, a manner learned in the old days but rarely practiced in the present. Nakamura, although participating in toasts, appears to be sobering up, especially when his eyes fix upon Olga's pneumatic Russian breasts. No sooner has she smoked a cigarette halfway than he lights another for her. He insists, grinning avidly. His attention encourages Olga to become frolicsome, so by the time Vera and Luckner rise to leave, she is calling him 'Michio' and chucking him under the chin. He insists grandly on paying the bill. Luckner wisely acquiesces with a bow of extravagant gratitude. Rising, Nakamura kisses Vera's hand. His lips, wet from champagne, nibble slightly across her knuckles. He grins openly at her for the first time, and Vera understands how deeply she loathes and fears him.

When Nakamura sits down again, Olga moves her chair close and grips his rough-hewn hand like a valued possession.

Eugenia. In this instant Vera thinks of the pampered girl. But for the Grace of God, as they say, here sits Eugenia Sudilovskaia. Does the girl snuggle with her British silk merchant in like fashion? Probably. Ah, but the difference!

While the two men are exchanging goodbyes, Vera stares with a smile at Olga, whose returning smile is winsome, startlingly innocent. Olga is going to do fine. She's girl who performs what she promises. It's merely a matter of making up her mind. Good girl.

From the exit Vera waves at the couple, who raise their glasses in a toast. The bull-necked Nakamura will make Olga a jolly companion until they are alone. What then? Vera is determined not to think about it.

Luckner, a little drunk, kisses her in the lane outside. 'Darling,' he slurs against her cheek, 'you were really quite wonderful.'

At the main thoroughfare they find a taxi (he leaves the limousine for Nakamura) and head for home. Vera watches the night recede, the night of Shanghai, whose garish neon continues to invite the seething crowds still looking for pleasure, solace, oblivion.

In the bedroom of their small house on Bubbling Well Road, a shaft of moonlight falls across Luckner's sleeping face. Although a few minutes ago they made love, his blond hair is still crisply parted, the sides of it, controlled by pomade, flat against his skull. Vera regards him curiously. Tonight he was more enthusiastic in his lovemaking than he has been for months. In his arms she felt a moment of hope. But awake now while he sleeps, Vera surrenders her expectations for the truth: Surely Erich was eager tonight not because of her charms but because of his success with Nakamura. She has noticed that the prospect of closing a business deal affects Erich sexually.

Agitated by such thoughts, Vera rises and tiptoes from the room into a hall that leads to the interior courtyard. The summer air is oddly cool, having swung in from northern waters past Korea; it is chilly enough to make her flesh tingle, but she doesn't put on robe – the cool sensation makes her feel alive, young.

Eugenia. That empty-headed creature with the little dog has remained with her into the early hours of morning. In the park, if seen together, would they have looked like sisters? She the older, of course, a matron? Less than ten years separate them, so they couldn't possibly be taken for mother and daughter. Even so, the girl looked young, very young. And herself? Not yet matronly. Not yet!

The moon is up. She hates it, the cold death of it shining down on a dead sister, on the vast winter steppes.

Turning from the courtyard, away from the moon, Vera reenters the house. Aided only by moonlight in the window, she finds the liquor cabinet and pours herself a glass of gin. It is good gin, the best money can buy, for let it never be said that Erich Luckner serves anything inferior. But without her he would have botched the evening's entertainment for Nakamura. Everything worked out finally. Or so she hopes. Olga. Briefly she imagines the girl in bed with the bull-necked man, who thought long and hard about what he was going to do there. Vera sips the gin and goes back into the corridor. On their return home tonight, she learned just how important Nakamura is: He's a Japanese government agent here in Shanghai to arrange arms shipments that will go to certain Chinese warlords. Ordinarily, Erich explained to her, the Japanese supply their own munitions for allies, but for reasons not yet clear they need foreign suppliers to help them fill the requirements. Erich has a good chance now of doing business with the Japanese, who always pay, unlike the Chinese, and pay well.

It is a chance Erich has embraced with all the anxiety of a dreamer – he still envisions retirement in Karlsruhe, the town house of a respected burgher, perhaps eventually a place on the town council, whatever a German expatriate dreams of. In recent months, however, he claims bad luck has plagued him. He delivered a shipment of arms to an old customer – a Kiangsu warlord – who was murdered before payment had been made. For the last month this story goes) Erich has paid his bills by actually selling the electric he uses as a front for the munitions business. But he can't exist long on electric fans, much less accumulate funds enough for Karlsruhe.

Now a lot of money is within his grasp; and Vera rather fears for him. Success often breeds jealousy, and in Shanghai jealousy can breed violence. She thinks of Hesse, a Swiss businessman who also dealt successfully in munitions. Hesse was a sandy-haired man with large blue eyes and the low, hesitant voice of a monk. Two weeks ago he was fished out of Soochow Creek just east of the iron bridge, nearly in the channel that would have floated him out to sea. A wooden stake had been shoved up his rectum, a chopstick protruded from one ear. Success, jealousy, violence.

Glass in hand, Vera shuffles down the chilly corridor; instead of returning to the courtyard, she enters her own room. It is a combination study and dressing room connected by a sliding door to the bedroom where Erich is sleeping. After a moment of hesitation she lights a lamp and sets it on her desk. Often when she can't sleep Vera comes in here to work at calligraphy or to look at her things. Kneeling, she lifts a floorboard under the desk and takes out a key. From a nearby closet she removes a small, inconspicuous suitcase of English leather and by lamplight opens it with the key.

Inside are her things.

She recalls the jade buffalo at the antique shop today. It burns in her memory like a star – and she must have it. Already tonight she began the process of getting it, too. While undressing for bed, she casually mentioned the need for money to Erich. She told him of new frocks, shoes, gewgaws discovered during a long day of shopping. She did not mention antiques – what man would want that sort of talk from a mistress? – but prated girlishly about the frivolities that charm men. Erich is no exception. She can see the pleasure in his eyes when she reverts to the giddy desires of girlhood. She'll say this for Erich: Unlike some men who like triviality in a woman, he gives her the money to pursue it. Like many people who anguish over their savings, Erich is absolutely negligent about the disposal of his own. If someone – it must be someone with no less persuasive power than a god – could teach him that daily extravagance pushes his Karlsruhe dream farther from reality, Erich Luckner might never again squander a *cash*. But, like a child, he sees his fortune coming from one swift and magical event: a bag of gold suspended on a silver thread that can be cut by a single sword thrust. Thrift is as foreign to him as patience. And a good thing for her, too, because when he has money or the expectation of it, Vera usually succeeds in extracting from him far more than he can reasonably afford to give. Tonight, for example, inspired by his promising new connection with the Japanese government, Erich has given her the lavish sum she named. He did it with a boyish smile, rather shy in its good intention, which suggests to Vera that in different circumstances the man might be not only generous but compassionate.

What Erich will never know or bother to find out is that has asked for ten times more money than the clothes and gewgaws are worth, just as he has never known or bothered to find out how she has managed almost daily, through manipulation of the household budget (a euphemism at best), to set aside funds for her private hoard. And it is to be hoped that Erich will never discover that she has robbed him in the pettiest of ways – midnight raids on his wallet, conducted with an intense assessment of how much can be removed without detection. Her hoarding and thefts, along with tonight's windfall, may enable her to buy the jade outright or at least make a substantial down payment after the initial haggling. Because she must have it. She must.

And have it she will. The overwhelming passion of the resolve heartens Vera, gives her confidence. She feels better than at any time today.

Squinting by lamplight into the small suitcase, Vera carefully – indeed, reverently – removes each object packed in there: A lotus-shaped lacquer bowl from the Yuan; a cinnabar landscape dish from the same dynasty; a brown cloisonné deer from the Ming with yellow enamel decorations – it fits neatly in the palm of her hand; a small but precious silk tapestry from the Ching, depicting flowering magnolia and peach trees and butterflies tremulous as blossoms in the wind; a *pi* disc in jade and a jade Kuan Yin, Goddess of Mercy, to whom she has prayed more than once, even as every morning she says a prayer to the Virgin Mary of her childhood; last, but certainly not least, there is a silk page of calligraphy, a poem copied by the great master Mi Fei of the Sung in his passionate Running Style.

Nothing she has bought is too large for this modest suitcase, its limits determining the parameters of her collection. Vera Rogacheva's life is here. All that she has managed to accumulate since coming to China lies in the confines of a little suitcase. Each object in it represents countless men in hot Shanghai nights, and scheming, and saving.

Moving the *pi* disc between thumb and forefinger, experiencing the coolness of regal jade, with her other hand Vera lifts the gin glass and drinks. It is sad how little pleasure the collection gives her. Perhaps this is true because what she owns forces her to remember what she once had. Years ago, at the outset of the flight from Petrograd, there had been other treasures – family heirlooms: A pair of earrings with pendant-shaped emeralds; an ivory locket with her grandmother's portrait inside; a small gold watch with a spring lid, among other things. And later, on the shore of a frozen lake, she had slipped the wedding ring from her dead mother's finger. All these possessions of worth and intimacy had been forcibly taken from her, here and there, during the terrible journey. She remembers the loss of each object, as if part of her own body had been ripped from her.

Her present treasures are not associated with memories either innocent or sentimental or tragic; even so, they are emblems of survival, and in a way represent all of the Rogachevas, every one of them, since she is the last alive.

Slipping each object back inside carefully, Vera locks the suitcase, returns it to its unobtrusive place in the closet, and hides the key again under the floorboard. Blowing out the lamp, she tiptoes down the corridor, passing the open doorway of the bedroom. She pauses to study Erich a few moments, arrested by the solitude surrounding him – like death itself. Vera shivers and continues to the courtyard, which is a small cobbled area enclosed by the four sides of the house. Erich has put little effort into decorating the house – he has no interest in art – but in the courtyard he has planted a lovely wisteria and for some reason, known only to himself, has set beside it a large and handsome replica of a Ming vase, whose smoky sides now gleam in the moonlight.

Sitting on a courtyard step, Vera drinks the gin and awaits exhaustion that will give her a few hours of protective sleep, safe from the waking nightmare, from tomorrow.

The tiny space reminds her of another, much larger courtyard.

The one in Qufu, where General Tang played Tai Chi Chuan. Perhaps she's reminded of that courtyard because tonight Erich had mentioned the man.

'Nakamura gave me some interesting information,' Erich said, while slipping into a dressing gown. 'There's to be a warlords' meeting on a mountain near Jinan.'

Vera had turned from the dressing table, where she was brushing her hair and looking stealthily for wrinkles. 'Is that important? she asked.

'It is to the warlords.'

'I see.' She turned again to the mirror.

'Remember General Tang? He'll be there.'

Brushing her hair vigorously, Vera said, 'Of course, I remember him.'

'The sonofabitch,' Erich murmured, not having forgotten his humiliation at Qufu. 'But he's getting what he deserves.'

'What is that?' Three hundred strokes – advice of her mother's that Vera still cherishes: If you want good hair, you must brush it three hundred times before going to bed, without fail. Two hundred twenty-two. Two hundred twenty-three. 'What does he deserve?'

'Losing face. Nakamura told me about it before you came in tonight. Tang has lost out to old Dog Meat.'

'I remember you telling me about Dog Meat.' Two hundred thirty. Two hundred thirty-one.

'The Japs are backing Dog Meat. That's why Nakamura knows about it.'

Vera glances through the mirror at Erich, who is sitting on the bed with a cigarette thoughtfully poised in his hand. 'Why do they back Dog Meat?'

'I told you.'

'I forgot.'

'Because he's so stupid they can control him. They got Marshal Chang Tso-lin to appoint Dog Meat to a big new post in Shantung.'

'Oh, Erich, spare me the details. I can never remember these Chinese generals' names.'

'But you speak the language beautifully.'

'That's different.'

'If you live in Shanghai, darling, Chinese politics mean something to you. Never forget it.'

'I won't. Thank you. So what's going to happen to General Tang?'

'I'm not sure, but I think he's through.' Blowing a smoke ring, Erich watches it dissipate. 'A month ago I thought the Japanese and Tang together would ruin me. The Japs were selling to my customers and Tang forgot to buy anything before galloping off. Now the Japs are going to be my customers and for good measure are going to ruin that bastard who pulled a crazy trick when I needed him most. A twist worthy of China, don't you think?'

Two hundred sixty-seven. Two hundred sixty-eight. Vera had smiled in agreement.

But now, gazing at the moonlit vase in the courtyard, Vera remembers the General with extraordinary vividness and hopes Erich is wrong. Few men have impressed her so deeply as the Chinese general on their stroll through the cemetery of Confucius.

Moonlight is detestable, she thinks; the color of death, of winter, of a dead sister's face.

Vera sips the gin, even while vowing to quit drinking tomorrow. Alcohol will age her more rapidly, and she needs her good looks a while longer. To settle her life. Tonight Erich showed ardor in bed, but its source was his impending success, and surely he intends to leave her soon. Vera looks at the glass; to her annoyance only a little gin is left. In the mirror tonight she noticed the ghost of a new line around the left corner of her mouth.

Eugenia. White arms, clear eyes.

And then Olga comes to mind: plump Olga like an innocent girl holding hands with the brute from Tokyo.

And Eugenia cuddling the dog, pouting her sweet lips.

And then Vera sees the General walking among the pines, his hair clipped short in military fashion. She has no affection for a soldierly bearing, yet there was something about the man – perhaps an odd blend of power and sensitivity that continues to interest her. Yes, that – interest her.

And the snow is melting on the steppes alongside a railway embankment somewhere east of Novonikolajivsk. She huddled all night in a shack nearby, watching the moon rise and hover and descend like a gigantic stone, almost symmetrical. Now the sun has risen over the snow. Dead bodies appear, like sea things emerging from white water, and young men from a nearby village come along. She watches them strip the female corpses of Czarist finery, of silk dresses and brocaded shawls and Muscovian hats.

She is glad to be wearing rags. Later, in the village, she notices the buxom girls wearing the pretty clothes, now cleaned and ironed. The boys had given them the finery as gifts.

But no nightmare, not tonight. What has just happened is something wayward, accidental, abruptly remembered. Not the nightmare, systematic, irresistible.

Vera tosses off the last of the gin.

Eugenia and the British boy friend, do they sleep together? Does Eugenia insist on having the dreadful pug dog in bed with them? Eugenia, that dog – she hates them.

' "I am like a felled tree," ' Vera begins to recite. It is from a poem by Li Po. Gin clouds her mind for a moment, then the words come readily:

> *'I am like a felled tree fallen in a well.*
> *For whom will my blossoms smile?'*

Oh, the man knew, she thinks. Li Po knew, he really knew. But she won't think about Li Po and the sad poem any more. She'll concentrate on the jade buffalo until she's exhausted enough to sleep. She recalls the way its swept-back horns fit the contours of its jade body. Then exhaustion finally begins to roll through her, slowly, like a mist. She's grateful for it.

Shuffling back to the bedroom, stretching out beside Erich, she lets the images come at her: foolish, beautiful Eugenia; the Siberian snow at dawn; Erich; the bull-necked Nakamura; sad little Olga who will not be happy tonight; Eugenia and the snotty-nosed pug; General Tang among the pines; Eugenia; Eugenia – until they all fade away and leave her finally at peace.

10

On the south bank of the Yellow River, at the junction of the Peking-Shanghai Railroad, lies the capital of Shantung Province: Jinan, more than twenty-five centuries old, source of a hundred natural springs. In a Dodge Tourer, high and square, with running boards and a canvas top, General Tang Shan-teh enters Jinan through Le Yuan-men Gate, near the precinct of the City God Temple. Another Dodge follows, and after it an old battered Chinese truck carrying a dozen soldiers.

The General sits alone in the back seat, his aide Yang next to the driver. In the accompanying car ride a division commander of infantry, a brigade captain of artillery, and a few other officers. Chief of Staff Colonel Pi has been left in Qufu, although the General knows he wanted desperately to mingle with high-ranking officers of other military organizations. It is precisely this desire that has influenced General Tang to leave him at headquarters. Tang wants no friendships made by his subordinates that may lead someday to intrigue or defection. His father once told him: 'Loyalty being all important in a soldier, if you don't have it from a man, at least restrict his scheming.'

The auto trip from Qufu has been pleasant in late summer. Along the rutted road there are ripening orchards of crab apples, hedges of nettles, beds of wild thyme, buckwheat and onion fields, cabbage patches, gardens heavy with beans and tall leeks almost ready to harvest. Leaves in a few elms have already turned, and smoke trees are aflame with autumnal red. Sumac in the undergrowth glows like coals in a furnace. The passing countryside has put him in a good mood. What is more comforting in life than the look of nature? His father might have said that, perhaps did, because the General feels the idea with the twin intensity of having experienced it and having learned it.

He has often thought today of his father, because yesterday he made a decision that his father would have approved; that in a sense, perhaps, his father made with him: He rejected the issuance of military currency to his troops.

Of course, his staff was aghast; everything had been done, and all that he had to do was sign the order. But when he picked up for examination a single note – the Southern Shantung Provincial Army Note for One Tael – the reality quite overwhelmed him. Each side of the printed note stated that it could be redeemed for silver 'After the War.' Under the image of a Buddhist pagoda an inscription declared that the One-Tael Note could be used for services and for payment of taxes by the forces of said army. It displayed the personal chop or seal of General Tang Shan-teh along with that of the 'Financial Bureau' of said army. Holding this fraudulent piece of paper in his hand, the General not only refused to issue the currency but ordered the corded bundles of it burned immediately.

Through the black lines of his personal chop he had imagined the stern visage of his father, who used to quote the Great Sage:

'Men of true breeding are ashamed for their words to go beyond their deeds.'

Tang has never thought of himself as an idealist. Surely, in the practice of life, deeds must detach themselves sometimes from the norms of behavior. Circumstances run counter to expectations, demanding of men, however eager to do what is proper, that they modify their actions. A sly argument which he has used more than once. But not this time. Not with his personal chop stamped on the fraud. Aside from philosophical discussions of moral dilemmas, what he knows is simple enough: He can't bring dishonor to the name of Tang. Not consoled as Christians are by a belief in eternal life, and without the Buddhists' faith in the promised mercy of God, he is committed ultimately to those who have gone before him, men and women of his blood, who have sweated and suffered and endured and frequently succeeded in living good lives. Nothing more tangible or spiritual than a sense of personal honor, therefore, has determined a course of action that can surely spell his ruin. Perhaps those attending the conference at Thousand Buddha Mountain will not yet know of his decision. If they do, they will comprehend the true state of his financial affairs and his unfortunate reluctance to seek the only way out of the difficulty. Sooner or later, like a pack of dogs who turn on their wounded, they may very well turn on him because of this decision. But it has been made; he is content.

At his command the little procession of vehicles leaves a sycamore-lined thoroughfare for a maze of streets hardly wide enough for the cars to navigate. At each corner he gives a direction to his driver, who has no idea where they are going. In and out of a thickly populated market area they proceed, vying for command of the dusty lanes with bleating herds of black goats, naked children, and coolies pushing wheelbarrows.

Finally the caravan stops in a muddy lane cluttered with tiny brick houses, their corrugated tin roofs held down by stone. Tang gets out alone and knocks at the door of one of these shacks. Pots of scraggly zinnias sit on some rocks near the entrance. A child sucking his thumb stares wide-eyed at the man in the plain cotton uniform of a soldier.

After the General's persistent pounding on the door, it opens a crack and a sunlit strip of human face can be seen in the tiny gap. 'Elder Brother is not at home,' says a high-pitched voice, trembling from age.

'Grandmother,' says Tang. 'It is your Second Daughter's Third Daughter's Husband.'

The strip of face vanishes, the door closes tight, but Tang waits, idly observing a column of ants climbing a weathered log that holds up a portion of the tin roof.

Again the door opens, this time wider, and a very old face peers into the sunlight. 'Are you a tax collector?'

'No, grandmother,' Tang says quietly. He repeats the information, adding that he is the husband of the granddaughter who died of typhoid some years ago.

The door opens wide. Still suspicious, however, the old woman regards him closely as he crosses the threshold. A candle sends out a thin thread of light, outlining a rickety table, a chair, the *kang* along one wall, a large grain storage jar, and a blackened stove with an old pot swinging above it by a chain.

'You are not a Bannerman?'

Standing just inside the door, Tang says, 'I am not a Bannerman. Be calm, grandmother.' He bows very low in respect.

Dressed in a shabby robe, barefoot, her hair pulled back into a white bun, a few hairs on her chin, her skin remarkably smooth for someone far into the eighth decade, she cocks her head sideways to enhance her concentration. Abruptly she utters a little cry and performs a *San Kiu Kau*: kneels three times and nine times knocks her head on the packed earth of the floor. 'Ah, your Excellency! I have forgotten! Excellency! I remember now! My ancestors are greatly honored!'

Tang does not attempt to shorten the performance, although the action is obviously painful for her arthritic joints. He lets her do what she must do – honor him as if he were the Celestial Emperor, Lord of Ten Thousand Years, The One Who Faces South, The Enthroned One, The Son of Heaven. A woman of her generation is bred to show elaborate respect.

In response the General bows again, deeply. His heart is moved by this meeting. Only this aspect of his trip to Jinan has appealed to him: a visit to his dead wife's grandmother, a chance to honor her.

She begs him to sit at the table. Clucking her tongue impatiently, she fills the pot with water and puts it on the stove. She will give him hot water, the peasant's substitute for tea. While the water is heating, Tang questions her gently. Does she have enough food and fuel for the winter? What does she lack? What can he get for her? To his questions the old woman waves vaguely, as the General has known she would. Why hasn't she gone to live with Eldest Son? He has asked the same question on every visit; and every time she has given him the same answer, with hands thrown up dramatically in the same way.

'Eldest Son would have me take orders from the shrew he married. Do I look like a fool? He's scheming to get my money.'

Tang suppresses a smile. Her eldest son got all her money a long time ago.

'Second Son – where is he?' She pauses thoughtfully, having forgotten that he died of heart disease a dozen years before General Tang ever met her. 'I think he has gone to Kaifeng. He bought a farm near there. Makes a fine living growing barley and melons. But how can I go to him if I don't know exactly where the farm is? What was I saying?' Refusing to sit at the table, she blows on the coals and fans them with both hands. Turning slowly, she eyes the General with increasing suspicion, then dread. 'What have you done, Younger Brother? Cut your queue!'

'Yes, it's cut, grandmother, but be calm. It's all right.'

'All right? How can you say it's all right with Bannermen prowling the streets? We must get you a false queue, Younger Brother, or you're a dead man.'

Tang realizes the old woman has moved back in memory to her youth, when the Manchus held China. They had filled her life then, those Juchen Tartars, just as they had filled the lives of her ancestors for three hundred years, ever since those wild men with their clan banners breached the Great Wall. They had ruled by terror and humiliation and until 1911 it had been mandatory for the sons of Han, the native Chinese like her father and brothers and nephews, to shave the front part of their heads and wear queues – a badge of servitude. The Manchus, mounted archers by heritage, believed that since the horse is man's slave, the Chinese by wearing a long strand of hair wear the tail of the horse. It was capital punishment for a Chinese to appear without this horse's tail. The old woman is reliving such history.

'Someday the Bannermen will slaughter us all,' she maintains while blowing on the coals. Waving her hands, she ignores the sparks that flare up on her palms and wrists. 'Those executed in the square last week? I knew some of them. The man two doors down was one of them.' Turning, with tears in her eyes, she leans toward the General and whispers, 'The Bannermen wouldn't permit their families to sew the severed heads back on the bodies. But that's the right of man, isn't it? What can the dead think? And the alley dogs lapping the pools of blood. They wouldn't shoo away. Kept coming back, the dirty *wonks*.' The old woman shakes her head in disbelief, in sorrow. 'But the Bannermen will pay now that the boy's gone. We'll hunt them in the streets.'

In her mind, Tang understands, the old woman has moved to the Revolution of 1912, to the end of Manchu rule with the abdication of the boy emperor.

She cackles as she takes a cup from a small shelf on the mud-brick wall. 'They can't hide from us. Do the Manchus think we don't know them by now? High collars, narrow sleeves, white linings in their robes. Sure we know them! I remember this one fellow. He came from another town and had us fooled until someone yanked his robe open and we saw the white lining.' She contemplates the remembered scene, holding the teacup chest high. 'That Bannerman was dead sooner than you could speak his name. I kicked him myself with this foot here. He was still alive too, when I did it.' She stares at the tiny lump of foot and smiles. 'No trouble with their women. We hunt them down easily. Won't bind their feet, won't they? Call it barbarian? They're the barbarians with their big feet! Now those Manchu bitches wish they had bound them!' Pouring hot water into the teacup, she brings it to the table and sets it in front of the General, whom she studies carefully. Suspicion lights up her eyes. 'Who are you, sir? Have you come for taxes? My husband is not at home.'

Tang has brought with him a large burlap bag. Now he sets it on the *kang*. 'For you, honored grandmother, in memory of your Second Daughter's Third Daughter.'

Looking from the General to the bag, the old woman smiles goodnaturedly. 'I remember her.'

Aware that she will remove nothing from the bag, Tang opens it and takes out everything: candles, boxes of matches, jars of tea, tins of spice from Shanghai, two pair of cotton shoes, a wool winter jacket, a bundle of money wrapped in paper, three packets of joss sticks, a half-dozen needles, a box full of buttons. At the table he lifts the cup of hot water and with a bow drinks. Then he calls to his bodyguards in the truck.

Four come running; in each of their hands is a five-gallon can of kerosene. Others drag in burlap bags of coal and grain. While the action surges around her, the old woman stares at the things piled on the *kang*. 'I remember her,' she murmurs with a smile.

When the bodyguards leave, Tang bows low again. He is making his farewells when there's a sudden uproar outside. In the lane every head is turned eastward in the direction of wailing sirens.

Standing in the doorway, the General shades his eyes from the glare. So old Dog Meat must be passing. Tang can visualize the boulevard lined with soldiers; a troop of White Russian horsemen trotting along in their smart uniforms, carrying tasseled spears; the limousine preceded by armored cars with sirens on. It's the customary way for old Dog Meat to get from one part of the city to another. Tang has always considered it ostentatious folly, but the fact remains that it is Dog Meat, not himself, who now occupies the seat of power in this province.

The caravan makes another stop near Pearl Springs, not far from the modern post office with its hundred-foot tower, electric generator, and steam-heating plant – pride of the city. Tang waits in the car while Yang goes inside the Municipal Building, an ugly pile of Edwardian stone. Soldiers wearing the green armband of Chang Tsung-ch'ang's troops lounge outside in the warm sunlight, their Japanese rifles slung loosely across their shoulders. From the car window Tang can see the upswept roofs of the nearby prefectural Confucius temple. Perhaps later there will be time to visit it. Coolies plod through the street pushing carts full of *feng chiu* wine in willow-twig baskets waterproofed with oil paper. As a small boy he often watched the same kind of wine being pushed along in similar carts. Nothing really changes, he thinks. The idea heartens him: order, design. But some things do change: Before the Great War, in this city German railroadmen strolled with Japanese mistresses; now, from the car, he can see Japanese businessmen strolling with Russian mistresses.

Yang returns with information from the Municipal Building. There will be a banquet this evening on the celebrated lake, Da Ming Hu. Tomorrow morning the conference will begin on Thousand Buddha Mountain. Governor Chang Tsung-ch'ang sends his compliments but regrets that a private meeting today will be impossible.

'Who told you all this?' the General asks.

Yang looks flustered; doubtless the clerks have treated him

shabbily – on orders, of course. 'An adjutant.'

'An adjutant.' Tang is glad that he didn't go inside himself to suffer the same humiliation. The situation is giving Dog Meat the pleasure he might derive from a new concubine.

Setting out again, the caravan traverses the commercial area of Jinan: silk and cake shops, lumber companies, small factories producing ironware and hair nets. They pass Hsing-hsun-fu, a soybean processing plant that Tang's elder brother once managed. His brother, Yen-chang. They never got along. Rising against the blue sky are thick black curls of smoke from flour-mill stacks. The Japanese own most of the mills nowadays in Jinan.

Across town, in a residential district once restricted to foreigners but now occupied as well by rich Chinese, the caravan halts, this time in front of a high wall lined with tall larches, their scaly upright cones on stunted branches looking to the General like grenades. Opening the front gate, he enters alone, but gives orders for a few bodyguards to take positions within the courtyard and rear garden and for the rest to patrol the street. These days it's unwise in Jinan for anyone with political interests to go visiting unprotected.

The General has been seen. The front door of the rambling house opens, and a servant bows very low. When the General brushes past him into the foyer, another man, young and in Western dress, bows too.

This is the General's nephew, Ping-ti, son of the elder brother who once ran the soybean plant.

· Amenities exchanged, the General follows his nephew into a large drawing room. As Tang expects, it's essentially a Western room with a few Chinese decorations, mostly in the form of table-leg scrollwork. A chandelier with smoky globes hangs from chains, and on the walls are displayed a series of Western landscapes. It is distasteful to the General, who sits in an overstuffed chair near a marble-topped table. This is no environment for a member of the Tang Clan. A chaise longue upholstered in damask catches his eye. Is this where Ping-ti's concubine stretches out? Is she Japanese?

'I am unworthy but honored that you've condescended to stay in my humble house,' Ping-ti says mechanically. He is serving notice that the old forms of polite discourse, though being followed by him, mean little – are a way of placating his uncle.

'Your generosity does honor to our family.'

Ping-ti nods briskly, but with a sour look that plainly expresses his impatience with urbane manners of the past. A servant comes with a silver tray and tea service. 'You did the right thing to come here,' Ping-ti says in a businesslike tone. 'The hotels are dangerous these days. Old Dog Meat has been a naughty boy lately.'

The General is shocked to hear such familiarity from one so young, even though the jocular contempt has been expressed for a scoundrel like Chang Tsung-ch'ang. Perhaps the young man's behavior is a direct result of four years of study in America.

'The first thing Dog Meat did as Governor General was execute Judge Nieh of the High Provincial Court.'

This is news to the General, terrible news. He had known the Judge well. As children they had played together, here, in the streets of Jinan. Nieh killed. Law murdered in the city of their childhood.

'Then two days ago,' Ping-ti continues, 'a Peking journalist disappeared from his hotel. He'd written an article criticizing our new Governor General.' Pang-ti pours two cups of tea. 'Even so, Dog Meat may do better than people think. He's harsh, but he'll keep the peace.' Ping-ti smiles. 'With your help, uncle. And he's on good terms with the Japanese.'

'That's commendable?'

'I believe it is, uncle. After all, they have their concession at Tsingtao and other interests here in Jinan.'

'For example, the flour mill you work for.' In reply to the General's letter about coming to Jinan, the young man had mentioned an executive job with a Japanese flour mill: his education in American finance has prepared him to be a comprador. 'Do you like the work?' Tang asks him.

'I am unworthy of the trust.'

'Any Chinese is worthy of a position in a Japanese company on Chinese soil.' The General lights a cigarette with fierce decisiveness.

Ping-ti dismisses his uncle's angry remark with a wave of his hand. It is startlingly rude. Aside from his eyes, the young man scarcely looks Chinese in his Western suit and leather shoes with laces. He wears tortoise-rimmed glasses, has a stickpin in his tie, and a loop of key chain is visible across his vest.

The General won't let his nephew avoid a topic by waving his hand. 'What's it like, nephew, to work for the Japanese?'

'They're quite good to work for. Anyway, we must learn to accommodate them.'

'We?'

'Everyone in this province. The Japanese have built a plant for making bailing machines and another for processing dried eggs. Right here in Jinan.' He takes a cigarette from a slim silver case in his suit jacket. 'They're building a sugar-beet mill. And they want to build roads.'

'Where?'

'From Tsingtao to Jinan and on to Techow, I understand.'

'Meaning they want to go north.' After a thoughtful pause, the General adds, 'Maybe to Tientsin, then to Peking. They'd dominate the coastal area from Tsingtao to Peking.'

Ignoring that possibility, Ping-ti suggests that they also might build some roads through the southern part of Shantung.

'Through my territory? Never. I won't let that happen, nephew.' He studies the young man, who seems honestly puzzled. 'Let me tell you about something that happened when you were too young to understand. You've heard of the Twenty-one Demands? Well, of course you have. But hearing is not always understanding. In 1914 the Japanese sent a kind of ultimatum to Peking, demanding outrageous concessions and privileges. Had we given in to all of them, today China would be a Japanese colony. As it was, they showed us the intense desire of the Japanese to have a foothold here. It's not difficult to understand the source of that desire: a growing population crowded into a few islands stares across a little sea at a huge land bursting with natural resources –'

'Which they could help us develop now, uncle.'

'Listen, please, to someone who was old enough to understand what went on. In 1918 they forced a military alliance on us, and at the Paris Peace Conference they managed to get the German Concession at Tsingtao. They hold it now like a base of military operations.'

The young man's eyeglasses glint in a shaft of sunlight coming through the window, giving him a metallic look, as though he were machine-made. When he dips his head slightly to sip tea, Ping-ti moves out of that scintillating light and resumes his human appearance. He seems physically soft to the General – quite vulnerable in that way. Tang realizes how much he wants to like his nephew, how deeply he fails to do so.

Before leaving Qufu, the General had the old diviner cast the Yarrow Stalks. The oracle said: A young man will come into your future and greatly influence it. In the presence of his nephew, Tang remembers the prophecy. He hopes the young man is not this one – of his own flesh and blood. In the lengthening silence he remembers the father of this young man, his own elder brother. They had been playing one day in the henhouse – they must have been about eight and fourteen – when Yen-chang tied him to a post. It was just to practice knot tying, Yen-chang said. Then Yen-chang took a surly old hen and held her inches away from his eyes; he can remember to this day the look of that cruel beak tentatively pecking at him.

'Tell me about Elder Brother,' Tang says.

Startled by the change in conversation, Ping-ti merely blinks.

'For example, is your father still in Hong Kong?'

'Yes, in Hong Kong.'

'Doing what?'

Again a dismissive wave of his hand. Ping-ti says, 'You know my father – eleven fingers in everything.' He leans forward, his face tense with a new thought. 'To get back to old Dog Meat. I'm afraid the Japanese think well of him, in spite of his vices.'

'Perhaps because of them.'

Ping-ti rises and starts pacing. This is unbecoming in a young man of family and education, yet he adds to the disagreeable impression by letting a cigarette dangle from his lips. The smoke from it causes his eyes to squint.

Is this a member of the Tang Clan? the General wonders in dismay.

'May I be frank, uncle?'

'As frank as you please.'

'Your future may depend on your willingness to cooperate with the Japanese.'

That is frank enough, the General thinks ruefully.

'The fact is, uncle, we must all cooperate with the Japanese. In the interest of progress.'

'Who told you to say such things?' Tang asks sharply. He assumes Ping-ti's boldness has its source in someone older, more powerful – in Yen-chang, whose eleven fingers must indeed be everywhere, including in the Japanese government's coffer. 'Are you expressing your father's ideas?'

Ping-ti sits down. 'Believe me, uncle, I speak for myself.'

238

That is possibly true, the General thinks. Perhaps times are changing faster than he imagines. Surely in this young man he sees a blend of Western impertinence and Eastern guile.

Crushing out his cigarette in an ashtray for emphasis, Ping-ti says, 'I feel it's my duty as your elder brother's son to warn you.'

A servant, poised in the doorway, comes forward to remove the ashtray and replace it with another.

'Warn me?' Tang says when the servant has left.

'We must all change with the times.'

'Yes,' the General says blandly. 'I think you've already said that.'

Again the dismissive wave of the hand. 'Do you read *The Three Kingdoms*, uncle?'

Tang is startled by the mention of a book that has been much on his mind lately. 'Do *you* still read our Chinese books after an education in America?'

'Before going to America I read it three times. Since coming back I've read it twice.'

A delicate rebuff: the General accepts it as justified. He takes more tea. 'There's no better study of loyalty and its consequences.'

'Among other themes.'

'Yes? What other themes in it interest you, nephew?'

'The need for flexibility. Just this morning I read the section in which Chang Sung comes to seek aid from Liu Pei.'

'I'm familiar with it.'

'Chang Sung says: "A man of noble ambition adjusts to his age." '

'I understand flexibility is characteristic of the Americans.'

'It is, uncle.'

'Do you miss America?'

Ping-ti pauses before replying. Perhaps he's calculating how far to go in his answer. 'Well, I miss American ice cream.'

Nephew has decided to be jocular – a good choice of tactics, the General thinks. But then the young man's father was always clever. Putting down the hen before untying him, Yen-chang had said, 'I did that to see how brave you are.' It had taken the General years to recognize the lie. Yen-chang had done it to break him down, and when he hadn't broken, Yen-chang had decided to placate him. Now the son of Yen-chang is amusingly describing the antic customs of America: the fast cars, the sports in huge stadiums, the cement swimming pools.

'And the people, do you miss them?'

Ping-ti shrugs. 'A friend or two. I'm content to be home.'

'I think I have a surprise for you.' The General, rising, goes to the front hall and calls out. One of the bodyguards in the courtyard comes running. 'Go inside,' the General tells him.

Ping-ti looks up in astonishment at the young man entering the room: blond, dressed in a soldier's cotton, with an ax stuck in his belt, an ugly scar creasing his forehead.

Sitting down, Tang says calmly, 'A recruit for my cavalry.'

Taken by surprise, Ping-ti studies the stocky blond standing at attention. 'Uncle, who *is* this?'

'A member of my bodyguard at the moment. I've allowed him to keep his ax instead of the sword carried by bodyguards. A concession to America.'

Ping-ti looks uneasily at the General.

'Ask him a question in Chinese.'

Grinning uncertainly, Ping-ti looks at the soldier. 'Please tell me who Kuan Yin is.'

At attention, eyes fixed at a distant point, Embree says, 'Goddess of Mercy. The historical merging of Avalokitesvara, the Buddhist God from India, with Hsi Wang Mu, the Taoist Royal Mother of the West. Kuan Yin lives in the Land of the Blest with Amitabha, Boundless Glory.'

This ready answer surprises Tang as well. 'Nephew, ask him something in English.'

After a brief exchange in English, Ping-ti looks at his uncle for further instructions.

'Now tell me,' Tang says, 'is he really an American?'

'Yes, of course. Did you think differently?'

'No,' says the General, aware that the foreigner understands them. The truth is, Tang hasn't been entirely sure. The fellow might be British, French – or Russian, for all he knows. Perhaps a secret agent? To his knowledge, however, the Americans haven't introduced spies into China. As far as the blond soldier is concerned, Tang can now relax. The young man is one of those boyish Americans who died so well in the last months of the Great War. He orders Embree to leave. 'I brought him,' the General says with a smile, 'to amuse them at the conference. Chang Tsung-ch'ang has his little army of Russian bodyguards. I have my one American.'

'Don't underestimate him, uncle.' Ping-ti lights another cigarette and blows the smoke out thoughtfully. 'Americans can seem rather simple, but I've known them to be formidable under certain conditions.'

'And Russians? I have a Bolshevik agent in camp.'

Ping-ti laughs. 'Keep *him* hidden. Chang Tsung-ch'ang's White Russians are everywhere in Jinan. A lot of them fought with Semënov. Dog Meat likes them for their mindless savagery. If they catch your Bolshevik, they won't return him in one piece.'

Tang wants to get back to their discussion. 'So you believe we must look for progress through the foreigners. I admit they gave us rifles, light bulbs, rubber tires. What else can they do?' He wishes to attack this serious question in a light tone.

'Roads, uncle.' Ping-ti leans forward tensely. 'They can help us with roads. Roads are the most important problem.'

'I agree roads are important. But the most important? Are they important enough so we must let foreigners loose everywhere?'

'Excuse me, honored uncle. It's not my place to discuss such matters of national importance. I work for a flour mill.'

For the moment he has both feet back in China, the General thinks.

'I'm intrigued by your opinion,' Tang says. 'Continue.'

It's a command that Ping-ti embraces. He leans far out of the chair, utterly devoid of Chinese reserve. The General decides that in America the young fellow lost his sense of the body, how it can reveal too much of the mind. An error.

So Ping-ti talks of roads. First he deplores the present system. Then he discusses them in terms of his own work in the flour mill. China grows enough wheat, he says, to maintain its mills at full capacity, but only a fraction of the crop gets to the mills cheaply enough to make it profitable for the mills to buy. Transportation across rivers, mountains, and rugged plains is nearly impossible, to say nothing of the expense of accomplishing it. 'Consider a Shansi farmer,' he says. 'We can't buy his wheat if we have to pay the cost of getting it here. It would be better to buy wheat in America and ship it across the Pacific! Yes, then bring it to the mill by rail, rather than take the Shansi farmer's wheat as a gift and have to haul it over our roads. Roads, uncle. We must have roads into the interior. But who will build them? Not us, not yet. We need the foreigners to do it.'

'In gratitude for your frankness, nephew, I'll tell you what I think.' Tang clasps his hands and lays them in his lap. 'I agree we need roads. But what goes with them if they're built by foreigners?

Why, the foreigners. And the goods of the foreigners. And what do foreign goods do to our country? Why, weaken it.' He pauses, waiting for a response.

'Weaken our country, uncle?'

'In the old times a farmer busied himself at handicrafts in the off season. What he made was sold in the towns to the rich, and this way he survived. But when foreign goods become available, the rich buy them instead of things made by the peasant. So the money that might have gone to the peasant goes to the British, the French, the Italians, the Americans, the Swedes, the Danes, the Germans, the Russians, and, of course, to the Japanese. Pleased at the good quality, the rich want more of what the foreigners offer. And to raise money, they raise the rent and taxes on the land farmed by the peasant. So what happens? The peasant can't count on selling his handicrafts to pay his debt on the land. He puts all his hope in the harvest – but it often fails. There's nothing for him to do but get off the land. And what's a Chinese peasant without his land? A miserable creature dying in the streets of Shanghai or Peking. That's what I think of foreigners building our roads.' Tang rises.

Rising too, Ping-ti accompanies the General to the front door, amid mutual exclamations of good will. It is settled that during the General's stay in Jinan he will occupy the east wing of the house. His retinue will share domestic quarters with Ping-ti's servants behind the garden. Ping-ti is self-assured while they make the arrangements. The General wonders how much of this confidence was acquired abroad and how much from a father who never fails to seize an opportunity.

What has their talk today meant to the young man? The General searches his nephew's face for a clue to his perception of it, but finds none. Ping-ti has planted both feet in China again.

Now it's time, the General thinks, to make the meaning of their little talk perfectly clear. In the courtyard, he stops to look at a large brass *ting* next to the moon gate. Four bodyguards, the American among them, stand under shadowed eaves running along the courtyard wall. Turning abruptly, Tang says to his nephew, 'Your father's now in Hong Kong?'

'Yes, uncle.'

'Convey to him my filial respect. I hope he's doing well.'

'That is my prayer too,' the young man says with mechanical piety.

'Aren't you sure?'

'Of what, uncle?'

'That he's doing well?' Sensing the young man's confusion, Tang persists. 'You seem unsure of your father's well-being. Isn't his business flourishing as usual?'

'Yes, uncle, of course, it is.'

'What business does he have in Hong Kong?'

Ping-ti starts to wave his hand, then drops it. 'Something or other. Forgive me, I'm not sure.'

No Chinese son is ignorant of his father's business, but Tang doesn't bother to make the explicit obvious. Instead he continues: 'This is a lovely house.'

'Thank you, uncle.'

Although the Japanese flour-mill owners may be wonderful to work for, Tang thinks, surely they don't subsidize houses like this for their Chinese compradors. Yen-chang must pay for it. The General halts and looks steadily at his nephew. 'I don't believe you told me about your father's business interests here. You're not sure about Hong Kong, but you must know about China.'

'Father doesn't confide in me, uncle.'

'Perhaps not, but you must be doing something for him or he wouldn't put such a house at your disposal.'

Ping-ti blinks rapidly. 'Father's most generous to an unworthy son.'

'Yen-chang is never generous. Road construction equipment.'

'Uncle?'

'Your father must be selling it to the Japanese.'

'Believe me, uncle –'

'Never mind.' Tang steps forward. 'It's a lovely house. Accept my profound thanks for allowing me to stay here while I'm in Jinan. Most generous, nephew. I'll try not to disturb your household.' He strides briskly through the courtyard, gathering his bodyguards on the way.

Catching the American's eye, he is seized by a strange idea: Perhaps this is the young man in the Yarrow Stalk prophecy. This American.

Or an American-trained nephew. At least he has learned from Yen-chang's son that the grip of the Japanese on the east and north of the province is even stronger than he expected. He knows, moreover, that the Japanese are willing to put utmost pressure on him to cooperate.

'Esteemed uncle!' Ping-ti calls from the courtyard.

Tang halts outside the gate and turns.

'Everything is at your disposal! My humble house is yours!' The shouted words convey a desperation rooted in poor judgment: Ping-ti is aware of reacting stupidly to his uncle's questions. It is too late to rectify the mistake. 'Everything, esteemed uncle, is at your disposal!'

Bowing curtly, the General turns to the waiting car. This is the bitter truth: His closest relatives, indeed, the only ones living, are aiding the enemy for profit. Has he come to Jinan, city of his boyhood and capital of the province he loves, simply to learn such terrible things? This interview, bad in itself, may be a harbinger of worse to come.

Shortly after sunset he arrives at the famous lake, Da Ming Hu. The shore is lit for its three-mile circumference with colored lights on lines hung from poles. Scores of invited guests – grain and salt merchants, Japanese officers, a few German business-men, bankers and industrialists from Tsingtao as well as Jinan – are seated already in the pavilions and teahouses, awaiting the pleasure boats that will carry them to little islands in the lake; banquet tables have been laid out there under the willows, their white linen visible from the shore. It will be a lavish gala, typical of Dog Meat.

The General has come here directly from Techow Arsenal. It employs seven hundred workers who use British and German machinery to make shell casings, grenades, ammo for small arms, and machine guns, all except the barrels, which are manufactured in Shanghai. The arsenal belongs to old Dog Meat, and the sight of so much weaponry frustrated Tang, whose troops lack rifles, let alone machine guns and grenades. He is in a black mood as he strolls alongside the lake with Yang, one bodyguard behind them.

Four elderly men in expensive gowns are playing mahjong by lantern light on a bench near a pavilion. Tang looks wistfully at them, envies their serene contemplation, their comfortable insignificance in a world of glitter and menace. Three men, approaching, wear bright smiles of false welcome. Halting to await them, Tang glances once more at the old men hunched over the mahjong board. Perhaps in the past they were active in the affairs of Jinan. Perhaps they knew his father, who served as a garrison commander here. But retired now, they seek the comfort of friendship on the lakeshore and pay no heed to the machinations of men bent on getting or holding power. It is a good end to life; he will be lucky to do as well.

One of the welcoming committee, bowing, introduces himself as Pao Yu-lin, 'Representative of his Excellency, the Governor General.'

What he is, as Tang knows well, is the brother of Dog Meat's favorite concubine. In Tsingtao he operates the drug traffic from the Pu Chi Hospital; for additional income, as if it were needed, he acts as director of the Wharf Administration, controlling trade – and bribes – for the entire province. Newly acquired wealth hasn't improved his appearance: tall, skinny, he has sloping shoulders and the hesitant gait of a drug addict. His obsequious welcome doesn't dispel the General's ill humor.

'We have anxiously awaited you, Excellency,' Pao exclaims, bobbing his head. He has sour breath, a hacking cough. He guides the General toward a boat waiting at a small jetty; a muscular oarsman, standing at the stern, braces himself with folded arms on the broad handle of a sweep oar.

'The Governor General awaits you on the *White Lotus*.' The skinny man coughs from deep within his chest. Tang suspects that he is tubercular. 'Eager to see you, Excellency. Honored by your presence. He is eager indeed.'

Tang turns, before getting into the boat, and looks at his aide. Yang has been singularly quiet all day. 'You look tired.'

'I'm fine, General.'

'You can go back now. Get some rest.' When Yang hesitates, the General says, 'That's an order.' It crosses his mind that the young aide has acted strangely since the General returned from White Wolf's camp. What happened to Yang during his absence? Did someone get to him, persuade him of something, put doubts in a youthful mind? Is Yang reliable?

These questions last the few seconds it takes the General to board the skiff.

Rhythmic splash of the oar. Drawing away from the jetty, Tang watches the lights throw a reflection upon the lake, like splinters of colored glass. Smoke in the air. Voices rising, falling like the easy motion of the boat. He concentrates on the look of things, the smoky smell, the sound of voices, while beside him the tubercular drug addict continues to express everyone's undying gratitude for his Excellency's presence.

Tang recalls something about this hacking toady, Pao. His sister, the concubine, has a reputation for intrigue and brutality. They call her Tzu Hsi, a nickname derived from the old Manchu Dowager Empress who held her emperor son captive in the Forbidden City and amused herself by having servants flayed to death. Perhaps the skinny fellow lives in fear of losing favor with his sister and therefore his income in Tsingtao; it may account for his nervousness, his terrible need to please.

Splash. Splash of the oar. Ahead, in the middle of the lake, resting placidly at anchor, is a large paddle-wheel steamboat with double stacks. It is a scaled-down model built a few years ago by a German company from designs of nineteenth-century Mississippi River steamers – a palace on wheels, old Dog Meat's pride, the *White Lotus*. The skiff reaches the gangplank; Tang climbs aboard. A number of Chinese officers, already drunk, stagger along the deck with giggling women on their arms.

'This way, Excellency. Please. If you will be so kind – this way, sir.' Pao beckons with a long, slim, feminine hand. 'Thank you, this way.' He gestures as if herding a wayward chicken back into the flock. Soon the General finds himself in an immense central lounge on the main deck. It reminds him of a lobby in an expensive Shanghai hotel: rugs, crystal chandeliers, hanging *chuan chou* of mountains and waterfalls. The floor is marble, the stanchions of wood painted a deep crimson. Waiters move among the potted plants carrying heavy trays. On a raised platform a Chinese orchestra is playing four-string moon guitars, flutes, large gongs, and circular drums. Western violins, trap drums, a trumpet, and a saxophone lie against the wall behind the musicians for later use.

A glass of wine is thrust into Tang's hand. The face smiling close to his, close enough for him to smell the bad breath, belongs to Pao, who keeps welcoming the General, eagerly.

A multitude of guests crowd into the great lounge. They lean against the gingerbread woodwork, curlicued and gilded, knobbed and flowered. They push and jostle for the trays of drinks. The women, even the foreigners, wear Chinese gowns, high collared, slit to the thigh. The men, both Chinese and foreign, are dressed in Western clothes or in uniforms. Among the officers there are many White Russians who have served Chang Tsung-ch'ang since the Revolution forced them from their homeland. Their uniforms are fancier than those of the Chinese; many of the foreigners wear plumed caps, gold piping, and massive epaulettes.

But no one can compete for finery with the tall fat man who now enters the salon. He seems to be a mountain of gold braid; a brightly colored sash a foot wide encircles his belly and rows of medals bedeck his chest. One white-gloved hand rests on the silver hilt of a ceremonial sword, while the other dispenses fistfuls of banknotes yanked from a trouser pocket. The money goes to the women who congregate around him, squealing in delight, reaching upward toward the pudgy hand held above his head.

Chang Tsung-ch'ang, Governor General of Shantung Province. Old Dog Meat. Born a coolie, migrated to Manchuria. After a stint there as a bandit, he joined Marshal Chang Tso-lin's army. Illiterate, stupid, vicious, but loyal. It has been his unbending loyalty to the Marshal that brought him along. Now he is first man in the province.

Bald, square-jawed, with a thick white drooping mustache, old Dog Meat towers above the crowd, surveying it now with an imperious gaze, while the women slink away with their loot. Seeing General Tang, he lets out a roar and shoves through the mob, which can't part fast enough. He embraces Tang in a bear hug. He smells of cloyingly sweet perfume and whisky, tobacco – and sweat, for his chubby face is bathed in it. Within minutes, after displaying utmost affection for General Tang in full view of the public, Dog Meat has maneuvered his guest into a drawing room off the salon.

There they sit at a table with cut-glass goblets, a decanter of whisky, a mahogany humidor, and heavy Sheffield cutlery beside a huge plate of sweetmeats. Tang looks around curiously: Upholstered Western furniture, hand-painted cuspidors, Persian rugs. He has been told that the *White Lotus* is worth a fortune; surely it is. They say the taxation of a million residents of Shantung over a ten-year period went to pay for it; that may also be true.

Refusing a cigar, Tang watches the huge man light one for himself.

'We won't talk seriously,' says Dog Meat, pouring himself a whisky. '*Gan bei*!' He gestures to the General and tosses it off. 'On a night like this we must follow the example of the ancients. Before battle they got drunk. After battle they got drunk.' He chortles and pours another whisky. There's a knock at the door; a tall pale man in a plain uniform enters. Without a word he sits down unobtrusively, behind Tang. Obviously a bodyguard, perhaps he's also an observer: Chang Tsung-ch'ang, already drunk, will need someone to tell him in the morning what happens tonight. 'Did you see my Russians out there?' he asks Tang. 'Darlings! No one's better at a bayonet charge. Once I had three thousand of them; that's been cut to a third. Their problem is they have no fear. Don't give a shit for their lives. Not like us, huh? But you should see them *charge* –' One gloved hand twists in air, as if thrusting a bayonet. 'You're too thin, General, too thin. One bad winter cold, you're finished. Have some of these.' He shoves the plate of sweetmeats forward. 'I survived more than one Manchurian winter without a warm coat. Know that?' He raises his glass. '*Gan bei*!'

'Who will be at the meeting tomorrow? My aide couldn't seem to find out today.'

'You and I. We'll be there. Are others necessary?' Dog Meat laughs and stuffs a cake into his mouth. His ears, flat against his skull, have an animal look: red, stiff, alert. But his eyes lack focus; they drift moodily in their bloodshot fields like clouds.

'Who else?' Tang asks patiently.

'Anyone who will come. How do I know? They say one thing, do another,' Dog Meat mutters silently. '*Gan bei*. Well, I know one you can expect. Chen Yun-ao. He's here tonight.'

Chen Yun-ao recently lost a battle to General Feng Yu-hsiang. Tang looks forward to a talk with the man who has that distinction.

Smoothing an end of his long white mustache, Dog Meat leans forward and pats Tang's knee. 'There are better things to discuss than a coward like Chen, who let that fucking bastard run him like a dog, right? I'm speaking of marriage. There! I said it plainly. Marriage.' Dog Meat belches and squints sidelong at the General. 'There are three things,' he begins, then pauses. 'There are three things.' He looks past the General to the man seated beyond. 'How in hell does it go?'

Quietly the man says, 'There are three things which are unfilial, and to have no posterity is the greatest of them.'

Dog Meat slaps his thigh. 'Confucius. The Master knew it all! Isn't that right? We must follow him all the way. Do you believe in the wisdom of Confucius?'.

'Yes,' Tang says with a faint smile, 'I do.' The quotation is from Mencius, not Confucius.

'So when are you going to remarry? I mean, playthings are

fine – I have about twenty myself – but a man needs legal sons for the future. Now listen to me.' Dog Meat leans forward: intense, ruddy, almost sober. 'I have a daughter. Unworthy of a distinguished man like yourself, naturally, naturally, but the girl's pretty enough and she'll bring a good dowry. You won't be disappointed.'

'I am deeply honored.'

'Well, then?' Chang Tsung-ch'ang tries to focus his bleary eyes. 'Is it settled?'

'An offer of such magnitude – it comes as a shock to someone as insignificant as myself.'

Waving off the traditional courtesy, Dog Meat laughs happily. 'Our families linked. Think of the consequences! What couldn't we do together, son-in-law!' He pours another drink. '*Gan bei*.'

Tang doesn't lift his own glass. 'I will give this exceptional offer the thought it deserves.'

'Good, fine, that's the way. Such a marriage is in everyone's interest.'

Someone else has used a similar phrase today: his nephew. It would be in everyone's interest if he kowtowed to the Japanese. He certainly has no intention of linking the name of Tang with such a creature as Chang Tsung-ch'ang. The marriage would give the scoundrel leave to demand loyalty from him on family as well as political grounds. A mad scheme, worthy of Dog Meat. Or did the idea originate elsewhere? Across the room, next to a Ching scroll, hangs a full-length portrait of Marshal Chang Tso-lin. He is Dog Meat's patron and adviser, the man who has just elevated Dog Meat to full command of the entire province. His thin, effete-looking body is draped in gold braid and medals and heavy epaulettes that seem to drag his narrow shoulders down. Above his small sallow face is a gaily plumed Austrian cap. The Manchurian Tiger. No one has survived the hardships of Chinese military life with more success than the Marshal, who has sired thirty-two legal children by nine wives. Has the idea of this misalliance come from that tiny, quiet, well-read, terrible old man?

'*Gan bei*,' insists Dog Meat, raising his glass again.

'*Gan bei*.' Tang drinks too.

'Then it's settled?'

'First I must find a way to repay such generosity,' Tang says, rising.

They exchange lavish farewells, with Dog Meat proposing one more *gan bei*.

No sooner has the General reentered the salon than a heavy-set Japanese in a Western business suit bows deeply to him. 'I am Fukuda Niwa. I have wanted to meet you for a long time, General Tang. I am overwhelmed by this good fortune.' He bows again.

His Chinese is good, Tang observes.

'Your nephew, Tang Ping-ti, is employed by a friend of mine. Your nephew has an outstanding future ahead of him.'

'That's good to hear. Thank you. Are you also in the flour business? Or in road construction?'

'I try to make a modest living as a banker.' On Fukuda's tie is a jade stickpin. 'These days it is difficult.' Frowning, he waves his hand for emphasis. 'There is insufficient trust for people to invest their money.'

Tang waits; obviously this man has more to say than that.

'General, I was on that train from Shanghai when the bandits attacked.'

'Please come outside,' Tang says crisply.

They go out on the deck of the *White Lotus*, where more skiffs are arriving with guests. The night air rings with laughter, with the sound of the orchestra – now playing Western fox-trots – and with distant gongs, probably from the opera on the south side of the lake.

'I will consider it a special favor, Mister Fukuda, if you tell me exactly what happened.'

Fukuda describes the ambush, the train halting, the bandits boarding the first-class carriage and rousting everyone out, including himself, some business associates, and a couple of Westerners. He was detained only a short time, then allowed to reembark.

'Your officers were less fortunate,' Fukuda declares with a little sigh of sympathy. He describes their deaths factually. 'I'm sure you wish to know they died like good men.'

'You are kind, Mister Fukuda. I welcome your words. Thank you.'

The Japanese bows but remains there at the rail; he seems reluctant to part from the General. Obviously there's more to come. While they watch the guests arrive alongside the steamer, Fukuda says with an apologetic dip of his head, 'Forgive me, General, but with your permission I have a question –'

'Of course, please ask it.'

Fukuda begins to stammer – deliberately – as a formal sign of his embarrassment. 'Rumors . . . you must be aware . . . Excellency, they sweep Jinan these days. It is rumored that the Financial Bureau in Qufu' – he does not say 'your army' – 'has issued new legal tender.' He pauses, glancing in the lantern light at the General. 'I'm merely inquiring if the rumor is verifiable. It's a matter of my poor curiosity. So sorry, General –'

'What you heard is nothing more than a rumor, Mister Fukuda. Such currency would not be legal.'

'Forgive my impertinent question,' Fukuda says, bowing with a smile.

When they separate, Tang has the distinct impression that the Japanese banker has been given the task of judging his worth. At their parting, Fukuda bows enthusiastically, as if things have gone well for the General. Perhaps the Japanese wish to approach him with a deal. Perhaps they prefer making it to a Chinese general more responsible than Dog Meat, although the old drunk has two outstanding assets: He is pliable and he is loyal. In assessing someone like Tang – he's fully aware of their difficulty – they must ask a crucial question: Can they ultimately control a general who is outspoken in his condemnation of foreign influence in China?

So the meeting was not accidental, but possibly an overture. He is wondering about it when a Chinese officer comes out of the darkness and grips the rail alongside him.

It is Chen Yun-ao, who lost the battle at Chengchow to General Feng Yu-hsiang.

'So here you are!' Chen exclaims with a broad smile. They exchange pleasantries and in the process Tang realizes that Chen is quite drunk. He has puffy cheeks, droopy eyelids, a small mouth hidden by a prodigious walrus mustache. Tang has known him for years, ever since their cadet days at Paoting Military Academy. Set in opposition to his observant eye and his intelligence is a tendency to complain and disparage. Tang likes him enough to wish it were otherwise.

Surrounded by gaiety, as the evening moves toward gluttony and license, on the deck of a Mississippi paddle-wheeler, the generals speak of warfare. Bluntly Tang begins it. 'I hope you'll forgive me, old friend, but what really happened at Chengchow?'

'What happened? I lost, that's what happened. I had one infantry brigade, one artillery regiment. Feng brought a whole army corps. I was outnumbered five to one.'

Tang nods politely, not altogether convinced of the numbers.

'He had trench mortars too. And three armored cars brought in by rail flats. My planes –'

'You had planes?' Tang is both surprised and jealous. Chen had planes? Does every warlord have planes these days except himself? 'What planes?'

'Only two Brequets.'

Obtained probably from Marshal Chang Tso-lin. The Manchurian Tiger has a habit of lending planes to anyone confronting Feng on the field of battle.

'They didn't do much,' Chen declares grimly. 'Fourteen-pound bombs aren't big enough to do much damage on trains unless they make a direct hit. And they flew too damn high, and they bombed while flying across the target at right angles. At *right angles*. Can you believe it?' His voice, slurred from drink, rises to a whining pitch. 'Then the young officers you get these days. Are yours like mine? Worthless except on the parade ground. I told them to create a trench system, but not one of the fucking roosters had the sense to go out and supervise.'

'You were digging rifle pits?'

'Well, it was all I could do,' Chen replies defensively. 'My troops were exhausted after a forced march.'

Tang suspects the explanation is an excuse. Following French theory, which Chen has always stubbornly preferred, he probably chose to fight a positional battle from trenches. For flat terrain like North China, Tang has followed the German solution: constant movement. He and Chen have never agreed on tactics.

'Then the sonofabitch used firecrackers.'

Tang laughs, but in fact likes the idea. It's one more indication that Feng makes a formidable adversary. Firecrackers: an excellent diversion.

'The firecrackers didn't fool me a minute,' Chen maintains gloomily, leaning both elbows on the ship's rail. 'But then he sent in dare-to-die units. They came yelling and waving their arms like African savages. Do you have a flask on you, Shan-teh?'

Tang shakes his head.

'Now about you.' Chen is grinning, his mouth barely visible under the huge mustache. 'What in hell is this about you and that bandit? I didn't believe the report. You led a company into Shansi because he killed an officer of yours?'

'Yes, I took his head.'

Chen laughs. 'Madness. You go bandit hunting while all of China is collapsing around us.'

'So you think China is collapsing.'

'Of course. And has been for three hundred years, ever since the Ming.' Chen passes one finger across the bushy mustache – he's that rare Chinese: hirsute as a Westerner. 'I need a drink. If Dog Meat is serving, I'm drinking. I've done enough fighting for a while.'

'Now that you've fought Feng, what do you think of him?'

Chen shrugs dismissively. 'He has a lot of Russian equipment that he got when he was close with Moscow. He's got those damn firecrackers. And he's got the dare-to-die units. Before battle he tells them they'll be tortured if captured and the fools believe him.'

'Well, sometimes it happens,' Tang acknowledges.

'Only to officers! What does anyone want with a peasant who's been tortured? What good is he? But Feng convinces them of anything, works them into a frenzy. They call him the Christian General because once he professed that stuff. I consider him a Taoist rabblerouser. Next he'll be using magic.' Chen shakes his head sadly.

'What do you think of Chiang Kai-shek? I understand Feng thinks highly of him.'

'Forget Chiang. The man to watch is Feng, even if he's a poor soldier. Wait a moment –' He reaches out for a girl who is passing down the deck holding a glass. Chen grips her arm. 'Beautiful lady, a sip, please?'

Staring at the medals on his chest, the girl purrs, 'Have it all, Excellency. I am honored.'

Tang takes this opportunity to slip away. He boards an outgoing skiff for shore. He has no desire to remain on the *White Lotus* into the early hours. For that matter, he wants to get clear of Da Ming Hu altogether. Before morning the entire lake front, every pavilion and teahouse, every island within its borders, will be strewn with stunned revelers, satiated on the monstrous hospitality of a governor general whose first official act was to behead a high judge who condemned him long ago for illegally seizing a rival's estate – a judge who had once played in the streets of Jinan with Tang Shan-teh when they were boys.

The bodyguard is waiting onshore. The General walks with him through the lakeside park, along cobbled paths under graceful willows, beyond Bai Ji Miao, a dramatic temple with a triple flight of stairs leading to its smoky altar – neglected tonight. The General reaches the main street, where his driver is asleep on the front seat of the Dodge.

Calling sharply, Tang wakens him and orders him and the bodyguard back to Ping-ti's residence.

'But, Excellency.' The young driver glances around in bewilderment. 'What will you do?'

'Even a general can hail a rickshaw. Go back, but first stop at a restaurant.' Tang gives each man a few taels. Speechless – generals are not supposed to indulge in such acts of generosity – the two drive away, leaving Tang in a crowded street. He is near the old extermination sheds for cattle and goats. He remembers them from childhood: beasts shuffling beneath the tin roofs to have their throats cut; the pungent, sickly-sweet odor of blood; the shrieks of final pain; the growing nervousness of animals nearing the door of death. In his drab uniform without medal or insignia, Tang is jostled by passersby who don't recognize in his powerful but plainly dressed figure the eminence of a general. He approaches one of four theaters in the district; he almost goes in, hearing the exciting whine of guitars plucked in unison. The bill advertises *The Monkey King*, one of his favorite operas, but a certain feeling of restlessness leads him farther into the maze of streets.

'Hello, Captain.' A girl in a dress slit to the hipbone calls from an open doorway. She has a small mouth, red and puckered. 'Goodbye, Captain. I had a wonderful time.'

Colored lanterns hang at the entrance of each brothel on the narrow lane. Girls in open windows smile or call or whistle softly as the General strolls by. The air pulsates with sound: the clicking of mahjong pieces, a thrummed guitar, the distant crash of porcelain, laughter, a voice raised in bawdy song.

Ahead, to his right, an elderly woman is bowing like a wound-up doll, her wrinkled face smiling brilliantly. For an instant he thinks of the grandmother and her smile when she said of her granddaughter, 'Yes, I remember her.'

'Soldier. Officer. I've been waiting for you, and here you finally are!'

Tang halts and looks at her with amusement. 'Has it been a long wait?'

Wiping both hands on a gown stretched tight across her paunch, the old woman laughs. 'Sure it has. I knew you were finally coming when my nose felt ticklish.'

'Is that how you conduct business? Through your nose?'

'This is no time for foolishness,' she tells him with a reproving frown. 'I have something here you've never tried before. A pretty flower from Soochow.'

Hands on his hips, Tang returns her frown. 'Then we won't have foolishness. But the truth is, I've tried more than one flower from Soochow.'

'Sir, there are flowers and there are flowers. Come in quickly. Don't lose your chance.'

Perhaps her outrageous familiarity is what decides him. Tang steps into the house. Its garishly striped walls – reds, golds, blues – are lit up by oil lamps. Three girls sit impassively on a bench. A serving girl comes in with a tea tray and sets it on a table. The old woman, pouring him a cup, brays at the General, 'Now I'm going to test you, sir! This is the Imperial Examination of the old days. Remember that? Men studied for years, then failed. Fortunes were made and lost on the ability to remember a phrase from the Classics. Yes, indeed. The Examinations – those were the days! Now here is your own test, sir. Which of these girls is from Soochow?'

Tang understands that whoever he chooses will claim to be from Soochow, so for perversity's sake he picks the least attractive of the three unsmiling girls.

Cackling, the old woman says, 'Now I believe you know the flowers of Soochow, because you have just picked one. That's the one!'

'A rare flower,' he says wryly.

'That's what I told you, didn't I? A rare flower.' Plucking him boldly by the sleeve, she draws him aside in a pretense of delicacy. 'Be gentle with her, sir,' the old woman whispers. 'She's new.'

'New?' It's difficult to determine the girl's age – perhaps fatigue and depression make her look older. But she is not new.

'Completely new, sir. Well –' She pauses, studying Tang. He realizes she's judging his interest in a maidenhead, therefore her insistence on the girl's youth. 'Not completely new,' she finally says, 'but not broken in, sir. Fresh.'

'And from Soochow.'

'Of course, from Soochow. You're a fine man, a man of taste.' The old woman's breath is surprisingly sweet – it smells of spice, perhaps from Szechuan. Perhaps she had been lovely in her youth, as grandmother must have been too. Lovely women, better than anyone from Soochow.

Leaning close, the old woman whispers the price, continuing the pretense of delicacy.

Shrugging, Tang gives her the money. Soon he is following the girl from Soochow upstairs. What is he doing? Lust hasn't prompted him to undertake this little adventure. Nothing has led him to this moment but accidental circumstance. The freedom of his action makes him feel wonderfully alive, especially after the lake and the *White Lotus* and Dog Meat and defeated Chen and all the false gaiety – the rotten tooth behind the smile. Having escaped the predictable orgy of Da Ming Hu, he has given himself to the streets of Jinan, much as he had done as a very young man. Without desire and yet with enthusiasm, he climbs the stairs, watching the slippers of the girl flash.

The room is surprisingly attractive: a smoothly made bed with clean sheets, a small filigreed table set with a wine jar and two earthenware cups, a few sweetcakes protected from flies by a linen cloth. On a hanging scroll are the large inked words: THE CHRYSANTHEMUM IN AUTUMN AND THE PEACH IN SPRING. A delicate touch. Could it have come from the old madam downstairs? A remnant of a better life, perhaps in Szechuan?

'Who put this here?' he asks, turning to the girl, who has slumped down at the table.

She's wearing a purple sheath, fastened at the collar around a slim, graceful neck. Not pretty though. Her face is as full as a melon. Her eyebrows, plucked, have been crudely penciled in; her mouth is small, withholding.

Tang repeats his question. 'Who put the scroll here?'

'The scroll?' She seems to awaken from a dream. 'Do you want a cup of wine, sir?'

Shaking his head, Tang sits opposite her at the table.

'May I have one, sir?'

'Of course. And cake too. As much as you wish.'

The girl, pouring wine, tosses it off.

Tang is not sure of staying. Coming here was perhaps a foolish thing to do, worthy indeed of the young man he had been twenty years ago.

'Would you care to play cards, sir? Do you want me to do magic tricks?'

'So you do magic tricks. Did you learn them in Soochow?' he asks with a hint of sarcasm.

'Yes, sir.'

'None tonight, thank you.'

'What do you wish? Shall I sing?'

'Yes, please. Do that.'

Without hesitation the girl pushes back her chair, folds her hands, and in a thin, reedy voice sings an old ballad with tremulous, startling conviction.

When she finishes, Tang smiles approvingly. 'I know that song. It's lovely.'

Flushing, the girl asks if he would like another. At his agreeable nod, she sings another and another. Pausing afterward, the girl murmurs thoughtfully, 'Sir, I believe you are an important officer.'

'Do you?' Tang smiles. 'Why?'

'Because you're old enough to be and you like the sad songs.' Lowering her eyes a moment, the girl looks up again with a new light in her eyes. The lethargy has gone. It's as if the singing has restored her will to live. 'Do you want another song?' She glances quickly at the bed, then at him, her hands still folded in her lap. Her delicacy surprises and excites the General. He wants her now.

'Perhaps you will honor me with a song later.'

Rising, the girl removes the sheath dress with confident, professional hands. Underneath is a silk chemise which clings to her body, emphasizing its contours. Tang is startled by the plump softness of the girl, as if the rind of a succulent fruit has been peeled off. The contrast between the metallic look of the sheath and this clinging chemise enhances his desire. He removes his clothes.

'Permit me?' she asks in a low voice. Tang understands she wishes to control what will happen, so, at her gesture, he kneels dutifully on the bed. She places a pillow under each of his knees, to make him higher off the bed, and then without hurry or hesitation she removes her chemise, assuring him by her graceful action of a competence to take charge.

'Something special for you,' she tells him with a smile. Lying down on her back, with her head directly beneath him where he kneels, the girl slowly raises her legs, knees far apart, until her toes touch the bed on either side of him, her body having flexed into the shape of a bow drawn to its extremity. In this position she offers herself for maximum penetration. He maneuvers slightly on his knees to place himself at her dark center, then enters with a single thrust, but gently enough to elicit from her only a sigh. After moving pleasantly a few minutes, he feels the girl grip his ankles with both hands, giving her purchase, so she can raise her head from under him to his scrotum. Her tongue begins licking, curving around each testicle. Aware that he is near, she engulfs each sac in turn with her wet mouth, pulling slightly to create tension, and he disgorges: Mind and body, like streams running from hill to plain, empty into sweet oblivion.

The oblivion is brief, however, and he comes back to himself. Stretching out on the bed, he watches the girl take a towel and rub from her belly the glistening sweat and from her thighs the rivulet of seed. Pausing, she gives him a friendly smile, as if to assure him they have both done as they should and, for her own part, she is content.

As they lie side by side in darkness, the General takes her hand and puts it gently against his cheek. 'I believe you really are from Soochow.'

Turning, the girl stares at him. They are bathed in moonlight. In the distance, perhaps from a late theater, a flute wails, its sound like smoke rising. 'Why do you believe I'm from Soochow?'

'What you did is a specialty of Soochow. At least a girl I knew once claimed so.'

'She told the truth. When my father died, I was sold to a house. I was still young and limber enough to learn it. They taught me how to bend around like that before a man ever had me. I practiced for months, but they waited until I was ready. And the house didn't lose money on me. Did you really like it?'

'It was a wonderful thing.'

'It was nothing, sir. My pleasure.'

Letting go of the girl's hand, Tang looks at the dark ceiling. 'I have always loved the city of Soochow.'

'Its gardens?' the girl asks quickly.

'Especially its gardens.' The girl can't know, of course, but the General's private dream is to retire someday and build a modest replica of a Soochow garden: a small, plain house but laid out to catch at every window and door a certain vista; a pond choked with lotus in the summer; an artificial hillock placed to suggest a mountain in the distance; perhaps too a coppice of scented trees; and even a few boulders washed and eroded by the celebrated waters of Lake Tai Hu. The dream of a lunatic – he hasn't the wealth to buy a single boulder from Lake Tai Hu, much less the funds to have it transported from there.

'My father was a caretaker at the Garden of the Forest of Lions,' the girl says, pride in her voice. 'I'm used to beautiful things.' She begins to whisper, as memory moves to the center of her mind. 'I went there every day as a child. It was allowed because of my father. I remember it all. The Hall of the Spreading Cloud. The lake with its stone boat and the island with the Eight-sided Pavilion. Trees along the east side of it. There's a narrow gallery running from it that connects with the Pavilion of Gentle Perfume and the Kiosk Where the Plum Tree Is Asked Questions. Beyond that, the Hall of the Two Scented Immortals.' Her voice fades, vanishes.

And for Tang she too fades, vanishes, although he cradles her head in his arm until she falls asleep. Her presence, he realizes sadly, has been illusionary in his life. He paid for release, got it, and that is all. For some moments he had felt a warmth experienced with his second wife. Is he getting old? The girl said he was old enough to be 'an important officer.' But for an instant he almost believed that he had found something more than purchased love.

Gently removing his arm, he turns toward the moonlit window. He can't see the moon, only its rays, like sea waves in a dream. It has been a long day, a disturbing day: the grandmother living in fear of Manchu Bannermen; his devious nephew hoping to profit from Japanese ambitions; Dog Meat lavishing the wealth of a province on an ephemeral evening; Chen, depressed and complaining, no longer a man of consequence; and this girl who cannot really exist for him or even for herself, except as a child who once strolled through a garden of the Sung.

He must think of tomorrow. He can't think of it, the convoluted intrigue. He thinks instead of an eighth-century poet, the great Tu Fu, who suffered exile and years of ill health, yet in the spirit of Confucius served the empire faithfully as official and poet. What really did Tu Fu feel? Neglected in his lifetime, he came to mastery of his craft with little encouragement. What had such a man of commitment really felt?

Lines tumble through Tang's mind in the few moments before sleep:

> *Floating, floating, what am I?*
> *Between earth and sky,*
> *I am a sea bird alone.*

11

South of Jinan, overlooking the plain of the Yellow River, lies Thousand Buddha Mountain in the Li Shan foothills. Leaving his Dodge Tourer at the bottom of the mountain, General Tang begins the long climb to the ancient temple, site of the conference, midway to the summit. He is accompanied by Yang and four bodyguards, three wearing the traditional execution sword and the fourth carrying an ax.

This July day, its air thick with heat, has the feel of deep summer. Insects buzz furiously. Paired-wing fruit is whirling off maple branches like so many propellers detached from toy airplanes. When a breeze sends a squadron of them his way, young Yang swats angrily. He has been in a grim mood since the General's return at dawn. When the rickshaw came into view, Yang let out a small cry at the gate, where he was restlessly pacing, and sent off a servant to rouse the nephew. The General had hardly dismounted from the rickshaw when Ping-ti was hurrying through the courtyard, rubbing his eyes and muttering 'profound relief' for his esteemed uncle's safe return.

'Last night at the gala,' Ping-ti exclaimed, 'I was troubled by your disappearance.'

The General couldn't remember seeing his nephew there. But obviously Ping-ti, who had left early for the lake, must have been aboard the *White Lotus* and from some vantage point observed him.

In the dawn mist, facing his nephew and his aide, the General was amused rather than annoyed. Their stern faces summoned in him a feeling long since forgotten – that of a child caught at mischief. The two young men, extravagant in their disapproval, struck him at the time as well intentioned and foolish. To his nephew the General might have said, 'After four years in America, you are still Chinese enough to worry about the proprieties? And at a party given by Dog Meat?' Instead he merely brushed past the two frowning young men and went into the house.

Climbing the footpath of Thousand Buddha Mountain, however, he is distinctly annoyed by Yang's sustained petulance. He wonders if Yang is bothered by the hard climb in the heat. But must a young soldier behave like an old scholar whose only exercise is turning pages of a book? Yang entered the General's service a year ago with excellent credentials, including a full stint at Paoting Military Academy, Tang's own school, and three years of administrative work in the Ministry of War in Peking. Tang had felt honored by Yang's decision to join him, but now, watching the young fellow struggle up the mountainside, swatting at winged fruit and brooding over a general's small act of freedom, doubts about his competence seem appropriate. Tang means to watch him.

Becoming steeper, the path winds through a grove of larches, and even within its shady confines his small party begins to sweat. At a sharp turn in the path they come upon another group of climbers, who are resting on stone benches. Three men rise respectfully at Tang's approach, the fourth remains seated.

This fourth man is Jen Ching-i, an old militarist of his father's generation. Old, but still active – and dangerous.

Tang is surprised that General Jen has come to this conference; it's a good distance from Hopei Province, northwest of Shantung. If Jen has come, perhaps the conference is in fact important. Jen rarely ventures from his stronghold any more, except to protect his territory from the encroachment of other warlords or to whip back in line any landlords or local officials who delay sending him tribute. Jen is a man with one foot still planted in the Manchu world of the past century. Bowing to the fat old general who squints up at him from the bench, Tang is reminded of the grandmother warning him yesterday of Bannermen.

Jen Ching-i's greeting is curt, bordering upon contempt; any general under sixty years of age he considers no more than a boy, an upstart. His own army apprenticeship was served under Yuan Shih-k'ai, the scheming president of the Republic against whom Tang's father had plotted. If old Jen remembers the extermination of Tang's clan because of that plot, he has never shown it. As they now begin to climb the path together, Tang suspects there is little room for memory in a life of such extreme violence. And shouldn't be. In any case, Tang harbors no malice against the old general, who was not responsible, although quite possibly as a division commander in those days he might well have detached a unit to track down and massacre some of the fleeing Tangs. Emotion expended in that sort of grudge is wasted. Tang knows that; and his father had often told him the same. At the moment General Jen is in firm alliance with Marshal Chang Tso-lin –between them there are eighty long years of soldiering – but the Hopei general, notorious for quick and treacherous shifts of loyalty, may well change camps tomorrow. Puffing up the footpath, the old man mops his fat, sweaty cheeks with a silk handkerchief and describes his perception of the current military situation. 'It's delicate, very delicate. Now this boy from the South, Chiang Kai-shek, has put his nose where it doesn't belong. What we must do is cut it off. That is, if you young fellows have the guts, which I doubt.' Halting at intervals to catch his breath, Jen continues to berate the poor leadership of every northern general except Marshal Chang and himself. His thick legs in knee-high cavalry boots finally get him to a clearing, beyond which, on the edge of the mountain, sits the first of two temples.

Followed by their entourages, Tang and Jen descend a short flight of steps into a courtyard facing the temple. Two bronze Ming lions guard the central bay. Saffron-robed, tonsured priests stand nearby to accept homage from the generals, who bow low.

'*Nan mo a mi to fo fuh*,' Jen mutters mechanically. He tosses spirit money into a brazier on a pedestal just inside the temple entrance. Then, taking from a priest an offered joss stick, already lit, he sticks it deep into the ashes of a huge porcelain urn. This temple houses a bronze statue of the God of War. It is said that the great warrior Kuan Yu – made the god Kuan Ti by the decree of a Ming emperor – became a Buddhist only after his death. He is now enthroned in a niche, wears a flowing imperial yellow robe, and holds an oblong tablet of authority.

This Devil Queller of the Three Worlds glares down fiercely on the fat old general, who mutters another short prayer and steps back, impatiently waiting for Tang, who takes longer in his obeisance here than at the temple entrance. Tang says no prayer, however, either here or at the urn; he pays silent and profound homage, for to him Kuan Yu represents the spirit of his own father, who also gave his life, as Kuan Yu did, for a cause. Staring at the angry visage of the bronze statue, Tang closes his eyes and conjures the image of a man slimmer and shorter than himself, whose bearing, however, is unmistakably martial and dominant: small chin, thin lips, wide cheekbones, flat nose elegantly flared, large, commanding eyes. A man, a soldier, a father who had tried to live by the values of a proud clan and in the attempt had destroyed it. Tang blinks away the memory and turns to the old general, who regards him quizzically.

'Behold Amitabha with all His saints appearing before you,'

General Jen recites rapidly. 'That's what will happen when you die – you see Amitabha and all his saints – if you repeat *Mi-to Mi-to Mi-to* endlessly. Strange I remember now.' The two generals turn and walk away from the temple. 'The Word is the Precious Sword that cuts down evil. I remember that too. Well, I suppose it's a good omen.'

Tang glances over his shoulder at the temple. In *The Three Kingdoms* Kuan Yu loses his head because of misjudging the loyalty of other men. It is something to remember this day.

As he and General Jen ascend a flight of steps toward the second temple on the mountain, Tang hears a bell ring behind them. The sound resonates above the treetops; it booms across a plain checkerboarded with ripening fields of barley and wheat. He absorbs the breathtaking view while General Jen grumbles about the inconvenience of holding a conference in such an inaccessible place.

'But that's Dog Meat for you,' he pants. 'He's even fatter than I am. How will they ever get him up the path? By elephant?' Imagining the scene, Jen cackles and wipes his face. 'When I die they will say of Jen Ching-i, "He was a man who ate the rice of one family only." ' He stares at Tang as they climb. 'Whose rice do you eat, young man?'

'My own.'

'I hear otherwise. I hear you eat the rice of Feng as well as the Marshal. And who knows? Maybe the rice of that southern upstart.'

'I think your Excellency knows better.'

'These days who knows anything? The situation is delicate.' Having made this rough sally against Tang, the old militarist seems happy with himself. It's easy to discount Jen, but only an innocent would do it. The old general has learned well the use of banality, how it can mask serious intent. Tang won't succumb to the temptation of considering Jen a fool.

The second temple is now visible: its lovely double roof of yellow tiles and ornately carved bays. Rising behind it is a steep wall of rock, honey-combed with hundreds of stone carvings, the sculpture of centuries ago. The two generals, halting before it, stare without comment. Even Jen seems moved by the sight of Buddhas and lohans and bodhisattvas appearing in the side of this mountain like spirits from another world. They have been here for fifteen hundred years, through the rain and snow of time, lifting their hands in the mudra HAVE NO FEAR, as witnesses of an inner paradise, deeper than stone, more amorphous than the clouds passing above them.

General Tang Shan-teh, Defense Commissioner of Southern Shantung Province, abruptly desires nothing more in life than to remain here in their presence, alone on the mountain, playing Tai Chi Chuan at dawn and dusk, existing on rice gruel and spring water, perhaps with time even hearing the god sounds fill his mind as they are said to fill the minds of hermits from time immemorial. But the brief reverie is broken by a cry of welcome.

A tall, thin officer comes rushing down the flight of stairs, arms outspread. Old Jen takes his embrace with disdain, turning away upon release. Tang is also surprised by such an effusive greeting from a man he hardly knows.

The tall man squints at the gallery of carvings. 'They were done in the Northern Wei period. But you know that,' he adds with an apologetic smile. Again he turns to view the massive wall of sculptures arranged above like a heavenly choir. 'This is the first time for me. My father would have loved to see them. He was devout,' the officer says in a low voice, as if the Buddhas bring his father into memory.

Tang understands, having felt the same way at the temple of Kuan Yu about his own father. He feels an instant bond with General Chu Jui, who speaks with the accent of Chekiang.

Old Jen has put his hands on his hips, as if giving orders to subordinates. 'Tell me, Chu Jui, what happened? How did Chiang Kai-shek defeat you?'

Taking off his officer's cap, Chu Jui scratches his head; it is shaven. He does not give Jen the courtesy of a look, but continues to survey the ranked Buddhas. 'I was not defeated, General. I retired from a military career before Chiang came into my province.' Now he looks at Jen. 'I had entered a monastery before Chiang ever set foot in Chekiang.'

'But you left it soon enough, didn't you?' Jen, patting his belly, guffaws.

'I left it because of the crisis our country's in.'

'Well, don't worry about it. Such retirement is traditional. If things go wrong, retire. Say your beads in a monastery, but keep one ear on the news. I did the same thing back in 1919. Sooner or later we all do it.' Jen has put two upstarts in their place and himself in a fine humor. Accompanying the younger generals up the final flight of stairs, he has a broad smile on his sweaty face.

The upper temple is larger than the one dedicated to Kuan Ti but is also built on the edge of the mountain. From its back windows there is a panoramic view of the Jinan plain and from its front windows can be seen another pantheon of sculpted gods, this one smaller but imbued with the same unearthly presence. Waiting in the courtyard for the three generals are a score of officers, perhaps half a dozen of them Japanese. There are formal greetings, bowing, smiling. Gloves look spanking white in the sunlit air, and the black bills of caps glisten. The Japanese are dressed more plainly than the Chinese officers; the latter, if they are majors and colonels, wear medals and epaulettes. The three generals alone wear holsters on their Sam Browne belts.

Chang Tsung-ch'ang is not yet here, nor Chen Yun-ao, whom Tang had last seen making a drunken overture to a girl on the *White Lotus*. But someone unfamiliar to General Tang has arrived. He is a colonel, the deputy of Marshal Chang Tso-lin – therefore the spokesman for the most powerful militarist, not only here, but in all of China. Deputy Wei looks remarkably like a young Marshal Chang Tso-lin: small, almost tiny, with sloping shoulders and a frail bearing, an ascetic face, lean and smooth, and a pencil-thin mustache under a pointed nose and very slanted eyes.

Clearly, fat old Jen from Hopei feels that the deputy is the only important member of the conference. He showers young Colonel Wei with compliments and calls the Marshal 'the august hope and salvation of our land.'

The assembled officers stroll toward the temple, although two major participants are still missing. The temple has been arranged for the conference: three long tables set end to end in the high-ceilinged hall. The Goddess of Mercy, Kuan Yin, a lovely work of gilded bronze, sits unobtrusively on a back altar, protected by two fierce wooden guards with swords in hand. Incense lends a pungency to the hot, motionless air of the temple. Sweating profusely, the officers group near the open bays, squinting often into the courtyard for a sign of their host, the Governor General of Shantung.

In conversation with Chu Jui, who is genial and responsive, Tang learns a number of things. For example, the British withheld aid, both military and economic, from warlords opposing Chiang Kai-shek's Northern Expedition, thus allowing the southerner to push forward unopposed in some instances or with little resistance. It is suspected that Chiang promised the British preferential treatment in the traditional ways: government contracts, shipping licenses, manufacturing sites. Tang also learns that Chiang's cavalry is inferior; that the troops of Hunan are unruly but extremely brave.

Barging into this conversation, old Jen says ruefully, 'We each had his own territory in the old days. Each respected the other's boundaries. Of course, there were squabbles, but they were settled easily enough. What, after all, was a battle then?' He spreads his pudgy fingers wide. 'You lost a few hundred men. Today you might lose five thousand in a single day.' Jen shakes his head sadly at the injustice of it. 'Now you take this upstart from the South. He isn't interested in coexistence. Chiang Kai-shek wants it all. He wants surrender.' Slyly he glances at Chu Jui. 'Or he'll take collaboration on his terms. Which do you prefer, young man? Whose rice do you eat?'

Chu Jui looks away, unable to mask his annoyance.

Obviously the two men do not get along – and Tang makes note of it. Old Jen is goading the general from Chekiang too hard, suggesting that he knows more about Chu Jui than is apparent. Taking this cue, Tang decides to watch Chu Jui more carefully.

A chorus of welcome rises from the temple bays, promising the arrival of the host.

But it isn't the host. It is Chen Yun-ao, the other missing participant, who enters the temple looking pale from last night's orgy, his whole face sagging, as if pulled down by the weight of his enormous mustache. Along with him is Chang Tsung-ch'ang's deputy, who brings word that the Governor General regrets the circumstances which prevent his attending the meeting.

Did old Dog Meat carouse so deeply last night that he can't get out of bed? Tang wonders. Or has he another reason for missing the conference? He is brutal and ignorant, but sometimes Dog Meat shows the cunning of a hunted animal. Tang glances around uneasily – this is a bad omen.

The deputy, a civil administrator named Ma Liang, assures the assembly that the Governor General will attend the afternoon session.

And so it begins.

Senior officers sit at the table; junior officers range themselves along the temple walls with the generals' bodyguards.

Ma Liang reads a prepared speech ostensibly written by the Governor General, although it is common knowledge that he can't write more than his signature. The speech lasts an hour. It is a paean of generalities concerning the Middle Kingdom – the greatness of China and its destiny, the latter vaguely associated by tenuous logic with this very conference. Apparently the brilliant minds here today will lead China to victory over the forces of evil.

The hot close room is a sea of bamboo fans stirring the heavy air sweet from incense. Waiters from the Jinan officers' mess replenish teacups and empty ashtrays. A dragonfly, among the last of the season, lights on Kuan Yin's bronze nose.

The morning limps along, getting hotter, affording little more than hollow rhetoric about patriotism and loyalty from a succession of young officers attached to the Governor General's staff. Tang notices two Japanese exchange glances when one of the young men declares in a blustery tone that the best soldiers in the world come from the province of Shantung.

Abruptly, old Jen interrupts the proceedings to demand time to stretch a bit outside and cool off. Ma Liang agrees to the break, although plainly he considers the sensible request an encroachment on his authority. People begin filing out of the hall. Tang, motioning to his bodyguards, rises and turns, but Ma Liang, waving at him, calls out: 'Excellency! A moment please!'

'Get out of here!' It is the blond American rushing toward the General.

Tang glances at Ma Liang, gesturing from the table, just as something hurtles through the air – the American – and knocks him off his feet, out through an open bay just seconds before the whole temple seems to rise off its foundation and with a tremendous roar surge over him like a tidal wave. Lying on the pebbles of the courtyard, he hears a ringing in his ears, as if a thousand temple bells had been set to clanging. Someone is sprawled over him, cheek to cheek – the American.

The acrid smell of burned chemical fills his nostrils. Through his smarting eyes Tang sees timber from the building spread out on the ground, scattered haphazardly among the bodies of officers who, like himself, lie just outside the temple. The American rolls off his body and sits up, breathing hard. Tang sits up too, hearing from within the shattered temple the dull thump of a rafter falling to the floor; then a cough; then a moan rising into a shriek of pain.

'You,' Tang begins, staring dully at the American, whose face, like his own, is covered with dust.

Philip Embree looks toward the temple bays; smoke billows, rolling out of them like a thick gray ocean wave. 'I saw him. Struck a match.'

The General shakes his head to clear the ringing in his ears.

'Fuse ran under a canvas.' The American spits dirt. 'In the corner over there.' Slowly raising his hand, he points toward the last bay.

Someone staggers from the temple, a Japanese officer holding his empty left sleeve. A few strands of flesh dangle from the shredded, bloody cloth. His face, evincing no pain yet, has the masklike stare of extreme shock.

The men in the courtyard, already there or blown out of the temple, are struggling to their feet. Both Tang and Embree rise too. 'Come,' Tang says, and they move, shaky from the explosion, toward the bombed temple. Standing in one of the bays, they can see the destruction: tables, splintered into countless small projectiles, have been hurled throughout the hall; some of the dozen casualties were probably killed by the flying wood, others by the trinitrotoluol, whose blast stripped every wall and demolished the altar, although Kuan Yin, lying face down in a pool of human blood, seems intact.

'Which one?' Tang asks thickly, looking at the bodies strewn across the floor.

Embree frowns, then understands, and helps the General search. Turning over a body near the central bay, Embree stares at the face of a waiter and says, 'This one. He did it.'

The General briefly studies a boy who seems fresh and calm above the neck; he is blown apart below.

'He didn't get out,' says Embree, 'because the fuse was too short.'

'We invented gunpowder,' says the General, 'but we don't always handle it well.' He moves among the bodies until he comes to one he knows – that of Chen Yun-ao. The dead general's head is untouched (pale cheeks, walrus mustache), save for a shaft of table wood projecting from the base of his skull. Old classmate, Tang says to himself.

Shuffling up is Chu Jui, looking rumpled but otherwise all right. 'Who did it, Shan-teh?'

Tang points to the dead young waiter. 'My man says so.'

'That child?'

Tang shrugs. 'I imagine with considerable help,' he comments sardonically and looks across the devastation: ripped wall scrolls, cotton uniforms, blood and flesh, dented gongs, shattered teacups, paper.

'Was this waiter from the officers' mess?' Chu Jui asks.

'We'll find out.' But such an inquiry, both generals know, will prove little. Waiters in a mess come and go; usually recruits or wandering coolies, they aren't regulars, attached to units.

'Ma Liang, that assistant sent by Dog Meat? He's dead,' Chu Jui reports, nodding toward the end of one upturned table.

'What does that prove?' Tang asks.

'That he didn't know it was going to happen. And maybe that Dog Meat didn't know either.'

'Or Dog Meat wants it to look that way.'

They hear a wounded man begin to scream in quick gusts, eerie in the vaulted temple.

'Where is Jen?' Tang asks suddenly.

'Halfway down the mountain by now,' Chu Jui says with a bitter smile. 'He was in the courtyard when it went off. I saw him get up and waddle away with his bodyguards trying to keep pace. How can such a fat man move so fast? But then "fear lends a man wings." Who wrote that?'

Tang looks at the tall man with the shaven head – his cap was blown away in the blast. Chu Jui seems unperturbed, not even tense. This is a man in control of himself. 'Who was the target?' asks Tang, looking across the smoky room. The hot summer air carries the stench of explosion into the courtyard where the two generals now stand.

'It could have been you or Jen or Chen Yun-ao. I think I'm exempt.' Chu Jui passes one hand across his shaven skull. 'I haven't been here long enough to make enemies. And just out of a monastery? A retired officer, without army or territory? Not me.'

Tang studies him; perhaps Chu Jui is less lighthearted than he appears. Coming toward them is Deputy Wei, kerchief tied around his head. A spot of blood seeps through the cloth over his right ear. Before he can reach them, Chu Jui says to Tang in a whisper, 'Meet me tomorrow morning. Come to my hotel – Stein's on West Gate Road. Please, without fail.' Stepping forward, he says in a voice of concern, 'Ah, here you are, Wei! Are you hurt badly?'

The young representative of Marshal Chang Tso-lin shakes his head stoically but his lips tremble.

The three men watch some priests, a few temple assistants, and officers attempt to help the wounded, lying now in the courtyard under the hot sun. Almost immediately Chu Jui says farewell and departs hastily with his own entourage. Clearly he wishes to avoid the Marshal's deputy. Tang suspects that the man from Chekiang doesn't want to answer questions about his presence here in Jinan. Earlier old Jen had looked dubiously at him, questioning his attendance. Chu Jui has something in mind; he has come to Jinan to do more than renew friendships and stare at old Buddhist carvings. Tomorrow, Tang thinks, I'll find out.

The General, having received one request for a private meeting, is surprised when Deputy Wei proposes a similar one for tomorrow afternoon. They settle for the Fountain Springs at the Hour of the Monkey. Chu Jui in the morning, Wei in the afternoon: an interesting plan.

'I seem to be in need of a doctor,' Wei says after they have agreed about the meeting.

'Let me help you down the hill.'

'I am honored, but my men will get me down.' The injured man calls an aide. 'Until tomorrow, Excellency.'

When Deputy Wei has left on the arm of a young officer, Tang looks around for his own men. The four bodyguards are waiting some distance away. Tang calls them. 'Where is Yang?' he asks the American when they come running.

'I haven't seen him, Excellency.'

The General is puzzled. Yang was not among the dead or wounded in the temple.

'Excellency.' Another guard steps up. 'I saw him leave.'

'When?'

'Not long before the explosion, he left the temple.'

'Not long before it? How long?'

The bodyguard, gripping his sword hilt as if it will help him remember, says nothing for a moment. They are turned toward the wounded lying in a row in the yard, away from the smoking temple. The guard brightens. 'Yes. It was just after General Jen Ching-i asked for a break to go outside and stretch. That's when he left, Excellency.'

Tang looks at the others. 'You haven't seen Yang since then?'

They shake their heads.

So it was Yang; he planned the assassination. No wonder he'd been so nervous this morning, pacing at the gate, hoping for the

General's return. Tang thinks: Yang didn't want to lose this chance of killing me today. 'Let's go down,' the General tells his guards and steps briskly into the midday heat. He glances once at the ruined temple, at the dead and wounded, then starts the descent.

Next morning he leaves his nephew's residence by taxi from the rear gate. His Dodge remains in full view on the main thoroughfare. His men, all but two , surround the house as if guarding him. One bodyguard now sits next to the taxi driver, the other with him in the back seat – the American. The General glances at the young man who saved his life yesterday, at the blond hair, scarred forehead, blue eyes. Perhaps this foreigner contrived to fulfill the Yarrow Stalk prophecy: he's a young man who has figured prominently in the General's life. But then, so indeed has Yang, another young man.

And last night the General had wondered about his nephew too. They had dined together, and although both had avoided those topics of conversation which might have resulted in argument – Yen-chang, the Japanese, the destiny of China – a strong tension had remained between them, enough to convince the General that this young man is persistent, energetic, intelligent, with the potential for affecting any lives that he confronts.

The Yarrow Stalk Oracle seems to draw in a number of young men, the General thinks. The old diviner earned his opium money.

While the taxi rattles through the early-morning streets, Tang speculates on yesterday's bombing. Surely he had been its target – his own aide planned it – but who was the chief plotter? Not Yang. It required someone in authority to engineer such a scheme. He can only be sure that Chen Yun-ao, dead from a piece of wood in his brain, did not do it. He rules out the Japanese as well. They wouldn't blunder so badly as to sacrifice four high-ranking officers of their own. Perhaps Dog Meat arranged it, knowing full well that he would lose a chief assistant in the bargain. Dog Meat has risen at the General's expense and might therefore view him as harboring a desire for revenge. So Chang Tsung-ch'ang wanted to strike first. This is possible. Or perhaps the order came from Marshal Chang Tso-lin, tired of a young general who has defied his Japanese allies. Or it might have come from Jen Ching-i, although his motivation's unclear. Still, the fat old general's actions were the most suspicious of anyone's yesterday. He called for an adjournment of the meeting, which may have been a signal for his accomplices, and he managed to get himself well clear of the temple before the explosion.

From the car window Tang sees Jinan's coolies; they get in the way of his analysis. Pushing and shoving and hauling, they move toward oblivion, without hope. They are China, his people. They seem in their squalor and drab lives to have no meaning, yet they do. They have centuries of glory behind them. They have a heritage of perseverance, a talent for happiness, a desire for love, a love of beauty. But they endured invasion for centuries; and in the last hundred years they have suffered the abuse of the Western Powers, who have robbed them not only of their land's wealth but of their confidence as a people.

Said the Master: 'Nothing can be done with a people who lack confidence. They are lost indeed.'

From the window Tang watches them plodding along like the beasts they lead or follow. He asks himself, How can a man look at them and not offer his life for their well-being? It's a question he heard long ago, asked often by his father. While mother did embroidery, father paced up and down, bellowing that selfsame question. His eyes turned upward as if expecting an answer from the Jade Emperor in Heaven. His fine soldier's face was contorted in the rage and frustration that attend an ideal forever doomed.

Roads. Perhaps Ping-ti was right – they are the most important problem, along with floods and droughts. And along with foreign domination. Ultimately – the General believes this – China must solve its own problems even at the expense of roads and industry. What, after all, do light bulbs matter when a flood can take whole villages with it, whole towns and cities, sliding them forward into the depthless sea? What will make his people thrive is something else, something the Great Powers can't provide – the Confucian verities.

On West Gate Road the taxi pulls up at Stein's Hotel, still owned and run by a family who remained here after Germany's 1919 loss of privileges in China. The car door, swinging open and held by the American, leads General Tang into another day of questions, lesser perhaps than the one asked by himself and his father, but all of which may add up to it in the end.

*　　*　　*

'Do you play Wei Qi? They say it takes forty years of practice to play well, and I believe it. I've struggled twenty years with the game. I took it up to sharpen my wits, but the game's outwitted me.'

They sit in Chu Jui's limousine, heading south out of Jinan. The two generals have the back seat; two bodyguards, one of them the American, occupy the front seat. They all have the appearance of a solemn delegation, whereas Chu Jui's chatter is hardly momentous. '– the secret of marinated squid is to boil it only until the tentacles curl. Let me tell you about jellied chicken –' Obviously he won't touch on important matters in front of the driver and guards. Chain-smoking, Chu Jui often removes his military cap and scratches his shaven head; it's his way of emphasizing a point. 'I read a recent article by Ch'en Tu-hsiu. I forget where. He wrote: "The six Confucian Classics are inadequate to provide leadership." Well, he's from Peking and Peking has always been anti-Confucian. I don't know why, do you? I read somewhere some students burned the Sage's effigy in straw. Little bastards.'

Tang likes him.

'Look there!' Chu Jui points from the window; they have traveled about a dozen miles from the city through the brilliant July countryside. Along a mountain ridge in the distance runs a low-lying ruin of blackened bricks. 'Isn't that the Great Wall of Lu? Built at the time of Confucius?'

'A century later.'

'So we're nearing the monastery.'

'Ahead to the left,' Tang says. 'We're almost there.'

The generals soon find themselves climbing a hillside path along a pleasant green valley. The bodyguards follow at a distance. Chu Jui glances back at them. 'Why do you keep a foreigner?'

'Well, he saved my life yesterday.'

'Do you trust him?'

'As much, perhaps, as anyone at the moment.'

Through a break in the tree-lined path they can see two stone lions below, guarding lower path. 'It leads,' Tang explains, 'to the cemetery of the monks. Beautiful stupas there. In ruins, of course.'

Chu Jui halts to light a cigarette. 'Can your foreigner be a spy?'

'It's unlikely. My aide Yang was an excellent one, though.'

'I suspect he'll turn up in someone's camp.'

'Of course. The question is whose.'

'When you find out, at least you'll know who gave the order to kill you. These are beautiful. They must be from the Wei.' Chu Jui stops near a wall of rock niched with statues; many of them are Buddhas, but some of them are stone portraits of pious devotees wealthy enough to have themselves immortalized next to gods.

'I believe they're from the Tang, not the Wei,' says Tang.

'Why does your foreigner carry an ax?'

Tang laughs. 'He loves it the way a child loves a top.'

'The Great Sage said: 'A powerful enemy is not so much to be feared as dissension in your own camp.'

Tang bows slightly. 'I won't forget that you and the Master have given me good advice.'

They are coming down the hill now toward the ruins of the cemetery. Half of a temple's rooftop juts from distant greenery on the hillside: the disembodied wing of a metallic monster glittering in sunlight. Reaching the valley they see the Pagoda of the Dragon and Tiger; it stands above scattered bricks of destroyed cloisters, surrounded by a few score stupas, most of them man-sized, with delicately carved pinnacles, like the ornate pawns of a giant chessboard.

'Also the Tang?' ask Chu Jui.

'The pagoda is. I believe the stupas date from the Yuan and the Ming. How many monks have lived in these hills!'

'I feel their presence,' Chu Jui comments simply. Glancing back to see if the bodyguards are far enough away, he says in a lower voice, 'In Shanghai, people feel that Chiang Kai-shek may hold all the territory he's taken.'

'But I hear he's not been tested.'

'True. His armies won by the mouth, not by the gun.' As they stroll toward the pagoda, Chu Jui describes the Northern Expedition that brought Chiang Kai-shek to prominence. Russian-trained propaganda units – this was before Chiang's break with the Bolsheviks – softened up many towns with promises of freedom and progress. Then the troops entered, brandishing placards proclaiming Brotherhood, guns strapped to their packs.

Chu Jui's description of the Northern Expedition confirms others that Tang has heard. Confirmation, repeated often, is necessary in China; rumor can become the sweet breath of truth before turning sour. But why, suddenly, is Chu Jui turning the conversation to Chiang Kai-shek? Tang knows the former general well enough now to understand that everything he does is fully calculated.

'That sort of propaganda won't work here in the North,' Tang argues, as they halt in front of the carved pagoda. Its stone façade, although broken and worn by centuries, still has on it a lively plethora of warriors, dragons, tigers, and serene Buddhas seated on lotus blossoms. In the presence of such carvings they lose the feel of their conversation.

Then Chu Jui takes it up again. 'I agree that sort of propaganda is wrong in the North – if it's brought by a southerner. That's why Chiang Kai-shek is looking for northern allies. He wants good men loyal to the idea of a unified China. He'd be overjoyed, for example, to have you with him.'

'You know a lot about his feelings,' Tang says coolly.

'Well, after all, they're obvious.' Chu Jui squints at the pagoda. 'As for me, I no longer care about politics. I'd rather chisel one of these figures here than win all the battles I ever fought.'

'Spoken like a retired gentleman,' Tang says with a smile.

Chu Jui ignores the implied skepticism. 'Let's walk over to the Four-Door Tower. All my life I've wanted to see it.'

They stroll across a small bridge; solid greenery rings them on hillsides soon to take on a variety of color. They absorb the brilliant day with its temples hidden by foliage and its hillsides loaded with a precious cargo of stone images.

Ahead are the yellow bricks of a square, windowless building, its lines wholly balanced and modest. 'Eastern Wei,' Tang says when they halt in front of it. 'Fourteen hundred years ago.'

Chu Jui nods silently as he studies its mortared walls and shapely pinnacle. Then they enter one of the doors and face a seated Buddha, palms up in a broad lap, the drapery stylized, the ears richly long, the eyes closed in contemplation, the entire figure dominated by an imperturbable smile. The two men walk quietly around the dim little room and examine in turn each of the other three Buddhas. Then, back in the daylight, they stroll under the shade of an enormous cypress.

Tang looks up at it. 'This tree is supposed to be nearly as old as the tower.'

'I believe it.' Chu Jui squints at the scarred, massive trunk.

'Why are you here in Jinan?'

Chu Jui turns with a smile. 'Marshal Chang Tso-lin invited me to come here. I was visiting Peking last week.'

'Then you represent him?'

Chu Jui throws up his hands in mock horror. 'I certainly do not.

He extended an invitation to an old warrior, that's all.' Glancing sideways at Tang, he adds, 'Are you disappointed that I don't represent him?'

'Of course not.'

'Anyway, I don't think he tried to kill you. I think it was Feng.'

'Feng? Why?'

Chu Jui glances at the guards, who are standing near the Four-Door Tower, out of range. 'I think he sees the thing this way – you're a vassal of the Old Marshal.' Chu Jui raises his hand to stop a protest. 'Whether you are or not. If he kills you – a public subordinate of the Marshal – he tells Chiang Kai-shek first that he's strong and second that he needs an ally to keep the Marshal at bay. That ally is Chiang Kai-shek.'

Tang leans indolently against the cypress, while Chu Jui, pacing, continues. 'Of course, his reasoning could be different. By killing you he'd deprive Chiang Kai-shek of an ally.'

This idea, new to Tang, interests him; he steps away from the tree.

Lighting a cigarette, Chu Jui blows smoke emphatically. 'Yes, it might be that. Feng knows your reputation for soldiering, and of course he knows Chiang knows it too. They could both use such an ally.' Chu Jui takes off his cap and scratches his bald head; walking to the edge of the shade, he squints at the hot greenery on the hillsides. 'Everyone in China knows what you did – tracked down a bandit who'd murdered one of your officers. That's loyalty, a special kind of commitment. That's the old style, out of *The Three Kingdoms*.' He turns to look at Tang. 'That's what Chiang Kai-shek is looking for, and Feng knows it.' He puffs his cigarette rapidly a few times. 'Men of quality have gone over to Chiang lately. General Li Shun and General Chen Kuang-yuan from Kiangsu. General Li How-chi from Fukien. General Nyi Tsze-ch'ung from Anhwei.'

'Does he bribe them?'

Chu Jui laughs, throwing away the cigarette. 'Chiang Kai-shek use silver bullets? I assure you, he's a man of honor, like yourself.'

So he has told me at last, Tang thinks. Chu Jui represents Chiang. He is Chiang's emissary. 'Are you suggesting I become Chiang's ally?'

Studying the General's face, Chu Jui becomes wary. 'I suggest nothing. I'm merely pointing out the obvious. If you two met, perhaps some mutual benefit might result.' After a pause, he adds something which, for Tang, is a powerful argument. 'Never forget this: Chiang Kai-shek will not cooperate with the Japanese.'

'That can be a rumor. There are rumors about him.' One that Tang recalls: The slightly built Chiang wears a long black cape, never moves one step without a dozen bodyguards, and carries a Pekingese everywhere in his arms.

'This is no rumor. He will not cooperate with the Japanese.'

'Does he know you're here?'

'Yes, he knows. But then, so does the Marshal and for that matter so does Feng, I suppose.' He opens his arms wide and grimaces. 'Shall we go back to the city? Or remain here in these pleasant hills, begging food each day, meditating, serving God?'

'By all means, let's remain,' Tang says; and they begin to stroll toward the waiting car, with the two bodyguards, one lightly fingering the blade of his ax, walking behind them out of earshot.

In the intense heat General Tang is walking under the larger willows for which Jinan is famous. Paths throughout the park lead to stone bridges over a pool of green water gushing from three natural springs. Three circles of watery agitation dominate mid-pool, but at one edge there is a hovering school of carp: blood red, ivory, cobalt blue, many speckled varieties. A piece of bread, a few grains of wheat, bring them splashing to the green surface, boiling it into a froth of brilliant color. Tang, standing within the shade of a pavilion, watches some schoolchildren toss bits of food to the swirling fish. He is reminded of his own childhood, when he too came to Fountain Spring and gazed down in perfect awe at an earlier generation of carp, whose vivid thrashings seemed no more magical then than those of their successors do now. It strikes him that his two sons, had they lived, would be older than these children. There's no one now, no one – only a scheming brother in Hong Kong, an equally scheming nephew here. Can there be a worse fate for a man than to die without sons? He thinks of the unbroken line of the Sage's generations: seventy-six. Whereas his own name will die with him. It is a bitter thought, calculated to make him recall, if not consider, Dog Meat's offer of a daughter in marriage.

Marriage – it's hardly the thing to occupy his mind today. He has a question to answer. Who bribed young Yang and conspired to blow up a famous mountainside temple, including along with it many army officers? Who did this simply to kill a landlocked general who can't even pay his troops?

Absorbed by the question, Tang scarcely notices the man approaching on the bridge. It's the deputy from Marshal Chang Tso-lin, wearing a bandage over his injured ear: small, frail, ascetic-looking.

On reaching the pavilion, Deputy Wei apologizes profusely for being late. He removes immaculate white gloves while speaking the rhetoric of a mandarin. Tang accepts the apology with interest, noting that the Old Marshal has sent an accomplished young man. Wei has come alone. Tang's bodyguards, like afternoon shadows, creep slowly behind him and Wei as they stroll to a bench under an old gingko. Wei waits for the General to be seated, then sits down beside him. They study the tree: its mighty trunk, huge crown of branches, two-lobed leaves like tiny fans. Tang is gratified to see that the young man observes the old style – courtesy, patience. But Deputy Wei comes to the point swiftly.

'Excellency, I suppose Chu Jui tried to recruit you today.'

'You know of our meeting.'

Wei modestly lowers his eyes.

'The basic trouble with our country is its lack of privacy,' the General says; it is the mildest rebuff. He glances at the young man, who has a catlike grace, reminding him of the Marshal. That old bastard – ruler of a territory as large as France and Germany combined. Someone making a speech in praise of the Marshal at a Peking conference once made that comparison; the old Manchurian Tiger had beamed from the speakers' platform. This young deputy has the same narrow face, pinched mouth. Perhaps the similarity suggests a close relationship between Wei and the Marshal. Could the young man be the son of a favorite concubine? The Marshal, it is rumored, keeps about thirty. At any rate, Deputy Wei will be carrying back to Peking his interpretation of this interview. What the Old Marshal ultimately thinks of the General may come from Wei; the General's future may well be in the hands of this young man – as the Yarrow Stalk Oracle prophesied. His aide, his bodyguard, even his nephew, and now this deputy from Chang Tso-lin: all of them young men, all involved in his life during the past day. The oracle mentioned only one; perhaps this is its little joke.

'May I be permitted to ask, Excellency, if Chu Jui made an impression on you?'

The General laughs. 'I don't know what you mean by "impression" or "recruiting." Why don't you tell me what you think of Chu Jui?'

'He's come out of retirement to act on behalf of Chiang Kai-shek.'

'Why? Because they're from the same province?'

'For Chu Jui it's a matter of keeping his estates. He either helps Chiang or forfeits them.' Deputy Wei shrugs. 'A simple and correct arrangement.'

'As a matter of fact, he did try to recruit me. He thinks Chiang and I have mutual interests.'

'The mutual interest of us all is to survive.'

Well put, Tang thinks. He gives the young man a closer look. Feet together, hands placid on his knees, back straight, Deputy Wei has the ideal posture of a military cadet. He must still be in his twenties. Had the General's first wife lived, they might have had a son this age. Had the sons of his second wife lived, they would now be slightly younger.

He fiercely pushes aside such thoughts.

'Chu Jui emphasized the good intentions of Chiang,' he says, to get a reaction from the young man. 'Called him honorable, loyal.'

'So you've been told, Excellency.'

'And a man who will always oppose the Japanese.' Tang notices a muscle twitch at the edge of Wei's mouth.

'The Marshal *also* opposes the Japanese,' declares Deputy Wei. In response to the General's skeptical smile, he adds, 'Marshal Chang Tso-lin has wanted one thing in his life – the same thing you want, Excellency: the unity and freedom of China.'

It is a glib declaration at variance with a fact that no one, not even a relative of the Marshal, can deny: For years the Manchurian Tiger has courted the Japanese, employed them, given them special privileges.

Wei is looking toward the bridge over which a soldier is now hurrying. Wearing the armband of Marshal Chang Tso-lin's Fengtien Army, he carries a brightly wrapped package. He salutes smartly upon reaching the seated officers and hands the package to Wei, who in turn, with a graceful nod, presents it to General Tang. 'Shall we stroll to the pavilion over there?'

The General stares at the gaily colored wrapping, the dainty ribbon.

They stroll to the pavilion and order tea. 'The Marshal wishes you ten thousand years!' exclaims the young deputy.

Tang unwraps the package. Inside is a handsome four-volume unabridged Ching edition of *Shui Hu Chuan*, *The Water Margin*, a story immortalizing the heroic exploits of Sung Chiang and his fellow brigands who put down a revolt against the throne during the Sung Dynasty. A tale of courage and loyalty like *The Three Kingdoms*, it is held dear by military men, and Tang is no exception. It is a splendid, thoughtful gift, worthy of the Marshal – as famous for his collection of manuscripts as he is infamous for his brutal treatment of prisoners.

'I believe, Excellency, there's something in the first volume for you.'

Tang finds a sheet of official stationery with a proclamation, followed by the Marshal's chop. It states that by this document and seal General Tang Shan-teh has been appointed Commander of the Bandit Suppression Army of Shantung Province.

The General smiles. It is a Chinese maneuver, at once sarcastic and practical: through this proclamation he is gently admonished for chasing White Wolf across the landscape during a time of crisis; and at the same time he is publicly acknowledged as the vanquisher of outlaws who dare to transgress territory under the ultimate control of the Marshal.

'If I may be permitted, Excellency, to speak on behalf of the Marshal – I shall attempt to use his own words, as he gave them to me.' The deputy waits until Tang nods his permission. 'Some people say that General Tang is too ambitious, therefore vulnerable. But I say this is not true. I admire the General's tenacity and sense of purpose, let alone his skill as a soldier. I share with him a vision of China. As for the military notes which the General has issued –'

Tang opens his mouth to deny their issuance.

'I am impressed by the courage and resolution which the General has displayed in handling a difficult financial situation. However, I am pleased to inform the General that he can recall the notes. They are no longer necessary.'

Tang waits, stunned.

'Those are the Marshal's own words,' the deputy continues. 'He regrets the delay in issuing the stipend for your troops. An accounting error. It will be forthcoming in a few days.'

The General attempts to regain his composure. 'Thank the Marshal. My compliments and gratitude.'

'The delay was unavoidable. The Marshal sends his deepest apologies.'

'I understand, of course. Please convey my limitless gratitude to him. I am unworthy of his kindness.'

'Governor General Chang Tsung-ch'ang also regrets the involuntary delay in issuing the provincial stipend as well.'

So the Marshal has pressured Dog Meat into giving up funds too! It's a victory for Tang, and he can't suppress a smile. Nor can Wei help but return it. The young deputy lifts his cup of tea with a sigh of contentment. 'I love Dragon Well in the summer. My favorite winter tea is jasmine. Your Excellency?'

Taking up his own cup, Tang says, 'I'm partial to black teas. Iron Buddha I find especially refreshing.' They toast each other in the shade of the pavilion, while Tang's bodyguards hover nearby, wiping their brows in the sunshine.

Alone in the Fountain Spring pavilion – young Wei has long since departed – General Tang contemplates the events of the past few days. His financial trouble has ended with the Marshal's decision to remit both the national and provincial allowances for his army. Why did the Marshal do it? Because the issuance of *zhun-yong-piao* would have disrupted the economy of southern Shantung? Unlikely. The Marshal would shrug at the plight of some thousands of soldiers and their creditors. Nor is the Marshal impressed by the 'courage and resolution' of a commander who issues worthless currency – it is, after all, the act of a desperate man. No, what the Marshal reacted to is the continuing threat of General Feng Yuhsiang, crouched on his western border, preparing to take advantage of any weakness in the Marshal's defensive alignment.

I am needed, Tang tells himself, sipping the last dregs of his Dragon Well tea. So I am paid.

What is not simple to understand is Chiang Kai-shek's overture for an alliance. Perhaps the southerner feels sufficiently embattled to seek help anywhere, or perhaps Chiang recognizes Tang's special geopolitical position. Astride the roadway between southern and northern China, General Tang is ideally situated for either invasion or alliance, as he well knows. Which alternative is pursued depends on the primary needs of his restless neighbors. Tang's mind quickens in anticipation of the days ahead and what they may bring – a grappling for power, the possibility of sudden defeat, or victory just as abrupt.

This much is obvious: He can now go to Shanghai and conclude the arms agreement with the German gunrunner. He can do it without using money lawfully belonging to his troops. And with new weapons he can stand against the forces threatening him everywhere: Generals Feng and Jen to the west; Marshal Chang to the north; old Dog Meat at his eastern doorstep; and Chiang Kai-shek to the south. The soldier in him delights at the prospect of strategy to plan, alliances to break or make, marches to undergo, and all of it in the service of the country he loves.

But it's not that simple any more. His strategy, alliances, and maneuvers are far different from those of his father's time. Surely there was as much intrigue then as now – perhaps more – but the alliances seemed less intense, more flexible. Officers who had known one another since military school went about warfare in the old days like gentlemen. They offered honorable challenges by telegram, and when a town was taken they gave protection to the families of their vanquished adversaries. Perhaps less was at stake then – a few hundred miles of territory which, in the next skirmish, might change hands. Today the whole country is at issue: Winner take all. And the armies have grown in size, in firepower, in destructiveness, so that battle casualties are tenfold what they'd been when his father took the field. Jen pointed all this out at Thousand Buddha Mountain. War is tougher. Ideas count more in the shaping of conflict. Once the Manchu had been deposed early in the century, there had been little to fight for except personal honor, a bit of territory, some wealth. Out of such matters, temporarily important but never urgent, the clash of warlords was not calamitous, overwhelming. In Tang's view ideas are now marching toward the battlefields of China: alien social doctrines from Russia; new philosophies of business and religion from the West; and now from China itself certain revolutionary concepts. These southerners under Chiang Kai-shek, for example, are professing to implement Sun Yat-sen's 'Three Principles': nationalism, livelihood, and democracy. Ideas, ideas at the forefront of the armies. There is – Tang senses it – a growing desire among military men to annihilate opponents rather than simply defeat them. The dour concomitant of belief in ideas. He has, in the waning light of a lovely afternoon in Fountain Spring Park, a terrible vision of conflict beyond anything his father could have imagined. It is like the crashing confluence of mighty rivers, a rage and convulsion of limitless power. It is China in the throes of ideologies at war. The land, and he alone with it, seem to be rushing toward cataclysm.

The vision fades with the light, and Tang tells himself it's nothing more than fatigue, coupled with the intellectual strain of piecing together the disparate elements of what he has seen and heard and thought and suspected during the past few days.

The General rises from the pavilion table. Seeing him do this, his two bodyguards, waiting under a willow tree, straighten their uniforms; and when he motions to them, they come at a trot.

Ten feet away they halt. Tang crooks his finger at the American. 'Come along.' The General turns and walks down a cobbled path into a garden. Hesitantly the young man falls into step beside him, but only after the General insists. Tang is gratified by the American's reluctance to take the liberty, even with permission. As they walk in silence, Tang glances at the blue eyes of his bodyguard. Unlike most eyes, they don't seem to reflect any mood, either of their possessor or of other people. They see without mirroring what they see, much like the sky on a cloudless day – without depth, shade, or gradation, but going on limitlessly, undefined, liberated, a broad waste of mysterious possibility. Tang doesn't like these eyes; they represent something new, raw, untouched by experience. They also intrigue him. 'I'm grateful for your quick response the other day at Thousand Buddha Mountain,' the General says finally.

'It was my duty, General. And . . . and –' Embree is seeking the appropriate words. 'A privilege for such an unworthy soldier to be of service to your Excellency.'

'Would it please you to be my permanent bodyguard?'

The blond foreigner's face sags, then stiffens.

Tang catches the disappointment. 'Would you rather do something else?'

'It would, of course, please me infinitely to . . .' Embree begins. 'I am deeply honored, but such an unworthy person –'

Tang waves aside the American's clumsy attempt to use Chinese rhetoric. 'Speak plainly.'

'General, I would like to stay in the cavalry.'

'Why?'

'I want to learn soldiering.'

Who can fathom the Western mind? Tang wonders. Yet looking

at the American he sees determination in the set of the jaw. The fellow has a bearing now, a discovered composure, a new presence that is in fact military. Perhaps it would be unfair, Tang tells himself, to deny such a request to someone who has just saved your life. 'Very well, Ax Man,' he says. 'Return to your cavalry unit.' Tang retraces his steps along the path. Glancing again at the American, he says, 'Who do you think planned the explosion?'

For a few paces the American is silent. 'Excellency, I heard it was Marshal Chang Tso-lin.'

'Do you agree?'

'I can understand why it might be the Marshal. He wanted to punish General Chen Yun-ao for losing an important battle.'

'Why not punish General Chen in a less crowded place? Especially at the risk of killing three other generals, to say nothing of a half-dozen Japanese officers, his allies? Why would the Marshal choose to bomb a temple?'

The American is glumly silent. Then, as they continue to stroll, he says, 'I also heard the Governor General might have ordered it.'

'Only with permission of the Marshal.'

Another silence. The General has received the response which he expected from a foreigner – something obvious and uncomplicated, without subtlety, without depth. It is somehow reassuring.

'There's another possibility,' Embree says.

Tang halts and looks at the young American, who thoughtfully fingers the livid scar on his forehead.

'I heard the servants in your nephew's house talking about it.'

'By all means tell me. We must take seriously the gossip of servants.' Tang is not altogether sarcastic.

'I heard them say it was Chiang Kai-shek.'

'Did they say why?'

'No, sir.'

'Can you think of a reason?'

'Yes, sir. Perhaps he wanted to wipe out as many northern officers as he could, with a single blow.'

Tang must concede that the hypothesis makes sense. Had Chiang Kai-shek succeeded and had Chu Jui, his representative, died in the explosion, blame would have fallen on others, not on him. Chiang might have done it. Servants whispering behind screens might well have outflanked the generals. And the American has just displayed rudiments of military thinking.

They start walking again. At a turn in the path – giving them a

284

final glimpse of the bubbling spring, the arching bridges, the children, a surge of carp – the General takes a different tack with the foreigner. 'What did you think of the Buddhas?'

'Excellency?'

'During the past few days you saw dozens of Buddhas on the cliffs. Wei and Tang sculpture. What did you think of them?'

For a moment Embree hesitates. 'Well, they were very old.'

'Yes. Very old.' Tang waits, but realizes after a few moments that the young man, this student with facts at his fingertips, has nothing to add. He has seen the antiquity of those stone faces, but nothing beyond it. He has not felt the inner life of the stone; he did not discover in the calm smiles an image of peace and fulfillment beyond rationality. The American is indeed a soldier, but of the sort that China has scorned for centuries – the military man who fights for profit or pleasure, not to sustain a world of beauty and justice. Such a man has always been rejected by China until now. Now it is different. A man without commitment may even have more value than one who lives with it. Ideas to start wars; men without ideals to fight them: the modern world.

Turning, he orders the Ax Man to join the other guard.

Continuing alone down a path lined by drooping willows, strolling through sunlight turning steadily into dusk, General Tang thinks of Shanghai, of going there in a few days. There are guns to purchase, deals to make, perhaps a country to win. And the Russian woman who came to Qufu, perhaps he will see her again. An odd thought.

He stops to consider it. And defying this wayward drift of his mind, he tries to conjure the image of Su-su. To his surprise and chagrin, her face is less memorable than the Russian woman's.

His mind turns like a heavy stone to the events of his stay in Jinan. Courted by North and South, formidable enough to assissinate, no longer desperate for money, he sees his star rising. Yet at this moment of reflection and satisfaction, to his astonishment he recalls a strange remark: 'I have never met a man who loves virtue as much as he loves a woman's beauty.'

He finds himself once again at the pool, where the carp are schooling in a great swath of color. The Great Sage, whose flights of wisdom have spanned the centuries, made that observation – a rueful one – about men and women.

A small boy tosses pieces of bread to the churning fish. With a sigh the General walks on.

12

'*Qing ni gei wo cha.*'

The boy, no more than sixteen, grins uncomprehendingly at Kovalik. Dressed in military cottons, with the addition of a dirty white scarf to give him the look of a house servant, the boy has been assigned to the Russian guest.

Kovalik repeats it with difficulty: '*Quing ni gei wo cha.*' When the boy nods eagerly but without moving, without the slightest light of comprehension in his face, Kovalik repeats it irritably, this time in Russian. 'Please bring me tea. Tea! *Cha! Cha!*' He makes the motion of lifting a cup and drinking from it. 'I want a – *yibei-cha. Yibei?* Is it *yibei* or *yiba?* A cup of tea!'

To each of Kovalik's frantic attempts at pronouncing the words, the houseboy dips his head rapidly in ecstatic approval.

Hopeless, hopeless. Kovalik, shaking his head, makes the motion with his big hands of shooing the boy out. Frowning, the puzzled boy leaves. For a moment Kovalik nearly yells out, '*Deng yi deng!*' to bring the boy back, but this will only cause more confusion, head bobbing, frustration. Kovalik used to hear that Russians are gifted linguists, but surely he's an exception to the rule. Perhaps if he had more opportunity to speak with the Chinese – but they avoid him or grin and nod approvingly to anything he says. Only Li Chung-lin has saved him from going crazy. Li and the cloud biting.

He glances restlessly from his room into the courtyard of the Kong Residence West Wing. In his garrison-blue pants and shirt he makes an incongruous occupant of this charming room which used to be reserved for guests of the Kong family. Moreover, he has grown a full black beard to match his flowing mustache. All the black hair on his face, coupled with pale skin and a fleshy nose, gives him a wild look that he covets. There's rebellion in it. For a revolutionary like himself, isolated from meaningful activity in this delicate prison with its vases and wall hangings, his slightest resistance to accepted patterns is a way of clinging to dignity. So he has told himself.

His stomach churns as he stands at the window, gazing at the lime tree framed prettily in a moon gate that leads into another courtyard. One pretty goddamn thing after another surrounds him. And lately he has suffered from knifelike pains and dull aching in his abdomen. Li claims it's caused by opium, but Kovalik, knowing his friend wants him to smoke less, doesn't believe it. True, in recent days his intake has leaped from a gram or two to more than five. He's also aware of early-morning sneezing, a sign of opium use, but it's all quite harmless ultimately, and anyway, he needs something to do. If he didn't go to the Place of Cloud Biting every afternoon, there would be nothing in the day. Colonel Pi has continually ignored his requests for permission to form a study group among the junior officers. The cold little bastard apologizes and assures him there may be a chance for such 'general discussions' when General Tang returns. When Tang returns, nothing will change, Kovalik has decided. Tang won't help the representative of a government that not only refuses to send arms but also avoids contact with its own representative.

Flopping down on the bed, Kovalik stares at his big feet in the cotton shoes. Feeling his flabby gut with one hand, he senses acutely his need for physical exercise, but lately he's felt tired, irritable, very tired actually, exhausted most of the day – until, that is, he sets off with Li for the Place of Cloud Biting.

Turning over on his belly in the hope of soothing it, Kovalik curses his friend for being late. They have a special meeting today, and Kovalik's pulse quickens when he thinks of it. At last some action, something to do! It is appalling how completely he depends on Li for everything, even for a diversion. He needs Li to translate, of course, but the dependency goes deeper. For one thing, Kovalik has begun to wonder if anyone in the world shares his opinions aside from Li Chung-lin. Cut off from Russia and apparently denied contact with his compatriots left in Wuhan – by their own choice or by Stalin's order – he has no idea what other people are thinking. Li is his sole contact with the world, and Kovalik is thankful that they agree on many things. Both believe, for example, that Borodin betrayed the Chinese Reds by helping in subtle ways to split them from the Nationalists just at the time when the Coalition, under Chiang Kai-shek's supreme command, had swept through the South and achieved victory as far north as Shanghai and Nanking. Moreover, both hate Stalin for supporting Chiang rather than the Chinese Communists. They despise him for opportunism, for backing Chiang because he has the money in China. Sometimes Kovalik wishes that he and Li disagreed on a major issue; it might add a touch of excitement to the boring life they lead.

A knock at the door. Turning on his back and lifting himself up on his elbows, Kovalik says loudly, '*Qing-jinlai!*'

Li comes in, exclaiming in Russian how well Kovalik has pronounced 'Please come in.'

The compliment is wasted on Kovalik, who understands his friend is encouraging the study of a language that might take him twenty years, fifty years to master.

Will I be here twenty, fifty years? Kovalik asks himself in momentary panic. In this terrible land? He feels his belly grind, a pain throb across his rib cage.

Li, dressed also in garrison blue, stands in the light and looks down at him. 'Have you eaten today?'

Strange, Kovalik thinks, I haven't thought of food. 'I asked for tea, but the boy didn't understand.'

'I'll speak to him.'

Kovalik laughs. 'That's just the point. I can't speak to him. Your speaking to him solves nothing.'

'There is a brief, tense silence.

'You must eat,' Li says finally.

'I know, I know. You think it's the *Ta-yen*. You think the *Ta-yen's* making me lose appetite. Yes, I know what you think,' Kovalik says impatiently.

'It's the *Ta-yen*.'

'Good. Then I won't get fat. I'm certainly getting flabby,' Kovalik says, rising from the bed and gripping a dollop of fat at his waist. 'In 1919 in Siberia you couldn't have found any fat on me, not as thick as a knife blade.'

Wearing a coolie's conical hat to hide most of his face and avoid notice on the street, Kovalik accompanies his Chinese translator from the Residence out to the dusty boulevard leading to the center of town. On the way they discuss once again – they do this at least twice a day – General Tang's place in current Chinese politics. They know of the bombing incident on Thousand Buddha Mountain, an event known throughout China, they suspect. In their opinion Chiang Kai-shek tried to kill him; motive: to eliminate a potential rival, although Tang clearly lacks support from other warlords. Li still believes Tang will turn to Russia for help.

'If Trotsky were in command,' Kovalik says, 'everything would be different here.'

'There's a chance he'll come back.' They are walking past the Drum Tower and turning into a side street.

A cobbler is coming along, beating sticks together to announce his arrival in the neighborhood. His tools and small workbench hang from ends of a thick bamboo pole across his shoulders.

'Who has leather shoes to fix?' Kovalik asks curiously.

'Shopkeepers, police, the landlords who live in town,' Li explains. 'And members of the Kong family, of course.'

'Do the Kongs really exist? I've never seen one of them.'

'They exist within a stone's throw from your room. The Residence is a complicated place.'

'How can they be so close and I not know it?'

Li smiles, unable to suppress his delight in the Chinese ability to live secretly in private splendor. Then he says, 'It's the way of the rich, those shitty bastards.' The obscenity atones for his having taken pleasure in the cleverness of aristocrats – it's hardly commensurate with his politics.

Feeling restless, suffering from abdominal pain, Kovalik glances moodily around the street. Two old men, smoking long brass pipes, sit erect on stools near a doorway and regard him aloofly. A herbal beverage seller, a bent old woman in rags, is squatting against a wall; in front of her is a sawed-off barrel on the top of which stand three bowls of thick black liquid. This is deeply foreign to Kovalik; and if he lives fifty whole years in this country, he will never feel at home. Never, he tells himself defiantly. Kovalik stops to sneeze. He glances sheepishly at Li, who is staring at him. 'All right,' Kovalik says. 'I know. It's the *Ta-yen*.'

'Yes. it's the *Ta-yen*.' Li points. 'This is the place.'

Kovalik looks at a jar shop, at the man inside of it who is dressed in a mandarin gown and black slippers. He leans indolently against one of the large earthenware jars – as tall as he is and four times broader. A variety of smaller jars are piled to the ceiling. Along with these utility vessels, for storing rice and water, the shop contains a few coal-fired space heaters, obviously for the rich, and a single tin bathtub hanging on the wall, reserved perhaps for the Kongs or for some foreigner who might come some day to live in the town of Qufu.

'Have they arrived yet?' Li asks the shopkeeper, who shakes his head and stares imperiously for a brief moment at Kovalik.

'Get him inside,' the shopkeeper tells Li. 'I don't want the neighborhood gawking at him.'

They go through the cluttered shop and enter a small, airless room without windows, lit by a single lamp on a table. There's a bench along one wall, a chair in the middle of the room. A powerful, nauseating stench pervades the atmosphere.

'What is that?' Kovalik asks, wrinkling his nose.

Li explains that the shop-owner has constructed a large brick trough in his back yard. Used as a latrine by the whole neighborhood, the trough supplies excrement for outlying farmers who bring their wagons in and load up and pay a handsome sum to the shop owner for his fertilizer.

'So our Communist shopkeeper is a capitalist who deals in shit,' grumbles Kovalik, who nervously kneads his hands. The gastritis has given him a touch of nausea – enhanced by the stench – which he fights to control. 'How many are coming?'

'It's hard to say. I talked to twenty, thirty, who said they were interested.' Li adds, 'Of course, it takes courage to come.'

'Will Tang have them shot if they come?'

'At least he'll have them punished. A good beating, I should think. And a good beating with us Chinese means a heavy stick laid on, the skin broken, perhaps a lot of bleeding, maybe something ruined inside.' Li studies him a moment. 'Don't worry, Comrade. I think more than a dozen should come.'

A dozen, Kovalik repeats to himself morosely. His aim as a Comintern agent was given to him before leaving Moscow. How grandiose it seems now: 'He must inspect and evaluate the army to which he is attached, paying attention to its military efficiency; he must encourage cooperation between high-ranking officers and the Russian leadership available in China; he must instruct both men and officers in the basic theory of the Marxist Revolution.' Of the three-pronged goal, one part no longer exists: There's no viable Russian leadership left in China with which to cooperate. As for analyzing the structure of Tang's army in terms of military efficiency, Kovalik has had the chance to visit the garrison only a couple of times and on those occasions he was surrounded by curious troops and watchful guards. What he has learned is scant indeed: Troops in general seem ignorant of the principles of firearms; they have no idea of a trajectory, but think a bullet goes straight from the gun barrel, travels a way, and falls abruptly to earth. His second observation: Troops practicing combat maneuvers tend to move in close ranks without taking full advantage of the terrain. And that's the extent of his military 'evaluation'. As for instructing the troops and officers in Soviet theory, today he'll begin with hardly more than a dozen, who probably have in mind the cigarettes that Li has promised them for coming. Li has denied Kovalik's charge of bribing them, claiming he simply mentioned a small gift for each one. But the fact remains that Li Chung-lin has brought along a hefty canvas bag filled with Capstans.

Kovalik sneezes. He studies the dim room, its uneven clay walls catching pits of shadow from the lantern beam. The soldiers are late. Hopeless, hopeless. A fine organizational meeting this is. A fine revolutionary endeavor.

But finally they shamble in. Four. One scarcely grown, another two in their early twenties, and one grizzled fellow who has the furtive look of a thief. They squat on the earthen floor until commanded by Li to sit along the bench.

'Where are the others?' Kovalik asks through Li.

The four smile and bob their heads like Kovalik's houseboy, even though they are asked the question in Chinese. Hopeless. He sees the oldest one, the thief, eying the canvas bag near Li's feet.

Yet when he rises in the stinking room to give the lecture that he and Li have painstakingly prepared for delivery to hundreds of avid listeners – in military camps, in factories, in village squares and union halls throughout China – Vladimir Kovalik does find his voice and in consequence forgets the four men who peer cautiously at him but all too eagerly at the canvas bag full of cigarettes; and he lets his resonant voice soar and ring through the stench-filled room in a fervent rendering of Russia's struggle for new birth, her triumph over the forces of repression and injustice.

He links the two countries in common cause, emphasizing their mutual suffering and their hopeful mutual destiny. He tells them that the Russian Revolution of 1917, which toppled Czarist rule, had its source in the same kind of autocratic tyranny that brought ruin to the Manchu Dynasty only a few years earlier.

'Russia is the true friend of China,' Li translates; Kovalik studies the men for their response. One yawns, one grins, one does nothing, and the old thief stares at the canvas bag.

Kovalik tells them he can prove Russia's friendship. In 1924 the Soviets renounced all treaties that infringed on Chinese sovereignty. They repudiated those unequal agreements which the Czarist regime, along with the Western Powers, had forced for a century upon this great nation.

Li's voice in translation sounds shrill to Kovalik's ear; but then he has always found Chinese shrill, even comical. When Li has finished, Kovalik begins pacing again. Russia, he tells his listeners, has always supported the revolution in China. 'And in the future,' he declares, raising his fist, 'Russians and Chinese will fight side by side for liberty and bread!'

Kovalik pauses to sneeze. His eyes are teary and a piercing cramp seizes his stomach. Yet he goes on, fired by a vision of brotherhood: The successful revolution in Russia proves beyond doubt that in a country as beset by imperialists as China a small group of dedicated laborers and soldiers can depose the privileged ruling elite. He speaks of *ko-ming* (a word given to him by Li, who continues patiently to translate his words for the soldiers, all of whom have colds, are sniffling and coughing), 'a change of mandate,' that concept dear to the Chinese mind ever since the days of Confucius. He explains to them (or do they know it already?) that *ko-ming* is a principle of Heaven, bestowing the right to rule on the best of men; this mandate can be recalled, however, if the rule proves unwise, for Heaven ultimately follows the wish of the people.

Kovalik pauses again, giving Li time to finish the translation. The four men sitting on the bench are politely erect, although their eyes seem glazed. A signal of their boredom?

Is it true? Kovalik wonders. Are they as indifferent as they look?

Slumping down in the chair, he places one elbow on the table and supports his bearded chin in his hand.

Hopeless.

His eyes fixed on the latrine door, Kovalik lets his mind drift awhile, pleasantly, as if he were biting clouds. Well, after all, what does it matter? he asks himself. He's alone now; there are people out there, but they don't really count. What counts is memory, the glory of the past.

The sudden change in the loud-voiced pacing man has a marked effect on the four soldiers, who regard him curiously. So does Li, who realizes he's going to depart from the prepared speech.

'On the twelfth of March, 1917,' he begins softly, aware of the meditative quality of his voice, the intimate tone. He begins again, staring at a spot above the heads of his four listeners. 'I was a young recruit in the Volynsk Regiment, when the Petrograd workers went on strike at dawn of the twelfth of March, 1917.'

Hereafter Kovalik pauses often for Li to translate, waiting almost indifferently, not caring whether anyone else hears his words. 'Seeing our officers shoot down the workers with machine guns, we soldiers revolted. We marched in perfect order – I will never forget it – we marched in perfect order while our regimental band played. As we went along, other units joined us: the Preobrazhensky, the Litovski, and others. Red banners appeared from nowhere. In windows, on poles, draped from balconies. Workers carried flowers, along with the pistols they took from Czarist officers. I was there. And on the night of April sixteenth, I saw Lenin return to Petrograd. He stood in the rain on the platform of the Finland Station, and he said to us, "Dear comrades, soldiers, and workers, I am happy to greet you. The hour approaches when our people will turn against the exploiters and crush them. Long live the International Socialist Revolution!" We carried him from the train on our shoulders. I touched his shoe. And I was there in November at the Bolshevik Soviet at Smolny when Trotsky gave orders to protect the printing plant. I was there when we took the Telegraph Building.'

Abruptly Kovalik stops talking. His cradling hand falls to his lap and he sits erect, staring at the four soldiers, who haven't moved during this reminiscence, although clearly they have understood scarcely a thing Li Chung-lin has translated. Hopeless. Yet for a moment Kovalik feels at peace. 'So there you are,' he says with a sigh.

The listeners take his sigh as a kind of command releasing them from attention. They squirm about, scratching at the lice inside their cotton blouses, grinning and stretching.

Kovalik regards them reproachfully: four ragged children let out of school. 'So there you are,' he says again, his voice heavy with despair. 'That's enough for today.' Turning listlessly, he stares at the bolted door leading to the latrine. Under his rib cage the intestines clench like a fist, unclench, clench. 'Enough,' he mutters.'

Li Chung-lin clears his throat and informs the four men that next time there will be a formal meeting with elections. Seeing little comprehension, much less interest, on their faces, he explains that they are going to form a Communist cell within the Southern Shantung Army. For this purpose they will select by vote an officer to represent them and someone to act as recruiting officer and as secretary.

'Vote?' one of the men repeats softly. He's very thin, his eyes hollow-looking from a bad cold, his narrow chest shaken by a cough. 'We're going to vote?'

'First,' says Li, 'we must find others who will come too. Enough to form a proper cell. Then we'll vote. Do you see? We are all equal.'

They stare at him, mouths thin and tight, while he explains to Kovalik what has been said.

'That's enough today,' Kovalik mutters wearily, staring at the latrine door. He scarcely turns when each soldier comes up and bows. But he does thank them – in Chinese – for coming. '*Xiexie. Xiexie.*' To Li Chung-lin he says, 'Now give them their fucking cigarettes.'

While Li goes outside with them, Kovalik continues to look at the door leading to the latrine. He can imagine the swirls of flies busy at the trough, the capitalistic shithouse. Hopeless. China is hopeless. Those four today – peasants lured by the promise of a smoke, willing to risk a bad beating for a few puffs on a cigarette. Absolutely hopeless.

When Li returns, he is smiling. Holding up a piece of torn paper, he says to Kovalik, 'What do you think of this? A poem dedicated to us.'

'What?' Kovalik, puzzled, sits erect and gazes at the Chinese characters on the smudged paper. 'Who wrote this? One of them?' he asks in amazement.

'No, not one of those four. Someone who was going to come but couldn't.'

'You mean wouldn't.'

'He was sick in camp. Here, I'll read it to you:

> '*I am Rebellion's Opening Page!*
> *I am the Child of History!*
> *I am a Gull of the Storm!*
> *I am the Bayonet of Time!*'

Kovalik sneezes violently, again, three times, and wipes tears from his eyes on his sleeve. He wants to say, 'At least one man in this miserable army can write more than his name,' but such a remark would only insult Li Chung-lin, who is as much a Chinese as a revolutionary. So instead Kovalik says they must try hard to recruit this poet for the next meeting. He wants to feel hopeful; out there in the sea of tents beyond Qufu is someone whose revolutionary ardor is unmistakable, a chosen man who can read, who possesses the ability to influence others. But enthusiasm doesn't come to Kovalik, no matter how hard he tries to force it. Perhaps, he tells himself, his stomach keeps him from generating optimism – those cramps, those pains deep within. More likely, however, he can't deceive himself into believing that this meeting with four bored soldiers in a little room next to a capitalistic latrine has been anything but a joke, a lie, a miserable defeat.

Outside in the dusty lane Li Chung-lin gives him an anxious glance. 'I think we'd better eat.'

'No,' Kovalik says emphatically. 'We're going to bite clouds.'

'You need food, Comrade.'

'I need to bite clouds.' Kovalik claps his slim companion on the back, simulating heartiness. 'After all, who introduced me to this greatest of pleasures?'

'It isn't the greatest of pleasures.'

'Trying to tempt me with women? Fine. But after biting clouds.' Kovalik strolls along with hands thrust into his pockets, whistling merrily. 'Such leisure! Nothing like it! Now I know how Nicholas felt, and the bitch of a Czarina and their cruddy family – all that leisure in the Palace at Czarskoe Selo!' Halting, he reaches out and yanks at Li's shirt. 'Do you realize, do you have any idea,' he begins tensely and lets go of the shirt. 'Stalin has deserted me, left me here to rot.' Kovalik sneezes again, wipes the wetness from his eyes. He sniffles, looking around the narrow lane. A porcelain mender, sitting at work near a wall, spits on a beetle trundling near his foot. Kovalik stares at the beetle as it rights itself, goes on.

'I know a good restaurant.' Li says, taking the Comrade's arm.

Kovalik pulls away. 'No. I'm in charge of this mission, am I not? Assigned in Wuhan. You to assist me. Am I in charge?'

'Yes, Comrade, you are.'

'I really am in charge of this mission. This *mission*!' he repeats, guffawing loudly enough for people to turn and stare at the tall, broadshouldered stranger in a coolie's hat.

Soon they see the familiar weathered door facing the narrow lane. The old woman lets them in; they climb the stairs with an odor like burned cinnamon getting stronger.

When they are seated, Kovalik takes the pipe from the taciturn proprietor, prepares his own thumbnail gob of opium, and heats it over the spirit lamp. He prides himself on his knowledge of *Ta-yen*. He knows, for example, that the opium of Yunnan, best of the Chinese varieties, must take a long, circuitous journey before arriving in Jinan. First it goes from Yunnan Province by French railroad to Haiphong in Indochina, then to Hong Kong, and from there to Shanghai. It takes this route, not because the Chinese authorities would confiscate it, but because it's safer from bandits and warlords. Kovalik knows more; he knows that the first lancing of the poppy gives the highest percentage of morphia; this accounts for the high quality of Indian and Persian opium – in those countries the poppy is lanced only once. He knows that the finest opium in the world is Indian Malwa, which he has yet to try. It's often eaten or drunk. He salivates in anticipation of having Malwa someday. Having little else to do but think about *Ta-yen*, he has even learned the harvesting schedule in China. He has forced Li Chung-lin to inquire and sniff out the facts. He may know little about Tang's wretched army, but he knows plenty about *Ta-yen*. In Szechuan it's harvested in April; in Yunnan and Shansi in July. He knows how the four incisions are made in the flower. He knows the sap is collected in the evening when the exudate turns from a cream color to pink to dark brown to black. He knows *Ta-yen*.

After smoking one pipe, Li puts his down and quietly announces that he wants no more. 'I like it only to take the edge off a difficult day.'

Filling his second pipe with the gooey substance, Kovalik laughs. 'I like it the whole day, any day.' He leans toward the lamp. 'Every day.'

After two hours, Li kneels beside Kovalik, who is stretched out on a bench with a wooden pillow under his head. 'Aren't you hungry? By now the *Ta-yen* should make you hungry.'

The Russian nods lazily. 'Yes, I'm hungry. But I need another pipe before we go.'

'So much will make you hungry. Too much will take your hunger away.'

After four hours and five pipes, Li says, 'You must come now.' He repeats the demand until Kovalik, half asleep, sits up and mutters, 'I'm no longer hungry.'

'But we're going anyway.'

On the street the late sun is slanting across low-slung rooftops, on tin and ceramic tile and thatch. Kovalik, holding his companion's arm, is taking quick, shallow breaths. 'Listen to me,' he urges impatiently, then says nothing.

They sway down the lane to a boulevard that leads to the center of town.

Kovalik lurches, nearly topples over. Li guides him to a wall beside the wide road and tells him to sit awhile. Blowing his breath out with a sigh, Kovalik obeys. 'I thank you, my friend. I have no Russian friends now. They left me to rot in this place. I don't even have anything to read.' He squints up at Li Chung-lin, who is staring down the earth-packed roadway. 'What are you looking at?'

'Cavalry. A small detachment.'

Propped against the wall, Kovalik allows images on the road to pass by him in their own pleasant order: cart, wheelbarrow, women carrying bundles on their backs; one, two, three, four, five coolies with poles on their shoulders; then an endless stream of people and animals no longer in logical procession, but a fluid motion continuous with the road itself.

The clopping of hooves gets louder. A file of cavalrymen approach; they pass the standing Chinese and his seated companion in the big hat.

One horse, reined in, turns and comes back.

A rider with straw-colored hair and an ax blade visible in his belt glares down at the two men. Pointing at Kovalik he says harshly in Chinese, 'Is he sick?'

'Yes,' Li replies with a curt nod, 'he's sick.'

Embree studies the fellow slumped against the wall, legs splayed out, spittle on the mouth; he can't see the eyes shaded by the hat. 'Sick? Or drunk?'

'He is not drunk.'

Hesitating, his horse prancing a few impatient steps, the American says, 'We can put him on my horse and take him in.'

'Our profound thanks for your generous offer' – Li has shifted into Chinese formality – 'but a thousand pardons, we will get back ourselves.'

'Is he the Bolshevik?' Embree leans forward in the saddle to get a better look at the pale face with its black beard, only partly visible under the coolie hat.

'He is Comrade Vladimir Kovalik,' Li announces with dignity.

'Why's he still here? Haven't the Reds been thrown out of China?'

'There's a Russian mission in Wuhan. Consulates in Shanghai and Canton,' Li says coolly.

'But there's no embassy in Peking, right? They threw the Reds out of Peking. And they're going to throw them out of Wuhan any moment. Am I right?'

Li looks up at the horseman without a word.

'What does General Tang want with a Bolshevik anyway?'

'Comrade Kovalik is here to help the General. As an adviser.'

'Does he speak Chinese?'

Li doesn't answer.

'Are you a Bolshevik too?'

'Yes, I'm a Bolshevik.'

After a long pause, the blond rider says, 'What are you two doing here in the town?'

'Nothing.'

'Nothing,' Embree repeats thoughtfully. 'Nothing but getting drunk, right?' For another moment he hesitates, as if ready to dismount, then jabbing the flank of his horse briskly, he heads down the road at a dustraising gallop.

Li kneels beside his comrade. 'The cavalry is gone now.'

Kovalik turns his watery eyes in Li's direction. 'I saw him, that American.' He smiles briefly, then his bearded face becomes blank. 'Does he really sleep on the horse?'

Now it is Li's turn to smile. 'I didn't ask him. For a moment I wasn't sure if he'd get off the horse and kill us or touch us to see if we're real.'

'Americans. They have not recognized my government. They are assholes.'

'Are you ready to go?'

Kovalik stares into the distance, then lowers his eyelids. The *Ta-yen* is really working. 'Almost ready,' he tells Li Chung-lin. But it's all hopeless, really hopeless. It's too pleasant now to think of the hopelessness, so he lets his mind drift through memory like a cloud. His brother's chubby face. Someone or other plodding through the snow. Now, now he has something in mind; he attaches himself to it, getting free of hopeless China. He is remembering the Far Eastern Russian Empire after the Civil War, its capital at China. Three years he was garrisoned there in the cavalry. It's worth remembering, and surely he has the time needed for such a memory. With utmost clarity he can see the taiga, the Siberian forest with its enormous pines ranked silently and endlessly in snow bluer than this summer light lapping around him here in China. He recalls, though with less vividness, the taste of *braga* and the homemade brandy they called *samogonka*. He and his mates swilled the stuff happily in dirty little inns while the wind whistled through cracks in the great logs, and they warmed their hands at a roaring fire smelling of pine cones. *Shanga*: Siberian pancakes. The name itself is good to remember. And *Kalach*: a thick black bread. He has seen reindeer and caribou dashing among the trees in that Land of Darkness, that dark mystery at the end of the world. He once lived in a house with walls three feet thick and triple windows to keep the cold out. He remembers the look of Yakutsk horses, squat and rugged, with cowlike faces and round bellies, snorting white geysers into the icy blue air. And the great Trans-Siberian Railroad – he has no difficulty remembering those rusty streaks of iron traveling across nothing to the extremity of nowhere. The trains, the trains – he can recall endless variations on the theme of trains: arriving at stations in the blue dawn, the constant hiss of steam; on the platform a virtual sea of fur, white leggings, billed caps; and the waiting there, the hollow sky sucking up the hours like smoke. Trains – he remembers as if it were yesterday that he boarded them in Perm, in Sverdlovsk, in Krasnoyarsk on his way to war. Once on a train somewhere he had peeked into a first-class compartment that had always been reserved for the aristocrats, but at the time served as a military command post; still intact were milk-glass lamps, an upright piano, lace-covered chairs, tapestries, gilded mirrors, lush sofas, plush curtains. He had half expected a white poodle to prance out of the room followed by a lovely woman in jewels; but instead, an officer in a great hide coat and black boots staggered drunk into the corridor and for fun emptied his revolver into the walnut panels before urinating on the red carpet.

'Good day, grandfather.' He was seven or eight, in a village outside Petrograd on a festive summer outing with his parents. He remembers what they wore – or thinks he does. His father, a mill worker, wore a felt hat with a jaunty feather in it that day. Mother wore beads that caught the sunlight and glittered. The man he called 'grandfather' was an old peasant they met casually in the street. Big and shapeless in heavy sheepskins, although the summer heat was stifling, the old man wore a tattered linen cap jammed over his broad forehead. 'Good day, little brother.' He insisted that the family come to his house for tea and bread. He wouldn't accept their refusal, but laughingly pulled father along. Kovalik can still remember the lean cattle in the street, the straw-heaped stalls in the market, the lichen-covered gate leading into the warm, musty, odorous dark hut. Tiny windows curtained by drab rags, floor of hard-beaten earth, a few sheepskins thrown down for rugs. A huge blackened stove, a greasy table, two rough benches. During tea the old man and his squat wife never spoke a word. But when the family rose to leave, the peasant suddenly became furious and accused them of robbing him of his meager store of food. As the family hurried away, he stood at his door and shouted at them. 'I invite you here, I give you everything, but you give me nothing in return! You city trash!'

Walking away, Kovalik's father told him – he has never forgotten – 'Remember this day, son. You have just met the Russian peasant. The wonder of your country. The despair of your country.'

Now, today, Kovalik has looked into eyes that remind him of the old peasant's – mild but unpredictable, indolent but alert, childlike but dangerous – although the eyes of the four soldiers were slanted instead of round.

Perhaps all peasants are the same, Kovalik thinks from somewhere deep within himself, where the *Ta-yen* works vigorously through his veins and cushions his mind. His bones seem to be rocking in a soundless cradle. It is a sensation he never wants to end.

Are peasants different from the city workers he'd known as a child? He'd always been told they were different, yet he no longer knows. He has seen too many people, seen them fight and suffer and die; dead, they are all the same.

Perhaps people are all the same, except the enemies of Lenin and Trotsky. They are different.

'Come on.'

He hears Russian words spoken softly against his ear. Slewing his head to the side, he meets a steady pair of slanted eyes.

'Come now,' the voice murmurs. The voice belongs to Li Chung-lin. 'It's time to go.'

Glancing past Li he sees a ring of other faces, all with their slanted eyes, all tense from curiosity. He fumbles in his pocket for one of the wooden dolls he makes, but can't find any. Maybe one of the children standing there would like a doll, only he doesn't have any at all. He hasn't carved for a while. No. Has he lost his knife? Does he have a carborundum stick to sharpen it on? Well, no matter.

'Come, get up, Comrade.'

'Yes, I will now,' Kovalik mutters, allowing Li Chung-lin to help him to his feet. In his nostrils, amazingly, is the smell of Russia: damp sheep's wool, fresh rye bread, and pungent Muscovy butter. But then it is gone.

13

This is his world, the army camp. He has no other. Nor does he want the memory of another. When his comrades, sitting with him in front of their tent, ask him about life in America, he shrugs and mutters slowly, like a man who finds recollecting things difficult, 'Well, I remember a lot of motor cars. And paved roads. Glass in the store windows,' he tells his listeners. 'Irving Berlin's songs. The telephone. And food: roast turkey with cranberry sauce, pancakes with syrup. I remember Christmas – that's a big festival.' Then his memory shuts down. Or he makes it shut down. He works hard at forgetting the past. He tries to rid himself of it in the same deliberate way that he wipes off the grime of a day's ride through the Shantung countryside.

This isn't the first time he has tried to forget the past.

He also did it at thirteen, not long after his mother's death, when he ran away. On the bus leaving New Haven, he made sure nothing in his clothes or small duffel bag identified him. He wasn't concerned about other people finding out who he was; he just didn't want to be reminded himself. On the way to Bridgeport, he started to call himself Nameless No Name. If people asked him, that was what he would tell them. And he had answers for other questions too. Where was he going? Anywhere, everywhere. Did he go to school? No, never did go to school. Who were his parents? Didn't have any.

Because the weather was mild when he reached Bridgeport, he slept that night in the park behind some bushes. Next day he spent a dime on a hamburger, then walked around the city, looking at strange faces, exulting in his freedom, hoping that someone would ask him who he was so he could say, 'I'm Nameless No Name.'

All day he dreamed of meeting gangsters who would ask him to join up. Maybe he'd just wander across the country in search of something. That evening he spent fifty cents at a local carnival and almost won a Kewpie Doll at a booth, throwing balls at painted tenpins. It got chill, the wind blew hard, so he slept that night on a bench in the bus station. Toward morning two policemen shook him roughly and asked his name. Embree told them immediately, 'Philip Embree,' and he went home to a baffled, subdued father who never discussed what happened but intensified the prayers for his son's soul.

Embree has cherished that experience all his life. He recalls the purity of feeling associated with having no past: Nameless No Name. Now, in this Chinese army camp, he allows himself only the barest images of life back home: the Old Campus fence at Yale; his father's study with its ranked books in the orderly shelves; the simple gray stone marking his mother's grave.

Controlling his memory is not always easy. Sometimes at night, lying in a sweltering tent filled with the odor of garlic, he imagines hearing in the far distance the long, mournful, assertive call to worship from the bell in the church steeple. At fewer intervals he is touched by guilt for what he has done – vanished without a trace, without a final testament from Philip Embree, without a curt note, much less candid letters informing father and Ursula of his decision to change his life. Nameless No Name. The guilt stays awhile like the dull ache of a rotting tooth; then mercifully something happens in camp to draw his attention beyond himself into the life of a Chinese army.

Once again he becomes the Ax Man.

It is now midmorning. Standing in the midst of camp, he looks down the dusty rows of tents. Most armies billet in villages or sleep alongside train sidings or in the fields, so these army tents are a rare sight in China. They represent a gift from Marshal Chang Tso-lin when last year General Tang defended Shantung Province from invasion by the Kiangsu warlord, General Sun Ch'uan-fang. The Marshal, in turn, had procured the tents as a gift from the Italian Embassy in Peking, and Philip Embree understands enough now about the intricacies of Chinese business – and its essential component, bribery – to guess that the Italians offered the tents in exchange, say, for a timber concession in Manchuria or an assignment of waterfront property in Tientsin Harbor or the right to make an archeological dig somewhere in the Northwest. After half a year the canvas of many tents has been weakened by

302

monsoon soaking and mildew and ripped by gusts of wind sweeping in from Central Asia.

Still, Embree and his companions are lucky to have this much shelter, to say nothing of millet gruel every morning. Now he fully appreciates the Chinese greeting. 'Have you eaten today?' It's more than polite; it's a real question, a vital one, the only one for countless Chinese. Most of the men in his unit have joined the army as an alternative to starving in their villages. Only a few know more than a couple dozen written characters; fewer yet can read a newspaper. They are happy to have a canteen, a blanket, straw sandals, a paper umbrella – all standard issue – and some kind of weapon, even if it is a rifle with a pitted barrel. Many recruits will never discover if their guns work until the moment they face the enemy – shortage of ammo excludes target practice.

Walking down the row of tents, Embree watches some of the men cleaning their weapons, playing dice, fanning themselves, or munching on apples with the vigor of ruminating cows. They aren't much. Even so, Embree feels wonderfully close to them. They mean more to him than his classmates at Yale ever did. He envisions going into battle with these men, living or dying at their sides. The intense friendship of soldiers is what he seeks. Moreover, he likes them for their qualities: acceptance of life as it is, endurance, and common sense. They ask what something costs; they never ask is there a god or what happens to me when I die. After a lifetime of grappling with lofty questions that don't seem to have answers, Embree welcomes his daily encounter with a single issue, pure in its simplicity: how to survive.

Wherever he goes in camp, he feels the constant regard of curious eyes. Not only is he a foreigner, which makes him fair game for bold stares, but he's also the man who saved their general's life at Thousand Buddha Mountain. Although showing a restraint derived from native cautiousness in handling foreigners, they still manage to treat him as something of a hero. Little things mark their respect: two hard-boiled eggs (a rarity in camp) set outside his tent the morning after his return from Jinan; a better saddle awaiting him when he went to see his horse; two clean pairs of cloth puttees laid on his grass mat inside the tent.

But saving the General's life hasn't made Embree a hero to himself. After all, what he did at Thousand Mountain was nothing more than the result of father's exhortations and training. To any public distress – so went the law of Embree's boyhood – he must respond in such a way that his action can be labeled 'doing good' or 'helping out' or 'performing a Christian duty.' Saving the General, therefore, doesn't have the stamp of his own decision; for that matter, he isn't even sure if he likes Tang Shan-teh. Of course he admires the man's strength and energy – qualities he also admires in his father – but at the same time he feels uneasy in the presence of someone with so much authority. In conversation with the General he's reminded of past times with his father, when he was never sure how far he could go in expressing himself. Implicit in both men, however, is the freedom to say whatever comes to *their* minds. They carry conviction; they're both the defenders and the purveyors of the truth – their own. So do you mean to save someone you fear more than you like? Embree doesn't know.

This morning he hears an old trumpet sounding through the hot, bright air, summoning the men to the parade ground, an uneven area of packed earth on the edge of a wheat field. Such gatherings are frequent, a way of fighting the boredom of camp life. Aside from drill and forced marches, the men work half-heartedly at weaving or tailoring; or they simply pick lice from one another's head. They like athletic contests for a break, and today a long-distance race has been arranged. Each battalion has selected one man to represent it. Preparations have been underway for a few days, and within minutes of the bugle call more than five thousand cooks, soldiers, animal tenders, gunsmiths, and petty officers have assembled to hear the rules explained.

Fifteen contestants, chosen by their units, shoulder through the gathering crowd to the middle of the parade ground.

Embree is one of them.

His selection has been yet another mark of respect from the men. Touching the raised scar on his forehead, shy and proud of the invitation to represent the Third Battalion, he had said to his comrades, 'I'm unworthy of you. You're all stronger and faster than I am, yet humbly I accept your gracious offer. Forgive my incompetence.'

Now he stands at the starting line, a stick-drawn line in the parade ground dirt. A group of officers, wearing peaked garrison caps, order the onlookers to form two lines, thus making a corridor through which the runners can begin the race. Next to Embree stands the contestant from the Fourth Battalion. He's from the Big Sword Company, the best horsemen in the army. In view of their favor with the General, they wear a patch on their shirt pockets; the characters sewn on it read: 'We fight with a gun, then a sword, then a fist, then with our teeth.'

The Big Swords had made the morning raid on White Wolf, and one of them doubtless had killed Fu-fang, had shot her face off.

The Big Sword runner, removing his shirt and throwing it to a comrade, stands with one bare foot toeing the line, his broad face set in concentration. The parade ground is a mass of blue-uniformed milling soldiers for whom such an event is the only diversion they will probably have this month. Many of them are betting the few *cash* they possess. The merits of contestants are loudly debated with good-humored bravado. Through the din of voices Embree hears 'the foreigner' and the 'Ax Man' being wildly praised by someone; it thrills and frightens him. He is lean, in better shape than he has been since his rowing days, but some of these runners, the Big Sword, for example, are heavily muscled men who have been toughened by years of outdoor work.

Embree is spared more anxious comparisons because a sergeant, lifting his pistol high, fires into the air. The race is on.

The fifteen set off at a dog trot between the two lines of men screaming encouragement to their favorites. Stripped to the waist, wearing knee-length shorts, Philip Embree begins to relax by the time they reach the end of the corridor and enter a fallow wheat field, as yet not ready for autumn planting. Running in the middle of the pack, he crunches into the dried stubble and nearly stumbles from the surprise of sharp pain – his bare feet at each step are bruised, cut by stalks as hard as jagged rock. The other runners don't seem affected, but continue through the field as if running on a smooth track.

Midway across it, thrown off balance by pain, Embree pitches forward and crashes down. A wheat stalk, shorn off inches from the ground, grazes him swordlike below the rib cage and opens up a cut at least six inches long across his belly. Had his rope belt not deflected it, the stalk would have impaled him. Shifting in the stubble – it sounds like crinkled paper – Embree sits up and examines the wound. It looks superficial, in spite of the bleeding. Rising to his feet, he sees the whole pack far ahead, beyond the wheat field now, and approaching a clump of trees. If he turns back, onlookers still massed on the parade ground will see him – his total defeat. Better to quit beyond their judging eyes, somewhere in the trees ahead or even beyond.

So he starts running or rather stumbling through the field, with the pain in his feet less insistent than that in his side. Glancing down, he sees blood welling out of the long slit; it's not copious, not sufficient to bring him to a halt.

So he goes on and finds himself out of the field at last, running along a dirt path toward the woods into which the other runners have already disappeared. Once on firmer ground, without the stalks pricking his feet at each step, Embree feels more confident of running a respectable distance before quitting. He should have run with straw sandals. It was allowed. Perhaps half the contestants wore them, but he had to prove he could withstand as much as men who'd gone without shoes for most of their lifetimes.

A noncommissioned officer is standing at the edge of the woods; he's a referee stationed there to indicate the path. Seeing Embree limp along so far behind, he grins and waves him on with a comic gesture, as if urging a reluctant mule.

They all want to see the foreign devil lose, Embree thinks, as he plunges into the cool shade of the forest. Goaded by that certainty, he tries picking up the pace; to his surprise, as well as relief, Embree manages to go a little faster. For the first moment during the race – perhaps a mile of it run already – he feels his lungs and muscles easing into a rhythm. Although his feet hurt at each step (they trail blood in their wake), the generation of rhythm enables him to overcome the pain; he keeps going. Elm, poplar, white-barked pine flow past him, as his arms and legs pump him along the serpentine path and then beyond it, out into the sunlight again.

The plain stretches toward the haze of a horizon broken by distant hills. Closer, to each side of the path in planted or fallow fields, rise smaller mounds, the graves of local families placed in the midst of their precious land – too sacred for plowing, even in time of famine. Embree sees them dotting the plain, a host of ancestors supervising seed times and harvests. Counting the burial mounds helps to pass the time as he runs, but pain makes him lose the count.

Ahead is a river flowing swiftly between high banks, which seem to have been sheared off by immense scissors, perpendicular to the brown water; it is thick with silt, moving at terrific speed. The river isn't wide, perhaps only a hundred yards, but the contestants are struggling desperately to cross it. All but a few are holding on to foot-long logs with one arm and trying to navigate with the other. They are being carried downstream much farther than the river is wide.

Limping up to the shore, Embree ignores the heap of prepared logs to which a squatting referee points with a smile. This is where Embree can make up time – by swimming across.

He dives into the water and with a powerful stroke (perfected during summers at the Cape) battles the current. It draws him inexorably downstream, as if a vacuum, unseen beneath the clay-colored roiling water, is sucking him toward a subterranean destiny. Yet he makes far more headway than the men helplessly gripping their logs. It occurs to him they have never learned to swim, yet here they are, crossing a dangerous river at great risk for nothing more than a foot race. But perhaps it's more than a race, he tells himself, stroking for shore. Perhaps it's everything.

Glancing downstream, he sees a few contestants who have reached shore groping up the steep bank. They fall back, unable to get footholds in the slippery earth. Others are being pulled farther downstream by the relentless current. Fired by the challenge, Embree starts fighting the water, his arms flailing.

Careful, he tells himself.

Don't fight, *use* the water.

Stroke.

Stroke.

Something flashes in from the past. It's summer on the Cape. He's fighting the breakers, trying to get in, hoping to save his life, while father paces along the shoreline, waiting to punish him for disobeying the order to keep out of a storm-swept sea.

Stroke.

He sees his father's angry face on the shore and the sight of it urges him to win, to live, to prove his worth.

Embree sees the bank ahead. Reaching out, he grabs at the slick earth; his hand pulls free, as if the water's a rope tied round his waist, yanking him clear. Again he grabs, his fingers hooking like talons into the loam; this time they hold on until his other hand makes its own grip, secures its purchase. Then he's scrambling up, moving from one fugitive grip to the next, until one hand covers the top of the bank, six feet above the surface of the ferocious river.

Pulling himself up and rising to his feet, Embree looks westward at a wheel-rutted road along which about half the runners have begun to jog. The other half are still in the river, a few of them far downstream.

A frowning referee, using his garrison cap for the purpose, signals Embree to start down the road.

Now it's Embree's turn to grin. His feet hurt, but they take him across the hard-packed dusty earth. The water has washed the blood off his belly; it's starting to bleed again, but just a little, only enough to make a soft, wavy line, as if a loaded paintbrush has dragged across the skin. There's no question now about quitting the race. He has made up considerable distance because of the river; and it'll be recrossed on the return leg of the course, giving him another chance to gain. Embree nearly shouts from exhilaration as he moves along the road not more than fifty yards behind that bastard from the Big Swords.

Ahead is a rocky hill, one of those outcroppings of earth that were thrust out of this plain long before men ever trod it. Embree can see Big Sword begin the climb, and from the man's abrupt slowing down, as if he were slogging through invisible mud, Embree can judge just how steep and difficult the climb is.

He soon finds out for himself. Not until now has he felt the full weight of the day's heat. It lies on his shoulders like a heap of smoldering wool as he forces himself upward through scrub weed, across pebbles. The legs of a runner a dozen steps ahead of him catch Embree's eye. They display a network of veins, muscles, tendons, all ballooning out and collapsing at each push forward. Embree concentrates on the pulsing look of those legs. They seem independent of the upper body – parts of a machine gone awry, awkward pistons churning to detach themselves from the solid foundation of the body. He wants to keep watching them, but heat and fatigue demand his attention. Everything below his chest feels insignificant, even the pain. Only his breath has meaning on this hill; it goes in, it goes out, painfully. He keeps his eyes on the wildly oscillating legs, fearful of estimating how much farther he must go.

Embree passes a runner who has collapsed. In the delirium of his own exhaustion he sees for an instant not a man but a dog. Perhaps the transformation takes place because the man is panting violently, his gaping mouth rigid, his dull eyes half closed, like those of a dog overcome by the heat. Embree glances back, seeing a man with legs splayed out, hands lying Buddha-like in his lap. The man hasn't even seen Embree go by, but remains deeply concentrating on his own anguish.

The legs that Embree has been following abruptly vanish. That runner has reached the top, and Embree's right behind him.

A referee sitting on a boulder motions at a large rock propped

308

nearby like a gravestone. 'Touch it,' he orders Embree gruffly.

Bending as he passes, Embree does. He halts for a few quick breaths before starting the descent. Then he plunges downward, trailing small avalanches of pebbles in his wake, trying to control his progress so as to prevent a headlong pitch down the hillside. He's too busy watching his step – a turned ankle would mean disaster – to notice how the other runners are doing. But reaching bottom he counts five men ahead of him, trotting along the road leading south. It will take them back to the raging little river, where he can make up time. Because he is not only going to finish this race, he is going to win it. I am, he tells himself, heading after them. Glancing at his stomach, Embree notes with satisfaction that the bleeding has completely stopped. Little gouts of congealed blood hang from the slitlike wound like berries on a bough. Berries on a bough? Christmas? 'Fuck Christmas,' he pants aloud in English. The defiant obscenity buoys his spirits. Did you hear that, father?

Below his knees is a mass of generalized pain that seems oddly to come from the road itself. But there's pain elsewhere too – in thighs, lungs, shoulders – so much of it that the sensation forms another presence. So what does that make him? A friendly companion. Pain is what runs.

Not clear thinking, he realizes, but for the lapse in clarity he's grateful. Better numb, right? He wants to giggle. A certain fogginess helps him get down the road to the riverbank, where he half dives and half wades into the flood. A paroxysm of current sweeps him away. Embree feels as though he is riding the back of a huge, leaping animal – one of those dragons seen everywhere in China. His arms flail, trying to control the dragon, but this time he has much less strength. After a few clumsy strokes, he treads water and gasps for breath, swallowing the tepid muddy liquid that makes him cough like a beginner. Buffeted in the current, he is carried downstream with the others, all of them clinging to logs taken from the riverbank.

Embree feels himself weakening, getting sucked down, but then his strength renews itself when he watches a man lose hold of a log to tumble free in the channel. Stroking with energy, he watches at each turn of his head how the man goes down the river. The log moves faster, bobbing like a cork, while the drowning man stretches out his arms, grabbing at empty air above his head. Embree has a final glimpse: the round eyes filled with the sight of death, his own; fingers of both hands raking the muddy surface of the river; shoulders rolling in a circular motion like the log he'd gripped and lost. On the way to Qufu at the flooded Yellow River a horse had gone down, Embree remembers. Horse, man: the same in death, Where is God?

For an instant, struggling himself, Embree wonders if he should go after the drowning man. Perhaps he might catch up a few hundred yards downstream, haul the fellow to shore – and lose the race. No one else is stopping; the race continues. Besides, just ahead now is the bank. Embree hauls himself up the embankment, the mud as slick as ice, and finally gets over it. Flopping down, he lies full length and stares at another man, not six feet away. Panting for breath, they watch each other in stupefied pain. Then Embree sees a strong emotion come into the man's eyes. The exhausted runner begins crawling toward Embree.

He's going to push me over the embankment.

Embree doesn't move, but pretends to a helplessness he's not feeling.

When the man reaches him, Embree rises suddenly to his knees, makes a single fist with both hands, and swings it like a sledgehammer. The blow, delivered sharply and accurately, knocks the man over the bank into the river. For a moment Embree sees nothing, then the man's head appears in the muddy water, but without any accompanying motion. He's unconscious, a nonswimmer in a flood.

Staggering to his feet, Embree stares at the road that will take him to the finish line. To his left he sees Big Sword swinging onto the dusty path at a slow but dogged trot. Another man is not far behind the leader, and Embree realizes he's within ten or fifteen feet of catching them both. Yes, he is moving too. He has been running after them without knowing it. There is nothing much left of him to know with. He is hardly more than eyes and a pumping heart. He is conscious of two things: the two men ahead of him and the feel of his heart beating within his rib cage, like a trapped frantic bird. But it's all right, everything is, because he's definitely going to do it. His feet take him forward while another thought occurs to him – somewhere in his skull, the thing he really is is sitting. It knows he is going to do it. It is smiling in there, knowing he will win. His eyes register the poplars lining the narrow road, and something below his waist is moving, and he knows where God is – inside his head. Not more than four or five feet in front of him now is a man.

They are even.

Giving him a furious glance, the man reaches out to hit Embree, who hits back. Staggering close together, they collide. Embree, being heavier, succeeds in making the man stumble, lose stride, fall behind.

Embree feels as though he has just urinated. A wetness seeps through his shorts. But it is blood, blood from the wound that reopened during his struggle in the river. The bleeding quickens; a bright red ribbon of it winds sluggishly down his leg. 'Fuck the bleeding,' he says aloud. It doesn't matter. All that matters now is catching Big Sword.

It's going to be all right. He's going to do it. Calm pervades him when ahead, not more than a couple of hundred yards, he sees a moving mass of blue on a flat surface – thousands of soldiers crowding the parade ground. Above them, rising like a gallows, he notices the tall wooden frame and climbing ropes hanging from it.

I'm going to win, Embree tells himself, when finally, not more than ten feet behind Big Sword, he enters the corridor of yelling men. To his dismay, he realizes that the other runner hasn't lost speed, but on the contrary has begun a final sprint. They both stagger between the rows of screaming men. Not many yards to go. Embree has gained a couple of feet, with perhaps five or six still between them. The thickly muscled legs of Big Sword keep going, keep going – and in frustration Embree sees him leave the ground.

Big Sword has begun to climb ropes.

Seizing a hemp rope almost instantly thereafter, Embree starts hand over hand up the twenty feet of snaking line. He feels nothing but the swaying progress of his arms, the tremendous pull of bicep and shoulder; the rope vanishes below him, as his eyes look up at the decreasing length of rope above him. Now ten feet, now maybe six.

A roar from thousands of throats tells Embree he has failed.

When his hand touches the overhead plank of the frame, Embree glances to the left and meets the weary eyes of Big Sword. Slowly the man begins to smile and Embree can't help but smile back, as they both cling for an extra moment to the ropes twenty feet above the yelling mob of spectators, sharing the solitude of pain and exhaustion and endurance.

*   *   *

Embree is honing the ax blade against a borrowed whetstone. The keen-edged blade catches the light, flashes in his intent face. He works on the ax every morning after drill. From inside the tent come voices, one raised in triumph, one groaning in defeat. Men are gambling in there. Patiently Embree draws the blade across the whetstone; it's his chief activity, his sole amusement. What had he done to pass the time at Yale? Read novels. Jack London, H.G. Wells. He recalls the overstuffed chair near the window, where he sat to read his novels. Embree rids himself of the memory by pushing the blade hard against the whetstone.

Yesterday he killed a man.

That is also a memory he wishes to avoid.

So he listens to the gamblers arguing inside the tent. Soon they'll be telling stories. Often they exchange tales of the exploits of great generals of history. Perhaps, once again, they'll conjure up more of the cunning of Yueh Fei, who fought against the Mongols in the twelfth century. Yueh Fei – their Stonewall Jackson.

Embree hones.

But if I hadn't killed him, he'd certainly have pushed me into the river. It was a matter of life and death.

Embree pushes the blade rapidly across the stone.

And anyway, I didn't mean to kill him; I only wanted to prevent him from killing me.

And anyway, there was the race to win.

His father never tired of a quote from Ecclesiastes: 'Whatsoever thy hand findeth to do, do it with thy might.' And that is what Embree did yesterday.

He hones vigorously until a shadow crosses his light and turns the burnished blade in his hand a darker, metallic gray.

Looking up he sees the Big Sword who won the race. Like himself the man has a scar on his face; only unlike his own, this scar is on the cheek. Embree regards him curiously, up close. He wears crossed bandoliers and leather boots, the latter his prize for winning.

Embree stares at the boots. His own torn feet can hardly endure straw sandals, yet this man wears new stiff leather on feet that had run more than fifteen miles over wheat stubble and rock.

Embree, rising, stands beside the man, who's somewhat shorter but as broad in the chest. Their eyes meet warily a moment. Then Big Sword makes a typical Chinese disclaimer of personal excellence: His winning was accidental, for it had been obvious to everyone yesterday that the Ax Man was stronger and faster.

In turn, Embree denies his own ability and praises his opponent.

Amenities completed, the man introduces himself as Fu Chang-so. Behind him stand two other men, also wearing Big Sword patches. Fu explains that he and his companions wish to speak with the Ax Man on a matter of importance. They beg only a moment of his time to ask with due respect if he will consider their humble proposal. The captain of the Big Sword Company of the Fourth Battalion has given them permission to ask him to join.

Join the Big Swords? Embree controls his excitement by staring at the ground, as if considering the idea judiciously.

Fu explains further that they must wait officially until General Tang returns from Shanghai – he alone can make the final decision on such a transfer – but if permission's granted, the Ax Man can keep this permanently. Fu holds out a shirt patch.

Suppressing the desire to seize it, Embree says, 'You do me too much honor.' Patiently the trio wait. 'Nothing in this world,' Embree continues in a carefully measured voice, 'could give so much pleasure to such an unworthy person. I humbly thank you.' Then he reaches out and accepts the patch.

After the trio bow curtly and stride away, Embree experiences a feeling that amounts to exaltation. It occurs to him to sit down and write father a letter. A foolish idea, quickly discarded. Sitting cross-legged, feeling a stitch of pain in his belly, he picks up the ax and fingers the keen blade. The idea of such a letter amuses him, and he plays at composing it.

Dear Father:
Sorry I haven't written, but I have been quite busy living with mountain bandits and making love to a camp whore and avoiding death by TNT. But I do think you will be interested in an honor paid to me today. I have been invited to join a special unit of Chinese cavalry in the army of a general whose life I have saved. I earned that honor by following your injunction from Ecclesiastes to do with all my might whatsoever my hand finds to do. In this instance, it was to push a man into a raging river.

Yours in the service of the Lord,
Philip

Of everything in this imaginary letter, he enjoys most the complimentary close.

A few days later, returning from maneuvers at noon, a column of horsemen passes through a patch of woodland smelling of late summer flowers.

Near the rear, guided by Fu Chang-so's example, Embree reins in his horse; turning, they gallop together back up the road, telling their companions they are going in search of a missing canteen. A couple of riders in the column glance over their shoulders, but their attention is quickly redirected to the wheat cakes waiting in camp.

Around a curve in the road Fu urges his mount into deep undergrowth, with Embree following. Side by side, unseen in the thicket, they wait.

Another column of horse rounds the curve. Three men, breaking from the column, tell their companions essentially the same story: They are going to look for a pistol that must have slipped from a belt and fallen onto the road.

The three men wait until Fu and Embree, coming out of the thicket, join them. Everything has gone according to plan. Two Big Sword sergeants have been bribed so the five can be missing for the rest of the day without report.

Yesterday when Fu asked him to come along, Embree didn't hesitate, although warned that they'd be committing an act of desertion, according to Standing Orders, and in consequence would be executed if caught. 'Don't expect sympathy if they shoot us,' said Fu. 'The company will get extra pay for watching. You don't mind watching a comrade die if it's worth a few *cash*. That's the army way.'

Shocked by the practice, Embree said, 'Is that Tang's way?'

'Few generals are as good as Tang Shan-teh,' Fu declared loyally. 'If he gives a bonus for executions, he does the same for weddings. Lose a leg, he gives you a monthly pension, if he has the money.' The Big Sword shrugged. 'So we take our chances tomorrow. But believe me, we'll have fun.'

As they ride now at midday down a rutted lane, he explains what 'fun' means. They are going to visit a certain landlord in a nearby town. This landlord is an important landlord. Head of the Rain Making Society. Leading official of the Temple Association. A story goes with this landlord, Wang Nan-fang. The story concerns the father of a Big Sword. It seems that the father, being a peasant, once borrowed some money from landlord Wang to buy medicine for his sick wife. To guarantee the loan, the frantic peasant indentured himself for three years at Wang's insistence.

Embree interrupts. 'Three years? For a little medicine?'

Fu explains that in small towns and villages a peasant will often sell his labor to a landlord – as much as three or four hours daily – to buy the barest necessities. The length of servitude depends on the desperation of the peasant and the greed of the landlord. Wang was a greedy man. And the father of the Big Sword was desperate. So daily he worked for the landlord two, sometimes three or four hours. At the end of three years, Wang claimed that tools had been broken and stolen during working hours. It was a claim that the peasant failed to refute in front of a magistrate who was Wang's brother-in-law. Consequently, this father of a Big Sword owed many times the original debt. To earn his freedom at the end of the fourth year, he sold the timbers of his roof. Wang was furious, having contemplated the continuing arrangement for a longer time. So on his orders the peasant was thoroughly beaten by toughs. The landlord defended his action by arguing that destruction of town property, even to raise money to pay a debt, was sinful, a crime against the gods.

'Our comrade is dead now, killed in battle last year,' Fu explains as they ride along. 'So is his father dead. But there's a debt still to pay.'

'Whose?' Embree asks.

'Landlord Wang owes a debt to father and son, and we are going to collect it for them,' Fu says with a smile.

'Do you mean to kill him?'

'Oh, better than that.' Fu points toward the horizon. 'There, you can see the town where Wang Nan-fang lives.'

Snuggled in a park of trees stands a high clay wall, crumbling in many places. Behind it can be seen tiled and thatched roofs.

As the five horsemen turn into a side road leading to the town, Embree asks thoughtfully, 'Won't this landlord report our visit to headquarters?'

Fu shrugs. 'If he does, of course we die. But if we do, other Big Swords will pay him a visit. We'll explain that to him.'

'I was merely curious,' Embree says defensively. He doesn't want to leave the impression he's afraid.

Fu glances at him. 'I never thought anything else,' and spurs his horse into a canter.

When Embree enters the town, images register, then vanish: Rows of adobe houses without windows facing the street; a hut-sized mud temple ('They keep the Harvest God in it,' explains Fu); a pond green with slime; rutted tree-lined lanes leading out to the fields; a town vista of reddish clay, half crumbling, hardly shaped enough to mark it as the work of men. Fu asks directions along the way from peasants with loads of produce strapped to their backs. A few, smoking pipes, squat under eaves out of the hot sun and watch impassively as the five uniformed soldiers file down the street.

They ride into a better part of town, where artisans and merchants have removed wooden slats from their storefronts to expose their goods to public view. A coffin maker is at work. Embree studies him as they pass, craning his head around to watch as long as possible. The coffin maker on one end of a saw, his assistant on the other, work it back and forth across a log lying against a sawhorse. Piles of coffins and stacked funeral canopies fill his booth and flow out into the street, along with huge red-lacquered funeral poles. Farther along the street Embree notices the open-air forge of a blacksmith; sparks fly in red profusion from the blows he gives a piece of iron. Suddenly Embree wishes that he had someone from home to share all of this with. Not father, not Ursula either. Someone, anyone off the streets of New Haven. An American like himself. They'd exchange glances, assuring themselves their eyes have seen what is actually here – like sticks of incense drying in rows on wooden benches or wet sheets of paper drying on the walls of nearby houses.

Ahead is a wall in good repair, its top capped with lime and straw to prevent crumbling in the rain. The gate is thick planks held together by iron stripping. Here, silently, they dismount, and Fu confirms from a passerby that this is the residence of Wang Nan-fang.

For good luck – it has become his custom – Embree touches the blade of his ax.

After Fu pounds hard on the gate, an iron window on it slides open and an old voice asks irascibly who is there.

'A contingent from the army of General Tang Shan-teh, come to pay respects to the honorable Wan Nan-fang.'

'What's that?'

Fu, smiling, patiently repeats his words. He has a certain flair and dignity. Embree wonders if it was acquired during Fu's visits to an uncle who worked as a gardener for a great clan in Wuhsi.

The gate window slides shut, and the men wait in the stifling heat. After a long while the window slides open again and the old voice says, 'Master sends his regrets. He is presently ill in bed. If you will kindly leave your address in town, he will be delighted and honored to send for you later in the day. Master says further – '

'You turd, open the door,' Fu is holding a pistol at the window, pointed directly at the wrinkled face framed there.

The heavy gate swings slowly back and the men enter, facing a spirit screen and the old servant, who backs away, mouth open in fear.

'Come here, old man,' says Fu. Turning to one of the Big Swords, he says, 'Show him our invitation.'

Walking up to the old man, the Big Sword takes out a small knife, then looks for confirmation at Fu, who nods approval. The keen blade moves lightly against the withered cheek, cutting a small gash in it, enough to make blood flow down cheek and jaw; the old man whimpers.

'That's our invitation. Something to show your master.' Fu watches the servant clap one hand against his bleeding face. 'When you take that to Wang, I think he'll jump out of bed, sick or not.' He shoos the old servant around the spirit screen. 'Tell your master we humbly await his pleasure!' When the servant is gone, Fu whispers to two of his men. 'Watch the rear. Wang may try to escape.' Then to Embree he says, 'How do you feel, foreigner? Do you still want to have fun?'

Embree hesitates. *With all thy might.* 'Yes,' he says, hoping no one will see his hands trembling. To steady them he puts one on the ax, one on his belt. If Fu had asked him to cut the old man, would he have done it? Maybe someone from New Haven could tell him. An odd thought, but there isn't time to dwell on it, as he follows the others around the spirit screen into the courtyard.

The house seems well made but neglected. Only a single potted plant sits in the yard. No trees. The main door and windows are wide open, so the rising cries of fear and dismay inside are clearly heard by the incoming Big Swords. Halting in the yard, they wait. Around a corner of the house Embree has a view of a side compound, a couple of other houses set at angles to one another, and a gowned figure running with a mincing gait, vanishing into one of the buildings.

There's a commotion at the front door. A short, plump, but sturdily built man in late middle age comes to the entrance. He is wearing a mandarin robe, a black skullcap. From his shirt pocket protrudes a Western fountain pen; on his wrist is a watch and his shoes are leather, with laces.

On seeing the three men, he grimaces in fear, possibly anger, then gives them a bright smile. 'Ah, honorable friends! Please come in! Please! You are welcome to my poor humble house! Welcome! Come in! Please, please – ' Bowing, hands in opposite sleeves, he ushers the three soldiers into the house with elaborate ceremony. In the dark foyer, salted ducks hang from the ceiling. Beyond is the main room, rather small and airless, but with lotus chairs, an incense stand, a sandalwood table. There are no scrolls on the walls, no vases anywhere, a dozen or so wine pots are stacked in a corner. It is a peasant's hut elevated by haphazard expenditures into the residence of a country landlord.

'Sit, sit, honored guests!' Wang is saying. 'Tea! Cakes! Everything! Everything I have is yours!' He shouts roughly at servants who come bumbling in, wide-eyed, fearful, confused. 'You heard me! Tea and cakes!'

Fu, smiling, sits down in a chair. On his face there's a look that Embree recalls having seen before, only on someone else's face. The same icy resolve, the same merciless fury kept under control with great effort, it being marked by tension at the edges of the mouth, in the nostrils. It's the same look he saw on Chin's face before the bandit ordered the execution of Tang's officers at the train. Embree remembers. He watches, fascinated, as Fu smiles that way.

'So you are representatives of the great General Tang,' says the landlord, giving a short cackle of pleasure. 'What a great spirit he is! Favorite of the gods, though I won't say it too loud' – he puts one finger to his lips – 'for fear they hear me and do him harm.' Wang begins rocking back and forth at every word. 'We are fortunate in having such a worthy successor to Kuan Yu right here in our poor district. How fortunate to have him. He has done nothing but good. Yes, good. Yes . . .' Landlord Wang's voice trails off when he looks at Fu's smile.

'I see you still wear a Manchu queue,' the Big Sword says in a pleasant voice.

A grimace crosses Wang's face. Obviously he thinks it's a curious question. 'Well, Captain, it really has nothing to do with the Manchu.'

318

'I'm not a captain,' Fu says icily, but maintains his smile.

'Yes, yes, of course. What I mean is, I wear it because our family has done so for generations.' Continuing to rock, Wang says, 'It means nothing.'

'Of course it means something. It means filial respect for your ancestors.'

'You have it there, sir! Filial piety. As the Great Sage tells us: "Respect for our ancestors is the glory of our land"!'

'Naturally you have sons to carry on your name. May I ask how many?'

Warily the stout man eyes Fu, before replying in a softer, less ebullient voice. 'Yes, sir. I have two.'

'Here?'

'One in Peking.' Wang pauses.

'But the other, he is here?'

Wang doesn't reply, but turns at the sound of servants rushing in with trays of sweetmeats and teacups. 'Here, here we are! Best tea in the district, if you permit me the immodesty of saying so. Serve them. Serve them,' he yells tensely at the serving girls.

'Give me wine,' Fu says, frowning for the first time.

Holding a teacup, Wang seems startled by the sudden brusque demand. He repeats it in a faint voice. 'Wine.' Turning to a servant, he mutters quickly, 'Wine, get it. The best yellow.'

'And daughters?' Fu asks, holding the teacup without drinking from it.

'Sir?'

'Do you have daughters?'

'But not here!' cries Wang, putting his cup down hard on the table. Rocking violently in his lotus chair, he says, 'One in Peking, another visiting her grandmother in Jinan. That's all. Two daughters, but not here.'

Fu throws the teacup on the floor, splintering it. Looking steadily at the landlord, he says, 'Forgive my clumsiness. I deeply regret breaking it.'

'Honored guest, it's nothing. Really nothing, that cup.'

'Yes, I suppose you have so many, it really is nothing.'

Wang, staring at the soldier, begins shaking his head. 'Oh, but I don't have many. No, sir. Essentially I'm a poor man. On my last legs, really, if the truth be known.'

'If the truth be known.' Putting out a hand, Fu Chang-so taps the sandalwood table. 'Our host is poor,' he tells Embree, and to

319

'Sir – '

'Sit back and live, Wang Nan-fang.'

The stout man sits back.

'We don't want your filthy bribes, your shitty cakes and wine, we want your women in payment of the debt.' Fu removes his pistol and lays it in his lap. 'Now where's your son? Get him here if you want to live. Get him!'

Wang has started rocking again. 'Is this my lot, is this my fate?' he complains.

'Get him!'

'I will. Yes, I will. Girl!' A servant appears in the doorway, ashen with fear. 'Bring Little Brother here.' To Fu he says, 'Don't kill him. I beg you, honorable soldier. Have anything you want – all the women – but don't kill him.'

'We're not going to kill anyone. Stop whining,' Fu tells him. To Embree he says, 'Have you ever seen anything more disgusting?' And to Wang he says, 'We'll have your women and cause you some pain and your son will watch, but that's all. It will pay the debt, do you understand?'

Embree, hearing something, turns to the door and sees a boy standing there, about ten years old, his small mouth set firmly to endure what must be endured.

Embree is sitting against a wall, hearing Wang in the sheep hut screaming as he sways back and forth, hanging from a rafter by his queue. The son, obeying Fu's orders, sits mutely beneath his helpless father. Embree doesn't know where Fu is, but obviously he has the girl in a room somewhere within the compound. Wang's wife, unharmed (an aged woman in black silk, hair dressed in seed-pearl pins, hands wearing fingernail guards in a parody of Manchu aristocracy), has gone off to weep in solitude for her daughters. The three Big Sword horsemen, generously sharing their bounty, are inside the master's bedroom with three girls: another of Wang's daughters, a concubine, and a pretty servant.

Embree is sitting in the second courtyard, near the pig trough, against the wall. Through open slats in the bedroom window come the sounds of men laughing; and at intervals from that window Embree hears a girl sobbing and moaning.

A girl is slumped against the wall not far from Embree, who glances often at her, furtively, guiltily.

Entering the servant quarters, where all the women were held, he had chosen this one, a concubine. He picked her for her pale skin and youth, and pulled her from the room, away from the communal wildness. He wasn't going to do anything to the girl. Turning, as he pulled her along, to look at her pale skin and dark hair falling below her shoulders, he felt only a kind of numbing bewilderment. In his entire life he had made love to one woman only, Fu-fang. Now another was his for the taking. Shoving her – not too roughly – against the grain-bin wall, Embree looked at the girl in the late-afternoon light. He only wanted to talk to her, get to know her; so Embree asked her name.

To his surprise and chagrin, the girl burst into laughter.

'Hairy boy.' She thrust her hand under his tunic and rubbed her hand over his chest. 'What are you like down here?' Playfully she grabbed at his crotch.

Backing away as if she'd hit him, Embree stared at the girl in disbelief. She was not afraid. This was nothing more to her than a game, an afternoon diversion that might prove a source of amusement later on in conversation with the other girls, who were now getting brutally fucked by real Chinese men.

Embree was furious.

Pulling the ax from his belt, he backed her against the wall with one hand and with the other raised the blade to eye level, not six inches from her terrified face. 'Are you afraid of me? Are you? Are you afraid to die?' He shoved the ax closer. Then he saw in her eyes what he had put in them: terror, fear of death. The ax, held horizontally less than an inch from her nose, trembled in his hand and caught the rays of a late sun; the blade's color was gold; it looked molten to him. Again he studied the girl's eyes.

Tossing the ax aside, he slumped down against the grain-bin wall.

No one from New Haven was there to confirm what happened, but it had happened: Philip Embree, graduate of Yale Divinity School and missionary attached to the Harbin Mission, had just threatened the life of a defenseless girl.

Her sobs reach him as he thinks about it. She is sitting against the cowshed, not more than a few feet away, too frightened to move.

Is this freedom? he asks himself. That night in the smoke-filled speakeasy, when his sister Mary gave him his first wine, freedom had seemed an uncomplicated deliverance from the past. He was going to have adventures and learn about life. Douglas Fairbanks with his flashing rapier. Jack London in the wilds of the North. And Charles Lindbergh making his solo flight across the Atlantic only a few weeks before Embree took an ocean liner across the Pacific.

But here in this Chinese courtyard he hates a freedom that has so debased him. A door opening in his mind had let out a nasty demon to throw a tantrum. If this is freedom, he doesn't like it. Moreover, he fears worse demons are lurking within, waiting for freedom.

Glancing at the girl, he realizes that she has stopped crying. She sits with her back against the cowshed's peeling wall, her legs parted as if in sexual readiness. In the nearby muck pigs are grunting, excited by the household commotion.

'The Lord testeth the righteous; but the wicked and him who loveth violence his soul hateth.'

An awful dread fills him. It's like the horror felt in childhood when father described to him the hellish fate of sinners. Turning to the girl, Embree mutters an apology – as he used to do after confessing a aggression to father. Only this time 'Forgive me' is in Chinese.

Crawling over and kneeling in front of the girl, he says it again: '*Duibuqi . . . duibuqi.*'

She stares at him; fear goes out of her eyes, replaced by a mingling of contempt and curiosity.

Someone is shouting from the sheep hut. Embree is being called to the sheep hut.

He has only a few *cash*, but taking them from his pocket Embree presses them into the girl's hand. '*Duibuqi.*'

For a moment her open palm remains motionless, then her fingers close like a clamshell around the coppers. She gives him a jaunty smile. 'Thank you, nice boy,' she says coquettishly.

'No, don't thank me,' Embree says, getting to his feet. 'Forgive me, forgive me,' he frets.

But it's no use; the girl continues to smile invitingly.

He turns and crosses the court, while memory rushes at him. 'For the Lord knoweth the way of the righteous; but the way of the ungodly shall perish.' He curses his memory, hates it.

Then he remembers something else – the ax lying on the ground back there. Returning and stooping to get it, Embree looks again at the girl, whose hand tightly grasps the coins.

He is appalled. She is still smiling.

Standing in the entrance to the sheep hut, the Big Swords are looking inside. Embree joins them. Hanging from the rafter by his long queue, Wang Nan-fang twists; his screams have dwindled to a steady moan. The boy sits almost directly below him, staring fixedly up. Pressed within a pen, the sheep are bleating softly.

'Landlord Wang, we are going to leave now,' Fu says. 'You were lucky today. Nothing lost but a maidenhead. Only one. I can assure you that one of your daughters managed to lose hers without my help. Wang Nan-fang, your mother was a cruddy whore. You are a Manchu pimp, a filthy bully. But the debt is paid. Be at peace. You, boy – ' Fu is speaking to the son, who turns his head slowly, tears in his eyes. 'Remember today. Not just because your father screamed like a pig all afternoon, but because you learned something. You can't cover the sky with one hand.'

When the Big Swords mount and ride away, leaving the devastated household behind, Embree turns to Fu Chang-so and asks what he meant by not covering the sky with one hand.

'You can't cheat forever without its becoming known. The boy won't be like his father. No, I'm sure of it.'

They ride toward the center of town in silence. Then Fu says, 'In China today there was justice done. Something important happened,' Fu declares.

'Wang paid his debt,' Embree says.

At twilight, as the Big Swords leave town, tables are lined up side by side in the street, and farmers returning from their fields now sit at them. Women come out of their kitchens carrying bowls of millet gruel and plates of unleavened pancakes fried with garden vegetables. The silent horsemen wave, the farmers wave back. The riders pass alongside a shed with a platform on which itinerant carters, filled with food, already sleep. Children, holding bowls, glance round-eyed over the rims. It is a peaceful scene, timeless in its essentials: faint light in the western sky, food in the communal street, weary bones, a little talk, and sleep to come.

During the ride, Embree creates a scene between himself and his sister. 'Mary,' he says in his mind, 'here I am, having my adventure.'

'Why did you threaten the girl with that ax?'

'She had to know who I was.'

324

'Do you know who you are?'

'At least I'm not who father thinks I am.'

'You mean you're not a missionary, you're not a Man of God?'

'I mean father's not going to live my life for me.'

'Keep going. I did. And I don't regret it.'

As the horsemen reach the main road, Fu Chang-so turns to Embree. 'Did you have fun? Are you glad you came with us?'

'Yes,' Embree tells him. 'I'm glad.' Justice has been done, just as Fu Chang-so claimed. Has it really? A man was tortured, his son forced to watch; the women of his household were abused and Embree himself threatened a girl's life. In spite of what he did, Embree is glad: he has seen within as he has never seen before. He is capable of doing far more than his father could ever imagine. But the demons within him, will they come out and throw other tantrums? Perhaps what comes out won't be demonic. The thing is this: He is a man of possibilities. Glancing over his shoulder, as if he can still catch a glimpse of the girl clutching the coins near the cowshed, Embree has another twinge of regret and shame. Then forcibly he turns his mind elsewhere; he will think of food, of sleep, of the simple things just as those villagers are now doing. Good. His mind feels suddenly cleansed of memory, doubt, and guilt; it is left calm and silent like the Shantung countryside after a great wind from Central Asia has blown through it.

14

This is what the General thinks: It is not a Chinese city, it is a foreign city.

Thirteen flags are flying today in Shanghai. Inside the French Concession and the International Settlement (their limits marked by barricades) the police, law courts, and municipal council ignore the fact that this is Chinese ground. They conduct themselves as if it were London, Paris, Berlin, Rome, Tokyo; and indeed, in certain sections, without the ubiquitous rickshaw to indicate otherwise, the street signs and storefronts suggest the cityscapes of other nations. In the Shanghai Club, No. 3 the Bund, sunburned British taipans in their white ducks stand at the longest bar in the world telling jokes about Chinese incompetence. When Tang was late here, attached to the iron fence at the gate to the Bund Gardens was a printed injunction: DOGS AND CHINESE NOT

ALLOWED. WORK COOLIES EXCEPTED. In both Chinese and English.

Yes, this is a foreign city

Too restless to remain seated on the velvet-covered bench in the waiting room, General Tang Shan-teh paces between chunky pieces of Grand Rapids furniture, silver plated spittoons and pedestals on which stand fabulous Ming vases. He has an appointment to meet Dou Yu-seng, leader of the Green Circle Gang – called King of the Golden Mountain.

Waiting in this palace of Victorian massiveness, tucked away in a residential area of Frenchtown, the General reflects on the irony of the Greens. They are gangsters whose principal racket is protection. No shop or restaurant or casino dares open without their permission. Yet in today's China, riddled by corruption and shaken by anarchy, the Shanghai Greens represent one tribunal that can actually enforce the law. Punishment for breaking its rules is simple, uniform, and swift: first, unbearable torture, then execution.

Perhaps, Tang reasons, the Green Circle Gang allows Shanghai to retain a Chinese image – bitter irony. For it is not Chiang Kai-shek (present master of the city) or British taipans or Japanese bankers or German importers who control the destiny of Shanghai, but rather these hundred thousand outlaws with their blood oaths and rituals of terror. It is from disciplined criminals that the street coolie derives his hope for tomorrow, his pride in today. Shanghai is still Chinese as long as the Greens entangle it in their web of intrigue and fear.

A bitter irony.

Tang has come to pay his respects to the Green leader because he fully appreciates a cardinal fact of life today: No warlord, however strong and confident, can ignore Dou Yu-seng and do business in Shanghai. Turning his Western felt hat in his hands (part of basic Shanghai dress, even when a Chinese robe is worn), the General thinks beyond this courtesy call to his meeting with the German gunrunner. He has the money now, but has Erich Luckner the weapons?

A servant in spotless white comes in with a low bow, then leads the General down a marble corridor to a windowless room strikingly small for such a mansion. It is strictly Chinese, a secret cubbyhole packed with sofas, chairs, pedestals; it is hidden from the public enormity of halls and stairways and drawing rooms that identify Dou Yu-seng to his foreign guests as a man to be reckoned with.

326

A slight figure sits in a chair, his silk gown, of a plum color, without adornment. On each finger, however, he wears a ring. Although he has the cool bearing of an official from the last century, he has risen to such eminence from the Pootung wharves.

There's a polite exchange of greetings – Dou has a thin, high-pitched, unimpressive voice – then his apology for the oil lamp. Powerhouse workers, still on strike, have cut off all the electric power in this section of Frenchtown. An extraordinary fragrance fills the small room; Tang wonders if Dou selected it. The little man gestures toward a mahogany table. Placed on it are utensils for opium smoking. He excuses himself from joining the General by explaining that he gave up the habit last year because of poor health. The General declines with equal courtesy; he too has given it up for the same reason – a sensible lie; he has never used opium. But from Dou's frail appearance Tang suspects the Green leader is telling the truth about his health. How could he ever have been a wharf coolie, even as a young man – hauling cargo all day on the Pootung docks? Now he's president of several banks, a director of numerous corporations. He had once been the Director of Detectives for the Frenchtown police, who reasoned that by giving him this honorific title they were better able to solve the worse crimes in the Concession, since a phone call from Dou was suffi-cient to get anything done – the criminal was dumped either dead or alive (depending on the French police's wish) on the station doorstep.

A young woman enters, bearing a tray for tea. She is a large-eyed, very pale beauty. Tang recognizes her as a well-known Shanghai film actress. Dou doesn't introduce her, however, so Tang masks his recognition of this famous woman now acting the part of a serving maid. After pouring the tea, she surprises Tang by showing outright affection for the old gangster. She coos at him outrageously and even draws her long thin fingers across his sallow face. She's wearing an emerald choker, a wide bracelet of jewels that sparkle in the lamplight. Her reward for serving tea? The incense is her choice, Tang decides; and probably Dou gave up opium for romance. The actress pats the old man tenderly on the shoulder – apparently Dou demands a public display of affection in front of guests – and leaves the room. The two men drink their tea in silence.

Abruptly Dou claps his hands, and a servant rushes in. 'Bring it,' the old man says in a reedy voice.

Almost immediately the servant returns with a small, framed painting and holds it waist-high toward Dou, who waves him on to Tang.

Tang leans forward to study the painting. In the foreground are a few scraggly trees clinging to meager soil. In the middle distance is a modest little hut, and in the far distance some bald hills leading toward a whiteness which is either sky and earth or neither – the horizon of infinity. This is all. The finely graded ink washes are rendered with a dry brush; the artist has featured shaping lines of the Broken Band Style.

Tang recognizes it as the work of Ni Tsan, a very great painter of the Yuan period. Ni Tsan was noted for inimitable elegance and a starkness of design that turned minimal lines into the vast poetry of suggestion.

'Yes, it's an original. Like it?' Dou asks with an amused chuckle. 'I thought you would. I heard you're even more of a connoisseur than old Dog Meat!' He laughs outright at the crude joke, displaying for the first time his lowly origin. 'I bought it because Ni Tsan came from Wuhsi. I like to have paintings by men of Shanghai or thereabouts. No Cantonese stuff for me. None of that Northern Sung either, I don't care what it's worth. I'm a Pootung man,' he exclaims proudly, one ringed hand lifted as if in defiance. With no perceptible change of expression, he says, 'You are here to buy guns, General?'

Tang admits it without hesitation. 'Yes, sir. To buy guns.' There would be no sense in lying to this man. Undoubtedly the answers to most questions Dou Yu-seng ever asks are already known to him.

'Who will you buy them from?'

'I was thinking from the German, Luckner.'

Dou nods approvingly. 'He's reliable. You get what you pay for.'

'Your approval, sir, lightens my heart.'

'I understand you have a fondness for the foreigners.'

'Me, sir?'

'You have a Bolshevik and American in your camp, don't you?'

'The Bolshevik is harmless. The American is a mercenary, a good one.'

'I understand the Marshal gave your stipend back. That was an intelligent move. He needs you against Feng.'

Tang might add against Chiang Kai-shek as well; but the Green

328

leader has made a strong alliance with the southerner. It's common knowledge that when Chiang waited at the outskirts of Shanghai, ready to enter it, he made a deal with the Greens, who agreed to rid the city of Communists and labor agitators for a price. They went at the task with such zeal that there were untold hundreds, perhaps even thousands, of murders in the back streets and alleyways. In the hotel where he is staying. Tang overheard some men discussing it last night in the dining room. One man – by the looks of him a businessman – was explaining to his foreign dinner companion: 'All day long there was shooting; it sounded like champagne corks popping.' It was, in Tang's view, an obvious effort by the Chinese to make light of the slaughter in front of a foreign associate.

'You were not the target,' Dou declares in the precipitous way he has of catching a listener off guard.

'The target?' Tang knows what the gangster refers to, but wants time to collect himself for this shift in conversation. 'Do you mean at Thousand Buddha Mountain, sir?'

'You were not the target. Don't you believe me?'

'Of course I believe you. Permit me to ask, then, who was the target?'

'General Chen Yun-ao. At Chengchow he lost the battle to Feng. It was a disgrace. Or at least that's how the Marshal would see it.'

'You think, then, the Marshal ordered the explosion?'

'Losing that battle was enough reason for the Marshal to punish Chen Yun-ao.'

Tang chooses to treat the subject lightly. 'All of us were nearly punished.'

'No one will change Marshal Chang Tso-lin. A reckless, malicious man. At least he has sense enough to stay clear of Shanghai.' Dou grimaces, giving a look to the opium utensils. It's a look of longing. Tang wonders how much power the beautiful actress holds over the old gangster.

Dou Yu-seng, probably aware that the General won't discuss the Marshal seriously, alters the direction of their talk once again. He deplores the electrical workers' strike, but only mildly; it has little effect on his organization. He turns then to a tram drivers' strike in the Settlement, but with the insouciance of a man speaking of the weather.

He's either bored or thinking of the actress, Tang decides – that lovely woman who might be waiting supine on a velvet divan in another room deep within the marble labyrinth.

It is time for the General to leave. He has fulfilled his obligation to the Grand High Dragon of the Greens, so he's free to make the first move. Dou responds to the leavetaking with verbal elegance, proving again that the dock worker and the businessman fit nicely together in his narrow, weathered skull.

Tang parts with him on excellent terms. The General can now pursue his own plans in Shanghai, a great city that belongs in many life-and-death ways to a Pootung coolie.

Climbing the rickety stairs to the second-floor office, Tang wonders if she will be there too, the Russian. He can't restrain his anticipation or his disappointment upon entering the office and finding only a Chinese secretary. She asks him in a brusque Western manner to have a seat.

Tang glances around curiously. There are large posters on the peeling walls, advertising Stuttgart electric fans in two foreign languages and Chinese. Not much lies on the secretary's desk; there's only a single filing cabinet in the room. Apparently the electric fan business isn't thriving.

The inner-office door opens, and the tall blond German comes out smiling, hand extended.

'Delighted to see you, General,' Luckner smiles hard, his intensity turning it into a grimace, as if he doesn't know what emotion to project.

As they enter the little office, he says, 'I hardly recognize you out of uniform.'

'In Shanghai a uniform has little importance.'

Although Luckner continues smiling, his sun-tanned face has no warmth in it for the General. 'You think so? Chiang Kai-shek dashes everywhere in full uniform with a high collar, a long black cape, and gray gloves.' Briefly, indeed vulgarly in Tang's eyes, he appraises the brown cotton gown (as common in Shanghai as the wheelbarrow) that the General is wearing.

'I must say' – Luckner sits back in his swivel chair – 'I was surprised to get your letter.'

'We didn't complete our business in Qufu.'

'Complete it? We certainly did not!' Luckner laughs. 'As I remember, you galloped off without a word. I read later in a Shanghai paper you went headhunting.'

The bitterness of that laugh and comment startles the General. Surely the German knows why their meeting in Qufu ended the way it did – all Shanghai knows – yet he harbors deep resentment. The General doesn't expect a foreigner to be sensitive to Chinese honor and justice, although in retrospect his own behavior must have seemed both arrogant and incomprehensible to Luckner. Nevertheless, he won't remain in this office unless treated with more civility.

Luckner seems to understand that. 'But I'm pleased, General,' he says in a conciliatory tone, 'you've come today. Now we can get down to business. I'm privileged to have you as a client.'

Back on a formal footing, they begin to discuss weaponry. It doesn't take the General long, however, before he realizes his antipathy for Luckner is as great as Luckner's for him. The German has done him no harm, yet from his first look today at the slick blond hair, suntanned craggy features, and icy blue eyes, he has felt an intense dislike for Erich Luckner – for the man who keeps the Russian woman.

Yes. That's it, that's the reason.

'Some new weapons are available. At least they are to me,' Luckner says. Sleeves rolled up, displaying strong forearms, he leans forward and with intensity describes the latest Revelli design in .50-caliber heavy-barrel ground-type machine guns. 'My suppliers are the best in Europe,' he claims proudly.

Tang has forgotten their mutual antagonism, his own jealousy; as he listens, another emotion grows in him – desire. Desire for new fieldpieces by Krupp and by Gruson, for the Mannlicher 6.5-millimeter rifles, for a Citroën armored car with turret and three machine guns. He is fascinated by the German's description of the new Thompson submachine gun, weighing only ten pounds and firing .45-caliber bullets from circular drums holding fifty rounds. He yearns for trench mortars, for wireless sets of field design, and above all for the new aircraft: British Moth scouting planes and Corsair bombers. Given today's confused alliances and uncertain battlefield strength, a good general with such weaponry, no matter the size of his army, might well achieve victory by default. At the least, a few planes would enhance his bargaining power. General Tang has wanted few things for himself, but he feels now a burning desire for new weapons, wireless sets, aircraft. His head swims with a vision: His Shantung troops rolling toward Peking with mountain guns and 75-millimeter cannon; each division equipped with the newest Danish Madsen light machine guns and Thompsons and the heavier Revellis!

Sweating on this hot day, Luckner falls abruptly silent. He leans back in the swivel chair and folds his arms behind his blond head. In spite of the tan, he looks excessively white to the General, contemptibly alien. 'Well, that's about it. Not all of those things are available yet, but I don't suppose you'll want *everything*.'

Tang ignores the sarcasm. He can think of nothing but the weapons. Asking for a price list, he broods over it a long time, while the fan rattles and drones in the close little room. Luckner goes out, leaving him alone with his desperate dream. He makes out a tentative list of items, excluding armored cars, planes, and Thompsons. Even so, he has listed more arms than he can afford to buy.

Luckner returns and slumps down in the swivel chair. Tang has rather expected him to supply some refreshment – a Chinese would have – but the German sits there, smiling faintly.

Looking at the list, Tang says, 'I'll order what I have here now, but I'll want more.'

'More?'

A rude way of putting it, yet Tang ignores this sarcasm too. The German has access to the finest weapons, and he wants them. 'I'll need credit.'

'I see. How much?' The German's tone is flat, neutral, hard.

Tang knows the credit he requires will far exceed what the arms dealer will provide. Goaded by desire, he says it anyway. 'Fifty, maybe sixty thousand dollars Mexican.'

'Excellency.' It's one of the few times today that Luckner, who fawned over him in Qufu, has addressed the General properly. 'I can manage five thousand, no more. It's deeply regrettable.'

'Never mind. Credit may not be necessary,' Tang declares. 'But I'm going to order more than I have on this list. Much more.' He hears in his voice a boastfulness uncharacteristic of him, yet the dream of glory sweeps him on. The German's weapons may well lead him to the seat of power. His entire life has come down to a question of money.

'I'm delighted to hear you want more, but in the meantime what am I to do?' Luckner asks coldly. 'Shall I wait to fill this order?'

'No, don't wait. Fill it as it is. I want the arms as soon as possible.'

'And so we'll wait for the rest.' Again the curl of Western lips.

'But not for long.'

'I see. Whatever you say, Excellency.' Luckner swivels a little, catching the breeze from the rattling fan – his blue eyes blink, but the blond hair remains unruffled, slick against his long skull. 'Now, I can put in the initial order with my supplier very soon. If you would be good enough to give me a draft on any Bund bank, the process can begin.'

'The Central Bank of China.'

'The Central Bank is fine,' Luckner says with an approving nod.

Tang is aware that they both understand how completely in command of negotiations Luckner has become. It is a function of Tang's greed, and goes against the grain of a life's training, for all the sages have warned that greed is the destroyer; following its trail, a man goes down to defeat. Yet he wants those weapons.

'I want the order as soon as possible,' he repeats.

'Of course. And if I may have your check at your earliest convenience.'

'You'll have it,' Tang says briskly.

'So we don't have another Qufu.'

Tang takes a deep breath, controlling himself. He wants those weapons.

With a smile, Luckner picks up a pencil and poises it over a pad on his desk. 'May I know where you're staying?'

'At the Palace Hotel. Under the name Po Ming.'

The German looks surprised. Most warlords stay in the private residences of officials and militarists when in Shanghai; they move around in limousines with a retinue in tow. Tang's independence seems to rattle him momentarily. Then he says, 'We can discuss the little matter of credit at our next meeting, General.'

Tang feels sure the arms dealer won't give him credit, but instead will toy with him, humiliate and tease him in revenge for Qufu. He can go elsewhere – many gunrunners sit in airless rooms like this one all over Shanghai. But Luckner is reliable – the Green Gang leader confirmed that – and he has the finest merchandise.

They arrange to meet in two days – Tang bringing the money draft and Luckner providing the details of shipping.

For a moment Tang nearly asks, 'How is Miss Rogacheva?' But he thinks better of it. This is not the desperate salesman of Qufu, who brought along a woman as an offering if necessary. In the interval since that Qufu meeting the German has doubtless found other customers, and his increased sense of well-being has proportionately lessened his desire to be accommodating. It is useless to be more than barely civil; for that matter, any Chinese show of excessive courtesy might be construed as weakness.

And he doesn't want the German to know that he even remembers the woman.

After they part with cool valedictions, Tang descends the creaking stairs and enters the narrow street. He breathes a sigh of relief. Up there in the German's office he had wanted the weapons with a passionate urgency that he knows is foolhardy. And up there in the small office with an electric fan trying to fend off the great swamp of Shanghai heat, he had thought idly of a woman, a foreign woman at that, when quite possibly his entire future hung in the balance.

What would father have said? Father, that rigorous man who never for an instant forgot who he was and what he must do.

Next morning, sitting in a rickshaw heading into the Native City, he is thinking again of his father, of the stern man's admonition: 'Look around you, if you wish to serve China.'

Three black storm-warning cones have been hoisted above the towering meteorological observatory on Edward VII Road. Glancing up at them, Tang is plunged the next moment into a maze of warrens in a poor district. As the rickshaw puller jogs farther into the maze, a noxious smell hovers in the air. Mud huts line the crowded street, their roofs often nothing more than rags or crossed-string rushes or bamboo trellises covered with tattered oil paper. Now and then he sees a hut built of packing cases or kerosene tins – a mansion in this fetid steamy slum.

Factory hooters are blaring in the silk filatures nearby, and night-soil carts rumble through the lanes, heading for fields on the outskirts of Shanghai. During the gently rhythmic ride General Tang looks at the various shops, crowded together like shoots in a rice field. They display umbrella frames, hot-water bottles, electrical cable, spring scales, foot basins, sulphuric acid in huge slim-necked bottles, galoshes, and soap. And there are people everywhere, hurrying toward their destinations of survival: mill hands, wheelbarrow coolies, merchants, cake vendors, astrologers, runners, messengers, beggars.

Getting out of the rickshaw, he walks the rest of the way. He enters a side lane too narrow for the smallest vehicle. Voices in the alley rise to a crescendo, but being Chinese the General is accustomed to loud noise – it is his heritage. At night here, he well knows, the sound of coolies' yelling will be replaced by Buddhist gongs and firecrackers. He comes out of the alley at a sharp turn and finds himself in a vacant lot, piled high with refuse and stacked with many coffins, which have been left here for days awaiting an auspicious time for burial. Beyond the lot he sees a jumbled warren of ramshackle buildings cinched up against a ditch beyond which is city swampland and beyond the stench-filled muddy waste still more rows of huts and shelters, all breeding cholera, typhus, tuberculosis.

He walks on, jostled in the choked pedestrian traffic of the alleys, until finally, on a somewhat better lane, he comes to a small but sturdy dwelling, windowless on the street, with a thick wooden door and a steel grate over a caller's box. He raps with a dragon-shaped knocker and almost immediately the box swings open. Coolly suspicious eyes regard him a long time – although these same eyes had studied him the previous afternoon.

Again Tang repeats his name and waits. Slowly, as if with considerable reluctance, someone extends a hand through the box and takes Tang's calling card. The box closes, just as it had done yesterday.

Waiting, aware he must wait as long as yesterday, Tang turns and looks aimlessly at the street. He feels a tug at his sleeve. A little girl, perhaps seven or eight, is staring up at him. On her thin body hang a torn shirt, gray shorts. In these rags, so filthy they seem as brown as her unwashed skin – flesh and cotton inextricably mingled on her bony frame – she is utterly drab save for the brilliant whites of her eyes. On her practiced hip she holds a naked baby, maybe a few months old, his eyes set in fatalistic patience, as if he has endured a hundred years on earth. The little girl briskly sticks out her free hand. Still young enough for optimism and too small to be thrashed for impertinence, she is probably more successful than the tattered beggars who scuttle up and down these lanes; they are like crabs, heads askew, gap-toothed mouths fixed in perpetual grimace, hands out, mumbling from the nightmare of their Shanghai lives.

Tang reaches into his pocket and holds out a couple of *cash*.

The child snatches them without a sound. After a brief examination of the lead-and-copper coins with a square hole in the center, she turns on her heel and runs away, the naked baby jiggling solemnly against her hip. A couple of passersby regard Tang with

Tang with amused smiles. They think he's a stranger from the provinces who hasn't yet understood the hopelessness of such gestures in Shanghai – or perhaps he's a new Christian convert, one of those attempting to gain favor with the foreign carpenter.

The heavy door swings open, and a silent boy conducts the General through a tiny court into a two-story brick building. Seated in a reception room, he feels again in an alien land. The room is heavily curtained against the daylight and cluttered with overstuffed Western chairs, all of them smothered in white slip-covers. He stares at a gilt-framed painting of pink-cheeked women in bustles, twirling parasols on the bank of a river and gazing across it at the spires of a European city. He deplores the foreign atmosphere of Shanghai.

Yet when a tall thin man enters the lamplit room, so does China. He wears a black skullcap, a parrot-green gown of shimmering Chekiang silk, and a dead-leaf-brown jacket with long sleeves.

He is a usurer who calls himself Banker Shao.

His greeting is traditionally profuse, and when they are seated opposite each other, he says, 'Your distinguished presence lends honor to my poor house. A thousand pardons, Excellency, for being late in receiving you.'

'I am honored that you find time to receive me at all, Banker Shao.'

Tea comes. Banker Shao waits until the General has sipped from a cup patterned with flying cranes, then says with a sad shake of his head, 'The tea is Dragon Well, honored guest, but I fear it hasn't been properly brewed.'

'Exquisite,' Tang remarks and means it.

Banker Shao, sipping from his own cup, purses his lips in appraisal. 'It is not an altogether impossible tea, Excellency, but for you my humble household should have done better. I apologize.'

I will not get the loan, Tang thinks.

While they drink tea, Banker Shao sighs repeatedly and comments on the rising price of silk, now nine hundred taels a picul, which will surely lead to uncontrollable inflation.

Tang tells himself to relax. There is no longer reason to feel anxious; he will not get the loan.

Abruptly the usurer claps his hands; a small boy in a blue gown appears in the doorway. 'The box, please,' the banker says quietly. 'In celebration of your visit today, Excellency, I would be overjoyed if you would consent to try one of these – ' He points to the aromatic wooden box that the boy has rushed into the room.

Tang takes a cigar from the box.

Soon they are both smoking. The cigar is stronger than the tobacco he ordinarily smokes in a water pipe, but the General is heartened. Yesterday Banker Shao had offered him a rather thin tea and a cigarette. Will I get part of the loan? Tang wonders.

'These cigars are Havana cigars,' Banker Shao explains. 'Havana cigars from the island of Cuba.' Blowing a large cloud of smoke into the lamplit room, he leans forward. 'I have spoken to my unworthy colleagues – '

Tang knows he has only one colleague, Dou Yu-seng, the Green Circle Gang leader.

' – and we have been trying to locate the funds you request, Illustrious Sir.'

Tang awaits the blow, composing his face. He tries to puff on the cigar calmly.

'But I regret to say that given the present state of affairs – ' He pauses for Tang to supply an interpretation.

Tang does, gallantly. 'A chaotic state of affairs, yes, I agree, Banker Shao.'

'We have managed to procure only fifty thousand dollars Mexican. If the other twenty thousand, which you requested, becomes available, be assured we'll send a wireless to Qufu.'

So most of the loan has been granted. Tang is stunned by his good fortune. Obviously this is the decision of Dou Yu-seng. Yet the Green leader has also served notice, by withholding a significant amount of the loan, that he is not altogether sure of Tang's future. It's a warning that the General must use the money wisely in order to survive the 'present state of affairs.' But it indicates too what the Shanghai community thinks of his chances for power in China: cautious optimism.

For the next half-hour he discusses interest terms and a payment schedule with Banker Shao, who is surprisingly generous. This too is the work of Dou Yu-seng.

When General Tang Shan-teh leaves the house, he has in hand a Shanghai bill which is cashable throughout China for fifty thousand dollars Mexican.

In a small restaurant tucked away on a little street near the Great

World Amusement Center (stage plays, miror mazes, storytellers), General Tang waits for Chu Jui. The retired general who acted as recruiting emissary for Chiang Kai-shek is supposed to meet him here. Tang has requested the meeting.

His wait is short. The tall man from Chekiang comes into the smoky room bareheaded, his shaven head looking decidedly monkish, especially in this place of laughter and loud talk.

Having shared the experience of Thousand Buddha Mountain so recently, Tang and Chu Jui move quickly past the formalities.

'Have you read today's paper?' Chu Jui asks over a dish of sweet-and-sour squid appetizers. 'Ho Chien has taken Wuhan.'

Tang had met Ho Chien some years ago in Peking. They were both colonels then, wary of each other's potential for higher command. A few years ago Ho Chien went to Canton and joined the staff of Chiang Kai-shek. He is now a trusted confidant of the southerner.

'As usual, the paper doesn't say much,' Chu Jui continues. 'Not only has Ho Chien put the city under martial law, but he's banished Borodin from Wuhan. The Soviet agent's gone up to Lushan.'

'Then Ho has finished the Russians in China.'

'And started executions.'

'Of Reds?'

'Not only Reds. Political agitators of any sort, and union members.' Chu Jui adds, 'And anyone else who has something Ho Chien and his thugs want. I know Ho Chien. He's a murderous bastard.'

Tang knows him too: Ho Chien is a steadfast Taoist who depends on geomancers and astrologers for his opinion on anything from the position of his bed to the alignment of troops in battle.

Tang asks, 'Do you feel Chiang could have stopped him?'

'In two days he's slaughtered over five hundred. That's the rumor. I suspect the estimate is low. I'm certain Chiang would *like* to stop him.'

'Perhaps he's carrying out Chiang's orders.' Tang's suggestion is an attempt to get from Chu Jui an opinion about Chiang's intentions.

Chu Jui lays down his chopsticks. Glancing around at the noisy diners, he leans toward Tang. 'Believe me, it's not Chiang's fault. His grip is not yet strong.' Chu Jui makes the motion of grabbing something in air; the knuckles of his hand whiten. 'It isn't only Ho Chien who gives him trouble, either. There's a pack of young officers in Nanking who squabble night and day. It's not Chiang's fault.'

'I asked you to lunch today,' says Tang, as they both pick up their chopsticks and reach for dumplings in a bowl, 'because I'm interested in your suggestion. In Jinan you talked of mutual benefits. In that regard, I'd like to meet Chiang Kai-shek.'

Chu Jui nods, but without the enthusiasm he had shown in Jinan. Something has happened or is about to happen. 'I'm delighted my insignificant efforts have helped to bring about your decision. It's a wise one.'

He means that, Tang thinks; yet something holds him back. 'When can the meeting be arranged?'

Chopsticks poised over the bowl, Chu Jui gazes into the distance of the loud, smoky room. Then he shrugs impatiently. 'Difficult to say. But I'll relay your message. Believe me, it will be welcome.' The chopsticks descend and secure a dumpling – waves of heat simmer on its boiled surface. 'Please don't be discouraged, my esteemed friend.' Popping the dumpling in his mouth, Chu Jui chews noisily. Then he leans forward and says in a half-whisper, each word measured for significance, '*Do not be surprised at anything that happens in the next few weeks.*' Chu Jui, with a sigh, reaches out for another dumpling. He has said as much as he will on the subject, that's clear.

Tang eats a dumpling too and washes it down with a cup of yellow wine. He won't ask Chu Jui for an explanation that will not be forthcoming. Moreover, he gets the impression that his Chekiang friend has probably said more than is wise.

They eat awhile in silence. Then suddenly over steamed fish Chu Jui exclaims, 'Must we have Americans in China? What arrogance, what nonsense! This morning I had tea with one of them. Do you still have your American bodyguard?'

'He's still in my camp.'

'Sun Yat-sen had an American bodyguard too.'

Tang is startled. 'I didn't know that.' His opinion of Doctor Sun has always been mixed. He admires the revolutionary fervor of a man who fought for the Republican cause before this century began. He is also in basic agreement with Doctor Sun's threefold political program for a new China: first military rule; then a provisional constitution; and at last the full apparatus of democracy. On the other hand, the General is suspicious of someone who spent so much time among foreigners; Doctor Sun's close friend was a British physician with whom he studied at an English medical school in Hong Kong; he lived in London, traveled widely through Europe and America; and now the General has learned that the 'Father of China' had an American bodyguard.

'Yes, Doctor Sun had an American bodyguard,' says Chu Jui with a little laugh. 'Just like you. But the fellow I had tea with this morning isn't like your strong fellow with an ax. This is a big, fat red-faced diplomat. Such a big nose,' he adds, grimacing. 'Where do foreigners get their noses? I wonder if they know how ugly they look.' Chu Jui is slurring his words. Over lunch he has consumed a half-bottle of strong *mao tai* along with the table wine.

Two foreigners in my camp, the General is thinking. I buy guns from a German. And since coming to Shanghai I have not gotten the Russian woman out of my mind. Is it the times? Is it impossible for us to live today without foreigners somehow in our thoughts, affecting our actions?

So absorbed is the General in such reflections that he scarcely follows his friend's account of the morning's tea. The American from the consulate complained of Russian influence in China, blamed it on Sun Yat-sen.

'This American waits until today,' Chu Jui declares with an angry toss of his head, 'until *today*, when the Russians are finished here, to lecture me on their influence in China.'

'Did he have another purpose in doing so?'

'You're thinking like a Chinese about a Chinese. I said he's an American. No subtlety there. I told him something, however. I told him that Doctor Sun Yat-sen turned to the Russians only after the Americans had rejected him. He'd accused Doctor Sun and the Cantonese politicians of falling into the Red trap. I asked him would the American trap be any better?'

Tang laughs; he can never resist a story that makes fools of Westerners.

'He didn't like it, of course,' Chu Jui continues. 'I told him, as far as our falling into foreign traps is concerned, don't worry about us. We only pretend to do it; it's our little joke on the rest of the world. He got so furious he spilled tea on a pair of white trousers.'

And thus does the luncheon come to a pleasant end.

From the restaurant they walk to an intersection where a turbaned Sikh policeman directs traffic. Standing on a high platform, he moves his white gloves imperiously above the throng of rickshaws, pushcarts, and trams.

The two men part here with bows, but not before Chu Jui once more mystifies the General. 'I think perhaps I'll be back in a monastery soon. Most likely we will meet there.' And with a drunken smile, mischievous and conspiratorial, the tall ex-general from Chekiang climbs into a rickshaw and draws away, waving one thin hand indolently in farewell.

Entering the Palace Hotel lobby, Tang lets his eyes grow accustomed to the dim Victorian interior. It is lit by chandeliers high overhead and yellow-jacketed wall lamps, giving the large space a murky, undersea ambience. The General halts a moment to let some chattering foreigners, carrying walking sticks and parasols, flow past him into the overcast afternoon. Another flash of color – deep crimson edged with white – catches his attention. It moves out of a shadowy corner into the circle of pale light beneath a chandelier.

It is the Russian woman.

She approaches at a brisk, rolling walk. The white ruffles of her blouse, flounced high, frame a pointed chin, a white face rising into widely spaced green eyes. She is extending a pink-gloved hand. 'General Tang. General,' she says.

He holds her hand briefly; for an instant her fingers seem to tighten on his own. Then her hand is gone, back to her hip, lightly settling on it. 'I do hope you don't mind, but I've been waiting here for you. I heard from Erich Luckner you were in town.'

She talks so rapidly, Tang thinks, even in a language not her own; and without fear, much less shyness, to a man she hardly knows. What has he answered to her rush of words? He can't be sure; something like her own version of inconsequential courtesy – without Chinese extravagance, but just as unrevealing. Why has she come here?

'In Qufu when we last met,' the woman continues, while people move around them like a stream, 'we talked about calligraphy. Remember?'

'Of course. I promised to show you a store here in Shanghai.'

'But only after I showed you mine, a worthless, little place in Old Town.' She gives him a brilliant smile.

Clearly Miss Rogacheva is proud of her calligraphy shop and this cheery emotional openness charms him. At the moment it seems natural, if astonishing, for them to leave the hotel together and keep their mutual promise to visit calligraphy shops.

Standing outside, at the intersection of Nanking Road and the Bund, he looks at the line of taxis at the curb and a single low-slung cabriolet with a faded old Chinese driver mounted on the dickey behind.

'General, please, let's take the hansom cab,' Miss Rogacheva exclaims. For an instant, to emphasize her appeal, she touches his arm, unheard of for a woman (surely for a Chinese woman) to do on the street. He glances around to see if the familiarity has ben noticed. Three foreigners, waiting to cross the street, have seen it perhaps, but don't seem disturbed.

Moments later, seated in the hansom cab, the General moves away a few inches, having come up against her thigh. They exchange a brief look; it's clear to him that she has also been conscious of the contact. He stares resolutely at the sway-backed nag clomping down the broad pavement of Nanking Road, but senses powerfully her presence beside him.

Almost immediately the rain, having threatened all day, comes down in pounding sheets. Through the open windows they see an ocean of big, black, British umbrellas undulating along both sides of the road. They speak enthusiastically – she begins it – about their good fortune in getting the cab before the downpour. Their eyes meet. His memory of Miss Rogacheva has been accurate, although perhaps she's somewhat older than he remembered – and more beautiful. While she squints at the writhing skeins of rain coming down outside the cab, Tang steals appraising looks at her: Black hair cut now in bangs across her round forehead; her straight nose (but not too long, Chu Jui, and definitely not ugly); her full, generous lips; her wide cheekbones, almost Chinese in their breadth; and her white skin, given a touch of poignancy by the tiny crow's-feet at the edge of green eyes. He can't deny her loveliness; nor can he deny his keen interest in this woman he doesn't know, a foreigner. These are two realities he should resist, but there isn't time for resistance; he has been swept up like flotsam drawn toward a whirlpool.

Abruptly the rain stops; a brilliant shaft of sunlight slants down on the glistening street, making Shanghai a marvel of color and freshness. Like an omen, he thinks; the sudden beauty of the day allows him to relax, to remember there are things in life that must run their course.

When they reach a little street in Old Town and debark, Tang tells the driver to wait. He follows Vera Rogacheva into the calligraphy shop; he understands, watching the crimson skirt and white flounced blouse disappear ahead of him, that he's committed to this afternoon, committed during it to this woman.

The store owner, unaware of the General's identity, seeing only the simple gown and felt hat, shows immediate contempt for a Chinese man entering with a foreign woman, although to her he's excessively polite, even for a merchant. Clearly he must often extract from her exorbitant prices for rice paper and ink sticks.

To the General she whispers that the store is quite reasonable, although small and difficult to find. What she considers reasonable are Western prices; even so, Tang is surprised that a European woman has ventured this deep into Old Town, much less located within it a rather decent calligraphy shop. He is fully appreciative, moreover, of her knowledge of the art – quite remarkable for a Westerner, proof of intelligence and persistence. Listening to her discuss calligraphy with the shop owner, Tang knows she has not come to such an understanding of it without steady application. This accomplishment in a woman – foreign *or* Chinese – is too strange for the General to judge objectively her understanding of the art's finer points. He merely surrenders to his awe, watching her examine the scrolls that are delicately but firmly thrust into her hands by the owner, a bent little man eager for sales.

Later, in his own favorite store (smaller but cheaper than hers), also in Old Town and not far from the one they have just left, the General is once again held by her childlike enthusiasm for an art deeply rooted in a culture alien to her own. Would a Chinese woman do this in another country? Would a Chinese man? Would he himself?

Remarking upon a reproduction of the calligraphy of Hui Tsun, a twelfth-century emperor, Vera says, 'What I like most is his control of the brush. You can see it. Right here. The way the hairs change direction with exactly the right pressure.' She stares at the *hsieh* with genuine love. Perhaps in another life she has been Chinese. It's the sort of observation Tang's father used to make of foreigners whom he met and liked.

As they start for the door to leave, Tang notices her give a long, curious look at a table display of tea caddies, vases, bowls, cups, and plates. This is the only art, aside from calligraphy, in the shop.

'I'm partial to small things,' Vera Rogacheva says in explanation, as they stand at the tables. 'These are quite beautiful,' she says, pursing her full lips as she leans over the three-and-five-color ware.

The General turns toward the wizened shop owner. 'Are any of these from the kilns of Ching-te-chen?'

The old man rolls his eyes in frustration. 'Honored sir, I only wish they were! These days it's impossible to find anything from Ching-te-chen.' He adds with a frown, 'What you're looking at are imitations of Yung Chen and Ch'ien Lung periods.'

Tang smiles at Vera. 'An honest man.'

She bends closer, her full breasts swelling the white blouse. 'Is this also *juan ts' ai* enamelware?' She's looking at a jar decorated with peony blossoms.

For confirmation the General glances at the shop owner, who nods.

'This is especially lovely,' she explains, pointing to a blue-and-white porcelain plate.

The design of it is the Willow Pattern. A Ming-roofed mansion in the right foreground is connected by a bridge to a cottage; beyond that is an island and a building in flames. Three figures appear on the bridge, two together and one following. Ascending into the sky above the burning building are two doves.

'I know the story,' Vera says. 'Two lovers escape from the house. They are chased across the bridge by the girl's father. That explains the three figures.' She points with a forefinger carefully manicured, polished a rusty red. 'They reach the cottage, where the girl's old nurse lives. She helps them get to an island by boat. They settle there, but finally their home is set afire by her angry father's men. Dying in the fire, they rise to Heaven as two doves. Am I correct?' she asks with a smile of anticipation.

'Correct,' Tang says, aware that the romantic story appeals to her. She's a mature woman, yet for a few moments Tang has had a glimpse of the girl she must have been: spirited, generous, frank.

'This is from the Ching, isn't it? Is it an original?' she asks the shopkeeper, who for an answer shakes his head and glances nervously at the General.

'It can't be an original,' the General tells her.

'Can't be?'

'The Manchus destroyed all the Willow Pattern plates.'

'All of them?'

'I doubt if there's an original left in the world. What you see here and abroad are copies. Most of them have been made in England. They're common now.'

The woman laughs. 'England.'

'The design was smuggled into England in the eighteenth century; it came back to China in the nineteenth.'

'How strange.' She looks at him thoughtfully.

He is fascinated by the size and roundness of her eyes, their expressiveness: eyes that have seen a great deal, have shed many tears. Her face in this moment of concentration has extraordinary appeal for the General. To suppress his emotion he picks up the plate and tries to study it.

'You seem to know about the Willow Pattern.'

Tang glances at her, then quickly at the shop owner, whose eyes, meeting his, turn away. The old man shuffles behind the counter, unwilling to share in this discussion. 'I know very little about it,' Tang declares with an indifferent shrug.

'Why did the Manchus destroy such beautiful things?'

'They considered this design revolutionary.' He is watching the old shopkeeper. 'They thought it contained a code.'

'Really?' Vera raises her eyebrows. 'A code?'

'Signs and symbols of Chinese defiance.' He adds, 'Against the alien Manchu government.' Tang is speaking to the woman but watching the shopkeeper, who has extricated himself from the conversation with some busywork behind the counter. 'The Manchus thought the Willow Pattern was the work of a secret society.'

'Was it?'

'That's the rumor. Certainly to have the Willow Pattern in your possession was a subversive act. To have it on a plate, a teapot, on anything, meant death.'

'Now I see.' Her face relaxes with the full explanation. Gone is the intense look which has made her both mysterious and vulnerable. To the General she's once again merely beautiful. 'Only the Chinese would think of using art to foster revolution,' she observes with a smile.

'Do you think it's foolish?'

'On the contrary. If you commit people through beauty, you commit them to the best.'

'I've not heard it put better,' Tang declares with feeling.

They leave. When they climb into the hansom cab, the General slaps his gown pocket and claims to have left something in the shop. He asks her to wait for him in the cab.

Returning to the shop, he asks the owner the price of the Willow Pattern plate. They both know this piece of *famille rose* porcelain is new – less than a hundred years old – and they have done business together in the past. So Tang accepts the price, a modest one, without haggling. He tells the shop owner to send the purchase to the Palace Hotel in the name of Po Ming. In past dealings with the shopkeeper, Tang has never revealed his true identity. While the man is writing down the name and address, the General studies him closely. Is it possible? The General decides to find out, so without warning he says, 'Where were you born?'

'Here, in Shanghai.' Their eyes meet. The old shopkeeper seems to be judging Tang with the same care that Tang has judged him.

'Where were you born?' Tang asks again.

'Sir, I was born in Shanghai.' After a long pause he adds, 'I was born under a peach tree in the Red Pavilion. Why are your clothes so old?'

'They were handed down by the Five Ancestors.'

The old man, smiling, bows low. 'The plate is yours, honored sir. It is a gift.'

'I accept it as a gift, but pay for it in the name of the foreign woman.'

The old man nods. 'Then I accept payment. Good day, honored sir.'

Tang bows. 'It has been a great privilege to visit your illustrious shop.'

Back in the hansom cab, Tang meets the woman's questioning eyes.

'May I ask a personal question, General? There are still a lot of so-called secret societies. Do you belong to one?'

As the old horse clops down the narrow lane, Tang laughs complacently. 'Of course not.'

The Jade Buddha Temple. They pause to stare at the magnificent yellow walls enclosing the temple complex; then they visit the Heavenly King Hall, the Grand Hall, and the storeroom for Buddhist scriptures. Passing through moon gates and fan gates into various courtyards, they admire upswept Ming roofs with writhing dragon ornamentation along the spines. They stand in front of the seated white-jade Buddha and the recumbent white-jade Buddha, both from Burma, the exquisitely sweet faces attesting to their origin.

Sharing this experience with her has made the General relax; they seem less strangers here than in the commercial shops. Yet, as they move from one area to another, he notices in her a new mood of agitation, as if she's struggling with a choice.

In a courtyard Tang asks her abruptly, 'Am I keeping you from an appointment?'

She looks steadily at him. 'I have no other appointment. Can we have some tea?'

'Of course. They have it here in the temple.'

'I don't mean the temple. I mean at your hotel.'

Tang tries to mask his astonishment by agreeing quickly. 'Yes, that would be my suggestion too.' As they head for the exit, he wonders how she can behave so indecorously. She is, of course, the German's concubine and doubtlessly has known other men, probably here in Shanghai (her Chinese is sometimes inelegant, as if acquired in part among people of the street), yet her bearing is dignified, estimable. Can such a woman invite herself to a man's hotel? Is it done in the West? Whatever the impropriety, he can't fail to recognize his own excitement. His attraction to this woman enables him to move beyond the borders of Chinese experience; he's at sea with her in a boat of their own making.

In the hansom cab, his thigh again touches hers, and in a spirit of inquiry Tang does not move away. Nor does she. Western or not, he has understood her. So Tang thinks at first, but has he? Their touching skin warms from the contact, until he can think of nothing else. But he does notice something – once the cab swung toward his hotel the woman's agitation vanished. Now that she has asked her bold question, Vera Rogacheva seems at ease. He has known whores who become content when their price is met. But this woman is no whore. Perhaps in the West there is less distinction between whore and lady than in China. He has heard stories.

It's just possible she means to stay only for tea. He could well be a simpleton for finding more in her suggestion to have tea at his hotel than is there.

That possibility makes him glum as they ride along. This is the truth and he knows it: He wants this Russian woman, Vera Rogacheva.

While she is talking of the changeable weather (the sky is a blank dome of shimmering blue after the earlier rain), suddenly she lays her gloved hand on his forearm. As they sway down the street, she doesn't remove it, so that a new spot of warmth – hand to arm – is created between them. Tang no longer thinks or even hears her chatter. He is experiencing the warmth against his thigh and arm. So intensely aware of the woman does he become – her presence seems to invade his – that he's scarcely aware of the erection. It is unobtrusive beneath the loose gown he wears, but the idea of its happening from the slight pressure of her hand on his forearm and their thighs hardly touching in a hansom cab is remarkable; after all, he's not a boy. Yet his mouth is dry, a sensation experienced when he used to lust for his first wife in their extreme youth.

He glances at Vera Rogacheva. Is she beautiful by Western standards? Surely not by Chinese. Her features are too large, too ruggedly dynamic. But he can't convince himself of her imperfection, and his manhood continues to embarrass him.

So he talks as rapidly as she does. He talks about Ni Tsan without inquiring if she knows of the Yuan painter. He tells her how Ni Tsan, as a young man, owned a great mansion, collected art, accumulated an impressive library, and ran a large household. Later, tired of the good life, he gave away his possessions and became a wanderer, living most of the time on a houseboat. In spite of a late start, Ni Tsan became an innovative stylist. Tang doesn't mention, of course, having recently seen an original Ni Tsan in the home of the Grand High Dragon of the Green Circle Gang.

To everything he has said Vera Rogacheva has nodded politely, convincing him after the first nod that she knows everything he can say about Ni Tsan. But he has talked himself back into physical control by the time they reach the Palace Hotel.

In the lobby Tang looks at her – he's slightly taller – and asks if she would like to have tea in his room rather than in the restaurant.

'That's what I was thinking we might do,' she replies without hesitation.

Tang's hand trembles as he opens the door of his room. The woman brushes past him into its interior.

While she's looking around, Tang picks up the phone. 'Would you care for some cakes with your tea?'

She turns with a grimace. 'I really don't want tea. Do you mind?

Can we have something else? Some "family harmony," perhaps?'
She uses crude slang for wine.

'Would you prefer whisky?' He believes all foreigners like whisky.

'No. I think *wei mei si* would be fine.'

While ordering, he watches her move restlessly around the room. Often she stops to gaze from the window at the Bund Lawns below and at the Whangpoo River snaking in a great curve eastward toward the ocean.

They sit in overstuffed English chairs in front of a glass-topped table, becoming as silent as earlier, in the cab, they'd been talkative.

All the talk was false, Tang decides. This silence is real. He watches her drum her fingers on the chair arm. They have nothing to say, but remain hopelessly apart, in spite of her excellent way with the language. As the moments plod on, he sees in her increasing agitation a mirror image of his own. This is all wrong, this is a mistake. They have played a foolish game, as if their pleasant afternoon together must end in bed.

Perhaps she too realizes the hopelessness of it all. Her embarrassment shows in her quick glances, the pallor of her cheeks, the fussy hand lifting to smooth her careless hair.

With a sigh of decision, Tang says quietly, 'I don't wish to hold you beyond your time, Miss Rogacheva. You've been most kind and generous to spend your afternoon with me. Mister Luckner – '

Luckner's name in the air is like a hornet. They exchange startled glances.

' – is probably waiting for you?'

Rising and pacing in the small room, turning a small jade ring on her finger, Vera doesn't reply. Then, halting, she says crisply, 'No, he's not expecting me. I imagine he's with a client. Probably one of his Japanese clients.'

Japanese? The German's selling arms to the Japanese?

Yet this possibility, no matter how interesting, can't hold the General's attention. He stares at the crimson skirt swaying about her knees, as the woman's pacing grows more agitated.

'I'm often alone,' she discloses. 'Sometimes all night.'

Tang nearly repeats it aloud: All night.

'Anyway, it no longer matters.'

Tang watches her pacing.

349

'Even when it did matter, I couldn't do anything. When his clients want pleasure, Erich obliges by getting it for them. That's his pigeon.' Again she uses the language of the street. How did she acquire it? From the German? But she speaks better Chinese than the German does.

'I no longer have any interest in what he does,' Vera declares with finality and sits down on the bed, just as there's a knock at the door.

Tang waits until she rises and sits decorously in a chair before ordering the waiter in.

In a few minutes, holding a glass of vermouth, again she rises and walks to the window. 'The Whangpoo is lovely at sunset.'

Taking this as an invitation to join her, Tang goes to the window. Down there in streaks of late sunlight the warships and steamers of many nations ride at anchor, while drifting along their strakes are little sampans and weathered tugs. A large junk, its batlike sail taut in a freshening breeze, turns toward the east, away from Soochow Creek and the Bund, heading for the Whangpoo's distant union with the immense Yangtze. Smoke from liner stacks roils in the sky, mingling with a few aimless clouds. The great harbor, at sunset peace, throbs with a subtle energy that the General has always felt only a Chinese can feel.

'Can you feel the river?' he asks her, following the thought.

'Of course. It's like the pulse in my wrist.' She holds it up for him to see, a smile on her face.

'I've thought of you often since Qufu,' Tang admits. He notices the dying light has given her skin a new glow, something vulnerable and affecting – white shading into lilac. She's exquisite. 'I regret leaving the way I did.' How often in his life has he apologized to a woman?

'I regretted it too at the time. But you got your bandit, or so we heard here in Shanghai.'

They are silent awhile, both watching the river fade into the dusk. For a moment Tang remembers the painting by Ni Tsan that he saw in the mansion of the Green Gang leader. The scene below the hotel room is blurred, as if a wash has been applied to the waterfront details.

The silence lengthens until finally Vera turns to him. 'It's difficult living in a foreign country,' she says.

The General is surprised to see her eyes filling with tears.

'Looking down there, I think: This is his river, his city. Not mine.'

'They are yours too.'

'Not really. The things that are mine,' she says with a faint smile, 'I'll never see again.'

There's radiance in melancholy, he thinks. The poets say it in many ways: a falling plum blossom, a tint of sunset on a calm lake, goodbyes waved from opposite shores. The poets would write too about this woman from another land. Yet for the moment she doesn't seem foreign. She might well be a Chinese woman standing beside him at this window, looking down at the soft dusk of Shanghai. His sudden change in thinking of her is accompanied by a hope so intense that it's more like happiness.

'They are yours too,' he repeats. 'The things of China.' He can hear the rising note of hope in his voice. She hears it too, he understands, because turning from the window she looks steadily at him.

'Do you really think so?'

Against his long-held conviction that one's country is in the blood, is an act of memory, is a commitment to tradition, is contact with the dead, is irrevocable and undeniable, he tells this woman the lie he wants to believe. 'This is your country now. You've become Chinese. I feel it.' Is the idea preposterous to her? She looks abruptly away, as if refusing it.

'Sometimes when I think of the past,' she says, her eyes turned again to the gathering dusk beneath the room, 'it seems to belong to someone else and I'm being told about it. It isn't mine. Have you ever had that feeling?'

'No,' he replies without hesitation.

'I've had it often. That I'm someone without a past. It's what I feel sometimes.'

Such a confession of loss, so easily made, is not Chinese, any more than is the idea of being detached from the past. Again she becomes a foreigner. It is not the way he wants to think of her, however, so once more he says, 'You're more Chinese than Russian now. This is really your country.'

'There is more to belonging somewhere than knowing the language.'

So, like himself, she understands the depths, shades, and energies of nationality. He admires her intelligent rejection of his claim that she has given up one world for another, yet his own struggle to believe it continues. He says, 'Where one belongs is a state of mind. You'll come to believe this is your land too.'

'Will I?' The tears continue to well up. She doesn't brush them

351

away, but lets them remain on her skin, as if welcoming them, as if they add to this moment of her intimacy with him.

For it is intimacy; the truth of it astonishes, then holds him. 'You must stay,' he says, reaching out and touching her arm.

Her eyes turn down slightly to regard his hand. Then she smiles. 'I have nowhere else to go.'

'I don't mean China.' Both hands touch her arms, remain there. 'I mean here, this room, right now.' His hands, feeling her warm flesh, begin to move with insistence, with authority. He pulls her gently to him.

It is done. So it is done for both of them – he can tell from her sigh, from the fading of tension in the body he holds. They remain this way awhile, savoring the realization that it's done, that they no longer need to analyze or judge, that what happens now is simple, inevitable. Against his body hers is familiar, without nationality.

Abruptly she breaks away and walks off a few steps, turning from him. At first he's startled, fearful that his understanding has been utterly wrong, but then he sees it is right: With her back toward him, modestly, she is undressing.

He too undresses in silence. Waiting for her – she is slow, deliberate, confident – Tang remembers the Soochow girl in Jinan who had known better things in the garden her father tended. And like that girl, shedding her clothes is like shedding the past for Vera Rogacheva, as she turns and walks proudly to him. Easing down upon the bed in embrace, they say nothing.

Then he hears himself murmuring, 'Heavenly Jade,' repeatedly against her ear, as she draws him into her.

In her passion she gasps foreign words, a language he can't understand, endearments learned far away in a land he will never see.

The alien words confirm for him the truth – what happens between them is hopeless – yet with joy, dismay, and astonishment he realizes there is no turning back.

15

Sitting in her bedroom with the shutters closed against the fierce heat and light of noon, Vera turns the little jade buffalo slowly in her hand, as if to warm her fingers.

She has done nothing this morning except moon around like a distracted schoolgirl. For the past three days she has neglected her calligraphy. Whenever as a child she failed to say her extensive morning prayers, she'd force on herself a punishing vision of hellfire. Is she capable of doing the same thing now with the calligraphy? Summon retribution? The nightmare?

When did the nightmare last come? Certainly not in these three days. She welcomes as much as a single day without snow piling up in her mind, without the gut-wrenching horror of the inevitable sequence: the bloated horse; herself prone against the frozen surface of Lake Baikal; her eyes, detached from her body, searching among frozen corpses for the Rogacheva family; and finally the severed head of her sister in a watering trough – images marching through her mind like a remorseless army, leaving in their wake a trembling survivor, wracked by thirst.

But why has she neglected the calligraphy? Has it to do with the General?

She refuses to consider the possibility. After all, she's no green girl swooning over a tall guardsman.

Around, nervously around, she turns the jade buffalo. It has been hers for a week now, purchased after stormy negotiations with the antique dealer, who, sensing how much she wanted it, exacted more from Vera than she could afford to pay. She's left without savings. If Erich decides to discard her, she won't have money for a hotel room. Of course, she could ask help from the General, but she can't, she just can't, although surely he must know that she's made a profession out of getting help from men.

Vera rises to pace, turning the jade in her fingers.

It's all Erich's fault, damn him. This morning she pretended to be asleep when he bent down and kissed her before leaving for his daily intrigues in the little office plastered with electric fan advertisements. If she felt secure with him, she'd never have started an affair with a Chinese general. Each day there are fresh signs of Erich's indifference. Almost every night he carouses with his new Japanese friends, who appear to have an insatiable appetite for singsong girls, whisky, and gambling dens. Erich has an explanation ready, of course: You can't do business with the Japanese during the day without playing games with them at night. It is probably true; yet what worries her more than his absence is his lack of interest in hers. At breakfast he may ask, 'Did you go to the movies last night?' Or the opera, or the ballet, or Rio Rita's? In the same mechanical tone of indifference he might be asking, 'Did you make love to a man last night?'

Turning the jade, Vera tells herself it will be soon. He is going to leave me.

Not that she cares much. Does she? Putting the jade buffalo in her purse – she carries it everywhere, just as she carried a small ivory figurine of Saint Nicholas in her girlhood – Vera opens the shutters, letting the daylight in. She has punished herself enough by keeping the sunshine out. Sweet air, touched by flower scents from the courtyard. Continuing to pace, she glances often at the floorboard under which she hides the key to her suitcase of treasures. She does care, yes, about losing Erich. Without him she'd probably not have survived Shanghai. He kept her from a terrible Chinese prison. He gave her things; the extravagance that nearly destroyed him has buoyed her.

Vera hears footsteps along the corridor. Her maid, Hsueh-chen, is broad-faced, squat. Her plainness is a main reason for Vera hiring her. She didn't want to tempt Erich any more than he is tempted every night in the dance halls. As if a man can be stopped from finding pleasure in this city! Yet Vera sadly realizes the tepid nature of her jealousy; she feels the emotion out of duty, like a matron of middle years who learns her husband has found solace elsewhere.

The footsteps slow in front of the door, continue. What is on Hsueh-chen's mind today? Money. Of course, money. Everyone in Shanghai, from comprador to coolie, is thinking of money, of the 'squeeze,' the innumerable illegal commissions that get each one through the day. Hsueh-chen is probably calculating her squeeze from a certain greengrocer for buying the house vegetables there; or when her mistress leaves the house, she will be careful to share the squeeze garnered by the porter when he selects a rickshaw driver for mistress at the corner. Vera envies them the schemes that keep them too busy to contemplate aging, sickness, and death.

Vera sighs, wondering if there's time for calligraphy. No, of course not. In a few minutes she must dress. She feels a little giddy in anticipation of meeting the General – as if they are young lovers. At the very least such emotion is foolish; it can be dangerous as well. With this man she can't look beyond today, mustn't. Her first reaction to him was surely right – in Qufu, fearing him, she wanted to run away. He's not for her; it's not possible. He is still the man who caged and tortured another human being. He is still Chinese, unable to enter her own world. And she has never forgotten the cold way he left her in the Kong cemetery, without a word, without even a backward glance.

Erich Luckner, a gunrunner. Tang Shan-teh, a soldier. Another of life's ironies: for she despises what they stand for, these purveyors of violence who for the moment absorb her life. War has accounted for her being here in this alien land, whorish and alone, without money or status. Guns have done that to her; yet she sleeps with the men who buy and sell them.

Even so, Vera can't stem the tide of excitement she feels at the prospect of seeing Tang today. The truth is she wants him. He has soft skin almost as hairless as Yu-ying's, yet beneath it move the hard muscles of a vigorous male. His tenderness enchants her; his sudden power overwhelms her at last, leaving her pure and mindless, swept clean of memory.

It is all madness.

But what shall she wear today? Perhaps that decision has kept her indolent in her room, the way girls were in Petrograd on the day of a great ball. Surely these last few days with the General have been romantic enough to qualify for adolescent fantasy. They have gone everywhere, like newlyweds, doing the romantic things so abundantly available in Shanghai: The Ta San Yuan Restaurant, the Sunrise Tea House, the Temple of Serenity, the Hongkew Street Market, the Garden of Yu the Mandarin, where like gawking provincials they stared up at the Jade Rock, most famous of Tai Hu stones.

It was in the Garden of Yu that he confided in her. A Chinese general. *Confided* in her. She'll never forget the strangeness of it. Unlike most men, he hadn't chosen the aftermath of lovemaking for a revelation, but instead had spoken intimately to her in a public garden. He told her of his secret ambition, but without prelude, without suggesting – as many men do – that their sexual relationship has entitled her to a confession. She liked him for the way he did it. They might have been together for a long time, establishing between them a deep trust, and in the course of events he had recognized something about himself and could now, knowing it, share it with her.

This was the admission: Although it was his duty to remain in public life, he didn't like it, had never craved it, but dreamed someday of retiring and building his own garden – Chinese style, with a modest house on the Soochow plan. He didn't look at her while describing this garden – didn't dare? He gave the impression therefore of describing it to himself as well. Rarely in her life had Vera felt closer to anyone. His quiet voice linked them in their stroll through the garden, held them tremulously together, and she understood that this man had never spoken of his dream to anyone before.

Now, while dressing, she remembers it vividly. And that was not all. When they halted on the Nine Bend Bridge with the Tower of Driving Rains behind them, Tang had turned and looked directly at her as he spoke of his parents. A Chinese general did this. From her experience of the Chinese, she never expects them to disclose anything intimate about their family lives. They build up walls around memory and live within them snugly, taking sustenance from the past in a way, Vera feels, no Westerner ever can. Yet this Chinese general, surely without prompting, without the impetus of sexual contentment either, had simply talked about his youth and by such talking had opened up his life to her with a frankness matching her own when first she gave herself to him.

His mother had been well born, the daughter of a scholar, and had taught him in boyhood a reverence for books. She had wanted him to become a scholar too, because 'Good iron is not used for nails.' In recalling the old axiom, Tang had looked away from Vera across the lily-choked pond. 'She didn't believe soldiering was respectable.'

'But she married your father.'

'The elders of her clan realized there was going to be trouble – revolution, possibly civil war if the Manchu fell. They decided a military man in the family might prove useful. It's done in China. You marry off daughters according to what the clan needs at the moment.'

'She married a soldier, but she wanted you to be a scholar.'

'I wanted the same,' the General admitted, looking down at carp swirling through the pond. 'My uncle, a wealthy man, would have supported me until I finished my studies.'

'But you still went into the army?'

'Because my father was a soldier.'

'He insisted?'

'Not my father. He wasn't the old tyrant you read about in Western accounts of Chinese life. He was Confucian. He believed in a man doing his own breathing.'

'But he'd have liked you to follow in his footsteps?'

'Yes, of course. Especially since the military was crucial, given the state of affairs then. He didn't think it was shameful to serve in the army. Far from it. But he wouldn't have stopped me from being a scholar.' The General turned to her. 'I had only to tell him my preference.'

'But you didn't tell him.'

'I couldn't. A scholar is honored far more than a military man. I couldn't bear to rise higher than my father.'

'Then you're Confucian too.'

'I'm afraid his brand of Confucianism was closer to the source. Mine – I know now – was filled with poorly understood ideas about piety and ritual. His had true feeling.'

'Do you regret your decision?'

The General shrugged. 'I had the benefit of his knowledge and experience. Studying the Classics, I'd have missed so much he could tell me about life. We shared our lives this way. He lived to see me do well in my chosen profession – and in his.'

Leaning against a railing of the crooked bridge, Vera murmured, 'None of us escape our birth.' Then she'd tossed her head in carefree repudiation of a remark which seemed too solemn.

Now, however, as she prepares to meet the General, as she applies makeup in front of the dressing-table mirror, Vera remembers her remark and fully appreciates it. She has never been free of her Russian childhood. Whenever she thinks of getting a job in Shanghai, every sort of complication rushes into her mind. Soon the idea has fled, and she's left with the Petrograd aristocrat's aversion to work. She is either a lady or a whore. Of course. What has she been raised to know? Art, clothes, horses. Better a bed in the whorehouse than a desk in the bank.

For the afternoon meeting Vera selects a tight lamé skirt, ending just below the knee, and a deeply bloused sleeveless bodice with a tight hip band. Most of her short black hair is hidden under a cloche of felt. She won't wear gloves today. A strand of pearls is draped between her breasts. The skirt is red – the Chinese color of happiness – and she will tell him with a brilliant smile that she wears it because of him. Her frank coquetry might well shock the Confucian in him, although Vera has discovered in the General a secret love of the iconoclastic – perhaps a function of his military desire for challenge. What, really, does she think of the man? What is he but a general? Yes, and a connoisseur of art; yes, a gentle lover. She lights a cigarette and puffs nervously, then grinds it out in an ashtray. It's been this way for the past three days – the same adolescent nervousness before she leaves to meet him.

Vera calls the maid, who sends the porter for a rickshaw. They are scarcer these days because of a tram strike in the Settlement, but 'scarce' means you can get one in a couple of minutes. Standing in the courtyard of the Chinese house, Vera stares into a cloudless sky. A touch of breeze stirs the single curl peeking at her left ear from under the bell-shaped hat. She feels the motion of the strand, knowing it will look just right when she sees the General.

Her parrot, Igor, sits on his stand in the shade of the portico. He's shelling a peanut.

This act seems so perfect in itself, so natural and skilful, so quietly integrated into the day, that Vera watches intently, almost jealously, until Igor has eaten the peanut. The shell lies on the ground under the stand in an accumulation of them. Igor, having swallowed, grips the stand with his big strong claws and cocks his head, attempting to locate the direction of a distant sound. The moment has passed, but while it lasted it held both the parrot and Vera in the grip of magic. A few times in her life Vera Rogacheva has been suffused by a wondrous feeling of unity with the world, as if everything has fallen into place, everything has been revealed, and God has whispered to her, 'You see now, child, how simple it all is.' Such a moment has just occurred for her again – a parrot has shelled and eaten a peanut. Both in gratitude and in confusion Vera crosses herself, muttering a quick prayer to the Virgin, and steps forward in the sunlight to go to her lover.

Past the Customs Building, coming into the hotel district, Vera sees across from the Cathay Hotel a large placard from the *North China Daily News*: BORODIN FLEES!

A couple of boys hawking papers scream into the hot afternoon: 'Stop Press News! Read all about it!' In English, French, and Chinese.

For a few exquisite moments Vera luxuriates in the sensation of victory. That arrogant Bolshevik has been tossed out of China. Stopping the rickshaw, she calls a boy over and buys a newspaper. Reading the English with some difficulty, she learns that Borodin, threatened in the mountain resort of Lushan by a local warlord, fled by train. He rushed to the headquarters of General Feng Yu-hsiang, a known sympathizer to the Red cause. But Feng, having shifted allegiance to Chiang Kai-shek – at least for the moment – turned away the Bolshevik leader and his Russian party. They had traveled by car and truck, after reaching the end of the rail line at Shen-chow. They had gone to Ningsia, the last city before reaching the Great Wall, and then – the Gobi. The news account stops here, noting that Borodin's destination will be Ulan Bator, in Mongolia. The paper claims Borodin is suffering from malaria.

Good, she thinks vindictively.

Vera tries to imagine the exhausted party struggling across the camel trails, encountering the shifting sands and the raging dust storms, the inferno of midday suns, the biting cold of desert nights. Good. Good, too, if the trip never ends for them, good if finally they lie dead in the silence and yellow sand of the Gobi. Why should the murdering Reds return safely to Mother Russia? Why? God in Heaven! When it should be Vera Rogacheva returning to the family estate outside of Petrograd, to the restocked stables, to the bright gardens and rolling lawns, to the great table laid with embroidered linen and sparkling silver, to the fireplace merrily aroar, to the entire clan of Rogachevas gathered in the main drawing room for a toast of plum-colored wine at the Christmas season!

When Vera enters the marble lobby of the Palace Hotel and sees the General rising from a chair to greet her, so intent is she on the Borodin news that she hardly notices his clothes, athough General Tang is wearing a British tweed suit, complete with vest and hat.

Waving the newspaper in the air, Vera exclaims, 'The Bolshevik butcher has run away!'

Only then does she fully realize how altered his appearance has become. In that suit he might well be mistaken for a European, aside from the eyes, whose skin folds make them seem slated – but moderately so. Vera thinks he can be taken for a stocky Italian or a Pole, even a Ukrainian. Her astonishment – and growing approval – is reflected in his shy embarrassment. He has done this for me,

Vera thinks. Or has he? Has he really? She feels the need to know; indeed, she must know, for somehow it assumes immediate importance. When they are seated in a taxi, Vera reaches out and lays one finger on the tweed lapel. Although they have lain naked together many hours, she has difficulty touching his sleeve in public, just as the General, spontaneous in bed, remains stiffly formal when they sally forth into the streets of Shanghai.

'The suit is attractive,' she comments.

Without a glance her way, the General shrugs, attempting to minimize his remarkable change in appearance. 'I thought you'd feel less conspicuous if I wore European clothes,' he explains after a long silence.

This is true, of course. A Chinese man with a European woman is a rarity in Shanghai, although the reverse is common enough in the pleasure districts. So he has sacrificed his Chinese image for her sake – a considerable sacrifice, given the man's commitment to his culture. Vera is shocked, delighted, and frightened by the implications of this gesture. She is overjoyed by his sensitive regard for her feelings, although in truth she has walked the streets of this city in the company of men too contemptible for him even to notice. Shyly Vera glances at his tweed jacket, and wonders at the will power he must have exerted in order to fit his bones and flesh within this framework of British civilization. Fear lies in her response: Such a man might demand of her more than she can – or is willing to – give.

At the race track Vera loses herself awhile in the excitement. Only recently has greyhound racing become fashionable in Shanghai; it is now the rage. The greyhound stadium in Luna Park can accommodate thirty thousand spectators. This afternoon the stands are packed, as usual, and tonight, under lights, they will be crowded with people in evening dress, fresh from dinner. Vera has come a few times with Erich, who predictably knows everything about the operation – even that the electrically propelled hare is called Cuthbert by the track manager, a retired British officer named Major Duncan E. Campbell. This is the sort of detail Erich accumulates. He knows, moreover, that the hare's speed is controlled by an operator housed in a tower above the track; that this operator can cheat by manipulating the hare's speed – encouraging the lead hound, for example, to slow down in preparation for pouncing on the little animal, and thereby allowing other contestants to gain or take the lead. Although Erich knows full well that gamblers control the outcome, he spends large sums anyway in the half-hour intervals between the half-minute race. Up and off he goes to the parimutuel windows, returning only in time to see the hounds paraded in the colored blankets of their stables.

But the General never leaves her side, reminding her of Russian gentlemen who at lawn parties and the race track used to vie with one another in showering women with attention. The General doesn't go through all that ritual posturing, but he does stay with her, as if his interest extends beyond the bedroom. And as each pack of a half-dozen hounds pursues the mechanical rabbit that makes a loud whirring sound, Vera is aware she has never felt this way since leaving Petrograd. What she feels, wonderfully, is safe. Perhaps contentment is the identifiable emotion, and the beauty of it suffuses her consciousness. Vera wishes to touch this man who brings it to her, yet she dares not in the fashionable but watchful crowd. By the time they leave the track, Vera is humming a half-remembered folk tune, smiling.

But then she notices the General is not smiling. Wrenched from her own happy mood, Vera can see he's especially grave – brooding – as he walks with hands fisted against his back, unconsciously Napoleonic. Does he regret the Western clothes? But he isn't a man for petty regrets. Has she displeased him? She said almost nothing during the races. She had simply luxuriated in the pleasure of being with this man, and in so doing had forgotten the need to communicate with him. She has broken a cardinal rule: Never relax with a man if you want to keep him. It's dangerous to stop calculating.

'Is everything all right?' she asks without modulating the bluntness of her question.

Tang nods, but Vera understands he has continued to walk headlong into his own thoughts. As they are leaving the broad acreage of the park, he turns suddenly. 'So Chiang Kai-shek is winning.'

This exclamation, unexpected, confuses Vera for a moment. While she's been thinking of them together, he's been thinking politics.

'With Borodin gone, the Bolsheviks are completely finished,' he continues, as if talking aloud to himself.

'Do you believe that?' Vera halts at the park entrance under a hawthorn tree.

'Yes, of course. The Russians brought their ideas here; now they're taking those ideas home with them.'

Vera shakes her head, wondering how to explain what she knows. She can't let him walk off in a cloud of innocence. So she tells him a story, kept fresh in her memory since her eighteenth year, when father sat her down and held her hand and in slow, measured phrases explained to her what for him was Bolshevism. In 1917 the Bolsheviks, as a political party, received only a quarter of the votes for the Assembly, whereas the Socialist Revolutionaries, generally more moderate in their politics, got more than half the votes. But when the Assembly convened in January 1918 the Bolsheviks demanded to be recognized as the government. When the other delegates rejected their usurpation of power, the Bolsheviks walked out. Next morning, when the rest of the Assembly gathered for the second session, they were barred from entering the hall by Red troops. The Bolsheviks, when they saw they were losing, simply took control with their guns.

By the time Vera has delivered her lecture – recalled with a vividness engendered by love for her dead father – they have reached the park exit. 'I remember my father's words,' Vera continues, head bent in contemplation of her own. 'He said such people have only one law, and it is power. So they don't understand other laws. Therefore, when they took the government by force, they merely carried out the law. That's what my father said. He was right,' Vera declares without looking up. She has an image of him in the study, holding a glass of sherry and wearing a black frock coat. A few weeks later, not fifty miles out of Petrograd, he would be dead beside the road, shot through the head by a drunken foundry worker using an officer's pistol on Czarist refugees who failed to salute him.

Glancing at the General, she realizes that he hasn't understood much of her story – voting in an assembly is not part of his nation's experience. 'I simply mean, the Bolsheviks here are still Bolsheviks.'

'Chinese Bolsheviks,' he corrects her.

'Does that really make a difference?'

'Better Chinese than Russian Bolsheviks in China.'

'But they are Bolsheviks whatever their country. They haven't left with Borodin. And from the Russian Reds they've developed an attitude. Let me tell you about that attitude. It's exactly the same that the Bolsheviks had in the 1918 Assembly.' Vera can tell by the set of his mouth that the General is not convinced; what matters to him is the nationality of the Reds. 'You must take them seriously,' Vera maintains, her voice trembling with passion. 'The Chinese Bolsheviks seriously.'

'Even if they number only a few thousand?'

'Even if they number a dozen.'

After searching her face a moment, Tang nods curtly and leads her to a waiting taxi. She's aware of her boldness; in his view, probably, a woman should never talk of politics, let alone warn a man of the consequences of his political thinking. Yet her spirits lift at the knowledge that his brooding has its origin in something other than their relationship. She didn't bring a frown to his face; politics did.

Glancing at him as they drive off in the taxi, Vera feels a sudden wave of fear. This man is a warlord of China, where each day the fortunes of men swing radically, like dragon kites in the wind. Tomorrow or the next day he may fall. But it won't happen to him, Vera tells herself, and for the first time she wonders in a moment of odd speculation if indeed she might fall in love with General Tang.

No, he can never pass for European, she thinks while they sit in a restaurant.

His earlobes, plainly visible now that he has taken off the felt hat, are much too long. And his eyes really are Chinese. And his color, that of weathered ivory, is a shade foreign to Europe. No, he can't be taken for a Westerner.

The faces of some Petrograd guardsmen return to mind: long pale faces with generous noses and wide-set blue eyes and a carefree wealth of curly brown hair. She dislikes the gold in the upper front row of the General's teeth. No, she can't fall in love with such a man, especially because they have little to talk about except art; and for that matter, she has discovered his knowledge of art outside of China is paltry. At least with Erich, who admittedly knows nothing about art, she has Europe in common. When in drunken despair he reminisces about Karlsruhe, she has never been there but she can imagine it; she has a childhood journey through Europe to sustain her imagination when it falters. But the General can't share that world with her, nor ultimately can she share his. The silence between them drifts sometimes until each dwells far from the other, hearing and seeing quite different things, thinking thoughts which are mutually exclusive and will remain so. Vera is certain of it. This very moment, as she looks at him across the table, she can almost hear the wind rushing between them, sealing them off from each other, a huge gap yawning between her mind and his, her emotions and his, her desires and his. Doubtless, as he fingers a chopstick and stares at his plate, the General is thinking of guns, soldiers, of raids, counterattacks, of cannonade, ambush. Or whatever it is that generals brood about. She will have none of it. And anyway, in a few days he'll leave Shanghai and return to his headquarters in Qufu.

No, she can't love this man. With a sense of relief Vera picks up her chopsticks to plunge them happily into a bowl of squid.

He is in the bathroom, and Vera, lying in bed, awaits him. How quickly the world spins in an hour, how quickly life changes. They have been in his hotel room (a little world of its own) only half an hour, yet it has been time enough for her to view the General in a wholly new way.

In began when they entered the room; he gave her a gift, wrapped decoratively in bright rice paper.

The Willow Pattern plate.

They sat on the bed, looking at it, and he reminded her of the charming story that goes with the Willow Pattern: Young lovers run away from an irate parent and after dying in a fire of vengeance ascend as two doves into Heaven.

'Now I must tell you the real story of this design,' he said gravely. And Vera listened, one hand on the plate, one hand lightly on his thigh, as he explained the true meaning of the Willow Pattern. In the early reign of the Manchu invaders, the monastery of Shao-lin was extremely powerful. Wanting to break the hold of Buddhism on the conquered Chinese, the Manchu sent imperial troops to burn it down. Five monks escaped and founded the Hung Society under a peach tree – a society for the preservation of the Chinese nation.

The General told her that the plate must actually be read in an order opposite to that of the popular story. The lovers' house that burns is in fact the Shao-lin Monastery. Souls of dead monks take a boat to the Isle of the Blest, which, in the popular version, is merely the home of the old nurse. On the bridge, as depicted on the plate, are not the fleeing couple and the girl's angry father in hot pursuit, but actually three Buddhas awaiting the dead souls: Sakyamuni the Buddha of the Past, Maitreya the Buddha of the Future, and Amitabha the Ruler of the Western Paradise. Beyond them is the City of Willows – Buddhist Heaven – although in the popular version it's the girl's home from which the couple escape. The doves are the monks' souls on the journey from human to immortal life. The house in which the lovers finally die is the monastery in which the heroic monks die – that is the correlation. And the house which the lovers leave is the paradise to which Hung heroes go. In this pictorial way the secret society defied the Manchu tyrants; they celebrated their martyrs and reminded Hung members of their pledge to defend Chinese and Buddhist values.

Tang had taken her hand in his. 'I wanted you to know.'

She thought then: He trusts me, he is telling me I have his confidence. 'There is more to China,' she said, 'than I can ever know.'

'Than any of us can. But I'll show you more of it than you can imagine.'

She sensed then that he had done something extraordinary; that he had told her what foreigners shouldn't know; that he had betrayed one trust in order to create another; that he had overstepped the limits set not by him but by many other men, over centuries – his brothers in this society.

Waiting naked for him now in his bed, Vera links the story of the Willow Pattern to his tweed suit and to his admission that filial piety rather than personal choice had determined his military career. He has moved farther toward her than any man ever has. Acknowledgment of it gives her again the mingled emotions of delight and fear. One hand slides down her hip to stroke her belly; soon he will be stroking it. Her hand moves to the edge of the Triangle That Drives Men Wild, fingers the soft hair. She wants him now in a spasm of gratitude, perhaps even of heartfelt dumb desire. Why does he remain so long in the bathroom with the water running? Vera knows enough about men to guess – and her guess drains away the gratitude, the desire. He is standing at the sink, staring in confusion at his mirrored image, asking himself repeatedly what is he doing with the Russian whore in the next room. Poor man, she thinks. And a Chinese man at that, a Chinese general. It is altogether possible that by wearing the

European suit and by speaking of his youth and family and by divulging secrets about an old plate, this poor Chinese general has just screamed out an impossible love. Impossible. Yet he is in the bathroom studying his anguished face, trying to understand what has happened to himself here in Shanghai, when he came only to buy guns – and to buy them from her lover at that. Erich. What would Erich think if he knew? Nothing much. Nothing. And she won't tell him either, because he'd take revenge on the General. Not because of love for her, but because of some twisted remnant of male honor he still possesses after all these wandering years, after the uncounted humiliations he endured as a prisoner of war in Russia, then as an electric fan salesman doubling in guns. She will tell Erich nothing. Because she knows nothing.

So many men..

A gray despair comes over Vera Rogacheva. She feels numb in the bed, as if her body has become mixed with the dead cotton of the sheets. So many, many men. For a few sad moments she imagines herself to be the young Russian girl met in the park a few weeks ago, a girl waiting for her lover with trustful innocence. So many men. They have entered her life, briefly, all of them for a price, none of them with her heart's consent. Only Yu-ying was deeply welcomed, only a drug-besotted girl of the Shanghai streets.

So many men. Vera fingers the soft down at the edge of the Triangle That Drives Men Wild. She and Yu-ying used to laugh about their sexual skills – naughty little girls exchanging whorish secrets while giggling and touching each other. 'If he does that, you do this –' amid peals of scornful laughter.

So many men. Yu-ying, where did you drift to in your opium dream? God in Heaven, to have nothing to show for all those men but a single suitcase packed with objects. She touches herself, imagines what pleasure the anguished man staring now in the mirror will anticipate when, opening the door, he sees her lying here, legs apart, supremely accessible. She ought to have given her virginity to one of those handsome young guardsmen who used to flock around her at Petrograd galas; one of those lovely boys in shiny buckles and gold epaulettes. Instead of the three grizzled Czech legionnaires who agreed to let her sick uncle remain in a heated train compartment if they could have her; the four grinning beasts who took her honor in a freezing train station on the way to Omsk. On a bare cold table.

So many men. Do I love this man, this Chinese general, this strange foreigner I can never know? Vera asks herself repeatedly. 'Do I love him?' in a silence of increasing fear and bewilderment.

The bathroom door opens; the man comes out, naked and smiling. Whatever he saw of his deepest self in the mirror he has put away; he has conquered it, Vera thinks. Without a word he strides toward the bed, and in this instant Vera recalls the White Hawk of the painting: muscular, alert, a predator serene in its fierceness. Fascinated, unable to speak or move, she lies there, half raised on her elbows, watching the thickset man move toward her. Vera has the odd sensation of not knowing him at all. But her unsettled feeling vanishes when, reaching the bed, he bends down to kiss her lips. His knee crushes the sheet. His weight, shifting onto the bed, seems abruptly added to her own, becoming part of hers. Reaching out, when he touches her hair, Vera slides her fingers across his arm and shoulder. Why do they talk of a woman's curves when men have them too? Yu-ying flashes into her mind: a bead of sweat on the girl's smooth forehead hovering above her. Every time Vera has gone to bed with this man, she has remembered Yu-ying. Why? Their mutual gentleness? There's no time for thought. None. Vera's hands take command and move at their own volition, exploring the hairless texture of chest and belly. Smooth skin like Yu-ying's, smooth as her own. But when he takes her fully into his arms, the muscles flexing, it's with a man's force and insistence. She awaits his entry, her head flung back to the side, breath lodged in her throat. She feels herself suffocating in the anticipation until deeply he thrusts with a motion neither brutal nor gentle, but determined. Vera, sighing, moves until her own rhythm coincides with his. Do I love him? Is it possible?

He is whispering in her ear. Lost in sensation, she can't recognize for a moment the language he is speaking. Then she hears the desperate whisper, as if the words had been dammed up for a long time and are now suddenly released. 'Come back with me to Qufu.'

Their rhythm quickens, the exquisite motion becoming almost unbearably keen, as she replies with her lips against the long, strange earlobe, 'Yes, I will, I'll go with you. Yes, I'll – anywhere.'

367

PART TWO

16

A few things always give him comfort: the distinctive smell of oiled gun metal, for one; the decisive clunk of a shell being chambered, that sound; and the report – but more than the report – the ultimate aural beauty of metallic impact. He has loved them since childhood, when in the Kraichgau hills outside of Karlsruhe his father introduced him to the rifle.

Professional respect for weaponry has aroused his contempt for the Chinese, who often lack the basic skills in using firearms, let along display a tactical regard for their employment. For example, General Tang has ordered a number of machine guns; yet if he follows the Chinese pattern, he'll move them up with an attack instead of deploying them on the flanks and rear for fire support. To arm a Chinese warlord is to throw good money after bad.

Luckner smiles grimly as he stands on the bow of a launch, watching the brown water of the Whangpoo ripple in an offshore breeze. From the Pooting side of the channel, where the warehouses are, the stink of offal and naphthalene hovers over ramps of godowns that store bales of pressed duck feathers and rabbit hides.

At least there's this to say for the General: He came up with more money than Luckner had expected him to find in Shanghai. Rumor had Tang's star falling, but apparently someone still believes in him enough to supply funds for additional weapons. The fellow came back for more, slapping down his bank check with that hungry look Luckner has seen on the faces of men at a brothel. He doesn't like the General, one of those arrogant Chinese whose troops often go into battle carrying pitchforks and clubs, but whose Confucian attitudes make them feel superior to foreigners who offer them modern weapons. Tang was desperate for more arms, yet this time he had not asked for credit. Pride. Confucian stupid fucking pride. Life hasn't yet forced him to get rid of that useless posture.

The tall blond German attempts to light a cigarette on the lee side of the launch, but there's too much wind eddying about, so he gives up trying.

The only Chinese good with weapons are the Shanghai gangsters. Unfortunately he can't sell to them, although a Mauser automatic bought in Hamburg for an equivalent of $30 U.S. will bring $120 in Shanghai. He could name his price for a .45 capable of being fitted with a rifle stock. Street hoodlums go wild for a Belgian pistol of the Colt type. But he can't do business with them, because the Green Circle Gang controls gun sales to the locals. If he let a single gun go and the Greens learned of it – and they would – he'd be floating right here in the Whangpoo within half a day. Perhaps the time's coming when the Greens will trust him enough to use his services, but at present he's still under scrutiny. It may take years for the Greens to make a decision about him; for such a bloodthirsty crew, they're as cautious as bankers. Right now they do all their buying from a Dane quartered in Canton with solid connections in Macao.

Sighing, Luckner shades his eyes and squints in the morning light at a rusty tramp steamer ahead. It rides taut on a bower anchor just off the east side of the channel, a lazy curl of smoke rising from its stack. Booms fore and aft on king posts are swung over hatches, the winches humming. Lighters are receiving cargo. Ragged, knobby-kneed coolies pause in their work to look at the launch pulling alongside the accommodation ladder.

Climbing aboard, Luckner needs no help finding the captain's cabin – he has been here many times in recent years, when this coal burner with a Lloyd's registry from Panama steams into anchorage on the Whangpoo and awaits people like himself who have quick orders for cargo.

The skipper, a grizzled Norwegian who speaks German, is sitting with booted feet on a desk in his cabin. He doesn't rise when Luckner, appearing on the threshold, grins and waves a wrapped package.

'So it's you,' the skipper mumbles in a coarse, deep voice.

Luckner rips the paper off and holds up a bottle, a fine cognac.

'Sit down,' says the captain, rubbing his unshaven chin. His blue eyes in a weathered face seem unfocused. He is already drunk, but Luckner knows that at sea the sobered Norwegian is one of the best coastal masters in Asia.

Two dirty glasses stand on the littered desk, next to a bottle of Hollands, half full. Luckner pours liberal amounts of brandy into each filthy glass (wincing at the look of them), lifts his own, and toasts the skipper, who he knows will not return the courtesy. The cognac bites, bringing tears to Luckner's eyes. With a slow grin the skipper raises his own glass and drinks it off without changing expression.

'Got business?' he asks almost pleasantly, wiping his mouth.

Luckner explains he has a shipment for pickup in Manila.

'Goods already there?'

'My ship from Hamburg is due in there today, as a matter of fact.' As a matter of fact, Luckner is telling the truth. He has tons of gelatin, fuses, nitro, black powder, ammo, Thermos flasks, rifles, and machine guns on the way. Driven in sealed Czech trucks from the Skoda plant in Pilsen, the military goods arrived at Hamburg, were put on lighters and loaded on a freighter bound for East Asia. He has a wireless to that effect in his pocket, but doesn't show it to the skipper, who would jeer at proof.

'You're telling me,' says the drunken Norwegian, 'your goods aren't in Manila yet.'

'I said they will be. Today. Captain Schulz will get them there on schedule.'

'Kurt Schulz?' The skipper leans forward heavily and grips the bottle, pours the glass full. 'Yeah, Kurt will get there on time all right. At the usual warehouse?' When Luckner nods, the skipper drinks half the glass, his Adam's apple pumping. Luckner is glad he came early – by afternoon the man will be stretched out in his bunk, pickled.

'Got to take on cargo here first,' the captain says after a long brooding silence. He raises his voice to be heard over the clanging noise of deckhands chipping rust on the wheelhouse bulkhead nearby. 'Will take time.'

'When can you leave?' Luckner asks, watching him finish off the glass of cognac and pour another.

'What?' When he wipes his mouth with the back of his hand, the skipper displays a forearm covered by tattoos: crossed anchors; a heart with initials in it; a dragon whose head takes up most of his left hand, fire from its nostrils leading down his thumb and forefinger.

'I said, when can you leave Shanghai? When can you be in Manila?'

The skipper blinks sleepily. 'Next week. Leave next week. In Manila by late August.' He stares a long time at a torn calendar pinned on the far bulkhead; it is a Chinese calendar with a pretty singsong girl showing a curvaceous leg through the slit gown. 'By twenty-sixth for sure.'

'That's fine. But no later.' He has promised Tang the arms by the first of October – plenty of time. 'I may have a double shipment to pick up.'

'Don't matter. We got room.' He sips the cognac, this time almost cautiously, as if two full glasses have given him respect for its potency. 'Don't you worry. Always worried. I pick up anything you got, anything.'

Luckner decides it's necessary to assert himself with the contemptuous Norwegian. 'You better have room,' Luckner says in a voice loud enough to be heard over the chipping hammers.

'What?'

'You damn well better have room! If my clients are disappointed, you'll answer to them.'

'Rough assholes, huh?' The skipper grins, then opens his mouth into a large red oval and bellows out his laughter. 'Well, you go tell these rough assholes they haven't got enough money to fill up the holds of my fucking ship.' These are more words than Luckner has ever heard him put together. 'Chinese assholes, who do they think they are! You hear me?' He's becoming belligerent, a man nearly six and a half feet tall if he can rise out of the chair, and nearly three hundred pounds, enough muscles still in them to cause someone plenty of damage.

Luckner rises. 'I'll tell them.'

'Goddamn right you tell them.'

'I'll tell them.'

'Where're you going?'

'I'll come back tomorrow and arrange the details.' There's no sense talking more business with the sottish Norwegian today. Luckner will return shortly after dawn tomorrow, when the skipper's had only a drink or two. Bringing the brandy was a mistake, except that without it he might not have got this far with the man, who is capable of doing infantile things, like refusing to recognize clients he has done business with for years or deciding that he doesn't want to move cargo he's always accepted. Dealing with coastal skippers is one of the headaches of the weapons business.

Outside, in the clear air of the hatchway, Luckner breathes deeply before yanking out a comb – the freshening wind has mussed his hair. Lighting a Chesterfield, he returns to the launch and soon is rocking in the swells of the Whangpoo, heading north toward the Bund past the ocean liners, the foreign warships, the Chinese gunboats, the stubby tugs and tankers, junks and sampans, world steamers and trawlers and houseboats, all wrapped in a matrix of odors: fish, smoke, oil, excrement, and the tang of ocean spray blown in from the east.

The florid, hulking man is awaiting him at the long mahogany bar of the Bankers Club. John Haversham, manager of the British China Match Factory.

They shake hands, and in German the Britisher asks him what he will have to drink.

Luckner, always the tactful guest, replies, 'What you're having.'

'I'm having a tot of whisky.'

'Excuse me?' Luckner says in German, for the Britisher has lapsed into English.

'Whisky. Sorry, I forgot.'

'I'm sorry my English isn't better,' Luckner says in apology.

Several men in seersucker, with ruddy English faces, turn to stare at the two who are speaking German.

'I'm pleased to practice your language,' says Haversham, but moves Luckner away from the curious group. They find a table in the dark-paneled dining room. Haversham sighs when they sit down. 'This is not the Shanghai Club, but I thought for our purposes it's a bit quieter. They do a nice lunch. None of your fancy Chinese dishes, but good beef-and-kidney pie and beefsteak.'

'This is a splendid club,' Luckner replies, raising his whisky-soda for a toast. The Britisher joins in, after which there's an awkward silence. They are only slight acquaintances, brought together by shady business. Haversham, representing an organization of local foreign industrialists, wants to purchase weapons for their employees. But the nature of his business with Luckner isn't why Haversham has chosen the Bankers Club for their meeting; he simply doesn't want to be seen in the more prestigious Shanghai Club with a German. Luckner understands the man perfectly well. With a smile he repeats the remark, 'This is a splendid club.'

Over soup the Britisher opens the discussion. 'I want you to know we trust Chiang Kai-shek to set things right. I want that straight.'

Luckner nods benignly.

'But some of the people he does business with –'

'You mean the Greens?'

373

Haversham glances around to make sure they aren't overheard, although they're speaking German. 'I must say the Greens have made us a bit unsettled about the future. If things get out of Chiang's control, if there's rioting and looting, we do feel we must protect our equipment.'

'Naturally. You have an important investment here,' Luckner agrees, lifting a spoonful of soup.

'That *is* the point, isn't it. We, that is, the Association, felt you would understand and perhaps agree to help.'

'Agree to get you weapons, you mean.' Luckner wants him to pay a little for meeting him at this club, not the other. But Luckner doesn't force his bitterness on the man. Quickly they proceed into the details – prices, time and place of shipment – details which make the Britisher nervous enough to drink more whiskies than he can handle. His face, now fiercely crimson, and his bloodshot eyes, straying in their focus, begin to remind Luckner of the Norwegian sea captain he has just left.

'I say, this is going to cost,' Haversham mutters gloomily after a while, staring at his untouched coffee. 'Boy! Whisky-soda! Another, Mister Luckner?'

'I've had my share, thank you.' Luckner lights a cigarette and waits for the Britisher to resume the discussion. Plainly the man doesn't want to pay very much for protecting the factories. Luckner feels no anxiety about the sale; the Japanese have freed him from his recent financial worries, or at least sufficiently for him to sit back and wait until people like General Tang and John Haversham make up their minds about meeting terms. It is a wonderful thing to be solvent. It will be a still more wonderful thing when he has accumulated enough money to go back to Karlsruhe, where he'll prove to Vera that it's as beautiful as he claims. Hail to the Japanese.

'Excuse me.' Luckner realizes he has been lost in his dreams; consequently he has failed to catch Haversham's last question. 'Would you repeat that?'

The Britisher eyes him sullenly, a glass of neat whisky in a big hand. 'I asked about renting the weapons.'

'I'm sorry. That's out of the question.'

'Rumor has it renting is done now in Shanghai.'

'The rumor is partly correct. Renting is done by the Greens, who lend guns for a percentage of the take from a robbery. I believe the percentage is now thirty. And a time and place are fixed for return of the guns. Only you do not have robbery in mind, and I doubt if you wish to deal with the Greens.'

Haversham, grunting in agreement, downs the whisky. He looks now like a smaller version of the Norwegian – glum, suspicious, quick to anger.

Searching for something innocuous to say, Luckner comments on the man's German. 'I admire your command of my language. If I didn't know otherwise, I'd have said you lived much of your life in Germany.'

'I learned some German in college, but most of it I got as a prisoner of war. In 1916.' Their eyes, British and German, meet steadily until Haversham looks away with a sigh. 'Yes, in 1916. Were you in the war?'

'Yes,' Luckner says.

After another brooding silence, Haversham abruptly pounds the table with his empty glass. 'Goddamn the Green bastards! Why does Chiang do business with the cutthroats anyway?'

Luckner knows. Years ago Chiang Kai-shek had worked as a stock-broker's assistant in the Settlement. With guidance from a Green Circle boss and with money from a financier, he made a quick fortune on the stock market which he promptly lost. Returning to Shanghai, he has found the old ties with mobsters and businessmen of great help, more help than he can get from traditional militarists. To the Britisher's outburst, however, Luckner replies with bland obtuseness, 'Chinese ways are mysterious.'

'Not that we don't expect great things from Chiang. He's a cut above the other warlords.'

Luckner smiles; Chiang Kai-shek would have this Britisher scourged for calling him a warlord, a term he denies with vehemence has anything to do with his noble aims for China.

'Chiang got rid of the Reds and brought order to Shanghai,' continues Haversham, as if trying to prove to himself as well as to Luckner that he has faith in the Nationalists.

Chiang did get rid of the Reds, Luckner thinks, but only after they organized the general strike that crippled the city of Shanghai so Chiang could take it over and then slaughter his erstwhile allies. Luckner recalls the fury of the Nationalist attack against the Reds, once Shanghai was secured. He saw the row upon row of Reds and their sympathizers, bound hand and foot, laid face down in alleys and calmly shot by Green Gang members or by KMT soldiers –

375

southern boys in cotton trousers, flapping puttees, and grass sandals. Standing over the corpses, they had grinned at Luckner. The executions were done with more style later. Bolsheviks had signs reading TRAITOR strapped to their backs, and when they fell they collapsed on their sides, curled up like sleeping street urchins. Beheadings took place with fodder-chopping knives. Student Reds were torched with kerosene. Bullets were fired up the vaginas of Bolshevik girls. Luckner recalls the order brought to Shanghai all right. 'That's true,' he agrees reasonably with the Britisher, who has ordered another whisky. 'Chiang brought order here.'

'Something I haven't sorted out,' Haversham says in a low, conspiratorial voice. 'Just how illegal is this business of yours? I mean, how *seriously* illegal.' He guffaws drunkenly. 'I can't get the answer from anyone in the Settlement.'

'The Arms Embargo Agreement was signed in 1919,' Luckner explains, although uncertain if the man is sober enough to follow. 'That made it illegal for governments to sell arms in China. But the agreement said nothing about individuals.'

'I see.'

'The nationals of the governments could do as they pleased. All that interferes with gunrunning here is the Chinese police, if they decide to raid a warehouse or a cargo ship when they have nothing else to do – on a whim. That's all.' Luckner shrugs. 'The only real danger is from the Greens, if they decide to shut down a particular sale. Certainly there's no trouble from the American or the British or the Italian or the Dutch or the French or the German government here in China.'

The cynical explanation seems to please Haversham, who chortles again over his whisky. In a more relaxed mood, he lights a cigar. 'You mentioned .38-caliber Smith & Wessons. Aren't they more costly than Lugars?'

'You'll do better with them. The 7.65 Lugar shoots high-velocity bullets.'

'Isn't that good? High velocity? Pardon my ignorance, but even in the army I was a poor man with guns.'

'High velocities go through the target with only a small perforation.'

'Go right through a chap,' Haversham says in English, then repeats it in German.

'Exactly. Your soft-lead medium projectiles, the kind used with

376

the Smith & Wesson, tend to mushroom on impact. They tear great ragged holes and do a lot of damage in human tissue, believe me, before they go out again. If your men don't know how to handle arms well, they'll get more from the Smith & Wessons.' Luckner has enjoyed giving the little lecture.

'I think for the price we'll take the Lugars.'

'As you wish,' Luckner says coolly, and the meeting is finished. It's a small order, hardly worth his time, yet it has opened a source of income that may prove significant in the future: private individuals and companies trying to protect themselves in this city of chaos. Maybe in two years, if Luckner can curb his spending, he and Vera will leave this doomed country and head for Germany, for Karlsruhe, for the Rhine . . .

Outside, in the sunlight, Haversham blinks at the long line of rickshaws queued up in front of the club. 'I'd very much like the guns as soon as possible,' he says pleasantly. 'One never knows in Shanghai when they'll come in handy.'

Luckner explains once again that a ship will be going out in a few days; within a month or six weeks the Association will have the guns.

'Come to my office tomorrow, we'll complete everything,' says Haversham.

'You'll have the money?'

Haversham makes a wry face. 'I wouldn't play cheap, sir, with someone who has done his soldiering too. Tell me,' he adds, studying Luckner's handsome features, 'what the deuce *did* happen to you in the Great War?'

Having closed the deal, Luckner feels relaxed enough to tell him. 'In 1915 I was with Mackensen's Eleventh Army in East Prussia.'

'I've heard of the Eleventh.'

'In June I was captured near Jaroslav by troops of the Grand Duke Nicholas.'

'You were a prisoner of the Russians?' the Britisher asks in open astonishment.

Luckner understands. Veterans of the war are amazed that anyone could have fallen into the hands of the inept Russians, who had contributed little to the Allied cause before withdrawing altogether after the Revolution. In French and British eyes the Russians had done nothing more than divert German troops from the Western front for a time. How could a German of self-respect allow himself to be captured by Russians? That question darkens the ruddy face of John Haversham.

'I spent four years in Russia,' Luckner says anyway. He doesn't add (complicated war stories rarely hold the interest) that in 1917 he escaped from a Siberian prison camp after the October Revolution, and in spite of harrowing trials made his way back to the German lines. There his own troops threatened him, for German POWs from Russia were suspected of Communist leanings. Returning to Russia, many of them actually joined the Bolsheviks, although others, Luckner among them, were afraid of the Red labor battalions in which foreigners were literally worked to death. He had joined the Czarist forces, served as an orderly, then as a guard herding Red prisoners to Siberia – more than seven thousand kilometers of fighting and suffering across frozen tundra, often at forty degrees below zero, corresponding to a march five times across the breadth of Germany. No, it isn't something he can explain to a rich Britisher, tipsy, at all odds a staff officer who never saw combat in the Great War.

'Four years in Russia,' Haversham mutters and jams a Panama hat on his sweaty head. 'Terrible, terrible. See there?' He points to the line of rickshaws. 'That's order. The club demands it of them and they obey. Anywhere else in this godforsaken city the yellows trample you to get the fare. It takes a European mind to establish a bit of order,' he says with a wink before hailing the first puller in line.

Watching the Britisher move into the stream of traffic, a beefy figure behind the frail coolie, Luckner repeats to himself several words just laconically pronounced: 'In 1915 . . . Jaroslav . . . captured.' In a few seconds he had described the most significant part of his life. What he can never relate to anyone, not even to Vera, who of all his acquaintances understands him best – having experienced similar things herself in the vast wastes of Russia – what he can never form into messages fashioned by civilized men to express their emotions, is the perfect horror and misery of his own imprisonment. Sixty days without shoes in a cattle car. On sidings without a view of sky for all the time or rattling along the clicking tracks toward deeper winter. A little soup writhing with tiny worms. Beatings with the knout by drunken guards. Hair eaten away by scurvy. His good friend Klaus dying beside him in the putrescent straw.

Klaus.

Flesh of a gangrenous leg swelling to monstrous size, a thick black fluid oozing upon the straw, freezing into dollops of incredible stench. The boy whining, then screaming, 'I want to live! Cut it off, I'll walk with a crutch! Don't let it kill me! I want to live! Oh, God, it's unbearable!' And then the croaking howl that filled the wooden prison car until some fellows wanted to toss him on the tracks. One night Klaus ripped off his trousers, clawed and shredded them with bleeding fingers, trying to cool the burning flesh. Next morning, dead, Klaus had presented to his comrades a face distorted beyond recognition by the insufferable agony.

Luckner climbs trembling into a rickshaw. It is never really gone, that time.

Most of the afternoon he spends with his Japanese hosts aboard a pleasure cruiser on the Yangtze. Coming upon its immense brown estuary from the Whangpoo, he stands with beer in hand on the boat's bow. In the distance he hears stevedores on the bank, chanting their '*Hai-yo-hai-yu.*' It is music, a faint wail of rhythmic sound from the far shore. He's alone for the moment, and like a tourist is enjoying the great river – its muddy strength roiling beneath the strakes, the haze above its water that obscures the meeting of sky and river at the horizon. Behind him a few Japanese businessmen and military officers are laughing, toasting one another. Always laughing, always toasting. Where do the little fellows put all that beer? He drinks one for their two, yet still feels sodden, a little drunk. They have asked him to continue the partying in Hongkew. He knows what that means: vegetables fresh from Kyushu, Japanese crabs and pungent soybean paste, the music of a samisen drifting from their paper-walled houses in the heart of a Chinese city, Japanese phonograph records, bowls of flowers in little alcoves – set there like shrines. And women. And sake, more beer, at last whisky. He admires their tremendous energy if he distrusts their good humor. Selling arms to them, so they can keep their Northern Chinese allies well stocked with weaponry, has given Luckner a fresh perspective on the Japanese. He used to think they were pushy and intelligent, but fun loving. Now he thinks they are all those things, yet multiplied beyond reckoning. In the old days he only knew the Mitsui taipan who used to give a riotous cherry-blossom party in his Frenchtown garden each spring. Now he knows the militarists and the bankers intimately, and they frighten him in a way he can't quite understand. Perhaps it's that energy of theirs. He has never seen a pleasure boat so uninhibited as this one commandeered by the Japanese: their toasting and playful cuffing, their spontaneous dancing, their coarse laughter, the mad intensity of their faces as they share dirty jokes.

With them milling around him, getting wilder on beer in the hot yellow currents of the Yangtze, Luckner draws within himself, as if it's urgent that something gets settled in his mind. He's been drifting of late, secure in newfound prosperity, lulled by resurgent hopes. To his sense of well-being he has sacrificed that alertness a man needs in the violent world of China. He thinks of Vera. Ever since boarding the cruiser at the Bund, he has seen images of her in his mind: the pale lovely face, the short black hair, the wide-set enormous eyes – she has loomed in his field of vision, blotting out the toothy grins of his Japanese hosts.

He has seen little of her recently. They have not slept together often. Has she been sleeping with someone else? Not a new question, an old one. It has come to his mind ever since they first met and he brought her home from the police station. Yet the question is more a matter of curiosity than of concern. He asks it often when she wears a smile. He asks himself in the morning had she encountered a man at the opera, at a hotel bar last night, and casually gone to bed with the fellow, while he'd been taking hot baths with Japanese whores? A question of mild interest, the answer to which he doesn't require. After all, they understand each other. Russia gave them something to share that few people ever experience singly: total despair, total horror, total fear, so that the human mind is transformed awhile into the reflexive little brain of an escaping rat. They share something greater than romantic love; they share Russia in 1919.

Luckner sips his beer, hearing a wave of wild laughter crash behind him – chairs skid across the deck, opponents breathe hard, spectators giggle and encourage a brief struggle, then up goes a cry of triumph and the inevitable call for another toast. He doesn't look around to have a view of their antics, but watches a cloud-bank start to roll across the water, heavy and cumbersome as a thick quilt, covering the late afternoon.

Again Vera intrudes. It doesn't matter if she has found someone temporarily; after all, he's been fully occupied with business. In fact, a brief love affair might do Vera good. Yes. Of course. He smiles at this proof of his common sense. Erich Luckner of Karlsruhe is not one of those credulous fools who sit in judgment of the world. Let Vera enjoy herself for a while. Yes. One thing about having a former prostitute for a mistress, he doesn't have to worry about her conscience or wearisome feelings of guilt. She has gone through all the moral questioning long ago; in a way, she has come full circle and reentered a state of purity like that of a young virgin – it is an odd thought not unfamiliar to him, especially when he kisses her sometimes in the morning while she's still asleep. So Vera might have a new man for the moment; she won't suffer from it, and consequently no one else will either. Vera was pure the day he first saw her, a vision of hapless purity as she scrambled out of that getaway car with three Chinese policemen leveling pistols at her and backing her against a shop wall in the dingy Chinatown street. With her dark hair falling to her shoulders (a policeman had knocked off her hat), she stood impassively beside her accomplices, motionless, resigned, a withdrawn look in her eyes that told Luckner everything he needed to know. Later he located her in the Chinese prison – it was the misfortune of these robbers to commit their crime in a section of the city under Chinese, not European law. The three White Russian men, for whom the woman acted as guide and lookout, had learned that a Chinese jeweler kept his valuables in a French Concession bank. Each morning he brought them back to his shop in a little cart. So one morning the three armed men attacked the cart on the street, tossed the bundles and jewelry chests into the back seat of the car, and, with Vera guiding them, sped off through Chinatown. Their luck proved terrible, however, for it so happened that another shop in the vicinity had just been robbed and the police had gathered there when the getaway car turned a corner. The woman, though unarmed and an accessory, would get the same treatment as the armed men – probably worse in a Chinese prison.

Luckner had some faint idea of what that really meant, enough to know it meant a glass of unboiled water, a thin rice soup, and some wormy vegetables once a day; disregard for sanitation; no blankets in winter, no sunlight in summer, only a dank and crowded cell. Through bribery he managed to get into the women's section of the prison. She was sitting against a damp clay wall in a tiny flyblown cell with a half-dozen other women prisoners. There was not enough room for a person to walk two steps in any direction. A stench rose from the foul straw. Incongruously, on one wall were tacked two frayed posters of American film stars whom Luckner recognized: Buddy Rogers in front of his Hollywood mansion and a seminude pose by Mae Murray. In front of the cell door sat an excrement bucket, above which the flies buzzed fiercely in a thick cloud, their iridescent bodies caught wriggling in a shaft of light entering from a window the size of a human hand.

'Yes, that's my sister,' Luckner told the guard, pointing to the disheveled foreign woman. He had explained that the prisoner was a member of his family, a fact guaranteed to arouse whatever sympathy a Chinese prison guard might feel.

Out in the bright air the freed woman squinted down at her sandaled feet. Flies were still clinging to her Chinese trousers and blouse.

'Why did you do it?' Luckner asked.

The woman shrugged. It was a gesture indicating the same tough fatalism he'd seen in her vacant stare when the police herded her and the Russian men against a wall.

'It seemed like a good idea for about ten minutes. After that it was just an idea I couldn't get rid of.' Her answer was so honest, yet so feckless too, that he felt drawn to Vera Rogacheva instantly.

Later Vera claimed she'd met a Russian waiter in a cabaret who needed someone familiar with Chinatown streets to guide a Russian businessman on a tour of jewelry shops. She was innocent of the heist. Luckner didn't care whether her story was true, and to this day he isn't sure. Within a few hours they'd become lovers; and Luckner believed – as he still believes – their similar experiences during the Russian Civil War made them companions for life.

His reverie is disturbed by a sudden downpour that envelops the boat in midchannel of the Yangtze. The pleasure craft comes about in lashings of rain that hammer down on the tin overhead of the wheelhouse. The guests crowd under the deck awnings to watch the descending clouds grip the cruiser in a churning grayness as palpable as the rain that comes from it. The frenzy of nature subdues the festive Japanese. They aren't themselves until a half-hour later, entering the Whangpoo channel and heading home. The sun, breaking through, washes the shoreline and passing vessels in a mysterious purple light. The guests move beyond the dripping canvas awning, holding new beers, to watch their entry into Shanghai waters.

A newly painted tug comes alongside when the cruiser is opposite the storage tanks of the Cal-Texas Oil Company. Japanese crewmen from the tug wave up, and one of them is shouting something.

A Japanese colonel, standing near Luckner, clicks his tongue in surprise and displeasure.

'What has happened?' Luckner asks him in Chinese.

'The man on the tug says some Red bandits have escaped from Nanchang.'

Luckner recalls reading in the paper that the Reds were under siege, in danger of being annihilated.

'They outmaneuvered the Nationalists,' the colonel explains with a disdainful smile. 'Now they're loose in the South.' He shouts at the tug sailor who bows low before shouting back at the officer on the receding cruiser.

'He says,' the colonel tells Luckner, 'the Red bandits are led by Chu Teh. Let *me* have a regiment, I'd finish him in a week.'

Luckner had heard of Chu Teh, a general of remarkable skill for a Chinese. He had for a time supported the Nationalists, so his defection from them may well mean the Reds still exist as a force. they say Chu Teh doesn't believe in the mass charges for which Chinese are notorious – fanatical assaults carried out to the cry of *Hsi-shen tao-ti!* Sacrifice to the last! Although he saw the destruction of thousands in Russia, Luckner is revolted by Chinese readiness to trade human lives for a show of courage. Their generals disregard the wholesale loss of troops who might have been withdrawn in the face of hopeless odds to fight another day. He once read something funny and wise: 'Soldiering is the coward's way of attacking mercilessly when you are strong and keeping out of harm's way when you are weak.' Had it been translated from English? He thinks an Englishman wrote it. In his opinion, those words define the essence of strategy.

As the boat eases down the main channel toward the massive skyline of the Bund, he wonders idly how General Tang conducts a battle. Fanatic or tactician? How is the man *in extremis?* It's hard to say from having met Tang. Like most Asians, he doesn't give himself away, at least not to Westerners, whom he obviously despises. Past the Garden Bridge arching over Soochow Creek, Luckner sees the Palace Hotel's tall spire come into view. Mister

Po Ming, who recently purchased arms from him, must have left the hotel by now for Qufu. Luckner suspects that in a land of such chaos General Tang Shan-teh, alias citizen Po Ming, will have the chance soon enough to show what he can do on the battlefield.

At the end of this long day, filled with too much alcohol, he feels exhausted, squeamish. He has begged off from continuing the fun with his Japanese friends and returns home nearly staggering from fatigue. Entering the house, he calls out loudly, and Hsueh-chen comes running to the foyer, an apron around her thick waist, her broad cheeks glistening with sweat.

'Where is Mistress?' Luckner asks.

'Gone out, Master.'

'Will she eat at home?'

'She had me go buy things at the store. When I came back, she was gone, so I don't know where she went or what she wants. Cook doesn't know what to do.' The girl regards him.

Sensing her curiosity, Luckner asks if Mistress left a message.

'No, Master.' Hsueh-chen wipes the sweat from her forehead with the apron. 'I am scrubbing floors.'

'At this hour?'

'Mistress said scrub them until she said stop. When I came back with a new brush, she was gone. So I keep scrubbing until she says stop.'

Luckner studies the flat, broad face and detects the faintest smile of sarcasm. The girl has tried more than once to make Vera out to be an irresponsible fool. It's just possible the girl is in love with me, Luckner thinks. 'That's enough scrubbing for one day,' he tells her. 'Have cook prepare dinner.'

'For two, Master?' Her expression is alert, expectant.

'For two. And bring me a glass of plain soda.'

Wandering into the small courtyard, he sits on a porcelain taboret, one of Vera's extravagances. One of his own, his silver cigarette case, he takes from a pocket. While smoking, he listens to the plaintive song of a thrush that Hsueh-chen has placed in a cage under the eave. Pity the girl is so plain, Luckner thinks; she would make someone a good concubine. He knows an Italian newly arrived in Shanghai who would appreciate an honest, dutiful, simple girl like Hsueh-chen. She is everything that Vera isn't; maybe the Italian wouldn't want anyone that predictable.

The soda comes, the girl leaves. Too much alcohol today has given him a headache. He kneads both temples with his fingertips, seeking relief in the waning sunset. Toward the east somewhere a clock strikes, its measured strokes, on the vibrating metal coil, twanging loudly. It reminds him of the churches of Germany, the enormous clock towers in medieval towns. So much reminds him of Germany, even in this City of the Muddy Flat, as Shanghai is called. Everything he reads in the newspaper assures him of his nation's renewed prosperity. The aged, magnificent Paul von Hindenburg – a leader of genius – has stabilized the currency, thereby encouraging foreign investors to make loans that in magnitude outstrip Germany's payments of reparations. Luckner, missing his homeland, envies his countrymen their new hope.

The pounding of his temples grows in intensity. Pacing the cobblestones, he sips the soda water and wonders where the hell she is. Lately he's caught her smiling a brilliant but inward smile, her eyes softly fixed on the distance. A definite sign. Of course. It is a sign; not that it matters. Yet he begins to question the good sense of letting Vera get away with an affair. After all, he's been busy with the Japanese, forcing himself to match their energy. Perhaps in the process he's neglected her – but for the sake of business. Is that reason for her to climb into another bed?

'Shut up,' he mutters at the singing thrush, who ignores him.

It's unfair of her. It's unfair although in recent weeks he has often stayed out all night with his Japanese companions – perhaps fucking a little Osaka whore now and then. It really is business. Most of the time he wishes to roll over and get a night's sleep, having no desire for a bowlegged girl who can't even speak Chinese. But he performs anyway for fear she'll tell his hosts; conforming to their perverse sense of honor, they might very well withdraw their account from a man incapable of or adverse to copulating with their countrywomen.

Unfair of Vera. Wasn't she willing to sleep with a Chinese general for his sake? They are not two naïve bourgeois citizens. What both of them want at any cost is security, then the chance to escape from this Chinese maelstrom of violence and confusion. It's unfair if she judges him for his last month with the playful Japanese.

Where is she? Panic edges for a moment into his consciousness, then withdraws. Not that a fling matters. They have something together; nothing can destroy it, damn it. Odd, Luckner thinks (the idea so odd that he halts in his pacing), but we've never discussed our Russias, hers and mine: she a fugitive, I a prisoner, struggling through frozen Siberia toward our mutual destiny in Shanghai. We should talk about what we share; we take too much for granted.

Tomorrow I'll begin, Luckner vows out loud; the pledge makes him feel better. He calls the girl to add some more soda and to put a little whisky in the glass. The headache isn't going away. He sits down again on the taboret, hunched forward, his hands clasped, dumbly watching the last shred of daylight tug loose from the cobblestone.

'Everything is all right,' he says aloud.

When the drink comes, he gulps down half of it and scowls until the watchful girl hurries away.

'Foolish,' he mutters aloud, but goes anyway into Vera's room to check her closet. Why? He isn't sure. It's full or at least there are enough clothes there to prove she didn't send the girl away on errands, then pack and leave. Foolish even to look. When Luckner returns to the courtyard, Hsueh-chen has lit a paper lantern, its candle glowing like smoldering ivory through the grained tissue of rice paper. The servant girl is making it obvious that she's interested in him. Well, why not tumble her, he asks himself sullenly. After all, the mistress of this house is neglecting her duty.

Panic edges back, expands in his mind until Luckner can't control his impatience longer, but rushes back into the bedroom to fling hatboxes and suitcases aside in the bottom of another closet.

Her treasure suitcase is gone.

Perhaps she has shifted everything to a new suitcase. She might do that, fearing he had discovered her secret. She might do that, a pack rat hoarding against bad luck. No sooner does the thought enter Luckner's mind than his hands grapple with and open the other suitcases. All empty.

Dropping to his knees near the dressing table, Luckner pulls off the floorboard and wildly feels around for the key. Hsueh-chen had reported its existence to him months ago.

The key is gone. Key and treasure gone.

Luckner sits wearily beside the pried-up board and looks at the little hole in the floor – a pathetic hiding place, worthy of a child. Has Vera been so blind? Hasn't she realized he knew of her petty thefts, her hoarding, her shabby avarice? Out of affection he has the other Big Sword he says, 'Essentially our host is on his last legs.' The man guffaws. Embree smiles awkwardly, unsure of what's happening.

'Poor but not yet finished. For you' – Wang leans forward, staring earnestly at Fu – 'I might be able to cement our friendship with a little gift.'

'I don't want your gifts,' Fu says with his fixed smile.

The serving girl enters with a pot of wine and cups.

'Let me pour!' Wang is on his feet, grabbing the pot from her. 'Let me do it for our guests!'

'I don't want your wine either,' snaps Fu, and leaning over the table, he sweeps the tray on the floor.

Wang sits down as if hit.

'We are not thieves you can bribe,' Fu tells him sharply. 'We are honorable men, we are soldiers.' The Big Sword draws his cotton sleeve across his mouth. 'Our dead comrade came from your town.'

'Ah, from here? I am honored! Truly honored!'

At this moment one of the men guarding the rear entrance comes into the room. He bends down and whispers to Fu, who begins smiling.

'Good. Go outside,' Fu tells him and turns to Wang. 'You may have known our dead comrade's father – Li Feng.'

Wang's eyes grow round, but otherwise his face arranges itself into a mask of effort, as he makes a show of trying to remember this Li Feng. 'I regret, I am deeply sorry, but I don't recall a Li Feng from this town. Perhaps another town?'

Fu waves his hand dismissively. 'It doesn't matter. I didn't come here to talk of Li Feng.'

With a smile Wang sits back.

'My comrade who just came in? He met two of your daughters just now. Apparently they've returned from Peking and Jinan.' Fu raises his hand to stop Wang from replying. 'We came here to collect a debt you owe.'

'A debt? Sir?'

'In payment of your debt to Li Feng and his son, our comrade, we will have your women. I will have one of your daughters.' He looks toward Embree and the other Big Sword. 'And they have come for your wife, if she's worth it, and your concubines. Other men are waiting outside for their share of the payment. You see, they've herded all your women into a compound behind here.'

let Vera play her little game. Out of affection, damn it. He has always understood her need for this secret cache. He knows Vera, her fear of losing everything, her deep sense of insecurity.

Once in Russia, while plodding along a winter road with fleeing White troops, he saw a horse-drawn wagon approaching. Piled high on it was meaningless treasure: antique furniture, wooden crates doubtless filled with heirlooms, jewelry, paintings – not a thing of real value out there in the middle of trackless Siberia. Seated on a filthy mattress a young noble-woman, as delicate as porcelain, was nursing a newborn infant.

The image has never left him, and in imagination Luckner has added awesomely to it: the eventual loss of each valuable item, one after another, either forcibly taken or bartered for crusts of black bread, until the young woman has nothing left on her back, not a last strip of fur, not even a wool coat or a threadbare jacket, but in nothing more than a cotton shift she lies beside the road, the baby dead in her arms, her legs frozen, the skin of mother and child as pale and brittle as eggshell. No morbid fancy, no romantic indulgence, Luckner feels, but a simple reconstruction of something that happened often then. Even today, during those moments awakening from sleep, when the mind is most vulnerable, he sometimes imagines the young woman dying beside the road. She had Vera's face, Vera's hair, Vera's mouth, Vera's wide-set, brilliant eyes.

Now gone, she's gone. She has taken the paltry treasure, accumulated so painstakingly on those little raids, and run off.

Vera has run off with another man.

Luckner stand up, touching one finger to the tip of his nose. He remains in that attitude a long while, stunned by the probability. She must have run off with another man. Vera would not willingly step alone into the abyss of Shanghai. Someone has persuaded her to go to him, and in a blind moment of temporary panic or attraction or greed or despair – God only knows what emotions govern that Russian woman – Vera has taken her treasure and like a schoolgirl run away from home.

This is serious. Luckner begins pacing, running his fingers through the slicked-down hair. Really serious. '*Die Närrin!*' he says aloud, irritably. Halting in the room, he cocks his head as if listening for her footsteps. The fool, little fool. How can she run off in a schoolgirl passion this way, giving him trouble at a time when he needs all his wits for them both? The little fool will destroy them with her pranks. Much more of this sort of business, they won't see Karlsruhe. Where is the little fool?

Luckner hurries to the courtyard. It is dark now except for the single lantern and a full moon rising over the tiled roof. Ran off with whom? That's the question now. He looks around as if hoping to spot the seducer lurking in the shadows. It can be anyone in Shanghai. In this City of Sorrows there are lonely men who'd give anything to have such a woman.

Looking at the round, watery moon, he remembers she always hated it. One of her caprices. Well, let the fellow have her, whoever he is. Vera will lead him a merry chase!

Luckner guffaws. 'Girl! Girl, come here!' he shouts.

Hsueh-chen rushes into view. She must have been waiting just inside the door for him to call.

'Whisky-soda!'

'Yes, Master.' She is gone.

'Whisky-soda,' he repeats in a low voice. Rumpling his hair, Luckner tells himself that wherever she is tonight, in the arms of whatever man, she won't give a damn if the moon's shining down on them. The slut, fool. 'I'll find out who the bastard is,' Luckner tells himself. It's a vow he says aloud into the night air. 'If I have to search all of Shanghai, I'll find him.' Shaking his fist at the moon, continuing the vow in a voice of rage, he says in German, 'Whoever you are, bastard, I'll find you. I'll make you sorry you ever met Vera Rogacheva.'

17

She once fled from this place and the man it represented. Now, after three weeks in Qufu, she wonders if she ever lived anywhere else or with another man.

Each morning at dawn she accompanies Shan-teh to a courtyard where they play Tai Chi Chuan. Or rather she first watches him play, then he gives her a lesson. He is teaching her Yang style, a version easier to learn than Chen. But she doesn't find the exercise at all easy. Not those hundred and eight postures, none of which ever reach a point of completion – even as she moves one way, she is already supposed to be moving in another, a contradiction typically Chinese. And the slightest inattention leads to failure. 'What am I doing now? Am I doing this or that? Did I already do it? Isn't that this?' Shan-teh explains rather pedantically: The progression of Tai Chi forms is so ordered that the mind must concentrate on it to the exclusion of everything else.

Poor Shan-teh. What she can't admit is her inability to concentrate only on Tai Chi. Because there is the morning to think of too. Because the light is changing night into day within the closed courtyard. Everything is shifting, just like the exercise, turning one thing into another. Behind her a wall rises like the diaphanous mist in a Sung painting, but later, with a change of light, the wall shimmers like a vast unbroken sheet of gray steel. The roofs undergo mysterious transformations: At one moment they seem to be floating in air, rising by the wings of their curved corners; then later, when a keen light summons a different vision, the roofs seem to crush down on the stanchions of hall and gallery by the sheer weight of their tiles. She gawks, fascinated, at the huge rocks, set strategically throughout the courtyard, coming out of the aquamarine dawn; something writhing and gelatinous like sea creatures, they become the scarred, pitted shields of old warriors. a few contain large holes through which she can see a distant world, that of a white plaster expanse of building, dotted by bursts of crimson – a potted rosebush that with later light will appear drooping, anemic, in the last throes: a sad commentary on the progress of all life.

Poor Shan-teh. He continues his instruction patiently: Remember now, each motion is always becoming something else, always moving toward its opposite. She pretends to give her attention to the correct design of Snake Creeps Down or Needle at Sea Bottom, while in truth she has surrendered grandly to the whole morning: to her lover, to Tai Chi, to the changing light, to things magical turning into wall, roof, and stone.

It is the best part of the day for Vera, who after breakfast must give him up to his staff and army. Then comes calligraphy and a walk or ride in town before she sees him again at lunch. It is at lunchtime of her tenth day in Qufu that Vera notices a wireless message in his hand. He pushes it toward her. It reads: 'Chiang Kai-shek has stepped down. No longer heads the Nanking government.'

Vera doesn't like Chiang Kai-shek, who cooperated with the Bolsheviks for years. Perhaps the rest of China is in an uproar about his fall from power, but certainly she is pleased. Or is it a fall? At lunch that day Colonel Pi, the chief of staff, eats with them. She overhears Shan-teh discuss with him Chiang's resignation; both feel it is nothing more than a tactical withdrawal. Chinese politics, she thinks: labyrinthine, without apparent direction, wearisome, treacherous.

Yet since hearing the news Shan-teh has seemed preoccupied, although he tries to appear otherwise when they're together.

Sometimes they get away for a ride to the Kong cemetery or a stroll in the Great Temple grounds. On these little forays she always wears a Chinese gown, while Shan-teh is usually in uniform. It seems incongruous that he takes a military bearing and appearance into the contemplative center of the temple precincts. In soldierly clothes here, he looks less comfortable than he did in a Western suit in Shanghai. Standing before the Hall of Great Achievement, gazing at the marble columns with their dragon designs, her lover conveys an impression of profound attachment to this place of quiet beauty. He belongs here, not among troops. As much as perhaps any foreigner can, Vera responds to it also: the leafy shadows playing about the edges of crimson pillars, the glinting gold roofs, old cypresses in the wide park, the pavilions into which the energy of air and thought and time all seem compressed, their force made visible. Sometimes in the afternoon, alone, carrying a sketch pad, inkstand, and brush, Vera returns to study some of the stone tablets there. More than two thousand years of Chinese writing cover the worn surfaces, from the Warring States period through the Han and the Sung and the Tang and the Ming right through to modern times. Most of the steles are too defaced by weather, the characters too ancient, for her to decipher the messages they hold, but at least she tries to duplicate the strokes incised there, as if through this method she can enter the world Shan-teh inhabits by blood.

It is after one of her long afternoons with the stone tablets that Vera meets another foreigner in the town of Qufu. She has expected it to happen – knowing of the Bolshevik and the American – but when the rider comes into view around a corner, Vera stiffens with dread. Often, since arriving here, she has asked herself what she will do when she and the Bolshevik meet. She halts, feet apart as if braced for attack, as the horseman approaches.

A blond man. It isn't the Bolshevik. She knows from careful inquiry that he has a long, black, filthy beard.

The blond rider must therefore be the American. She relaxes

while he comes toward her with a faint smile on his square, ruddy face.

In Chinese, very formally, he says, 'Good afternoon, Madam.'

Vera wants to reply in English – she'd had an English governess for a year – but she's ashamed of her accent. They exchange pleasantries in Chinese; his fluency surprises her. She tells him she understands he's in the cavalry. He tells her he understands she's visiting the General.

Visiting the General. Quaint, she thinks, and smiles up at him.

The meeting lasts only a few minutes, then the American rides on, his own awkward boyishness shortening the interview. In spite of his shyness, Vera is sure that behind the bland young sunburned face she detected a familiar tension. Perhaps in the narrowing of his blue eyes she found it – an interest in her. Not that she welcomes it, but proof of her continuing charm tends to lighten her step on the return stroll to the Residence.

She needs a good mood for the return. She must face Yao and other servants, many of them soldiers assigned to the General's quarters. Aside from their dawn Tai Chi and their meals and their short excursions into town and their lovely nights together, Vera has learned that her life with the General will be spent in a hostile world. Vera knows enough about China to expect precisely this, so it hasn't come as a surprise. The senior officers were shocked by her arrival; even with a Chinese talent for masking emotions, theirs showed when she stepped off the train. They were appalled not because their general had taken a new concubine, but because she was a foreigner. Not only that, but they must have been scandalized by his decision to pay off the Chinese woman, Su-su, and live exclusively with this new one, as if they were married in a Western way, disregarding the tradition of concubinage. From the outset it has been painfully clear to Vera that such a liaison can only do him harm with his associates. After all, she's aware that a chief asset of the General has always been his loyalty to the nation, coupled to an antiforeign attitude. This personal lapse must carry for many observers the stamp of a grave mistake, perhaps a fatal one.

Has he jeopardized everything for her?

Vera hopes not. Fervently. Because every day reveals the depth of her feeling for him. She doesn't want her lover's downfall on her conscience, so Vera looks around for another rationalization of his reckless act that will absolve her of guilt. She gives it much thought; there's plenty of time for that in the silence of her room. It occurs to her finally that, along with any other attraction she has for him, her foreignness might well have played a role. For one thing, he can never marry her. That is certain. And therefore, by taking her for his companion, Shan-teh has protected himself from marriage. But why would he do that, especially since he has no children? Given her own history, Vera doesn't search far to find an answer. Like herself, he's the last of a family, the survivor of a clan that's been wiped out. Like herself, he must feel guilty that they are all dead while he lives. For this transgression – for living – he must be punished by punishing himself. This argument, so familiar to Vera, comes with ease. Living with a foreign woman he can't marry, Shan-teh remains without a legal heir, socially defiant, irresponsible in a Confucian sense, and continues to humiliate himself in front of his disapproving ancestors. All this is theory, a combination of muddled Western and Chinese thinking – of this she's aware. It's a theory she does not altogether accept or want to believe. If she believed it completely, Vera would have already returned to Shanghai and fallen at Erich Luckner's feet, begging forgiveness. But experience has taught her that nothing is simple between man and woman. She has clear indications from the General that he cares for her deeply; indeed, sometimes she worries that her love for him is superficial compared to his for her. Moreover, his defiant handling of their affair, in spite of his demonstrable intelligence and ambition, seems oddly in character. Having decided on a course of action, he's a man who won't deviate from it; there comes a time in his progress through events when Shan-teh abandons reason and follows the impulse of his heart. At that time the Tai Chi player takes command. The man who gapes like a child at the Kong Temple takes over from the sensible public figure; and when this happens, doubtless his courage displaces his common sense too. He has not brought her here, Vera decides, merely to protect himself from marriage and to cultivate guilt. Or he has brought her here in part for those reasons. Coming this far in her analysis of Shan-teh, she tells herself to forget it, to bury the argument like a sad memory. Nothing good between man and woman ever comes of cold reason; that has been her experience. To brood over a lover's motives is the first step in losing him, and she doesn't want to lose Shan-teh.

So instead she concentrates on old Yao, the servant who has

been with Shan-teh for many years and before that with Shan-teh's father. Yao has become a formidable person in her life. When she arrives at the quarters each afternoon, his presence is felt even before she puts one foot on the threshold. He has placed a mirror above the entrance, so if a demon happens along it will see its own image before slinking in; being frightened by itself, it will run away, leaving the house unharmed. That's Yao. A strong-willed old peasant with centuries of superstition guiding each arthritic movement he makes during a day fully devoted to his master.

Vera, sighing, glances up at her distorted image in the glass of the round mirror, then opens the door. 'Yao! Yao!' she calls out, although certain the wily old servant has seen her coming and by now is a few courtyards away, withholding from her the menu for dinner, so only he can tell the General what will be served.

It is the twenty-seventh of August, the birth date of Confucius.

On a walk that afternoon Vera watched a column of schoolboys pass by on their way to the Great Temple to pay their respects to the Teacher of Ten Thousand Generations. They wore gowns like little scholars and carried 'blinding' wands to hold before their eyes at the altar, so they wouldn't impolitely stare at the wooden face of the sculptured saint.

This evening Shan-teh has feasted with his staff in another part of the West Wing. No women, of course. Vera has accepted it with the patience of a Chinese woman. Eating alone in the General's quarters, she turns that idea – passive humility – around in her mind like a piece of jade she inspects in her hand. The prospect of becoming a Chinese wife – or mistress – horrifies her. She has seen too many of them: heads lowered, following their men like wagons of goods purchased at market. No Russian woman raised in the salons of Petrograd could possibly accept a life of such abject submission. But then the question of marriage doesn't exist in her relationship with the General, does it. Love seems to drag behind it a cumbersome way of thinking, like a nurse pulling by the hand a fat, foolish child who whines always for the same treat. Vera drinks another glass of wine.

That's when the first gong sounds. The deep boom so fascinates her that she goes to the front door and stares into the courtyard, lit by lanterns in festive acknowledgment of the auspicious day. A second gong sounds, the heavy brass sounding deep in its throat, sending the low full thunder of beaten metal across the upturned eaves and ceramic tiles of pavilions, halls, quarters, throughout the vast Residence. The sound is coming from the East Wing, where the Kong family will assemble.

Then other gongs commence from the southwest, from a temple where tonight the ceremony will take place. The night air, slashed by torches, vibrates to the slow tempo of the tolling. Vera feels the hair on her arms and the back of her neck actually rise, as though she were startled. She feels abruptly cold – the emotion sweeping her has a physical component. SHE GOES BACK INSIDE AND SITS DOWN, CLASPING HER ARMS, KNEES TOGETHER, BENT SLIGHTLY FORWARD IN A STRAIGHT CHAIR. The heavy thud of measured notes from many gongs has gripped her; she can't move, but holds herself, while the tremendous sound courses through the night and this room and through her mind. Nothing has been more mysteriously overwhelming in her life. She can't understand it. Perhaps it's so many of them sounding together and in the nighttime. Or perhaps it's the deep timbre of the huge metal disks, when they're struck, that sends something unearthly through the air.

She is sitting like this when Shan-teh enters the room. Rising, she runs to him and embraces him hard. She can't tell whether it's from excitement or fear. 'I've never heard anything like it,' she says, when they sit beside each other on the couch.

'It's the same throughout China tonight. But more important here, Black Jade.'

Black Jade: his nickname for her. Taken from *The Dream of the Red Chamber*. Black Jade, the book's heroine, is beautiful and independent, a symbol of purity. So Shan-teh tells her, without adding what Vera already knows – Black Jade dies brokenhearted on the day of her lover's marriage to another woman.

'You're fortunate,' he continues. 'At least we Chinese would say so – to be in Qufu on the Sage's anniversary.'

'I think the Kongs have been getting ready all day.'

He laughs at her innocence. 'It's more like a month. The ceremonial robes must be cleaned. Frayed threads replaced. Ritual utensils polished. Musical instruments repaired. And enough other details to keep a small army at work.'

'Is it true they sacrifice animals?' She overheard the servants talking today.

'A pig, a cow, a goat. They're already killed.'

Vera grimaces.

'It's no more barbaric than killing them for our dinner,' he tells her sharply. 'They're killed and cleaned and put near the main altar as offerings. A missionary once told me you Christians drink blood.'

Vera is startled by the way he puts it. Then she explains with an indulgent smile that Christians drink wine to represent the blood of Christ.

'So you could say you drink the blood of your god.'

That's a comment she will ignore; it is true and untrue, but if he can't – or is unwilling to – comprehend the ritual, she won't let it become an occasion for unpleasantness between them. So Vera says, 'Will you go to the ceremony tonight?'

Tang frowns, as if she has committed an impropriety by asking this question. 'No. I am not invited.'

'How can the Kong family *not* invite you?' Vera feels it's a sensible question. He is the chief official in Qufu, with an army under his control sitting on the outskirts of town. Of more importance to Vera is the next question. 'Is it because of me?'

Shan-teh answers both questions while gongs boom through the evening air. Had he insisted, Tang tells her, the Kongs would have invited him. But traditionally, for such ceremonies, only scholars are invited. Living with a woman not his wife does not disqualify a qualified man from attending. 'And anyway,' Shan-teh continues, 'this sort of celebration is not really Confucian.'

'But it's for Confucius.'

Shan-teh says more, while staring at the nub of candle still burning. In none of the ancient writings available to the Sage was there a precedent for sacrificing to any mortal. The Sage never added any himself, but taught that ritual was a means for unifying a family through time, not to sanctify a claim to power or appeal for favors or aggrandize the memory of an important man. In the early days of the Republic, politicians rushed to Confucian temples with their ostentatious piety, hoping through it to promote their claims to greatness. The Sage would have despised them. And he would think the country has gone mad in its wholesale celebration of his birthday. It should be done by his family, by the Kongs alone, and by them solely for their health of mind. The value of ritual is for the living; by bringing the dead into their lives they live better lives. It shouldn't be used to placate or plead; it mustn't be used to wheedle something out of gods who may not exist. Confucius was a humble man who felt that no one, surely not himself, deserved adulation and worship. Moreover, he once said that acts of the deepest reverence are without display. 'So it is a ceremony,' Shan-teh concludes, 'I have no interest in attending. Listen.'

A great drum is booming from the direction of the East Wing, signaling the start of a procession that will take the Kong celebrants to the Great Hall. Their rituals, Shan-teh explains, will last until dawn: the offering of three sacrificed animals, the speeches, the music, the dancing.

'Do you resent the ceremony?'

The candle has guttered, gone out. 'Do you want another?' he asks.

'Let's stay in the dark.'

'Of course. Darkness enhances the sound.'

'That's what I think too.'

'Do I resent the ceremony?' Shan-teh repeats the question. 'I resent what men have done with his ideas.'

'Tell me.'

He does. With the huge sound enveloping their room, Shan-teh admits that men have used the Sage through the centuries for their own ends. Those professing belief in him, Shan-teh admits further, never abolished the eunuch system in the great houses or stopped the practice of footbinding or revoked the use of judicial torture. Sometimes the teaching of Confucius has even been used as an instrument of oppression, a philosophical means of establishing approval for tyranny. None of these things belongs to Confucius, who believed in the eradication of four conditions that cause misrule. Shan-teh counts them on his fingers: a biased mind, arbitrary judgment, obstinacy, selfishness. Confucius believed that human-heartedness is the first rule of life and therefore the first condition of a good leader's nature. He believed that men need to govern their relationships, but flexibly, without the dogma that smothers good judgment. He believed that men are essentially equal, therefore that they deserve equal opportunities in education. He believed that the chief role of government is to help people in distress.

While listening to Shan-teh's patient explanation of an alien creed, Vera thinks of the religion in which she was raised. It had not been so reasoned, so centered on what people do, but in her mind had dwelled upon the numinous and ineffable, drawing from her not admiration but ecstasy. Since leaving her country, Vera Rogacheva has never entered a church, yet the faith of her childhood has never left her – so she tells herself each morning without fail. And in the darkness, with gongs sounding in the distance, she listens to Shan-teh speak of one wise man while her mind shifts to the image of another, of Jesus plodding the dusty roads of Palestine, chasing the moneychangers from the temple, taking common fishermen for his disciples, making war on hypocrisy.

Vera takes Shan-teh's hand. They hear the sound of the great drum changing direction, as the celebrants move from the Residence toward the Great Hall of the Temple. 'Does it bother you I'm Christian?' she asks after a while.

'I admire Christian initiative.'

'Initiative?'

'Well, they preach against idleness. They believe in getting things done.'

He gets his entire impression of Christians from missionaries, Vera thinks. She also notices that he has not answered her question. Listening to the gongs, holding his hand, Vera says nothing in response to either of her perceptions. Yet moments later she can't help saying, 'Christians also believe in love and mercy.'

'Oh, I believe that,' Shan-teh replies nonchalantly, as if it hardly mattered. 'So do the Taoists and the Buddhists. But the Christians have this extra thing –'

'Aggressiveness.'

'Yes. That.'

'And you admire that?'

'I do. Buddhism has crippled my people by teaching passive acceptance.'

'But I thought you were Buddhist.'

'There's much of Buddhism I appreciate.'

'That's a strange way of putting it – you appreciate something about a religion. I was raised to look for belief, not appreciation.'

'You were not raised Chinese.'

'Do you appreciate Taoism too?'

'Of course. Some of it. I appreciate the Taoist's search for truth within. In times of crisis it's helpful. Men turn for comfort to themselves, to their internal strength.'

'I can see it doesn't bother you that I'm Christian. It wouldn't bother you whatever I believed.'

'You sound annoyed, Black Jade.'

'No, just unprepared for so much tolerance.' After a pause, withdrawing her hand, Vera adds, 'Maybe a litte annoyed. You see, I really am Christian. I believe in it more than I appreciate it.' When he doesn't respond, Vera feels that she has gone too far. Their different childhoods have put a gap between them that can widen at any moment into a chasm. Leaning against him, she smells ginger on his breath, the faint scent of light wine. 'I saw another Christian yesterday,' Vera remarks. Her tone of voice, carefully neutral, has lost all trace of annoyance. 'I saw the American in town.'

'What did you think of him?'

Vera shrugs. 'He sits a horse well. Shall I light a candle now?'

'Yes, I think so. He sits a horse well and apparently can sleep on one.' Shan-teh adds, 'When you met, did you talk about God?'

'No.' Vera is startled. 'Why should we?'

'When I speak to him, I feel he wants to talk about God, although with me perhaps he's embarrassed.' After a pause, Shan-teh adds, 'But I suppose it's true of most Westerners.'

Vera, lighting the candle, looks at his Chinese face, which she has come to regard as ruggedly handsome. 'What's true? That Westerners talk of God?'

'Yes. I thought they always did when they met.'

Vera laughs. 'You've met too many missionaries.'

'Perhaps so. But I've heard you Westerners can never speak of life seriously without speaking of God.'

'Seriously?'

'Of man's purpose on earth, in the universe.'

Vera thinks through his remark before replying. 'What you heard may be right,' she decides. 'Yes, to speak seriously I think we must speak of God.'

Now it is Shan-teh's turn to laugh. 'But we Chinese can speak seriously without speaking of God. We don't need God when we think of man on earth or in the universe.'

'I don't understand.' .

'Then listen to the Chinese talk. It's simply so, Black Jade. What else did you think of my strange American cavalryman?'

'I like Americans.'

'Why?'

'Because they never recognized the Bolshevik regime. They're generally loud and brash and naïve and I imagine under stress they can be cruel, but they've never recognized the Bolsheviks.'

398

Shan-teh says nothing in reply. Vera wonders if he's thinking of the other foreigner in Qufu – the Bolshevik.

'Yao,' he calls out suddenly. In an instant the old man is bowing in the doorway. The General orders tea. A little breeze has come up, rustling the window curtain, carrying with it the throbbing boom of the drum. The sound comes now from the southeast, but its ultimate destination is the southwest. Briefly, Vera recalls the American, but then fixes on the Bolshevik. She and the General no longer mention him, although shortly after her arrival in Qufu she'd asked if the fellow was still around.

'Do you want him to leave?' the General had asked in a rather indifferent tone.

Vera said, 'Yes,' immediately, but after a few minutes changed her mind. 'No,' she said. 'Let him stay. I want him to stay.' Vera knew the Bolshevik lived with his interpreter in a section of the West Wing, but rarely went out. They were virtually isolated in their quarters and only ventured into town for opium. It occurred to her that Shan-teh, out of an abiding hatred of foreign interventionists, was taking revenge on the Reds by letting their representative rot here – a humiliating fate, especially in the eyes of the Chinese, who have contempt for that idleness which results from a forfeiture of duty. So Vera decided to connive with the General in the destruction of this Bolshevik.

'Yes, I want him to stay.'

'Are you sure? It's your decision.'

'I want him to stay.'

She has never reopened the matter of the Bolshevik, although sometimes she wonders what will happen the day they meet.

The drum sound has shifted to the southwest and remained there. Added to it now is the wail of flutes, the strum of stringed instruments, and cymbals and gongs of various timbres – all coming out of the far darkness into their bedroom, where they lie naked on the warm sheet under moonlight.

Yes, moonlight. She has not yet told Shan-teh of her hatred for the moon, just as she has not told him the full story of her life. She's grateful that he has never questioned her closely, but has allowed her to explain as much or as little as she wishes. Perhaps her worst memory of the brothel is of her relaxed clients grilling her, wanting to know every detail of her degradation. Of course,

Shan-teh must divine the essentials of the story. Anyone in China can do that. What life could there be for a Russian girl who escaped from the Reds with nothing? He seems to make no judgment at all, an unsettling response in her opinion, for it can signal up his indifference.

Bad thinking.

With every man Vera has gone through a similar process – suspecting him of callous disregard, no matter what he says or does. Each time, however, she has fought against her apprehension and conquered it; that is, until the end has been in view. Then the suspicions return with good reason. It was all quite true of her time with Erich: first distrust, then trust, and in the end a return to the suspicion that he was going to leave her. Now with Shan-teh she tries to move past the early doubts and believe in him. Perhaps she knows the truth – that he's tolerant of her past, whatever it may be. Yet the strict demands of survival, a habitual concern of hers, encourages Vera to distrust him longer than perhaps is necessary. Each day she commands herself to wonder if he'll turn her out by nightfall.

Given their mutual reluctance to build on history, they go to neutral ground for conversation. It is often through a discussion of art that they share the moment. Over tea this evening they looked at a folio of copies from the Southern Sung – especially four paintings by Ma Yuan. They bent close together, their heads nearly touching, as their eyes fixed on details of the landscape, the intensity and unlabored crispness of tree and mountain captured in a few confident brush strokes. Shan-teh spoke of the Chinese gift for working from memory. Images held in the mind are transformed over a period of time before actual commitment to paper. He said: To look for likeness in a painting, especially of the Sung, is to show ignorance of its aim; it's not to show something but to be something.

On Vera's part, she commented on the neglect of human love in Chinese art. Seldom do you find lovers in a landscape. If the artist does place human figures there, they're likely to be old scholars who, meditating together, share a flagon of wine.

And so while the drumbeats led the procession to Confucius' temple, Vera and her lover sat over tea and a folio of paintings and let art bring them together.

Now they are together in another way, here in the moonlit bedroom, naked in the heat. His left earlobe is clearly visible to her – long, like a frozen drop of water, a feature striking in its prominence. She recalls enough of Buddhist iconography to know that a long earlobe is a sign of spirituality. Chinese Buddhas and lohans in art often have pronounced earlobes. But Vera sees nothing spiritual in Shan-teh's. She finds in them a symbol of sexual power; often in bed she slips one into her mouth, savoring the hard cartilage within the incredibly soft skin. Now, with the wailing of flutes and the gongs' thunder filling the room, she desires him. Lately her lust for him has been keen, although Shan-teh is not physically the heroic measure of her girlhood dreams. He lacks Russian height and carriage. His pelvis is broad, his legs thickly muscled in proportion to his chest, which is narrow in comparison to that of a well-built guardsman. Yet he enthralls her. Perhaps in his appeal there's an androgynous component. His chest and abdomen are as hairless as a girl's, his skin as smooth as plate. Yet at the groin, within the scant silken forest, she finds the pulsing hardness of a male who wants to penetrate her.

Her fingers touch his earlobe while moonlight dies in a cloud, returns in time to guide her touch from cheek to neck. Awakened by this signal, he reaches out and brings her nipples to a tingling alertness. It is he who starts to move. His lips, skimming her breasts, travel the contours of our body with a feathery touch that reminds her of Yu-ying. She is splayed out now, arms flung wide, eyes open. At her groin he stops to kiss her, his tongue to enter her for a brief time, but though she arches slightly to encourage him, to signal her desire for more of this, his lips move away to the inner softness of her thighs – and thereby end his journey. She understands his reluctance; without anger she accepts her frustration. Few men have any knowledge of a woman, Vera decides. A Danish lover had once tried diligently to satisfy her with his tongue and had technically succeeded, but without truly arousing her. A man loving her this way does it from curiosity or gratitude, Vera thinks, but lacks the real passion: the real passion of someone like Yu-ying, whose skill and ferocious ardor resulted in lovemaking quite beyond the comprehension of any man. No man, not even this wonderful Chinese general whom she deeply loves, will ever take her as Yu-ying did. Yu-ying, whose tongue lapped like fire, like the breath of a dragon –

Vera, easing away from her lover, decides to give him pleasure orally on this night of the Sage's birth, invoking for him a special ecstasy (unlike the monotonous practice countless men have paid her for) which she shared with Yu-ying in the hot Shanghai nights, their nostrils filled with the perfume of Triangles That Drive Men Wild, their tongues mutually poised and flicking, enslaving them both.

Reversing her position now and hovering above him, Vera takes command of Tang Shan-teh, kissing his face, his chest, his muscular abdomen, moving in slow progression down his body. What lies below, what she is heading for, is at other times such a childish vulnerable thing, flaccid against his thigh, but now, through her machinations – her tongue trailing sluggishly to his groin – that harmless tab of flesh is indeed formidable. Out from a cloud the moon illuminates the massive helmet, the thick veins. So elementally compelling is the look of it that she draws it into her mouth almost as if to pacify its brutal force. One hand, to control his motion, clasps his buttock, which tightens as the warmth of her lips intensely focuses his entire body. As she works slowly, his hands go to her shoulders, grip them, then cup the back of her head. His fingers weave into her hair like the gesture of a child. There is something wonderful for her in the trusting way he holds her head in his trembling hands. He arches in surrender to her machinations, as she had done to his, but unlike him she doesn't stop and won't until completion. She loves him. And in this moment, his open innocence and posture of need and trust overwhelm Vera.

Stringed instruments in the distance scratch out to her Western ear a cacophony of sound; cymbals crash and flutes wail, but always in the background of the night the huge gongs continue their resonant booming. Clouds blot out the moon altogether, blackening the room. Unable to see him now, Vera can only feel him beneath her. She senses him coming apart, unhinging himself from everything in life but the sensation she gives him.

Gladly she will drink the essence of this man, while the sultry night air, trembling from ancient music, holds them gently in its dark web.

Calligraphy.

The hapless stroke, the fortuitous stroke, the bold and arrogant stroke, the hesitant stroke, the tremulous stroke – all of life is under her hand in the swaths of ink she makes on a piece of rice paper. Vera is so absorbed in her practice that she doesn't hear him enter the room. He has to speak her name softly – 'Black Jade' – before she turns from the desk. Looking up, startled, she receives an immediate signal from the look on his face. The compressed lips, the pinched brows tell her their idyll has ended.

Sitting on the bed with a letter in his hand – it is from his Shanghai friend Chu Jui – Shan-teh begins the explanation in a calm low voice.

It is enough to make Vera smile. Men often try to give bad news in this patient and reasonable manner, yet anyone can see from the faces of women listening – thrust forward, harshly aware – they've already guessed the content. Even as Shan-teh tells her he must leave Qufu, she is recalling the words of her father, just as falsely soothing, when it was necessary for him to tell mother what she already knew – the Reds were overrunning the country; Czarists must flee or be slaughtered.

Shan-teh is going to meet Chiang Kai-shek in the southern province of Chekiang. He will travel incognito. The length of his stay is as yet undetermined. He leaves in two days.

In two days.

Shan-teh is explaining something, much of it convoluted politics, but she retains this much: Chiang Kai-shek, having stepped down from government because of internal squabbles, has gone into a monastery near his home town in Chekiang. From this retreat he's maintaining contact with politicians and military leaders. He has ordered Chu Jui, a former warlord and now one of his deputies, to invite Shan-teh to the monastery for a meeting. It is important. It could decide the fate of China, Shan-teh tells her.

He also told her two days. He will leave me in two days.

Hoping by indirection to suggest that she go too, Vera asks if he will take anyone along.

He shakes his head.

'Not even a bodyguard?' To lighten the effect of her questioning, she adds, 'Not even your precious American?'

'That's a possibility. They say Chiang is pro-American now that he's given up the Russians. But traveling with a foreigner would be conspicuous.'

'Are you afraid of being recognized?'

'It wouldn't be a good idea,' he says with a smile.

'So it's dangerous.'

'If recognized and held, I might be ransomed. It happens today in China. But nothing worse than that.' He looks down at the

403

letter a moment. 'I wouldn't want to waste the time and money on a ransom, so I'll travel in disguise.' Shan-teh forces a little laugh. 'In the old romances traveling in disguise was often done by the heroes. It's a tradition.'

Poor Shan-teh, she thinks, he's trying to be lighthearted. And she thinks: He will be gone in two days. Now he's explaining more of it, all leading to the end of the idyll: Japanese troops have entered Jinan; they claim they have done so to protect their nationals from Chinese violence; Dog Meat has welcomed them rather than resisted. 'Naturally, I don't want them in Jinan,' continues Shan-teh, 'but their presence there might help me bargain with Chiang Kai-shek.'

'Yes.' In two days the idyll ends.

'If he returns to power – and he might – Chiang will want to know who in the North will stand against the Japanese. We could make an alliance on that point alone.' Shan-teh falls silent, crumpling the letter.

'Yes,' Vera says, glancing at him from her desk. Two days. We've had this time together, now it's ended. She stares at the black strokes she has put on the ink paper. Vera, clearing her throat, is determined to be as calm as a Chinese woman. 'I'll pack for you,' she says.

Shan-teh, sitting on the bed, looks at her.

'Shall I begin now?'

'Pack for me?' His eyes widen in surprise. 'No, Yao will do it.'

'I will pack for you.'

'Yao always does it. You needn't bother.' He adds, 'But thank you.'

'I am going to pack for you, not Yao.'

Then Vera does something unusual. Indeed, she'd not have thought such restraint possible in a Russian woman until she came to this place. Turning from him, after a polite nod indicating their business together has been transacted to mutual satisfaction, Vera coolly picks up the brush and continues her work.

The military man in Shan-teh will admire her containment, Vera knows; but such Chinese discipline can never give a hot-blooded Russian any real comfort.

Well, he is gone.

At the last moment she lost her admirable self-control and flung herself weeping into his arms. His obvious delight at her display of affection surprised Vera. He naïveté amuses her. Sleeping with a man doesn't guarantee a keener understanding of him. At their parting he was not the austere Chinese, far from it, but kissed her tenderly. In fact, the depth of their feeling seemed to embarrass her, not him. Trying to hide a portion of her sadness, Vera asked him with a laugh if he had advice for her during his absence.

He took her seriously. 'Have you ever killed anyone?' he asked.

'Of course not.'

'Then stay clear of the Bolshevik. Otherwise you might kill him.'

She laughed. 'Anything else?'

'You'll be lonely, but don't confide in Colonel Pi.'

'Unnecessary to tell me. I don't trust him any more than you do.'

Their eyes met, like those of two children developing a conspiracy. She'd think of these new moments as magical.

'Yao will be loyal in my absence.'

'Yao will be insufferable in your absence.'

'He will be loyal.'

'You believe that?'

The General nodded emphatically. 'And do your Tai Chi.'

'Yes, Master. Yes, Illustrious General.'

Shan-teh blinked in confusion. Her use of the extravagant honorific, acceptable in a Chinese woman, is something else in her. He can't adjust immediately to the ironic use she makes of traditional address.

Aware of her victory, Vera smiles – and in acknowledgment of his defeat Shan-teh smiles too.

Magical. She never loved the man so much.

And now he is gone.

At least he didn't gallop off without a word as he'd done a few months ago in the Kong cemetery. Loneliness has already gripped Vera, although he left only yesterday. She must occupy her time sensibly. It's what mother would have told her. She can imagine the reedy but firm voice: 'Vera, we won't have your self-pity. Occupy yourself.' That was always mother – using the imperial 'we.' As if an invisible array of relatives, both dead and alive, stood at her elbow. Odd, but mother had a Chinese way of enlisting generations of ancestors to edify a wayward girl.

Yet in spite of good intentions Vera does little during the first few days of her lover's absence. She leaves the quarters only for a short turn around the adjacent courtyards. Often she wonders if she might suddenly encounter the Bolshevik. If so, will she try to kill him as Shan-teh suggested? Nonsense. It is unlikely they'll meet anyway, the Bolshevik living as he does in a far section of the West Wing. He'd have to make a deliberate effort to meet her, and surely, not even under the influence of opium would he risk that. Not if he wishes to remain, damn him, in pleasant surroundings with a supply of his precious drug within a stumbling half-mile of his attractive quarters. Vera wants nothing to do with him, yet she can't help but ponder his strange fate. A few weeks ago, a clever young officer, Captain Fan Chen-wu, confided to her during a brisk ride in the countryside (the General had assigned him to escort her on such excursions) that the Bolshevik had once tried to recruit a few soldiers to his cause; failing that, he'd abandoned himself completely to opium. She can't imagine it. Having fled from the Bolsheviks at an impressionable age, Vera has developed a fanciful picture of them; and at this remove of time she thinks of them as inhuman automatons, much like the painted nutcrackers given her at Christmas: You wind them up and set them in wooden motion and they never deviate from the prescribed path until they run down or crash into an unyielding obstacle. Precisely – the Bolsheviks. She can't imagine them succumbing to the temptations of ordinary mortals. She can think of one committing murder in the name of Lenin or some other scoundrel; that's easy enough. But not making love or holding a child's hand or weeping at a grave. Surely not turning to opium, like a hapless coolie, out of personal disappointment. It is fascinating for Vera to contemplate the Bolshevik staggering around Qufu in sufficient despair to behave like a man wounded by fate. Curiosity, tinged with dread, forces her to hope that someday she will see him.

Meanwhile, she keeps close to her quarters. Monotony before noon is broken by her practice with the brush. After lunch she spends a long time translating Chinese poetry into Russian. Shan-teh, before leaving Shanghai, presented her with a collection from the Tang and earlier dynasties. She has vowed to work through all fifty poems with the aid of a dictionary, and to this labor she devotes herself in the late afternoons – at that particular time in the secluded gallery of her courtyard, because the light changes swiftly then in the nearby flowering catalpa, whose heart-shaped leaves and spotted white flowers accept the brilliance, then let it go, and move deep within shadow, while she glances up frequently from her work to watch this progress of sunlight.

Today she's reading a poem by T'ao Chi'en of the fifth century. He was a man of simple tastes who loved his modest plot of land, which he farmed and about which he wrote brisk, realistic accounts of the joy of rural life. Sometimes his homely descriptions achieved a kind of mystical passion when he suggested that everything merges – sky, land, animal, human – without ever mentioning divinity itself. Ensconced today in the courtyard, working on the poem, she recalls that afternoon in Shanghai when she was waiting to leave the house to meet Shan-teh. Her parrot shelled a peanut, the most insignificant of actions. For a few moments, however, perhaps she felt as T'ao Chi'en had felt fifteen hundred years ago, when he plucked ray flowers from a chrysanthemum at sunset and looked beyond his garden to see a few birds homing toward a distant wood and told himself, wine cup in hand, 'I know once again the real meaning of life.' It's like that for her now in recollection; she had known the meaning of life, its absolute unity, its seamless merging of one thing into everything else, for those few moments on a day in Shanghai.

Tears fill her eyes as she looks at the characters of T'ao Chi'en's poem. She's grateful to T'ao Chi'en for reminding her that she too has experienced the final awareness. Fifteen hundred years disappear in a moment, as she remembers the parrot shelling a peanut, while she reads of a man plucking some chrysanthemum petals. She's grateful to China for bringing the poet to her across a vast chasm of time. She must love a country that has nurtured in herself such a moment.

The next day Vera walks extensively through the West Wing. She's in search of chrysanthemums, like the one mentioned in the poem. T'ao Chi'en had plucked it to make an infusion of wine. The Taoists of ancient times considered the flower a life-prolonging elixir. Ironic, she thinks: in the midst of shoring up his own personal existence through a potion, T'ao Chi'en experienced himself as nothing more or less than all existence. The chrysanthemums are starting to bloom in the Residence now. She finds many of them sitting in pots. Bending down, she studies the toothed leaves clustered at the base of stems; the prominent disk of cushioning yellow; the rows of white rays leading out from it. T'ao Chi'en said in a poem that the sun won't be shining where he finally goes. He said you can't compare today with yesterday. He said each day dawns only once and the best of times don't come often. He said it's all gone quickly. He advised us to use for pleasure whatever money we have before the years drag us down. In all the utterances of T'ao Chi'en, she concludes, there was a gallant defiance of fate, and she admires that, but abruptly she feels depressed. She wishes for her lover, who never terrifies her like this strange poet, this deceptively simple and bucolic poet who pulls her toward the abyss, holding her head over the edge so she must gaze into it. That afternoon, fearing T'ao Chi'en will bring the nightmare in his verbal wake, Vera forgoes the translation of his poems and moves on to Hsieh Ling-yun, whose spirtuality is untainted by glimpses into old age and death.

And the next morning, as if the act can bring Shan-teh closer, she goes at dawn to a distant courtyard and plays Tai Chi. Feet are the root, Shan-teh said. Vera, wearing a loose blouse and baggy trousers, begins Grasp Birds Tail Right. He said, Energy moves upward through the legs and control is in the stomach. She tries to feel something happening in her stomach – a sensation of warmth, perhaps. Instead, she merely forgets the placement of her hands. Which hand should be coming forward? The left? Didn't I just do that? Am I repeating Grasp Bird's Tail Left?

Abruptly Vera feels that someone is watching her. Swinging around from her crouched pose – certain she will at last confront the mysterious Bolshevik – she looks into the frightened eyes of a child standing in the shadow of a gallery.

No more than five or six, the little girl wears a knee-length tunic with long, flowing sleeves, a skirt reaching to her ankles, and white cotton shoes on tiny feet obviously bound. Her thick black hair is coiled tightly into two braids above and behind her ears. She clutches a small porcelain doll with a fat wide face, vermilion lips, and hair braided exactly like her own.

'Good morning,' Vera calls out.

The child remains motionless, guarded, ready to bolt.

'My name is – Black Jade. What is yours?' After a long wait, Vera says, 'Do you know what I'm doing?' She waits, then: 'Do you know I'm playing Tai Chi Chuan?'

The child nods slightly.

'That's a very pretty doll you have.'

The child holds the doll closer to her silken chest.

'Her hair looks just like yours.'

The child stares.

Vera motions for her to come closer. 'Will you show me your doll?' When Vera takes a single step forward, the child grips the doll tightly and hobbles away with surprising quickness.

Not until evening does Vera think of the child again. Then the recollection of those large eyes, the small grave mouth, and the fastidiously done-up hair all bring a smile to Vera's lips. Will the child be in the courtyard tomorrow?

At dawn the next day, before starting Tai Chi, Vera glances around; she feels disappointed that the gallery is empty. But a half-hour later, in the midst of practice, she has the same feeling as yesterday. Turning, Vera notices the girl in the shadows.

This time she wears a headband of black silk embroidered in pearls. The doll is missing. The girl's hands, ensconced within long sleeves, can't be seen.

'Where is your doll this morning?' Vera asks briskly, as if they've been deep in conversation.

'Home.'

'I see.' Vera moves slowly through another pose before saying more. Then, stopping, she looks at the girl. 'Does the doll have a name?'

The girl shakes her head.

'But you have. Do you know my name?'

'Black Jade.'

'You have a good memory. Will you talk to me awhile?'

The child shakes her head but doesn't leave.

'Do you live around here?'

The child nods.

'In which direction?'

A sleeve, without the look of a hand in it, rises and points.

'Are you of the Kong family?'

The child nods.

'But I don't know your own name.'

'Bright Lotus.'

Vera purses her lips as if judging the quality of that name. 'Yes, I like that.'

The child remains watchful.

'Will you come to see me tomorrow? I'd be pleased.' Vera kneels to put their heads on the same level, but the child, misinterpreting the action, bolts. A blur of blue silk, she is gone.

But next morning she is there again.

'Good morning, Bright Lotus.'

The conversation resembles yesterday's. Then, from the pocket of her loose trousers Vera takes a tangerine. Holding it up, she studies it gravely a few moments. 'I brought it to eat after Tai Chi, but it looks too big for one person. Will you help me eat it? I think it would be a shame to waste it, don't you?'

Nodding, the child steps out of the gallery into the courtyard. She is wearing the silk headband again, with pearls mounted in gilt. Vera can see a touch of rouge on her round cheeks. Kneeling, Vera peels the tangerine and holds out half of it.

The child has halted beyond arm's reach. Cautiously she eyes the fruit, then with a few mincing steps on her bound feet she comes forward and flips back the long sleeve to reveal a plump hand with dimples at each knuckle.

'Good, isn't it?' Vera says a few minutes later, when they have finished the tangerine. 'It's been nice of you to come this morning. Shall I bring another tangerine tomorrow?'

'Yes.'

That evening, before falling asleep, Vera in the drift of her thoughts has a sudden image of the lotus flower; it recalls summer heat, the calm and silence of a secluded pond in late afternoon. She thinks lazily of fields of their waxen green leaves rocking in the wind above ruffled water. Lotus – that lovely flower with a fragrant scent. They did well to name the little girl after it.

Next morning, midway into the exercise, Vera turns expectantly in the direction of a sound, but instead of Bright Lotus a young woman is standing there. She wears the plain blue cotton of a servant, her hair in a single thick braid down her back.

In response to Vera's stare, the young woman bows deeply.

'Yes?'

The servant, back hunched in the pose of humility, steps forward into the courtyard. 'Most Illustrious Madam –' But she halts and says nothing more, eyes properly downcast.

Studying the maid, Vera says, 'Where is Bright Lotus?'

'She hasn't come today.'

'You mean, she hasn't been allowed to come today.'

The maid bows her head lower.

'I'm sorry she hasn't come. You see, we talk together. And share a tangerine.'

When the maid doesn't reply – perhaps doesn't dare – Vera tries a new approach. 'Are you her personal maid?'

'Yes, Illustrious Madam.'

'These past few mornings she got loose from you and came here?'

'Yes,' the girl says hesitantly. 'She got away. We didn't know where she was.'

'But now you know. And it's perfectly safe for her, isn't it? I wish you'd tell her family that it's safe. That I'm a guest of General Tang. That I play Tai Chi here in the morning. That I'd welcome the chance to speak with Bright Lotus now and then.' After a long pause, she adds, 'That the General would be most happy to know of my friendship with the little girl. Will you tell them what I've told you?'

'Yes, Illustrious Madam.'

Next morning no one comes to the courtyard, and Vera is crest-fallen; indeed, she is surprised at the depth of her disappointment. Having finished Tai Chi, she walks slowly back to her quarters, thinking of children. Thinking of those deliberately killed in her womb. One of them might have been the same age as Bright Lotus. All day she broods on the past, hating herself and giving in to the self-pity her mother would not have accepted. Where is Shan-teh? Why didn't he take her with him – say, in a disguise of her own? Is he in danger? Of course he's in danger. When will he return? Why haven't his deep thrusts put life into her body? She drinks *mao tai* that evening at dinner and nearly fails to rise next morning for Tai Chi. But forcing herself to practice, Vera senses once again that someone is watching.

It is Bright Lotus.

And beside her stands the young maid. And behind them, to the side in shadow, is another woman, scarcely visible in a dark gown.

By the time Vera has finished practicing, the woman is gone, but Bright Lotus and the maid remain.

'Good morning,' Vera says, hearing the tremor of excitement in her own voice.

The maid bows, while Bright Lotus returns the greeting in a high, firm voice. 'Good morning to you, Black Jade!'

That evening Vera sends for young Captain Fan Chen-wu.

'Can you tell me how to interest a child?' she asks the Captain. 'A little girl of noble family?' She explains what has happened.

Fan Chen-wu, a sturdy and good-natured young man, beams happily. 'It's very nice, very fine of the Kongs. Their little girl will benefit from knowing you.'

Vera, warmed by her success today, wants to believe his flattery.

After discarding boyish things like kites and hoops, the Captain suggests a book. It's appropriate for a daughter of the Kong, too, because of its religious import: *Journey to the West.* 'What she'll like, however, is the mischief of Monkey King. All children love Sun Wu-k'ung.'

'But perhaps she's already had it read to her.'

'No matter. Children can't get enough of Monkey King. I'll bring you the book tomorrow.'

And Fan Chen-wu does. In succeeding days, after Vera plays Tai Chi in the courtyard, she sits with Bright Lotus (the maid hovering in the background) and over a tangerine they laugh together at the wild pranks of Sun Wu-k'ung, and although Bright Lotus seems to know them by heart already, she listens to Vera's reading with the zest of someone who has come upon the mischievous fellow for the first time.

And so does Vera Rogacheva pass her days in Qufu.

18

He is traveling under the name Po Ming again. Citizen Po is a Shanghai merchant, an importer of English leather goods, who has just visited his ancestral home in Taian. He has papers to prove his identity, although it's rare for Chinese police to ask for papers, much less examine them.

The General is taking a long route to Shanghai, eschewing an easier train ride through Jinan and a boat trip from Tsingtao. Dog Meat in Jinan and the Japanese in both cities would be interested in his going to meet Chiang Kai-shek: Tang and Chiang are both known for a strong stand against Japanese intervention in Chinese affairs. And traveling incognito makes sense after the bombing at Thousand Buddha Mountain. A forthright official journey, complete with entourage, might encourage another assassination attempt. And the truth is he likes to travel in disguise. It gives him a chance to observe his fellow citizens in a way denied to a high-ranking officer. He can travel alongside them as they crowd into the stuffy trains with their wicker baskets and their bad jokes and their tales of greed and sorrow as they embark with a few wheat cakes on distant pilgrimages.

By oxcart he travels from Qufu to the small depot at Tzeyang, where he catches the southbound local. He wears a faded blue shirt, black trousers, cotton shoes, and a Western-style felt hat with a gray hatband. He carries a suitcase, battered but with its straps intact. Fellow passengers eye the suitcase with envy, but his brisk manner guarantees him decent treatment. At least he's no longer subject to the excessive courtesy of his staff. Here, sitting on a wooden bench in a smoky train carriage, smelling the stench of garlic and sweat, he feels that the principles which dominate his days at Qufu are transformed into action. It is for these exhausted peasants swaying in the compartment that he works. All his efforts, his defeats absorbed and his victories counted, are for them alone. He must never forget it. As a Confucian and the son of his father, he must never for one moment believe that what he hopes to achieve is for himself. It's a hard doctrine.

At the border town of Hanchwang he leaves the train and heads along the bank of the Grand Canal by foot. In this way he avoids the station at Xu Zhou, a town within the province of Kiangsu, where warlord troops have been reported on the move – for everyone is restless now that Chiang Kai-shek has stepped down and added to the national confusion. For a day he joins a little caravan of merchants and their loaded mules in a journey along the ancient banks of the placid canal, with fish nets hovering on poles above the brown water and weathered old sampans dragging through a channel that has been traveled for centuries. At the village depot of Yunho he catches a train off the main trunkline for the seaport of Lienyunkang. Here he books passage on a small coastal steamer which makes a sluggish run along the low shore; the coast is slashed by tributaries of the great rivers, carrying silt to the ocean and turning it for miles from deep green to muddy brown. In two days he reaches Shanghai.

That afternoon, when he checks into the Palace Hotel, Citizen Po looks bedraggled from his long, circuitous trip. The desk clerk eyes him suspiciously, this rather seedy merchant, although a reservation has been made in the name of Po Ming. An older desk clerk pushes him aside. 'I will take care of Mister Po. Good afternoon, Mister Po.'

Tang nods wearily, wiping sweat from his brow. It's a hot day in Shanghai, one of those final days of heat before autumn brings its crisp weather from the Asian plains.

'I remember your last stay, sir. It was only some weeks ago.'

'That's right.'

'In fact I remember your room number. Would you like the same room?'

'No.' He doesn't want to be there without Black Jade. He doesn't want to stare at the empty bed. 'No, thank you. Give me another.'

'Sir.' The clerk hesitates, giving Tang the impression he has something special to say – unconnected with the job. 'A foreign gentleman came to the hotel recently.'

'Yes?'

'And showed me a photograph of a woman, a foreigner too. It wasn't a good photograph, but I recognized the woman.'

From the faint smile on the clerk's face, Tang understands it isn't necessary to admit what they both know: that the woman had often come to the hotel with him and had accompanied him to that room which the clerk is so eager to give him once more, as if they are colluding to get the assignations underway again. Tang is angered by such impertinence, yet also curious about the man with the photograph. He asks the clerk.

'Yes, he told me his name, sir, I have his card here.'

He takes a card from a drawer behind the front desk and lays it on the counter. It's in three languages, one of them Chinese. *The Good Luck Corporation. Importer of High-Quality Electric Fans. Erich Bruno Luckner, President.*

'Did you tell Mister Luckner you recognized the photograph?'

'I did not, sir.'

'Did he say why he was showing it to you?'

'He wanted to know if she came to the hotel.' The clerk pauses judiciously. 'In the company of a man.'

'And you told him she never came to the hotel.'

The clerk purses his lips. 'I think I told him I wasn't sure.'

'But if you remembered, you would call him?'

'I think so, sir. I believe that was the arrangement.'

'Did he have a particular man in mind when he asked if she came with one?' Too exhausted to play this game any longer, Tang adds, 'Did he mention my name?'

'He did not, sir.' The clerk is emphatic. 'May I offer an opinion?'

'Of course.'

'I think he was going everywhere, asking everybody. In the hope of finding the right man.'

'Why is this your impression?'

'Because he was nervous. Of course' – the clerk smiles – 'a lot of foreigners are, but Mister Luckner was very nervous.'

'I see. Thank you.' Tang takes money from his pocket and hands a good sum from the rolled bills to the clerk. 'If I can depend on your discretion, the next time I'm in Shanghai we'll discuss the matter again.'

'Thank you, sir. Honored.'

'By the way, I'm expecting someone – Mister Shih.'

'I'll take care of it, sir. You may count on that.' The clerk, leaning forward, gives a little nod of respect.

Tang doesn't trust him, yet there's no alternative. He surely doesn't want Luckner to know he has taken Vera away – the arms shipment's en route. He has no idea what Luckner might do with the discovery, but at stake are weapons for an army. Any circumstance that jeopardizes their delivery is serious. In his room the General has the solitude to reflect upon this doleful fact: from the moment he took Vera Rogacheva to bed, his entire future and perhaps those of many other people were put in jeopardy.

It's significant that the Great Sage had little to say about the love of man and woman, he thinks.

While Tang confronts the problem of Luckner, the desk clerk informs him by room phone that Mister Shih awaits his pleasure in the lobby.

The Nationalists are wasting no time getting him in tow. Shih is his contact in Shanghai, a KMT agent mentioned in Chu Jui's letter. Shih will arrange for him to get to the monastery where Chiang Kai-shek is playing the role of monk.

Shih Fu-lai is a tubby man in his mid-thirties, a fancy dresser in business suit, vest, and shoes with white spats. He greets the General with an expansiveness that's suspicious. Surely an honest reaction to one of Chiang's potential rivals would be caution, but Shih is jolly beyond good sense. Throwing an arm around Tang's shoulder – a gesture of outrageous familiarity – he ushers the General from the hotel into a waiting taxi. He describes a new teahouse, the best available in Shanghai, which serves the finest *dim sum* north of Canton. Throughout the ride he talks of food. The General catches phrases: shark's fins in silver netting, Hopei chestnuts, monkey brains. And opinions: Fukien soy is the best soy; Hunan peppers are barbarous; so are the odorous stews of

Mongolia. 'The egg,' says Agent Shih, 'is a perfect illustration of *yin* and *yang*. In the round shell you have the yellow and the white, eternal opposites. They're combined, yet each retains its separate character.' Tang gets the feeling that Shih often makes this comment to impress people with his philosophical turn of mind.

Not until they're halfway through the *dim sum* at the teahouse does Shih stop talking about food long enough to mention Chiang Kai-shek. He refers to Chiang as 'Eldest Uncle.' Tang knows this is bravado; at best the fellow's a distant relative. Pouring another glass of wine (Tang notices he's a hard drinker), Shih claims that Eldest Uncle's retirement from government has thrown the whole country into chaos.

This is an exaggeration – half the country's never been under Nationalist control – but Tang lets it pass. Shih continues. He maintains that people are grieving as if in fact a great leader has died. He throws out the names of heroes from ancient dynasties, linking them to Eldest Uncle. Nanking is alarmed, being left now in the hands of squabbling politicians who so exasperated Eldest Uncle he felt he had to leave. Canton is horrified. Shanghai is depressed.

At least the General accepts the last claim: Shanghai business-men have counted on Chiang to help them strengthen their hold on the national economy.

Now the Kuomintang agent is talking about an outbreak of cholera in Shanghai. Vaccine is being administered on the streets of Frenchtown from a white medical car. And 'I think it's barbaric the way foreigners cut their noodles. The other night in a Chapei restaurant I saw a table of them sawing away. It killed my appetite. General, I hope for great things when you and Eldest Uncle meet.'

'Do you? Why?'

'Because you both command the loyalty of your troops. Let me give you an illustration of loyalty to Eldest Uncle. At the battle of Lungt'an – of course, you're familiar with it.'

'I am.' He is. It was fought between the Nationalists and the troops of warlord Sun Ch'uan-fang for the possession of Nanking some months ago.

'General Sun wanted to control the railroad station there. He threw a lot of units at the spot and would have taken it and probably won the battle, except for two hundred Whampoa cadets. They'd been taught by Eldest Uncle at the Academy. They volunteered to hold the station and died to a man, but held it. They held it long enough for reinforcements to arrive and win the victory. That's what I mean by loyalty. Sun Ch'uan-fang has never recovered from the defeat. Have one of these, they're good.' He points with his chopsticks to a pork-filled bun.

'So Chiang Kai-shek is your father's eldest brother?'

Shih hesitates, then drinks off his cup of wine. 'Not really, General. It's a term of intimacy we use together.'

'Because I didn't think he had an older brother.'

Shih smiles; being caught in a lie doesn't seem to bother him. 'I'm the nephew of his uncle's second son's wife.'

'And as for Sun Ch'uan-fang, although he suffered a defeat, he's prowling the countryside north of Nanking right now. Please have some more.' Tang motions to the decanter of wine. He's encouraging Shih to drink in the hope it will turn him from political speeches and foolish lies to disclosures of some value.

Shih pours another glass. His jowls are ruddy, his eyes bloodshot. 'The Generalissimo says' – it's no longer Eldest Uncle – 'Love your comrades with the purest honesty.'

'A nice sentiment.'

'It's printed on banners, it's painted on walls. And he's loyal too. He says we must follow the teachings of his teacher, Sun Yat-sen.' The agent drinks and grimaces. 'Even though Madam Sun Yat-sen has run away to Moscow.'

'I didn't know.'

'Yes, off to the Bolsheviks. She's run away.' Shih pours more wine. 'But then, to be perfectly candid, General, her husband was tactless and autocratic. Sun Yat-sen was blinded by his own importance. He couldn't work with people. He said: "To make the nation free we must give up individual freedom." The only worthwhile thing he ever did was give the Generalissimo a chance.' Now plainly drunk, Shih has forgotten about following the teaching of Sun Yat-sen. 'Thank the gods he's dead,' Shih mutters. Leaning across the table, spots of color in his cheeks, Shih says, 'It was predicted hundreds of years ago – well, more than a thousand – that the Generalissimo would lead China.' With a smile of triumph he adds, 'Let me explain.' In the Book of Prophecy, he maintains, it is clearly stated that someday a general will rule the country. This general will have grass on top of his head. 'The "chiang" in the name Chiang Kai-shek, you see, is part of the word for "general," but in this instance, with a few extra strokes at the top of the character, it resembles the sign for "grass." There you are: general with grass on top of his head, and the prophecy's fulfilled.' He waits for a response, but when none comes he drinks his wine. 'They have Ponay tea here from Yunnan. It's a reddish-black tea combined with chrysanthemum buds. You must have fruit puffs with it. I'll order. General, we want you to join us. Look who have already. Li Pao-chen, who used to be Sun Ch'uan-fang's deputy. He's now Defense Commissioner of Shanghai. Did you know that?'

'I'd heard.'

'It's an example of men of ability rising. And there's Chen Tiao-yuan and Chen Yun-ao –'

'Not Chen Yun-ao,' interrupts the General. 'He died on Thousand Buddha Mountain.' For an instant Tang recalls the puffy cheeks, the walrus mustache, the shaft of wood projecting from the shaven skull.

Bewildered a moment, Shih smiles in acknowledgment of his error. 'Yes, of course. The gods were with you that day, General. The Manchurian Tiger nearly got you.'

'Really? You believe Marshal Chang ordered the bombing?'

'Everyone in Shanghai knows it.' Shih waves his hand as if concluding the matter.

'Why would the Marshal want to kill me?'

'He was afraid you'd come over to us.' The tea arrives, but Shih pushes his cup aside and pours another wine to drink with the fruit puffs. 'Don't worry about the Marshal any more. With men like you on our side, we'll finish him quickly.' It's a boastful remark, improper from a man of Shih's position. He has indeed let wine get the better of him.

Tang smiles encouragingly; the man's tongue is now loosened. 'Is the Generalissimo so optimistic? After all, he's not even in office.'

Shin waves his hand through the air. 'Office means nothing. Do you think Wang Ching-wei and Sun Fo and hotheads like some of those southern generals and that womanish T'an Yen-k'ai will stay in office long? Do you think they'll make anything of their Special . . . Central . . . Supervisory . . . Committee?' He repeats the name of the emergency council of the Nanking government in a measured tone of scorn. 'Special . . . Central . . . Supervisory . . . Committee!'

'When will the Generalissimo take office again?'

Shih, shrugging, downs another glass. 'When he does, you'd

better come with him.'

'Is that a threat? It sounds like a threat.'

Shih, reaching out as if to touch the General's sleeve, thinks better of it and withdraws his hand. For a moment he looks sober. 'Believe me, Excellency, the Generalissimo wants the same thing you want.'

'Which is?'

'A unified country.'

'Without foreign interference?'

Shih blinks thoughtfully. 'Is that what you want, General – no foreign interference?'

'I thought everyone knew my position on foreign intervention in Chinese affairs.'

'We thought we knew your position. Until recently.'

Tang stares at the drunken man, who seems to be struggling toward a new subject in their conversation. 'You *thought* you knew my position on foreign intervention in Chinese affairs,' Tang says slowly. 'Do you think it's changed recently?'

Looking down at the wine, Shih pushes it aside. 'My dear General, we just don't know. We'd like it clarified.'

'What's there to clarify?'

'Your foreign commitments.'

'I have none.' But then it strikes the General. 'Are you referring to my guest at Qufu?'

'Yes, Excellency.'

'She is not a Bolshevik.'

'I believe you, General.' Shih takes up his wineglass again and drinks.

It occurs to Tang that the Kuomintang agent, charged with bringing up Vera's presence in Qufu, has drunk so much out of nervousness.

'Every man is entitled to live as he pleases,' Shih continues. 'No one is more faithful to that principle than the Generalissimo. But – a Russian. And at this time.'

'She is not a Bolshevik.'

'We don't doubt you.' Shih wets his lips, glances around. 'The Generalissimo knows you wouldn't take a Bolshevik into your confidence.'

Tang restrains an impulse to say that for years Chiang Kai-shek took Bolsheviks into his confidence even as they often took him into theirs. 'Do you also object to the Comintern agent?'

'Oh, him. That's quite different,' Shih says with a laugh.

Chiang Kai-shek has a competent spy in my camp, Tang thinks.

'What we'd worry about,' Shih continues, 'is the influence of a woman. I mean, Excellency, it's the sort of relationship –' He pours more wine, drinks. 'We'd like your assurance she won't interfere. I mean, influence you.'

'That's assurance you won't get.' Their eyes meet. Tang puts down his teacup and leans forward. 'It is insulting. How dare you ask such a thing from someone whose country is his life? My entire clan was wiped out because of my father's convictions. I've taken them from him. Don't speak to me of assurances and interference and influence.' Tang rises.

So does Shih, unsteadily.

At the entrance he apologizes for his impertinence.

'Don't apologize for doing your duty,' Tang tells him, as they wave for separate rickshaws. 'Is the meeting still scheduled?'

'Of course, Excellency. Someone will come for you in the morning.'

They part – and Shih seems pleased, in spite of the bad feeling toward the close of the evening. It occurs to the General that he has given Shih an assurance anyway. But he is furious. Had he taken a Chinese girl, a Eurasian, even an Italian or German woman for his concubine, no one would have questioned it. Chiang Kai-shek's own guilt about his past relationship with the Russians has made Black Jade an issue.

Riding back to the hotel in a rickshaw, Tang realizes a question was left unasked – one he's almost afraid to ask himself. If he had to choose between an alliance of importance and Black Jade, what would he do? The alliance must come first, yet he will not let her go. It is the kind of dilemma often set out by the Yarrow Stalk Oracle. He arrives at his hotel in a black mood.

Lying on his bed in the hot night, hearing the overhead fan whirl like a great tireless insect, he lets his mind turn to a childhood event. It was one of the few times he ever defied his father. Relatives had come and during their conversation they mentioned Shan-teh's grand-uncle. Someone said he'd been instrumental in winning the Battle of Nanking in 1864 that ended the Taiping Rebellion. But after the relatives had gone, father told Shan-teh to forget that grand-uncle, even though the man had been a military commander. Father explained why. Shan-teh disregarded the admonition, although father had warned him if he thought about grand-uncle he might grow up to be like him.

A terrible fate – to be like grand-uncle.

Because at the age of thirty-six, when Tang's father was a boy of five, grand-uncle had run away with a singsong girl. He left name and honor behind, forsook the ideals of his ancestors, discarded his right to memory in the clan. Ran off with a mere girl, probably to Southeast Asia, and disappeared with her into Singapore or Djakarta, unknown, without prospects or hope. Ran off with someone not good enough to be a servant in the Tang household. Across the years Shan-teh has often extended his sympathy to the hapless lover, wandering with a girl through strange cities toward doom. He has done it in defiance of his father's wishes.

Lying in bed in the Shanghai hotel, he understands his grand-uncle, who forgot his duty when touched by passion.

Next day, in the company of a different KMT agent, the General leaves by steamer for Ningpo. This agent, a short fellow from Wuhsi, is as reticent as Shih had been garrulous. At the wharf they stand in line for steamer tickets and watch the clerks toss each coin on the wooden counter to judge, from its ring, if it's counterfeit.

The trip south takes all day. They reach the Chusan Archipelago off the coast at dark and anchor in the channel. At dawn they enter the harbor of Zhenhai, where they change to a smaller craft for the trip to Ningpo. Tang stands on the bow, watching the muddy water slide along the curved stakes. Gulls are soaring and swooping and he wishes Black Jade were with him. Ningpo comes into view, the City of Calmed Waters, at a confluence of rivers. Ringed by hills, within smelling distance of brackish swamps, Ningpo, the General sees, is blessed with few elements of beauty. A seven-story pagoda rises stylishly above the brown city walls, but otherwise there are factories, most of them processing tins of bamboo shoots, their names in faded crimson above the doors.

At the dock the launch takes on two new passengers, one of them a stout Westerner in pith helmet and khaki. The other is his Chinese interpreter. When they move toward him at the bow, Tang doubles back and goes to the stern. That Westerner has the inquisitive look of a journalist.

Tang soon learns he's correct.

Not a half-hour out of Ningpo, while the launch is chugging through a weed-choked stream, he's confronted by the beefy

421

Westerner on the stern. The interpreter, bowing, gives traditional apologies for breaking into his privacy.

The General turns to the KMT agent. 'Did you know they were accompanying us upriver?'

The agent hesitates long enough to confirm Tang's suspicion: this interview on the launch has been arranged. 'No, Excellency,' says the agent.

Arranged by Chiang Kai-shek.

'I'm as surprised as you are,' says the agent.

Planned by him to publicize his meeting with a prominent northern general.

And without my consent, Tang thinks. Furious, nevertheless he manages to shake hands with the American journalist. Furious.

Deck chairs appear. The two men sit next to each other on the stern of the old launch. The interpreter has to shout their replies over the noise of its engine.

First the journalist wants to know about Thousand Buddha Mountain. Who did the bombing and why?

Tang draws his face into the so-called mask of Chinese inscrutability; he knows the Western journalist expects it. Tang also knows, from the man's keen eyes, that he's experienced enough to ask good questions. The General replies that he doesn't know who did the bombing. Why it was done is obvious, however.

The journalist leans forward expectantly.

'Someone,' Tang says, 'wanted someone killed.'

The journalist wipes his sweaty face with a rumpled handkerchief, trying to hide his annoyance. 'It's rumored you were the target, General.'

'Yes, I've heard the rumor.'

'They say some northern officers didn't want an alliance between you and Chiang Kai-shek.'

'I don't know who they could be.'

'General Feng Yu-hsiang?'

'At the time of the bombing, General Feng made public statements suggesting it was he who wanted an alliance with Chiang Kai-shek.'

'Marshal Chang Tso-lin?'

'The Marshal is my superior – and patron.'

Coming at them through the heavy air is the clatter of the engine, the journalist, annoyed at the difficulty of translation, looks forward toward the source of the noise. Then, turning, he says, 'Do you agree with your patron and superior that the Japanese should be welcome in Shantung Province?'

Tang has correctly assessed the man: he is knowledgeable, bold, persistent. 'By law the Japanese have a concession in Tsingtao.'

'But now they've sent some troops to Jinan.'

'I understand it's at the invitation of the Governor General.'

'They say to protect their nationals from local agitators.'

'You must ask the Governor General about that.'

'Is it true he's called Dog Meat because he likes fried dog?'

'I won't answer such questions.'

'Do you hold him responsible for the increasing Japanese presence in your province?'

'How can I? He's the Governor General and assigns responsibilities to others.'

The journalist wipes his sweaty face in frustration. Tea comes. The agent from Wuhsi has engineered its appearance. Now he stands behind the two men as if acting as host.

Tang is furious. This interview is linking him with Chiang Kai-shek. Whatever happens at the monastery, the world at large will suspect him of making a deal with the Nationalists.

The next question is easy: What is the General's opinion of Chiang Kai-shek. Tang provides a conventional answer. The southern general is a man of honor, a soldier of talent, a citizen dedicated to the ideals of Sun Yat-sen – freedom and prosperity. It's therfore a pity, the General adds with a touch of mischief, that Chiang Kai-shek has chosen to retire from public life.

'If he's retired, why then are you visiting him, General?'

'To exchange views.'

'Will he return to government?'

'That's his decision. I believe at the moment the Nationalist Party has a committee running things. But I wouldn't know about that.'

'It's said of you, General, you believe in innovation.'

'If it brings us closer to Confucian ideals. Good conduct in leaders brings harmony to the people.'

The journalist smiles. 'That is Confucian, isn't it?'

'The right man in power determines the success of government.'

'Are you that right man, General?'

'I think China has many good men.'

'Chiang Kai-shek?'

Tang is cautious here; he mustn't allow political courtesy to seem like enthusiasm. 'I believe he's one of them.'

'Because of this meeting with Chiang at the monastery, I think people are going to speculate about your joining the Kuomintang.'

'I'm visiting him to exchange views.'

'Does that include the possibility of an alliance at least?'

'Exchanging views includes a lot of possibilities.'

They regard each other warily in the midday light. The journalist seems unnerved by the inconsequential nature of their interview. Tang is still furious at Chiang Kai-shek's blatant use of him for publicity.

After a brief exchange in English with the journalist, the interpreter turns with a deferential bob of his head and asks permission to pose a military question. Tang gives it and relaxes; for him such questions are easier to handle than political ones.

The journalist wants to know if the General, like Chiang Kai-shek, believes in the practice of *lien-tso-fa*.

It's a question, the General realizes, designed to elicit a sensational reply, the kind sought by the West. In this instance, however, the General wishes to be unfailingly clear, as explicit as the reporter desires. His aim is not so much to satisfy the press as to warn his adversaries. So he replies that, in fact, he fully believes in *lien-tso-fa*, the principle of collective responsibility in war, as it was first promulgated by Ch'i Chi-kuan in the sixteenth century. If, for example, a platoon leader retreats with his men without orders during battle, he will be executed. The same policy holds for commanders of larger units who retreat without orders; they too will be executed on the field. There is more to the law, however, Tang tells the listening journalist, bent forward with a pipe burning in a gnarled hand. If the commander stands his ground, but his officers and men flee, then every subordinate officer will be executed.

'Without exception?'

'Without exception. If the officers hold their ground, but the men run, then a certain proportion of those men, usually ten percent, will be executed.'

'You follow such a policy?'

'I do.'

'Have you ever put it into effect?'

'On occasion.'

'What were the circumstances, if I may ask?'

'You may not.'

'But you agree with the Generalissimo?'

'On this matter, yes.'

'And on others?'

'I can't say yet.'

'But you imply a disagreement on others.'

'I imply nothing. I'm only visiting Chiang Kai-shek in a monastery. We will talk, and that's all.'

'That's all?'

'That's all.' At least he won't enter the monastery as a proven supporter of Chiang Kai-shek, who will get a careful report of his interview from the interpreter and the KMT agent. Lighting a cigarette, he sits back to enjoy a breeze coming across the tidal waters that take them deeper into the marshland south of Ningpo. There are mountains now to the west, and clouds in them seem like ocean waves in paintings – frozen at the crest. The interview peters out, although Tang ends it with excessive courtesy. During their final exchanges he's deliberately enthusiastic. Actually, he's pleased with the outcome of this unsought interview. His replies have asserted his independence.

The florid journalist seems vaguely disgruntled, aware perhaps that the interview contains a nuance of meaning as yet lost on him. He doesn't understand that the General's replies, far from being devious, were in fact clear signals of his military confidence and his political freedom. But the meaning won't be lost for long on this reporter, Tang knows. He's tougher than the usual foreign newsmen who leave the bars of Shanghai and Peking only long enough to file a few lively quotations for the papers back home. Blowing smoke into the freshening wind that hurls it behind the stern, the General tells himself that if all Westerners were like this one, they'd be a greater threat to the autonomy of China than they are now.

At the village of Chikou they leave the motor launch and proceed in sedan chairs borne by coolies who wear tinkling bells around their necks. Footpaths rise into foothills, a sudden rain squall inundates the trail, but the tinkling continues. From within his chair, covered by rattan strips, the General watches his two forward bearers lean into their work. The rain forms a ring of tiny waterfalls around the rims of their broad field hats. They haven't traveled five miles before the sky is clear again, a pristine blue as blue as the sea. In a small village they come on a festival – paper lanterns of fish and animals, cymbals clashing, the children dressed in holiday gowns and intricate paper crowns. Again he wishes Black Jade were here with him.

The path ascends on a stoneway leading up a mountain. The little caravan passes a grove of bamboo, then of pine; buffaloes drag stones over grain to mill it as buffaloes did thousands of years ago. The air, cooling, is ladened with the fresh scent of fir trees as the path winds upward along the rim of an extinct volcano; glimpses into the abyss alternate with views of mountain brooks. The trees are filled with birdsong as the party descends into a valley, then moves upward again. On the steep climb the pace slows to a sluggish trudge; the General can hear the labored but rhythmic breathing of the coolie bearers as they bring his chair out into an open space on the mountainside. Ahead is a stone bridge, beyond it a gurgling stream, and at the far end of the clearing a low building in monastery precincts.

The chair behind Tang's comes alongside, and the American journalist leans out to say something. They wait until the interpreter's chair reaches theirs. The General is told that the journalist wishes to thank him again for the interview. The square, florid face of the newsman is beaming.

He knows I'm not a subordinate of Chiang Kai-shek, the General thinks; the knowledge has come to him during the climb.

'One other point,' the journalist says through the interpreter. 'I'm still interested in your policy of *lien-tso-fa*. What if your men retreated – in some order, but without specific command – from a much larger force? What would you do?'

'If the enemy's clearly superior, I'd not use *lien-tso-fa*. To apply it rigidly might lead to excessive losses.'

'Meaning you'd let them get out of there without telling them they could retreat.'

'If the odds are impossible, it's unreasonable to stay and die.'

'So you wouldn't apply *lien-tso-fa*.'

'Under those circumstances, no.'

'I believe the Generalissimo would call that a grave error in discipline.'

'Let him call it what he pleases. I call it good sense not to waste your forces on a hopeless cause. Regroup them for another day.'

'Do your men understand you'd apply *lien-tso-fa* in one case but not in another?'

'They do.'

'That means the use of individual judgment.'

'Yes, of course. If they behave like cowards, they die at my order. If they retreat because they clearly see nothing can save the situation, they don't die by my order.'

'Then it isn't quite correct to say you agree with the Generalissimo, even on his point of *lien-tso-fa*.'

'He must speak for himself. Men have minds – even soldiers do,' Tang says with a smile. 'I want my troops to use theirs.'

'An unusual view. Especially, if I may say so, in China.'

'I've read of your Western battles when men stood their ground against all odds. Unnecessarily. You celebrate such stubbornness. An unusual view.'

The journalist, when he gets the interpretation, breaks into a laugh. 'I've enjoyed our interviews, General. Particularly this second one.'

As they proceed by chair to the monastery, Tang realizes that he has publicly defied Chaing Kai-shek by contradicting the policy of *lien-tso-fa*, which the Nationalists boast of as proof of their discipline and sincerity. Tang went at it with zest. Father always told him pride is a dangerous thing – to give way to it is an error of judgment. Yet at this moment, journeying toward the monastery where Chiang Kai-shek resides in full command, pride in self is a matter of survival for General Tang Shan-teh.

He doesn't see Chiang that day. He's not surprised, because delay enhances the power of the host. Chu Jui is not at the monastery, which does surprise him, because the former Chekiang general and now aide to Chiang Kai-shek had expressly promised in the letter to be here.

KMT staff people are in the dormitories where monks used to live, and the monks have been moved to a monastery down the mountain. The General has been given private quarters in a lovely grove of bamboo. Through their closely ranked trunks he can see the wood hut that the American journalist shares with a few other Western newsmen. Beyond that hut, in a prayer hall, are three emissaries from the Nanking coalition. Down the mountain, in a small village on the eastern slope, a detachment of Nationalist troops is billeted. Although a staff member claims that the Generalissimo is here to meditate, obviously the retired head of the Nanking government has brought with him the trappings of government.

That evening Tang is joined by a half-dozen staff officers for dinner, which is served privately in his quarters. Clearly Chiang wishes to isolate him from other guests – no more interviews. The meal (strictly vegetarian in accordance with Buddhist principles) is dominated by the staff officers' eulogies to their leader. They vie to outdo one another. Yet Tang listens carefully, sifting through the praise for kernels of information. He learns, for example, that Chiang has sent away his wife and his concubine. The reason offered by an ecstatic staff man is Chiang Kai-shek's desire to implement Sun Yat-sen's program for equality of men and women. Tang also learns that Chiang insists his initial reason for breaking with the Reds was military. The Communists believe in dual command within the army – a political commissar in tandem with an officer at each echelon of organization. Chiang, on the other hand, believes in unity of command under one military leader. Dual command, in his opinion, leads to battlefield disaster.

Tang agrees. In this decision he sees the mind of a soldier at work, and by the end of dinner he feels amicably disposed toward the southern general. He goes to bed hoping they will cooperate, at least for a while. Sleepily he allows himself his dream of Chinese unification: Feng and Marshal Chang and Dog Meat and others like them removed from the warlord scene; good leaders first aligned and then absorbed into a truly national armed force. What of Chiang Kai-shek? Time will take care of placing him in the order he deserves. He is formidable – events have so far proved that – but he's not the man China needs.

China needs me, Tang thinks.

Secure in that conviction, his mind turns before sleep to Black Jade. Is she all right in Qufu? Can she endure the isolation? Does she miss him, love him? Can she love the Chinese man he is?

It is amazing, he tells himself, lying on a mat in the monastery hut – amazing that her smile is with him at this very moment. A smile, nothing more. But everything.

Temple bells booming shortly after dawn. The General is escorted by a staff man to a broad veranda behind the main temple building. Chairs have already been arranged, a dozen of them in a semicircle with one chair moved out of line to indicate its importance. Along with the journalists and General Tang come the three Nanking emissaries and a few gentlemen in business suits, who are introduced as representatives of the business community of Hangchow. The American journalist and another from Britain attempt to sit by him, but the KMT agent politely if firmly positions the General between two of the Nanking dignitaries – harmless officials from the newly formed Special Central Supervisory Committee. Oranges, cakes, chocolate wafers, and tea are served to the assembled guests, while bells continue to toll through the soft blue air of early morning.

They have finished and are drinking third cups of tea before their host appears in the temple doorway, flanked by bald priests in saffron.

Tang regards the southerner closely: a man of average height in a long gray monkish robe. He wears his hair cropped, giving his small face a youthful look, although Tang knows he is forty. He greets everyone with quiet efficiency, eschewing heartiness and warmth, which seems proper in this contemplative setting. He sits with the ramrod posture of a military man, with long thin hands planted on his thighs; they never move. He's obviously a man of considerable control – or one who wishes to appear controlled. Tang is aware of his own disappointment that Chiang Kai-shek looks so impressive: the thin lips parting in a smile of benign criticism; the eyes steady, perceptive; the entire slim frame emanating a kind of animal awareness.

Chiang makes an opening statement while the guests finish their tea. He takes nothing. His plans are to go abroad, he says in a rather high-pitched voice, where he will study economics for three to five years, preferably in America, which is a country he longs to know better. Chiang says this with a slight nod in the direction of the American journalist. It is all translated into English.

Having therefore declared his intention to leave China, he asks for questions.

The British reporter asks him in Chinese why he broke with the Communists.

His answer is delivered in a thin, precise voice without hesitation: The discovery of documents in the Russian Embassy of Peking convinced him, as well as his colleagues, that Moscow wanted to overthrow the Chinese and make the country a vassal state of Russia.

A predictable answer, Tang thinks. Chiang adds to it a call for Chinese democracy on principles outlined by Doctor Sun Yat-sen.

Another journalist, beginning hesitantly, as if afraid his question is too bold, wants to know if Doctor Sun was actually a Communist, as some people claim.

'*Some* people *claim* he was a *Communist*.' The Generalissimo repeats the words with heavy sarcasm. 'Some people claim I am too. But am I? Let Shanghai and Wuhan and other cities, where the Reds have been, answer that. Ask the Reds – *if* you can find any.' He smiles. Many in the circle smile back.

The journalist appears surprised – Chiang Kai-shek has referred with open pride to the slaughter of thousands of Reds in the past few months.

'Other questions?' Chiang glances around the semicircle of chairs in the shaded light of the veranda.

The American asks why he left government.

'To give others their chance.' Chiang looks at each of the three men from Nanking. 'These illustrious gentlemen visiting here are better qualified, I'm sure, than I to tell you what is intended by Nanking in the future.' One hand lifts into the air; having remained motionless so long, Chiang gives this slight gesture a dramatic importance – the skill isn't lost on Tang. 'I hope the government finds a way of establishing a unified country, free of Communists.'

'Can they do that?' the Britisher asks crisply.

Chiang stares at the emissaries, who return his look with embarrassed grins. 'Ask them, not me. You see me here in a monastery, attempting to cleanse my soul. They have only to cleanse our country of Bolsheviks.'

A polite titter.

'What is your opinion of Wang Ching-wei?'

'He's a man of distinction, a statesman of long standing.'

'He says you wish to be called back to Nanking.'

Chiang glares at the journalists. 'I will not discuss what Ching-wei says.'

Tang likes this bluntness, especially with a foreigner.

Chiang is then asked about his political philosophy.

'That's quite simple,' he says. ' "The virtue of the prince is the wind; the virtue of the people is the grass. The grass bends in the direction of the wind." '

After a silence, the Britisher leans forward and asks in correct

Chinese, 'Do you think of yourself as the prince?'

Chiang blinks, as if someone has struck him – lightly, but struck him. 'I am quoting Confucius, not myself. Prince is the Sage's word.' The veranda is silent; Tang wonders who is the better newsman, the British or the American, both of whom attack boldly; there's no tradition for this sort of interviewing in China. Tang considers their behavior a sign of Western strength. He will remember it for the day when he has power; Chinese reporters will be able to pursue truth with the same aggressiveness.

Chiang is looking past the seated guests into the temple compound with its pines and bamboo and twittering birds; someone is laughing far away, perhaps from a dormitory on the wooded slope. 'This is what I will tell you about my political philosophy,' he say finally. 'China's ills can be cured only by example from those above. Confucius taught us that without a pure leader the people can't be pure. Those who oppress the people must be regenerated. That doesn't mean changing the system radically, as the Bolsheviks want. Reform must be voluntary. Each man must come to see the error of his ways. Landowner, businessman, judge, and soldier must cooperate in carrying out reforms. These reforms must be designed to lessen the power of powerful men. Yes, you heard me correctly – lessen their power to exploit and oppress. And they must do this by their own volition.' Stopping, he looks around the circle until he comes to the American. 'I believe the Christians are correct in their emphasis on example. They appeal to the better instinct of men.'

Tang considers this a gratuitous flattery of Christians; and coming after Chiang's defense of Confucian principles, it is a surprise. What's the reason? To please the foreign journalists? There must be a reason for him to single out a foreign religion for special praise in a carefully staged interview. The next moment Chiang, rising, concludes it with an apology: He would like to remain for more of such stimulating talk, but the temple priests desire that he place himself at their disposal for the recitation of sutras.

Chiang disappears inside the temple, and the assembled guests disperse, most of them strolling in small groups through the pine forest.

Tang returns to his quarters, but he scarcely has time to absorb his initial impression of Chiang when an aide comes breathlessly to the door to tell him that the Generalissimo would appreciate sharing his illustrious company for a while.

The recitation of sutras didn't last long, Tang thinks.

He finds Chiang Kai-shek sitting in a courtyard behind a hall removed from the central grouping of monastery buildings. Chiang has changed into a KMT uniform without insignia. Below his neatly pressed pants are Western-style white socks and patent-leather pumps. He is hatless but wears a Sam Browne belt and holstered pistol. In the uniform he looks slimmer than in the gown; indeed, the belt cinches his tunic around an extremely small waist and causes his breast pockets to wrinkle over a narrow chest. But the eyes are those of a soldier. Tang and Chiang exchange formal pleasantries as they stroll out of the courtyard toward a distant promontory on the mountaintop.

'I've looked forward to our meeting,' Chiang says. A man in a simple monk's robe follows at a discreet distance; under the gown he is undoubtedly armed. ' "The tree for shade," ' Chiang quotes, ' "the man for reputation." Reputation is, after all, what we have.'

Tang nods in agreement.

'I heard of your punishment of the bandit White Wolf. Was he a Tartar?'

'I'm not sure. We didn't talk. I only went to take his head.'

Chiang smiles. It isn't a pleasant smile, Tang decides – more like a grimace, like something grudged.

As they stroll, Chiang lifts a long hand and points into the distance. On Mount Yu, he explains, there is a temple said to contain a relic of the Buddha. 'My mother was devout Buddhist,' he observes in a voice unusually low. 'She was truly devout. She could recite the sutras for hours. 'Yes,' he says pensively, 'truly devout.'

For an instant Chiang seems to have lowered his guard, and in this instant Tang sees a good son, dutiful, adoring. Once again Tang is prepared to like him, to come to terms with him, but Chiang, halting on the path, turns with a cold stare. 'I find it hard to believe you told that foreigner you'd relax discipline under certain circumstances. Dedication, which is another way of saying discipline, is the soul of military life,' he declares and sets out again. The thumbs of both hands are stuck in his gun belt.

'I didn't say relax discipline. There's simply no need to execute troops without a clear reason.'

'We must have loyalty from our men.'

'One way to get it is to be just in dealing with them.'

Chiang shakes his head impatiently. 'I'm afraid, General, you miss the point. For years we've looked foolish to the world because so often our soldiers run in battle. Why do they run? Because by and large they're mercenaries who don't care who wins as long as they get paid. Having only wages to lose, they run under fire.'

'That's often true of mercenaries.'

'But my troops don't run,' Chiang declares with sudden heat, as if he'd just been challenged. 'They are loyal, and if they aren't, I have them shot.'

'The question is: Are all men who run disloyal?'

'Those circumstances of yours!' Chiang guffaws scornfully.

In silence they walk to the edge of the mountaintop. Across a deep chasm is another mountain down whose slopes a waterfall spills. They can hear its music. Behind them the temple bells are tolling again, calling monks to prayer. The steady boom echoes across the valleys and peaks of the region. It is beautiful here, beyond politics, Tang thinks.

Chiang turns, his expression less angry. In a calm voice – Tang suspects he might have made a good schoolteacher – Chiang explains that the Nationalist Party must stand above personal feeling or aspiration. The highest duty of a Kuomintang member is to consolidate and expand the Party's hold over China; in this way the country will be saved.

Tang, returning his stare, doesn't comment.

Chiang's lips tighten into a thin line. 'Loyalty is the soul of communal effort.'

'A fine phrase.'

'Thank you, General, it's mine. As a father to his sons, so is a commander to his troops. That's also mine.'

'Sometimes I wonder if the family tradition is a hindrance today.'

Chiang looks at him in open astonishment.

'We're taught to believe the family is everything. But we also teach that our country is everything – especially today. But can both be everything – family and country?'

Chiang shakes his head slowly in disbelief. 'I heard you were a steadfast Confucian.'

'And do consider myself.'

'Then how can you slander the family in this manner?'

'I question the emphasis on it. If the Sage lived today, he might feel the same.'

'Circumstances again,' Chiang says derisively. But then he smiles. 'You're strong, General. Good, that's good – not easily led.' He's smiling broadly now. 'Well, neither am I. Who said it?' Pursing his lips, he tries to remember something. 'Anyway – we Chinese, someone said, are too arrogant to work together.'

The sudden change in Chiang is heartening; Tang feels as though finally they are meeting on common ground.

'Do you drink?' Chiang asks suddenly. Before Tang can reply, he continues at a rapid pace. 'I don't, I don't believe in it. Or in smoking. I need all my strength for the work. This morning I was up writing letters before dawn.' Grimly he looks across the ravine to the waterfall ending in a ground mist. ' "Man's mouth is two bits of skin," ' he murmurs, giving Tang the impression he's thinking of another time, place, and companion. Then, turning with another smile to Tang, he says, 'I think the Seventh Corps won a fine victory over Sun Ch'uan-fang at Lungt'an. Li Tsung-jen followed my advice about the deployment of each battalion. Took twenty thousand prisoners. I call that loyalty and discipline.'

He wants me to think of him, Tang realizes, as a talented general, not a politician.

Thumbs stuck in his gun belt again, Chiang says, 'You mustn't let the Japanese have their way in Shantung.'

'I'm not the governor general of the province.'

Chiang paces near the dropoff. He has a springy step, typical of a wiry, almost frail man. 'Marshal Chang Tso-lin is the fault. He's playing into the hands of the Red bandits as well as the Japanese invaders.' Tang, watching him pace, wonders if this is the rhetoric he uses with his staff and financial backers. 'Until the Marshal gives up his Japanese allies and corrupt subordinates like the Governor General of Shantung, we won't get anywhere in this country.' Turning, he looks at Tang. '*You* should be governor general – a man of honor, a man who avenges his chief of staff massacred by Tartar bandits. You should control that province instead of a degenerate puppet.' Chiang stares at his leather shoes, their polished surface dusty now. 'But then the Marshal has always shown terrible judgment,' he declares with a blunt ardor rare among Chinese discussing their peers. ' "Don't fret because men don't know you, fret because you don't know men." '

Tang isn't sure how to interpret the quotation (the last time he'd heard it was from the Kong Patriarch). To whom does Chiang mean it to apply: The Marshal? Chiang? Myself?

Pacing again, Chiang halts at the edge of the precipice and stares into it. 'General Tang, do you believe in the Three Principles of Doctor Sun? I do: nationalism, livelihood, and democracy.' Before Tang is able to comment, the Generalissimo adds, 'He had a bodyguard from Canada named Cohen. *Kuo han*. This man was a big man. Doctor Sun was always impressed by size. *Kuo han* was what they call a prize fighter and a cowboy. In the United States in San Francisco this year they are raising money to erect a statue of Doctor Sun. I understand it will overlook the Bay. The committee writes me they will chisel this on a plaque: *Father of the Chinese Republic and First President, Champion of Democracy and Lover of Mankind, Proponent of Equality, Liberty, and Justice for all People, and Friendship and Peace Among Nations.*' He recites the inscription with the ease of someone with a sure memory. Thumbs hooked in the gun belt, he turns again to Tang. 'I believe in equality of man and woman. Women should be free, not held in bondage. For that reason I have given up my concubine.'

Tang nods noncommittally, unsure of Chiang's intent.

'Have you, General? Have you given up yours?'

'A woman lives with me,' Tang replies coolly.

'May I ask about her?'

'What do you wish to know?'

'Her nationality.'

'I think, then, you already know it,' Tang says. 'She is Russian.'

'Russian,' Chiang repeats.

'She fled from Russia, as many people did, when the Bolsheviks took over.'

'Russian.' Chiang is pacing rapidly. His thin figure jerks each time he turns; his hollow-cheeked face is thrust intently forward, as if he's searching the ground for something. 'Inequality is a major weakness in our country. I was divorced in the tenth year of the Republic and gave my wife back her independence. People say that's a lie, but they are the liars. She sits in Wuhan giving out lies to people only too eager to believe evil of me.' Chiang stops pacing. 'Sacrifice, commitment, discipline,' he says, 'these are the watchwords of the future, General.' He paces again, again halts. Tang is astonished by the man's physical energy. 'We as leaders must set the example.' He stands at attention, as if commanded by

435

an unseen voice. 'Never give up! In the name of the Sage, work for our country!' He rushes to Tang and holds out his arms. 'Will you do that, General? Work in the spirit of the Sage?'

'I will, I do,' Tang replies uncertainly, as the slim Chiang embraces him. He can feel the bony arms, the quick strength of the fingers that grip his arms, and he smells the heavy scent of jasmine – the scent of a dandy – as Chiang's cropped head brushes against his own.

On releasing him, Chiang steps across the clearing and moves into a dark stand of pine trees. Almost before Tang realizes it, the slim figure has vanished.

Slowly Tang walks back to his quarters, shaken by this extraordinary interview. He has met few men as complex as Chiang Kai-shek, this intense and mercurial man who seems possessed of both a crystalline intelligence and the heart of a child, a deceptive man, wholly unpredictable, alarmingly hidden, but a man of exceptional discipline, perhaps too a man of vision, surely a brave man but foolish as well, a man of impulse who acts on intuition, quite possibly a man who is somewhat mad, in full control of his public bearing yet prey to private fits of emotion, a man other men will follow even when they doubt him, a man uncertain of nearly everything except his own overwhelming ambition, except his sense of personal destiny.

An ambition perhaps even greater, Tang thinks, than my own.

That afternoon Chu Jui arrives on the mountaintop, but Tang doesn't see him right away. What he does see is the departure of the three minor Nanking offcials and the journalists, the latter being taken on a side trip to Hangchow for a look at the wooded islands and willow causeways and mansions of West Lake.

So Chiang is clearing out the camp, thereby making room no doubt for a new contingent of visitors. Tang is sure of it when from his prayer hut he watches arrivals trudge along the paths, like guests at a busy hotel.

He's unsure what to do, although the presence of Chu Jui will keep him here another night at least. He suspects that Chiang has been deliberately vague about the length of his stay. He isn't sure what to think. Should he join Chiang and gamble that together they can defeat a coalition of other warlords? He's certain that is Chiang's goal. The embrace on the path, in spite of their obvious differences, attested to Chiang's belief in their potential alliance. Sitting on a monk's stool, while the afternoon wears quietly away in this cool mountain air, General Tang admits to himself that the prospect suits him too, for through such an alliance – with the luck of Heaven and a shrewd handling of Chiang Kai-shek – he may yet achieve his own goal.

Filled with such thoughts, he's hardly aware when the tall familiar figure of Chu Jui approaches through the pines. After an exchange of amenities Chu Jui sits down on a bench. Together they watch another trail of guests disappear into the temple compound.

'A lot of people are flocking to the foreign concessions in Tsingtao and Peking,' Chu Jui says after a while.

'What people?'

'Petty officials, local warlords. People who've squeezed the peasantry enough to have the money for a good life behind the concession walls.'

'Who frightens them?'

'Chiang Kai-shek, the Old Marshal, Feng.' With a laugh he adds, 'You.' He lights a cigarette and watches the smoke drift lazily upward. 'Have you visited the neighboring temples? Buddhism is strong in this region.'

Tang remembers his religious interests. 'Are you still planning to go back to the monastery?'

'You mean – like Chiang?' The ex-general frowns. 'I think I'm ready for a trip abroad to study.'

This remark brings a smile to Tang's lips. 'To study abroad' has often meant among Chinese politicians 'to escape a purge.'

'Come, it isn't that bad,' Tang says. 'Have you talked to Chiang since you got here?

'I have. He's impressed by you – but not favorably.'

Tang is startled.

'I didn't understand much of his reasoning.' Chu Jui spreads his hands in frustration. 'You spoke insultingly about him to a foreign journalist.'

'Not true.'

Chu Jui holds up his hand. 'Something about military discipline – how you dislike it. And then you don't believe in the Three Principles of Doctor Sun.'

Tang ponders the last strange charge. To his recollection he never replied to Chiang's question about whether he believed in the Three Principles.

'And the mistress. He's especially incensed about her.' Chu Jui chuckles ruefully. 'He calls her a traitorous act.'

A detachment of soldiers is walking down the path, having come from prayers at the temple.

'He said something about its being all right to have a British or American or Italian woman or whatever, but not a Russian. An act of treason on your part.' With a sigh Chu Jui takes a silver flask from the KMT uniform he's wearing and drinks from it, grimacing. 'Want some *mao tai*? I seem to be addicted to it lately.'

'Are you telling me cooperation between Chiang and me is no longer possible?'

'That's right.'

'I didn't get that impression from him.'

'I'm sure you didn't,' Chu Jui observes with another laugh. 'When I left Shanghai to carry a message for him to Canton, I'm sure I felt secure in his friendship. Now that I'm back, I feel in need of a trip abroad.'

'Where will you go?'

Chu Jui shrugs. 'Out of his grasp, if possible.'

'Is it really that bad?'

'I won't take the chance of finding out.' Chu Jui takes another drink from the flask, showing his long teeth after swallowing. 'I'll be frank, because I don't expect we'll meet again. If ever you decide to use these words against me –' He raises his hand again to prevent Tang from denying the possibility. 'I won't be around to suffer from it. I like you, Shan-teh. I respect you. Perhaps I even believe in you. That's why I'm saying these things. Listen carefully. This man is changing the way things are done. The intrigues and inconclusive skirmishes of yesterday are gone. Gentlemen soldiers no longer have a place. Because this man is deadly serious and tremendously forceful. He interest is power, its increase for himself, its temporary distribution among others. In the past our way of fighting was to pit two weaks against one strong – that kept a sensible balance. But with Chiang there's no balance between opposing forces; there's no coexistence with anyone who's against him. He's changing the pattern. His is two strongs against one weak; then one strong against the other. His is a war of annihilation. His goal is absolute power, with no distribution of it beyond his own two hands.'

For a long time they sit in silence.

All of a sudden Chu Jui begins talking again, this time in his usual jocular way. Has the General tried the wine of the region? The best is from Shao-hsing, and that means the best in China. What makes it so good is the lake water with which it's made. (Tang feels as though he's listening to Shih, the KMT agent.) The wineries are only a few hours' ride by horse – worth the trip. 'Ah, but I forget,' Chu Jui says merrily, 'there won't be wine here as long as Chiang Kai-shek stays – he never drinks. The monks will bring it back when he leaves. Shan-teh, *you* leave tomorrow.'

'You think I should?'

'There's nothing but trouble here for you now. Go while he's in a happy mood.'

'What makes him happy?'

'The Reds in the South are being routed. They've lost Nanchang and Chuchow in rapid succession. Swatow has repelled them. They aren't strong enough to undertake action now, but they keep fighting. Perhaps they want to get it over with. So Chiang's happy today. He sees an end to the Red bandits. Mao Tse-tung has been caught – the agitator from Changsha?'

'I've heard of him.'

'I suspect they've shot him by now. Chiang is pleased today, so it's a good time to leave.'

'I'll leave in the morning.' Tang adds, 'My dear friend, I thank you.'

Chu Jui shakes his head, refusing the gratitude. 'If I were still in his favor, perhaps I'd have told you none of this.'

'But you told me. You are risking it.'

'Yes, I suppose that's true. Are you sure you won't have a drink?' Chu Jui looks at the silvery side of his flask, glittering in sunlight through the pine trees. 'If you are near ink, you'll become black. I'm talking about myself, you understand. And Chiang Kai-shek.' With a sigh he looks closely at the General. In a voice now slurred from *mao tai*, he turns to another subject: the leftist politician Wang Ching-wei, whom he has just left in Canton.

Tang once met Wang Ching-wei at a conference in Peking. Many years ago, as a youthful rebel, Wang tried to assassinate a Manchu prince, but the bomb didn't go off. Later he was an ardent follower of Sun Yat-sen, became head of the Propaganda Department of the KMT, deferred to Borodin when the Russian came to Canton, but never himself became a Communist. He has always wanted to walk in Doctor Sun's footsteps, but in spite of excellent qualities as a public speaker and a politician, he has lacked the personal magnetism of his mentor, perhaps because of a tendency to be irresolute.

Chu Jui explains that Wang Ching-wei, his aspirations still intact, is interested in talking to a northern warlord of importance. Wang has therefore extended an invitation through Chu Jui for the General to visit Canton. For their mutual benefit.

'What benefit could there be?' Tang asks.

'Wang is cautious. He won't criticize Chiang Kai-shek openly, but I think he wants an alliance with other men in case Chiang goes down. And he thinks Chiang will go down – through weakness in judgment.' Chu Jui, sitting back, leans against the wall of the prayer hut. 'Will you go to Canton and see him?'

'I'll think about it.'

'Would you need an interpreter?'

'No, I can speak enough Yue. I learned it when my father was stationed in Canton. But I should get back to Qufu. I don't trust my chief of staff.'

'And you wish to see the Russian.' Chu Jui slaps his thigh. 'Forgive me. I shouldn't have said that. It's the *mao tai* speaking.'

Tang likes the man's natural responsiveness. Food, drink, love, an interest in the peace of a monastery – Chu Jui is not complicated, a welcome relief after Chiang Kai-shek. 'I do wish to see her,' Tang admits with a smile.

'If you go to Canton, at least you'll not have wasted the time and effort of coming all this way.'

'It's not been wasted. Now I know Chiang Kai-shek.'

'And it's important to know him.' Chu Jui grins slyly. 'But do you really know him? Did he tell you he's given up wife and concubine on principle?'

'To promote equality.'

'But did he tell you of the beautiful young lady, educated in America, who belongs to one of the great families? Did he tell you an alliance with her will give him the best business contacts in the land and also bind him to the house of Sun Yat-sen? Did he tell you all that?' Chu Jui laughs, taking out the flask again. 'Did he tell you he's going to Japan?'

'He told us yesterday he's going abroad for five years to study economics.'

'He's going to Japan. He's going to meet the young lady's mother and persuade the old lady, who's vacationing there, that a divorced Buddhist is good enough for her Christian daughter.' Chu Jui, face darkened by drink, leans toward the General and shows his long teeth in a wide grin. 'The Generalissimo wants to marry a Christain.' He gets up unsteadily. 'Walk slowly, my friend.'

Next morning General Tang Shan-teh is southward bound on a coastal steamer, heading for Canton.

19

Each morning Embree looks at himself in a broken shard of mirror borrowed from a soldier in a nearby tent.

Nameless No Name.

Perhaps now he has really earned the name, for who is this tanned, blue-eyed stranger with the blond beard and the ugly purple scar across his forehead? Nameless No Names? Or the Ax Man? Or Philip Embree? Perhaps least of all the last.

Each day he hones his ax and trains with the Big Sword Company of the Fourth Cavalry Battalion. Like the other men, he retires soon after the evening meal and rises at dawn. Like them he accepts the camp monotony as a soldier's lot, although unlike them he has memories of another sort of life to sustain him through the long hours. Earlier he'd tried to forget his past in order to fully enter his new world, but now he conjures up visions of America: not because he misses it, but because such memories are a way of maintaining alertness. In consequence he doesn't flag on the prolonged marches and remains free of the common grumbling. His companions, Fu Chang-so among them, look at Embree with a mixture of admiration and wonder, for the Ax Man seems to thrive where they merely exist. They can't know that sometimes he thinks of himself as Douglas Fairbanks, a film swashbuckler who comes to China under the name of Embree and keeps an ax shoved in his belt.

Recently Embree's recall has been stimulated by happenstance: A soldier, buying something in town, came back with it wrapped in newspaper. Noticing it was not a Chinese paper, the men brought it to the Ax Man to see if he knew the language.

It was English – an edition of a Peking newspaper.

Avidly Embree read – no, devoured – it, surprising himself by his passion for news. Poring over the torn, soiled paper, he exulted in the shape of English words, the twenty-six signs in their subtle combinations, instead of the endless scratchings of Chinese. The first American item he came upon was about St. Louis, Missouri, where a tornado killed ninety people on 30 July 1927. The second had to do with President Coolidge, who starkly announced on 2 August, 'I do not choose to run for President in 1928.' The name Coolidge brought a flood of memories – Coolidge was father's idol. He remembered father at dinner, after a long, solemn prayer of thanksgiving, pounding the table until the plates jumped, exonerating Coolidge from any guilt in Teapot Dome and barking out the presidential watchword: 'Thrift!' Next to Coolidge the names of household gods were Mellon, Hoover, Kellogg. And with a little effort Embree can hear his father boom across the mashed potatoes, 'As the President has said time and again, there's no right to strike against the public safty by anybody, anywhere, any time!' Perhaps that's why Embree has never developed a political conscience – father sucked from the atmosphere all of the politics in it, leaving none for Embree to breathe, as the minister opposed entrance of America into the League of Nations, disapproved of government relief to farmers, and put his stamp of approval on any utterance coming from the White House.

Coolidge. Father.

Now Coolidge is out. Embree smiles. A twinge of fear – will he ever see father again? It hasn't yet occurred to him that his failure to communicate with father might end in *irrevocable* separation. He still has something to learn about adventuring: That the adventurer doesn't live by the same rules others do; that he accepts as temporary what others believe is permanent.

Then another item in the English-language Peking paper: a printed attack by Fundamentalist missionaries against their Modernist brethren in China. They dub the National Christian Council, largely Presbyterians and Congregationalists, 'ecclesiastical Bolsheviks.' So communism has come to religion, Embree thinks. He reads on with delicious amusement: 'Satan's adaptation of Christianity has put into the lead of the Modernist movement a band of ecclesiastical Bolsheviks who work on the principle of boring-from-within, feeding on Christianity to destroy it.' A certain reverend (Secretary of the Christian Endeavor Union) lets the idea gather steam: 'The Council has a large army run by well-trained officers and a marvelous intelligence department with secret codes, wireless communications, and well-equipped training camps right here in China. It is liberally financed and secretly allied with other great subversive organizations that also have abundant funds.'

This is not flagrant burlesque, Embree realizes, but a serious attack. He's thankful for having moved beyond the limits of a fate that would have made such squabbles central to his life. Not that he despises them all, the missionaries, but he can't understand them. Never could. Starting with his own father. And as for fate – how did he come to his? Embree refuses to tackle that question. Shaking off theology, he goes riding with Fu Chang-so and other comrades from the Big Swords. Or sometimes he has a little rice wine and dinner in town with a young artillery officer, Fan Chen-wu. He's the aide who replaced Yang, the treacherous young officer at Thousand Buddha Mountain. Embree perceives why the ambitious captain wishes to befriend him – his knowledge of the West – and indeed, most of their time together is spent with Captain Fan asking questions, Embree answering them.

Fan's especially interested in the cinema. He fairly beams while Embree describes, almost scene by scene, such movies as *Safety Last* with Harold Lloyd and *Raffles* with John Barrymore. The young Chinese adjusts his glasses tensely and listens to yet another rendition of Douglas Fairbanks in *The Black Pirate* fighting off eight swordsmen at once or James Pierce, as Tarzan, rescuing Dorothy Dunbar from crocodiles.

It is Fan who one day invites him for dinner at Qufu's best restauran – to which Embree hasn't yet gone – to meet Madam Rogacheva, a friend of the General's up from Shanghai. Fan doesn't seem to know that they've already met by accident in town. But surely Fan knows that he knows the woman is a concubine.

Embree struggles with the knowledge that his own idea of concubinage is un-Chinese. For him the word 'concubine' conjures up the slatternly companion of a fat merchant. For the Chinese, however, it also means the imperial women of ancient times who were treated at court like queens instead of mistresses. To have a girl from your family taken into royal concubinage was to reach Heaven, and all that Heaven implies to the Chinese: money, prestige, unlimited power. Grandmothers of such girls basked in the honor. Little nieces stared in wonder at their heroine aunts who shared the royal bed.

'What languages does the lady speak?' Embree asks, smoking a bamboo pipe – he has taken up the habit in camp.

'Very fine Chinese,' Fan claims.

'And English? I don't speak Russian.'

'She speaks only a little English.'

'If she's Russian, she must speak French.' Embree puffs energetically. 'I hope my French is good enough. Otherwise we'll have to use Chinese.'

The idea of foreigners talking together in his language rather than their own appeals to Fan. He guffaws loudly and orders another earthenware jug of yellow wine.

From the street this restaurant looks no better than others in Qufu, but Embree knows that in China it's impossible to equate the appearance of a restaurant with its food. And anyway, he's not interested in food. All day he's been thinking of the Russian woman – and of how little he knows about women. Most of his childhood was spent in a boy's school; then he went to a male college and a divinity school without female students. Until the age of twenty-three he was a virgin, and his time with pretty Fu-fang, unlucky Fu-fang, was dismally short.

Entering the small candlelit restaurant, he blinks to get his eyes accustomed to the dimness. In the far corner he notices Captain Fan and the Russian woman. Fan rises. The woman smiles in the flickering light. Embree's aware of being overwhelmed by that smile – stunned by it. He goes toward them, murmurs a few words of polite Chinese, and sits down, timidly.

Captain Fan beams. The woman is saying something, leaning forward with that smile.

Embree ins't sure what she is speaking – it's not Chinese and doesn't sound like Russian. After she repeats it a few times (looking more and more uncomfortable), he understands the English phrase: 'I regret not speaking better English.' He feels young, stupid, and hates himself for glancing sideways at her, lugubriously. With effort he forces a smile and attempts a non-chalance he doesn't feel. In Chinese he asks if they may speak French, a request she refuses with a vigorous shake of her head.

Sensing that the foreigners are ill at ease, Captain Fan brings up the subject of food. Embree agrees impatiently to all his suggestions while stealing glances at Madam Rogacheva, who is turned to the Captain and his Chinese enthusiasm for certain dishes served here. She wears a high-collared, plum-colored

Chinese dress. Embree wants to look directly at her, as if to memorize what he sees, but this mustn't be done. He's appalled by the effort it takes to stop staring at the woman, who suddenly turns to him and asks something.

America? She's asking about America. Fired by her curiosity, he talks at breakaway speed about everything he knows, taking up suggestions from her and explaining at considerable length what he knows of a subject and guessing at what he doesn't: the American fashions, the American museums, the American automobiles. Slowly he realizes that her questions are those of a European aristocrat, concerning aesthetics and the stylish life, about which he knows little. Still, he tries to recall details and fabricates the rest. Yes, glass-bead necklaces are still fashionable in New York. No, headbands are going out. He agrees with her that Frank Lloyd Wright's slab-constructed skyscraper (she read about it once in a Shanghai magazine) is really quite ugly (he has no idea what slab construction is).

Embree's better on movies. When Madam Rogacheva maintains that all Shanghai awaits the showing of *Ben Hur*, he's able to assert – truthfully – that he saw it before leaving the States. Their eyes meet as they lean toward each other across the little of dishes. He describes energetically the M-G-M spectacular with the great Ramon Navarro and the even greater Francis X. Bushman and the lovely young Myrna Loy (though to his mind, this woman is lovelier).

He decides Madam Rogacheva is an intelligent listener. It's all in the way she leans forward, full lips slightly parted, green eyes expressively fixed on him. He feels depressed, though, that the woman is older than he is – perhaps as much as four or five years. yet she's still young. And that's what makes the difference of age so depressing. If she were really older, perhaps ten years, he'd never think of her this way. What way? He can't think of her any way. Gloomily ending the description of another film he saw before leaving America, Embree turns to the food, as if hungry.

They eat awhile in silence until Madam Rogacheva asks him in her deep voice, almost mannish in its resonance, why he has remained in the General's army instead of continuing to Peking and taking up his studies.

So they've discussed me, Embree thinks; he's flattered.

Boyishly – later he'll recall with disgust his open enthusiasm – Embree speaks of his need for adventure, his hatred of a staid life. Without considering his words, Embree brags of the whole family's love of roving, and comes within a hair's-breadth of admitting he comes from generations of Christian missionaries who've traveled the world. He tells her, at any rate, that his ancestors have lived everywhere, under the most difficult circumstances. 'My father is the wildest of them all,' Embree lies proudly. 'But I intend to outdo him.'

'So fun, not principle, keeps you here,' the woman comments coolly. 'From the General's estimate of you, I had thought you believed in his value to the country.'

For the first time Embree looks at her appraisingly – to judge her motives rather than appreciate her beauty. He has the distinct feeling she lies about the General's discussing him. What she wants is his opinion of the General.

She cares only what I think of General Tang.

Embree is now cautious. 'I do believe in the General,' he declares with civility. 'And his value to the country.'

'Are you a student of art, Mister Embree?'

He admits that art has never much interested him. Now she takes up the burden of their conversation – he's impressed at her quickness in sensing his change of mood: from warm to cool. While he finishes a course of bean curd and pork, Madam Rogacheva relates a story that in her opinion illustrates the originality of Chinese aesthetics: something about ancient scholars at the game of composing poems while their wine cups, released by servants upstream, float gently down the current; the poems must be finished before the cups reach the scholars sitting on the bank. 'Of course,' she says, 'losers had to drink the wine as a forfeit.'

'That's interesting.'

'Yes, isn't it.'

I don't interest her, Embree thinks. She thinks I'm young, inexperienced. I should never have crowed about staying in the army for the sake of adventure. She doesn't think I'm serious.

And now, he realizes, she is on to something else – a child, a little girl from the Kong family.

I should have said I believe in the General's politics, his hope for China, a country I love. Effusive. It would have impressed her.

'Naturally I realize the Kong family allows me to see her only because of the General.'

'Because of the General?'

'Yes, because he gives them protection. Bright Lotus is a delight.'

Her comment, made with childlike enthusiasm, allows Embree to forget his frustration; he listens, admiring her, while Madam Rogacheva describes the child and what they do together. Bright Lotus and sometimes her five-year-old brother come to the courtyard every morning with a nursemaid. Sometimes they bring cages of fighting crickets. Bright Lotus is very good at arousing the insects by touching their antennae with a long mouse whisker, but nevertheless, she won't let them at each other for fear they'll get hurt. Madam Rogacheva laughs.

She is beautiful, Embree thinks.

'If the General thinks it's a good idea, I'm going to buy them a dog. I think a dog's a much better pet than fighting crickets, don't you?'

Always the General.

'They shave the little boy's head, and I've heard the uncle calling him "turtle" and "*wonk*." '

'Aren't those terms of abuse?'

'Of course, Evil spirits hear him called insulting names; they think he's worthless and leave him alone.'

'Do you think the Kongs, educated people, actually believe such nonsense?'

'No,' After a pause (she presses forefinger against lower lip) Madam Rogacheva adds, 'But I suppose they want to make sure.'

There's something innocent about her, Embree decides. And sad too. He realizes he's staring at her; instantly looking away, he seeks the attention of Captain Fan, who has hardly uttered a word, but sits beaming, enraptured by the success of the evening.

Madam Rogacheva finally brings it to an end. She offers Embree a ride out to camp in the General's car.

'I have my horse,' he explains with pride. 'I call him Marengo after Napoleon's white horse, although mine's brown and no thoroughbred.'

'I don't care for Napoleon,' she replies curtly with a frown, which is immediately followed by a rather embarrassed smile. 'But I love horses. Apparently you do too. I hear you sleep on one.'

Although he takes this for an oblique compliment, Embree tries not to show it; regret for his earlier boyishness has made him suddenly rigid. Clearing his throat, he thanks Captain Fan for the evening.

As they rise to leave, Madam Rogacheva says with a smile, 'My name is Vera.'

Rejecting the invitation to offer his own given name, Embree merely nods. He won't appear young and foolish at their parting.

At the entrance she turns again to ask if it's true the soldiers call him the Ax Man.

He acknowledges, coolly, it is true.

'Where's the ax tonight?'

'I left it in camp,' Embree tells her, hearing the defensiveness in his voice. He tries to soften his tone. 'It's the first time I've been without it in months. Since I first got it.'

'With the bandits?'

She knows everything. So they *have* discussed me, Embree thinks. 'Yes, with them.'

'And what is your name?'

Instantly he tells her, with appreciation for her persistence. 'Philip. I am Philip.'

'I enjoyed our dinner, Philip.'

He detects in her pronunciation of his name a strong French accent.

'Life in Qufu can be dreary with the General gone,' she continues with a smile. 'You've been kind to entertain me this evening.' Turning to young Captain Fan: 'Both of you.'

Philip Embree watches as the beautiful woman drives into the night. Mounting Marengo, galloping off in the direction of camp, he fells exhilarated and depressed. What he can't understand, given his background, is how this European aristocrat can sacrifice everything, the world of Shanghai and surely the attentions of many Westerners there, for a Chinese general who lives in an outlying town. How can she? He doesn't ask himself a similar question: How can he, a missionary's son assigned to a mission in Harbin, remain here too at the call of that same general? Trotting through the dark streets toward camp, Embree not only wonders why Madam Rogacheva – Vera – could have taken such a step, but feels angry with the General for allowing her to do so.

The next few days Embree carries his resentment everywhere, at the same time dwelling on the memory of her loveliness. He feels as lovesick as a boy and hates himself for it. Even so, this embarrassing infatuation has taught him, so Embree believes, that he never really loved Fu-fang; he had merely wanted her. What he does want someday is a woman like Madam – like Vera Rogacheva. He can't get her out of his mind: the straight hair cut in bangs across her white forehead, her full lips, her swelling bosom from which he could hardly take his eyes, the silk Chinese gown containing a softness that makes his mouth dry when he brooks on the mystery there. He pictures her in the flagrantly romantic terms of those penny romances so popular among churchwomen whom father used to excoriate for their silly pastime.

And her deep-set green eyes.

He'd noticed a liquidity about them, as if tears were constantly edging toward their corners. Stupid, stupid romance. Yet the image of her drives him through the day, and thoughts of her, like worrisome flies, keep at him in the night, when in the dark garlicky tent he tosses and turns and hates the tumescence which prevents him from sleeping.

And it's not only her beauty that torments him, but her aura of mystery as well – the suggestion of sadness, of terrors endured beyond anthing his puny imagination can conceive. On horseback or by a campfire or inside the smelly tent, Embree endows her with mythic resonances: the lovely woman, inaccessible, historied in pain and suffering, turning to him with a wan smile, unable to unburden herself of a past that has led her somehow to this bondage in a Chinese town.

In constructing his fantasy, Embree thinks of another woman too. It is not Fu-fang. It is not the girl he nearly raped in Landlord Wang's courtyard. It is surely not his fiancée, whose name he has nearly forgotten.

It is his siter, Mary.

For she too is a woman of mystery. She left home for New York and husbands and lovers and life in Greenwich Village among the speakeasies and artists' lofts, when Embree was still in his teens. She was a free spirit, unashamed, an adventurer like Douglas Fairbanks and Jack London. Like Vera Rogacheva. In his brooding mind Embree mixes the two women, American sister and Russian emigrant, until from the caldron of his thoughts he fashions a startling creature, unattainable but dazzling and fearless, the wished-for emblem of an adolescent dream.

So overwhelmed is Embree that when he's given permission to

ride into town for an afternoon, he heads straight for the restaurant where they'd dined. He reins Marengo in and stares at the entrance, wryly aware that in boyhood, smitten by a girl from the next block, he'd once stood under an elm and gazed at the upper window where she played after school with some girl friends. Looking at the barred entrance of the restaurant, but in truth seeing Vera inside it, leaning toward him, her slightly pointed chin resting on one white hand, Embree at last wrests himself free of the romantic indulgence, brutally kicks his horse into a fast trot, and weaves through a crowd of frightened porters in the narrow street.

Coming to the main road, he notices under the Drum Tower, which dominates the broad intersection, a huge man – too big for a Chinese – shambling along beside someone who is gripping his arm.

The Russian. Led by his Chinese Bolshevik companion as if he were a performing bear.

Embree hasn't seen the pair in weeks, but they're often the butt of sexual jokes in camp. Soldiers are amused by the big Russian's addiction to *Ta-yen* and contemptuous as well – they boast that no foreigner knows how to handle the stuff. A few have sworn off their own weekly pipes, not out of fear of the General's standing order that opium smokers will be severely punished, but out of the desire to prove they don't need it like the foreigner does. In effect, the Bolshevik has become a moral force in the army.

From the look of him now, however, Embree judges his deterioration has been swift, furious: dirty pants and shirt; immense black beard and shaggy hair framing a haggard face with rheumy eyes; the powerful frame hunched; feet bare in the dust; trembling hand gripping the shirt, chest high.

A dying bear led by his little Chinese master.

Embree decides to avoid them by riding down the opposite side of the road. But then he sees, approaching the pair, Vera Rogacheva mounted on a spirited roan. Embree reins in and watches.

Vera is wearing high boots, riding breeches, a silk blouse – perhaps this Western habit was tailored locally – with her dark hair hidden beneath a wide-brimmed straw hat which does not, however, obscure her face. She's more beautiful than Embree's fantasies have allowed, and the sight throws him into confusion. Shall he cross over to greet her? Or ride quickly away?

Meanwhile, she has pulled up in front of the Russian, who is doing something inexplicable.

He is holding out one hand, palm up, in the attitude of a beggar, while the little Chinese, yanking at his other hand, tries to lead him away.

The woman on horseback must be communicating her nervousness to the stallion, because he keeps shifting in the dust, his powerful haunches quivering above the dainty hooves.

As the roan moves in this agitated manner, the Russian man attempts to follow it, his hand still outstretched. Embree can't hear from this distance, but he sees the lips moving in the bearded face. Kovalik stumbles but keeps moving around to match the skittish steps of the horse. Above him Vera Rogacheva stares contemptuously, her facial muscles set with such tension that Embree can see them across the road. She's holding the reins with both hands, a riding crop gripped between them, in her attempt to quiet the stallion, but he continues to jitter sideways, rolling his huge rump.

Now she is saying something. The words are louder and clearer than the Bolshevik's, but Embree can't understand them – they are Russian.

Suddenly the woman's arm is raised, the riding crop descends and strikes the man on the shoulder. It goes up and comes down again and again, slashing at his face, while ineffectually he lifts both arms to ward off the blows. The horse, wildly agitated, rears and stutters in the dust, but in spite of it Vera Rogacheva, leaning far out of the saddle, strikes furiously, without pause, even after Kovalik loses his footing and slumps to the ground. Again and again the crop descends, wielded so blindly that most of the swings miss and a few hit the stallion whose prancing above the fallen man threatens to crush him.

The Chinese companion, grabbing one of Kovalik's feet, begins to drag him out of striking range.

It is at this moment, impelled by emotions too deep for him to understand, that Philip Embree kicks Marengo into a gallop that brings him quickly across the road. He goes directly to the fallen Russian and the Chinese, who is still hauling the big fellow back, toward an earthen wall near the edge of the broad road. There's blood on the Russian's clothes; two long cuts, bleeding profusely, mark his forehead and left cheek. He's breathing heavily, his parted mouth revealing yellowish teeth.

Embree calls out harshly, 'Get him out of here! How dare he bother Madam Rogacheva!'

Li nods and continues pulling Kovalik toward the wall.

Uncertain for a moment, Embree follows on horseback, one hand on the ax. He feels a sudden righteous fury, and in retrospect he'll ask himself if he might have used the ax had the injured Russian said one word. Li, having got the big fellow to the wall, says nothing. Kovalik, looking sleepy rather than in pain, licks the blood from his lips and stares into midair.

'If he ever does that again –' Embree begins in strident Chinese.

'No, don't!'

Embree whirls around to face the woman.

She repeats it, 'No, don't! Leave him alone!' Under the straw hat her face looks pale. A stray beam of sunlight reveals tears in her eyes.

'I'm sorry,' Embree says, as if this encounter has been his fault. 'If he's done anything –'

'Done anything!' She laughs and draws one silken arm across her eyes; they are filled with the tears of anger. 'He and his dirty kind have done everything that can be done!' Reining her house and heading it away from Embree, she answers his question before he can ask it, before he can even think of asking it. 'No, don't come with me. Thank you, I'll go alone.' With the riding crop she points at the Russian sitting against the wall. 'Better get him to his quarters. Can you do that? Thank you.' And without another word Vera kicks her mount into a steady trot, leaving the trio of men and a gathering crowd behind.

Turning to the Chinese and the Russian, Embree says to Li, 'We will put him on my horse.'

'Please, sir, it's not necessary,' Li protests. 'I'll take care of him.'

'I said we will put him on my horse. You heard Madam Rogacheva.' Turning a moment, Embree glances at the receding house and rider. There are two sweat circles visible on her silken back where her arms join her shoulders. I love her, Embree tells himself. I love her, I really do love her.

'What did I say to her?' Kovalik asks numbly, looking up from the bed at Li.

'You asked for money.'

452

Kovalik shakes his head. 'No, I could never have done that.'

'Yes, you could, For *Ta-yen.*'

'I could not.'

'You hadn't money for more pipes, remember? So you asked her.'

'I could not.'

'You'd have asked anyone for money, my friend.'

'Not that Czarist bitch.' Kovalik glances around the room, then sits up. 'Did she say anything?'

'She asked if you were the Bolshevik.'

He laughs gruffly. 'Did she need to ask?'

'And you kept asking for money.'

Kovalik shakes his head. 'Ridiculous. It could never have happened.'

'Friend, you will have scars to prove it.'

Getting up unsteadily, Kovalik staggers to the small mirror nailed on the wall; he had put it there in their early days, a measure of his past vanity. Staring at the haggard image with two deep cuts, Kovalik lets out a groan of shame and anguish. He begged from a Czarist bitch? Let her whip him like a dog? Kovalik shuffles back to the bed and throws himself down, sprawling there with his eyes fixed on the ceiling.

All he can remember is the white face with the aristocratic chin, delicately pointed, and the two large holes under the wide-brimmed hat from which she watched him like a snake. Begging money from a Czarist bitch? Impossible. She said something, called him something in their own language. Was it traitor? Yes, it was traitor. What a thing to say! She thought of him as a traitor to the Czar! Kovalik shakes his head in wonder. All he can remember of it then is the whip descending. He can't even remember the terrible pain of stretching his hand out to beg from one of them, the venal Czarists who bled his country of wealth and dignity for centuries.

Aroused from his reverie by Li, who puts a wet compress on his head, Kovalik brushes it aside impatiently. 'How did we get back? I remember a horse. Was I lying across the saddle?'

Li, nodding, puts the cloth back; this time Kovalik lets it stay.

'Whose horse?' Kovalik's appalled by the possibility that the Czarist bitch got off her house and helped to throw him across her saddle. 'Whose? Whose horse?'

'The American's. You remember him?'

'Oh, yes. Him. The one with the ax who sleeps on horses.'
Kovalik sighs with relief: Thank God it wasn't hers.

During a long silence he tries to think clearly. I've got to, Kovalik tells himself. 'I know this is a strange question, friend, but I don't know where we get money.'

'Now and then I get some from an officer.'

Kovalik raises himself on his elbows to took at Li. 'From one of Tang's officers?'

'Yes, a Captain Fan Chen-wu. The General's aide.'

'Why does he give us money?'

Li shrugs. 'He says we're the General's guests. It's the General's pleasure.'

Kovalik lies back, sighing. The Chinese general, whose Czarist bitch it was who beat him, also enjoys humiliating him. He would be better off if the woman had shot him instead of cutting his face with a whip. Glancing at Li, he murmurs, 'Why do you stay with me?'

Li wrings out a compress and places it on his brow. 'Because we were assigned together to this mission.'

'You call this a mission?' Kovalik laughs ruefully.

'And because you're my friend.'

Kovalik stares at him. 'You put that much faith in friendship?'

'It's a Chinese tradition.'

A correct Bolshevik should point out that it's against tradition their Communist movement is directed. But he can't tell Li that; perhaps friendship's the only good thing in this forsaken land.

'Do we have money now?'

'We've spent it.'

'You mean I've spent it.' I've spent everything, he thinks: my hope, his, our mutual courage. I've spent his will to live and work as much as my own, and if there was a god to pray to, I'd do it – for forgiveness. But there's another way to make amends, isn't there. 'When you get money from the Captain, don't give me any.'

'You mean it?'

'Don't let me have it whatever I say or do – or threaten. Don't give me money under any circumstances.'

'Are you sure of this?'

'Yes, I'm sure.'

'Friend, look at me.'

Kovalik does.

'*Ta-yen* is a hard master. He'll make you pay for disobeying him.'

'Don't give me money. Ever again. But save it.'

'Save it?'

'Until we speak of this later. But we won't speak of money until I'm out of *Ta-yen's* grip.'

'If you wish.'

There's a strong note of doubt in Li's voice that troubles Kovalik. Even so, he replies, 'Yes, it's what I wish.'

So it begins, the withdrawal, and Kovalik has no illusions about the difficulty. In the Qufu den, while he lay on the bench after smoking, he has often heard through Li's translation the other men talk of *Ta-yen's* possessiveness. They laughed and called *Ta-yen* 'the landowner who gives up nothing.' While the cinnamon-scented smoke drifted through the room, they'd exchange stories of their own fruitless attempts to break away. 'I was free of him,' an old man once said with a laugh, 'for a whole week. I was lying there trembling like a cold dog, proud of myself, when he came out of nowhere. I saw his true face for the first time.' 'What did he look like?' another man asked. 'Like a demon from hell, believe me. Like every demon you've seen carved in a temple, only worse.' 'What did you do when you saw him?' 'I screamed, naturally, and he laughed. He leaned close and whispered in my ear – I felt the heat of his breath like fire. 'You asshole,' *Ta-yen* said, 'if you think it hurts now, wait a few days, but by then you won't be able to stand the pain, and you'll crawl to me, crawl.' And *Ta-yen* said, 'I'll take you back, fool, but think of the suffering you'll have done for nothing!' 'And what did you say?' 'I told him to go to hell. I was young in those days and tough. I said go fuck a turtle. He just laughed and went away and I kept free of him a few days.' 'And then?' 'It was like he said. The pain was unbearable, so I crawled to him. I crawled out of the house with my wife screaming at me not to go, and I crawled in the snow to *Ta-yen's* house, this house we're in now, and I crawled upstairs where we're lying now, and *Ta-yen* took me back, just like he said he would. And when I smoked then, I saw his face once more, only it wasn't demon's face.' 'Whose was it?' 'It was the face of Kuan Yin.' Both men cackled, their ancient dreamy eyes seeing in the smoke that day the image of the Goddess of Mercy.

Kovalik has not forgotten that, while he starts to feel the initial restlessness that will lead to the stomach cramps. They will nudge him toward the door and a stroll to the house of cloud biting. He waits; yes, the cramps soon come. But instead of leaving the room, he tries coolly to estimate his state of addiction. He has learned to calculate the number of pellets in a gram, the number of grams a user can take. He had begun with about one and a half grams. Most experienced users required three or four a day. No one used twenty grams for long and lived. How many has he been using? He estimates about fifteen to eighteen a day during six or seven hours period of smoking.

He sneezes.

Already he desires the dried opium gum with the look of a cake of cow dung. Lately, like an Indian or a Turk, he's been licking it before heating a pellet in the pipe bowl. They say Afghans often drink it. Thinking of *Ta-yen*, his nose running copiously, Kovalik knows if he had it now he would bathe in it, put it in his ears, up his ass, he'd take it anywhere. Sneezing and yawning, but with increasing agitation, he sits up, then walks around the room. Li won't leave, but sits unobtrusively in a corner. Within two days Kovalik forgets which corner, forgets Li. He's obsessed with grams, with the number of pipefuls he'd get from so many grams. He's obsessed with his companions at the den, their traits – how they hold the pipe or scrape the bowl or suck the smoke in – and how many pellets they use each day. He works desperately at recalling the exact number of every man's daily pipes, although they've never told him how many they smoke. Just the same, the attempt to reconstruct precise details of the House of Cloud Biting renders him capable, for short intervals, of forgetting the chills and the sweat oozing from his pores and the violent cramps that are now twisting his guts, wrenching from him, pitiful groans which sound disgusting to his ears. Virulent diarrhea keeps him most of the day in the outhouse behind their quarters. The last flies of late summer flock around him for a feast; soon he's too weak to brush them away from his eyes, his lips. Vomiting comes next. He lies on the boards of the outhouse, his slack mouth awash in blood and bile, his eyes filled with vibrating lights, as beyond the stinking wall poor Li crouches and whispers encouragement.

Kovalik tries hard to remember the Ten Cannots which an old smoker once taught him about opium. At the time he'd laughed; now, swimming in his own fluids, too weak for crawling much less walking, Kovalik goes over each commandment slowly, precisely. One – you cannot enjoy sleep. Two – you cannot rise early. Three – you cannot plan anything. Four – you cannot walk far. Five – you cannot enjoy wealth. Six – you cannot help others. Seven – you cannot get credit. Eight – you cannot wait patiently for your pipe. Nine – you cannot be cured if you fall sick of something. Ten – you cannot escape from *Ta-yen*. It is during one of his many recitations of the Cannots that he sees *Ta-yen*. It is like the old man said, the face of a demon: the huge red eyeballs, the enormous mouth filled with fangs, the flared nostrils smoking. And the old landowner tells him he must stop this foolishness and crawl home with rent money in hand. But Kovalik won't do it. What in hell does torture mean to a man like himself? He was in the Revolution and the Civil War. The memory of what he'd endured doesn't make the stomach cramps less painful, but it assures him of one thing – such horror passes, just as it passed for him in the old days, when he'd been taken prisoner by the Whites in 1919. Lying on the fouled boards of the outhouse, Kovalik in his anguish runs his fingers along the bumps of his back and arms – they are reminders of the old pain, ugly welts received long ago on the train ride. Compared to it this contest with old landlord *Ta-yen* is nothing.

On that train he and his Bolshevik comrades, stripped naked in the winter weather, had been tied to benches in the car. White guards, armed with whips – to the ends of which bullets were tied – strolled up and down the windowless compartment and slashed at the strapped prisoners. At the fourth or fifth cut the guards were ripping out gouts of flesh; after fifty or so, many men died. Those who fainted were doused with cold water that quickly froze on them. There were slits in the floorboards, allowing water and blood to spill out. Such trains felt crimson trails between their tracks for hundreds of miles through Russia, as Bolshevik prisoners were transported to labor camps and death. He remembers the station where the car, uncoupled, stood on a siding for a whole day – unaccountably the Whites gave them some blankets, and of the original hundred, twenty-five or thirty staggered into the noon light, wrapped in those blankets. It was a miracle to be alive, to be in the bright air. Refugees were moving alongside the track, clinging to the rails of sledges pulled by skinny mules. Then Kovalik had been something he has never forgotten, that he remembers even now, with his face lying in vomit on a latrine floor.

First came the Cossacks in their yellow-and-red-striped trousers and their fur hats, riding their sleek horses. They were followed at a brief interval by a line of elegant troikas.

At the window of one troika sat a beautiful woman, swathed to the chin in costly furs.

Kovalik has never forgotten the bored and indifferent look on her splendid face: the pouty lips, the painted eyes, the spit curls hanging negligently over her white forehead.

Now he has begged from such a woman, held out his hand and pleaded for money from such a monster. A fresh seizure of gastric cramps bends him fatally on the reeking floor. Now he experiences what the old man had felt when defying *Ta-yen*: unbearable pain. 'You will crawl home to me. Don't worry. I'll take you back, fool, but think of all that suffering for nothing.'

Kovalik struggles to get up, but finds to his dismay he hasn't the strength. Sinking down again, he tells himself to relax – well, relax as much as possible. Take the cramps, take the nausea, take everything. Hasn't he gone through worse? Of course, he assures himself. Speaking aloud, he says 'Worse!'

'What did you say?' Li asks anxioualy through the latrine wall. 'Did you say something?'

He soon forgets faithful Li. He thinks only of 'worse than this.' Worse, what was worse? He'd been taken from a labor camp – too many prisoners to feed – along with a few hundred other prisoners, maybe more. It was early spring; he has always remembered that. Patches of earth were visible in the snow, whose tendrils receded and left, incredibly, little enclaves of tender new grass. In a field with such emblems of rebirth, the Whites tied their prisoners together in rows, like beads on string. There must have been four or five rows of seated men – Kovalik never counted them – who watched silently while the guards set up machine guns with methodical care. Kovalik had watched too, as if curious about the efficiency of the guards. He recalls a very young guard unable to attach the ammo belt to his gun and an older man scolding him for his awkwardness. A few hundred bound men sitting on the cold spring earth, listening to the metallic click of bolts drawn back. Kovalik remembers the utter calm before the guns began rattling. Rows fell from the center, where the firing began, toward the left and right. The bodies fell against one another like tenpins. Soon there was a tangled heap filled with kicking arms and legs, and the spring afternoon was rent by a terrible scream compounded of many screams, and then by groans and whimpers so bestial that they seem to lose any connection with human sound. Cossacks, riding forward from a nearby hill, lowered their swords and lances to 'prick the ground,' as they called it in their regiments during the old days, finishing off what still gasped with life. Kovalik? Wounded, he'd fallen beneath someone. That night wandering peasants, who came to strip the dead of any valuables, were so surprised by someone still alive that they took whimsical pity on him; they not only pulled him from the mass of corpses, but harbored him in their village until a detachment of Red cavalry came along and rescued him.

Afraid of *Ta-yen*? A man who has known worse?

Yet his body seems in subversive alliance with the old demon. Retching helplessly, Kovalik feels as though a force is driving his eyeballs out of his head. Minutes later – is it minutes? – he hears something other than the fierce pounding at his temples. It is Li. It is Li asking through the outhouse wall if he can help.

'No,' Kovalik croaks, unable to life his head from the floor. The rhythmic cramps are whipping through his bowels like snakes.

'I'll get *Ta-yen*,' Li whispers against thw wall. 'It won't take long. I can go now.'

'Tell *Ta-yen* –' He pants, feeling new sweat gush from his face. How can there still be fluid in his body? He speaks again, weakly but distinctly. He tells *Ta-yen* to go to hell. He says it in Chinese: '*Qu-nide-ba*!'

When was it? Where? He can't remember, but the *dacha* itself remains vivid in his mind – a huge rambling structure with Russian minarets painted gold. Infantry had arrived, along with peasants from a neighboring village, so the looting was already in progress when he got there. He cantered up the long English lawn and dismounted at the colonnaded entrance, hearing from inside the mansion a crash of mirrors. Peasants were dragging clothes and furniture onto the lawn. Necklaces dangled from their sunburned throats. Others swung bottles of expensive wine through the air. In the study he found some boys diligently pulling down the books from shelves twenty feet high. A grizzled soldier, dead drunk, staggered by in a woman's feathered hat. Most of the plastered statues had been overturned and lay shattered on the parquet floor. In a drawing room a few peasants had started a fire with inlaid tables and damask chairs. They were dancing around the smoking heap, urging the flames up. On the back lawn Kovalik found a group of liveried servants herded near a bed of roses. Young soldiers were questioning them. 'What side are you on?' Before the servants could answer, the boys yelled out, 'We represent the side of revolutionary discipline!' and pushed the trembling domestics forward to join others, who were stripping near the stable. It was there they were shot, one by one, in the balmy air. On the west side of the house – he recalls that detail precisely, the west side, because the sun was low on the horizon, a soft golden glow – Kovalik ran into a crowd of peasants who were gathered around something. He joined them to stare too. It was or had been a woman, wearing shreds of a negligee. Doubtless they had surprised her upstairs in a bedroom, taking a nap. Out here, held down, she had been repeatedly raped; that was evident from the pool of blood between her outstretched legs. Then she had been disemboweled, her throat cut as well. From a few yards away she might have looked like someone wrapped in pieces of white cloth, lying asleep on the lawn, with a bucket of hog guts thrown across her belly.

A bearded soldier was wearing a silk scarf around his neck. He grinned at Kovalik and Kovalik grinned back in brutal conspiracy, for in those moments with smoke in his nostrils and drunken laughter in his ears, he hadn't felt sorry for the butchered aristocrat, who alive must have accounted for untold suffering among her serfs – nothing as dramatic as her own end, just small daily tortures that added up to hell. Looking down at the powdered skin, the coiffed hair, the carmine lips, he kicked at her bare feet. 'Czarist bitch,' he muttered to nods of approval from the assembled peasants, who later, when utterly drunk, dipped their arms to the elbows in her entrails and joked obscenely as they strewed the stuff about the lawn.

'Czarist bitch,' he says aloud in his room. Turning, he tooks at Li, who is seated by the window. 'I think I'm hungry. Yes, I'm hungry. I want to eat.'

'My friend, that's very good.'

Kovalik lies back with a sigh. He can feel the wet sheets against his back, his trembling legs. He must have soaked through dozens of them in these terrible days. 'Li, have you seen that captain for money?'

'Yes, he's given me a little.'

'Will he give you more?'
Of course, that's no problem.'
'I didn't think it would be. See him again.'
'Why? We don't need it.'
'Tell him we need quite a bit more, because my landlord *Ta-yen* wants the rent paid.'
'You're going home?' Li asks nervously.
'No. I've got his far, I won't go home.'
'This far, but there's tomorrow.'
'Don't worry about tomorrow.' Because Kovalik isn't worrying about it. He can hold out tomorrow and tomorrow and the other tomorrows. Nothing in the world can keep him from holding out now. Nothing, not the craving that squeezes his bowels, that turns his mind to jelly. He'll puke his guts out until death, but he won't go home to *Ta-yen* where the rent is too high – the price of two scars laid on by the whip of a Czarist bitch.

'How much money do we have now?'
Li tells him.
'Will it buy train tickets to Wuhan?'
'That and more. Is going to Wuhan what you have in mind?'
Standing at the window, Kovalik stares at a huge porcelain pot of chrysanthemums: flowers of the autumn. A gardener must have placed it in the courtyard at dawn, surely not much later, because Kovalik has been at the window all morning, looking for a sign of change, but of course there has been none. Same trees, same rocks, same portico, same pebble mosaic on the courtyard ground. Memories have drifted like clouds through his mind, wisps of recollection, mostly of the war. He keeps seeing a soldier in a 1915 Russian uniform: bedroll over left shoulder, billed cap with three fur flaps, blue epaulettes, heavy boots, sand-brown tunic and trousers. Who is the man? He can't see the face; it's obscured, as if thrown in shadow by sunlight in the background. Perhaps it's the face of a dead comrade; although Kovalik knows he won't ever identify the features, he keeps trying. It's a way of passing time. He has learned how to do that recently. Either he stands at the window recalling long-lost events that may have not occurred or he plays cards with Li, as they used to do in their early days together. For endless hours they slap down the cards on the table, while he fights to hold on. Now that he can walk and keep

461

food in his stomach, it's harder to hold on. *Ta-yen* is a sly bastard. He wants his rent; well, he won't get it.

'We are leaving here,' Kovalik says, facing the window. 'We're going to Wuhan.'

'Can we do that without orders?'

'I haven't gone through all this so I could rot here in comfort. If the movement's still alive, we'll find it in Wuhan.'

'You mean to stay in China?'

'Of course.' He doesn't add, 'Where else can I go?' They both know the truth – he has no country now, only an ideal. Come to think of it, perhaps that's better: to have only an ideal. In Moscow, during political training at the institute, he used to chatter a lot about communism, how it must become a worldwide movement, not simply a means of satisfying Russian interests. He used to brag about his commitment to Trotsky's ideals. Now he has the chance to prove it by working for the cause in a country that seems doomed. China today, perhaps India tomorrow. Then someday France, Germany, all of Europe. Perhaps the world. Regained health has infused Kovalik with wild optimism.

'We'll make plans now,' he tells Li.

'Can you travel?'

'I can. I will.'

Li is fingering the worn deck of cards that Kovalik had brought from Moscow. 'The General might not let us leave.'

'You think he cares if we stay or not?'

'Remember, he's looking for deals. When the generals start offering things, exchanging gifts Chinese style, we may be included as a present.' Li cuts the cards, gazes solemnly at the top one. 'Chiang Kai-shek might be interested in you. Give you a public trial, accuse you of Russian mischief.'

'And you would be summarily shot.'

Li keeps busy with the cards.

'If I'd gone home to *Ta-yen*, what would you have done?'

Li looks up from the cards. 'I would have stayed.'

'In Moscow, training to come here, I was told the Chinese aren't trust-worthy. They're more cunning than loyal. If I ever see Moscow again, I'l go to the school and tell those instructors to go to hell.'

Li shuffles the cards to hide his embarrassment.

Outside nothing has changed, except that three new leaves are lying on the ground, blown there by an early autumn wind.

Everything else is in its ordered position. If he stands at this window until his beard turns white, nothing out there will change. He hates this place. 'I think we must forgo any farewell banquet the General might want to give us in appreciation for all we've accomplished here,' Kovalik says. It's been a long time since he's tried to be witty; the effort is invigorating.

'So we are going.'

'As soon as possible.' Looking at the yard, Kovalik understands now how beauty can be a prison. He hates this place.

'Then I'll find out about trains to Wuhan,' says Li. 'I believe they stop at Tzeyang, about a hundred kilometers from here.'

'How do we get to Tzeyang?'

After some thought, Li shakes his head. 'By foot, Maybe by cart. We must be careful.'

'Who will I be?'

'Well, an exporter. But not Russian.'

Kovalik laughs. 'Hardly Russian. I speak a little German.'

'Then you're a German exporter.' Li cuts the cards again, cuts them again thoughtfully. 'You're in the region looking over this season's crop of soybeans. Shantung soybeans are very fine.'

Kovalik turns to the window. He can't help staring at the court, watching for something to change aside from light and shadow and the placement of fallen leaves. Boredom brings with it a peculiar anxiety, a terrific anticipation of something about to happen.

'Comrade?'

He turns to Li, who is looking up from the cards.

'I have never seen anyone do what you have done,' Li says.

Kovalik stares again at the courtyard in its autumnal stasis. '*Zai jian*,' he says to it. Goodbye.

Wuhan, collective name for three cities at the junction of the Han and Yangtze rivers. Last time Kovalik arrived here he'd looked on its turbulent activity with the benign gaze of someone convinced he is looking at historical change.

He feels different now, as the train pulls into the northernmost city, Hankow. To get a sense of the new mood here, he insists on riding through its streets before going to Communist headquarters. The tall smokestacks of the Liuhokou Ironworks are belching gray columns of smoke; it is clear to Kovalik that the workers, no longer striking for freedom, are again laboring in conformity to the old rules of the bourgeoisie. He had once linked the industrial energy of Hankow to a socialist future: the bean and flour mills, glassworks, metallurgical plants, cigarette factories, match factories, an arsenal, bristle and tallow factories, plants for the processing of goat skins – all at the service of singing Communist workers. Business seems to thrive more than ever, yet the workers are silent. Gloomily he looks at the packing plants and their water tanks feeding automatic sprinklers into hot godowns in an effort to prevent fires that otherwise will lessen the profit of businessmen sitting in New York and Paris. The revolutionary ardor that had impressed him a few months ago has disappeared from the city. At the end of Han Chun Road they come to a large gray building – Borodin's headquarters. Getting out of the rickshaws, they walk up to the heavy wooden door; it is bolted. From some workmen nearby they learn that the building has been purchased by Italians – a few say Danes – for business purposes. The Russians, where are they? The workmen shrug, as if they've never heard of Russians or of a man named Borodin, who less than a year ago had been welcomed to the city by a quarter-million people lining the boulevards, wearing red stars on their shirts, giving the clenched-fist salute. Kovalik stares a long time at the locked building, at the boarded windows, at the blank facade. He had spent many hectic days inside this headquarters before orders sent him to Qufu. Wandering through the rooms, he'd watched the presses run off political leaflets a spirited Wuhan wished to read. Upstairs the great Borodin was receiving everyone important in China. Chain-smoking, running his hands through unruly black hair, the tall and muscular Borodin had dazzled them all – yes, Kovalik too – with his energy, his flamboyance, his dedication to the cause. 'Let's get the hell away from her,' Kovalik mutters to Li and walks back to the rickshaws.

So they return south to the crowded dirty streets of the native quarter, looking for familiar faces. What Kovalik sees everywhere, plastered on walls and storefronts, are anti-Borodin posters condemning the man who had been worshiped here six months ago. Some of them offer money for his head. All of them ask for help in capturing this traitor to the cause of nationalism and Chiang Kai-shek, who six months ago had been his collaborator and friend. What Kovalik sees is young women in the streets with their hair grown past thei ears; when last in town, he'd seen them with their hair bobbed for the revolution. Today fortune-tellers are playing fiddles and tambourines to stir up business. One explains to Li that a bunch of Reds are living in the brothels on Dump Street; but rushing there, the two men discover it's only a rumor. They go to Rosie's, a dance hall run by a Chinese woman married to a Portuguese. Months ago it had been a revolutionary hangout; now it's filled with sullen taxi dancers who swear at them when they ask information. Standing outside in the squalid lane, watching a tailor pressing a shirt with a flatiron filled with charcoal, wondering where to go next, they are called into a tiny herbal store by a girl. She has sneaked out of Rosie's to tell them some Reds are hiding in Hanyang near the freight yard; they should go there and inquire.

So they cross the Han River by sampan, with Tortoise Hill and the Lute Terrace rising above crowded shacks wedged between water and rocky ascent. They walk through the damp little town to the Iron and Steel Works with its great blast furnaces and piles of coke, and find behind the freight yard's heap of limestone a group of hovels, where Li's comrades from the old days are holed up with opium, girls with medium-length hair, and naked children.

A half-dozen crowd around Li, asking for news, and when they see he has none – in fact, has come to them for news – they back off silently and let him and his big foreign companion into their tin-roofed shack, pungent with the smoke of opium.'

Kovalik waits patiently while they look him over and listen to Li's explanation of the journey.

'What do they say?' Kovalik asks, someone motions for him to sit down on a bench.

'They say at least you're not Indian.'

Kovalik laughs heartily. They certainly don't want an Indian. Anyone but an Indian like the tubby little Bengali Communist, M. N. Roy, who in panicky judgment had released a telegram from Stalin proving that the Russians were playing politics in China for their own benefit. Roy's act helped to bring Borodin down, and Borodin's fall led to widespread persecution of Chinese Reds associated with the Russians. Kovalik figures it will be a long time before these men what to see an Indian again.

When a pipe is offered to him, Kovalik refuses, seeing for an instant the alarm in Li's eyes.

'We've come down a long way,' one of the Communists observes grimly. His explanation of the fate of Wuhan's radical activity is short, relentless. When Borodin left the city, a neighboring warlord declared martial law, then put hundreds, maybe thousands, of Reds and unionists to death in the name of the Nationalist movement, even while derogatory posters of Chiang Kai-shek were being put up by warlord troops on the walls of the tricities. Since then the warlords – now this now, now that one – have marched through Wuhan, taking what they wanted, making grand pronouncements, gathering loot for their concubines, hauling treasure away in mule caravans. Agitation among workers increased during the chaos, which only frightened city officials, who came to fear unruly unionists and incoming peasants more than they did the warlord troops. Therefore they cooperated fully with rascals like General Ho Chien who whimsically pardoned the Reds one day and hunted them the next. And yet at the same time, still attempting to obey a Comintern order to be patient, many Communists were trying to mollify the worked-up peasants, who, pleading for law and order, wanted to overthrow the local government and establish soviets in outlying districts immediately. The Red agents, trying to placate these irate farmers, were often murdered by them on the spot, thereby dying for the advantage of their common enemy, Chiang Kai-shek.

'Is it any wonder we take this?' the man says, holding up a pellet of opium. He adds that Ho Chien, a ruthless scourge – who says he's a Nationalist but whose claim no one can substantiate – has been systematically combing the hills of Hunan, south of here, for leftist peasants, slaughtering them without stint. Few radicals are left in Wuhan, as can be imagined. Many of them defected to the Nationalists; many have been killed.

Li asks about old friends. Kovalik watches his comrade's face get smaller and tighter when at the mention of each name the men shake their heads.

'If you want a pipe,' Kovalik tells him, 'have it. Don't worry about me.'

'Thank you, my friend, but no.' Li asks more questions and tells Kovalik that some Red commanders, farther south, have struck out on their own to act independently against the Nationalists. He mentions Chu Teh, who is leading a few thousand troops. Rumor has Ho Lung and Yeh Ting swinging their columns toward Swatow. Mao Tse-tung, in command of a small force of peasants, was defeated by local militia mear Changsha. They say he was captured at Hengyang and executed.

'Executed? I remember him,' Kovalik says. 'We argued one night. Ask these men who is heading the Russian delegation here – if there still is one.'

Li discovers that Soviet Russia is now represented officially for the moment by a man called Besso Lominadze. He's somewhere here in Wuhan.

Lominadze is an arrogant young Georgian, lazy and incompetent, whom Kovalik recalls only too well. They drank authentic Russian vodka together one evening in Wuhan. Obtaining good liquor and rare edibles was the fellow's only virtue, in Kovalik's opinion. Now Besso Lominadze is in charge of Russia's destiny here – quite a task when his address is virtually unknown – while his world-famous predecessor, Mikhail Borodin, must be sinking into a vast bureaucratic quagmire of obscurity, pushed into it by Stalin, who surely doesn't want to give the opposition loyal to Trotsky a political advantage because of the fiasco in China. So the mighty fall, the worthless rise, even in a socialist society. It's a proposition Kovalik has always resisted until now. For a moment he stares longingly at the pipe held by one of the drowsy men.

Days lengthen into weeks in the shantytown of Hanyang at the foot of Tortoise Hill. Kovalik watches some of the men wander into an opium world too far ever to emerge from it. Infrequently, Li has a pipe; he is one of those people who, by some miracle of character, seem to escape addiction. As for Kovalik's reaction to so much smoking, he can now watch it without pain. Something has come between him and the old urge. It's like the early days of the Revolution, when he strolled with comrades through the streets of Moscow, flowers thrust into the barrels of their guns, as they bawled loudly, 'All power to the workers' soviets!' Now he squats at the entrance of the mud-and-corrugated-tin hovel where he and Li are staying; instead of paying rent to the demon landlord, he conjures his own dreams, while around him push and shoulder the emaciated poor of Hanyang. He begins to recall the good things about his country: say, a modest little restaurant in winter, with the windowpanes frosted white and scraggly tree limbs tapping the glass in the wind; people hurry by with scarves over mouths, earflaps down, icicles in beards and lashes, while inside at the white-clothed tables the diners enjoy the rosy glow of squat stoves, whose blackened flues rise to high ceilings, mingling there with laughter and the scrape of fiddles. The hot soups, the black breads, the heavy cheeses. Little things, too: say, striking a match against muddy boots or smoking Mallorca cigarettes as acrid as burned rubber or grinning over tall slim glasses filled with vodka. He doesn't need *Ta-yen* to give him ease of memory. And he remembers the immense resonant sound of church bells ringing on spring days through Petrograd, his parents holding his boyish hands in theirs on the way to service. His country was once beautiful, in spite of the aristocrats and their ravages. But he will never set foot on Russian soil again. That is clear; it's what *Ta-yen* used against him. Now this, China, is his country. And with the realization comes a commitment typical of Vladimir Kovalik. He'll struggle to set free another people. Like a man married once who wants to be married again, Kovalik finds his determination easy to come by; indeed, he welcomes it. And amidst the gray sooty drabness and squalor of Hanyang, he dreams of working for his adopted country, nurturing the resolution in silence and alone, while inside the tin-roofed hut remnants of Borodin's great Bolshevik organization sit in the sweet smoke and let go of their lives.

Sometimes Li sits with him outside and relates the news. The Secretary General of the Chinese Communist Central Committee, hiding out in Shanghai, has been ousted from his role by whoever is left in that city to give him the telegram from Moscow. Because Stalin has dismissed the Secretary General through the Comintern. Kovalik smiles grimly when Li adds that the man has been accused of Trotskyite errors; on his shoulders alone do the Stalinists place blame for the China debacle.

'It no longer matters,' Kovalik says mysteriously.

Twice they shift quarters in the native district, when warlord troops, as if for a lark, prowl through the streets on the lookout for Reds. Meanwhile, Kovalik eats and sleeps and watches as tired coolies lug their immense loads through the narrow lanes. All he must do is wait patiently, and the day will come – Kovalik feels it with a certainty that amazes him – when China will need his services.

That day comes sooner than expected. Flushed with excitement, Li sits beside him outside their shack and explains that Mao Tse-tung had not been executed at Hengyang, but in fact had escaped and joined others in the Hunan hills. Moreover, Red general Chu

Teh was still loose in northern Kwangtung, leading the forces of warlords and Nationalists a merry chase.

'So to the south our people are still fighting,' Kovalik observes.

'Our people?' Li repeats quizzically, for Kovalik has put it in a national context. He never has before. 'Well, yes, of course.'

'I mean *our* people. My people too.' Reaching out, Kovalik pats his comrade's shoulder with a big hand. 'They are now my people. It's true. You'll see it's true.'

Li smiles faintly but doesn't comment.

'So now we go south.' kovalik takes out his knife to whittle a piece of wood. He is fashioning a stooped coolie laboring under a huge sack. 'Can you arrange that?'

'Perhaps we should go to Changsha. I hear comrades are there, hiding out. We can learn from them what to do next.'

'Arrange it,' Kovalik says as if speaking of a dinner menu. He whittles expertly into the wood. 'Let's not waste any more time. There's work to do.'

Next day they cross by motor launch into the southernmost of the three cities of Wuhan. Having worn the clothes of a peasant for months, Kovalik has begun to move like one – shuffling along with short, mincing steps and a stooped back, arms held in to the sides, as urban Chinese learn to do in childhood in the crowded thoroughfares. On his head he wears a broad-brimmed coolie hat, pulled low on his forehead. The dramatic beard, shaved in Qufu before departing, has been replaced by the grizzle seen now and then on Chinese faces. Aside from the eyes, obscured by the hat, he might well pass for an uncommonly big peasant, in from the country-side to buy a sack of grain.

Here in Wuchang they stay with an old radical who had known all the leaders and experienced the glory of former days. He has gone back to work in a hemp factory, but talks incessantly of revolution. 'We'll do it yet,' he claims to Li's annoyance and Kovalik's satisfaction.

'He's an old fool,' Li whispers their second night there, but Kovalik defends him.

'The man is right,' Kovalik declares. 'We'll do it yet. We'll bring socialism to China. It's true, you'll see it's true.'

And the next day, leaving his comrade sullenly behind, Kovalik accompanies the old Communist to the battered headquarters used during the 1911 revolt from the Manchus. From there they go to the Peasant Movement Institute, where Bolshevik cadres had been trained until a few months ago. They are speaking Russian, which the man learned from his days at headquarters. 'I knew the director of the Peasant Movement Institute,' he claims. 'A young Hunanese named Mao Tse-tung.'

'They say he's escaped execution in the south.'

'I'm glad of that.'

'Do you think he's worthwhile?'

'Definitely.' They are sitting near a three-story pagoda at the western foot of Serpent Hill. 'Mao is right about the peasants. The big officials never understood him. China's revolution lies in the hands of the peasants.'

'Kovalik doesn't offer an opinion, but during the Russian Civil War he remembers the peasant armies as nothing more than disorderly mobs who went into battle not by political conviction but by abject fear of the retreating Whites, who were under the command of brutal Czarist generals like Atamen Annenkov. After the war the Red Army had to destroy the peasant forces. Had to. The peasants were a rabble who could never understand it was wrong to loot the villages of their own people. Kovalik remembers them lying frozen by the roadside, with the innocent faces of big woolly children, makeshift weapons cradled in their arms, their blackened feet, having been gnawed by wolves, looking like the staves of battered casks. Peasants? The soul of revolution?

'But Mao won't get far,' the old Red says in afterthought.

'Why not? You say he's right.'

'He's not strong enough to fight in the hills. It takes a powerful man. He's too delicate.'

'Yes, a scholar,' Kovalik adds, recalling his own impression of the fellow with full cheeks and soft hair parted in the middle and limpid eyes. An intellectual. A dilettante of revolution.

'Somewhere we'll find a man strong enough to lead us out of the hills into the cities. Someday that will happen,' the man declares, never suspecting that this shambling foreigner next to him is convinced that such a strong man goes by the name of Vladimir Kovalik.

Next day, leaving the Wuchang train station, Kovalik thinks for a moment he has seen a familiar face in the crowd – General Tang. That's not possible. And the man, soon lost in the flood tide of humanity, wasn't in uniform but wore a merchant's gown.

It doesn't matter, Kovalik decides. Such things no longer matter. Only one thing matters: fighting for China. This is the tranquil, assured mood that accompanies Kovalik southward into the region of rice paddies, into the hilly land of tobacco and tea, into rich country of cedar forests and peanut fields and the slashed red earth of zinc mines. Kovalik whittles; more often, letting his gaze stray over the vast countryside, he immerses himself in a dream of struggle, even while he looks, without seeing, at the thousands of water birds settled on the calm blue surface of the immense lake of Dong Ting.

When they arrive at Changsha, yet another city on a river bank, it is raining. Long curling sheets of rain veil the paper mills and eiderdown quilt factories, muffling the noise within riverside tea shops where Li and Kovalik locate the remaining Bolsheviks. Defeated by their military losses, homesick, disillusioned with policies made in Moscow and Shanghai, they sit over tea like men starved for sleep.

Yet they also tell wonderful stories about Chu Teh, the KMT commander who not only disobeyed his superior's order to suppress a peasant uprising but actually joined it – dragging along elements of his own regiment into the Hunan hills. Allying himself with bandits led by a wild young radical student, he finally linked up with a local warlord who tried to murder him, but in the confusion of this night attack, Chu Teh managed to escape by claiming he was only the cook. Now he is slogging somewhere with less than a thousand men who call themselves the National Revolutionary Army, with one machine gun among them, a little ammunition, and a few Marxist slogans.

'He was once an opium smoker,' Li explains to Kovalik. 'That was before he became a revolutionary. He took the cure in Shanghai and began the study of Marxism.'

'Let's go to him,' Kovalik suggests eagerly.

But they can find no one in Changsha who has the slightest idea where Chu Teh is now hiding.

After three days in Changsha, changing rooms each night in fear of a rumored KMT crackdown on local Communists, Li has further news of Mao Tse-tung. He takes Kovalik to a former Red soldier who knows first-hand what was happened.

They sit in the back room of a noodle restaurant over tepid beer. Passing them in a loud downpour are the people of Changsha holding their famous umbrellas – gaily colored, in startling contrast to the shop fronts turned gray in the sooty rain. My people, Kovalik thinks.

'Mao,' the ex-soldier begins. Pronouncing the name is enough to draw a laugh from him. 'He had this bunch of peasants he thought could be soldiers. That was his first mistake. Then he went to Hengyang to recruit coal miners. That was his second. Some militiamen captured him there. They were taking him off to be shot when he escaped.'

'How did he do that?' Kovalik wants to know how an intellectual escapes from a firing squad.

'Just did. Jumped off a path into a swamp.'

Not an intellectual way of escaping, Kovalik decides. 'Maybe he bribed the troops and they let him go.'

'They didn't let him go because he didn't have any money to bribe them with, you can be sure of that. They searched for him and got some farmers to look in the swamp too. Mao hid in the weeds for hours till they got tired and went away. Then he returned to his troops – what was left of them.'

'Where is he now?' Li asks.

'That's what I'm getting to,' the ex-soldier says with a smile. 'But let me say this: I was in one of the army units that split off from the Nationalists. You see, I'm a Communist going back to 1923. I joined Mao's bunch when he returned to them, and you've never seen a sadder bunch of so-called soldiers. Not one in five was a Communist. They had no politics. They were just a shitty bunch of peasants with nothing to do because their fields had been burned by the Nationalists. You understand? So anyhow, because Mao was a Communist, I decided to stick with him when he started for the hills.'

'Why did he go into the hills?' Kovalik asks through Li.

'You want my opinion? He didn't know where he was going. He just went and kept talking all the way. He'd stop in a field somewhere when it was raining and tell us his plans. I'm sure not half of those people understood a word he was saying.'

'Then why did they follow him?'

'It's what I ask myself. Why did they? I followed because I understood what he meant by revolution, by democracy in the army, by political comradeship, by a Marxist world.' The man sips his warm beer. 'I think they followed him because none of them had any idea what they wanted, and he seemed to have an idea about what *he* wanted. Something like that. Of course, we all knew he was in disgrace. Being defeated all over the fucking province of Hunan, he had this bad reputation with the local Communist Party – what there was of it. We knew the Hunan Provincial Committee, his own people, you understand, had thrown him out of office. We knew Mao was on his own.'

'Yet you followed him.'

'When I think about it now, it's crazy,' the man admits, shaking his head. 'In the town of Wen Chia, near an old temple, he got us to gather round – in the pouring rain. Then he told us we were going into the mountains where we'd fight like the heroes of old. You can imagine how much of *that* the peasants understood. He was quoting from *The Water Margin* – that old book. You understand? Telling us how the brave rebels held out exactly the same way we were going to do. He just didn't tell us how many centuries separated them from us. Anyway, I think what the peasants got from him that afternoon was his stubbornness. Any man who can stand in a downpour and shout above the heads of a thousand men and be heard for an hour, well, he can be a man to follow, even if he's as confused as everyone else. So we trudged after him, barefooted, without food, crawling with lice, listening to his wild stories every time he let us stop to get out breath. Finally I had enough. I just had enough. I came home. Fuck Mao.' The man orders another beer and stares broodingly at it. 'That madman with his head in the clouds telling stories about heroes – what in hell *are* heroes? I told myself, I said that fool will lead you to your grave. People who had any sense felt the same way and deserted too. He must have started from Wen Chia with twelve hundred men, but when I slipped away he couldn't have had nine hundred left.'

'Where is he?' Kovalik asks through Li.

'According to Mao, but that sure can change, he was going to Ching-kangshan.'

'I don't know the place,' Li admits.

'You don't?' asks the man, smiling. 'It's on the border of Hunnan and Kiangsi. It's just a mountain near a road between Jian and Ganzhou. You wouldn't know those towns either unless you came from the area. Ching-kangshan is nothing.'

'Perhaps,' Li says. 'But it might be a good place to lick your wounds.'

The man nods in agreement. 'Let me tell you, Mao has got plenty to lick. I'm sure glad I'm rid of him. You understand? He'd only get me killed.'

Later, when they are alone, Li says to Kovalik, 'What do you think?'

'Mao's wrong about the peasants. His theory won't work.'

'But we know where he is. And he has an army.'

'What there is of it,' Kovalik notes with a sigh. But it doesn't matter if the army is small, ill equipped, led by an impractical scholar. What Li says is true: Mao has an army, which by now is on top of an obscure mountain. It's a start for everyone.'

'So let's get ready,' Kovalik says.

'We're going there?'

'That's right. To join a peasant army on a mountaintop.'

20

The sky cannot have two suns.

It's a saying that comes often to the General's mind during the south-bound journey by steamer. He should have thought of it at the monastery, but pride blinded him to a grim truth which had been recognized by Chiang Kai-shek with perfect clarity: A man of superior power must keep a man of lesser power but comparable ambition in his place or remove him altogether.

So the journey to Canton is now vital; Tang must find an ally against the powerful enemy he has made. Perhaps he'll find what he's looking for in the southern politican Wang Ching-wei.

By the time they are approaching Swatow on the southern coast, he has put behind him the meeting with Chiang. At least he knows that cooperation with the Kuomintang – surely with the clique devoted to Chiang – has become impossible. He stands at the ship rail and stares at the marshy shoreline. Flights of geese in V-shaped formation skim above the tidal rivers opening to the ocean, where fishermen on bamboo rafts spread their black nets. He wonders if the southern language will give him much trouble. Listening to Cantonese passengers on shipboard, he can recall his childhood fluency with the tongue and can decipher most of what they say. Even so, the language uses double the tones of his own Mandarin. He hasn't practiced for years; he will speak Yue badly.

Before they have the port of Swatow in sight, a sailor rushes on deck to say that a wireless message just received has warned of Red troops grouping on the outskirts of the city. Tang and the other passengers therefore expect the steamer to bypass Swatow and put in farther south, perhaps even in Hong Kong; to their surprise the captain increases speed and runs for Swatow. They arrive at the fan-shaped port in late afternoon. Two men, joining Tang at the rail, begin to talk about the city. A few years ago a typhoon and tidal wave swept much of it away and left rows of remaining houses so shaky they are braced by bamboo poles crossed over the streets. The men seem familiar with Swatow, so Tang, trying out his Cantonese, asks them why the ship's putting into harbor if there's a chance of attack.

One of the men, a tall fellow, after registering his disgust (a quick grimace) with Tang's accent, replies that the steamer is the property of Ch'en Chiung-ming, a warlord controlling the eastern half of the province, including Swatow.

Having been courteous enough to offer this explanation, the men turn away from the northerner. In silence Tang watches the ship chug into the wide harbor; it fronts a flat, colorless city ringed in the far distance by granite hills. So Red troops are threatening Swatow – a contradiction of Chu Jui's claim that the city had repelled them. But that's hardly the fault of his friend. In wartime China, rumor quite readily substitutes for fact. It is commonplace for armies to be reported hundreds of kilometers from their actual positions. Such confusion has worked to his own advantage in a campaign.

Having learned that the steamer belongs to a local warlord who'll decide its destination. Tang faces the possibility of being stranded in Swatow in the guise of a Shanghai merchant. It is probable that Ch'en Chiung-ming will load it up with his own goods and leave before the Reds enter. Tang could find himself in a Communist-occupied city without means of getting away.

The harbor is feverish. Every vessel capable of getting underway is already in the channel. Docked ships are loading and unloading as quickly as possible. He sees heaps of cargo strewn about the wharf: casks, bales, sacks of tea, sugar, raw cotton, and bamboo going into steamer holds; and coming out of them clothes from England and Italy, paraffin from America, matches from Japan. The General notices a ship unloading pressed bean curd from Manchuria for use as fertilizer in southern rice fields. Coolies haul them – these cakes as hard and weighty as grindstones – off the gangplanks and at the end of the dock take tally sticks from the wharf clerk.

So he will be a bean-cake merchant – Po Ming of Shanghai.

No sooner has the ship eased into its berth, alongside a crowded pier, then local constabulary climb aboard. Tang doesn't like the look of them; one, obviously drunk, lurches and nearly falls into the water. The General knows only too well that any crisis – flood, famine, or military attack – enables local police and soldiery to profit from people willing to pay for escape or protection. Tang tightens his grip on his valise and follows the other passengers to the gangplank, where the police are assembling them. A score of people crowd around, while a stout officer wearing a garrison cap at a jaunty angle begins to harangue them. He's bragging that the people of Swatow will break the yoke of the foreign imperialists and of the Bolsheviks too, so anyone on this ship who has reason to hide his true intentions in coming to this illustrious city had better step forward and confess; in the long run it will go easier for him if he does.

No one steps forward, and the harangue continues, while the harbor noise seems to increase with the lowering of the sun, as if everything movable must be shipped out of Swatow before morning, when the Red troops enter. Three of the policemen are passing a bottle and gawking at a woman passenger, a rather pretty one holding the hand of a small child. At last, after lengthy consultation with his men, the police captain orders all the passengers to form a line at the gangplank.

The questioning of each one begins.

The captain and his two assistants don't bother with papers, but simply ask questions and study each traveler, as if judging his financial worth. Tang notices that they dispense quickly with the few peasants aboard, who rush down the gangplank and vanish into the crowd on the wharf. Other passengers, once questioned, are sent down the plank and herded into a group under guard at the bowlines. The three policemen are ogling the young woman as she approaches the head of the line. One of them says something under his breath, the other two giggle. Tang, next to the woman, smiles down at her anxious little girl, who, sensing something is wrong, grips his mother's wrist with both hands.

The police captain begins an indifferent examination of the woman, obviously intent upon her figure, not her answers. His eyes stare boldly at the swell of her breasts in a silk blouse. 'You stay aboard for more questioning,' he tells her gruffly.

'Pardon me, honored captain,' Tang says with a low bow. 'But I know the woman's uncle in Shanghai.'

Both the captain and young woman look at him in surprise.

'Forgive my impertinence, honored captain, but I fear if she's detained you may have trouble later.' Tang bows a few quick times, obsequiously. 'Her uncle's a powerful man. He's well connected with the Greens.'

The captain, a slack-jawed man, rubs his chin thoughtfully. 'Who asks you anything?' he snarls at Tang. 'You say you're here for a visit?' he asks the woman. She repeats her story: She and her daughter have come to visit her in-laws, residents in Swatow. The police officer waves her roughly on; when she remains, confused by the gesture, Tang tells her, 'He means go. Now go.'

Watching her descend the gangplank with the little girl hanging on her arm, the captain of police turns furiously to Tang. 'A bean-curd merchant?' he says, looking Tang up and down, after a few questions.

'Where's your luggage?'

'This is all.' He holds up the valise, which the captain immediately seizes and throws to one of the assistants who have been waiting for the young woman. 'When it's searched, you'll get it back. Go down there.'

Tang doesn't hesitate. He knows that by defending the woman he did enough to put himself in grave danger. To argue about the loss of his valise would guarantee it. These fellows are desperate to use their advantage while there's time – before they must vanish into the rice fields and hope the Reds will withdraw soon or be defeated, so they can return to Swatow as symbols of law and order.

Tang goes down the gangplank and stands with the others, while a young policeman, hardly more than a boy, holds a rifle on them. Soon more than half of the passengers are sitting on bales or leaning against crates on the wharf. They've not yet been robbed, but their luggage has been taken from many of them, ostensibly for a search. The captain of police wishes to make a show of legality, but when they're herded down to the station and beyond sight, he can do what he wants. Surely the rich will never see their property again.

Not that Tang worries about what is in his valise – no more than clothes, a book, some ginger candies that he likes, a bar of soap.

But he carries enough money for the police to give him a closer look. Surely they will discover the letter of introduction from Chu Jui to Wang Ching-wei sewn into the lining of his gown, just below the left armpit. What might happen then is conjecture, none of it good.

None of it good enough for him to risk discovery. He must escape here on the dock, but there isn't much time for it. The constabulary aboard the steamer are taking the passengers' luggage off and loading it into an old truck on the dock. He slips over to the young guard, who, seeing him approach, raises the gun threateningly.

'Don't shoot, young sir!' Tang pleads in a frightened voice, coming up to him.

The young policeman, bemused by his demonstrated authority, smiles and then frowns.

In low, quick, precise phrases the General then tells him that soon the passengers will be taken to the station, probably stripped and robbed; that a young policeman, however, won't see any of the money because the older officers will take it all; that he could do better for himself by letting someone escape for a price, especially because the captain is too busy aboard the steamer to worry about the exact number of prisoners here on the dock.

The young man prods Tang with his rifle as a response. He has a runny nose and tired eyes and he keeps moving his tongue nervously over his lower lip.

'Think about it,' Tang whispers, backing off. 'But think fast – there's not much time.'

Next moment the piercing wail of a siren rises above the harbor noise. Like ships struggling in a stormy ocean, three cars make their way through the throng of porters, dodge piles of stacked crates, knock over wheelbarrows, shove aside carts, until the three of them – the last a limousine – come finally to a halt in front of the steamer. Soldiers leap out and form a cordon at the bottom of the gangplank. A man in uniform, wearing a chestful of medals and a plumed cap, emerges from the limousine and approaches the ship. He hesitates a moment, as if appraising his property, before climbing the gangplank.

Ch'en Chiung-ming, *tuchan* of eastern Kwangtung, come to take charge of his ship. He'll want to get clear of the harbor before Red troops arrive. Doubtless he has left a couple of junior officers to make a last-ditch stand, promising them rewards if they succeed in fighting off the invaders. At midships he meets the police captain and the ship's captain. They bend together in a hasty, earnest conference.

Now is the time.

Removing some money from his gown, Tang walks rapidly toward the young policeman. If the bribe doesn't work, he'll shoot the guard with the sub-nosed .32 held under his gown and run. The young fellow, seeing the General's fisted hand with the money, turns a grimace into a smile and lowering the gun steps aside, allowing Tang to brush past him and press into his hand the bunch of taels.

Walking a few paces straight ahead, wondering if the young guard may have a change of heart and shoot him in the back, Tang slips behind a tall pile of crates. In an instant he passes beyond view of the ship, where Ch'en Chiung-ming is arranging with the captain and the police chief for the trio's departure from Swatow. Tang once met Ch'en Chiung-ming at a military conference in Wuhan; it is therefore likely that the Swatow warlord would recognize the General now. A cutthroat addicted to sweet cakes and Japanese whisky, Ch'en Chiung-ming would like nothing better (except, perhaps, to have the ship already clear of the harbor, than to have a northern general in his grip, an object ripe for barter or ransom.

The three-masted junk is clear of Swatow. Harbor when the first light of morning streaks the water, enlivening its muddy skeins with a warm pink color. On the elevated poop General Tang watches the city vanish slowly from sight. He can make out the distance outline of the steamer, which still lies alongside the pier. It has not left Swatow because Ch'en Chiung-ming is continuing to take cargo aboard – possessions from his mansion and office, the treasure of a corrupt rule. He's gambling that his young officers will fight off the Reds or delay them until his ship finally gets underway. Greed has put his safety at risk. If he hasn't cast off by noon, if the Reds do break through the outer defences, they'll be swarming like ants over his cargo.

Last night after making his escape from the pier, Tang had slipped into the center of Swatow, losing himself in the stream of coolies that flowed down every street. It is always the coolies, buffeted by fear and rumor, who flee last at the approach of an enemy. They hope for advantage until it's too late to hope for escape. The rich leave first or brace themselves for cooperation with the new power. In a teahouse, where Tang sat late, he overheard two merchants discussing the Red advance. The troops were commanded by Ho Lung, a former Hunanese bandit who at sixteen years of age had led a gang of outlaws in the mountains. He had fought during the August uprising against the Nationalists at Nanchang – and lost. He has force-marched his troops from Nanchang to Swatow, hardly pausing for rest or food. One merchant said, with a sigh of experience, the Red soldiers would therefore be tired and hungry and furious tomorrow. By morning the teahouse merchants (Tang has seen it elsewhere) would be cringing in the street, waving gaily at the incoming troops in the hope of salvaging their property from the general pillage, of keeping their women hidden, of saving their lives until another army brought temporary order.

Ah, my country, Tang thinks. The merchants are shrewd enough but lack both the courage and the power to bring to such a life any more than resignation.

When Tang had returned to the wharf, coolies were still working desperately to load vessels for departure. He managed, for an exorbitant sum, to book passage on a large old junk with its lug sails so patched in their ribbing that they had the worn look of a clothesline in a Shanghai shanty-town. Even so, he was lucky to get aboard anything leaving Swatow.

This morning he is tired, having slept only an hour or two in his tiny cabin at the stern. His bed is a plank attached to one bulkhead with hardly more than a foot separating it from the opposite bulkhead. He prefers to stand on deck rather than remain below in that cramped hole smelling of fish. On the poop deck, raised high above the clutter of shipboard lines, rope slings, cargo nets, and wicker bales of cargo, he feels the wind freshen from the sea, bringing a tangy moisture to his lips. He peels and eats a Swatow orange, none better in China. Through the slow hours aboard the junk, he will have time to think of his plans. And of Black Jade. Her image eases into his mind and stays there awhile, calming him and letting him bring into manageable perspective what happened yesterday.

His valise is gone and he's traveling to Canton on a weathered old junk, but he still has his money and his freedom – double proof of a traveler's luck in China. In part his luck has resulted from good judgment. In Qufu he had seriously considered bringing Black Jade along (a measure of his infatuation), but had finally rejected the folly. It would have been madness to travel in the company of a woman, a foreign woman, a beautiful foreign woman. Her image fades a moment, replaced by that of the young mother. Is she all right now? And her child? In China there's no mercy for the vulnerable. It gives him satisfaction to know that Black Jade's safe in Qufu with her ink brushes and her poetry books and Tai Chi, with the rockeries and gardens at her disposal (though not those of the Kong family, of course), and with good food to eat, with a wise servant to help her (even if Yao growls while doing it), and with the calm hours bringing her deeper into his world, edging her farther into the life of China. For he hopes, dares to hope, that Black Jade will stay with him and with her intelligence and passion transform herself into a woman of his people. This dream stays with him through the long, slow day as he sits on a keg or leans against the peeling rail, gazing down at the gray strakes lapped gently by a freshening sea. He gazes, gazes, letting his mind empty out into the vast blue water, merge with it, roll like the ungainly but powerful junk, become part of the wind, the sea, the sunlit salt air. He shares a meal of fish and rice with the crew, hunkering with them amidships under the flapping shade of the main mast. As he studies the rough-hewn faces of the sailors, all of them quite indifferent to his presence, Tang Shan-teh understands why men go to sea.

It is a magical day, and timeless, although it passes all too quickly for him. He sleeps well that night on the hard narrow shelf in the smelly cabin and rises the next morning refreshed, strangely heartened, full of optimism and the memory of love, as he watches the creaking ship lumber south of Hong Kong Island. He notices the Hakka boats with their high, flared bows, swallow-tailed stems, and immense triangular sails. In the distance he sees the numerous rows of brown sampans moored in the hill-ringed harbor of Aberdeen. Then they pass Waterfall Bay, Telegraph Bay, and Sandy Bay, leaving Hong Kong behind to enter the Pearl River estuary. It waters the fertile delta stretching from Canton to the Macao Peninsula. The General watches, enthralled, trying to remember his childhood in this hot, fecund country. Behind him on the poop three men, standing on a cleated plank, manipulate the huge stern oar. They are enclosed by loop-holed plate iron – 'pirate' armor. There is, in fact, a barricade of heavy iron sheet around the entire poop, for these are dangerous waters the junk now enters.

Tawny islands, their hills gashed by centuries of torrential rain, lie to the east. It's from them, from their salt-water caves which serve as lair and harbor, that pirate boats rush into the channel and attack the packet steamers, junks, and coastal launches that run the gantlet. Tang remembers his father describing the rivr pirates: Mozambique blacks. White Portuguese Timoristas, Goans and Sikhs from India, mixed breeds including Japanese Christians and Dayaks from Malaya in breechclouts and rattan caps, all of them slipping in and out of the islands in their small quick boats, armed to the teeth, merciless, renowned for their tortures and their toasted melon seeds that they munch back in the gambling dens of Macao, where they spend the blood-stained loot.

When they lived in Canton, father used to tell him stories about the pirates. He had been twelve or thirteen when he began dreaming of being a pirate himself, free and daring on the South China Sea.

Now, of course, he hopes the junk stays clear of them. It's hard to believe such pretty islands could harbor cutthroats known for eating the livers of their bravest victims. The hours pass languidly while the junk runs before the wind. By sunset the islands have given way to flat delta, purple in the distance, fringed with bamboo and palms. In the darkness, to warn other vessels of the junk's approach, a sailor beats a large sheet of iron, attached to the foremast, with a blacksmith's hammer. The prevailing wind brings in the scent of fish from villages fronted by nets. They pass the ruin of a steamer beached on a sand bar where the estuary has narrowed. That night the General sleeps on deck with the crew, eschewing the hot little cabin. In the morning he rises to see the estuary narrow enough for both shores to be visible, the banana palms and mud villages and paddies golden in the early light. Already the plowmen are wading knee-deep in the fields behind their buffaloes. Geese rise in heavy flight above the lovely flowers, the rhododendron in scarlet bloom, the bushes of red roses. All along the shoreline are loquat trees with bunches of yellow fruit. Trios of men holding a horizontal rod are at work on their treadmill waterlifts which feed the insatiable paddies. Field after field stretches back from the shore, flat, olive green, sparkling towards a distant ridge of blue hills. Looking down at the water, Tang recalls another childhood story, one he often begged his father to tell him. His grandfather had been invited by foreign business-men to accompany them on a pleasure trip by paddle steamer. While they made way at full speed, at some distance a sampan, heavily ladened with bricks, was in midstream; four coolies were rowing wildly to get out of the larger vessel's path. Grandfather and others on deck awaited the whistle signal for a stop that would give the struggling coolies a chance to row clear, but none came; The British captain held both course and speed. When the mate asked, in response to the coolies shouting in the sampan, if he should order the engines stopped, the captain replied, 'No, go ahead.' There was a shout, a swaying motion on impact, and then the steamer continued on its way. Grandfather, rushing to the stem, could see only one of the coolies and he lay motionless on the water, an arm severed by the paddle. Leaning over the rail, the captain and mate satisfied themselves that no damage to the steamer had occurred and returned to the bridge. The wind carried the captain's voice back to the assembled guests, many of them Chinese, rendered speechless by the incident. 'They must learn to give way, damn them.'

Tang had often requested this story; it kept his anger hot. Although the incident took place many years before his birth, it has always signified for him the psychology of foreigners.

Then he thinks of Black Jade, also a foreigner. But not any longer. Any more than the blond American is a foreigner. They belong at Qufu, part of a larger scheme of things in which ulti-mately all races will find their union in the Tao. He comforts himself with this dream of unity, knowing it's his need at the moment, but also knowing it leads him toward a brighter vision of the future, perhaps not only the future of China but of the outside world as well, the world beyond the Flowery Kingdom. He enter-tains the dream as other people imagine themselves rich – for him an idle comfort, not to be cherished.

River traffic bound for Hong Kong is beating down the channel. A junk much like their own passes by, with a round eye painted on the bow to watch out for evil water spirits. Both crews wave. So does the General, who for these precious hours has allowed his landlocked mind to float free and dream of beauty as amorphous as the water on which he sails. They overtake a packet steamer, the *Yue Ping Wa*, rolling in the land swells, its stack pouring out a froth of white smoke. On both banks now the settlements are thick. There are wooden piers where duck herders hold bunches of fowl by the heads, like inverted bouquets of white flowers for sale. They pass a Bocca Tigris fort, its old brick crumbling, the crenelated battlements in ruin, but still witness of another age of foreign incursion into this country. They pass the town of Humen on the eastern shore, where scrub oak lies in timber stacks on the wharfs; coolies, wearing cone-shaped bamboo hats at least two feet across, wave at the junk's crew. Numerous small craft appear in the muddy current: *lorchas*, *yulohs* with fishtail oars, barber boats, lighters, barges, even bamboo rafts. There are cattails growing along that part of the shore unemcumbered by docks. Floating houseboats, as the junk proceeds toward Canton, become entire cities occupied by river people who live and die on their boats, never setting foot on land. In the midday heat music drifts across the water; rich Cantonese have left the crowded city for seafood luncheons on restaurant junks. Tang can now see the two pagodas on Honam Island and near the western shore an island where Chiang Kai-shek, with Communist help, started the Whampoa Military Academy. Tang shades his eyes to stare at the fort, the dormitories, the classrooms behind closed galleries. The sight of Whampoa jerks him away from the lapping dreams of the past few days – Chiang's school, which has supplied the Nationalists with brave young officers. How Tang wishes he had them! He looks down at his wrinkled gown. He must get clothes immediately in Canton. From the starboard bow he can see, rising above and behind the misty skyline of the city, the blue ragged peak of White Cloud Mountain. On the right now is Honam Island with its tall square blocks of masonry, pawnbroker warehouses, and mat factories. Houseboats, a dozen abreast, are tied up at the dirty waterfront. Scooting between ocean liners and coastal steamers in the harbor are sampans, fruit boats, peddler boats, and pottery boats with pots loaded up to the gunwales. Everywhere now are the flower boats with their cargoes of pretty girls for sale – the junk's crew yells down at them, they wave back – not one of them yet twenty, all in flowery silk blouses and skirts and coolie hats. Slipper boats ply from the Bund across to Honam Island, carrying anything, with small women sculling the dilapidated hulls in and out of traffic. From Canton itself the waterfront din is carried to Tang's ears: hammering, planing, chanting, and firecrackers celebrating one of the countless southern festivals. A launch, belching soot and cinders, brings the junk into anchorage. Soon the General is being taken by slipper boat toward the river front – toward the wild cacophony and vertigenous bustle of the City of Rams, named after the animal mounts of five genii clothed in radiant garments of five colors, great wizards who, before mankind knew enough to write of it, founded this heaven on earth at the mouth of a great river.

Having taken a room in a modest hotel on Tai Ping Road, the General returns to the street and strolls to the waterfront. He gazes awhile at the tree-shaded mansions and Victorian banking houses of Shameen, a tiny island attached to Canton by a single gated bridge. It's jointly owned by the French and British, with its own laws, council, and police. Tang remembers its isolated grandeur – no Chinese permitted on the island – from excursions taken with his father to its causeway and sentry box. Holding father's hand he would stare at it, while father, wearing civilian clothes so as not to be recognized by foreign officers entering or leaving Shameen, would tell him the story again of the four coolies run down on their sampan. Tang stands a few minutes under a banyan tree near the bridge – the same tree under which he and father stood, reliving in their imagination the death of the four coolies.

The roots of his hatred are deep.

Turning away from Shameen, from this reminder of his land's humiliation, Tang walks to a business district filled with other evidence of the Great Powers: banks, mission houses, Standard Oil tanks, the Customs Building. At the large intersection of Wing Hon and Wai Oi Roads he looks up at the Western clock on a brass pedestal. While he's looking at it, a black car whizzes past with a half-dozen khaki-uniformed soldiers on the running boards, holding cocked pistols. It could be Wang Ching-wei inside. Or one of the many politicians who have kept the City of Rams in constant turmoil these past few years. No city in China has suffered more from rioting, strikes, kidnaping, and murder. In an arcade he stops to buy a few clothes and a black skullcap. He strolls deeper into the hutungs, where overhead reed matting, supported by wooden frames, keeps out the tropical sun. Perhaps he hadn't felt the heat so much as a child, because it now seems a new thing about Canton. And the shops, the wonderful shops with their curios and wigs and false mustaches, all seem shabbier now. Coolies, bent double under rice baskets, pant alongside him. He notices the black ink stamped on the surface of the rice to prove on arrival that none has been taken. These are powerful, spirited men, the coolies of South China. He regards their hard bodies, as brown as steeped tea, with a professional eye. His father used to say they were splendid, if erratic soldiers. Someday Tang's army may come against men like them in battle, as Chiang Kai-shek leads his southern troops northward.

Now Tang comes to the bazaar he has been seeking. The hatred he feels for the Great Powers in deep, having been nurtured on these self-same streets by his father; yet he has come here, among the silk shops and ivory shops, to find a gift for a foreigner. What would she like? There are goldfish bowls made of used light bulbs – smiling, he thinks his people can make use of anything. He inspects the sandalwood curios, then walks down a street jammed with stores selling fans with mother-of-pearl ribbing. He looks at blackwood and pearlwood furniture, gewgaws of brass, straw sandals. On Tien Ping Street he comes to a shop specializing in ink stones.

Ink stones.

Minutes later he's on the street again, carrying a small parcel wrapped in rice paper, tied with string. A lovely ink stone. In the waning light of a Cantonese day he enjoys the satisfaction of making such a purchase. He tries to imagine her face when she unwraps the package – her smile, her eyes liquid with feeling.

It is late, the sun has dropped behind the storefronts, its last rays shooting toward a distant pagoda upthrust from the maze of hutungs, leaving the narrow lanes awash in blue shadow. Merchants are coming from their shops to shutter them; the clang of metal sheeting is resonant in the twilit air. From a nearby lane comes the sputtering roar of firecrackers, chasing away demons. Tang walks on, content in the belly of Canton. He knows in many households the old women are now presiding, just as his grandmother used to preside in his. As wrinkled as crushed rice paper, they are deep within the city here, bowing to the Kitchen God, caring for the ancestral tablets, telling old ghost stories, maintaining the honorific titles. It is that time of day when, as a boy, he used to feel the spirits everywhere, numinous and insistent, their voices clacking faintly through the centuries, and now he wishes for Black Jade beside him, so he can tell her that in their country – hers now too – it's not madness to listen to the dead as to the living. But the mood is broken by something earthly: the smell of food. He has come upon Wing Hon Road, where the restaurants are. Their specialties are described on vertical signs, and he chooses a snake restaurant. Inside the dim interior he looks at a number of cages filled with them, their tongues flicking. He has come here for old times' sake, because father dearly loved this specialty of the South. Once, feeling brave, Tang had accompanied him to such a restaurant. It had required as much courage as he ever mustered in his life, including battle, to take the first bite of a creature he had watched the chef skin: A thin knife blade was run the length of the body, head then severed, and the skin peeled back to reveal a white twisting carcass.

Tonight, however, he enjoys the meal without heroics. He orders snake-and-cat stew, a sweet soup made from constrictor, and a few stuffed rice balls in oyster sauce. While eating, he listens to some Cantonese businessmen at a nearby table. They're discussing the proposal for a radio station in Canton. Then they shift to the Telephone Commission, which purchased a hundred phones last year from the Chicago Automatic Telephone Company of America; because of local politics not one has yet been installed. They shake their heads in a show of consternation, as if unaware that such petty intrigue has strangled the city not for years but for centuries. Tang watches them drink the bile of snakes in *mao tai*; they giggle about its ability to stimulate sexual performance. This observation, with the third bile-and-*mao tai*, turns their thoughts to women. A man in spectacles remarks that these days teahouse waitresses pay a fixed tax to bullies so they won't be molested on their way home at night. Another man, shaking his head sadly, maintains that crime has taken a nasty upswing – in his father's day a woman could walk anywhere without fear.

In the day of that man's father, Tang thinks, a woman never left her house alone, for fear of being kidnapped one day, used the next, dumped with a slit throat into the Pearl on the third. It's always the same. But someday a leader must break the sequence. I will break the sequence, Tang thinks, paying the bill and leaving.

He take a rickshaw to the hotel. The puller, detecting his northern accent, mutters something under his breath – probably an obscenity. The trip takes much longer than it should, but Tang pays the high fare without complaint. This day in Canton has been like a day from his childhood; indeed, traveling in the rickshaw down the lantern-lit streets of humid Canton has made his link with Qufu seem tenuous. In his room, removing his travel gown.

Tang stretches out on the bed, mildly surprised by his exhaustion. But then he contemplates the strain under which he's laboring. In his search for allies he has traveled nearly the length of China, knowing that without help he is doomed, Black Jade doomed too, and his army, and perhaps the entire land.

The General is up early. After a bowl of *congee* in the hotel restaurant, he is out on the street, not long after the fish sellers arrive to bray the merits of their fish, kept alive in tubs they haul about in wheelbarrows. Tang has decided to walk to Wang Ching-wei's headquarters in a fashionable suburb. On the way a thunderstorm speeds across the city with tropical suddenness. He rushes under an arcade while coolies run about in the rain gear of a single large palm leaf. In a nearby shop men are gambling noisily; they are using too much rapid slang for him to understand much of what's happening. By the time he has sorted out a few phrases, the storm has ended and a patch of sky opens above the street. Sunlight plays across some noodles drying on raised racks of bamboo in the alley opposite the arcade where Tang stands. In a half-hour of steady walking he leaves the gray hutungs for the lawns of fine residences. Somewhat later, having stopped to ask directions, he comes to a macadam street lined with Flame of the Forest trees, all in crimson flower. There's an iron fence ahead with a uniformed guard at its gate. Here the General stops to present his name and a letter of introduction written by Chu Jui at the monastery.

Awaiting entry, Tang can see through the iron fence a broad Western lawn and a two-story villa with the porticioes and multi-paned windows of foreign consulates in Shanghai and Peking. It amuses him. Wang Ching-wei, long a Chinese revolutionary, lives in a European mansion. Theory and practice are usually far apart; their separation is as universal as men speaking of the good old days.

A swarthy young man in a business suit comes from the villa and walks rapidly down the cement walk to the gate, holding the letter of introduction in his hand. Bowing, observing the amenities, he escorts the General into the house and a reception room. Two other men are waiting there, dressed similarly to Tang in black pants, shirt, and skullcap. One is complaining of the housing shortage, the result surely of Red agitation in the labor unions. The other, looking preoccupied, rarely responds during the pauses left to him for that purpose. Finally both fall silent, their eyes crinkled with worry. They wait a long time. Finally a trio of men crowd into the doorway to peer inside – not at the worried merchants, but at the General. He's aware of it and responds to their curiosity with a disdainful look, aware they're perplexed by his behavior: a general arriving on foot?

A young man in seersucker comes at last for the waiting merchants. Time drags, while the overhead fan rattles like an old train. Twice more a few staff people come to stare at the General from the doorway. Finally the one in seersucker returns to the room with profuse apologies, scattering his phrases with 'eminent sir' and 'overjoyed' and 'illustrious' and 'most gratified,' all of which signify to the General that they have completed an examination of the letter and his person and feel assured that he is indeed Tang Shan-teh of Shantung, General and Defense Commissioner. Perhaps, too, someone may have recognized him from a newspaper photograph or seen him at a conference. At any rate, the young man in seersucker, leading him from the reception room, continues the apology at exceptional length. 'We have been quite upset all morning,' he explains, although it is still early morning. 'Excellency, we have just learned that Ho Lung and Yeh Ting are nearing Swatow.'

Wang Ching-wei must have a wireless in the house. The news about Swatow was not known at the hotel or hawked on the newsstands yesterday. Of course, Tang knows the Red generals were at the wall of Swatow more than forty-eight hours before the news arrived here.

'Please, Worthy General, here –' Tang is ushered into a Western room with overstuffed furniture and thick curtains drawn at the windows. An overhead fan whirls. A huge desk dominates the room, without an object or paper on it, save for an inkstand. This is Wang Ching-wei's desk, where he'll be sitting soon. Perhaps he hasn't finished breakfast or the suddenness of Tang's appearance has flustered him – a possibility that the General has deliberately created by coming so early, unannounced. He knows Wang's reputation for indecision. Had he sent a message here announcing his arrival in Canton, it might have been a day or two before Wang decided when, where, and how they should meet.

Behind the desk is a huge portrait painted in the coarse realism of the West. It is Sun Yat-sen, square-faced, with a thin, determined mouth, cropped hair, and wide-set, commanding eyes. People have told the General he bears a striking resemblance to 'The Founder of the Republic' and the 'Soul of the National Party.' Others have told him it isn't so – he's not as somber as Doctor Sun.

Sitting in a leather chair that creaks at every movement, Tang stares ahead; eyes must be watching to see if he touches anything in the room.

At last a very thin young man enters, sighing dramatically as if pained by his own tardiness. He introduces himself as Luk Fat; it's a fine southern name with its consonantal endings. He speaks flawless Mandarin. Luk Fat goes behind the desk and plummets down in the chair. Tang is startled to think an aide would dare sit in Wang Ching-wei's chair at Wang Ching-wei's desk.

Clapping his hand, Luk Fat calls out, 'Tea!' Then, turning, with the indulgent smile of a bureaucrat he says, 'To what may we pay homage for the honor you do us, Excellency?'

Tang, leaning forward, has had enough empty courtesy. He asks to speak without delay to Wang Ching-wei.

'I'm afraid, Exalted General, that will be impossible. He's in Shanghai.'

'Shanghai? But Chu Jui told me he was here. You know Chu Jui?'

'Indeed I do know him, General. I count myself blessed by the gods to be his friend.'

'Chu Jui said Wang Ching-wei would be here, ready to meet me.'

'I'm afraid he was called to Shanghai in great haste.' He repeats the phrase, 'In great haste,' thereby assuring the General that he's lying. An irresolute man, Wang did nothing in haste. Still, he might well have gone to Shanghai.

'Did you know I was expected today?' This is Tang's own lie: The hope for a meeting had been expressed by Chu Jui in behalf of Wang Ching-wei; the General's own sense of desperation had confirmed its certainty.

'I regret, Illustrious General, I didn't know, you were coming. Perhaps Honorable Wang kept it to himself for security reasons. Canton is full of trouble these days.'

Tang concedes that. Having seen the staff here exhibiting a blatant curiosity, he'd not confide in them if he were Wang. The question that interests the General is, did Wang ever intend to see him? Has he himself been lured south, away from northern politics, while Wang pursues other interests in Shanghai?

'General?'

In his haste to make credible sense of this latest twist of fortune, Tang has lost contact with Luk Fat. 'Yes. Go on.'

'I was saying, General, permit me to welcome you to Canton. I'm ashamed to see you've not been properly treated. I am completely at your disposal. Believe me, Honorable Wang would not have it otherwise.'

'Thank you. When will he return?'

Luk Fat throws up his hands. 'Who can tell? I don't know his business in Shanghai, but I suspect Honorable Wang may remain there several weeks.'

All this is senseless, Tang tells himself bitterly. He rises to leave. It isn't easy to leave – sensing an advantage. Luk Fat becomes fulsomely polite, using a range of rhetoric to apologize for Honorable Wang's absence. 'Is there something I can tell him when he returns? Will you remain in Canton? It is to be hoped you will, sir, so we can entertain you. Is there perhaps a written message you wish to leave with me? I'll see he gets it instantly on his return. Such a shame! Perhaps a slight misunderstanding –' To the questions and exclamations Tang merely shakes his head or waves his hand vaguely, aware the fellow doesn't expect an answer but is taking advantage of a chance to torment a superior. 'General, what can I possibly do, insignificant though I am, to make this situation good?' He continues in this infuriating manner until Tang gets free of the house.

Outside, on the avenue of flame trees, the General hails a rickshaw, feeling week from humiliation and anger. He returns to the hotel, determined to leave this southern quagmire as soon as possible and return to Black Jade, his dusty homeland in the north, and his army.

He spends a few hours at the train station, waiting in line for a ticket on the next train for Wuhan; it leaves at midnight. There is nothing more for him here. He sends a wireless at the telegraph office to Colonel Pi in Qufu: TEA SHIPMENT SENT. PO MING. He can't send a message to Black Jade. The telegraph company would be dumbfounded, rendered incapable of getting a wireless out to a Russian woman at a general's headquarters in the heart of Confucius country! But within hours everyone in the town of Qufu, much less the camp, will know he's on the way home.

Returning to the hotel, he has tea in the restaurant and goes to his room, where a large basket of fruit awaits him; the attached card conveys Luk Fat's officious compliments and false regrets. Tang is sick of the South; it's no longer the place of his childhood. And yet in the hope of recapturing some of the old feeling, he decides to ride through the city. He has a long wait before train time and no interest in seeking out the companionship of Luk Fat.

At the hotel curb stands a line of rickshaws. As the General is about to climb in the lead one, the doorman in uniform steps up and bars his way. 'Please sir, I know this rascal. Let me get you a better rickshaw.' Already from across the street another puller is trotting briskly. 'We keep a few good men for hotel guests,' the doorman explains with a smile.

Climbing into the rickshaw, Tang tells the puller to drive around.

'I can show you, master, the yamen of the Kwangtung Province Civil Governor.'

'No, just drive around.'

Shortly he sees on the right the twin Gothic spires of the Roman Catholic Church, they make him think of Black Jade, if she would want to go inside the church – and drag him along. Would he go? Of course not.

The puller, grinning, looks back over his shoulder. 'You got the right man, sir. Nobody knows Canton the way I do.' Then in the heat, pulling a wooden-tired carriage at six miles an hour through the uneven streets, he manages to give his opinion of the world and describe Canton as well. 'Yes, you're lucky,' he says in explosive little pants. 'You speak our language. Most northerners can't speak a word. What can I show you? I can take you to Wah Lam. You can see five hundred genii there. And it has a big statue of the foreigner with a feather in his hat. A disciple of the Great Buddha. I know what they call him too. Mako Paho. The foreigners when they come here go directly there to get his blessing.'

That monastery, Tang knows, is located in North Saikwan, far away. And he doesn't want to see a statue of Marco Polo. 'No, not there.'

'How about Five-Storey Pavilion? It once guarded the city from invasion.'

The rickshaw coolie is working for a large fare. Tang smiles. 'I'm afraid that's too far out.'

The puller leans into the long handles. 'Don't worry,' he says after a while, looking over his shoulder. 'Rates are fixed, but for you I'll talk price. You won't regret it. I don't know what they do up North, but here we pullers do as we please.' The trotting hasn't cut his breath enough to shorten his conversation. He's talking as if they are seated over tea. 'Fuck the government, that's what I say. All they do is make us work free for their damn armies. I don't know how many times some officer waving a pistol has stopped me and said, 'All right you, now you're working for the army.' And after a full day of running until I'm ready to drop like a dog, they don't give me a single *cash*, nothing. Bastards, right?' He spits as he trots along.

'You don't want to see the usual things. I can tell you've been here plenty before. No Temple of the Six Banyan Trees for you, right? No mosque, no Temple of the Chen, right? You've seen them all. But don't worry, I'll show you a good time. Don't worry abut the fare either. We'll talk about that later.'

He will charge an outrageous fare, Tang thinks, but swaying along in the rickshaw is pleasant, and from its vantage point he has yet another look at this hot jumble of a city, as dangerous as a snake, beautiful, tawdry. It occurs to him that without the meeting with Luk Fat he'd have liked Canton enormously. It is, after all, the lush, mysterious city of his childhood.

'Where are you going?' He notices the puller is heading at a brisk pace northward.

'White Cloud Mountain. I thought you'd like the temples there, Master. Temple of Strong Virtue, White Cloud Temple, and the others there, and the Nine Dragon Spring.'

'You can't be serious. That's too far, it would take hours.'

'Don't you worry, Master.' The rickshaw coolie increases the pace as proof of his ability to trot forever through the tropical afternoon. 'On the way we can see the Peasant Institute. That used to be the Temple of Confucius, but they changed it. We don't need the Sage any more, right? Today we've got an institute for training peasants. They caught that fellow Mao who used to teach boys how to be Bolsheviks. They got him and killed him.'

'Do you read?' Tang asks, thinking this is an intelligent coolie.

'Yes, I read,' he says proudly.

'Maybe you can take me to the Five-Story Pavilion,' the

General says, 'if you insist on going somewhere far. Isn't there a street of bookstores near it?'

'In fact, I do.' Tang wonders if he can find in the bookstores another gift for Black Jade, a book of poetry. In Qufu now it is chrysanthemum time. In the Residence they must be blooming in huge tubs, and at the tomb of the Great Sage an old pistachio standing there must be putting on its scarlet plumage after the summer green. Instead of waterweeds and bullfrogs, he'll return to persimmons heavy with orange fruit. He misses the northern gardens that allow a man to feel each season to its depth. He can hardly wait for the train to give him back to autumn, where the gardens and Black Jade wait. The nights must be chill; she sleeps beneath a light blanket.

He notices the rickshaw coolie has increased the pace, yet still manages to keep up the chatter as they pass alongside an old canal, fetid and covered with slime. 'They're going to dig it up. Put in a wide road. New city soon. That's what the government says. But we don't get a raise in rates. Roads are for the big cars, right?'

'Where are you going now?'

'Don't worry, Master.'

'But you've turned around, you're heading south.'

The puller has been staring at the sky, as if judging the time from the sun's position. Now he leans hard into his work.

'I asked you where we're going!'

'Don't worry, Master. It's late. I'm getting you back to the hotel. There's this short way –' He veers along a line of little shops, plunging into a muddy lane.

'We're not going back now! Where are you taking me?' He leans forward to grip the puller, when midway down the lane he sees a parked car, a big one, taking so much space nothing can pass around it except a pedestrain. Two men, lounging beneath the canopy of a shop, move into the late-afternoon light, pistols drawn. Two more leap from the car, pistols drawn.

Tang has only seconds to decide whether he should draw his own. The quartet have their guns aimed directly at him, so he leaves his hands folded in his lap, while the coolie pulls the rickshaw up to the black hood of the limousine. A few people, children among them, stand in the shadowy doorways and stare.

'Get out, please,' one of the men says. When Tang has climbed from the rickshaw, he says, 'Please give me your gun.'

Tang does, slowly. The man turns the sub-nosed .32 in his hand contemptuously. 'Is this what generals carry?'

Another man gestures Tang toward the limousine. A man sitting in the back seat holds out a long piece of black cloth; when Tang is inside, the man proceeds to wind it around the General's head. Before the blindfold leaves him in darkness, the last thing Tang sees is the rickshaw coolie standing beside the car, his hand out to be paid.

Nothing is said during the ride.

Tang welcomes the silence; it gives him time to adjust. Clearly he's being kidnaped, and one of the men mentioned 'generals,' so they know – or think they know – who he is. Yes, an intelligent rickshaw coolie. He could use such a fellow. These men who have him wear civilian clothes, but their way with guns seems professional.

The car stops. He hears the door open and feels someone roughly take his arm. Then he is led across crunching gravel. There's a whiff of mimosa. After a rather long walk – it must be through a big courtyard – he hears voices, two or three, raised in excited warning: 'Not there! Take him there!'

Someone shoves him, causing him to stumble. And then he feels cooler – inside a building – before a heavy blow across the back sends him sprawling. Then the blindfold's torn away. Blinking rapidly, he finds himself in a small bare windowless room. In the candleglow from a table, four or five men are looking down at him.

'Allow us to extend our humble appreciation for your kind visit,' one of the men says. 'Be seated, General.'

'You have it wrong. I'm Po Ming, a merchant from Shanghai. Papers –' He fumbles in his gown pocket.

'We don't want to see your papers. Be seated, General.'

Slowly he rises and goes to a chair near the wall. The men find chairs too. Tang notices on the wall to his left a blue-and-white plate with the Willow Pattern on it. It is the only decoration in the room.

'We regret detaining you in this manner,' says the man again. He smokes a cigar. The others sit in glum silence. 'Unfortunately in Canton these days we can't always observe the amenities in extending an invitation.' Puffing on the cigar, the man regards Tang a long time before continuing. 'You went to see Wang Ching-wei today.' When Tang remains silent, the man says, 'Why?'

'Permit me to ask who you are,' Tang says.

The man rises and walks to the table, where he stares at the burning candle. He's heavy-set, a man of middle years who wears the gown of a merchant. 'Don't concern yourself with who I am, General.' He speaks excellent but roughly accented Mandarin. 'Believe me, your life depends on your answers. Now again. Why did you go to see Wang Ching-wei?'

The curt, reasonable, yet ominous manner of the stout man is sufficient for Tang to accept the threat as very real. 'He wished to see me.'

'Go on.'

The General is sure he has only two choices: either resist or cooperate. The cigar smoker, impatient and serious, won't tolerate any rhetorical tricks, and his companions look like men capable of immediate, uncomplicated action.

'To discuss the political situation,' Tang says.

'Where did you come from?'

'From a talk with Chiang Kai-shek.'

'You're a Kuomintang general?'

'No. Nor an ally.'

Another man leans forward in his chair. 'But weren't you sent here by Chiang Kai-shek's aide? By Chu Jui?'

The General wonders where they got their information. It occurs to him they have a spy in the headquarters of Wang Ching-wei. Perhaps it's Luk Fat, whose question, although elaborately phrased, had been persistent requests for information. The General admits that Chu Jui suggested he come and talk to Wang Ching-wei about politics. To show good will, he even volunteers that he came for the purpose of finding an ally.

'What sort of alliance did you intend making with Wang?'

The General shrugs. 'That would depend.'

'An alliance between you and Wang or between Wang and Chiang Kai-shek?'

'Between myself and Wang. I wouldn't act for Chiang Kai-shek.'

The cigar smoker, who's been pacing, halts and looks at his companions. 'I don't believe one word he says.'

The men exchange glances, then file out, leaving Tang alone. He sits erect in the chair, looking at the Willow Pattern plate on the wall. He has a short wait only before the cigar smoker returns with a new companion – this one a thin fellow with a hard, taut face.

They sit down and maintain silence for a long time. Finally the cigar smoker says, 'Do you think we're serious, General?'

'Yes, I do. Permit me to ask who you are.'

'We do things our way in the South, General.' He claps his hands sharply. 'There's someone we want you to meet.'

The door opens and a dark man with a drooping mustache enters the room. He isn't Chinese; he wears a Malayan turban. The cigar smoker exchanges a few words with him. Tang recognizes the Hakka dialect, used widely in the South.

'This is Jacinthe Erodoza from Macao,' says the cigar smoker. Tang looks at him through the eyes of childhood, for this, obviously, is a pirate – one of those men father used to describe. He's a real pirate: shorter than average, with a Macanese name, a turban from Malaya, blood from Portugal among other places.

'Jacinthe Erodoza has come at our request,' the cigar smoker says with a kind of sarcastic formality. 'He has agreed to accompany you to a ship and transport you to some islands south of here. Do you understand, General? That's what Mister Erodoza will do if we say so. Perhaps he'll explain what happens if you go with him to the islands.'

In poor Chinese the little man says, pointing at the General's groin, 'If he's got something there, we start there.' With a sudden grin he adds, 'Believe me, he won't like it.'

The cigar smoker asks Mister Erodoza to wait outside. 'That's how we do things in the South, General.'

Tang has wondered before how he will die. Usually he imagines it happening on the battlefield or sometimes he's gunned down in the street or perhaps once in a while he dies in bed, looking at a tranquil garden. But he's never contemplated death by torture at the hands of the kind of half-breed river pirates he had dreamed of joining as a boy.

'Let's start at the beginning, General, and try to get at the heart of things. Otherwise Mister Erodoza is willing to take you off our hands.'

'I've told you the truth.'

'You come to our city, you try to make contact with someone, you say you're looking for allies. And you've just come from Chiang Kai-shek, but you claim he isn't an ally. It's all confusing, sir. Can you blame us for worrying about your presence among us?'

'Permit me again to ask who you are.'

The hard-faced man scrapes his chair a little closer. One eye droops slightly, giving him a rather sad expression to go with the bony structure of his face. 'Tell me, General,' he says in a thin, hoarse voice, 'will Chiang Kai-shek return to government?'

'I think he will.'

'Did he tell you that?'

'No.'

The hard-faced man clears his throat. 'But you want him to return to the Nanking government.'

'No.'

'Please explain why.'

'He isn't the man to unite China. He's not really Confucian. He lacks – human-heartedness.' The General has used a favorite term of the Great Sage.

'Why did he send you here to see Wang Ching-wei?'

'I told you he did not send me. I came for myself.' After a pause Tang adds, 'Why would he send a northerner like myself? Chiang has plenty of southern subordinates who could do the job better here.'

The hard-faced man purses his lips. 'I can think of a reason for sending you. He could show Wang that he has support in the North.'

The cigar smoker says, 'I don't think we've been very courteous, General. Here you are our guest, and we haven't given you a chance to express your opinion about things.'

'What things?'

'What you think of the Russians, of Wang Ching-wei. And what you think of the late Doctor Sun Yat-sen.'

'I will answer you truthfully. I don't want the Russians in China. I know Wang Ching-wei only by reputation – which is mixed, in my opinion. As for Sun Yat-sen, he was a man of high principles, but he found himself in a dilemma: to get rid of foreigners, he had to depend on them. He never worked free of the difficulty.'

The cigar smoker, having listened intently, his eyes on a spot on the floor, now looks up. 'Thank you, General. Permit me to say you are a fool. You don't want Russians in China, but Wang Ching-wei was ready on a number of occasions to give them the country. He talks a lot, he understands nothing. As for Sun Yat-sen, perhaps you must live in Canton to have really known him. You northerners never understood what a *fumbler* he was. He believed the last person to whisper in his ear. He didn't know where to place his trust. There was never as much corruption in this city as under him. He brought in mercenaries from Yunnan and Hunan who couldn't even speak our language. To pay them he sold public land, confiscated property. And all the while, just like Wang Ching-wei, he was fawning over the Russians.' The man glares at Tang. 'And then there was Bloody Wednesday. The Russians planned it, he carried it out.'

'Permit me again to ask who you are.'

Taking the cigar from his mouth, the smoker at last answers. 'We're what's left of the Merchants' Volunteer Corps.'

Both men, without another word, leave the room. Tang waits rigidly in the chair for Jacinthe Erodoza to come for him, but enough time passes for him to realize they aren't quite ready to give him up. They need confirmation on their decision. It's likely that they are waiting for their superior.

The Merchants' Volunteer Corps.

The General is familiar with the history of the organization. The MVC was a private army sponsored by the Canton merchants' guild. Every metropolitan business had been assessed funds to create and maintain the MVC as a military force in the early 1920s. Its mission was to destroy or at least control the roving bands of mercenaries who had been cut adrift from the provincial armies. Later the MVC, becoming a political force as well, opposed the pro-Russian policies of Doctor Sun Yat-sen. There was a showdown in the streets between MVC troops and Nationalist soldiers.

The General had read about it in the newspaper. He had also read about Bloody Wednesday. The victorious Nationalists, on orders from Doctor Sun at the instigation of his Russian advisers, then tracked down and murdered the surviving MVC leaders on Wednesday, October 15, 1924.

So the men who now hold him, Tang realizes, are remnants of that private army, and as such, they nourish an abiding hatred of anyone – Nationalist or Russian – connected with the massacre.

The question now facing him is the effect his answers might have on them. That he has come here to meet with Wang Ching-wei is surely against him. That he has come here from seeing Chiang Kai-shek is worse. Nor did it help him to have given Doctor Sun even guarded praise.

The General gets up to pace in the hot, airless little room. There is nothing he can do now but wait. It is useless – his father would have said cowardly and wasteful – to speculate further on the outcome. If he goes to Jacinthe Erodoza, he goes. He attempts to turn his thoughts to Black Jade, but there is something about the prospect of eventual torture – sexual torture – that thoroughly inhibits his ability to think of her. In his pacing seeking an anchor for his mind, he glances often at the Willow Pattern plate on the wall. It's a new one, a plate common today in China, but it reminds him of many things – of his past – and that's something to steady his mind. The blue-and-white plate and its symbols, which he had explained to Black Jade, once played a part in his life. He must have been seventeen – or was he eighteen? – when he was initiated into the Eight Trigram Society, a Shantung branch of the White Lotus, called the *Hung* here in the South.

He joined the Eight Trigram out of filial respect for his grand-father, who had once belonged to the Plum Blossom Fists, led by Chu of the Red Lamp. Chu claimed descent from the Ming emperors; at the time of the Boxer Rebellion, the Plum Blossom Fists along with other societies had fought against the foreigners at Peking. His grandfather died in an assault on the Legations there. Father used to describe the old man's ascetic life, spent in full service to the society. Tang had never tired, as a child, of listening to this account of a man who rose before dawn, meditated two hours, ate a breakfast of boiled vegetables, boxed all morning, and practiced sword dancing with curved daggers and three-pronged spears. It was such a spear that grandfather brandished while charging a British blockhouse, convinced that his incanta-tions and his talismans rendered him immune to gunfire. Father had one of those talismans (stolen by Yuan Shih-k'ai's men when the Tang clan was exterminated). Now Tang Shan-teh, prisoner in a windowless room in Canton, remembers that talisman with absolute clarity. Perhaps he can now, as he could in boyhood, draw it from memory: that drawing on paper of a creature without feet, but with a pointed chin and a crimson face, and four halos over its head. On the body were painted the characters for Buddha, tiger, and dragon. In the top left corner was printed: 'Invoke first the Guardian of Heaven.' On the right hand: 'Invoke next the Black Gods of Pestilence.' And so armed with his three-pronged sword and this paper charm, grandfather went to his death, no doubt positive of his safety until the breath left him and darkness filled his eyes, no doubt sure that the White Demons would never overcome the magic that protected him.

It was in behalf of grandfather that Tang had undergone the

ceremony: Removing his own clothes, he put on the white robe of the Mings, removed his shoes, and washed his face of the dust of the Manchus. He had put on a red turban and listened to the history of the thirteenth-century monks who defied the Mongols – and by extrapolation the later Manchus. Betrayed by one of the brotherhood, the monks at Shao-lin Monastery were surprised and massacred by imperial Mongol troops – all but five, who survived to take an oath of allegiance to one another. In the Red Flower Pavilion they taught their disciples the arts of war that would free them from heathen invaders. Afterward, Tang was given the password, then entered the 'gate' or doorway into the initiation room under an arch of crossed swords. 'Which is harder, these swords or your neck?' a member had asked. 'My neck,' he knew to reply. He was then in the City of Willows, the ritual lodge room symbolizing a Buddhist heaven. He was told, 'The barriers are open, the way is clear.'

Strange, but during the years he quite forgot the steps of that ritual; now they come back to him, almost sweetly, as if through them he recovers part of his youth.

Someone said in a ringing voice, 'The way is clear!' Then Tang burned incense to the gods and to the warrior brothers of the Three Kingdoms, one of whom became Kuan Ti, God of War, the soldier's god, tutelary deity of the White Lotus. Donning grass sandals, he knelt and swore to abide by the Thirty-Six Oaths. A rooster's head was severed, its blood mixed with blood from the middle finger of his left hand. He intoned the proper words: 'Henceforth I am one with the family. Where the Brothers lead, I will follow.' He was shown precious objects in the room: the sword to kill Manchus – and other oppressors; the pair of scissors to cut through heavy clouds hanging over China; a brush by which just laws can be written; a red lamp to distinguish true from false; a pair of scales to weigh the hated Manchu against the beloved Ming emperors; a white fan to revive the spirits of dead heroes; a rosary to pray for Buddhist protection; a yellow umbrella, symbol of imperial Ming authority; a small bush to represent the Peach Tree where the heroes of *The Three Kingdoms* swore their oath of eternal brotherhood many centuries ago; a small jade ruler to measure the time left before restoration of the Ming; a mirror by which to appraise inner strengths and weaknesses; a sacred bowl to stand for the one found by the five heroic monks; a wooden model of the Red Flower Pavilion; a pair of red candles whose significance he has forgotten; and finally tea and wine offered to the noble ancestors who fought for the return of good government. Throughout the ceremony there had been a mystical journey from darkness into light. 'Where did you come from?' they asked him in the glow of the red lamp. 'From the Red Flower Pavilion, where I was instructed to the bonds of loyalty and the five virtues.' 'How many roads could you have taken?' 'Three.' 'Which road did you take?' 'The middle road.' 'Why?' 'Because it was the broadest.'

He recalls not only the ritual but also his growing disillusionment with the society. It became evident to him that its members had lost or never possessed the inspiration that had fired its originators – those Buddhist monks in revolt against the Mongols six hundred years ago. He came to believe that the modern version of a society dedicated to liberty was fostering ignorance rather than enlightenment, superstition rather than spiritual force. Merchants instead of scholars took leading roles, especially in the cities, where membership was good for business, not the soul. And some of the branches – the Red Knives, the Yellow Spears, the League of Hard Bellies – often oppressed the very people they claimed to protect. Gathering their forces in the towns, they went armed into villages and terrified the inhabitants. Householders, in an effort to placate the marauders, sometimes placed red cloth over their door frames and set a bowl of water and a knife at their thresholds. The use of the society's old symbolism was rarely effective, as the members cleared everything they could find out of hapless villages. Thus did the White Lotus administer justice.

The General now accepts the reality of human weakness; surely more than he in those early days when youthful idealism narrowed his understanding of men. There hangs the Willow Pattern plate, symbol of an old China, of his own youth. It has helped him pass the time – and a lot has passed. He has changed the candle a number of times from a box in the corner. Hours must have gone by. His captors must be waiting restlessly for their leader, while Jacinthe Erodoza sits with far more patience, ready to accept the job or return unpaid to his boat. It's all the same to him. A man who lives only by violence needs little else to sustain him in life. Tang has seen it in the army – men who live to kill.

He figures it must be late at night when finally the door opens and the hard-faced man enters the room, accompanied by a stranger with steel-gray hair and gold-rimmed glasses. The newcomer, staring at the General, bows like someone at home with the protocol of high places. 'I regret the inconvenience,' he says in Mandarin. He doesn't employ the sarcasm that had roughened the voice of the cigar smoker. 'If you'd do so kind as to answer a few more questions, General. I think I may know your family. Are you related to General Tang Chi-yao?'

'I am not.' Tang Chi-yao is a Yunnanese warlord hated by the Cantonese.

The man doesn't seem to respond to the General's denial. 'I thought you were related.'

'Tang is one of the One Hundred Names,' the General says.

'Of course, a very common name, General, but I was sure you were related to him.'

The General feels a tug of despair. In spite of this man's appearance and bearing, he's no different from the others; they are all skeptical.

'If not Tang Chi-yao, then perhaps Tang Shen-chih. I must have been thinking of him. Your cousin, perhaps?'

'He is not.' Tang Shen-chih is a warlord from Hunan. It occurs to the General that the gray-haired man has mentioned two notorious warlords, scavenger dogs who've looted Canton whenever the city has been vulnerable. Why link him to such hated militarists from Yunnan and Hunan?

'You speak excellent Mandarin,' the gray-haired man says with a faint smile.

'I would hope so,' Tang says, meeting the man's smile with his own. 'It's my mother tongue.'

'I believe you.'

Then it strikes the General that Hunan and Yunnan are the two southern provinces where Mandarin is spoken. Perhaps the gray-haired man is implying that he's acquired Mandarin here in the South. An astonishing idea – that he's a southern Tang, working for either of two despised warlords. 'I'm fron Shantung,' he maintains as coolly as possible. 'I have nothing to do with the men you speak of.'

'Tea,' says the gray-haired man.

At this command – obviously the gray-haired man is the leader – the hard-faced man leaves the room.

'I don't want to hand you over to the Macanese,' the leader says to Tang when they're alone. 'Too much blood is spilled these days. But I will not be fooled. Let's start again. Who sent you to see Wang Ching-wei?'

503

Tang repeats his story, noticing with dismay that the leader never once nods in agreement; he maintains a steadfastly judgmental look. The General knows he must satisfy the man quickly that he's neither a Kuomintang agent working for Chiang Kai-shek nor a member of a southern warlord clan. Otherwise, there's no doubt of it, he will go to the islands with Jacinthe Erodoza.

Tea comes, brought by the hard-faced man. Thus far Tang hasn't seen any servants, a sign that his imprisonment is a secret. They can be done with him easily, without a trace. He watches the hard-faced man set down the cups and pot. The pot bears the Willow Pattern design. Common enough – the design is everywhere in China today. Yet uncommon in certain circumstances. The design has taken up unusual space in his mind during this captivity. The plate on the wall has taken him back to his youth, to the old ritual ruined for him by those who perform it. The hardfaced man lifts the pot gravely; the blue pattern wavers in the candlelight.

The gray-haired man says something, but Tang doesn't catch the words. He is staring hard at the raised teapot, at the design that has filled his solitary hours.

As the hard-faced man pours tea into the cups, Tang says, 'I will take the middle one.' He repeats his words in a loud voice. 'I said I will take the middle cup!'

The two men regard him curiously.

'We are all people from the Garden,' he says while taking the middle cup. Sipping from it, he points with the index finger to his left hand toward the ceiling, right hand toward the floor. Then with his right index finger he points to his heart.

For the first time the gray-haired man shows emotion: surprise. His eyebrows lift questioningly. 'Where were you born?'

'I was born under a peach tree in the Red Pavilion.'

'The first time?'

'No, the second. When I was reborn.'

'Why is your skin so yellow?' the leader asks harshly.

'I am troubled for my country.'

The two men glance at each other. 'Why is your shirt so old?' continues the leader.

'It was handed down by five ancestors.'

'Does your nose ever bleed?'

'Vast waters run from the channels of my nose.'

'What does that mean?'

'It means a revolution will come. The Manchu and their successors will be destroyed by the deluge and leave the Mings their rightful place in the Middle Kingdom.'

'You cannot pass.'

'Please, Chan Kan Nam –' He is calling the gray-haired man the Lodge Master. 'Give me more teacups.'

Then, struggling with memory, fired by the chance to save himself, Tang recites slowly, 'The changes with teacups are inexhaustible. My abilities are few, my knowledge superficial.'

'Get the cup,' says the leader.

While the hard-faced man is gone, Tang says nothing and neither does the leader. They sit looking steadily at each other. With each passing minute the General's hope rise. Yes, these men are *Hung* – southern members of the White Lotus. On other occasions this little room with its Willow Pattern plate must be the scene of ritual. For men in white robes the incense-filled room becomes celestial: the City of Willows, a paradise, a fortress of patriotic resolve.

When the hard-faced man returns with a dozen cups, Tang arranges them in various patterns, such as he recalls from his own training. Sitting back at last, he asks the men to test him. They do, putting seven cups in the following design:

```
  O        O        O
           O
           O
           O
           O
```

Without hesitation Tang moves the bottom cup to the top, forming a sword with its hilt.

The two men, rising, bow. The leader says, 'Do you swear on your oath of the Brotherhood that what you've told us about your visit to Canton is true?'

'I swear.'

'Then we believe you.'

Not only is he released, but next morning a car is placed at his disposal. He leaves the mansion in the suburb of Pak Wan Shen – he remembers from childhood its mulberry groves, cemeteries, great houses – and is driven to his hotel for his belongings, then to the train station.

Sitting at the compartment window, he watches his escorts depart, men who might have driven him instead to Jacinthe Erodoza's boat had it not been for his youthful association with a society whose rituals awed him but whose practices he has long since disavowed. It is something to think about, but certainly not now. Perhaps when he's an old man, if he lives to be old. Meanwhile his senses are refreshed by the landscape of Kwangtung that passes by his window all day. Along a lake he sees a line of willows that mark the watercourse: the willow tree, symbol of woman. Black Jade. She's beside him, supine, naked, open. But as the day wears on, its monotony returns him to the past, as if the *Hung* ritual room with its Willow Pattern plate has drawn him deeper into memory, into corners where he once stored facts now long forgotten. He recalls them, one by one, with delight: 108 is the number of postures in Tai Chi Chuan, of beads in a Buddhist rosary, of yogis who attended Sakyamuni's birth. Seven's the number of death. The least important number is six. Fifteen surpasses all other numbers: three (birth) plus five (life) plus seven (death) equals fifteen. Fifteen is the number of souls uniting in the body to form man. He remembers a magical arrangement of numbers that add up to fifteen in any straight line:

$$
\begin{array}{ccc}
4 & 9 & 2 \\
3 & 5 & 7 \\
8 & 1 & 6
\end{array}
$$

He recalls other matters, generally Taoist in origin, which few people attend to any more except priests and old women of the household, yet wayward trivia now tumble back gaily into his mind and fill him with good cheer. There's no need, he tells himself, to believe or disbelieve in them; he can merely accept them as formulas of a history he's now part of, at this living moment.

The watery province of Kwangtung slips by. Egrets as white as clouds stand at the edge of paddies. Clumps of pine forest present themselves, recede, leaving a faint whiff of their perfume in the train. The leaves of bamboo in the distance look like raindrops clinging to bare limbs. There are lakes, streams, ponds; the endless paddies march along, their color, he is certain, like nothing else under Heaven. The green of young rice shoots is a green beyond green, a green lighter and more iridescent than jade, darker than the reef water through which the junk sailed in the South China Sea, a perfect green. He remembers the line of a poem, maybe from the Sung: 'The green of rice shoots is a green to make the heart sing.'

He loves this land.

And that night, sleepy, he leans his head against the side of the window and watches the rivers and fields under moonshine; thick palm groves are lit deep in their interiors by candles in solitary huts, little pricks of light in the vast darkness of China.

Such reveries never last long, however. Surely not in this land, where meditation is a short respite from struggle. Next morning the train breaks down on the Hunan border. Nonpaying passengers drop like ripe fruit from the top of boxcars into the lush undergrowth along the tracks. The inside passengers mingle with them soon enough, all heading northward like mountaineering trekkers, lugging their valises, packages, and burlap-wrapped boxes. Tang picks up his own small bundle and starts in the direction of Wuhan. They've been lucky that the train merely broke down. A few years ago, during a fierce warlord upheaval, someone exploded a cask of sulphuric acid in the third coach from the end of a Canton-Changsha train going forty miles an hour. It burned down to the framework in minutes. If Tang remembers correctly, almost a hundred people died before they brought the train to a standstill.

So along with the other passengers, moving alone or in groups, the General sets out for the North. He goes by cart at times; once a long stretch by hired pony; more often by foot, crossing streams on rocks; and over broad riverways by flat-bottom scows. There are daily rain squalls. He sleeps on boats, in temples, under sheds for a few *cash*. Hearing on the road that Changsha is under siege by a local warlord or the remnant of a Red army – it's unclear which – he turns northeast and at Chingchiang gets an inland junk to Nanchang, continues by river boat to Wuhan, arriving there two weeks after leaving Canton.

He stays in the tricities only long enough to get a train ticket. There's time to read in a local newspaper that Chiang Kai-shek has gone to Japan for 'consultations' with General Tanaka, the Prime Minister. on a back page he discovers an item about Red armies in the South. Ho Lung and Yeh Ting have been driven from Swatow (so the brave leader Ch'en Chiung-ming can turn his ship around

507

and bring his loot back home); that the whereabouts of Chu Teh is uncertain; and that another Red bandit, Mao Tse-tung, has escaped execution by Hunanese troops and is now hiding out with a detachment of Bolsheviks in the mountains somewhere.

At the Wuchang train station, the General has a strange experience. As he climbs into the rail car, he notices among the milling crowd a very tall, massive fellow who pushes his field hat back for a moment, revealing a foreigner's face.

Getting to his seat, the General leans out of the window for another look, but the man is gone, vanished in the noisy throng. It couldn't be: The man was clean shaven, not heavily bearded. And he was no opium addict, shuffling along. It couldn't have been the Russian, but there he was, strapping and purposeful in the station of Wuchang.

Yet this odd possibility commands his attention less than the thought of going home. Craning his neck farther from the window, he looks in the opposite direction, toward the locomotive that will take him there.

21

Out of direct sunlight the days are chill now in Qufu, the nights cold, and courtyards crackle with the leaves of autumn.

Only yesterday Vera was informed of a wireless message received at headquarters days ago from a certain Po Ming in Canton: TEA SHIPMENT SENT. Captain Fan told her. Had she waited for Colonel Pi to send word of the General's eventual return, she'd have waited until Shan-teh walked in the door.

His eventual return. No estimate of arrival given. Yet she's relieved to know he's coming back. Often – more frequently as time passed – she'd imagined him imprisoned by political foes or captured by roving bandits or maimed by an accident the nature of which can never be anticipated in China.

It seems to Vera that most of her life has been spent waiting for men; that has taught her patience. Yet this time she has suffered greatly, for the man she awaits is a man she loves. In consequence she has tried to keep busy. Playing Tai Chi at dawn has helped to give shape to her thoughts and calm her fears. So does her work at translation in the afternoons. She has moved inside to work now, feeling the chill of the courtyard when it's in shadow. Through daily persistence she has managed to translate thirty-one of the fifty poems in the collection Shan-teh gave her. The monotony of evenings is broken now and then by dinner with Captain Fan and the American cavalryman, both of whom are pleasant companions, attentive as she could want. In a restrained way they flatter her with the knowledge that she's sufficiently desirable for a man like Shan-teh when he returns.

But her greatest comfort during the long wait comes from her daily visits with Bright Lotus. They meet usually in a courtyard with the maid waiting in a shadowed gallery. But sometimes the little girl, taking Vera by the hand, leads her into the Kong compound, into the sanctified area of the Residence. Here they play or read together in one of the women's pavilions. In her trips through the compound Vera has little glimpses of Kong life: of old women in silk gowns with their hair dressed in seed-pearl pins, ivory guards on their fingernails; of elegant studies (the doors ajar in the last warmth of autumn noons) with their raised platforms and low narrow tables. She has seen the shelves with books in their thin covers lying flat, piled one on another, the tall water pipes, the ivory incense holders, and the writing materials – brush, ink stone, paper – all in an instant. Only yesterday she'd seen a Kong gentleman rounding a distant corner, wearing a squirrel-skin overcoat, leggings, wide-brimmed hat, and carrying a firebox with coals to warm his hands. Each of these glimpses into the secret world of Chinese royalty thrills Vera, lifting her from her own time into an ancient Tang painting, where poetry ruled the tranquil days and where, by tiny streams in a feathery grove of bamboo, people in rich gowns had their tea.

In a room off to themselves Vera and Bright Lotus inspect the fighting crickets in their little cages. Although the girl has developed her talent for rousing the insects to fighting ardor by tickling their antennae with a mouse whisker, she still refuses to let them fight. Vera likes this in the girl – curiosity modified by tenderness. Bright Lotus is as appealing a person as she has ever known. Sometimes it seems to Vera that Bright Lotus and Shan-teh can provide her with a total world, although the next instant she's just as certain it can't last. For one thing, she knows that with age Bright Lotus will be increasingly cut off from contact with everyone outside of the family. Her young brother will fare better, although at present he's more isolated. Vera saw him for a while, then he never came back, and neither Bright Lotus nor the maid will offer an explanation. Since then she's seen him once, while she was reading the adventures of Monkey King for the third time to Bright Lotus. They were sitting in a room near the women's kitchen. From where Vera sat she could see the shallow tubs, lanterns, jars, and baskets on the kitchen's back porch. Looking up from the book, she abruptly saw the round-faced boy staring at her. He was wearing a silk gown and a black cap adorned with a pearl-studded ornament shaped like a fan – an heir of Confucius. A sleeve, then a hand came from behind the door frame in the courtyard and whisked him away by the arm.

Vera is sure these are the happiest moments of her life – of her adult life, at least – here with Bright Lotus. Along with the maid they fly brightly colored dragon kites over the rooftops of the Residence (even though Captain Fan warned her the Kongs might not want a daughter engaging in such an activity) or they boil eggs and color them or they play hide-and-seek, little Bright Lotus stumping along at considerable speed on her bound lily feet, her braids bouncing. They stand for long solemn minutes and watch the sparrows twittering in a gnarled pomegranate or in one of the many cedars, their tops brown now, withered, and the trunks white with dust. More than once Vera wakes from sleep, trembling from fear that something has happened to her little friend; that the Taoist bag worn around her neck won't ward off evil; or that the curved roof of Bright Lotus' quarters won't cannonade bad spirits back into the air, as they're supposed to do when demons alight. But the moment passes, and in the cold darkness Vera is left with a comforting image of Bright Lotus in her tunics and skirts and with her hair coiled into two black glistening braids and her dark eyes brilliant, at once solemn and mischievous, The girl has returned Vera to a better day, when her own hair wore a yellow velvet ribbon and her father's big vest watch pressed against her thigh as he lifted her up for a hug. Bright Lotus has given back to her some memories of Russia far different from those of the nightmare: Chopin played in salons with snow falling softly at the windows; the sight of fur hats and muffs as big as Chinese melons from Kiangsi; waltzes from Austria and elbow-length gloves in the glittering ballrooms; and sleighs with gracefully curved runners; and horses wearing their musical bells in the nights as clear as crystal.

Often in these midnight reveries, fostered by thoughts of a little Chinese girl, Vera recalls the religion of her own youth and recognizes with mild surprise how deeply, deeply, the rituals had

510

suffused her daily life in Holy Russia, the third and final Rome. The other afternoon Bright Lotus carried in her pudgy hand a little ivory of Kuan Yin, Goddess of Mercy, and the sight of it has remained with Vera, whose patron saint had once been Nicholas of Myra, protector of children and young women; in legend he gave a poor man dowries for his three daughters to keep them from a brothel. 'If God dies, we still have Nicholas.' Her mother used to say that on the way to communion, where deacons swung their censers, pouring clouds of perfumed smoke into the great domed church, and the male chorus lifted their voices in ringing affirmation of eternal faith.

'Christ in his meek love is the way to salvation,' Vera mumbles sleepily in the dark night, quoting her mother – alone with her memories and her delight in Bright Lotus and her desire for the return of Shan-teh.

He has returned.

When she recognizes him in the doorway, rumpled and wan but smiling, Vera understands in an instant how dreadfully frightened she has been. Running beneath the gaiety of her hours with Bright Lotus and the gentle memories of a sweet childhood has been a flood of anxiety and fear. Life has taught her that anxiety and fear are usually justified. They are harbingers of truth, never to be dismissed or scorned. Only later, when she has assimilated his return, will Vera suspect that her memories of Mother Church were in fact a form of prayer, her good times with Bright Lotus a shoring up of her mind against the nightmare.

But now she simply rejoices at his return. Vera scarcely hears a word of his brisk, almost curt rendition of his adventures during the weeks of travel. She hears the names of people and places, but concentrates on the set of his lips, the look in his eyes. It occurs to her that he looks strangely unfamiliar; her memory had given him the square chin and big nose of a Russian. She had forgotten the slant of his eyes, the stained-ivory hue of his skin. While he speaks, Vera concentrates on the long Buddhistic lobes of his ears. He has not yet touched her. She wonders if for them this is right – the shyness, the restraint – when with little effort she can trade upon her brothel skills and transform their decorum into full-blown desire. Yet he talks and she replies; they converse like two people married for years. Gradually she feels the calm his return gives her, the full awareness of her attachment to him, and she senses it's the same for him. Vera accepts, then welcomes the place of this calm in their lives.

Then the ink stone, his gift from Canton.

It is a plain oblong of white jade. Shan-teh tells her with a smile that the contemplation of white jade expels evil from the mind. 'A steel point won't touch this jade, it's so hard,' he explains, as Vera tests its grain with her thumb. 'I imagine the workman used crushed garnet as an abrasive. It's highly polished and a fine-grained stone. That's what drew me to it.' He reaches out to touch the jade too; their fingers graze one another. 'White's a strange color for an ink stone. But I thought when the ink stains the trough, you'll have the light and dark.'

She looked at him. '*Yin* and *yang*.'

'Exactly. It's almost too finely grained for an ink stone. It will take a long time to grind your ink sticks on it.'

'The ink will be smoother.'

'True.'

Vera turns it in her hand and studies it. She can almost see the lamp-black ink stick grind against the sloping little wall of the stone, hear the scraping in the hollow become muffled as the ink absorbs water; as she dips and lifts the brush, the ink runs like sluggish oil. 'I love you, Shan-teh.' She warms the hard mineral in her hand as if it were his body.

Later, long after dinner and another wait while he confers with his staff, they touch, and the touch of their bodies quite overwhelms Vera. Their lovemaking takes her to the heart of myth, the *yin* and *yang* of separation and unity. Next morning they play Tai Chi Chuan, extending their intimacy beyond the bedroom. Then she introduces him to Bright Lotus, who is shy but dignified, pleasing Vera. As for Shan-teh, when he kneels to look at the child, he is rigid, nervous, curt. Vera whispers to him, 'She won't bite.'

'It's been a long time –'

She realizes he's thinking of his dead sons. 'I want,' she says, 'to buy Bright Lotus a chow puppy. That's better than fighting crickets, don't you think?'

'Be careful. Don't spoil the child – and don't praise her too much. It's dangerous,' he adds with a smile.

'Why dangerous?'

'The gods could become jealous and harm her.'

10

'I've heard that superstition,' Vera says. 'Do you believe in it?'

'I would first have to believe in the gods.'

'Well, do you?'

'No. But it's better to please than annoy them.'

Next day, changing his schedule to conform with Vera's time with the child, he joins them in the courtyard. 'Come on,' says Vera cheerfully, 'we're going to the big garden.'

'The Kong family garden?'

Vera takes the little girl's hand; a maid waits in the shadowed gallery. 'Of course, we go all the time.'

The General shakes his head. 'I have not been formally invited.'

Vera stares at him: the strong face, the tip of a gold tooth showing between his slightly parted lips, the long earlobes, the vigilant eyes. It is, at the moment, a severe and determined face; yet she has seen it break into tenderness, the eyes express mischief, the mouth humor. 'May I say this, Shen-teh?' She puts her free hand on her hip, while the little girl, holding the other, stares hard at the General. 'You're a strange man. Open one moment, closed the next. A man caught in the middle of his convictions.'

'Just the same –' he begins.

'Come.'

He does. Sheepishly, he follows them into the central part of the Residence, along the west side of the women's quarters to the great garden in the north. Vera and the little girl lead him in triumph – his hands fisted self-consciously at his back – into forbidden territory. And in succeeding days Vera takes him alone to the garden with its pavilions, bridges, and deep pools fed by an underground spring. They even go at night and sit upon the rocks to view the moon's image, either motionless or wavering on the pond's surface. She tells him of the moon that looked down on her family's annihilation; but in his company she no longer hates it.

'Tonight,' she says once as they sit on a large rock, 'the moon doesn't remind me of snow. Maybe I'm becoming free of all that.'

'Time will take care of it.'

'I don't think time can. Something has to replace the memories. That's what you're doing for me – replacing them.' After a long silence, she says, 'Tell me about the gods.'

'What makes you think of them?' he asks in surprise.

'The moon, the night, the quiet.'

'There's a saying: To watch the moon washing its soul.'

'And the gods?'

Again he speaks in amusing paradox. He tells her to stay clear of the gods if they exist, because they're spiteful when mishandled. Then, as she might expect, he talks of Confucius. The Sage never spoke of the gods, let alone answered people when they asked about monstrous births caused by comets or the meaning of owls hooting in the day. The Great Teacher let Heaven alone and focussed his attention on Earth.

'Is that all you have to say about God?' she asks, disappointed.

'I do have one belief about a certain kind of divinity,' he admits. 'We Chinese deify people who've led good lives. They're worshipped as if they are actually gods. For me, in this way, the dead live.'

'I knew you believed that.'

Shan-teh laughs. 'How could you?'

'I felt it. I knew the great heroes and your clan are alive for you. You don't speak much of your family, yet sometimes I know they're here in your mind, existing in a way I can't understand. Because for you, when we're alone, we're not alone.'

'Then you understand.'

'I told you I don't understand. But I know. And sometimes I feel God is with us.'

'For me I suppose your god is my clan.'

'So we have more than ourselves with us.'

They both breathe out a little laugh of agreement. 'I never asked you outright,' Vera says, 'but I'll ask now. Do you love me?'

'Yes. I love you.'

'Let's go home.' They rise to walk back through the moonlit Residence. She is touched by the evening and what they have said in the moon-drenched garden – touched, frightened, and exhilarated. She learned long ago never to equate a man's passion and his love; they always seem to be separate in his mind, or like one experience viewed by two men. Yet with this man his passion for her seems to become his love, and in a way she can understand, in a way she'd understood with Yu-ying. Such deep love is frightening, and she undergoes, as they walk toward their bed, a sense of melancholy. Can the world be so perfect? Of course not. Can it? she asks herself hopefully.

There is a drought, and the cold wind from Central Asia sweeps through Qufu; it rattles the skeletal trees and overnight it leaves a hard frost that kills the withering chrysanthemums in their pots. For Vera, in her warm bed with Shan-teh, it's a peaceful time. Between them she sense a deepening of intimacy, a lessening of tension. In such a calm atmosphere, however, the most offhand remark can take on significance – Vera knows this, as she knows that man and woman must search for complications. Or at least she does. For example, she can't let go of a casual remark Shan-teh made on the evening of the hard frost. They were discussing the immensity and decay of the Residence. When he's in charge of the central government, Shan-teh has said, he will have the archives of the Kong family filed and catalogued. There are no papers like them in all of China. They contain, among other priceless items, a list of Qufu temples and minutely detailed reports of restorations over the past five hundred years. They describe the civil adminis-tration of Kong estates and give a complete history of the family from Han times, along with biographies of local officials from the Ming and accounts of trade during that period. They contain chronicles of court life, even a record of floods going back as far as the Yuan Dynasty. They are unique documents, Shan-teh explained, but spread throughout the Residence in shelves, trunks, boxes, rotting and disintegrating, the witnesses of a civilization as well as the spokesmen for one of the great families of the world.

What did Vera hear? 'When I'm in charge of the central govern-ment.' Shan-teh said it – chief of state, the ruler of China. She is astounded. Their new-found ease of intimacy has uncovered his deepest ambition – and what an ambition! By following the impli-cations of it, she begins setting in place any observation he makes or any question he asks. How was she treated by his staff during his absence? Vera figures he wants to measure the extent and depth of his control over them: indifference or courtesy to her being the gauge of his assessment. Why does he keep the American in camp? To learn something about a country which someday he will deal with over a conference table. Where is she, Vera wonders in alarm, in the vast landscape of such ambition? The question won't go away, as she tries to find the answer to it within his most casual remarks. She listens carefully when Shan-teh mentions a point of military administration, not, surely, because she wants to under-stand the intricacies of managing an army, but because she must discover his way of fitting the world to his desire – and thereby discover her own place in his future. She must, she *must* know. 'When I'm in charge of the central government'? She must know.

And all the while Vera detects in herself the telltale signs of incipient distrust. It is only too familiar. In the past her suspicions, beginning the same way – a mundane remark setting off speculations – have rooted out of her her affection for certain men and planted in its place the meanness of possessive jealousy. She reins up with horror at the prospect of losing Shan-teh through an old habit. Yet she continues to pay attention to the details of his work, and encourages him to discuss it with her. One night in the Kong garden, she says, 'How long would you be chief of state – if it came to that?'

Shan-teh smiles. 'If it came to that, I wouldn't have the job long.'

'Why not?'

'I wouldn't be wanted or needed. Once the civil war ended and the government was strong enough, I'd step down. A military man as head of state? Not in China.'

Thank God, she thinks. At least he doesn't have the grasping mind of a Stalin – of a Bolshevik. It occurs to her that Shan-teh has never mentioned the Bolshevik agent who fled recently. But she remembers him all right. And this evening, when they're in bed, she tosses restlessly beside Shan-teh, unable to sleep because the Bolshevik is on her mind. She relives their encounter near the Drum Tower. She is yelling at him to get out of her path, although the truth is that ahorse she can get clear of him in an instant. He lifts his arm to protect his face when the riding crop descends; then her arm, having a furious life of its own, brings the whip down to slash at him and slash at him until she sees two long ribbons of blood appear on the face, above the yellowish teeth, the filthy beard. Then: the little Chinese dragging him away from her like a corpse from a battlefield. Then: the blond American, Philip, galloping up to threaten the beaten Bolshevik, who's too woozy from opium to understand that what he's feeling is pain.

Shan-teh, turning in bed, puts his cheek against hers. 'You're awake?'

'Yes. A little restless, that's all.'

'We both are. I'm curious,' he says in the darkness. 'Do women of your country take an interest in politics?'

'Some do,' Vera says cautiously.

'I'm not accustomed to it,' he admits.

'Does it bother you when I ask questions about it?'

'No.' He adds after a little silence, 'It's only different.'

'I've never been interested in politics until now. But if you're going to be chief of state –'

Shan-teh strokes her cheek. 'Do you think I'm attached to the idea?'

'What do you mean?'

'I think my duty lies there, so I will do it. But I prefer a garden somewhere with you.'

'Can I believe that?'

'Do you know me?'

Vera falls silent. She feels like a fool, yet a rankling within her prevents her from letting go of foolishness. 'You ask me if women in my country take an interest in politics. Now I ask you if Chinese men have contempt for women.'

'As you replied to my question – some do.'

'I've heard they do.'

'I've heard the same of Western men.'

'Then perhaps all men are the same.'

Shan-teh, laughing, takes her into his arms. 'In one thing Chinese and European men are different. Chinese want nothing but their own land. Europeans want everyone else's. No, I don't have contempt for women. How, really, can you ask?'

She kissed him to avoid the troubling answer, unable with good reason to explain that every day brings her closer to the old anxieties; they lurk in her mind like shadows, bringing with them the old creatures: fear, suspicion, panic.

A few days later a traveling acrobatic company comes to Qufu. Performances are arranged for the troops at camp, and one evening, by torchlight, the group performs for the officers in a courtyard of the West Wing. Chairs and benches are set on the cobblestone. In a covered gallery sits the orchestra that has accompanied the troupe. Vera listens with deep interest to the music: to the dulcimer, castanets, drums and flutes, the pear-shaped guitar, the bronze bells and cymbals. During these moments, with Shan-teh seated next to her, with members of the senior staff ranged nearby and with junior officers standing against the walls (among them Captain Fan, who has brought the American), Vera surrenders to the excitement of the evening, the music. It reminds her of another evening, the anniversary of Confucius' birth, when she and her lover lay in the dark secret of the night. When the acrobats enter, leaping the gallery, balustrades and somersaulting through the Moon Gate, she tells herself this time in Qufu is the best of her life.

'We've come to pester you,' a juggler says impudently to begin the show. The troupe is called One Hundred Entertainments, and does its best to emulate the name by introducing one act after another for three entire hours: parasol balancing; long-knife and sword juggling; bicycle balancing – ten of them on a single bike; jar balancing, with the narrow rim of the heavy utensil touching its edge against a small girl's forehead. One man fights as two in a voluminous costume. Gongs and lutes accompany three men who, quacking like ducks, waddle across the courtyard. Once a young juggler drops a plate. The manager, striding briskly into the performance area, cuffs him hard on the side of the head for his mistake; then they both walk off as casually as if strolling in a garden. The performers, their faces painted bright colors and their eyebrows thickly blackened, accept the faint applause (Chinese don't applaud much, but Vera claps vigorously) with deep bows. Then they come forward, their spokesman winking as he declares, 'An acrobat is lucky to die with the price of a coffin in his pocket.' Vera turns to see if Shan-teh is getting out *cash* for a donation, but then remembers that during the performance someone had called him out.

He still hasn't returned when the acrobats, having moved through the crowd of officers with hats extended, leave the courtyard and everyone else starts leaving too. Waiting discreetly until it's clear the General will not return, Captain Fan comes forward and offers to escort Vera to quarters. A step behind him is the young American, whose blue eyes in the torchlight catch Vera's an instant in an appeal only too familiar, then break guiltily free. She accepts the men's invitation. They stroll through the courtyards and along sheltered walkways in the briskly cool night. Captain Fan, a chatterer at heart, does most of the talking. He describes acrobatic troupes in his native Peking, boasting of their superiority. Meanwhile, with only one ear on Fan's garrulous talk, Vera senses keenly the presence of the American on her other side. Though she never turns to him, keeping her full attention on the Captain, she accepts the blue-eyed adoration that seems to bore through her clothes, stealing through and warning her. Vera doesn't resist the pleasure of accepting his infatuation. After all, it means nothing – no more than flirtations at Petrograd balls, which also came to nothing, not even a kiss.

They leave her with polite bows at the door. Inside the quarters she calls loudly for Yao, who comes running. Shan-teh has been right about the old servant. During his master's long absence, Yao gave allegiance to his new mistress (by degrees), and with the General's return has served them both.

Vera asks for tea. When it is made and she has poured a cup, Vera doesn't drink, but waits for Shan-teh. The tea is ice-cold and she has fallen asleep on the sofa when he finally returns.

Rubbing her eyes, hearing her name called, Vera looks up at him. Instantly she reads in his pinched mouth, his frowning brow, what perhaps she has always dreaded.

'Tonight we received a wireless from Peking,' he says and sits down beside her. Taking her hand, he hesitates. 'Jen Ching-i has been making accusations. He calls me a traitor. He says I betrayed the Republic. He claims my staff is filled with Nationalist agents. He accuses me of harboring dangerous Bolsheviks.' With a pained grimace suggesting the worst is yet to come, Shan-teh continues. 'He blames me for the death of my father, the destruction of my clan.'

'But what does it all mean?'

'Mean?' He gives Vera a startled look, as if sure she must understand. 'It means war.'

Jen Ching-i, general of the northern province of Hopei (Tang last saw the fat old man sweating in the temple on Thousand Buddha Mountain, just before the explosion occurred), sent a circular telegram to the president of the Republic (a nonentity), to the *ta-yüan-shuai* of the ruling military body in Peking (Marshal Chang Tso-lin), to the cabinet, to every provincial governor, and, perhaps most important, to all the newspapers in the country.

'I, Jen Ching-i, regret that the task has fallen to me to make the following accusation against Tang Shan-teh, who once seemed to be an honorable and upright man, but whose corrupt behavior has forced me to speak out in the name of the Middle Kingdom.'

In the long propaganda missive, the old man concentrated on the following crimes for indictment: Tang's meeting with Chiang Kai-shek, at which the two plotted against those who rightfully protect the Republic; his issuance of worthless currency to his troops, his reprehensible practice of protecting unscrupulous foreign advisers under the pay of Bolshevik and Western governments; his immoral personal life; and finally his establishment of questionable allegiances during the time of Yuan Shih-k'ai, when his own father and clan were murdered for opposing a return to monarchy, their deaths occurring under circumstances detrimental to the honor of General Tang.

The rambling document, filled with invective and righteous denunciation, ended with a few phrases condemning the promotion of evil and the profanation of morality, along with a vague concluding reference to his own muddled philosophy: 'The troubles of China will vanish when the system is recognized on principles inculcated in the constitutional rules of democracy but with deep reverence for traditions of the past.'

It's the sort of challenge the General would expect from someone of Jen's generation. When the founding of the Republic encouraged countless little wars, they were usually started by someone firing off one of these circular telegrams; that way China was ready for the clash before it occurred. The General doesn't take the telegram from Jen seriously. He can dismiss all the charges but one: his immoral behavior. Clearly the old general is aware of Black Jade, and although he keeps a half-dozen concubines himself, they are all Chinese, so he feels justified in accusing Tang of immorality. Before Black Jade, the General might well have done the same to someone who took a foreign woman.

Behind Jen's moral posturing, however, there's an authentic intensity that indicates the old man is quite willing to do battle. But why? He has been the ally of Chang Tso-lin in recent years, and at Thousand Buddha Mountain he called the Marshall 'the august hope and salvation of our land.' It wouldn't be the first time, of course, that a warlord praised his ally one moment and attacked him the next. The wireless message with its furious allegations surely implies that Jen has changed allegiance; otherwise he wouldn't have attacked the Marshal's subordinate. Someone – probably Feng Yu-hsiang – has stirred up the general, an old man more concerned with personal honor than with the acquisition of territory. He has probably been told that General Tang of Shantung has contempt for his military abilities; that the Shantung upstart is spreading rumors about his lack of courage – perhaps even mentioning Jen's hasty departure from Thousand Buddha Mountain after the explosion. So challenged, the old man would forget alliances and politics, would button his tunic and yell for an adjutant, ready on the instant to go to war.

Feng Yu-hsiang could surely be behind this. He could only benefit from an outburst of hostilities between two northern warlords who, ostensibly at least, have been allied to his enemy, the Marshal. The whole affair, Tang thinks, reflects the tortuous cunning for which Feng is known. If Feng is in fact involved, then the Marshall will react in kind.

This inference is confirmed the next morning, when General Tang receives a wireless from Peking. He has been hastily appointed by the Marshal to a newly created post: Peace Commissioner of the Central North-east. It is a peculiarly designated command which includes Hopei Province, Therefore Jen's own territory. Tang's chief duty, broadly and vaguely described, is to suppress any incitement to disunity among officials of the entire Central Northern Region. In effect, then, Marshal Chang Tso-lin has given him permission to pursue Jen Ching-i, his public detractor, with military force. Less than an hour later a wireless from Jinan bears out Tang's understanding of the situation. The Governor General of Shantung Province – old Dog Meat – declares his readiness to send a brigade of troops southward if General Tang wishes to discourage General Sun Ch'uan-fang, the Kiangsu warlord, from moving across the border, *in the event that the new Peace Commissioner of the Central Northeast is busy elsewhere.*

So it is done. A familiar feeling pervades General Tang at the end of the morning – the anticipation of war. Father had described such a feeling to him when he was a boy; since then he has often claimed the feeling for his own, felt it to the core of his being: a heightened sense of life.

By the end of the afternoon a wireless has gone out to Jen Ching-i at his Hopei headquarters in the temple town of Chengting. Using a traditional format of invective, General Tang accuses him of betraying the Republic, citing as proof his support of President Yuan Shih-k'ai before that madman died of a stroke and saved the country from the embarrassment of pulling him off the Dragon Throne; reproaches Jen for shifting loyalties in a time of crisis, but without specifically naming Feng Yu-hsiang; alleges that Jen has misappropriated funds throughout his military career; and finally denounces Jen for colluding in the destruction of the Tang clan during the civil strife of 1915–16. 'I have been appointed,' writes Tang, 'Peace Commissioner of the Central Northeast and in consequence have the authority and duty to preserve order and to apply force within the region as I see fit against insurrections and incitement to disunity. In this capacity I therefore command you to answer the charges set forth herein and, in addition, to give proof in person of your loyalty to the authorized government in Peking.'

It's a message calculated to incense Jen and commit him to the fight. It also upholds Tang's honor as a man ready to answer an insult.

According to latest word from Chengting, Jen has about sixty thousand troops, twenty thousand more than Tang. But Jen won't commit that many to a battle as long as Marshal Chang Tso-lin remains poised with a larger force east of him, near Peking. On the other hand, General Feng might offer a sizable detachment to his new ally, especially because a good railroad links Chengchow, where Feng's main force is camping, with Chengting. Sending troops is problematical, nonetheless, because Feng has his forces scattered throughout three provinces and many of them are starving. A movement of troops away from the Chengchow area might also encourage an attack from his Shansi neighbor, General Yen Hsi-shan, with whom Feng has quarreled for years.

The alternatives are discussed eagerly in staff meetings. Tang senses that the challenge has come at the right time, giving him reason for tightening personal control over an army that has been garrisoned too long. His extended absence from Qufu has surely hurt him with junior officers, who've grown accustomed to taking their orders from Colonel Pi. Indeed, the General's guess that a battle will benefit his command finds substantiation in the ill humor of Colonel Pi. The Colonel understands that the destiny of each officer is now linked to Tang Shan-teh, not to himself, and that any secret ambitions he's been harboring must be put aside until the Southern Shantung Army confronts the troops of Jen Ching-i, one of the oldest but best generals in China.

Far into the night General Tang and his staff pore over maps and discuss strategy. He's especially impressed by a young major named Chia Ju-ming, who commands the Second Infantry Brigade of the First Division. It is Chia's premise that the army should move quickly into the field and engage Jen at a single stroke. Although Jen must be prepared to fight or the challenge wouldn't have been given, the old general has always been an exponent of positional warfare; as a consequence, from his habit of setting up forces with deliberate caution, Jen will not move southward at a rush or expect his opponent to move with like speed toward him from Shantung. The terrain lying between the combatants will be flat farmland, however, lending itself to the tactics

General Tang has always advocated – a mobile advance, featuring quick strikes and shock troops maneuvering in fluid patterns. Rapid engagement will also discourage Feng Yu-hsiang from sending reinforcements into the area: The outcome will be decided quickly, once the combatants meet, and long before Feng troops could arrive by rail.

Tang agrees, but with one qualification: Jen, a wily old man, may decide to move more expeditiously than expected. Colonel Pi's objection to the entire plan is made rather timidly, and then withdrawn; it's a sign that he means to support his commander fully during the campaign.

The discussion proceeds to the disposition of the army and its immediate mobilization for setting out to the Northwest. One division, the First, is stationed here in Qufu. Another lies in Yi Nan, in south-central Shantung. A full corps – two divisions – is garrisoned at Lin Yi, to the south. Tang decides to take all but three regiments from Lin Yi and count on Dog Meat to protect the border. He will leave half of the First Division at Qufu to look after the Confucian temple and the Kong family. The entire corps lying at Yi Nan will take part in the expedition. To get those troops ready for departure the General sends Colonel Pi, who is quietly furious at leaving headquarters while strategy's worked out. Both men know why the Colonel is being sent away. In Pi's absence the General will reestablish his personal authority, while serving notice to the other officers that he doesn't need his chief of staff for planning.

He puts a seasoned veteran in charge of logistics and recruitment of carriers. About 70 percent of the army – thirty thousand men – will be on the move, so for carrying supplies and guns they'll need about four thousand coolies. The recruiting officer proceeds through the districts, overseeing village headmen in their procurement of carriers. It's an easy task at this time of year, when farming no longer occupies the time of rural peasantry – they like the idea of getting paid for hauling weapons they don't have to use. The General truns down recruits for the army, however. There's no time to train them, and he remembers Confucius' admonition: 'To take an untrained multitude into battle is tantamount to throwing it away.' It's a warning some warlords have failed to heed, and they have lost not only callow boys but precious veterans as well.

Within a day peasants are trudging toward Qufu, where the

supplies are housed. One-third of the rice they will carry on their backs they themselves will eat on the march – it's a rule of thumb taught to the General by his father, and he has never known it to fail. The length of the march makes no difference; a third of the rice will be gone.

Each day from dawn to dusk the outskirts of Qufu are alive with activity, the sound of men and horses at training exercises. Astride a horse, Tang watches intently as young soldiers run their obstacle courses, polevault, yell at their tugs-of-war, climb fences, and bayonet imaginary foes on the wind-swept drill fields. They look good to him – tough, wiry, hardened by the spare life of the camp. They are ready to go now and wait only for enough coolies to assemble to carry their supplies.

The General's enthusiasm is marred by one troubling fact: The weapons shipment has not arrived from Shanghai. Or rather part of it has, about one-fifth, and only gun carriages, wheels, extra rifle stocks. No ammunition, no howitzer barrels, no breeches, no trench mortars, no machine guns. In short, what is unessential has arrived; what is essential has not. Of course, this sort of shipment is usually sent piecemeal: It's easier to pack, and it escapes the notice of bandits who might attack a wagon train or derail a locomotive hauling cars filled with munitions. What troubles the General is the selectivity of what has come and what has not. It's as if Luckner is taunting him by sending items of little value and withholding the essence. Tang hasn't been sure of steps to take; he lacks real evidence of the German's intention to break the contract. So far he's sent two wirelesses to Luckner in Shanghai, requesting immediate clarification of the status of the shipment. The reply to both: ON THE WAY. If Luckner is cheating him, the motive is plain enough. Surely by now the German must know that his former mistress is in Qufu. Yet Luckner is also a businessman – a cold one at that, who brought her to Qufu initially to seduce the General into a weapon purchase. Will such a man give up his reputation in Shanghai for jealousy? Are Westerners apt to throw themselves recklessly into acts of revenge? Tang doesn't know. He feels that the events of recent months have left him puzzled about the behavior of all foreigners. Luckner, Black Jade, the American, the Bolshevik – they haven't fit into the patterns expected of foreigners.

How could anyone surprise him more than the Soviet agent did? Struck by a woman with a riding crop, the fellow compounded his humiliation by slinking out of camp like a dog. Yet not quite like a dog; that's what amazes the General. Kovalik gave up opium first, *then* ran off. The man in the Wuchang train station was definitely Kovalik. In buoyant good health. Not someone fatally weakened by the treachery of his own government, as the General had assumed.

Tang is less surprised, of course, that Black Jade wielded the riding crop. Given her past she might well find it in herself to attack the Bolshevik. The intensity of her attack surely surprised those who witnessed it in the street. Colonel Pi, who reported the incident to him, seemed genuinely in awe of Black Jade; apparently eyewitnesses had given dramatic descriptions of it to soldiers from camp who in turn added details of mythic proportions to the accounts they gave to officers. For the General, at any rate, this woman is surprising in far more subtle ways. In Black Jade he finds the marked delicacy of response, the intuitive understanding – as well as the pure eroticism – that he's always associated with women of his own country, with them alone, having cherished the conviction that only in China do such women exist. Now at dawn (but not for the past few days) he plays Tai Chi at the side of the fair-skinned woman who, in her nightly passion, utters the words of another language.

And then the American. Watching units of cavalry wheel in columns or practice a charge in the fallow wheat fields, Tang has glimpses of him: ruddy from the sun, tendrils of blond hair slipping from under a Chinese cap, the ax stuck in his belt, while one hand holds the reins and the other a pistol.

The American looks older, but no less young. Tang has heard that foreigners can't estimate the age of Chinese; he has the same trouble with foreigners. They are ageless or rather many ages at once. The General watches the Big Sword Company at practice, jumping wooden rails set up in a drill field. He notices that the American fails to give his horse sufficient rein in midair during the jump. The bit could cut into the horse's mouth and make him bolt. Ax Man might break his neck before seeing a battlefield. The General has an aide call him over.

When the American approaches, Tang sees that in fact he does look older. The General points out the error and makes a few other suggestions: Ax Man should sit farther forward at the gallop, his weight as much as possible on the withers, giving the loins at the point of the animal's hip less to bear; that way his horse can bring its hind legs forward with greater ease and go faster for a longer time. 'And shorten your reins at the gallop.'

'Yes, Excellency.'

'Do you like army life?'

'Yes, I do, Excellency.'

'Would you like the command of troops someday?'

'Well –' The American hesitates. 'Yes, I think I would like that.'

The General knows, even if Ax Man does not, that they're both military men, committed to the life. Studying the broad shoulders, the cold blue eyes, the determined mouth, Tang knows that if this fellow doesn't fight here in China, he'll fight elsewhere, with or without a cause. This is a warrior at heart.

On his tour the next day, Tang notices the American working with the Big Swords at their battle formations: charging, regrouping, turning on signal. Ax Man is shortening his reins, Tang sees. Good, but although he sits a horse well, he still lacks control of it; he needs more work gripping the flanks with his thighs. Again he calls the American over and tells him. Again the young man seems to appreciate the advice.

'What do you feed your mount, Ax Man?'

'Grain three times a day. Not too much, of course.'

'How much is that?'

'My friends tell me.' He adds after a pause, 'I check his feed for dust and mold.'

'Why?'

'Moldy feed causes stomach trouble. Dust causes heaves.'

'Who told you that?'

'My friends.'

'In the company?'

'Yes, Excellency.'

'Let me see his shoeing.'

Ax Man dismounts and lifts the right front leg of his horse. Tang leans forward to take a good look. As it should be, the shoe projects slightly beyond the heel; there are the right number of nails, seven, in the fore-shoe. 'Do you watch the blacksmith?'

'Yes, I do, Excellency.'

'And tell him what you want?'

'Yes, Excellency.'

'Do your friends tell you what to tell him?'

Ax Man smiles. 'They do, Excellency.'

'Is your horse free of ticks?'

'Yes, Excellency.'

'Where do you usually find them?'

'In the tail head.'

'Do you still sleep on your horse?'

'Sometimes – to keep in practice.'

'Do you know why the Mongols did it?'

'They had to, Excellency. They lived on their horses.'

The General rides away. He watches other cavalry units at work and ponders their use against Jen Ching-i. He would like to use his cavalry in a classic way: strike, retreat, pester rather than charge, probe for weaknesses and circumvent a frontal assault in preference for disruptive sallies against flank and rear. It's how his father viewed cavalry, and father had learned his tactics from German instructors with the Yangtze Corps before the Boxer Rebellion.

But Tang suspects he won't be able to employ his cavalry in the most efficient way. Jen won't let him. Most likely the old general will try to manage a defensive position requiring a frontal assault – a boot-to-boot charge, wasteful of life at best. Many of the cavalrymen the General is watching on the drill field today would die in such a charge.

Next morning he again sees the American jumping – reins looser in midair. Good. And that afternoon, as the General is served tea under the canopy of a headquarters field tent, the captain of the Big Sword Company comes to him with a request. He needs a sergeant for the second platoon, because the regular sergeant, having come down with chills and fever, won't be ready for the march. Fu Chang-so, his color sergeant, has recommended the American for the post.

'Why?' Tang asks in surprise. 'Does it amuse your color sergeant?'

'With due respect, Excellency, Fu Chang-so is an experienced man. He says the American's clever, hardworking. And the men like him.'

'They do?'

'Yes, Excellency.'

'And I suppose he's a friend of Fu Chang-so.'

'He is, but that helps with the men.'

'The American.' Tang smiles. Ax Man doesn't fit the popular idea of a foreigner: austere missionary in his walled enclosure, mustachioed diplomat in his white linens. Ax Man is becoming Chinese. 'Send him to me.'

The General is munching a wheat bun when Ax Man rides up and dismounts. He stands outside the circle of shade, his hair blowing in a freshening wind. At the moment he looks terribly foreign to General Tang.

'Do you think the Big Swords are a good unit?' the General asks.

'Yes, Excellency.'

'Good riders?'

'The best –'

'Yes?'

'Well, that I've seen, Excellency.'

'And you've not seen a lot. Do you think they'll fight hard in battle?'

'I know it, General.'

'You seem very sure.'

'I am, General.'

'Yesterday you told me the Mongols lived on their horses. What else do you know about them?'

'They were great horsemen. Under Jenghiz Khan they conquered Asia and part of Europe.'

Tang laughs. 'Great horsemen? They were the greatest horsemen the world has *ever* known. They could have taken all of Europe, but they pulled back to compete for the succession, when the Khan's son died. You see, their Mongol titles were more important to them than European land. What else do you know?'

'They drank fermented mares' milk.'

'Gallons of it. *Koumiss*. Did you try some *koumiss* in White Wolf's camp?'

'I tried it.' Ax Man grimaces.

'Do you know the black-and-white signal flags you're using today are a Mongol idea? Mongols used them the same way you are – seven hundred years ago.'

'I didn't know that.'

'It's worthwhile remembering the past – for comparison. You Big Swords think you're good riders, good cavalrymen, but you have a long way to go, and you'll never be Mongols. For one thing we can't even comprehend their discipline. They were formed into precise units – more precise than ours, than the Europeans! There were ten thousand troops to a *touman*; that was their army corps. In the *touman* there were ten regiments of one thousand each, ten squadrons of one hundred each, ten troops of ten men each. Exactly. Do you understand? No more or less. They were kept at full strength. If they had too many men, they waited in the rear – too few, they broke up the *touman* and sent it to the rear also. In other words, to maintain their order, they'd risk going into battle with fewer men. I think of them often.'

The General looks past the Ax Man's shoulder toward the drill field. 'They must have been magnificent coming across the plain. All mounted, no infantry, no artillery. They wore armor of tanned hides, in overlapping lacquered plates. They carried a lance, a sword, two bows. They had three quivers each with arrows of different caliber. Do you understand? For different ranges and degrees of penetration. This was seven hundred years ago. Each trooper has a camp kettle and a watertight bag for extra clothes; it could be inflated for crossing rivers. They used a battle formation of five ranks. In the two front ranks the troops were heavily armored; the rear three had only bows. Approaching the enemy, the rear ranks advanced through the front ones and shot their arrows, retiring then to let the front ranks go to work. Fire and shock tactics – seven hundred years ago, Ax Man. When a superior force charged them – and they were usually outnumbered – they retreated by signal, regrouped by signal, turned and fired from a distance. Their tactics prevented wholesale slaughter of their own troops. They were never trapped, never annihilated, although sometimes outnumbered ten, fifteen to one. They never failed to execute any of their own who showed a moment of hesitation. They never spared the enemy, but killed their prisoners, cutting off the ears and sending them home to the Great Khan like tribute from kings. They were the greatest warriors of all time.' General Tang looks at the blue-eyed horseman. 'Do you know why I've told you about the Mongols?'

'No, Excellency.'

'Because seven hundred years later most of them live inside China as Chinese. The rest are scattered. We go on as we did then, for better or worse. You have just had a Chinese history lesson.'

The cavalryman nods with a smile. 'Yes, Excellency, that's true.'

'Are you still a student of Chinese religion?'

'There hasn't been time –'

The General studies him a moment. 'Why did you really come to China? Tell me the truth, it won't matter now.'

Ax Man hesitates – the General can see the struggle in the lines around his mouth and eyes. Finally: 'I came as a Christian missionary.'

For a moment longer the General stares at him, absorbing the confession, then leans back in the canvas field chair and roars with laughter. Calmer, with tears in his eyes from the effort, he sees the young horseman staring at him in bewilderment. Finally the General says, still chuckling, 'You told me you were a student interested in the gods of China. Remember that?'

Ax Man nods silently.

'Remember what I told you then?'

'Yes, Excellency. If I stayed in China long enough I'd see religion in a new light.'

Fresh laughter seizes the General, who can't remember when he's laughed so much. 'In a new light,' he repeats, shaking his head, trying to gain control. Finally he says, 'Well, Ax Man, at least you've seen *life* in a new light. Beginning in White Wolf's camp. And here in the army. Life and religion in China for a Christian missionary.' He chuckles, pushing the billed cap back on his head.

The blue-eyed horseman has begun to smile with him. 'And you said whoever comes into your country, Excellency, will be changed by it.'

'The Mongols –'

'And myself.'

They regard each other curiously. 'I asked you then what you believed in,' the General says. 'What do you believe in now?'

The young man, sitting on his horse, looks around. 'My friends, my horse. And I asked you, sir, what you believed in.'

'And I said China.' The General points to the pistol shoved under the cavalryman's belt, on the side opposite the ax. 'Can you shoot that thing?'

'I need more practice,' the cavalryman admits.

'What about the ax? Would you use it?' Their eyes meet.

'Yes, Excellency.'

'Tell your captain I consent. You'll act as temporary sergeant in the Big Sword Company, Fourth Battalion of horse.'

Philip Embree, holding the reins taut, salutes. But his mouth is open in surprise.

'We'll see,' the General says gruffly, 'if the new sergeant has been a good student of warfare. The battlefield will be your test.'

It is a test they will all face soon. General Tang receives word from his spy in Chengting that Jen has begun battle preparations. It would be characteristic of the old general to move slowly, perhaps down the Peking-Wuhan rail line, maintaining his transportational advantage. He would probably send out seasoned pickets by horseback each morning to reconnoiter with great care and daily dispose his infantry around hillocks and streams in defensive positions. It should take weeks before he comes into striking range, his army waddling along in a motion similar to his own. Even so, Tang again warns himself not to succumb to the temptation of laughing at Jen. What the old man has is abundant experience, courage, a resolute commitment to his reputation as a soldier. Tang recalls him huffing and puffing up the path on Thousand Buddha Mountain – stopping to complain of young officers and announcing haughtily that he eats the rice of one family only. In military terms the old fellow has a talent for deploying artillery. Tang's father once explained Jen's skill at gunnery: 'He studied tactics at Paoting when foreign teachers were there. It was just after the Russo-Japanese War, and the German and French instructors competed with one another in their knowledge of tactics, especially artillery. Jen sat in on those talks and learned more about artillery than anyone in China.' Father had told him that fifteen years ago, yet it may still be true today.

Tang worries about his own artillery, a worry that has deepened because of the arms shipment delay. His batteries are in the hands of young, mostly inexperienced officers. Moreover, in recent maneuvers he noticed the clumsiness of machine gunners in dismantling their weapons and reassembling them. He also needs mortars, the most vital group of weapon included in the shipment yet to come.

In spite of these drawbacks, Tang is confident. No one has a better cavalry in China. No one has instilled more discipline. And in his army thre are fewer mercenaries, fewer soldiers who have joined solely for pay. Not that reward isn't uppermost in the minds of his men, but he has tried to add another dimension to their service: a belief in the destiny of their country. Standing on the drill field and watching them, the General admires his men. Someday he wishes to reward them another way for their loyalty – with a strong government in Peking. And peace.

He works alone at headquarters.

Jen has moved with uncharacteristic speed out of Chengting to the rail junction at Shih Chia Chuang and then past Kao Chuang and Shulu eastward to the Fu Yang River. At least three divisions have taken up position there, according to Tang's far-ranging scouts. Tang reasons – his staff agrees – that from this point Jen can enter Hengshui and wait, either remaining there astride the railroad or moving toward Qufu through open country. The last thing Tang wants is a battle near Qufu, sacred home of Confucius, so he'll give orders in the morning for the corps at Yi Nan to set out for Hengshui. The divisional elements from Qufu and Lin Yi will follow in a day. There won't be a battle here, whatever happens.

Tang sips a cup of cold tea. If Jen wants to attack Qufu, he will cross the Grand Canal at Lintsing, follow it south to Liaocheng, thence across swampland to Tunga. Anywhere along the route a battle could be fought, but Tang feels that the old habit of caution will overcome any desire for innovation Jen might have. The old man will probably wait at Hengshui, straddling the rail junction, as commanders have done ever since foreign engineers taught the Chinese the efficacy of using iron monsters to transport men and guns.

Unless Jen becomes anxious for some reason, he will settle down at Hengshui and let Tang bring the battle to him. Of this strategy Tang is finally convinced, as he sits in the silent headquarters, gazing at a large map pinned on the wall. Today the old diviner cast the Yarrow Stalks for him and came up with an auspicious oracle: the upper trigram of thunder and the lower trigram of Heaven. Thunder in Heaven is the image of power and greatness. Nevertheless, the old beggar warned the General to act in accordance with established order and resist the twisted path. At the outset, Tang plans a simple line of march with three expeditionary forces following different routes to Hengshui. No twisted path, no innovation, no bold stroke. Perhaps this will be the most traditional battle he has yet fought.

With a sigh the General rises, giving the map a last thoughtful glance. Outside it is cold, and he wonders if tonight Qufu will get another frost. Overhead the moon shines like a sliver of ivory. He pulls the thin blouse — he has forgotten his coat – tight to his neck while leaning into a sharp wind. Ahead is the cosy glow of his quarters, where Black Jade waits. He hasn't seen her all day, all this fateful day, for not only did he learn of Jen's sudden move southward, but also by wireless of Wang Ching-wei – Wang is now deep in negotiations with Kwangsi warlords in Shanghai and may become the leader of the Nationalists, especially now that Chiang Kai-shek has left the country for Japan.

No wonder Wang Ching-wei had no wish to see a northern war-lord in Canton. He had better things to do in Shanghai; and he wouldn't want the fiery southern generals from Kwangsi to think he was on good terms with a northerner.

Weary of politics and preparations for war, General Tang enters his quarters, where Black Jade, wearing a robe of lavender silk, greets him with a smile.

'So you leave again,' she says, her lips against his cheek as they lie in the darkness.

'It will be a short campaign.' Tang laughs briefly. 'Indeed it will be. Neither of us has the resources for a long one.'

'Will many die?'

After a pause, Tang says, 'That can't be predicted.'

'A hundred?'

'Well, more.'

'A thousand?'

Again he pauses. 'I have no idea.'

'More than a thousand,' she declares, moving away from him, arms to her sides. 'A lot more.' They are silent awhile. 'Can you win?'

'I expect to. My men are well trained and armed.' He hasn't told her about the shipment from Luckner. Black Jade would blame herself for the loss of weapons his men need. Although she has shown recent interest in politics, Black Jade has none for warfare and seems to have forgotten the shipment of arms that brought them together. 'You should see Jen – fat as a pumpkin.' Turning at her, Tang makes a big circle with his arms.

'But he's a good general.'

'He's an old man.'

'But he's a good general.'

'How do you know?' Tang asks with a laugh.

'Captain Fan told me.'

'Did he? Fan's an adjutant, not a field commander.'

'Don't be annoyed with him.'

In truth the General regards Fan highly. Even so, the young officer shouldn't have told her about Jen. Perhaps Fan should be watched. He's too open with foreigners, too modern in the company of women. Tang catches himself in foolish jealousy.

'I understand from him,' Black Jade continues, 'the American has been promoted.'

'Yes, he has a platoon of horse.'

'You allow it?'

'Of course. He's Chinese now – as you are.'

She moves back to him, her cheek resting on his chest. 'It's true, I am. I dream now in Chinese. When I close my eyes and think of paintings, they aren't Rembrandt and Titian, but Hsu Tao-ning and Ni Tsan. When I think of children, I think of Bright Lotus. And I think always of you – your color, the shape of your eyes.'

'When I return,' Tang says gently, 'we'll go to the sacred mountain of Tai Shan. We'll climb it slowly and stop at each temple.'

'To give thanks we're together.'

Startled, he turns slightly and caresses her cheek. 'Exactly for that reason.'

22

Five passes lead to the scrubby, fog-shrouded southern mountain of Chingkangshan, at the base of which lies a cluster of primitive villages. Peasants have eked out an existence here as their ancestors did centuries ago, when bandits and thieves and fugitives from justice climbed the same pine-clad paths to safety. When Kovalik has his first look at Chingkangshan on a wet, chill morning, he understands immediately why Mao Tse-tung, a native of this province and therefore familiar with it, has chosen this sanctuary for his battered little army. Kovalik and Li have traveled through rich farmland, dotted with paddies and sweet-potato fields and groundnut patches, but arriving here they feel they might well have come to the end of the world. This is Chingkangshan with its fog and dripping fir trees and silent peasants who munch on soggy caraway-seed cakes or in winter eat their dogs. Up the mountainside the two comrades go, wearing black felt hats and straw sandals. They pass by groups of Mao's men who are heating food in old fruit cans or sitting beside the damp path with the shovels and iron bars they call their weapons. Kovalik looks at them curiously. All the way from Changsha he has heard about these men: how they fought through Nationalist traps; and how others, deserting to the Nationalists, had turned on old comrades and shot them down like dogs; how the survivors – some of them runaways, thieves, escaped criminals – had then fought against the defense militias of local landlords; how they had won less than they lost, but after winning had raped the daughters of the gentry, had broken the opium pipes of village headmen, had smashed sedan chairs in the courtyards of town mansions, had compelled local officials to walk through village streets wearing the tall conical hats of dunces. These bedraggled soldiers (Kovalik will learn they call themselves the First Regiment of the First Division of the First Workers and Peasants Revolutionary Army, under the command of Mao Tse-tung, Secretary of the Front Committee of the Communist Party of Hunan Province – a title almost as long as the column they must have presented on the march from Changsha) which often caught in fire fights along the way; those unlucky enough to be captured by the Nationalists or by local militia (sardonically called Associations for Beating Dogs) had their Achilles tendons severed so they couldn't crawl away from what would come later – castration or a heated bamboo stake thrust into the anus.

The survivors look to Kovalik like men he had known in the days of the Revolution: hollow-eyed, exhausted, as frail as children, yet carrying about them a palpable strength, a dangerous aura, which arrests his attention even as it did in those early days around Petrograd and Moscow, when he himself was such a man. They stand now – the Nationalist deserters and thieves and Anyuan miners and Liuyang peasants – grinning wanly at the thickset Russian and his small Chinese companion as they trudge up the mountainside, past ancient Buddhist temples from which hermit monks have been rousted and which now are being used as makeshift hospitals and offices. The travelers pause to see a spitted boar turning over a fire, and the hunters of it leaning on their spears like warriors of the Iron Age. Going up the path, they see men trying to wrest vegetable gardens from the rocky mountain, digging up sulphurous red earth in the hope of getting something planted and harvested before winter sets in – an impossible task. Kovalik, knowing winter like the back of his hand, can envision this place in a few months: troops ankle-deep in snow – no boots; their feet wrapped in dried grass – gnawing on roots, bracing against bitter winds that will find a swift merciless path through the leafless trees. Right now, however, he sees village merchants trundling up and down the mountain, doing what business they can – hauling up baskets of eggs and chestnuts, stopping long enough among the soldiers to clean their ears for a small price. Nearing the summit, Kovalik notices a large group of men digging a series of ditches ten or twelve feet wide. Other soldiers are embedding in the bottom of these ditches upright bamboo poles sharpened on the ends. Still others are soaking those ends in tung oil to keep them from rotting. Finally, half a dozen workers are gathering branches and scrub grass to place over the finished trenches to conceal them.

No matter how ragged and disorderly it appears, it is still a military camp, Kovalik thinks – a huge impossible fortress in the clouds. And in that regard, he notices near the summit a red banner planted on a high pole. It has a five-pointed white star crossed by a black hammer and sickle. Both he and Li halt for a moment to salute the banner with clenched fists. My home, my people, Kovalik tells himself with grim exaltation.

In a battered temple (hewn from pine and with its plaster chipped off) they find headquarters and inquire there after old mates from Wuhan who might have got out with Mao. They are sent for information to a nearby pine grove and discover Tuan, a Bolshevik from the early days in Shanghai. Li knew him in the past. It was rumored then that Tuan had been castrated in a torture cell by Annamese police in the French Concession a few years ago. At least other torture is evident: a misshapen nose, two fingers missing from his left hand.

Tuan greets them enthusiastically. He envelops Li in a bear hug, an uncommon familiarity for a Chinese. Soon he is sitting with them under a tree, sharing a jar of warm beer. 'These villages,' he tells them, 'make the worst beer in China. But then everything's the worst around here. Landlords, secret societies, bandits. Did you know there are still leopards in these hills? *Leopards?* Villagers hunt them with bamboo spears.' He shakes his head. 'But Mao's trying to set up councils and peasant associations anyway. We don't have two hundred rifles among us, and those fucking bandits with us have all but fifty of those.'

'Bandits,' Li asks, startled.

'Sure, bandits.' Tuan explains that two bandit chieftains, leading six hundred men, have joined forces with Mao, who in order to control them has made them commanders. 'Mao says bandits have five senses and two legs like anyone else – revolution can find a place for everyone. But the truth is, if he hadn't honored the murderous bastards with big-sounding titles, they'd have wiped us off the mountain.'

'Are these bandits Communists?' Kovalik asks when Li has translated.

'Of course not,' Tuan says with a laugh. 'But they've got rifles. And they sure know how to cut throats at night. Mao took a company of us and a company of them to a nearby town where some Nationalist troops were billeted. We killed a bunch there. These bandits are night fighters. Of course, we've got some good men ourselves – these miners from Anyuan. A lot of them are deaf because the dynamiting exploded their eardrums, but they're tough and mean. Anarchists all. We're trying to make Reds out of them. I sure don't want them on the other side.'

Tuan takes the new arrivals around the camp. In a wooden shed he shows them a printing press hauled from Liuyang. On it revolutionary slogans are being printed on the backs of confiscated Buddhist scrolls. 'Look – look there.' Tuan digs Li in the ribs as a man rides down the path on a mule. He is wearing a long mandarin gown and an English bowler. Trooping in his wake are at least ten women, their eyes downcast. 'That's one of them I was telling you about,' Tuan whispers. '*Commander* Wang Tso. A murdering thief is what he is,' Tuan adds with a guffaw. 'Mao has made him Commander of the Twenty-ninth South Hunan Peasant Regiment – whatever that means. At least it's a long enough title. Those are his women. All of them. I hear he's a real fucker.' Tuan digs Li in the ribs again. 'But he's got nothing on Mao. His wife, Yang K'ai-hui, is in Shao-shan with the kids, so the revolutionary girls here in camp are begging for his time. He sure is generous with it.'

Li, grinning, translates for Kovalik, who is not amused. There's a carefree atmosphere in this camp that he doesn't like. Or is the lack of seriousness a kind of desperation?

Tuan is scratching his cheek thoughtfully with the three-fingered hand. 'Sometimes I think Mao keeps these bandits under control because he and Commander Wang are such fuckers. Maybe they've got an understanding about women, I don't know. I can't figure out how they understand anything else about each other.'

When Li translates, Kovalik has his own doubts about an intellectual Marxist having anything in common with a mountain bandit. He doesn't know whether to admire Mao for controlling such fellows or to suspect him of relinquishing his ideals.

'Where is Mao?' Li asks.

'Down in one of the villages setting up Party cells.' Tuan shrugs. 'Then tomorrow the landlords or the Nationalists will come along and enlist the villages in local defense forces. So the poor dumb villagers end up Red soldiers who are supposed to kill Red soldiers. Do you get it? I don't. I don't think Mao does either. Anyway, between us I think the peasants are having fun. They've never had such excitement here, except when the wolves come around. Did you know in winter they have wolves? We'll have to worry about the fucking wolves coming into camp.' Tuan shakes his head in disbelief. 'There's not a morning I wake up I don't wonder why I'm here.'

He reminds Kovalik of the ex-soldier in Changsha; the only difference is this one hasn't quit yet.

'At least we're safer here than in the countryside,' Tuan continues. 'And we have a place now to train the men, get them ready for the long haul. Mao says a base is to an army what an ass is to a man – they're something to rest on.' Tuan escorts them farther into camp. Kovalik notices with increasing uneasiness that only one man in four or five has a firearm of any kind. They all wear red armbands but no other vestige of uniform, although some of them – enthusiastic youngsters – have tied pieces of red cloth to their spears, hoes, and axes. Tuan explains they are called Young Vanguards. Another of Mao's ideas. Other men belong to the Supervisory Massacre Corps, which is an execution squad ready to take care of miscreant landlords and captured Nationalists. Another of Mao's ideas – the women fight beside men in the ranks if they're young and if they're old they are organized into laundry and cooking brigades. Boys under sixteen operate as messengers. Everywhere Tuan takes the newcomers they see boards nailed to trees, designating the assembly area for battalions and regiments, although the truth is plain – on the whole mountain there aren't enough troops to form *one* regiment of full strength. When

Kovalik makes this observation, Li doesn't translate it for Tuan, who is too busy explaining the camp rules to want a translation anyway. The rules that seem to fill Tuan with a grudging pride are nothing new to Kovalik. Rules like them had been part of his own life during the Revolution: no rape, no prostitution, no reward for bravery but death for mistakes. Of course, when the Civil War took Bolshevik troops across the breadth of Russia, none of the rules applied any more. Even so, on the summit of this damp mountain in the middle of a Chinese nowhere, Kovalik draws from memory the fresh enthusiasm of his youth, when ideals were a substitute for comfort, and men really did live on hope.

That night at a campfire he eats his rice and vegetables with appetite, although his Russian palate dislikes the fiery Hunanese peppers that have been tossed liberally into the bland meal to give it spirit. He sleeps under a blanket on the bare ground, sensing the presence of these other fools, all locked together in a brotherhood beyond understanding, and by the time he and Li meet Comrade Mao the next day, Kovalik is prepared to give his complete loyalty to a man whom he had once considered a dilettantish intellectual firebrand who knew nothing of the real world. His opinion of Mao hasn't changed from what he has heard, but his own attitude toward China has.

Mao greets them from a cot on which he's resting after his return from a tour of neighboring villages. He wears a loincloth, nothing more, exposing a trunk that is slim but not muscular – the body of a scholar masquerading as a soldier, Kovalik thinks. And the man still wears his soft girlish hair parted in the middle. The eyes are the same too: clear, limpid, as direct as a child's. Yet he seems much older than the garrulous young man Kovalik recalls from the Wuhan tearoom where they argued politics only a half-year ago. Mao's nose is thicker. Cigarette smoking has blackened his fingertips, stained his teeth. Kovalik had forgotten the large mole under Mao's lower lip; it seems more prominent.

Mao doesn't get up from the cot, but waves his cigarette in greeting, all of which adds to the informality surrounding him in the small room in the rear of a temple – old tins and pans brought from a village; a row of bottles containing boiled water; a little table, a few chairs, embers in a hearth. 'I remember you,' he tells Kovalik through Li's translation. A broad smile display the teeth stained from smoking. 'I remember our talk in Wuhan. You said revolution must come from the cities. I miss Wuhan.' He draws on the cigarette, looking up from the cot at a pine tree framed in an open window. 'I used to walk on Snake Hill and compose poetry.' He glances at Li, waiting for the translation. 'I wrote about the Yellow Crane Tower in Wuchang. A copy's in a book on that table. Read it, go on.' Nodding vigorously at Li, he waits until the little Chinese finds the copy. 'Go on,' he urges.

When Li starts to read silently, Mao tells him to translate for his Russian companion.

'Now?' Li asks.

'Of course now.'

Kovalik listens patiently to the poem about a bird departing from the hills of Wuchang. Watching Mao's face with its boyish skin break into a contented smile, Kovalik recaptures his earlier disdain for this intellectual. What sort of revolutionary spends his time wondering where a bird has gone?

Finishing the translation, Li turns to Mao. 'I like it very much, Comrade.'

Only after the compliment has been delivered does the Ching-kangshan leader ask his guests to sit down. Throwing his cigarette stub on the floor, Mao lights another with his childishly pudgy hands. Sucking in smoke with a loud noise – Kovalik finds it unpleasant – Mao says, 'I wrote that poem last summer after my reelection to the Central Committee at the Fifth National Congress. That part about the tide of my heart "rising as high as the waves" is an allusion to my optimism about the future of our cause.' He shrugs dramatically. 'It was premature. What have you come for?' he asks Li.

'We want to join you.'

'We?' Mao glances at Kovalik. 'You mean him too? The Russian?'

'Yes, Comrade, both of us.'

'Ask him what he thinks now of Borodin.'

After Li translates the request, Kovalik replies that the Russian representative of the Far Eastern Bureau of the Comintern had a pernicious effect on the progress of revolution in China. By following Stalin's policy, which was to appease the moneyed classes, Borodin had discouraged the arming of peasants and in this manner hindered the Communist advance for months, maybe years. Kovalik feels as though he's back in Qufu at the first interview with General Tang, giving explanations that go nowhere, like throwing pebbles against a sheet of tin.

When the long translation's finished, Mao smiles but asks Li, 'Does he mean it?'

'He does, Comrade.'

'Are you sure? We Chinese are sometimes taken in. If our foreign comrades fart, we call it perfume.'

'He means it, Comrade.'

Kovalik asks for a translation of what they've been saying. Then he says, 'Please inform Comrade Mao my farts stink like everyone else's.'

Mao smiles in reply. 'Ask him if he thinks our task is to begin in the cities or the countryside.'

Kovalik responds guardedly. 'We must be flexible in our thinking.'

'Exactly,' Mao agrees, but this time without a smile. 'Our view of the peasant must be flexible. To get him going is not as hard as some people believe.' Mao rises and starts pacing in his loincloth. 'First we make him aware of his poverty. I've been doing it in the villages below the mountain. Listen to this.' He assumes an orator's stance and gazes into the distance, as if addressing a crowd. 'You there, who do you think you are? Third younger uncle? Second older brother? That's what you've been told. And your father was told and his father before him. And you believe that's who you are? Well, let me tell you who you are. You are *poor*. That's right, *poor* – and therefore *nothing*. How can I convince you of this? Easy, comrade. You owe the landlord a lot of money. You have debts you can't pay. Just as your father and his father did. You don't understand this is poverty, because you've known nothing else. It has always been the same – to suffer is your lot. But what if I tell you, listen here, you don't have to suffer this way? You don't have to pay these debts, they aren't fair? Now tell me, do you know who you are now? Of course you do! You are *poor*!'

Mao slaps his thigh, delighted with his rhetoric. 'That's the first step, knowing you're poor. Now you can do something about it. You must save yourselves, you can't look to gods and spirits and ancestors to do it. None of them ever told you the truth, the only truth worth knowing – that you're *poor*. Now you and I can start doing something about it.' Mao sits down, frowning. 'When we tell the peasant that, he will listen and learn. Do you see?' Mao has begun the speech by looking at the Russian, but ends it by staring at Li, as if he's the one who matters. 'I know people think of me as a rebel from an old romance, not a real Communist leader – well, let them.' His tone is sullen; the light goes out of his boyish face like a snuffed candle. 'Make yourselves at home,' he mutters indifferently and turns to the wall, curling his legs under his buttocks, a cigarette dangling from his mouth.

Outside in the temple compound, Li talks eagerly about their interview. It went well, extremely well, he keeps saying. But Kovalik senses the interview went badly, at least for him. By the end of it Mao was looking to Li not only for translation but for confirmation of his ideas as well. Kovalik had felt left out. He had been more of a stranger than in Wuhan, even more than in Qufu. And he doesn't like Mao, who is vain but insecure. All the time Mao is talking about people, he is thinking about himself.

Yet the next day (overcast, drizzly, with a keen chill in the air that presages winter) Kovalik feels better about Mao. Coming along the path, wearing a broad-brimmed peasant hat, Mao halts and stares at Kovalik where he stands under a tree, out of the rain, with Li.

'What do you think of this news?' Mao shifts his glance equally between the two men under the tree. 'Somebody comes into camp this morning saying the Nationalist Eighth Army's in the neighborhood, looking for us.'

'It could be a rumor,' Li suggests.

Mao winks, not at Li but at Kovalik. 'Well, let them come. I shit better when I'm fighting.'

Kovalik watches the tall man continue down the path at an awkward gait, as graceless as that of the peasants he claims for his own. Kovalik decides (warmed by the attention) that Mao is more than a stuffy intellectual. Even so, the fellow lacks physical strength and spends time writing poetry in what Li claims is some kind of classical form. Worse than the poetry, however, is Mao's belief in the peasant. Beginning with that visit of his family to a peasant's hut, when the man yelled insults for no reason, Kovalik has seen nothing good in peasants. During the war they were venal, suspicious, untrustworthy, and brutal. Only an intellectual could put his faith in them. And Mao is breaking with the traditional Marxist view: Revolution must have its source in an organized industrial proletariat. Does Mao think he can civilize the backward peasants of China with his damn poetry? Yet

Kovalik decides to follow this chain-smoking intellectual fucker (Tuan calls him that, being more impressed by Mao's sexual prowess than anything else). Kovalik will force himself to believe in a military leader who until a few months ago had no military experience, in a Communist now divested of all official status, in a political thinker whose theories surely run counter to his own. But if Kovalik vows to accept Mao as his leader, having no other choice, the question is, Will Mao, who has a choice, accept him as his follower? Kovalik feels edgy in the face of that question.

Li, on the other hand, has no doubts. Often summoned to Mao's side, he returns from these meetings enthusiastic about the future. Sitting under a tree with Kovalik, he repeats Mao's words. Li's reverence for this newfound leader reminds Kovalik of his canonization of Trotsky in the days when his own world was young.

'Mao said this today,' Li begins with feeling. 'When millions of peasants finally rise, they will become a flood more powerful than the Yellow River, and their force will be so fierce and swift that no power on earth can stop it. And when they rise, we must make them into new men, free of selfishness and imperialistic habits. He said the important thing is strength.'

Kovalik listens in polite silence, unwilling out of friendship to break in upon Li's ecstatic acceptance of such timeworn declarations, recalling his own idealistic passion in 1918 that allowed him to accept promises of glory for the certainty of truth. Continually on his mind now is his own part in this doomed – doomed, possibly doomed, of course doomed – strategy on a mountaintop. He has made a decision to die in this hopeless adventure because nothing else but Marxist revolution can be a cause for him. He has already fought of it, watched comrades die in its service. What else can there be for such a man?

Is it possible that the offer of his life will be refused?

'Today he said there is no Marxism,' Li continues. 'There are only Marxisms. Each adapted to its situation.' Li moves one small hand through the air. 'I thought I understood theory. I studied it. ut it was never like this.'

'Did he mention me?' Kovalik asks.

Absorbed in recall, Li doesn't reply. 'The old way to look at justice,' he continues, 'is to see it fixed, unchanging. Mao sees it always changing. Justice changing. Let me explain,' Li says, again waving his hand impatiently through the air, as if the gesture helps him to order his thought. 'There will be turning points along the way. For example, a time may come when equality will be a bad thing for society.'

Kovalik wonders if Li is becoming a schoolteacher too, his attitude as eager and as pedantic as Mao's own.

'So what we do we give up equality for a while. But in order to change we must analyze, study, analyze.'

What fascinates Kovalik is Li's ability to forget that he already knows what he now takes for revelation.

'Then, if we're self-critical and *really* honest, the people will follow. We win them by developing their trust –'

'Is there a radio on the mountaintop?'

Startled, Li stares at him. 'Radio? No, at least not that I've heard of. Why?'

'Having a radio, keeping in touch with the outside world, might help in analyzing what the enemy has in mind.'

'Yes.'

Kovalik is a little annoyed that his friend doesn't get the sarcasm, doesn't realize they may all be murdered while Mao is running a schoolhouse.

'Comrade Mao says we must change our method of fighting.'

'Drawing on his experience of warfare?'

'He has written a sort of poem about it.'

'Poem?' Kovalik is appalled.

'It's only a few characters, so the men can easily remember it. *The enemy advances, we retreat. He camps, we bother him. He grows weary, we attack. He retreats, we pursue.*'

'Not bad advice,' Kovalik notes with a petulant shrug. 'But can he get his peasants to follow it?'

'Tomorrow he's going to declare a People's Government here.'

'What?' Kovalik is shocked again. 'On this mountain?'

'Chingkangshan will be a self-governing district, independent of Wuhan or Peking or Nanking or Shanghai or Canton. With its own laws. Mao's going to redistribute the land.'

'What land?'

Li opens his arms to embrace the air. 'As much land as possible around the mountain. Landlords who resist the law will be executed.'

'First Chiang Kai-shek, now Mao.'

Now Li is surprised. 'What does that mean?'

'They both declare independent governments. Chiang had one while there was another in Peking. Then there was the provisional government in Wuhan. And Canton has always been more or less on its own. So Mao has added one to the crowd.'

'Please, my friend,' Li says in a voice of restrained anger, 'do I mention Chiang Kai-shek and Mao in the same breath.'

In the next few days Kovalik sees little of his comrade, who spends most of his time around the temple headquarters, where Mao composes manifestos and consults his men about training the neighborhood peasants in battle tactics. Kovalik tries to control his impatience by taking long walks around the summit camp. He looks down upon the checkerboard fields and beyond to the asymmetrical lakes and farther beyond to blue mountains in the Lohsiao Range astride the borders of Hunan and Kiangsi. At certain unsettling moments he thinks of opium, of old landlord *Ta-yen*. Fortunately, none is available on Chingkangshan by order of Comrade Mao. Punishment, even for the bandit allies, is death. That the bandit chieftains ever agreed to a rule against opium is proof of Mao's gift for persuasion.

Each day increases Kovalik's anxiety. He's especially vulnerable to depression because of his linguistic dependency on Li. Isolation deepens, while for hours he stares down at the Chinese landscape, unreal below the clouds, cleansed by distance of filth and drudgery and fear, the trio of specters that Kovalik has spent his life working to eradicate.

But do you understand that, Mao? Damn it, with your boyish cheeks and pretty hair and big mouth?

In the evenings, when Li finally joins Kovalik for their meal together, they no longer speak openly; it becomes clear to Kovalik that their friendship is in jeopardy. Once, glaring at him, Li says, 'You Russians were too easy, too weak. You worried about the Chinese middle class, about upsetting them. But if you read Marx correctly, you'll see what you really feared was the people themselves – the peasants. That's a bourgeoise instinct, to fear the people, and you brought it with you to China.'

Kovalik doesn't argue or even comment, but waits patiently. His future – for that matter, perhaps his life – is in the balance now. He mustn't tilt it the wrong way by losing his temper. Patience, the Chinese virtue. He must practice it until Mao recognizes him for the indispensable man he is, the experienced revolutionary, the battle-tried soldier.

Li says abruptly, 'Do you know what he said today?' They share a tiny cubicle in one of the numerous old goatherders' huts that dot the mountainside; it is night and they lie on the earthen floor. 'He said to us, I defy *The Communist Manifesto*.' Li waits, perhaps with the intention of challenging an objection to this heresy.

In the dark hut Kovalik says nothing.

'He said he defies the *Manifesto* if it means he must believe in the industrial proletariat.' Again Li waits hostilely before continuing. 'He says we must believe in the peasant, *always* the peasant. Where the *Manifesto* uses proletariat, we must substitute peasant.'

Not such flexible thinking after all, Kovalik decides, but says nothing.

'You must remember this is China,' Li adds after a long silence. His tone is suddenly contrite; perhaps he's aware of the gap widening between them. 'We have our own special problems.'

'Of course. I respect that.'

'That's what I told Mao.'

'But he didn't believe you.'

'I'm sure he did. He's a man with an open mind. You must understand him, my friend. He has taught me certain exaggerations are necessary.'

'And you must change, be flexible.'

'That's right. To right a wrong you must exceed limits.'

'I suppose Mao said that too.'

'Yes. Why?'

Kovalik falls silent. The silence lengthens, and the next morning Li is gone before he awakens. Looking at the cold gray day, hearing on the clay walls and thatch roof the heavy monotonous thud of autumnal rain, Kovalik wishes suddenly for a pipe. Just one. Then he tells himself what a fool he's becoming. Patience. That's all he needs, because it's certainly all the Chinese have needed for millennia to keep themselves above the ground rather than beneath it.

Even before Li reaches him, Kovalik can tell from the downcast eyes what his friend has in store.

Kovalik is sitting on a large rock overlooking the valley, which in the morning mist is half obscured. He is whittling a coolie from a chunk of pine. Already he has carved four and given them to village boys hauling goods for sale up the mountain.

I know what he has come to tell me, Kovalik thinks, but let him have his say in his own good time.

'That's a nice carving,' Li says cheerily, hovering above him.

'Thank you. Sit down.' Kovalik moves sideways on the rock, but the little Chinese refuses the invitation.

'The weather will get cold soon,' Li says.

Kovalik whittles.

'A man came in from Kanchow today with news.' Li explains that the former commander of the Nationalist Fourth Army, at the head of Red defectors from it, is now camped on the outskirts of Canton. Yeh Ting and Ho Lung, turned back from Swatow, are nevertheless still in the province somewhere. Rumor has Chu Teh in northern Kwangtung.

'So we're still alive in the South,' Li concludes with a bright smile.

Tell me, Kovalik is thinking. Tell me, he thinks, while his knife slices through the soft pine.

Instead, mumbling an excuse for leaving, Li hastens away. As Kovalik knows he will, he returns within the hour, his mouth tense, his brow furrowed, his shoulders cinched up by the strain of having to tell his friend that Mao no longer wants him on the mountain. 'He wants you to go,' Li says.

Kovalik nods calmly. 'I expected it.'

'He told me this morning. This is true! I have never been so surprised.'

Kovalik smiles up at him. 'You have found your Trotsky.'

'What?'

'Never mind. You mustn't worry. It's not your fault he wants me out. He just doesn't want foreigners up here.'

Li shakes his head. 'The truth is he doesn't want a Russian up here. I told him you could help with political training – military too. And he admitted if you were German, even British, you could stay. But as it is –'

'Wait now. Let me understand this,' Kovalik says in a low voice. 'I must go because I'm Russian?' He doesn't need confirmation – the answer is on Li's face. 'So that's it. He doesn't want a Russian.' Kovalik can feel the anger rising in him like fire; it burns his gut, his face, his eyes. Getting to his feet he towers above the little Chinese. 'No Russian, but he'd take a German.

Even a Britisher like those who've exploited this country for a hundred years. Does he think the world's actually watching this pathetic little game he's playing here? Will history care who died with him on this mountain? Take a German but no Russian. Who *is* the madman anyway?' Kovalik shakes his head in furious wonder.

'I don't think –'

'Wait a minute! *You* don't think? *Nobody* thinks around here! We Russians came here, we made mistakes, but we came *for the revolution*. Stalin, Borodin, they're only men. But we came with an ideal and *gave* it to you. We showed you how to fight, how to teach revolution. But this arrogant boy with his head in the clouds, this fucking poet with his "departing birds" and the tide of the heart rising and his stupid slogans, *he* is going to tell *me* – me, who's willing to die for him on a mountaintop because I think even if he's insane, his cause is not – *he* is going to tell *me* to get out because *I'm* Russian!' Kovalik stands with clenched fists, shaking through his huge frame.

Slowly, without haste, his old friend turns and walks away.

That night Kovalik has the goatherder's hut to himself. Next day he never sees Li, who obviously has found new quarters. Kovalik waits, fired into patience by self-righteous anger. Let him take his time to come see me, Kovalik thinks; I can wait, I have done nothing else since coming to this terrible country. Meanwhile, Kovalik works hard on a dancing bear, Russian style. Although it's small enough to put into a pocket, Kovalik endows the carving with intricate little curlicues and exceptional detail, etching in the claw nails, tufts of hair, whiskers on the bear's face.

That night, returning to the hut, he sees little Li hunched forward on a bench, waiting.

Li jumps up. When Kovalik is close, he says, 'I have missed seeing you.'

Looking at him closely, Kovalik replies, 'Then I suppose departure's tomorrow.'

'Someone is returning to Changsha tomorrow. He can help get a steamer to Shanghai.' In Li's voice there is guilt, embarrassment, anguish.

Kovalik is not going to let him escape those feelings. 'I don't understand,' he says, understanding perfectly. 'Why do we need someone else to get us to Changsha, when you can do it?'

'Me?'

'No one's released you from your assignment. You go with me.'

'Me? No, I – listen, I'm staying here.'

Kovalik stares at him, wondering if there's any point to this cruel little game. There's no point, 'You said Shanghai.'

'Is Shanghai all right?'

'Any place,' Kovalik says with an indifferent shrug.

'There are still comrades in Shanghai. You can find them and –' In the twilight Li looks up anxiously at his big friend. 'What will you do?'

'You said Shanghai. So I'll stay in Shanghai.'

'Doing what? What will you do?'

Again the Russian shrugs, feeling empty, as empty as the sky's darkness now engulfing them. 'I'll do what they do in Shanghai. Look for comrades, as you suggest. Don't worry, I'll get along.'

'I'm sure you can contact the Party there,' Li's voice lifts hopefully.

'Of course.'

'They can – get you back to Russia.'

'What for? So Stalin can have me murdered?' Kovalik guffaws. 'Let's sit down.'

They sit on the bench, watching the final light withdraw from the pines, changing the intricate spindly forms into tall simple poles. 'Don't worry,' Kovalik says, 'I'll be fine in Shanghai.'

'Will you contact the Party?' Li persists in desperate hope. 'It shouldn't be hard. You can work for them there.'

'Of course.'

'Then you'll contact the Party?'

'No. There is no Party any more in Shanghai.'

After a long silence, Li reaches out and touches Kovalik on the wrist. The Russian, although accustomed to bear hugs in his own land, is startled by Li's gesture.

'I didn't think we'd ever part,' Li says.

'Neither did I.'

'There's a poem –'

'Not one of Mao's, I hope,' Kovalik says gruffly.

'By the great Li Po. Someone in camp has a copy of his poems, and I read it today to refresh my memory of this one. It says:

'So let us vow a friendship beyond friendship
And meet again beyond the stars.'

*   *   *

Kovalik nods. After another long silence he says to Li, 'Now that I'm going, I have something to tell you. First, I envy you. I envy what you have coming – the cold, the hunger, the fighting. And you know why: we believe in the same thing. But I don't envy you Mao. He's an intellectual, no matter how hard he tries to hide it with his swearing and his women. He's not one of these peasants he's always yelling about, never was and never will be. And he'll break under pressure. The intellectuals all do. We had them in Russia and they broke.' For an instant Lenin and Trotsky, among others, come to mind – they didn't break – but he won't weaken the argument by making exceptions. 'They broke and Mao will too. His peasants will betray him in the end. They'll walk away when the going gets tough. And because Mao has got his head in the clouds, when they do betray him, he won't be able to take it. He'll crack wide open, just like a melon.' It is Kovalik's turn to touch his friend's sleeve. 'One thing more, friend. These Red commanders wandering around out there with their little armies? Someday Mao will link up with them, and when he does, you shift over to them. This fellow Chu Teh sounds good. Go to him. He's a soldier, and if anyone survives, he will. But give Mao up. If you do that, perhaps someday, well, it all might work.' Kovalik rises. It is totally dark now and all he can see of his friend is faint oval light where Li's face is.

'Thanks for that poem,' Kovalik says roughly and shoves the finished carving of the Russian bear into his friend's hand. 'Remember me.'

Turning and entering the hut, Kovalik lies on the floor, wide awake all night. In the morning, accompanied by a scowling, taciturn Red soldier, he begins the long slow meaningless trip to Changsha and to the steamer that will bear him downstream to the city of Shanghai, where he will do what is done there.

Often he tries to remember the words to that poem, but few of them have stayed in his mind.

23

Of the twenty-four *Qi Jie* which fix the seasons of the Chinese year, today is *Li Dong* – beginning of winter.

It is a cold day, the tenth of the march from Shantung Province, and the men are tired, having tramped sixty li a day – twenty miles – on rutted lanes and sometimes across fields, when the poor roads of Hopei disappear under the pounding of mule hooves, wagons, foot soldiers, and cavalry. Thirty thousand troops move forward, along with the four thousand coolies bearing supplies. Columns on the march carry their forest of rifles at an angle, like branches bent one way in a storm. Unwieldy, patient, chaotic, but irresistible, the regiments plod forward through the province of Hopei, past the bare willows and poplars, fording small muddy rivers, dragging past fallow wheat and cotton fields, down empty village paths, tramping through the mud towns of Poping, Lintsing, Tsingho, Nankung, and Hihsien to the broad flat outskirts of Hengshui. Jen Ching-i has been hunkered down here for two weeks, just as Tang expected, with his batteries dug in and concealed on two hillocks, his infantry commanding an expanse of wheat field, a transverse road, and the train junction which Jen obviously means to defend. Tang leads the mass of carts, pack mules, coolies, horses, trucks, and foot soldiers at a steady, almost brutal pace in an effort to prepare his army for worse hardships to come – for the battle itself.

Aside from rice doled out once a day by the quartermaster, each company has fended for itself, bargaining with farmers and villagers for bread and vegetables (when officers are watching, otherwise 'confiscating' the provisions), collecting firewood, and sheaves of straw to use as camouflage it needed. In the large towns officers have dealt with the *Chin Chang*, district supervisors, in obtaining supplies which are divided among company cooks and battalion supply sergeants.

As the army approaches Hengshui, facing winds that have picked up speed across the vast flat of the Gobi, scouts continue to confirm Jen's intention of waiting at Hengshui. It appears that the old man has no interest in petty skirmishes or clever feints, in the flashy maneuvering with which some young officers attempt to emulate the battles they've read about in Western military books. Jen has firmly positioned himself on dominant hilltops in command of a broad approach. As scouts report in more detail – breathless on their horses thickly lathered by galloping – General Tang fully appreciates his opponent's selection of terrain. These two hills are the only natural barriers within a day's march of Hengshui. North of these hills the approach is marred by a swampy lake and two streams which, although narrow, are quite swift and therefore a danger, especially to pack mules hauling cannon wheels and ammo boxes on their sides. Jen has seen to it the choice of battle-field will be his, and the style of combat as well, for although Tang favors swift maneuvering across a flat expanse, Jen has created a situation for bringing artillery into greater prominence.

Of course, Tang would like to use big guns too. During the march he overheard young Major Chia describing German 'hurricane barrages' that featured 155-mm. cannon, followed by an infantry charge and rolled-up light artillery. The General, hearing this, imagined the effect of 155's. There are so many things he would like for his army. A modern logistical system, for example; a proper means of transport and supply, with motorized vehicles replacing human carriers. He would like modern field telephones and wireless sets for speedy communication between pickets and command posts. He had ordered a score of phones and three wirelesses from Luckner, but since they never arrived, the forward elements must depend on a scant half-dozen crank-up phones and no wireless. Often the General hears his junior officers voicing a desire for modern equipment. He can't blame them, watching them bed down for frosty nights in town and village – lucky to find a vacant storehouse or a tax bureau for shelter.

One day out of Hengshui the General rides up on a little knoll; it gives him a view of the army stretched out before him in the early-morning light. The sun, just risen, has not yet burned off the frost, and it twinkles by the roadside in the trampled weeds, glistens on the slickers worn by some of the men and on the rumps of baggage mules and on the chinstrapped billed hats of officers, on crossed bandoliers, on rolled umbrellas, on cartridge boxes, on field packs and the cotton shoes tied to them, on wadded cotton trousers, on the flapping puttees wrapped around thousands and thousands of churning legs, as the endless brown column penetrates the cold dawn of Hopei, marching through the oceanic vastness of China as armies have done for thousands of years.

We Chinese are sand, the General thinks, lowering his field glasses.

Later that day a little airplane stutters across the horizon. It is a British Moth with a whirlwind Wright motor that sounds like a loud cough. The pilot flies high to avoid riflefire, although no one shoots at him. Many of the young soldiers and carriers gawk at the plane, having never seen one before. Tang remembers what happened when Chang Tso-lin once bought a Ryan-Mahoney Brougham for use in a battle near Peking: its motor giving out like a bad heart, the plane crashed into a pond; just before going down out of control, however, it released a bomb that killed no one but that provided curious soldiers with a special treat – they rushed to the shell crater and picked out smoking fragments for souvenirs. Tang had been a colonel then, stationed in Soochow, and the story made the rounds of the officers' mess.

The British Moth is now spraying a stream of leaflets into the windless air (the winds have not yet begun to blow, as if patiently waiting for the sun to get high off the horizon and clear of their path), and the papers float lazily down upon the heads of the startled troops. The leaflet turns out to be Jen Ching-i's call for desertion according to a sliding scale of reward: $20 Mex for a private (twice what a Tang trooper gets in a month); $40 for a private who brings a rifle with him; $500 for an officer who comes over with a machine gun; $1,000 for an officer who deserts with a piece of field artillery. The soldiers who can read explain the terms to those who can't. They all laugh, although Tang knows full well that many among them will stuff the offer inside their jackets in case the opportunity for defection presents itself. It is the way of Chinese warfare.

At dawn the next morning, forward elements of the Shantung army tramp around a lake and slog through a stretch of swampland, its frosted surface crackling underfoot like thin glass. Their pickets are taken under fire by skirmishers across a broad wheat field. To the northeast the troops can see the low-slung train station and the railroad tracks leading from it eastward and northward. The scouts had given General Tang an accurate report. Jen Ching-i commands two craggy hills, battery emplacements dug into them, with infantry drawn up behind them, so well concealed that an uninterested passerby might not be aware of an army of fifty thousand. On the north side of the lake there is a little rise in the flat farmland; here Tang sets up his field head-quarters. For hours his troops arrive and take up positions along the southern edge of a road running east and west in front of the wheat fields, facing the two hills and the train station. Through scouts the General learns that Jen has a command post behind the two hillocks next to a soybean field in a farmhouse. He learns further that all the countryside to the east and west, for one reason or another, is unsuitable for rapid troop movement; a flanking action in either direction seems inappropriate. Progress is therefore limited, aside from a frontal attack across the wheat fields by his infantry; that would lead to annihilation, since Jen has the overlooking hills bristling with guns.

What does Jen think I'll do? Tang wonders. Surely the obvious move would be against the train station. He could bring troops along the eastwest road to a wagon path that runs at right angles to the tracks coming from the east. The wagon path would lead right to the station. But according to intelligence – and so far his scouts have proved effective – the station and its environs are heavily defended.

All morning the General paces the tiny wooded hill, looking often through his binoculars at the fields, which are now dotted by puffs of smoke, as skirmishers from both sides engage in a brisk exchange of fire. At the outset Tang wants to maintain contact with Jen's forces, although a major clash won't come until tomorrow. The General's father once told him never to lose contact with the enemy: Have skirmishers out, have detachments in motion. Otherwise an observant enemy (and Jen is that) might push through untended gaps in the line and at the very least disrupt communication between units or throw incoming columns into confusion. A passive army is a vulnerable army. With this dictum in mind, Tang has his picket maintain a steady fire on the hills and the pass between them.

While his various units begin to wheel along the northern edge of the lake and the swamp, he continues receiving reports from regimental commanders as they take positions facing the hills. He consults often with young Major Chia, who has been brought into staff. On horseback, they watch the maneuvering through binoculars and agree that an initial frontal assault across the wheat field, given Jen's artillery strength in the hills, would be a disaster. Moreover, an attack on the train station is also a poor choice, although most commanders would go for it: China is a country of rail transportation; who holds the train stations and track holds everything. Jen knows this, of course, and in consequence will have heavily armed the station, which is a natural fort of brick and tin. A charge at it along a flat road and across open field would be suicidal. Yet Tang – and Major Chia agrees – has a feeling that Jen, a traditionalist, will expect him to go for the place of prime importance. At nightfall, when men on both sides are gathering wood for campfires, the General calls his staff to gether for a discussion of tomorrrow's battle plan. He will initially attack the southwest hill, nearer his own line, while feinting along the road that borders the wheat field – as if heading for the wagon path that leads to the train station. The hope is that the feint will draw fire from the farther hill and give his attacking force enough time to scale and overrun the batteries on the nearer hill. Once this objective is taken, he can turn the captured guns on the farther hill, whose artillery must then respond. That leaves the corridor along the wheat field free of fire. Columns heading for the train station, their feint ended, can wheel about and cross the field. He will have Jen's troops in the pass between the hills caught in a pincer.

That's the plan. But the General knows through experience it is the nature of a battle that such plans never unfold as they should. This plan's virtue lies in its emphasis upon the nearer hill; his troops will come under fire for less time than if the main attack begins elsewhere. Its weakness may well be in the trouble of men scaling the hill.

In *The Three Kingdoms* a general says before battle, 'The planning lies with men, the outcome with heaven. No man can force it.'

Recalling the words now, Tang moves with a few aides through the evening. He has left Major Chia with other staff members and commanders to work out details. Now he wants to be with the soldiers. Cooking fires dot the verge of lake and swamp, where men hunch at bivouac with their rifles stacked in tripods. They squat near their mess kits in a welter of teapots, umbrellas, field equipment. Sometimes he halts to ask a soldier his unit. The answer always comes back with the name of his commander. 'I'm from the Shih Battalion' – not the Third Battalion, Sixth Infantry Regiment. It's a measure of the personal command, traditional with the Chinese, that Western military observers scoff at. But Tang finds satisfaction in the bond between soldier and officer: It is Confucian. Some of the men wear steel helmets, taken on other battlefields from the corpses of enemy more affluent than they. In their padded uniforms and leg wrappings, with their thick cartridge belts and rolled blankets across their chests, they look in the firelight like great furry bears. Tang, halting at the edge of a campfire, overhears a sergeant exhorting youngsters about the coming battle. 'Look, children, it's very simple. What's going to happen is this. If you people go forward, we eat bread. If you people retreat, we eat sticks. That's all there is to war. Let no one tell you different.'

'A practical man,' Tang murmurs to an aide. 'I want his name and unit.' The General keeps a list of such reliable soldiers.

After a meal of vegetables and bread, he goes over the plan again with his staff, checking to see if they have handled the details. Colonel Pi looks crestfallen, rather than furious, at the obvious success of young Major Chia.

Looking once more at the field maps, Tang claps his hands down on his thighs decisively. 'So we're ready.' He tells his staff to get some sleep, then wraps up in a blanket in his tent. That night the wind blows hard, flapping the canvas, but it isn't noise that keeps the General awake, it's the test tomorrow. All the training, all the complexities of administration, all the motion and the thought and the expenditure of money, all the countless details that have gone into bringing thirty thousand fighters to this place in time, all of it comes to the test in the morning. In the cold darkness his mind is filled with images of the long day just ended: the caissons, the coolies, the line of troops all flowing toward two hills as common in appearance (sides rocky, tops flat, with a few scraggly trees perched there) as the wheat field they command. Yet tomorrow many of the men whom he has just strolled past tonight will be dead on those hills, their flesh and blood mixed with the soil of this insignificant acreage near a town called Hengshui. It is the same before every battle – his regard for the terrain where men will die. Tomorrow he will look through his binoculars at it and see movement to and fro, nothing more. Tonight, thinking of the landscape before him, he envisions a huge graveyard. It is always the same.

But it isn't of the land fronting Hengshui or the battle itself that he last thinks before falling into a fitful sleep. It's of Black Jade, her long white foreign face parted in a smile, her lips parted sensuously, her green eyes drawing him toward her, the white fingers – he can almost feel the warm little weight of them – as they circle and gently grip the back of his neck.

*   *   *

The day begins. It is remarkably hot, as if yanked from its proper season and mistakenly deposited here at the time of *Li Dong*, the beginning of winter. A day out of its weather, Tang's father used to say, is never auspicious. For a moment, muzzy from sleep, the General considers the possibility of postponing the battle, contenting himself today with skirmishes. Then his mind clears, and he is up, calling for a subaltern.

Within half an hour he is standing on the wooded knoll with field glasses fixed upon the commotion before him – the wheeling of 37- and 73-millimeter cannon and howitzers into place, unlimbered, their ammo laid out. Infantry are shuffling into position, adjusting on their arms the orange bands which distinguish them from the troops of Jen Ching-i, who wear purple. Such armbands, easily removed and changed, have saved countless men in tough battles, the General knows, but have also allowed for wholesale defections. He wishes in this last moment for proper uniforms, field phones, hand grenades (his troops have few; they were in the Luckner shipment), more weapons of every description, supply trucks, planes and heavy artillery for 'hurricane barrages,' and more machine guns and more rifles. He thinks with a military man's fervor of such advantages when he stands on the threshold of battle. Shaking off his rush of desire, General Tang watches some 65-mm. Italian mountain guns being positioned along the ditch south of the transverse road. Crackling small-arms fire lets the army know that their opponents have not overslept either, but are preparing too for today's business. Tang's troops, some of them holding 303-caliber Lee Enfield rifles a quarter of a century old, move into their columns. The cavalry, not as yet mounted, take up positions in the rear to either side of the lake. Behind these troops are other companies that are poorly armed. In fact, a third of them lack weapons and hope to get them from comrades fallen in earlier waves before making their own contact with the enemy. This is traditional, and they accept it, but once again General Tang wishes for that shipment from Luckner.

Giving orders to his staff, the General begins the operation. His batteries north of the swamp open fire on the nearest hill, which later will be assaulted. Batteries eastward, in front of the lake and the knoll where he stands, are rolled forward almost to the transverse road, between willow trees. They open at long range against the farther hill, hoping to soften up emplacements there and to keep Jen's artillery from accurate spotting. For this purpose General Tang calls for battery fire – guns firing in succession. Regiments of the First Division, from Qufu, once the artillery has established its rhythm of bombardment, move ostentatiously onto the transverse road, heading eastward toward the wagon path that leads to the train station.

They are not *kan-si-tui* do-or-die units – but today these troops may serve the same function, for it's the General's intention that they draw fire and divert Jen from what will become the major assault. And they do draw fire immediately from both hills, artillery shells lobbing into the road and along the line of willows. The companies break ranks and crouch in the ditches, then move again during loading intervals. They are out of infantry range, but the roar of cannonade suggests many casualties among troops who may not even see the enemy today but simply take their fire. Dust rises along the road, and through his binoculars Tang can see men opening their padded jackets, sweltering in the unexpected heat. The Second Division, from Yi Nan, emerges from the eastern side of the lake, around a stand of trees, and heads at a trot in a column of fours toward the wagon path. Tang smiles with satisfaction, aware that Jen must be viewing their emergence from the woods. The old man must be standing on the farther hill, looking down at the wheat fields. From his vantage point he'd not see the Lin Yi Division until the last moment, when they swirl out of the small forest and head for the train station. To protect it Jen will probably step up the barrage from that hill, and he does. A tearing racket of cannonfire fills the warm morning, and through his binoculars Tang watches a whole platoon dissolve after the smoke clears – they were there, some thirty men, and now they are gone. He looks down at his own batteries and is appalled to see gunners lax at their work: Fuses lie on the ground; shell casings lie about, impeding the operation of the guns. He yells at a subaltern to get down there and reprimand the battery commander.

The First and Second divisions, both heading for the wagon path to the train station, continue to take intense fire from the hill. Rank on rank, moving forward, are greeted by fierce volleys. Some men break away and start to run back, so Tang gives the order to herd them together and have them summarily shot – a practical application of *lien-tso-fa* which he had debated theoretically with the American journalist on the way to Chiang Kai-shek's monastery. He watches with great interest the behaviour of Jen's guns. The old man has made a mistake in using high explosive instead of shrapnel against troops in the open. And he's using time fuses instead of percussion. Or is Jen, like himself, simply using what he has available? It's difficult in China to distinguish between bad judgment and necessity.

Tang now unleashes the first assault battalions from north of the swamp; they will cross the road and a few hundred yards of uneven ground to the bottom of the nearer hill. Perched on its summit are batteries which, thus far, have fired only sporadically at Tang's staging areas. The General slews his binoculars away from the hill to see what's happening to his diversionary troops on the train-station road. From this distance their columns weave and twist, when shells hit among them, like ants deviated from their path by the pounding steps of human feet. Above them are tiny puffs of smoke – some of Jen's gunners are aiming too high, their shot exploding harmlessly in the air. The fuses aren't set right. What in hell's wrong with the old man? Tang wonders, even as he slews his field glasses around to watch his assault troops emerge from the swamp thicket and willow trees.

A rolling barrage from the nearer hillside sweeps down on them. The shot digs in. The earth shakes from it, the leading line is cut down as if by a sickle, and the forward battalion gives way, backing off a few yards to regroup. Tang's batteries answer, this time with salvo fire – every gun of the quartet in each battery firing at once – so that the following barrage from the hillside is thready, broken, lacking the punch of the first volleys. He can hear the attackers scream in full throat as they scramble toward the bottom of the near hill.

Then Tang sees them: circling the western edge of the near hill, Jen's infantry with bayonets fixed, coming on the run, within seconds of clashing head on with his own troops. There's no room for maneuvering, but tightly packed, the two forces hit with the impact of cement. A few of Tang's units break free and scrabble up the hillside, while below them the men with orange and purple armbands grapple hand to hand or fire pointblank at one another.

So Jen has held back this surprise: Instead of marshaling his infantry for a defense between the two hills, he has swung a large concentration of them behind the near hill to intercept Tang's charge. Even so, he has staggered, not halted, the assault; although what's left of it – a trickling of foot soldiers struggling up the hillside – can't take the summit alone. So in their support General Tang orders a full attack by the entire corps, without holding back reserves. It is a bold, irrevocable decision, made within seconds, while he and Major Chia pore over a map. Rank upon rank of two infantry divisions, nearly fifteen thousand men, lumber through the swamp – soft in the heat of this strange day – out upon the transverse road and head for the hill. Officers urge the men up the hillside, avoiding contact with Jen's troops, who are locked in combat with the first wave of Tang's infantry. As for that clash, it assumes an intensity which Tang recognizes as something his father spoke of in awe, along with retired officers who'd cluck their tongues at the memory of it – of battles that occur rarely but go beyond conventional limits, that move beyond control or logic, so that the combatants lose any sense of guidance on the field and, rendered blind by smoke and blood, wholly lost to reason, forgetting their objective, deaf even to the inner plea for survival, rush together in impossible tumult, hitting out drunkenly, and in primal fury go about slaughtering one another without stint. They are doing that now on this battlefield; they stand toe to toe and fire their guns or stab wildly with sword and knife, or lock arms and legs and teeth in total combat, prepared to hold on to one another until death.

But Tang's decision to commit the entire corps immediately does accomplish its aim, for in spite of Jen's resistance, the mass of Shantung infantry gets past it and moves up the hillside.

The decision is effective so far, but if Jen reinforces his troops at the bottom of the hill, he may turn the whole flank and roll up everything in his path, turning the battle into a rout. Aware of the danger, Tang needs to redirect his units in the east and get them back into action. This will force Jen to keep some troops between the two hills, to hold ground rather than reinforce the men already in combat: in other words, to make him shift from offense to defense. But in order to bring infantry from the east across the exposed wheat field, Tang must neutralize at least some of the batteries looking down on the field from the farther hill. He calls up two cavalry battalions for a frontal assault; their objective will be to gain the pass between the two hills and force Jen's infantry back there to protect it. Turning to a senior officer, Tang points with his binoculars down the road, where a few dozen soldiers are helping the wounded out of ditches. 'They're not fighting,' Tang observes sharply. 'When able-bodied men are busy with wounded, it means they're shirking. It's the commander's fault. Get these battalion commanders to control their men!'

The hillside assault continues, with men edging up the rocky slope while from its summit the defenders are shooting down at them, no longer with artillery – they can't get a low enough trajectory – but with rifles and pistols. Through his field glasses General Tang can see Mauser 68s, Mannlicher 6.5s – better weapons than most of his men carry, although not better than he should have received from Luckner. The cavalry charge begins and soon afterward the First and Second divisions wheel away from the wagon path, giving up the feint at the train station, and start across the wheat field. So much change of direction apparently confuses Jen's hill gunners, who break the rhythm of their salvos and resort to individual fire.

It'a a good sign, Tang thinks, but he can no longer get a clear look at the battlefield, which is now obscured by shifting layers of dark smoke.

'We must get closer,' he tells his staff, and mounts his horse. Soon they're all moving off the knoll and halting a quarter of a mile farther north, on the edge of the transverse road, under a willow, the top branches having been sheared off by a shell as if by giant scissors.

Dust rises from the warm earth where the cavalry units have begun their charge. The air is filled with the neighing of wounded horses, the cries of wounded men. But the fire from both hills is sporadic now, having lost the confident timing of salvos; and from the nearer hill, where the assault troops of the Second Corps have reached the summit, the firing of artillery almost stops. The tactic is working, Tang thinks. He feels the sweat pouring from his face. Looking at his officers, their faces blackened by smoke, the General smiles. The unusual heat of this day has certainly *not* been auspicious – not for Jen Ching-i.

But then to the east he can see the line of his two infantry divisions coming through the fallow wheat field. Batteries on the farther hill lash out with renewed salvos, spraying shell into the ranks, sweeping down and then rolling up the line with murderous fire. Lifting his binoculars, General Tang sees the tiny shapes of guns jarring back in discharge – toys at this distance. Those guns still command the approach to the pass between the two hills. Pressure must be put there, between the pass and upon the farther hill. Otherwise Jen could take the offensive again and outflank Tang's entire force to the west; from the rear, then, he'd catch Tang in a fatal crossfire.

'Another cavalry charge,' the General says. 'What's left over there?' He points to the far southeast, to the edge of the lake.

'The Third and Fourth Cavalry battalions, General.'

Tang blinks away the acrid sting of cordite. 'Send them in now – a mass charge. We have to free our infantry from the hill guns. Do it now!'

A subaltern attempts to crank the field telephone, but in his nervousness moves the crank the wrong way. Pushing him aside, Major Chia cranks up and yells above the battle din for the Third and Fourth Cavalry to attack – *Xi-shen tao-ti!*

Abruptly the sunlight moves behind a cloudbank that is building in the west. Within minutes a chill wind blowing in behind the clouds has turned the weather terribly around.

'Whatsoever thy Hand findeth to do, do it with thy Might.'

Embree has tried all morning to concentrate on those words, seeking protection from the fear that has been stalking him ever since he awakened on this warm, muggy day. Fingering the Big Sword patch on his jacket, he has tried in vain to rid himself of the shameful emotion. He even held a conversation with his sister Mary.

They sit in the same speakeasy Mary had taken him to on his visit to New York. 'Mary, the adventure has gotten out of hand! I'm going into a Chinese battle.'

Mary won't like that. She'll think he's a fool to mix so deeply into something alien and dangerous. But Mary won't say it. She will steel herself against disapproval. She will set her lips as he has seen her do many times. 'If that's where the adventure takes you, you have to follow it.' She'd say that, Mary would.

And in the conversation he tells her how much he loves China, not as a missionary would love it – as a place to conquer or at least to understand – but with illogical passion, so that he feels the men beside him are truly his brothers.

'Are you committed to their politics?'

'I don't have any politics.'

In the imagined talk Mary reaches across the checkered table-cloth and pats his hand. 'Then do it. Go fight beside them. Just do it.'

But now he isn't sure of doing it. The first casualties returned from the bombarded raod. He saw blood dripping steadily from the rear of a bullock cart in which a heap of wounded lay. One man held up a rag-soaked stump of arm in an effort to ease the throbbing pain. Embree hears a rumor that the army's sustaining heavy casualties, but his friend Fu Chang-so laughs.

'When you get out there,' Fu tells him, 'you'll think they're heavy, but afterward you'll figure the casualties were light. That's the way it is.'

But the way it is doesn't give Embree any comfort; nothing does. He had enjoyed the march from Qufu; being mounted, he didn't get the blistered feet of infantry. He liked singing the war songs and eating hard bread along the roadside with his companions, all of them wearing Big Sword patches.

Now, however, the battalion awaits orders beside the lake on a patch of unplowed ground near some trees. Earlier they passed near a small knoll and Embree had caught a glimpse of General Tang. Hoping for a sign of recognition, proud to be leading a Big Sword platoon, Embree was disappointed – the General, pacing in a plain uniform, had his eyes fixed on the hills.

Later, hearing the first barrages rend the warm November air, Embree spent the time grooming Marengo, who will take him into battle.

Into battle. Should he, an American, be fighting in a Chinese battle whose outcome has nothing to do with him? Certainly nothing to do with a missionary, a little late in taking up his Christian duties in Harbin! Do it, Mary said, because they are your friends. It's what he spoke for her, yet belief fades with the shells bursting not a quarter-mile away. And he hates the rumors that continue to multiply – we are holding ground or the enemy is holding ground or both are retreating; casualties are heavy, light, are heavy again, light again. Embree glances furtively at his comrades, many of them resting under their umbrellas, others splayed out on the bare warm ground like sunbathers on a beach. Are they afraid too? Is there anything to the idea that Orientals are insensitive, fearless, indifferent to fate? He tries to think of the Russian woman back in Qufu. That helps. He remembers her violent thrashing of the drugged Bolshevik. And he imagines her thinking of him here, now, preparing for battle. Perhaps she'd be surprised at his being here, admire his courage. The idea braces him, and he continues to groom Marengo. Often he stops to scratch inside his belt and under his arms where the lice congregate. 'If you haven't had lice yet, you can't understand

China.' Who told him that, a foreigner or a Chinese? Anyway, if it's true, he understands the country as well as anyone. Then he sees the ammo wagon creak forward, and with other sergeants he orders his own platoon to line up and receive their twenty rounds. For an instant, looking at the weathered cart with its canvas top, he remembers the white-wall tires and running boards of automobiles back home, where no one could picture Philip Embree keeping his horsemen in line to receive their ration of bullets near a Chinese battlefield. But it is so. And he will fight. The reality at last settles in him, like a hard plug of stale bread that feels uncomfortable but fills the stomach. He will fight. It occurs to him with mild surprise that there's no way out anyway; he's a sergeant in the Big Swords, and if he refused to fight, General Tang would have him shot.

Fu Chang-so, coming up with a smile, says to him, 'Hear that?' He has to repeat it for Embree to hear, because a tremendous surging of metallic noise rolls beyond the transverse road into this staging area. 'Some one's catching it.' Fu Chang-so steps back and shouts into the noon air, 'Mount!'

On their way from the staging area, Embree notices a machine gun set up to shoot deserters. A young crew member is slowly munching a piece of wheat bread. Stokes mortars, lashed to the sides of mules, are moving parallel to the cavalry battalion. Embree hears belt-fed machine guns racketing across the wheat field that has now come into view – endless brown stubble, wholly deserted for the moment. As the battalion moves out upon the transverse road, he has a glimpse of a field gun which, having recoiled and jerked backward, is now being pushed into place again by straining coolies, who have stopped carrying supplies to help with the artillery – doubtless volunteering at gunpoint.

And then Embree sees his first dead man of the battle. It is a coolie who has been cut in two, the parts within arm's reach of each other.

'That's what a high-explosive shell does,' Fu Chang-so remarks next to Embree. 'Jen has got German and Japanese guns, I hear. He's got heavy mortars too, the old bastard.'

Suddenly their captain shouts for the company to return to cover; they've been mistakenly pulled out. So for an hour they remain mounted at the edge of a small woods, while the sunny day fills with yellow acrid smoke. They watch two battalions of cavalry, farther to the west, disappear into that smoke while the earth shakes beneath their own horses, who shift about nervously. At last they're ordered forward again. This time the wheat field is filled with soldiers, the First and Second divisions, who have wheeled away from the train station and are coming westward across the field. The entire line of men seems to melt away under terrific fire from batteries on the far hill.

'Soon,' Fu Chang-so says under his breath and taps the side of his holster.

Embree speaks a soothing word to Marengo. He watches in dismay how his hand on the reins is trembling. Do the others see it? He glances at Fu Chang-so, who's looking ahead where the air is lit up like lightning from a massive barrage of shells bursting in the wheat field. A cloudbank wipes out the sun, leaving a cold gun-metal gray light on everything. Embree hates the queasy color of his trembling hand. He speaks soothingly to Marengo, who is nervous under him, the great flanks shifting weight at each fresh blast of sound.

The company commander, sporting three gold bars on his jacket, rides up with a grim smile. 'It's going to be a boot-to-boot charge for that pass between the hills,' he tells his sergeants.

What pass? Panicky, Embree can't see anything in the direction of the captain's vaguely waved arm. What pass? He can't see anything except smoke hovering above the wheat stubble and fallen bodies turned gray under the cloudy sky. By companies the battalion moves forward in a long skirmish line along the southern edge of the wheat field. With the color bearers leading the way, the charge of the Fourth Battalion begins at the sound of a half-dozen bugles blowing out a tinny series of rapid notes.

Philip Embree, the defiant sound of '*Sha! Sha! Sha!*' – 'Kill! Kill! Kill!' – in his throat, spurs his chestnut into a gallop. He's alongside Fu Chang-so, literally boot to boot in the *xi-shen tao-ti* charge. They plunge into the wheat field. Almost instantly the entire line is met by withering fire from the hill. Embree yells '*Sha! Sha! Sha!*' into a suddenly chill wind and brandishes his pistol, while beneath him the bullets rip through wheat stalks, snipping them off like pieces of paper. On either side men are yelling, bugles blaring, horses snorting on the gallop. Shot plows up the earth in front of him, causing Marengo to rear and nearly throw him, but the interruption of his forward motion saves Embree's life – ahead of him a dozen yards now, Fu Chang-so's horse, along with two others, is struck by shell fragments at full gallop and crumples in midair, rolling to the ground with Fu Chang-so underneath. As Embree bolts past them, he can see his friend beneath the animal, chest crushed, the light gone from his eyes. But this is an instant's sight for Embree, who leans forward against his lathered Marengo, no longer yelling *Sha!* but intent on keeping the target of himself small. Men from the iron-gray hill – it is large now – are sniping down at the charging line. Cavalry just ahead of him are still getting battery fire; one burst drops a half-dozen men. Embree's eyes register a terrible fact: The field is becoming red. When he looks back to see how many are behind him, a metallic crimson covers the stubble. And even more horrible, he watches Marengo step down fully on a fallen comrade. But he spurs the horse to catch up with those ahead. The sound comes out of his throat again – '*Sha! Sha! Sha!*' They are nearly across the field, yet Embree hasn't fired a shot. Ahead, facing the charge, is a detachment of Jen's infantry who are lightly dug into the ground between the pass. A few kneel, but most of them lie in shallow trenches, sighting at the horsemen with their rifles.

Now Embree shoots and shoots and shoots at the prone snipers. There's a low breagtwork of timber, and a few of the infantrymen race for it to get out of the way of the horses. Machine guns, set in front of the infantry, take the brunt of the cavalry charge – guns, belts, and carriages are bowled over. The Fourth Battalion jumps the little breastwork and strikes at the foot soldiers. Looking at a haggard frightened face – the man has risen uncertainly to one knee from the shallow trench he dug for himself – Embree shoots and the face breaks apart like a melon. Riding on, at a slower pace, Embree picks off a man swabbing out a Stokes mortar that has just been fired. And in the next moments (how long they last will always be beyond his comprehension), Embree moves up and down, swirling about, shifting his weight from one side to another, reloading, bringing Marengo around in circles. He fires his pistol until out of bullets; holstering it, he yanks out the ax from his belt. Leaning far out of the saddle, he brains a fleeing infantryman. For the rest of his life he won't forget the impact, the resistance of bone, the giving way.

The Fourth Battalion of horse has broken the defense of the pass and annihilated most of the defenders, but could in turn be annihilated by the main body of Jen's troops behind the hills, except that they are drawing fire from the southwest hill, which is now in Tang's hands. Glancing up, Embree sees the orange armbands on men peering down at Jen's infantry; it is stepping back from both hills, being concentrated by the heavy smallarms fire into a slowly retreating mass.

The Fourth Battalion, its charge completed, swerves aside as the First and Second Infantry divisions slog out of the wheat stalks, firing from the hip. The cavalry begins to regroup under the shouted commands of their officers. The exhausted horsemen look dully at one another. Many of them cough. A black greasy smoke clings to their skins, leaving a gray film as if they have come out of a slimy hole. Embree looks for Fu Chang-so, then remembers his friend was crushed under the fallen horse. Everywhere he looks are the signs of tremendous battle – artillery wreckage, corpses, broken wagons, shell casings, rifles, and sickles shaped like half-moons – he has seen the sickles used by some of Jen's men to hack at the oncoming horses. Sweat pours from him, yet he realizes with surprise that the temperature has dropped precipitously; his breath is pluming in the air.

Firing continues, but most of it now on the northeast hill, which Shantung troops have also scaled and where they're wiping out remnants of artillery units. The crackle of gunfire above Embree shifts his attention to the hillside, dark with bodies and casings. Forming up what is left of his platoon, he is shocked to find only eight men left of thirty-seven. Dead or wounded? Or have they run from this terrible place?

Someone rides up to shout that Jen's troops are retreating fast – he points west and north – into the town of Hengshui.

Details are going across the battlefield collecting weapons and ammo from the dead and wounded, even before the smoke has cleared. Jen's soldiers hug the ground, too terrified by the noise of battle – still with them in imagination – to get up and run. They are captured or shot or bayoneted, according to the whim of Tang's men. Scavengers are already searching the corpses for stray *cash*, tobacco, anything. This continues while pockets of resistance hold out across the entire battle area.

The Fourth Battalion, formed up in loose order, rides toward a rim of trees along a soybean field. Embree keeps looking down for fear of Marengo stepping on a body still alive. The acrid odor of smoke is mixed now with another smell – blood? death? He watches a file of officers canter by, the General among them, all heading for a distant farmhouse that earlier may have been Jen's headquarters. Embree shivers; the sweat on his body is chilled by freshening gusts from the west.

Fighting is now desultory; Jen troops retreat out of range and make for the safety of houses in the town. Tang troops don't pursue, having no orders from the General to do so. They are glad of it, many slipping to the ground and stretching out there, beside the dead, to rest. Embree leads his men back toward the morning's staging area. As he approaches the wheat field again, he hears a new sound, distinct from the sound of battle. It takes him awhile to understand its meaning, this low thick wail, like the sea beating against a distant shore. Coming closer to the battlefield, Embree shakes uncontrollably, hoping the men don't notice.

The dreadful sound is the unceasing cry of thousands lying wounded, untended, on hilltop and field, in roadway and hillside. Their agony is a massive harrowing chorus that accompanies the rest of this day, then the long cold night, and the next day, continuing until some of them are removed and others die where they have fallen. The rail station of Hengshui is packed with their litters, while both armies, having rested, move out of the area toward the north in a series of minor engagements, leaving in their wake more wreckage of war.

On that first evening of battle, stunned by the events of the day but especially by the whine of terror and pain floating across the darkness. Philip Embree hunches over a ration of hard bread, his hands almost numb from the cold that has rushed out of Mongolia, and he thinks, this is madness, madness, this is madness.

When Vera hears that a train carrying wounded into Qufu has arrived, she continues her daily horseback ride into the windswept farmland. From Captain Fan she already knows that Shan-teh has won a great victory and, more important, that he has emerged unharmed from the campaign. That's all she needs to know; and yet, cantering along a dirt road some kilometers out of Qufu, she begins to think of the train in the station. Just beyond the gate of the Residence she had seen a lorry filled with men going past, and the guard there had told her about the train with at least a thousand aboard.

A thousand wounded men.

Glancing up at the overcast sky, Vera shivers and draws her fur jacket closer to her neck. A thousand wounded men lying in boxcars in the cold. The thought of helpless people in the cold moves her to memory, to the Siberian crossing, the endless days spent by refugees traversing its trackless waste in midwinter. Each night men froze to death at their campfires and were found the next day as stiff as boards, with their naked feet, pointed toward the ashes, charred black. She remembers long stretches of time when nothing else entered her mind but the thought of warm clothes. She used to imagine Cossack fur hats like great soggy loaves of bread. On that trek through the Siberian winter she recalled the feel of homespun wool on her back, encapsulating her like an oven. That was the time she wore only a shabby cotton jacket and a thin dress and wrapped a single threadbare blanket around herself in temperatures below zero. Only the young could survive a few days in such clothing, and she'd already managed five. She dreamed of shiny leather jackets, fur-lined, and peasant woolens, and many varieties of fur – thick, sleek, with the pungent odor of the animals still in their softness. When the Czarist troops plodded past her own pitiful line of refugees, she envied them their heavy uniforms as she'd never envied anyone anything.

Now, mounted on a Chinese horse, Vera recalls them marching along with rifles on their shoulders, the fixed bayonets looking like sharp ugly growths coming from their bodies; and she stood by the roadside gawking at the woolly backs of their Imperial-issue greatcoats, at the scarves wrapped around their ears, at their huge furry gloves as big and unwieldy-looking as bear paws. She would have given herself to any of those soldiers for a single article of winter clothing – for a single glove. She calle out, but their fear of freezing was greater than their desire for a young girl, and so the column vanished in swirling snow. She trudged on, perhaps with only a few hours left before she'd begin to freeze. But within an hour she stumbled on the corpse, not yet rigid, of a young soldier who must have staggered out of the column, ill from disease, and died quickly. Stripping him bare – she recalls to this day the curiously pathetic look of his pink shriveled penis, like a child's crooked finger – she wrapped herself in his underwear, trousers, blouse, jacket, greatcoat, fur cap, heavy boots, and until Vera Rogacheva dies, she will never forget the sensation of warmth those clothes gave her, the ecstasy of it. Then she woundered if the young soldier had strayed out of formation in the throes of fever – of black typhus. Is so, it was likely that she had wrapped herself in a terrible death: the rash, the black sores, the strangulation, the pain beyond imagining. Yet she luxuriated in the heat of the dead boy's uniform, ready to accept typhus if only she could have a few exquisite hours of warmth. She had drifted out of the line of refugees and so lost them. But that didn't count either – only the warmth did; it moved across her skin like the comforting fingers of her mother when she'd been sick as a child.

I'll go to the train station, Vera tells herself. She wheels the horse around, heading back into Qufu.

A thousand wounded on the train platform? Snowflakes are starting to fall in the gray air, huge feathery globules that to her practiced Russian eye will soon become sheets of snow. Falling on helpless men. She can't stay away. What can she do at the station? Vera doesn't know, but she can't ride in a leisurely fashion through the countryside, while down there at the station the wounded must be cold and getting colder, colder.

It is worse than she imagined, when Vera turns the final corner and comes upon the little square in front of the Qufu station.

Under the lightly falling snow, not in rows but in haphazard profusion, on straw mats or on the ground, lie the wounded Chinese soldiers, so close together it is nearly impossible for medics and nurses – what there are of them – to step between the bodies. It looks as if they had been dumped like coal.

Few people see more death and suffering over an extended time than Vera has, yet such experience has never helped her to accept them in the past, and it doesn't now. Dismounting, moving slowly toward the square behind the train station, Vera feels as though she's looking for the first time at such misery. There they lie in their dumpling-thick padded uniforms, many with badly tied swathes of bandage about their heads, leaving only fixed eyes and open mouths visible. The odor of blood is heavy in the cold air. She notices Chinese Red Cross workers helping a few wounded into a mule-drawn wagon. Other people move around with swastikas, the symbol of a Buddhist first-aid organization, on their arms. Moving closer, Vera sees the orderlies trying to make some pattern of the chaos, while the train, empty now, begins to pull out of the station. Oh God, Vera murmurs in Russian, Oh God, Oh God. How many trains has she seen heaving and chugging out of stations, while troops sang old Russian marching songs and a thousand refugees struggled to get aboard the departing cars while a thousand already on board attempted to shove them away. Her exclamation, so utterly spontaneous, is proof, if she needs it, that a scene like this can bring the horror back – perhaps even the nightmare.

Moving still closer, Vera stares down at the pallid faces, at the mouths gasping fishlike for breath, while from the dark sky white snowflakes descend on bloody uniforms plastered against stomach wounds, on stumps of arms and legs. In Shanghai – it must have been seven or eight years ago – she had once seen a troop train leaving for a front somewhere or other. On that bright summer day the train had looked like a great yellow dragon, each open car canopied by the oiled yellow paper of umbrellas, which were held up by smiling young troops to protect them from the sun. Vera had smiled back. It had looked so much like an outing, not like real war, not like war as it was fought in Russia.

But they fight real war here too. It occurs to her, oddly and yet with terrible insistence, that somehow she has never thought of Shan-teh allowing, much less ordering, such destruction. He has always seemed to her more of a diplomat or perhaps a philosopher than a general. She can't connect him with the horror in front of her. She can't believe in Shan-teh speaking the words that would bring people to this fate. A thought even stranger occurs to Vera: Since she has lived in Qufu she has never once remembered it was Shan-teh who tortured a man in a cage.

Squaring her shoulders, Vera moves on. A tall Chinese, standing near the station where most of the activity has its origin, seems to be in charge. Stepping gingerly among the bodies, Vera reaches him and says, 'I want to help.'

Looking at her with grim surprise, then disapproval, he asks if she's a nurse.

'No, I am not.'

'Help them then.' He points to a half-dozen people bending over the wounded, dragging them into three different areas in the square.

'Help them do what?'

'Ask them.' The harassed doctor turns away from her.

So for the next few hours Vera in her Chinese trousers, jacket, and furlined topcoat helps to move the wounded. She is told what to do by a tired young Buddhist – she notices the swastika. He bends down and inspects each of the wounded, probes a little, asks questions if the man is conscious. 'Put him in that group,' he tells

571

Vera. 'Put him in that one.' Sometimes Vera is able to help the wounded man rise and get there himself, but often she simply gets hold of both hands – if both are there – and pulls him bodily toward the designated area. At first when they moan or cry out, Vera halts, but after sharp rebuffs from the Buddhist medic, she keeps yanking and dragging no matter how much the wounded yell in pain. At dusk, when torches are lit in the square, Vera notices that her clothes are splattered with blood, reeking too of a smell familiar from her march through Siberia: the fetid smell of flesh going bad. But Vera works on. Under the Buddhist's orders she washes the wounds with gauze wet from a single bucket of water that quickly becomes crimson. Noticing a few townsmen lounging nearby, idly watching the proceedings, Vera yells at them to go get more buckets. They saunter away with some reluctance, but of course never return with buckets. The Red Cross workers, paying some children, get buckets.

As time wears on, Vera notices the three groups of wounded are treated differently. One group is left utterly untended; another group is given some attention; the third, where the Buddhist medic assigns her to clean wounds, gets nearly all of the medical care. Before leaving that evening, thoroughly exhausted, she learns that the wounded have been placed in groups according to their chance of survival. Group One wounded are likely to die in spite of care, so they get none; Group Two are likely to live without it, so they get only a minimum; what medicine is available goes to the Third Group, whose recovery depends on it.

Practical, Vera thinks, as she rides home; the night is silent and motionless now that snow has ceased falling. Practical like the Chinese. And horrible.

In spite of fatigue, she awakens at dawn, bolt upright, but instead of going out to play Tai Chi, she dresses quickly, calls Yao to make tea, and in the grim light of another overcast day Vera rides back to the station. She is wearing coolie clothes, secured for her by old Yao, who resisted the request bitterly until she threatened to tell the General. This day is like the last – and to her dismay another train pulls into the station, another load of wounded is deposited on the cold platform and in the square, which is beginning to look as if someone had painted it with a broad brush in vermilion. The smells of blood and stinking flesh grow stronger this second day, but at noon the sun comes out, warms the earth, melts yesterday's snow.

She learns that the Red Cross and Buddhist medics have come down from Jinan. They were sent by their organizations at the first word of the battle and General Tang's victory.

Victory? It is clear to Vera that the casualties are enormous. Of course, the wounded from the other two garrisons are coming here to Qufu too, because there are no medical facilities there. And *here?* she wonders, appalled. A medic tells her that the two hospitals, both military and civilian, are already crowded beyond any capacity to handle more patients. Yet they keep coming into town, streaming in not only by train but by oxcart and lorry as well. The medics use a nearby school and two temples to house those who otherwise will die of exposure. Already, Vera realizes, the wounded are dying in large numbers. Yesterday in the square at least fifty must have died before they could be removed. Today is worse, because they have lain unattended in freezing weather for more than five days now, between Hengshui and Qufu. They are a woeful sight, worse than anything Vera can recall in Russia. Or is this true? Perhaps then she'd been isolated from the pain of others by her own pain. Here there's no personal suffering to get in the way of a pure experience of the horror, and throughout the long cold hours of washing wounds and dragging shattered men into the three fateful groups, Vera confronts the horror raw, with memories shooting through her living of it to add another dimension. At times the breath seems to ball up and clog in her chest. She feels dizzy, hoping to scream and release what she feels.

The next day is the same. Only now she has learned more about what is going on. There are food, bandages, and medicine for less than a third of the arrivals in Qufu. In the hospitals, let alone the makeshift aid stations, there are few surgical instruments, and aside from the medics from Jinan almost no trained personnel to handle the patients. She keeps asking in frustration and growing anger, 'Where is the General's medical unit?' The answer is usually a shrug or a gesture which means the dozen shabby soldiers who walk up and down the row of straw mats – the Southern Shantung Medical Corps. There's no blood for transfusions, almost no anesthetic, and the death rate from shock alone seems terribly high to Vera, as she transfers from the train station to the field hospital on the outskirts of town. It's a low building which was once an officers' dormitory. There is, consequently, no actual hospital for the army. On her fourth day, slumped at dusk against the outside wall of the hospital, trying to fight her exhaustion enough to go back inside and dress more wounds, Vera is joined by the tall doctor she had met the first day. Sitting with their backs against the wall, they watch the sun setting, its cold red light letting go of some ragged branches in a winter tree. There's a smell in the air – more snow? Vera wonders. She asks the doctor if he thinks it will snow.

Listlessly he nods. 'There's a lot of pneumonia now, and dysentery.'

She knows about the dysentery all right – the stench even out here in the air is overwhelming.

'Tetanus,' the doctor continues in a lazy voice, as if still talking about the weather. 'Ulcers covering a third of the body.' He shakes his head wearily.

'Is it true all the wounded come here because there aren't other facilities?'

'Yes,' the doctor says. 'The Second Corps has only an aid station. There's not even that at Lin Yi.'

'So these really are the facilities.' Taking his silence for affirmation, Vera says out loud what she's been thinking all day. 'I heard that but couldn't believe it. How can the General allow such a thing? Only you and three other doctors for an entire army? And a dozen or so medics who don't know much more than I do? I can't believe it, I won't believe it.'

The doctor clears his throat. 'That's four more doctors than some armies have. It's the Chinese way.'

'But there's medicine in China. And the missionaries –'

'Yes, the missionaries. They taught me medicine, though I never became a Christian. I'll always be grateful to them.'

He is drifting from the subject, as if uninterested in it, Vera thinks. 'But before the battle, didn't you – didn't the General think of casualties?'

'Of course. But not this many. General Tang is a compassionate man. You mustn't blame him.'

'But – I do.'

'Medicine takes money. That's the problem. He can't fight without equipment and equipment takes money, so what money he has goes into equipment.'

'You're defending him?'

The doctor looks at her in the twilight. 'He is a general.' the doctor offers in explanation. After a pause, he asks, 'Do you speak French? I learned French in the French Hospital, Shanghai.'

'I do not speak French.'

'But I think you understand it,' the doctor says with a smile. 'I'll tell you in French what I'd need to make this hospital capable of taking care of these casualties. I will tell you in French because I learned the terms in that language. For my hospital I would like some X-ray machines, quartz lamps, oxygen cylinders, extension tables for diagnosis, Erkameter Precision blood-pressure manometers, and steam sterilizers and Pacquenlin's cauteries, grope instruments, artery forceps, dressing scissors. We need twenty thousand English pounds of absorbent cotton. We need dozens of splints, rubber gloves, hypodermic syringes.' The doctor's voice, weary before, takes on new energy. 'Surgical catgut, glucose, codeine, iodine – ah, tons of that – alcohol, hydrogen peroxide. . .'

Abruptly he falls silent, common sense catching up with the dream, and Vera understands he won't talk any more. Rising, she returns to the moaning rows of patients, a pitiful scene under torchlight. Bandaged heads turn expectantly her way. Thank God they've found a potbellied stove, she thinks; it keeps the ward almost warm. Turning, she sees the doctor reenter the room, his tall figure moving slowly down the line of mats where the men lie. Some of them wear caps with the earflaps tied up like the folded wings of insects; the caps make them look so young, innocent, like Bright Lotus in her winter furs. At the far end of the room Vera picks up the water bucket and a handful of bandages that have been washed for reuse. Thank God for the stove. At the first patient Vera kneels and looks critically at his bandaged chest; it will need washing. With a sigh Vera begins to untie the bandage, seeing from the corner of her eye the tall doctor move slowly down the aisle, past the wounded soldiers on their woven mats.

During the Hour of the Rat, when a hoarse wind shouts through the darkness, she awakens suddenly, having seen swollen corpses blacken in the sun. Sitting up, Vera blinks away the nightmare, relieved it is new, not the old one with its unalterable pattern.

But the next night, when she awakens, it is from the old nightmare and its inevitable sequence, ending with the decapitated head of her sister in the horse trough. The old ferocious thirst returns. Vera rushes for the table decanter, gulping every drop of water in it and wanting more. Soon the headache will begin, so she rummages through a drawer for the Tiger Headache Cure Powder

575

she brought from Shanghai. Sometimes it works; she got it at Eng Aun Tong, where the Chinese get their traditional medicines: the roots, fish bladders, hog testicles in cloudy liquid, jarfuls of odorous plants and herbs. Without water to mix the powder, Vera pours herself a little drink of *mao tai* and shakes the medicine in.

So the nightmare is back.

Next day, to break the routine that's encouraging its return, Vera plays Tai Chi in the morning and then visits Bright Lotus, who has been unhappy during her absence and who greets her with untypical squeals of delight. Vera feels better as they play hide-and-seek through the courtyards, but then the snow begins falling again, this time heavily, and after muttered apologies, she leaves the disappointed child and the astonished maid in the portico and goes for her horse. Today she remains at the train station until after dark, helping to unload and sort out another five hundred arrivals, probably the last bunch and in terrible shape, who lie patiently under the falling snow and wait for food, for blankets, for medicine, for something that will tell them they might yet live.

That night the old nightmare comes again, but this time Vera's prepared for it – she has grimly lined up three decanters of water on the table, along with the Tiger Powder. Next morning she rides to the train station, which is empty at last, in fact, desolate. Two old women are picking up spilled rice from the railway platform that will keep its dark stain forever. Then she goes out to the hospital for a full day's work.

That evening Vera hears a noise at the door. It is Shan-teh. It is the man for whom each night she has said prayers to the Archangel Michael – patron saint of Russian princes who go to war. It is the man she loves.

But during the late Hour of the Ox, she wakes again in a sweat, filled with nausea by the nightmare. She withdraws her arm from the sleeping man, who has shown in his lovemaking tonight the eagerness of a boy. The moon, shining hard and crystalline through the window, illuminates Shan-teh's face. For a moment, juxtaposed upon it in her aroused imagination, is the image of the White Hawk in the painting: predatory beak, head thrust cruelly forward. But shaking off the strange moment, a result surely of the nightmare, Vera rises quietly, careful not to awaken her lover, and drinks down three decanters of water before slaking her thirst. Not until the Hour of the Tiger, when China's moon has crept beyond this part of the sky, is Vera calm enough to sleep again.

24

General Tang Shan-teh has won a victory.

In retrospect he feels the assault on the near hill, coupled with the two cavalry charges, proved decisive. Jen went oddly wrong in his use of artillery. The ammo and fuses were designed for battering down walls and earthworks rather than scattering troops. He may have lacked the proper ammo and fuses, but surely there was no excuse for Jen's poor tactical judgment. He should have maintained pressure on troops assaulting the near hill; timidity in committing reinforcements there was a grave mistake. Moreover, someone – either Jen or a subordinate – should have kept back the machine guns rather than placing them forward with the infantry; they were bowled over by the horse charge. Perhaps Jen has reached the age of retirement; the thought saddens Tang, who admires the cranky old man's military career.

General Tang recognizes the part played by luck in his victory. Jen had prepared a surprise that might have won the day, if an engine hadn't broken down: An armored train had been scheduled to come down from the center of Hengshui to the station, where it could have taken the Shantung rear under fire with cannon and machine gun. To nullify the train's effect, Tang would have had to commit reserves otherwise used in the main battle. Moreover, cavalry and troops crossing the wheat field would have dealt with fire from three sides, a murderous difficulty. Fortunately, the train chugged to an abrupt halt only a hundred yards down the track and was left stranded, like a whale on a sandbar. Surrounded by Tang's troops when they entered Hengshui, the train commander, without hope of escape let alone usefulness, surrendered.

Tang pursued the defeated army through Hopei into northern Shensi, not seeking another full-scale engagement but maintaining pressure in an effort to move Jen Ching-i far back, out of contention. During the initial days of pursuit, Tang captured three Citroën armored motor cars with turrets and windshield slits. He took cannon, a few heavy machine guns, and numerous thirty-calibers of Italian and Danish make. He was able to round up a lot of pack mules, horses, and more than two dozen camels from distant Kansu (Tang guessed the old man got them as gifts from Feng Yu-hsiang, who controls that country), which are excellent at transporting heavy boxed ammo. He rummaged through Hengshui warehouses under Jen's jurisdiction and found supplies there: field telephones, wireless sets (like those ordered from Luckner), cartons of food including smoked ham and salted fish, a few cases of medicine, and many piculs of high quality opium, which if handled by the right dealer should net a considerable profit in Shanghai. Tang's army is no longer poor or ill equipped, a condition which prompts the General to continue the pursuit, even though his men seem exhausted. As they move forward, approaching them on the trail are many deserters who shuffle along without the purple armbands marking them as members of Jen's army. To a man they swear that they are peasants. The General takes only a few of them prisoner, those who might serve as artillery gunners or look intelligent enough for other specialized work. A file of these captured men follow the army, their hands tied behind their backs. Many of them don't need to be bound, for they want a new job. Many of those who are rejected for imprisonment plead to be taken, so they can eat. All of those not chosen begin to head for home, looting on the way in an effort to get something from their military adventure.

Tang stops the pursuit a few day's march from the Great Wall, which Jen has crossed at an old arched gateway, one that barbarian invaders from the icy steppes passed through centuries ago. The defeated army will settle down on the windswept Mongolian plain and like a great animal lick its wounds before returning to Jen's province. Tang might continue the pursuit – he considers it seriously – and eventually destroy Jen in another pitched battle, but his problem is now a stretched-out supply line.

More than logistics calls him back. He has left the town of Qufu unprotected too long. Also of great importance is the weariness of his troops. And of greatest importance now is the casualties he has sustained.

He has won a victory all right, but at a major loss of men, the size of this loss as yet unclear. After reports from most of the units, he roughly estimates 30 percent of the army fell at Hengshui: one of three dead or wounded. The finest unit in his entire army – the Big Sword Company of the Fourth Cavalry Battalion – lost nearly three of four horsemen. Since the battle, there have been other losses to skirmishes, to the cold, and to illness incurred by weary men. In the excitement of pursuit, Tang hasn't allowed casualties to hamper his determination. When finally he halts and turns back, the problem of casualties takes on increasing importance. He has forgotten his father's warning: 'We Chinese tend to think of battle in terms of honor, so we keep throwing men into the fight to protect it until there are no more men – and no honor.' By the time General Tang rides into Qufu, finding it turned into one huge hospital, he is deeply troubled.

It will take days to assess the full extent of his loss, both militarily and politically. Politically too, for although he has routed Jen Ching-i by his battlefield tactics, it will soon be widely acknowledged that his once formidable army – well trained, if not large – has been crippled, if not mortally wounded. His gain in equipment is no compensation for the loss of those veteran soldiers.

Victory starts to look like a major defeat.

At headquarters on his return, there is other news of vital importance: Chiang Kai-shek has not remained in Japan or gone elsewhere to study, but has returned to Shanghai. It is reported that Chiang has cast aside all pretensions of retirement and engages daily in politics. If Chiang succeeds in his new plans, most likely the northern push of the Nationalist Army will resume – and the army of Tang Shan-teh lies in the way.

The General spends two depressing hours at headquarters, receiving fuller casualty reports from various commanders and learning of the latest political developments (Wang Ching-wei is also in Shanghai, no doubt in touch with Chiang), before going to his quarters. Bone-weary, haggard, brooding, he moves through the doorway and into the arms of Black Jade. What happens then is familiar to him – it has happened after other campaigns with his wives and concubines: absolute physical urgency, which leads to a fierce coupling, as if it can bring to life what blood and death have killed in him, the feeling of life killed in men who survive battle. And Black Jade responds with like intensity, proving she is fearless in love, imaginative, generous. On this night of his return, so tired and worried, Tang Shan-teh adores her as if she is the Black Jade of the old romance: *The Three Kingdoms*.

Yet in following days he notices a difference between the woman he left some weeks ago and the woman he finds now. Each morning, after they play Tai Chi together, Black Jade mounts her horse and rides to the hospital, where she works until lunch, then returns there and works until the evening meal. It is unseemly. If his officers resented her in the past, what will they think now? The

General's woman emptying slops like a coolie, dressing wounds like a peasant girl who, hearing of a battle, comes to town to make a few extra *cash*. When he brings up the subject, her attitude in response is intransigent. Black Jade lets nothing interfere with her hospital schedule and on occasion she speaks of individual patients with deep compassion – and with bitterness too, for she keeps asking why there isn't medicine for them. Black Jade is not soothed by his answer, eminently sane to him: After the purchase of arms and other war supplies, there's little money left for such things.

At dinner she asks suddenly, 'When you see the wounded lying in the cold – not for hours but for days – what do you feel, Shan-teh?'

'I think about the men I must still lead.'

They say no more about it, but that night, sleepless, Tang realizes he has been closer to this woman than to anyone in his life. It is miraculous, and he wants to cling to the miracle, yet as he looks upon her sleeping moonlit face, Tang feels sudden anger. She has accused him of not caring for his men, but in a sense she is an origin of their loss. Luckner denied him the firepower that would have lessened the casualties – because of her. To stave off such thoughts, he whispers her name. In response, she murmurs his sleepily. Later, easing into sleep, he is content again, secure in their mutual trust.

In succeeding days General Tang has other worries. Still reeling from the campaign, his officers and troops show a reluctance to reorganize. Units in disarray remain in this condition – easy enough to do with the cold winds blowing out of Asia. Men sit in their tents brooding, stunned in the aftermath of such an effort. Tang spends much of his time on inspection tours, attempting by cheerful example to impart new enthusiasm to his men; to look at them, an impartial observer might feel they had just come out of a bitter defeat. He walks slowly between the rows of tents, stopping for a chat, or he watches men at their exercises or joins them for a meal at a camp kitchen. He oversees the construction of some new dormitories, controlling his temper, for during his absence little work was done on them in spite of winter's coming. He visits the cavalry every day, especially those battalions gutted in the two charges. Tang learns that the American acquitted himself honorably, charged with the others, fought hard. The battalion commander recalls having seen him cave in a Jen trooper with that ax. Tang is pleased at the report: Black Jade and the American are both capable of living fully like Chinese.

The greatest restlessness comes from the general staff. Colonel Pi had received a minor shrapnel wound in the arm and nurses it with unmanly grumbling. On the other hand, Major Chia not only showed a gift for tactics on the battlefield but since their return to Qufu has demonstrated an ability to reorganize his own command. In the uneasy atmosphere of Qufu, the General is grateful to have an officer like this Paoting graduate.

Through it all, the General thinks of his fellow militarists in China watching him on every side, slinking around like wolves, sniffing at the edges of his territory to learn how badly he has been injured, to ascertain if it's time to go in for the kill. While in this mood he receives a letter from Wang Ching-wei in Shanghai. Wang expresses ornate regret for missing the General in Canton. To rectify the situation, Wang invites him to Shanghai. The General doesn't take it seriously. Wang must know he will not enter a city controlled by the KMT when Chiang is reassuming power. If the visit is not convenient at present, Wang's letter continues, he would be honored to send a small delegation to Qufu to pay respects and offer whatever services he can to the General. Tang reasons that if the shrewd politician really wanted to discuss an alliance, he'd come himself. This way nothing would be resolved. It is possible that Wang is making the overture at the behest of Chiang Kai-shek, who would like to know through such a delegation the full extent of Tang's disorder. Replying with old-fashioned flattery and self-deprecation, Tang refuses to have Wang's people in Qufu.

Next a letter comes from General Feng Yu-hsiang. It never mentions the battle of Hengshui, although Tang had it confirmed through a captured officer that Jen had offered the challenge on the encouragement of Feng. In the letter Feng suggests that with Chiang Kai-shek and Wang Ching-wei in Shanghai, a new look at the political situation is needed. 'Men of good will should discuss it.' He proposes a meeting with Tang for this purpose. If such a meeting is impossible at present, they can send representatives to neutral ground for a discussion, the aim of which will be to arrange for the two generals to meet in mutual safety.

In Tang's opinion it's a reasonable idea and so he treats it seriously in his reply. He agrees that they should make contact through delegates, perhaps in Peking, which is accessible to both parties and constitutes neutral ground. Tang sends this off by wireless.

A new development in the region heightens the General's anxiety. Reports from the southern border indicate new troop movements by the forces of General Sun Ch'uan-fang. In a small battle last year – nothing to compare with Hengshui – Tang had defeated him roundly by a tactical surprise. General Sun has doubtless heard of Tang's recent losses; given his character, reckless and opportunistic, he might well storm across the border for another attempt on Shantung. In support of Tang, old Dog Meat might send a few regiments; on the other hand, he might stay at Jinan and let Tang take the brunt of Sun's attack. That might serve Dog Meat's purpose anyway – finish off his provincial rival and also cripple Sun. What stands between Sun and Qufu is the garrison at Lin Yi. For the Hengshui campaign, however, Tang drew all but three regiments from there, and those that followed him were badly mangled. The Lin Yi garrison is not strong enough in itself to handle an attack by Sun's forces. Tang must therefore gather what troops he can spare from Qufu and send them to Lin Yi. Sending them may forestall any adventure that Sun may contemplate.

This means, however, that Qufu will be dangerously vulnerable, a town of wounded soldiers defended by a remnant of its usual garrison. After a discussion with his staff, Tang decides the gamble is worth taking; he'll send troops to Lin Yi anyway. The decision poses yet another problem: How to protect the Kong family in Qufu. Few militarists would dare to touch such a distinguished family, but Sun is one of them. He would ransom them at least; given his mercurial and vengeful personality, Sun Ch'uan-fang is capable of more.

So Tang makes another decision: he will try to move the Kong family out of Qufu temporarily. He wins the Duke Patriarch's consent easily. 'It is Heaven's will,' the Duke says during the audience, as he faces the General in his far corner. 'I must admit I'd like nothing better than a stay on Tai Shan, even if it is cold. I'm shut in here with all my responsibilities. It will be a relief to get away from them awhile. And, of course, there'll be ceremonies at the Tai Shan temples.'

Tang reasons that the Kongs can go as a merchant's family by palanquin with a couple of armed riders. That is not an uncommon way for rich pilgrims to make the journey to Tai Shan, the most sacred of mountains. They won't be regarded as suspicious. Tang will have them leave some morning before dawn, so they'll be far from prying eyes around Qufu by sunrise. The servants in the Residence will perform their duties as if nothing has happened. He will assign two officers to make sure of it. As for the two-day journey by palanquin, along with mounted guards Tang will have two platoons of infantry front and rear, dressed like common traders, so there will be plenty of protection. He sends an aide to make arrangements for the Kongs to stay near the summit at the Temple of the Princess of Colored Clouds.

His thoughts then turn to Black Jade. She too will be in danger if Sun ever breaks through and gets to Qufu. She isn't a national treasure like the Kongs; they are worth bartering, she is not. Moreover, she'd represent to General Sun the property of a man who had defeated him once in a battle – something to be confiscated and disposed of in ways only Sun might devise. So Tang decides to send her away too. He discusses it with her when she returns from the hospital.

'You want me to leave?' Her initial question is asked in a tone of astonishment, fear. Later, when she has understood, Black Jade sits quietly, hands folded in her lap. 'I see it. If General Sun got hold of me, he'd use me to take revenge against you. Yes, I believe that.' Rising, Black Jade says, 'Then I will pack.'

'It can wait until morning,' Tang says gently.

'No, I will pack.'

He follows her into the bedroom, where she puts a suitcase on the bed and opens the dresser. Pausing to look at him, Black Jade says, 'How long will I be gone? I need to know for the packing.'

'Not long.'

'How long?'

Tang shrugs. 'Days.'

'No, I think you mean weeks.'

'Perhaps a few.'

'A month?'

'No more than that.'

'How can you be sure?' she persists.

'I know Sun Ch'uan-fang. He never plans, he acts. If he hears I'm weak up here and I've sent some regiments to Lin Yi to discourage him from coming over the border, he might try something reckless. Either he'll do it at the moment or do nothing. It's his rashness I fear. He's capable of rousing twenty or thirty thousand men out of their sleep and running them up here, bypassing Lin Yi or simply leaving a suicide force behind to meet my men there. The Qufu garrison's in no condition to resist a wild rush, the kind Sun Ch'uan-fang can make. He might capture the town for a day or two before his exhausted men collapsed or rebelled – they do that sometimes with Sun. But a day or two would be enough. He could rout me, destroy the Residence, take you –'

'I understand. But he'll do it soon or not at all.'

'Within a month.'

Black Jade pauses thoughtfully, a shoe in hand, then slumps into a chair. 'I'm a little tired.'

In her loose robe Black Jade looks small, her skin ashen white. 'We haven't had much time together,' she murmurs.

'But we soon will,' he assures her.

'In a month?'

'No longer, I promise.'

'Will you come to see me in Peking?'

Tang doesn't reply.

'All right then, I'll see you back here.'

'Within a month. Sun will either move or not move by then.'

'And it's necessary I leave?'

Tang nods. 'I'm sending the Kongs away too.'

'To Peking?' she asks hopefully.

He knows she's thinking of the little girl, Bright Lotus. He explains the plan for their trip to the sacred mountain, Tai Shan.

'I'd rather go with them,' she says firmly.

With equal conviction he tells her it's impossible. Her presence in their party would attract attention all along the journey and especially on the mountain, which is rarely visited by foreigners. The secret would be out immediately.

While he gives her this explanation, Black Jade sits with her head bowed, hands clasped between her knees. When he finishes, she looks up at him. 'Why haven't we talked about our life together?'

Tang has often wondered about the same question, so his reply comes without hesitation. 'Because we haven't known what it is.'

'Exactly.' Black Jade smiles. 'But it *is* a life together, isn't it?' She cocks her head, frowning at him. 'Can a Chinese general do what you're doing?'

'I'm doing it.'

'But at the expense of everything you hold dear. Is that true?'

'If that's true, then what I hold dear isn't worthwhile.'

'Is life with me worth your reputation?'

'I won't lose my reputation as a man who loves his country and will fight for it.'

Black Jade reaches out to him, so he rises and comes to her chair and takes her hand. 'I don't want to hurt you,' she says. 'You're a Confucian. You're expected to act in certain ways.'

Their clasped hands at once separate them and bridge the gap between them. Tang looks down at her haggard face, at the anxiety showing in the tension around her mouth and eyes.

'You're not yet Chinese.' he says gently, 'if you believe Confucian thinking is only one thing. It's many things. Is there more than one way of being a Christian?'

'I think so.'

'There's more than one way of being a Confucian. And the Sage himself seems to change. His ideas speak differently to me from the way they spoke to men in the past. What remains is a simple little core. The five virtues, for example, are part of it. Kindness, honesty, dedication, knowledge, faith. You see? The impossible heart of Confucius. Is there a core to Christianity?'

'There are ten commandments.' Vera smiles up at him, still holding his hand. 'Impossible too.'

'Men mistake rules and rituals for the ideal. Because it's impossible to follow. In this I suppose we are all alike.' Kneeling beside the chair, he looks into her eyes, bloodshot from fatigue, a hint of anguish still in them. 'China has a place for us,' he says.

Leaning toward him with a little sob, Black Jade puts her cheek against his. 'If you believe it, then so must I.'

But the next afternoon the General's outward show of optimism is not matched by the dismay he feels as they wait in the depot for the Peking train. Captain Fan, playing the role of tourist guide, will accompany her. A few other staff officers (Colonel Pi remains at headquarters) have come to the station and with excessive courtesy (perhaps a measure of their relief to see the foreign woman go) flatter her during the hour they wait for the train.

Black Jade is wearing the clothes of a Western tourist: tweed skirt with a waistline dropped to the hips; argyle socks like a hearty British or German hiker (she got them from Captain Fan, who got

585

them as a gift a few years ago from a niece, who got them in a Hong Kong shop); frilly blouse and man's jacket; all of it topped by a full-length seal coat (purchased in Shanghai during the last frantic day there before leaving Luckner and all the other men of memory); and a bell-shaped hat, fitting close to her rich black hair and framing her face with its pointed chin, its high cheekbones, nipped by the frosty air into a healthy tinge of color.

Tang watches her glance around the train station; she squints with a frown, as if expecting to see a crowd of wounded men shivering in the cold. He looks at the skirt, the brogues, the stylish coat, the felt hat like a cocoon wrapped around her head. The sight unsettles him. She looks totally foreign, a woman whose name might be Vera Rogacheva but not Black Jade. He nearly shouts, 'Don't go!' But he knows his decision is right. Until Sun Ch'uan-fang moves his troops back from the border and settles down, these dear lives – the Kongs, hers – must be out of harm's way.

'Remember, you're a tourist,' he says, as they move to the platform at the sound of an approaching train. 'Be sure to act like one.'

'And how do tourists act?' she asks with a smile. 'I'm not used to your Chinese disguises.'

'Point at things. Ask too many questions. Laugh loudly. You must act a little rude out of ignorance.'

'How do you know so much about tourists?'

'As a very young officer in Peking I was given the task of escorting some dignitaries around. They were British or American, I don't remember. In those days I considered them the same thing. One of them spoke Chinese and that's how we fared for a whole week. It was horrible.'

'But how do I ask too many questions? I'm not supposed to understand Chinese.'

'The way tourists do. Wave your hands wildly in the air.'

They laugh, dreading the departure.

'Must I play that role?' Black Jade asks, seeing the train chug into view. 'Why can't I be myself?'

He knows she really doesn't want an answer. He has already explained to her that in today's chaos, it's better for someone like herself – a foreigner involved with a Chinese general – to keep her identity hidden. She's talking out of nervousness. And so is he, as once more he tells her that Captain Fan speaks a little English. The train has arrived. He is staring at a compartment window; soon she will be looking out of such a window, her face pale and drawn from so much hospital work. 'So you speak English back to him. You said you know some English.'

'Not much. And anyone hearing me will know I'm not English.' She is staring too at the train. They are speaking rapidly in a distracted way.

'That doesn't matter.' Tang says. 'You don't have to be English to speak a little. The passport's your insurance.'

'Yes, isn't it.'

People are debarking while others are crowding toward the compartment doors, waiting to get on.

'You have the passport?'

'Of course I have it.' She laughs nervously, tossing her head back. 'It's not as if I'm going overseas.'

The General knows she carries a forged German passport, obtained for her by a friend of Luckner's from the Shanghai consulate. Tang feels the frustration of being unable to provide her with a passport from his own country. Vera Rogacheva with a Chinese passport? A poignant joke. Glancing at her, Tang can see the woman really is a foreigner. It surprises him how effectively he has managed to sidestep this obvious fact. During the campaign, riding hunched into the snowy wind, whenever he conjured her face to comfort him, Tang had seen in his mind the shadowy features of a beautiful Chinese woman.

The train whistle blows, startling them both. Black Jade takes a step forward, as if prodded by an invisible rifle butt.

'Wait,' the General tells her, but when she turns expectantly, his hands remain stiffly at his sides. It is impossible for them to embrace in front of the officers. An account of it would run like wildfire through the common ranks of his army. Already dispirited by their losses at Hengshui, they might think their commander has been mentally weakened by the terrible victory if he makes such a public display of affection – and with a foreign concubine – yet his need to reach out at this final moment is so strong that he repeats the word, 'Wait.' Without touching her arm, Tang leads her with his eyes to a spot out of earshot of the officers, who huddle together and try not to show their curiosity.

Bending slightly toward her, he says, 'You asked me if I care about my men, about the wounded. In my way I do care. In the way of a soldier.'

'I know that. I knew it then, only I didn't want to believe it in my anger.'

'Black Jade.'

'Don't keep me waiting in Peking. I want to come back. To Qufu. To you.'

'No longer than I must,' he says. 'Black Jade.' He looks at her steadily, then his eyes move away to Captain Fan, who is dressed in the worn topcoat and shabby fedora of a Chinese guide trying to appear European.

Fan, understanding, comes forward with a bow and with a gesture of his arm indicates the compartment door to Black Jade.

Tang doesn't wait for a longer goodbye but turns instantly away. He looks around for an aide, calling harshly for his driver to get the car started – he had it driven to the depot for this occasion. At his back the General hears the train engine's cylinders plunge forward, the steam pour in galvanic hisses upon the track, and the whole line of cars rattle into motion, like the bones of an old beast getting to its feet. Tang doesn't turn to see the train move out of the depot, but remains with his eyes fixed on the square. Again the whistle, a screeching trail of sound like a bright thin ribbon rippling in the wind. He doesn't turn, but calls again for his motor car. Only after the train has chugged out of the station and beyond sight does he finally turn and look at the empty track leading to a distant point of blackness on the flat horizon.

In his mind he says the words of Po Chu-yi:

At midnight she comes
And at daybreak she leaves.
She comes like a dream of spring, but for how long?
She leaves like the dew of morning, without a trace.

But it is foolish to worry; it is love's foolishness, he thinks.

The aide returns, announcing the car is ready.

Nodding, the General turns and with long vigorous strides goes to his work.

Waking from troubled sleep – but not, at least, from the nightmare – Vera looks out of the train window at the passing countryside, lightly dusted with snow. Wheat stalks, shorn ankle-high, peep from the white cover to look cold in the sharp morning light. She will get up soon and comb her hair; there's breakfast to eat and in a few hours the train will be arriving in Peking. She feels an urgent need to urinate. Checking her clothes in which she slept in the chill compartment (empty but for her), Vera goes down the corridor to the toilet, pulls the latch down firmly, closing herself in. She squats over the hole shaped by tin into a funnel. Once in a Shanghai beauty parlor she overhead two Frenchwomen deploring sanitation in China. Ever since leaving Petrograd, Vera has endured the worst of conditions and has quite forgotten the fastidiousness of ladies of her class. This morning, however, squatting above the toilet hole, she feels oddly self-conscious, uncomfortable. It occurs to her that she has urinated very often in the past few days.

Back in her compartment Vera slumps down on the seat, as exhausted as if she hadn't slept at all, whereas she had fallen asleep almost instantly after getting on the train. She had slept nearly the whole way to Peking. Vera plays with her skirt, getting it straight. She hasn't worn Western clothes in Qufu, and the skirt feels strange, even awkward on her body. She recalls her first tube dress. In 1923 the tube dress had the entire foreign community of Shanghai excited. Dress shops along Nanking Road couldn't keep them in stock. She bought her first tube dress and also a deeply bloused sleeveless bodice with a tight hip band the week after she'd aborted herself. The purchases were a kind of reward, self-given, for having gone through the abortion, her second since working in the brothel. When she walked out of the shop that day with the package under her arm, Vera had vowed never to have another. But she did.

Vera sighs and feels queasy. And the urination – its frequency – occurs to her. But she can't be pregnant. Using chopsticks as Yu-ying had taught her, Vera injured herself the last time she tried it and nearly died – chills, high fever, kidney failure. She had been saved by a Chinese doctor who spoke French to her, like the Qufu military doctor, but even half dead she'd pretended not to understand. No, she couldn't be pregnant; she had torn herself to pieces inside. Hadn't she? What had the doctor said? She can't recall or rather she recalls it had been vague – he said the things doctors say: 'We'll have to wait and see.' At the time she hadn't wanted to see anything like a pregnancy again. And now? What about now? When did she last menstruate? Vera tries to recall that too, but can't. Confident that she can no longer conceive, Vera hasn't paid attention to it for a long time. But she is very regular; that's true. So when was the last time? Vera concentrates on the question, while the train shakes rhythmically along the track. Finally she tires of trying to remember. It's a vain hope anyway. But a hope? That she's pregnant?

If she could have a child like Bright Lotus, she'd be happy. That little girl. Vera sighs at the recollection of their parting. Wrapped in a big fur coat, Bright Lotus had the look of a seal cub – bright black eyes, twitching nose. She carried a brass firebox to warm her hands and wore a leather hat with Mongolian earflaps. Precious. For a parting gift she had the maid give Vera a box of almond cakes.

Having acquitted herself with admirable decorum, Bright Lotus suddenly asked, 'Why can't you go with us?' Her face screwed up in resentment.

Vera knelt and, taking the firebox from the child, held in her own hands the small pudgy fingers roughened by the wind to a faint pink. 'Because I have somewhere else I must go,' she explained, sensing a fullness in her eyes. Would she cry in front of the child? 'You won't be foolish now,' she told Bright Lotus, 'and worry about me.'

'Yes, I will.'

'Bright Lotus, I –' She wanted to tell the little girl how much she loved her, but was it done among Chinese aristocrats? Would the strangeness of it alarm the child? In the covered gallery, shielded from a bitter wind, stood the maid and two priests: a Taoist in black, a Buddhist in saffron. Perhaps they were going to take the child to a religious ceremony, to pray for a safe journey to Tai Shan. 'Bright Lotus,' she began again, 'I will miss you very much.'

The girl stared at her from a round face marked by two spots of crimson. 'Who's going to play with you when I'm not here?'

'I'm afraid no one,' said Vera, touching the girl's cold cheek. 'I must wait until we're together again.'

'I don't want to go to the mountain.'

'You'll like it there.'

'If you're not with me, I won't.'

Vera gathered the child into her arms, hugging her until she heard a little expulsion of breath. She kissed the girl's cheek, nose, forehead; she kissed those pudgy fingers and again embraced her, seeing past Bright Lotus' head the two impassive priests, calmly waiting, and the maid, her mouth parted in sympathy.

Now while the train rumbles through the snowy countryside, Vera wonders if she ought to have insisted on going with the Kongs to Tai Shan. But perhaps they didn't want the foreign mistress of a general. Perhaps that's why Shan-teh decided to send her elsewhere. Would he have acted differently had she told him she might be pregnant? But she isn't pregnant.

A knock at the compartment door, a head thrust in, a waiter asking if she'd like breakfast.

She tells him, 'Only tea,' before remembering she isn't supposed to understand Chinese. Well, she's made the mistake now, so when he asks if she wants anything else, she tells him again, 'Only tea.' She feels nauseated. Perhaps the swaying of the train causes it. For a moment her hope rises – perhaps it's not the train; perhaps it's the morning sickness that accompanied four previous pregnancies.

Another knock at the door. This time it is round-faced Captain Fan in his ill-fitting Western suit. He whispers in Chinese about their plans for Peking, playing his role of tourist guide with relish – he's proud of the city of his birth. He is wonderfully considerate. Vera doubts if she's ever met a man as gifted at divining someone's mood. He quickly realizes, for example, that she has no desire for conversation this morning, so after a few minutes the Captain excuses himself and leaves. Yet she doesn't like him. Perhaps familiarity does breed contempt, for the longer she knows Captain Fan the less she likes him, trusts him. There's about him at times a suggestion of the cringing obsequiousness of Shanghai pimps; she wonders if he might also display another side of the flesh merchants: often they beat their girls once the customers have gone. Pregnant? No. On the day of her third – it was the third abortion – Vera had strolled into a Taoist temple with the strange idea of getting comfort there or at least the courage to go through with it. Instead she found the depiction of Chinese hell in graphic temple paintings: men struck by thunderbolts, thrown into a pit of poisonous snakes, ground to pieces in huge mortars; men tortured with the intricacy of modern surgery without the anesthetic; disembowelment, castration, slicing, sawing – it was horrible, a Chinese nightmare to go with her Russian one. At the brothel she'd heard that by Chinese standards abortion is one of the worst crimes, because it might destroy a man child, killing a girl fetus was less crucial. For the male child you got boiled in hot pitch and oil. Vera had searched the paintings until she found that scene, and for minutes she stared at the crudely drawn woman, her mouth opened in an O of agony; then Vera walked out and did the abortion herself. She never looked for the sex of that child or for any of the four. Thank God for that.

Vera lights a cigarette, but quickly puts it out because the smoke sickens her. Above her on the luggage rack is a small, unobtrusive suitcase of English leather. Inside is her treasure, all of it. She has brought it along, although she won't be gone more than a month. He promised a month, no longer than that. Only a month at most, because General Sun Ch'uan-fang is a reckless fool who will attack soon or find other diversion. She'll return soon to Qufu, no need for her to drag along the treasure on this trip. Yet she feels especially vulnerable without her treasure, the thing that gives Vera her identity. What if something happened to Shan-teh – another battle, say, with General Sun on the outskirts of Qufu or inside the Confucian temple, men dying near the ancient steles, gasping their lives out under a pavilion where the Great Sage once taught? What if she's really pregnant, carrying the child of a man fated for a lifetime of battle?

This is incipient panic; she recognizes it all right. Vera blinks rapidly, as if the physical act can rid her of the sort of questions that build in her mind into terrifying obsessions.

Another knock at the door. Thankful for it, Vera calls out, 'Come in, please,' again forgetting she's not supposed to know the language.

Captain Fan enters, his smile of reproach as broad as a smile of approval. 'Illustrious Madam, excuse me for mentioning it, but I think English must be our language now. And this –' He waves his hands wildly through the air. 'Come now Peking,' he says in English, pointing to the window.

Vera stares at it, having forgotten the window, the train, her destination. Snow hasn't fallen here in the outskirts of Peking. Under the winter glare lie huts indigenous to all Chinese cities; tight curls of black smoke are rising from the glittering tin roofs, leaving a dark sooty cloud above the residential clutter. Vera recalls hearing that the most common cause of death in Peking is asphyxiation from charcoal smoke. Little children dying in the night from smoke. Why am I always thinking of death? she asks herself. And children? Vera stares fixedly at the scene out there: blue hills in the distance; a temple roof the color of rust; vegetable patches among the huts; and dirt paths filled with Peking carts, mere wooden slabs on wheels. The steadfast observing begins to dispel her panic. She looks, looks. There, in sudden lonely splendor, a rambling mansion with court yard lined by lilac bushes, now meager, but which in spring must turn the whole area fragrant. Look, she urges. Yet the panic keeps nudging forward, like a child pestering for attention. She wants Shan-teh, she wants Bright Lotus, she wants Qufu, and she wants the morning court-yard where playing Tai Chi Chuan is like praying in the church of her girlhood.

Clearing her throat, Vera turns to Captain Fan and begins to ask questions in halting English – a tourist entering the capital of China. He nods approvingly.

The train labors through the South Gate, then enters the Chinese City, first of five walled sections, the Captain tells her. Paved streets with electric lamps recede past the window. Wooden trolleys move with reckless speed down thoroughfares choked with mules, hooded carts, and camels. At Fan's urging, Vera leaves the compartment to look eastward through the corridor window. She has her first glimpse of the Temple of Heaven, sitting on a huge marble platform, its immense three-tiered dome of Prussian blue dazzling in sunlight. The emperors came here once a year to pray for a good harvest, using a broad processional road – the Emperor's Avenue – for this occasion. Otherwise its cobblestone were forbidden to everyone on pain of death, Fan explains. Glancing at him, Vera sees his pride in the history of his land.

Soon the train is pulling into the noisy station at Chien Men Gate on the border of the Chinese and Tartar cities. Vera rises and hauls her treasure suitcase from the rack, in spite of the Captain's attempt to do it for her.

Outside the Peking Hotel she looks at the sky above Chang An Road and searches for the pigeons, who are making a wailing sound like a siren. They belong to temples and have whistles attached to their wings. Throughout the city, all day long, they create this strange music.

Each morning for the past week, standing outside of the hotel, Vera has looked up for them before accompanying her guide, Captain Fan. They have been touring like other visitors to Peking.

She visits Bei Hai Lake, the White Dagoba. She visits Coal Hill, where the last Ming emperor hanged himself on a silken cord after dismembering his daughters and slaughtering his concubines so the barbarian invaders wouldn't have them. She visits the zoo and great mosque in the southeast. She spends a whole day at the Summer Palace, where the Dowager Empress, nicknamed without affection 'the old Buddha,' slowly poisoned her emperor nephew and once set ten thousand birds free on her birthday. Vera goes aboard the marble teahouse built at the old Buddha's order in the shape of a Mississippi paddle steamer topped by an Italian loggia. It had been built with appropriations meant expressly for the Chinese navy. While climbing around its marble excesses, Vera is spoken to softly by a foreign gentleman who doffs his homburg. When she doesn't respond to his elegant greeting in English, 'Good morning, my dear lady, I hope you are having a pleasant tour of Peking,' he tries it in German, then French. When she remains adamantly silent, he doffs his hat again and walks away.

Later, standing on the dun-colored road leading to the Ming Tombs outside Peking, she looks at the huge granite guardians in a row there and then glances at the Captain, whose face is suffused with pride. She agrees it is lovely, with fruit trees (bare now) on the blue slopes of surrounding mountains, and groves of pine, and nearby temples, the ochre roofs flashing. When they arrive at Yung Lo's Tomb, she is reminded of Qufu. And as she looks at the temple beams, faded by centuries of weather, and the ramp leading into the cool interior of the crypt, her heart yearns for her own courtyard and for Shan-teh coming through the Moon Gate, smiling, his brisk military walk concealing the tenderness of his hands when he caresses her in the night. Of course, at the Ming Tombs there are also, along with the beauty, the grinning caretakers; unpaid now that China is a republic, they go around hawking wine and pulling down roof tiles from the temple buildings to sell for souvenirs.

She looks at the snaky pathway of the Great Wall from a distance, but passes up the chance to climb its windswept battlements, icy at this time of year. On the other hand, Vera spends many hours among the art treasures of the Forbidden City; it is open to the public now, except the Presidential Palace (occupied by Marshal Chang Tso-lin, who controls Peking), and the residence of the former Manchu emperor, Pu Yi. The Captain takes her to the rear entrance of the Forbidden City, where green-paneled carriages used to wait for Pu Yi's loyal visitors. After the dynasty fell and Pu Yi had been proclaimed an ordinary citizen, Manchu noblemen would visit him at night and accept proclamations from him stamped with the interlocking eight pieces of jade that formed the royal seal. Now the deposed emperor, Captain Fan explains, has fled for his safety; he lives in Tientsin under Japanese protection. While Fan is speaking near the wall, an old lady comes through the gate, followed by an entourage.

'Manchu,' the Captain whispers in awe. 'Come to look at her former glory.'

She is wearing platform shoes on her unbound feet. Her cheeks are pallid from applications of rice powder, with patches of bright vermilion daubed over them. There's also a spot of scarlet on her lower lip and a small mirror dangles from her neck.

'She wears her hair in the Black Cloud,' the Captain observes in a low voice. Her hair, parted sleekly, rises at the back into a fanlike shape as stiff-looking as brocade.

But what commands Vera's attention is the absolute hauteur with which the old woman walks along, her hands far away from her sides, as if kept there by invisible blocks fastened to her hips. Watching the Manchu lady, Vera glimpses another world, another era, when strange images and stories had been the stuff of imperial life: hundred-course dinners; silk robes lined with sea otter and hats adorned with peacock feathers; divination by a study of cracks in a tortoiseshell; a scrupulous daily record kept of the emperor's sexual performance; persistent flogging of servants with clubs of split bamboo; eunuchs wearing diapers but ruling the Forbidden City with iron cunning – brutal, elegant, superstitious, mysterious Imperial China. The Captain, who is describing some of these things, can't know that she had first heard about them in the arms of a brothel girl who had a childlike enthusiasm for tales of splendor and extravagance.

'I want to see the Legation,' Vera tells him. What she really means is the Russian Embassy.

When they get there, she stands on Canal Street in front of the gray pile of somber architecture and feels gratified to see the windows boarded up. Silently Vera thanks Chang Tso-lin for having shut down the Red government here. The embassy stands next to the British, who rent theirs from a Manchu nobleman. On the stone wall outside it, painted in English, are the words 'Lest

We Forget,' a reminder of the Boxer siege a quarter of a century ago. Throughout the whole Legation area there's a smug atmosphere, visible in the confident faces of foreign dignitaries getting in and out of their limousines. This area had once housed the envoys of vassal states; now it is home for the arrogant diplomats of the West. A bitter irony she knows has not been lost on a patriot like Shan-teh. But he isn't here telling her about it. Vera is tired of her plump, considerate escort.

'More,' she tells the Captain, 'I must see more.' It's a way of escape from her restless thoughts.

He takes her to the Russian Church, called Pei Kuan here, built in 1900 to replace the one destroyed in the Boxer Uprising. Staring at the blue minarets, she decides finally not to enter. It might remind her too vividly of her childhood church, and for a few moments, lost in concentration, she thinks of her tragic country and its strange history, a sketchy, incoherent, discontinuous history unlike that of China, which has been minutely documented for hundreds of years. Even though the Hanlin, China's great classical library, had been fired and destroyed during the Boxer affair, there's still more Chinese history extant, far more of it, than Russian. Her people live, die, are forgotten.

'Let's go to the markets. I love the markets!' she exclaims with false gaiety.

So they go to the markets on Lantern and Brass streets, to the curio district, to the Thieves' Market, to the vegetable stalls that had once been the royal execution ground. Ignoring the ill-disguised exasperation of Captain Fan (not *always* considerate), who admires the monuments of his country but hates its daily life, Vera wanders everywhere, her anxieties giving her a remorseless energy. She takes in the sights – the red marriage candles and toy cranes dangling from sticks – along with the noise of barbers clacking their metal clippers, the knife sharpeners blowing their trumpets, the old-clothes merchants tapping their little mallets on thin wooden discs. 'Come now, Captain!' she cries over the din, as they are buffeted in the narrow streets. 'This is Peking too!'

She pulls back the heavy doors (they are padded with thick cloth to keep out the cold) and enters the fur shops, which are everywhere. A variety of magnificent furs hang from the rafters: sable, marmot, yellow Chinese mink. Shan-teh has given her enough money for a lovely coat – he shows the generosity of someone who has never been in real want, just as Luckner had thrown money away like someone who had never been out of debt. But Vera accepts Shan-teh's money only to play the role of tourist. She won't spend it as a reward for sexual favors, as she has done so often in her life. In her treasure suitcase, however, she carries the ink stone he had brought her from Canton. That is different – like a man's gift to his wife. It's a distinction Vera chooses to make, and therefore, to Captain Fan's surprise, she visits one fur shop after another without asking for the price of a single item.

Trudging through the winter streets, the Captain asks gloomily, 'Where now?' He has lost the role of guide. In his weariness he seems to have forgotten (Vera has not) that they are speaking Chinese all the time.

'Somewhere very special.' Vera tells him.

'Where?'

'We'll know when we get to it.'

So they walk on, passing the letter writers crouched under awnings with their writing materials spread on overturned boxes; passing umbrella makers and confectioners; passing the dentists who proudly display the strings of teeth they have successfully pulled. To all of them Vera gives a bright smile, feeling in herself an uncontrollable gaiety, no longer false. 'At last,' she says, halting. 'We are here.'

'Where?' asks the confused captain.

Vera walks into a bird shop, kept warm by a charcoal fire. Inhaling the acrid smoke, she thinks of the children asphyxiated in their sleep. Everywhere she looks in the smoky little shop are cages and birds: dwarf siskins, brightly plumed Japanese nightingales, brown larks, yellow canaries, gray thrushes. The tiny store vibrates with birdsong, and even Captain Fan can't hold back a smile. Assuming the role of foreign tourist, Vera asks him to find out prices for her. The shopkeeper, grinning, has them on his tongue. 'Tell him I come back,' Vera says to the Captain in English.

She will buy a songbird for the General before returning to Qufu.

Outside the shop, Vera notices some children playing in the lane. She looks at them as intently as if they were Ming scrolls like those displayed in halls of the Forbidden City. Seeing the children in their quilted jackets, their hair cut as if a bowl had been placed on their heads, Vera thinks of Bright Lotus, and when they roll their wooden hoops along the dusty ground, she thinks of herself, of the possible life growing within her body. Is it possible? It is possible.

Captain Fan, misinterpreting her smile, comments on his own happiness. 'You have made me happy, Madam, because the tour of the markets has made you happy!'

From the window of her hotel room, Vera can see east of the Legation to the polo grounds, where Europeans and Americans wield their sticks and strike the willow ball and make their backhand saves – she watches part of a game – astride Mongolian mounts that would be disdained in capitals of the West. Evenings she eats alone in the dining room, unless she specifically invites Fan – something she does less often with time. More than once she is accosted by foreign men who bow and offer her an aperitif. She refuses them and avoids anything but a quick glance into the ballroom, where a tinseled Christmas tree, harbinger of that season, stands in the middle of the dance floor. She carries away from this single glance the vivid impression of thin-stemmed wineglasses raised in toasts and feathered fans and some couples – maybe Slavs – dancing the polka.

One evening, sitting in the lobby for want of better to do, Vera overhears the conversation at a nearby card table. Two men, two women speaking French. They are discussing a recent midnight party at the Peking Club. They are sipping lemonade through straws and gossiping about an unfortunate acquaintance of theirs who has been punished recently for his indiscretion with a Chinese singsong girl – he has contracted syphilis. Titters. Vera turns quickly for a look at them. Both women are wearing tight skirts enlivened by wisps of chiffon – the bottoms are drawn closely around the ankles, *tres chic*. The inch-high collars are buttoned demurely. In their hair are festoons of pearls, as if in imiation (conscious or otherwise) of Manchu ladies. One of the men, gray-haired and wearing tails, has caught her eye. He smiles. Vera summons up a contemptuous smile in response, which brings from him an instant frown – a frown of surprise and humiliation. He fixes on his cards and doesn't look at her again.

It is small enough triumph, but a triumph nevertheless for someone who once contracted syphilis herself and went through a long, difficult medical regime to get rid of it. It is a triumph Vera savors again that evening, late, while she stands naked in front of

598

the mirror, hefting her breasts to judge if they are enlarging. Next morning she vomits and lies on the bed a long time, waiting for the nausea to subside. While lying there she recalls the young Russian woman she met in a Shanghai park some months ago: rich, spoiled, innocent, in love. Well, we are now even, Vera thinks – I am also in love. Running her hands across her belly, Vera wonders if it's possible, a child. Anticipation is quickly followed by fear. A child? In China? She, a general's concubine, pregnant with a child who will have no name? She feels as though time has coiled back and left her in her Russian girlhood. The thought of having a bastard child would have horrified her then; so it does now, while she lies in a bed in Peking, as if nothing had intervened between adolescence and maturity – no brothel, no abortions. She prays for deliverance from sin, mouthing the words as she might have done as a young virgin in Petrograd. But the moment passes. She laughs at her fragility, telling herself it is fake. And anyway, she is not pregnant; it is not possible.

That day the Yellow Wind comes out of the west, the dust it carries settling like a thin grainy veil across every surface of Peking. Usually a phenomenon of the spring, this is a strange December wind. Dense clouds of fine yellow dust blow along the streets, while overhead the currents of air whirl the powdery dust upward, then downward, then upward again in fierce drafts. Finally the dust settles, covering eveything in sight, moving into hidden places, sifting into every crack. The sun has the glow of a burning coal obscured by dense fog, and throughout the day great solid clouds of dust move across the sky like rolled casks. Everyone on the street has bloodshot, watery eyes.

'I don't like it,' Captain Fan admits. 'The Yellow Wind at this time of year is a bad sign.'

Vera is amused. He's as superstitious as his ignorant countrymen (she knows he despises them), who see in nature signs of human destiny. The Yellow Wind lasts for three days, long enough to depress Vera and encourage her to pester Captain Fan for news from Qufu. He claims there is none. When she urges him to telegraph, he manages to worm out of it. The Captain seems relieved to see her infrequently. She gets the impression he is busy in Peking, although his entire family now lives in Tientsin. A woman? Or contact with one of the numerous politicians who roam the Legation halls? Experience suggests to Vera that he's busy with a politician. She can't envision the Captain going out of his way for a woman, in spite of his impressive show of consideration. He's the kind who used to buy her in the brothel – a busy, ambitious man for whom sex was a tea break between meals of power.

When the Yellow Wind vanishes, he accompanies her into the market place again. In a street noted for brassware and gems, they see a solid phalanx of people approaching between the shops. Men are running, yelling, craning their necks to stare at a slight, unimposing figure in their midst. Two immense bodyguards in Mongol attire are shouldering aside those who get too near him. Captain Fan whispers it is a renowned female impersonator from the Peking stage; when he appears on the street, pandemonium breaks loose. Flattening herself against a wall to let the crowd by, Vera feels one of those rushes of joy that come upon her at odd moments in China. The racket, the motion, the color and sweep of the Peking mob seem to include her in a design of momentary delight. And the child! It is possible!

Flushed and taken by the tumult of her emotion, she is unprepared for Captain Fan's behavior. He reaches out and touches her arm, plucks her sleeve insistently. Above the noise he shouts into her ear that they must return now to the hotel. 'It is time!' he yells. 'A surprise awaits you!'

They return in a creaking old cart. The Captain, grinning and triumphant, refuses to say more about the surprise. He touched her sleeve. Amazing, Vera thinks: Captain Fan's striving for a new familiarity, as if he shed his Chinese decorum when he put on Western clothes. She glances curiously at him. He's a man who loves to orchestrate events. He'd rather plan them for others than be in them himself. Now she knows him; she has got to the core of Captain Fan, who rides beside her with a round beaming face. Vera is struck by a wonderful possibility: Shan-teh is waiting at the hotel. Is that the reason for the Captain's boyish teasing? He won't tell, of course, his pleasure at the moment seems almost sensual. Huddled in her coat, Vera tries to control her anticipation during the long, bumpy ride. When the cart stops, however, she rushes into the hotel.

The man rising from a leather chair is not Shan-teh. Wearing a business suit too tight for his broad frame, smiling uneasily, the blond young American comes toward her.

25

The battle was fought a month ago, yet it clings to him like a powerful smell, the memory remaining as close as yesterday, as this afternoon.

He remembers the bloated horses stinking in the wheatfield; what he especially remembers is the way their legs went out straight; if you set them upright, they could be standing. And the dead men lying in a ditch of melting snow, each head to the side in the attitude of sleep; they had looked peaceful, childlike. But not the ones blown out of their clothes by cannon blasts; they were meaty, hideous. He remembers the many fires consuming the carcasses of horse and man, the greasy smoke going up, leaving a terrible ash on everyone's uniform, on hair and eyelashes. In the view of all this he can't understand Napoleon, who viewed the carnage of Borodino and observed, '*C'est le champ de bataille le plus beau que j'ai encore vu.*' Embree, obsessed with the French general during a college history course, had memorized many of his phrases, but none more remarkable than this one. Then it had fascinated him to think that Napoleon could describe such destruction in aesthetic terms. He is no longer fascinated, he is appalled by it. In the aftermath of Hengshui he is horrified, and this sense of horror deepens in succeeding days, when the wounded, not the slain, take precedence in his mind.

The day after the battle, before his unit sets out with the rest of the army in pursuit of Jen, he watches four wounded men, obviously dying, shoveled into the ground with a heap of dead bodies. They are pleading with the burial squad to let them live. 'Can't be helped,' an onlooker tells Embree. 'They haven't a chance anyway. Gangrene will get them in a few days or the cold or dogs. Believe me, it's better to bury them now. Shovel them in, be done with it. Their ghosts will thank us.'

On the homeward march, ten days later, Embree sees the sampan coolies at a river crossing take equipment and horses first; they leave the wounded in the freezing mud for last. He notices how decisive the coolies are; they move without hesitation, selecting the most valuable things first. No one has to tell them what order to follow. He sees other things that will remain with him always. A Chinese medic uses torn bandages, already soiled,

601

that he takes from a battered old suitcase. Dying soldiers lie on doors pulled off farmhouses. Wounded officers, riding in wagons, drunkenly brandish bottles of rice wine. Embree passes through villages that have been looted. By Jen's troops or Tang's? It is never clear. With the General still in the North – he has remained a few days longer with some detachments – there's no one sufficiently in command to stop the plundering. Embree understands now what is meant by personal command in Chinese armies: It means the top officer, from general down to captain depending upon the unit. No one else will do; subordinates are ignored, and there is hardly any such thing as chain of command. He is amazed by the efficiency of the looters. In one district yamen they took anything they could move: light bulbs, brass fixtures, door and window casings, even the copper wire along the baseboards. Each night Embree dreams of his friend Fu Chang-so in the wheat field; Fu is trampled not by one horse but by battalions of them, endless hooves reducing his happy, generous face to a pulp.

The vividness of warfare remains with Embree, yet his response to it undergoes a transformation. He will never be sure when the change started, but one morning, shortly after his return to Qufu, Embree recalls the excitement of the boot-to-boot charge. He sees himself galloping across the wheat field, screaming into the wind, brandishing his ax. The emphasis of memory shifts from the dead and wounded to the battle itself. Napoleon's comment about a beautiful battlefield no longer shocks him; he begins to understand it. He thinks of the great surge of men through the billowing smoke, moments intense enough to fill up a lifetime. He has a desire again for more adventure, like a drunk wanting whisky after a hangover. He feels disappointed that the Big Swords, nearly demolished, were sent back early with other ripped-up units. He'd have wanted to go on across Hopei, snapping at Jen's heels.

Embree wonders, however, if he acquitted himself well in the battle. He thinks so, but his performance needs verification. It comes in a surprising way from an unlikely source. The General calls him over during one of the first inspections since the army's return to Qufu. They are facing each other across their horses. The General nods curtly and asks him to accompany a small military delegation to Peking; it will be led by Major Chia, to whom the sergeant will be responsible. Without another word, the General rides on. A delegation isn't war, but it will keep him close to the feel of war, Embree thinks. And his selection is proof that he performed satisfactorily at Hengshui. He is eager to do more, to prove more. He is eager even on the delegation train from Tientsin to Peking, although the unheated compartment is shot through with a piercing wind. He shivers with a traveling rug wound about his legs. Fine yellow dust sifts through window-casing cracks and through ventilators and under doors, piling little ridges of powder on everything. Embree's companions call it the Yellow Wind and feel uneasy, not so much because of the yellow powder it leaves everywhere, but because it has come out of season. Each time Embree moves, the rising dust causes him to sneeze.

'You don't like our Yellow Wind?' Major Chia asks, open in his sarcasm. He heads the delegation of five. It is his reward, everyone knows, for having displayed a gift for tactics at Hengshui. Chia is small, blocky, thick-necked, with a shaven head. Prominent bags under his eyes age him a little, but Embree figures he can't be more than thirty. He doesn't like Embree. Once, deliberately in earshot of Embree, he said to another delegate that the American's foreignness was his only qualification for the mission. That may be the truth, Embree knows. It is common knowledge that General Feng Yu-hsiang is partial to foreigners: an American on Tang's negotiating team would be taken as a favorable sign. And Embree has heard that in negotiation the Chinese often put faith in foreigners – trusting not their honesty but their lack of skill at dissimulation. Perhaps Tang has followed that reasoning, yet at the train depot, on the delegation's departure, the General had drawn Embree aside and said with a smile. 'You fought like a Chinese. I will treat you as Chinese. You will represent me as one Chinese representing another.'

It is ironic, that after the battle Embree was no longer sure he wanted to be Chinese. And in the intervening weeks this doubt has grown, until now, when he enters the capital of China as an official representative of a powerful Chinese leader, Embree feels less Chinese than he did when boarding a train months ago to take up a missionary post in Harbin.

What has happened to him is the battle. He saw men rush forward to die for the General because they must. Whereas he rushed forward to experience a challenge. And after the battle, seeing the wounded, Embree began to realize that this was their destiny, that they couldn't escape it, whereas he had the right to quit any time – except in the heat of battle. He was free, they were not. Fighting for him was optional, for them it was unavoidable.

He has come to a conclusion both sad and exhilarating: He has it in his power to be a stranger on this earth, to live unencumbered by the ideas and duties which bind most men, to be free and therefore to live without conviction, to observe rather than participate, even though during the observation he might well lose his life.

His sense of alienation from Chia and the mission is increased by something that happens when they reach the house in Peking where they will stay. The dust storm having stopped and the day being warmer than usual at this time of year, Embree sits in the courtyard under a locust tree. The house owner, a distant relative of Major Chia, has kindly supplied him with newspapers in English, featuring items from abroad. Avidly he consumes what news there is from America.

Calvin Coolidge has again insisted he will not run for President in 1928. Embree can imagine how disappointed father must be.

On the first of October Babe Ruth hit home run number sixty on southpaw Zachery's third pitch.

A new film, called a talkie, has just appeared. *The Jazz Singer*, according to the article, will bring in a new era of sound. Embree doubts it.

On the twelfth of November the Holland Tunnel under the Hudson River, connecting New York and Jersey City, was opened. In the first twenty-four hours 52,000 vehicles traversed it. That's more cars, Embree estimates, than can be found in all of China.

In an editorial, written by a Chinese educated abroad or by a foreign resident of China for years, Embree reads the following:

'Fancy a Chinese Buddhist mounting the roof of a hansom cab at Charing Cross or Wall Street and preaching Buddhism to the mob in execrable pidgin English. That's the effect on a Chinese crowd when – I have seen it – a missionary perches on a cart outside the South Gate in Peking, haranguing a crowd of gapers in bastard Chinese.'

Fu Chang-so, who knew so many things, used to tell stories about the Christians in China, though the absolute truth of them was questionable. He said there was an execution ground in the southern quarter of the Chinese City in Peking where Chinese priests waited to baptize criminals. They put a medallion of the Virgin Mary (Embree gathered that's what Fu Chang-so meant) around the man's neck, said words over him, and made the sign of the cross. Meanwhile the shackled man knelt, arms tied behind him, while soldiers argued for the chance of earning a few *cash* for performing the execution. The priest would step back among the curious children and all would watch a soldier blast a huge hole in the victim's back. Beggars rushed forward then to fight over the trousers; Fu Chang-so explained they fought less over the shirt, because it was torn and bloodied by the shot. This story and many like it, often of pointless violence involving Christians or tales illustrating the common belief that Christianity is a rich man's religion, Fu Chang-so told with much guffawing and knee slapping, while other grinning Big Swords studied their foreign brother for signs of approval or disapproval. Embree never flinched, but sat there with a neutral smile, denying a lifetime. In an internal voice of cool logic he told himself that Confucianism had worked no better for these Chinese than Christianity had worked for him.

Amen, father. So be it. I am free of it all.

Embree turns the pages awhile, reading ads for machine tools, Western boots, and cars. He wonders if he's truly free of America. Sitting beneath the hard sunlight of Peking, he lets himself drift in memory; the images pass by like flotsam in a stream: knickers and high-top boots, cigarette holders, open-sided trolleys, the plaid golfing cap of his roommate in college, his own light-blue hat with a broad band, Greta Garbo in *Flesh and the Devil*, spit curls, the glass-bead necklace that Mary wore in the New York speakeasy. It all comes at him lazily, nearly lulling him to sleep, the combined memories of his life before this life: oval mirrors and Tiffany lamps, suspenders and vests, stickpins, wool scarves, fat men smoking Robert Burns cigars and wearing red carnations in their buttonholes, the song 'Am I Blue?,' striped barber poles, his father's study with the rows of leather-bound books. The images come along without order, without logic, drawing him deeper into the memory of his past. America, is he free of it? Then the images vanish with brutal swiftness as if he has willed them away. He's left in a strange mood, both homesick and resolved never to return. Return means enslavement to ideals and duties that he no longer believes in. He wants to be free.

Embree throws the *Peking Gazette* and the *Daily News* on the ground. From somewhere close by come the wailing of a flute, the pounding of a drum. He goes to the gate, opens it, and stands in the entrance to watch a wedding procession go by. Musicians wear green robes. Wedding gifts in gold-lacquered boxes are carried on poles. Coming up behind him, Chia explains that the bearers all belong to a beggars' guild. Next is a red palanquin, fronted by two huge umbrellas of embroidered silk and ceremonial fans sparkling with mirrors and bright banners. The palanquin curtains are tightly drawn. In mild irony Embree thinks of Ursula in such an ornate chair, big plain busy practical Ursula seated within such outrageous splendor. They were supposed to marry next year or the next. What must she think? Not a word of his whereabouts in half a year. Considering him dead, good Ursula must include him every night in her prayers and climb chastely into bed.

He thinks of the Russian woman, of her bed, of her in it, writhing beneath the General.

'We will talk now,' Chia declares, so they turn away from the noisy wedding procession. Inside the house they sit near a fireplace, the fire laid but unlit, in deep easy chairs and look at each other across a stone floor strewn with Mongolian rugs. Chia's relative is a rich man who mingles the feeling of East and West in his house. Chia goes over ground already familiar. At the meeting this afternoon with Feng's men they will refuse a conference between the generals in Peking – it is a site controlled by Chang Tso-lin. Chia will lead the delegation and no one else must offer suggestions. Final decisions will be his.

Embree listens without any desire to challenge Chia's authority. This is not the sort of fight that interests him.

That afternoon, when the weather turns colder, they motor to a village called Pao Ma Chang, west of Peking. Here are the weekend cottages of prominent officials and businessmen. Nearby is a golf course (sliced up by railroad tracks), a horse-racing stadium, and a duck blind for the Peking Hunt Club. They stop at a cottage surrounded by a high brick wall. Feng's five delegates are there. They are sitting around a crackling fire near a low table crowded with delicacies and a bottle of Scotch. Feng's men are obviously pleased to find an American among Tang's representatives. Often during the discussion they study Embree's face for a clue to the effect of their proposals – they don't waste time on Chia, whose features are mask-like. In response to the challenge Embree tries to show nothing. The General must have known he would try not to disgrace himself – Chinese to the bone. So he works hard to compose his face during the endless talk. He finds none of it important enough to draw emotion anyway. They argue such matters as the number of courses each general will supply when he gives a banquet. They get stuck on this issue of hospitality, each side wanting their man to make the most impressive show. They debate for an hour the site of the conference and decide tentatively on Sian, the capital of Shensi Province. At present it's in the hands of a local warlord who is politically neutral and who would be honored to be the host of two distinguished militarists. Exhausted, the delegates agree to meet the next day.

On the way back to the city, Embree turns to Chia. 'That young man with the bushy eyebrows? I know him. His name is Yang. He was once the General's aide. He was at Thousand Buddha Mountain and disappeared just before the bomb went off. He betrayed the General.'

Chia nods with a smile. 'I never knew him. I joined the General after he was gone.'

'But that's *Yang*,' Embree says impatiently. 'I know he recognized me.'

'I believe you.'

Embree is startled by Chia's lack of interest. 'Why has Feng sent him here, knowing he'd be recognized?'

Chia lights a cigarette.

'It's proof Feng planned the bombing,' Embree declares.

'Yes.'

'Then he sends the assassin to plan a meeting? That's flaunting it!'

'You don't understand,' the Major says coolly. 'By sending Yang he's saying to our general, "I once tried to kill you, but things have changed. I admit my error in the past. I do it openly. Now let's talk." '

'I think the General will be furious.'

'That's not for you to judge.'

They remain silent during the rest of the ride. An old acquaintance of Embree is waiting at the house – Captain Fan, in his baggy Western suit. Over tea the Captain alludes to being in Peking on 'official business' too. Chia asks rather sharply how Fan has discovered them in the city.

'I know your nephew quite well, Major. Or rather my second-younger brother does.'

'But I thought your family lived in Tientsin now.'

'They do. My brother wrote me here and suggested I visit your family and pay my respects.'

Chia looks skeptical, and Embree understands why. There is something makeshift about Captain Fan's explanation; most likely he found out about their being here from someone else. Or am I becoming suspicious like the Chinese? Embree wonders.

Suddenly the Captain invites him to dinner. Embree looks for approval from the Major, who grants permission with a slight nod. Minutes later, in a taxi, the Captain laughs. 'Between us, my friend, Chia doesn't like me.' It is a Western thing to say, making Embree relax. 'Chia has a huge family here in Peking. He'll be seeing them tonight. He won't admit it but I'm doing him a favor by taking you away. Now he can see them without you along.'

'Would he take me along if I had nothing to do?'

'On second thought, I don't think so. Not Chia. He keeps all that wealth to himself.'

'So the family's rich?'

'His is and so is his wife's.'

'I didn't know he was married.'

'It's something Chia wouldn't think of telling you,' Captain Fan observes cheerily.

'Then his wife isn't in Qufu?'

'She's here in Peking.' After studying the American, Fan adds, 'You look surprised. The fact is Chia won't let her live in Qufu. Her father likes it that way, and Chia does what his father-in-law likes.'

Embree is fascinated. He has progressed far enough into Chinese life to be privy to gossip. Fan rattles on about Chia's wealth. Apparently Chia joined the army to honor his maternal grandfather, who once served as the superintendent of Paoting Military Academy. Once the debt is paid, according to the Captain, Chia will leave the army and jump into business, accepting yet another family obligation – to become richer.

They dine at a Mongolian restaurant that features bits of lamb cooked in boiling water and dipped into various sauces. Sitting over beer before the meal begins, they hear a commotion outside. Curious, Embree goes to the entrance and stands in the doorway. In the twilight he sees a long column of troops in field gear, wearing Mongolian fur hats with earflaps. They tramp along with canteens slapping their thighs. After a brief look, Embree returns to the table. They eat the lamb, then a vegetable soup made with the broth in which the lamb was cooked. Now and then Embree goes to the door and looks at the column still trudging down the street. When the Captain suggests they go to the Wagon Lits Hotel for an after-dinner drink, the column is still moving along by torchlight. When the two strolling men turn a corner, they see more columns filing beneath the great arch on Hatamen Street, their numbers vanishing into the darkness like the long body of a dragon inching its way toward magical encounters.

'Whose troops are they?' Embree asks in wonder. 'Since we went into the restaurant, there must have been many thousands going by.'

'They're the troops of Chang Tso-lin.' The Captain laughs. 'My friend, you've been deceived since coming to China.'

'How is that?'

'You thought our illustrious general had a large army.' The Captain shrugs dismissively. 'Chang Tso-lin can muster more army corps than our general has battalions. Chang Tso-lin – there's *real* strength.'

In the gloomy dining room of the Wagon Lits, hunching over imported brandy, Embree is glad to have the Captain for a companion again. Major Chia makes him uneasy. Captain Fan has an insouciant, cheery manner rare in the Chinese. After the second drink, Embree considers himself lucky. Ever since coming to China he has managed to find good men for companions: first the bandit Chin, then the Big Sword horseman Fu Chang-so; and now Captain Fan proves once more that the Chinese, when they wish, can be staunch friends. He feels emboldened by the good brandy to ask what 'official business' has brought the Captain to Peking.

Turning his brandy glass, the Captain gives Embree a sly little smile. 'Perhaps we can both explain why we're here.'

'That's simple on my part. I'm here on a military matter, but I can't discuss it.'

'You're here to set up a meeting with General Feng.'

Laughing, warmed by the brandy, Embree shakes a finger at his chubby friend. Embree has never felt more American since being captured by the bandits.

'Don't tell Chia I know about the meeting or he'll lose sleep.' Waiting for Embree to chuckle briefly, the Captain then adds, 'I'm here with the Russian lady.'

Embree is stunned. In camp there had been a rumor that the foreign woman, no longer pleasing the General, had been sent away. She was gone, gone home, and wouldn't come back. This was the story Embree had heard from the troops, who were happy their general had thrown the woman out; now he could get himself a few Chinese girls to bring luck to the camp.

Captain Fan here with the Russian lady? Embree hears his voice go thin when he asks, 'She's here? In Peking?'

Fan nods somberly.

'With – you?'

The Captain, lifting his hands in mock horror, denies it vehemently. 'No, my friend! Not that! I'm with her only in the sense I'm making sure she's comfortable and safe. It's my mission. The General sent me.' He explains that General Tang wants her out of Qufu for a while. The Kong family has been sent away somewhere too.

Embree scarcely hears. In his mind is Vera's image: the black hair, limpid eyes, sensual mouth. His secret feeling for her, lately arrested by hopelessness, floods back in an instant. 'So she's here,' Embree murmurs with a smile that does not escape the little captain's notice.

'Yes,' Fan says happily, 'right here in Peking.'

Negotiations next day deal principally with the sites for banquets. Two sites in Sian are finally selected: the Temple of the Town Gods and the Temple of the Recumbent Dragon, both about equidistant from the Bell Tower, where the generals will meet. The problem is, which temple is more desirable? The Town Gods Temple is in better repair and features two stone lions from the Ming at its entrance. The Recumbent Dragon Temple, on the other hand, is an older structure and possesses a fine library which includes a famous Buddhist text from the Sung. Another problem proceeds from the first one: Which general shall get which temple? Prestige is at stake. The discussion lasts well past noon, then adjourns until the next day.

Chia and the three aides take a car back to their residence. The Major seems relieved that Embree professes a desire to do some private sightseeing. Embree even refuses a ride back into Peking, and insists on taking a cart – he has time to kill before an appointment with Captain Fan at the hotel. So in a creaking old cart he rattles slowly back into the city. He notices that pullers have tied mittens to their rickshaws' handles in anticipation of a sharp drop in temperature, but right now the weather is merely crisp, invigorating. A file of heavily laden camels shuffles down a lane past him. They conjure in Embree images of desert country and distant mountains. The vision is sharpened when he passes a makeshift market where a Mongol caravan has stopped. He stares at men who remind him of White Wolf's bandits, although these seem better fed, richer. Indeed, spread around the marketplace are wonderful things from Mongolia: saddles of red leather, figured saddle carpets, stirrups of chiseled iron, pleated robes of rust and tangerine hues, peaked hats of fur with floppy brims. The Mongol women stand motionless beside the horses, wearing silver earrings, red jackets, and green turbans. In these moments, while the cart hobbles by, Embree thinks: Adventure. Later, when the cart is passing the Wagon Lits Hotel, he sees another vision – a beautiful European woman. She's obviously no tourist, but perhaps the wife of a Legation diplomat. She wears a leopard coat and sits in a low barouche; beside her, panting, is a little white dog that wears a tiny leopard coat, matching hers. The coachman, shaking the reins, is in a green uniform and a crimson mandarin hat. Briefly Embree's eyes meet hers; hers are smoky gray – he can see them clearly in the bright winter light.

But she is not as beautiful as Vera Rogacheva. And he has the opportunity to confirm his judgment when, an hour later, he rises from the chair in the Peking Hotel lobby and watches her come toward him.

Surrounded by rich Chinese and foreign tourists and porters in the bustling lobby, they exchange pleasantries in Chinese. Embree notices an elderly foreign couple staring at them. Leaning forward he says in a low, conspiratorial voice, 'They think we're scandalous for speaking this heathen language.'

Vera laughs. The image remains with him: green eyes crinkling at their edges after her face has regained its calm. She is obviously glad to see him; it shows, it shows. Encouraged by his estimate of her good will, Embree asks her to have dinner with him – he includes Captain Fan too, with a quick nod.

That evening they renew their Qufu relationship, when the trio gathered in General Tang's absence. Fan beams throughout the dinner, a benign spectator. Vera talks of Peking sights while Embree sits there happy in her presence, absorbing it the way a man coming from the cold absorbs the warmth of a fire. After dinner, at their departure, Embree shakes her hand, holding the soft warm flesh a moment longer than propriety dictates; she blushes slightly. It is a girlish reaction that charms him. Long after he and Fan have left the hotel, he thinks of her still being capable of the delicate emotion of modesty. Would she have reacted the same with any man? Of course she would. Or perhaps she's especially sensitive to him, anticipating more advances. That assumes he is embarking on a possible seduction. Impossible. Yet like a log jammed in a stream, the thought remains. Captain Fan is chattering on. What's he saying? Embree feels impatient with him, as if the fellow's breaking in on a private meditation.

With a sigh the Captain says, 'Too bad you won't be long in Peking. We could do this again.'

'I'll be here longer.' Embree doesn't want to suggest such meetings should end.

'You haven't finished your mission?'

'No. So far, we've only discussed where to hold the banquets.'

'In Sian?'

'Yes.'

The Captain laughs. 'You must forgive us Chinese. Gluttony's our chief vice. Perhaps it's the result of famines – we think constantly of food. So you'll be here longer?'

'I think so.'

'You haven't set the date for the Sian meeting?'

'That won't be decided,' Embree explains, 'until the last moment.'

'Why is that?'

'I'm surprised at you, Fan: to keep it secret. It will be an important meeting.'

The Captain looks at Peking from the hackney cab. Torchlight intermittently glides past the window. 'I'm glad you'll be here. There are many things I must do. You know, personal obligations which I can't discuss. For my family.'

'That's understandable,' Embree replies cautiously.

'What I mean is,' Fan continues, 'if you're here, perhaps you'll do me a favor and see the Russian lady. Entertain her in my absence. Your worthless friend would be indebted.'

Embree studies him. Is the man joking? 'If you wish,' Embree agrees as calmly as possible.

'Good, it's settled.' The Captain sighs with relief. 'Shall I tell Madam Rogacheva you'll come by tomorrow?'

'As soon as the meeting's finished. If it's like today's, perhaps shortly after noon.'

'You're a generous friend.' The Captain leans forward and shouts at the driver to stop. 'I'm getting out here, it's just a short walk to my hotel.' He shakes hands in a Western manner before leaving the coach. At the window he pauses to say, 'One other thing, my friend. Keep our little scheme from Chia.'

'Our scheme?' Embree laughs, but without humor, sensing the truth of the word 'scheme.'

'Chia's strict, as you know. Too serious for his own good, if I'm permitted such frankness. Leave him out of it.'

'I agree. It's better that way.' And they part with Embree feeling both conspiratorial and elated. Tomorrow. Alone with Vera. Of course, it means nothing, it simply can't mean anything, yet the anticipation blinds him to the route that the hackney driver takes through the Peking evening.

At the meeting next day there is more wrangling about the disposition of temples for the Sian banquets. But Embree begins to see behind the squabbling to a more important issue – the two delegations seem to be establishing a familiarity with each other that may lead to trust. The genealogy of all the negotiators (excluding Embree) is discreetly revealed during the discussions, and he watches them search for promising connections, not only among relatives but among mutual friends as well, and even school mentors and commanders with whom they have served. The negotiators seem to spin a web of relevance from such information, attempting to bring everyone there into psychic accord and thereby pave the way for good will between the generals. Moreover, each team of negotiators vies for moral advantage. All the participants strive for a rhetoric unattached to belief, as they deny ambition in their generals and claim their only goal is unity. They defer at great length, as if they never initiate but only respond to ideas, as if they wouldn't dream of creating difficulties but in all humility react to problems. Embree is now sufficiently aware to catch them at another game: Feng's men inquire about the recent battle, knowing full well their own commander had encouraged one of the opposing generals to fight it; Chia, resisting the probe, merely claims total victory for Tang. When asked about casualties – the question comes at the end of a labyrinthine discussion of chicken dishes – he replies by describing an influx of new recruits who wish to be part of the triumphant Shantung Army.

Meanwhile, Embree sits in almost complete silence – as does Yang, opposite him at the conference table. Sometimes they hand each other the Scotch bottle with faint smiles. They are, Embree comes to realize, symbols for each side: he is Tang's concession to the pro-Western sentiments of General Feng; by the same token Yang represents Feng's admission of guilt for the Thousand Buddha Mountain incident. So a relaxed Philip Embree (as a symbol he is quite free of responsibility) enjoys the unveiling of a code based on mutual interests, common values, and fraternal relationships.

The meeting ends with the negotiators agreeing to have a banquet for themselves; therefore it ends on a note of calculated merriment. A few joke about who will drink too much.

When they are leaving, Major Chia stops Embree. 'Have you seen the Captain?'

'You mean Captain Fan? Yes, that once,' lies Embree. 'Not again. Why?'

'Keep away from him. I don't trust him.'

'Major?'

'I said I don't trust him.' With a glare of disdain, Chia walks away.

So Embree is again left alone. He finds a hackney coach – there are plenty of them in this fashionable Western Hills. It is past noon, so he urges the driver forward. Embree fears she might go out alone. Aware of his lover's anxiety, Embree forces himself to sit back against the leather. He tells himself it is only a favor for the Captain, nothing more, but getting to the hotel, Embree races into the lobby.

She is waiting in a chair.

He never imagines that she may look so radiantly expectant because of her loneliness and because she misses her real lover. What Embree sees is her smile, her shining eyes, her proffered hand, and he takes all these signs as ample proof of her pleasure solely in him.

They go to the famous Feng Tse Yuan for lunch. It is far too expensive for someone like Embree, who has his soldier's pay and an allowance from Chia to spend in Peking. A lunch here will nearly break him. Yet he's driven to give Vera the best Peking has to offer.

They take a private dining room of little distinction: overstuffed furniture, a table with a plain white cloth, an old screen in dark gloomy colors, thick curtains at the window. He realizes too late that what they should have is a cosy place for conversation, not a gourmet lunch. Even so, Embree insists on house specialties: duck marrow soup, chicken puffs with shark's fin, braised fish in brown sauce, stewed cuttlefish eggs – far more than they can eat. He's grateful that she doesn't protest or remark on his obvious error in judgment. To move past the mistake he begins to talk at a fast pace. No longer constrained by the presence of Captain Fan, he speaks quite boastfully – acutely aware this is not like him – of his horsemanship, of his promotion to sergeant, of his close relationships with the men. He is grateful once again for her good will and polite attention, even as he knows much of what he's saying is silly. By the time they have finished half their lunch, he tells himself once again, hopelessly but with undiminished enthusiasm, I am in love, I am really in love.

Rattling on, he pauses suddenly to confess that he had thought of her just before the battle, that thinking of her had given him courage.

Silence fills the room.

Vera puts down her chopsticks. Her face has grown pale. 'Tell me about the battle,' she asks softly.

He does, and his enthusiasm in giving an account increases as he notices the effect it has on her – she seems riveted by the details. When he describes the suffering of the wounded, Vera winces visibly. Interrupting him then, she leans forward and tells him of her own experience in the Qufu hospital: the look of this man, the fate of that one, the sounds and smells of death, the horror. . . . Her absorption in the memory is so deep that Embree wonders if she hasn't gone past it into other memories as terrible. Her face seems wrenched by recollection into despair, into a vulnerability that makes it almost intolerable for him to sit quietly and listen. In fact, he should be holding her in his arms, Embree thinks, soothing her, stroking her hair, as his mother had done for him in his childhood. Without thinking about it (in retrospect he will think about it endlessly) he begins to link the agonies resulting from that battle to General Tang. In recalling that afternoon, Embree will tell himself it is true: Necessity is indeed the mother of invention. For as he talks he manages to implicate the General in every death, in every wound. By making objections to the battle having been fought – objections invented on the spot – he puts forward the General as someone impatient for glory, who had been strongly advised against the campaign. As he speaks, Embree becomes more subtle in his denunciation, granting that the General is 'a good man' and 'honorable' but led by 'unscrupulous' officers who catered to 'a certain vanity' common in Chinese warlords. Coupled to this criticism of the General is Embree's judgment of Chinese medicine – the treatment of wounded is inhuman.

Her face quite flushed, Vera agrees that the treatment of the Hengshui wounded was inhuman. 'Inhuman,' she repeats, twisting a napkin above untouched food on her plate.

Graced by the temporary shrewdness of a man in love, Embree is fully aware that he has made her an accomplice: they are colluding against General Tang.

She too becomes suddenly aware. It is obvious in the way Vera sits up straight and declares, 'But all war is inhuman. The General can't be blamed. Such things are complex.'

Embree nods in agreement; the cunning of love tells him the damage has been done. 'I agree.'

'He can't be blamed for the lack of medicine in China, even if he did have the money to buy what there is. We are being unfair.'

Yes, you're right. I agree.'

'He's a great man.'

'He certainly is,' Embree agrees with an emphatic nod. 'Or I wouldn't have given him my allegiance. If I've let you think otherwise –'

'No, of course not.' She smiles, as if reassuring them both. Yet Embree – sharp-eyed in his love – detects a slight tremor of doubt around her mouth.

Before calling for the bill, he says, 'The General has been one of the great men in China. But to remain great is another thing.'

'What do you mean?'

Embree is astonishing himself with his own daring. 'He's hemmed in by enemies.'

'That's been true for some time,' Vera comments with a smile.

'But Hengshui was a defeat he can't afford.'

'Hengshui was a victory.'

'When a general loses so many men, victory is defeat.'

Gravely she nods.

'We would all – his men, his officers – like to help him if we could. We don't want to see him go down.'

'Down? Of course not. He won't go down.'

Embree shrugs again, developing a little mystery from the gesture. When the bill comes, he sees with dismay that Vera is rummaging in her purse. An argument ensues. He won't have her pay! His pride nearly results in mutual ill feeling, but, exercising control at last, Embree allows her to split the bill – with the understanding he leaves the tip. As they prepare to go, the waiter, having counted the money, steps to the doorway and in traditional fashion calls out the amount of his tip so that everyone along the hallway will hear. He adds, 'A gift of munificence from a great gentleman!'

Vera laughs, and the tension between the vanishes. 'Do waiters do such things in America?'

'Never!'

'You must tell me about America.'

'That would give me pleasure,' he replies formally, but dares to take her arm when they leave the dining room. The soft flesh of her upper arm seems to burn his hand. He is sick with desire and hopes the intense emotion is not transmitted through his trembling fingers.

During the next two days, although the Yellow Wind doesn't return, the Great Cold sets in, and a low gray haze composed of charcoal smoke hovers above the red-tiled roofs of Peking.

A banquet for the negotiators is held in a restaurant called the Pavilion for Listening to Birds Sing, inside the grounds of the Summer Palace. There's much drinking, elaborate toasting, and feigned drunkenness, but Embree has enough experience now to recognize in the relaxed antics of the banqueters a studied good cheer, a dutiful response to ritual. He is bored and waits for tomorrow when he will see her again. Lucky for him the Major is too busy with family to pay attention to his comings and goings. That evening, when the delegates return to the house where they are staying, Embree strolls in the little courtyard by himself. Under the influence of rice wine, he conducts another conversation with Mary.

'I thought I loved the girl in White Wolf's camp. I was a virgin. I took gratitude for love.'

Mary in her wisdom would agree. She'd probably say, 'That's

something many of us do.'

'But Vera means something more. I can see spending a lifetime with her.'

'Careful.'

'Why?'

'What about your love of adventure?' Mary might say.

Embree understands the need for sacrifice in love. 'I'll give it up gladly.'

'Will or would?' It's the kind of distinction Mary would make.

'I will. I will give up everything for her.'

'And what does the General say?'

Embree has given that question to his sister for good reason – it plagues him relentlessly. He devises more than one scenario to answer it. General Tang, aware of the unbreachable gap between cultures, accepts the inevitable, wishes them Godspeed, and says goodbye. Furious, he pursues them. Cunningly, he plans revenge. Poignantly, he begs Vera to return to him. Aloofly, he regards them with indifference. As the scenarios unfold, Embree develops a strong dislike for the romantic adversary he has created in his imagination: Tang becomes a symbol of unmitigated authority, a counterpart to his own father. Embree intertwines the two images – Chinese general and American minister – into a dreadful portrait of repression and tyranny. His hatred of the General grows in mathematical progression to his desire for Vera Rogacheva. He contemplates gloomily the injustice of a world that denies him her love. For she does love him, or will love him as soon as she has freed herself of the General. He is younger – but that's of no importance. Of vital importance is their heritage. It's something she can never share with the General, who is thoroughly Asian. And Vera dotes on stories of America – it appeals to her far more than China. *Of that there can be no doubt.* Perhaps someday he'll take her there, perhaps to New Haven, and they'll stroll down Chapel Street with her arm in his, oblivious to the admiring glances of men who had once been his classmates or his teachers at Yale. He feels the frenzy, the effort it takes to control his impulses, to draw himself back from fantasy into the world of Peking.

He sees her the next afternoon for tea, for a look at some scrolls in the Forbidden City (aware that his enthusiasm must seem to her the counterfeit it is), then back to her hotel, where they shake hands in goodbye. He goes from her to the Wagon Lits Hotel bar, where, according to Vera, the Captain will be waiting to see him.

Fan is there all right, smiling, cheery, suave in a Western way in spite of his baggy suit. They sit in the dim bar over Scotch. After a long silence the Captain says briskly, 'Well, my dear friend, you certainly look troubled.'

Embree decides to be candid; it is intolerable to carry such emotions around in solitude. 'I suppose it shows,' he says. 'Yes, I'm troubled.'

Fan laughs. 'I hope it doesn't show enough for Chia to notice.'

'He has his relatives.' Embree waves his hand dismissively.

'He has a sharp eye, too. If he learns why you're troubled, he'll become a source of still more trouble.'

'Do *you* know why I'm troubled?'

'That's none of my business, dear friend. What I must speak about is our mutual concern – General Tang.'

'What about him?'

'Don't you know? Surely you must know.' Captain Fan leans forward so as not to be overheard. 'He is finished.' The round face pinches into a thoughtful frown. 'Let me explain.' The Captain then outlines an argument for the General's sure and imminent fall: Battle losses have crippled his army for at least six months, a dangerously long time in volatile China; his failure to make a secure alliance has hurt his reputation politically; his attempt to ally himself with General Feng, pro-Russian until recently, has further damaged his name; moreover, it is rumored in Peking that Chiang Kai-shek has singled him out as a treacherous northern warlord who must be eliminated; finally, his refusal to accommodate the Japanese is a direct insult to his superior, Chang Tso-lin.

Embree is surprised by such a clear, pragmatic analysis from someone who most of the time beams at him across a dish-laden dinner table. Embree's next reaction (he will later view it as a measure of romantic fantasy's hold on him) is to believe every word of it.

'I have spoken so frankly,' Fan says, 'because of my deep regard for you.'

'I'm aware of it. I appreciate that,' Embree says, trying for a response of dignity.

Fan smiles in approval. 'Then you understand my concern for your future, as long as it's linked to his.'

'I understand. I am grateful.'

'Your generosity encourages me to be even franker. May I?' When Embree nods consent, the Captain says, 'I don't believe you have considered your position here in China if you're left in the army of a defeated general, a disgraced general, who will have no friends whatsoever, no one to help him or anyone connected with him.'

'Surely an American national –' Embree discards the argument of immunity; it is dishonorable. 'What would happen to a cavalry sergeant under arrest?'

Fan smiles briefly, then shrugs. 'If he was lucky enough to be arrested, he'd go to jail or end up in a Manchurian work gang. Whatever happened, it wouldn't be nice. Most likely, a foreigner wouldn't reach jail or a work gang.'

'I see. He would die in some kind of accident before getting there.'

'Regrettably. I believe when General Tang comes down, the reprisals against his men will be swift, complete, bloody. I'm talking, of course, about his staff, officers, noncoms.'

'You and me.'

'Permit me to ask, dear friend, do you have money?'

'None at all.'

'If you wanted to leave China, how would you pay for travel? Where would you go without money?'

For an instant Embree thinks of the Harbin Mission, of a scarred American with an ax in his belt showing up there for duty. 'I have no idea,' he says.

Fan nods as if pleased by the answer. 'My friend, one thing you need, given the circumstances, is money – a lot of it.'

Embree feels himself drawn to the Captain's reasoning. Fan seems to have access to his deepest secrets and desires. 'Yes, I admit I need money.' Once said, the words come again with the emphasis of sudden, public conviction. 'I really do need money. Definitely.'

'Travel for one is expensive enough, but for –'

'What?' Embree says sharply. 'What is that?' He asks himself if Fan's imprudent enough to mention the lady's name.

Fan recovers hastily. 'But for traveling beyond the borders of China it is very expensive indeed.'

'Yes,' Embree says; he's relieved, for if Captain Fan had mentioned Vera's name, he would have got to his feet and left without another word.

'What I'm trying to say,' Fan continues, 'is you needn't worry.' He leans back in the chair with a smile, looking more like his usual relaxed self. 'Everything can be arranged.'

'Arranged? What can?'

'Everything you need. A friend here in Peking will help you, and believe me, he's a powerful friend.' Fan, leaning forward again, winks as he must have seen foreigners do. 'Chang Tso-lin.'

Embree laughs uncertainly.

'Sure, I mean it. Don't think I am making light of your troubles.' Fan calls the waiter and orders two more drinks. Tourists are coming to the bar, talking in loud voices. His eyes glittering in lamplight, the Captain studies them. Turning back to Embree, he says, 'So that's why our mutual concern is General Tang. Once that matter's taken care of, everything can be arranged.'

'Please say what you mean.'

'What I mean is, General Tang has annoyed Marshal Chang by disloyal, rebellious behavior. He must be punished.'

'You mean, defeated?'

'Punished first. Defeated later. Right now some kind of public humiliation will be enough.'

Not sure of Fan's intent, Embree says nothing.

'If you're thinking the General will be personally harmed, he won't be. It will be public humiliation enough if the meeting between him and General Feng does not take place. Am I clear?'

'You are now.' Embree wets his lips with the Scotch. 'You're saying if I help to wreck that meeting, Marshal Chang will have his revenge. And I'll be paid for it.'

'Then you agree?' Captain Fan holds up his glass expectantly, for a toast.

'No.'

'But my dear friend, why not?'

'I don't know.' But Embree knows. It comes at him like a booming voice at his shoulder – his father's voice at the height of an impassioned sermon: *To betray someone is tantamount to sinning against God.*

'If I may be permitted – you owe General Tang nothing.'

'I just won't do it,' Embree says gloomily; he can't seem to rid himself of the scruple.

'Very well,' Captain Fan says briskly. 'I understand.'

What does he understand? Embree wonders.

'You need time to think about it.'

'I don't need any time. I tell you I won't do it.'

Fan, his glass still in hand, lifts it high again. 'Let's toast anyway. To our friendship.'

They toast, and Embree is somewhat disappointed by Fan's easy acquiescence to the decision – as if he wanted the man to continue trying to convince him.

Leaving the hotel, they walk toward the line of waiting rickshaws and hackneys. Before getting there, the Captain halts. 'One more thing, my friend. Speak to Chang Tso-lin.'

'About what? I said no!'

'Otherwise he will think your decision is my fault – that I persuaded you not to agree.'

'Then I'll talk to him.' The Captain's ensuing smile makes Embree add, 'But my mind's made up. I mean what I say. I can't betray the General.'

'You need only tell Chang Tso-lin exactly that, and we're both clear of the matter.'

'Then arrange for me to see him.'

They agree to meet in front of the French Legation tomorrow at the Hour of the Snake.

'You'll have no trouble with Chia?' asks the Captain.

'No meeting's scheduled for tomorrow. He'll be busy with his family.'

'Then tomorrow you will meet the Manchurian Tiger.'

Embree is waiting in front of the French Legation at the Hour of the Snake. Annamese soldiers wearing blue berets stand guard at the entrance. Behind them in a courtyard someone is practicing bugle calls. Kicking dust in its wake, a blue automobile turns the corner of Chang An Road and speeds down Customs Street. It is a 1925 Lancia Lambda – Embree once saw a full-page ad for one in a New York magazine. The car screeches to a halt in front of him. In the front seat, grinning, sits Captain Fan, and behind the wheel a thin young man with arched eyebrows, wearing a Western suit and a felt hat with an alpine feather stuck jauntily into it. A beautiful Chinese girl, wrapped in fur, looks sullenly at Embree from the back seat.

The introductions are curt, offhand, the way Embree remembers them from America. The driver of the sports car is Chang Hsueh-liang, son of the Manchurian Tiger.

Embree sits in the back with the pouty girl whose name he didn't catch, and the car's large whitewalls spin in dust before getting enough purchase to send the blue chassis at great speed down the quiet street. It becomes a wild ride through Peking, with coolies scattering in front of the big blue open car that honks incessantly. Embree has glimpses of old men staring from dark doorways, shaggy gray mules shaking their heads and making their neck bells rattle, ducks squawking angrily in their cages as the Lancia Lambda weaves in and out of the narrow streets. Behind him, when Embree looks back, swirls or dust rise like miniature whirlwinds. On the outskirts, when traffic thins, Chang Hsueh-liang slows down a little. Often taking his eyes from the road, he talks about automobiles with Captain Fan. The wind carries the conversation past Embree's ears; he hears something about the Type 35 Bugatti with eight cylinders, how it can be fitted with a hood and running boards. The easy familiarity between the two young men convinces Embree that Captain Fan is a long-standing friend of Chang Tso-lin's son – perhaps has been so for a longer time than Fan has served in General Tang's army. Embree glances at the girl, but she keeps her eyes fixed on the road, her mouth small and compressed. After a half-hour Captain Fan turns and hands Embree a silver flask. Embree wonders where he is – China or America? Back in New Haven? Where his classmates used to pile into Tin Lizzies or Essex Sedans and go larking after girls, brandishing their flasks of bootleg whisky.

Embree takes the flask, hesitates to see if the girl will turn and share it, then drinks.

Chang Hsueh-liang looks over his shoulder with a grin. 'Don't worry about her. She's like that. She's angry at me for not buying her a new coat when she's only got about a dozen. She'd better watch out or I'll give her away.' He adds in English, 'Maybe to you, Mister Embree.'

They pick up speed again in the countryside north of Peking. Fan passes the flask around while discussing with young Chang the gambling dens of Tartar City, near the Eastern Peace Market. Embree is shocked by Fan's familiarity with the dissolute life of rich young Chinese in Peking. A grove of crab-apple trees, spiny and harsh, and then a persimmon orchard flash by the car, giving way soon to a vista of bare plains and mountains beyond, blue in the distance like the sea, their shoulders runneled by skeins of new snow. Fan, leaning back, explains to Embree they are heading for

Badaling Fort on the Great Wall.

They drive for another hour, passing horse-drawn carriages filled with tourists wrapped in fur robes. They come at last through the winding dirt roads into sight of the old Ming fort. Embree forgets about the two young men so similar to the Yalie classmates who left him – a minister's son – out of their seductions and drinking bouts. He looks up in awe at the immense stone walls, at the top roadway that's wide enough, he estimates, for five horses abreast to gallop from one battlement to another. The great stone dragon with its gateways and ramps and watchtowers undulates across gorge and mountain for a distance (it's a fact he brought with him from America) equal to that from New York to San Francisco. Seeing the Wall has the effect on Embree of interesting him in the Manchurian Tiger. Until now Chang Tso-lin hasn't supplanted Vera in his thoughts. But staring up at the huge pile of serpentine granite, he turns his attention to the tyrant of Peking, Marshal Chang, in whom flows the blood of the Liao, the Chin, the Tartar, the Mongol, the Manchu, those hard-riding invaders who came in successive waves from the harsh northland and crossed the Great Wall into the fertile plain of China.

Chang Hsueh-liang and the girl have remained in the car. Embree's last sight of them from the steep roadway is of the young man trying to light a cigarette in the steady wind, the girl hunching in her fur coat against the cold. Embree and Fan labor up the roadway, a hard climb that has them both a little short of breath. Approaching a watchtower, they see some officers, wearing Prussian-style shoulder cords, idling at the crenelated wall. Farther along, at the entranceway of the watchtower, stand two soldiers, each wearing the sword of a bodyguard. Fan, leading the way, asks their permission to enter the watchtower. One leaves, comes back, waves the Captain in.

A tiny man is sitting on a wooden stool. He wears a double-breasted greatcoat with a broad fur collar. On his small head, fitting it squarely, is a billed cap with a five-pointed star in the colors of the Republic: red, black, white, blue, and yellow. His mustache is pencil-thin and curls around the edges of his mouth. In his Mongolian eyes there's a dreamy look, belying his reputation for bold action.

Although Captain Fan is in civilian clothes, he salutes and holds it until the little man nods slightly. With a gloved hand Chang Tso-lin signals and the half-dozen men who are there quickly leave the watchtower. Chang's skin is that of a young man, Embree notices, but his gestures make him seem old, brittle.

Fan makes the introduction, Embree bows low. In a soft, almost delicate voice – appropriate to his physique – Chang says, 'Young Fan here is a good friend of my son. Have you met my son?'

'Yes, Excellency.' Embree thinks it's an odd question to begin their interview.

'And?'

'Excellency?'

'Have you seen his car, his women, have you been to his opium dens?'

Confused, uncertain, Embree smiles. Perhaps the old man on the windswept battlements has been thinking about a wayward son.

'He's not what he seems,' Chang asserts in the little voice. 'I let him enjoy his wildness now, so in the future he'll act in a way to make me proud.' Chang sighs, as if remembering his own youth, and slowly rises. He is not five feet tall, Embree decides. 'Have you seen the Wall before? I come here often to think.' He walks to one of the small, square windows. 'There is no place like it on earth,' he murmurs, staring at the snow-flecked barren slopes.

Embree wonders how the old man can enjoy the cold blast of air funneling through the window.

But for the wind there is silence. Embree has the feeling that Chang Tso-lin is capable of remaining silent a long time – hours – for as long as he pleases. Here's a man, Embree thinks, who is in full control of his world, or if not, is quite ready to do what is required to bring it under control. Does that apply also to controlling his son? In the damp and gloomy watchtower, Chang Tso-lin seems to dominate the entire space, standing with his back to them, staring at a landscape as bleak and powerful as himself.

Turning after a long while, he begins talking as if they have been deep in discussion. 'I'm prepared to demonstrate my regard for you, young man, if you're prepared to help me.'

'Excellency,' Embree says.

'I want to know when Tang will arrive in Sian.'

'My regrets, Marshal, but I don't have that information.'

'But you will have it.' Chang sits on the stool again, his knees wide in a posture of authority. 'When you have it, I want it.'

Such raw directness in a Chinese startles Embree. But then he reflects that Chang Tso-lin isn't really Chinese. He's a man whose ancestors may have ridden the Mongol ponies of Jenghiz Khan. He's the cold, shrewd, remorseless fighter that White Wolf – of similar blood – must have been before taking to opium. Frightened by the fixed stare of the little old man, Embree can feel the hair on his arms lift. Unable to think of a reply, he says nothing.

'I admire you,' Chang says with a quick smile. 'Your Chinese is excellent, very unusual. I understand you distinguished yourself in battle. You are now Chinese, in fact.'

'Thank you, Excellency. It's more than I deserve.'

'But if you're really Chinese, you want this country run by the best man. Don't you?'

'Yes, Excellency.'

'That man isn't Tang Shan-teh. The battle of Hengshui ruined him. And his alliance with that bastard Feng – all China would suffer. Apart they'll fall sooner, and the rest of us can go about the work of unifying this land. Do you understand what I'm saying?'

'Yes, Excellency.'

'Tell me when the meeting will take place.' Chang Tso-lin lifts one slim finger like a schoolmarm issuing instructions. 'Do that, you will have what you want.'

'Thank you, Excellency.' Embree is deliberately ambiguous.

This stratagem is obvious to the old man, who smiles and calls for an aide. 'What a pleasure it has been,' he says listlessly, his mind already elsewhere, 'to meet a young foreigner who speaks Chinese so well.' His small eyes fix Embree for an instant. 'Prove now you have common sense – the chief virtue of our people.'

On the return trip the same seating arrangement is followed: the two young Chinese chattering in the front seat; Embree sitting beside the sullen girl in the back.

Fan and Embree get out at the Gate of Heavenly Peace when they reach Peking. Chang Hsueh-liang speeds away, reminding Fan to meet him at a casino that evening.

The Captain suggests a stroll in the Forbidden City.

Why here? Embree wonders as they enter the first courtyard. It is getting toward twilight, and the late sun upon the red walls turns them a strange liquid color, like melted amber. Embree watches these walls detach themselves optically from the long black shadows of the courtyard – as he vows to detach himself from Captain Fan. He won't go along with the scheme. Not because he believes in General Tang, but because he doesn't want to lose his self-respect. Yes, father is still with him – the best of father, Embree thinks, as they stroll along. Coming to the Hall of Supreme Harmony, they pause for a look. Fan explains the significance of a carved marble ramp leading up to the hall. The stylized clouds represent the heavenly nature of the five-clawed dragons who protect the Night-Shining Pearls situated here and there along the enormous ramp.

Why is he telling me all this? Embree wonders.

'The emperor used to carried up this ramp,' Fan continues. 'Believe me, my friend, Chang Tso-lin will be carried up this ramp too.'

'Meaning he will be emperor?'

'I'm sure of it.'

'In the Republic?'

'This is no republic.' Captain Fan is staring at the Hall of Supreme Harmony. 'In fifteen years we've never functioned like a republic.' He turns to Embree and smiles. 'It's not in our blood.' He opens his arms to encompass the buildings and courtyards of the Forbidden City. 'But this is. The Great Within, The Violent Enclosure, here where I've brought you so we could stroll awhile and you could think about this place, *the seat of the Celestial Empire.* That man you met today, he will mount the Dragon Throne and create a new dynasty.' Fan opens his arms even wider. 'It is our way. We can't change.' He drops his arms; and on the round face, so often beaming over food, comes suddenly an expression of such determination that Embree is shocked. 'We won't change. Men like me won't let it change.' And then he smiles. 'Chang Tso-lin is a generous man. Believe me, if you help him in this matter, he'll arrange everything. Your passage out of the country – hers too. And enough for you both to start out elsewhere.'

'It's time to leave.' Embree stares past Captain Fan across the courtyard, watching the twilight draw back from cornice and roof; a strange idea overtakes him: If he doesn't get out of the

Forbidden City before it gets completely dark, he'll be trapped in here forever.

'Did you hear me?' Fan asks anxiously.

Embree swings around, determined to get out of this vast complex of halls and courtyards. 'I've got to leave.'

'Yes. You're wanted at the Peking Hotel.'

Even the Captain's impertinent reference to Vera – this one and the others spoken a moment before – have no effect on Embree. He strides forward, wanting to get free of this place; it is foreign to him, a place where he doesn't belong. It's as if he has awakened from a long dream into a waking nightmare that might hold him forever unless he moves at great speed. Emperors and Dragon Thrones, what are they to someone whose father will be disappointed because Calvin Coolidge won't run for President in 1928? Embree increases his pace, so that Captain Fan, trying to keep abreast, has to break into a little trot.

'You must make your own decision,' Fan says, as they head for the main entrance. 'But if you agree, if you cooperate with the Marshal, you'll never regret it. Leave China. Take her with you!'

Embree glances at him without slowing up.

'Your life is elsewhere, dear friend. Believe me, I say it as a *friend*.'

Embree sees in the last of blue twilight the Gate of Heavenly Peace.

'What's here for you now?' the Captain asks breathlessly. 'Tang's finished. So are you. And what about her?'

Embree glances at him again.

'Without money you can't help her. Think of that.'

Almost at the gate, Embree halts abruptly and puts his hands on his hips. 'I'm not going to do it. But even if I were, I wouldn't even know what you want of me.'

'Information. Just this –'

Embree begins walking again, with Fan at his side.

'Date of meeting,' Fan says as they approach the gate. 'Time of train's arrival. And train number. Will you do it?'

Embree gives him a quick contemptuous smile. 'What kind of a man do you think I am?'

'A brave man, a good friend. Believe me –'

Coming to the gate, Embree sees a squadron of Peking carts lined up.

'Wait!'

Embree turns and stares at the Captain.

'Date. Time. Train. Write the three numbers down. You have that?'

Embree says nothing.

'Give the paper to the houseboy, Kun. They call him Kun in that house. Do you know Kun?'

A powerful young man with fat cheeks, not unlike those of Captain Fan. Embree knows him, but says nothing.

'Give the three numbers to Kun!'

Turning, Embree strides toward the line of Peking carts, leaving Captain Fan breathless in front of the Gate of Heavenly Peace.

Next morning at the negotiators' meeting, Embree scarcely hears a word of their interminable discussion.

He is thinking of last night – dinner with Vera. Later they walked past the polo grounds where (he'd overheard Chang Hsueh-liang tell Captain Fan) a famous British polo team would be playing the French tomorrow. They strolled along Legation Row, past the high forbidding stone walls and iron fences between whose spikes they could see the flagged courts and the fruit trees, now leafless, in lamplight that shot across the granite walls belonging to England, Russia, Holland. Vera stood awhile silently in front of the barred Russian Embassy, then they turned the corner of Canal Street and came to the American Mission. Two armed marines stood stiffly at the gate. Looking at them, Embree began bragging about his country. He swore to take Vera there someday. He meant it, but apparently Vera hadn't been sure, because she laughed. Or maybe she laughed at his helplessness in the face of her own dilemma: a penniless White Russian, adrift in this mad country with its thrones and emperors and treacherous men vying for supremacy. Returning to her hotel, they drank tea until late, sitting through long silences, until the question seemed to hang palpably between them: Would she invite him to her room? Embree had been in a panic of confusion, wanting to speak the right words but not knowing what they were, the words correctly spoken that would put her hand in his, that would move them up the stairway to her room.

And she had been beautiful, tossing her head in a way that made the rich black hair catch the light, the strands of it seeming alive. Once he had been astonished to feel his fingers curved slightly, as if flexing in anticipation of touching that hair. He felt self-hatred and frustration at his inability to move them toward the stairway; and then, finally, Vera rose to her feet. For an instant he had been sure of her reaching out to him; the thought had been there on her face – of this he was absolutely certain – then her lips lost their tension and she gave him a smile that said no. At last they parted, there at the bottom of the stairway, with only the tips of their fingers touching. They said unimportant things of goodbye, and then he said, 'Must you go?'

'Of course, it's very late.'

And he followed her with his eyes up the stairway until she had disappeared from sight.

All the way in a Peking cart to his own quarters, Embree had clenched his fists in a rapture of fury, asking himself why he hadn't said, Let me come with you, I must come upstairs with you, I will come upstairs with you!

At the meeting now he hears something that shifts his attention from last night. Chia and the chief Feng negotiator have just agreed that the final details are complete.

The two generals will hold their conference in the Drum Tower of Sian on the fifteenth of December and for three days thereafter. General Tang will arrive in Sian on train number 30 at eight in the morning. He will proceed by car directly to the Drum Tower. General Feng will be waiting to receive him. Embree remembers that Buddhist and Taoist priests will be there to bless the meeting.

The delegates part with bowing and compliments. Back at Chia's house Embree sits disconsolately in his room, looking at a light snow falling past the window. In the courtyard there's a miniature stone garden where the flakes settle whitely for a moment, then dissolve on the rocks into an iridescent liquid. He has been watching this happen for some time. He has not been thinking of Vera but of people in America. He is stricken with guilt for having failed to write his father, Ursula, a few friends. During the battle of Hengshui there had been a moment when he sat on his horse in wonder at being alive. He had vowed to himself that if he continued to live, he would write them, at least relieve them of the conviction that he was dead. But he hasn't kept the vow. Guilt overwhelms him as he sits alone, watching the snow flutter down upon the rocks.

He will write father first. 'Dear Father,' he writes in his mind, but nothing else comes.

So he begins a conversation with Mary in a speakeasy (it is always the one she took him to in Greenwich Village). 'Mary, I want to come home, but I never will. By my conduct I have made myself an exile forever. What I want to do is take my dearest Vera to Hong Kong, away from this mad country. But to do it I must raise money and to do that I must do something dishonorable.'

He envisions Mary interrupting him impatiently.

'Look, my dear brother, you managed to cut loose from father and you lived with Chinese bandits and made love to a camp girl and joined a Chinese army and killed a man during a foot race and fought in a fierce battle, so what in the hell do you need me for? To confirm what you already know? Namely, that daring's essential to a life worth living? Don't bother me again. I love you. But you no longer need me.' It is exactly what Mary would tell him, Embree decides.

So there in the quiet house (Chia has gone to relatives, and the others are playing Wei Qi in the next room) Philip Embree tells himself this has been his last imaginary conversation with Mary. He feels free; by his own choice he takes a piece of paper and a pen from the desk. Calling out, he waits until a stout, fat-cheeked young man has come to the door.

With a little snort of decision, Embree dips the pen in ink, writes characters on the paper, and hands it to Kun.

In a row down the paper –

Fifteen, eight, thirty: 15 December, 8 o'clock, Train # 30.

26

He has learned more Chinese since coming to Shanghai than he ever did when Li was around to translate and verbally protect him. He is sometimes amazed at how well he gets along with facial expressions, gestures, his elementary Chinese. Now and then, in this cosmopolitan city, he runs across a Chinese who knows a little Russian, and at these times Kovalik gets as much information as possible. For example, he once found a newspaper with a picture of Trotsky staring at him, and the wonder of his hero returned in memory: the beard, the glasses, the amused smile, the alert eyes, all of which Kovalik could recall better than the features of his own father. But there was nothing for him to do until he found someone who could tell him why Trotsky's picture was in a Shanghai newspaper. For two days he lived with soaring expectations. Had Trotsky overthrown Stalin? That was possible on the basis of Stalin's deplorable China policy. Stalin had been wrong to encourage the Chinese Communist Party to cooperate with Chiang Kai-shek. Stalin had been wrong to reject Trotsky's idea of setting up Red soviets in the interior. Stalin had been terribly wrong to stop the Red peasants from taking military action. Stalin had been abysmally wrong to trade off the ideals of international Marxism for the temporary gains of Russian diplomacy.

When Kovalik found a Chinese merchant able to translate the article, he was appalled to learn that Trotsky had been expelled from the Communist Party – Trotsky, true successor to Lenin, had been humiliated beyond plausibility. Kovalik wandered through the noisy Shanghai streets, unable to focus his mind on anything but the defeat: Trotsky's, Russia's, his own.

A few days later Kovalik crosses the Soochow Creek over the Garden Bridge and approaches the Russian Consulate. It is a huge structure which flies the hammer and sickle from a tall pinnacle. He has come often to look at it and to reflect on his duty to report here as a Soviet agent. Now, as at the other times, he understands the emptiness of such a gesture. If he stepped up and presented himself to the Red guards at the door, within a day he would either be under arrest or floating dead in the Whangpoo. Until the fall of Trotsky he has simply been expendable in the scheme of Stalinist politics. Henceforth he is a marked man, no better than a Czarist traitor.

On this particular afternoon, when he stands in the square fronting the consulate, Kovalik sees a great many red flags flying, limousines lining up at the entrance, soldiers at attention on the steps. A band is playing Russian folk music. Milling in the square – held back by Chinese and Sikh policemen from the building itself – are many people in threadbare clothes, angrily shaking their fists at the floral bouquets displayed in the large consulate windows. They are Whites. This is the closest he has been to Czarists since the Civil War, and then they were dead and wounded Czarists, or those captured by Kovalik and his Red comrades. Yet curiosity drives him farther into the crowd.

Suddenly he understands. It is November, on the new calendar. The Russian Consulate is celebrating the anniversary of the October Revolution.

Sidling up to his old enemies, Kovalik listens to them. They are grumbling – all of foreign Shanghai is turning out to drink Red vodka and eat Red bread. Have the British, French, and the others no shame? As the afternoon fades into sunset, electric lights go on in the building; people arriving in limousines soon appear in the high-ceilinged ballroom. From where Kovalik stands among the furious White Russians in their shabby coats, he can see handsome men and lovely women whirl past the windows to the beat of faintly heard waltzes. A few of the Whites, approaching the cordon of Municipal Police, begin to shout taunts and throw rocks, one of which breaks a window. The Chinese and Sikh police, guns drawn, move across the square and soon clear the area.

Hunched deeply in his coat, Kovalik trails after the Whites a little way beyond the Garden Bridge, then breaks contact with them – they are defiantly singing Czarist songs – and ducks into a tiny food stall. Awkwardly he asks in Chinese for a bowl of noodles, but it's some time before he makes himself understood. Glancing at the solemn Chinese faces, recalling the Soviet consulate in its red gaiety, Vladimir Kovalik has never felt so lonely. Those men in the square, whom he would have tried to kill eight years ago on the plains of Siberia, are now closer to him than his own comrades. Like them he's trying to survive in a city known for its heartless way with strangers.

In following days Kovalik becomes so intent on survival that he forgets politics, the loss of everything he holds dear: country, ideals, self-respect. He understands the true nature of his situation. He must hide his connection with the Reds not only from the White Russians but from the Chinese as well. He discovers that Chiang Kai-shek has given orders to the gangs of Shanghai to wipe out any remaining Reds. Dou Yu-seng and his Green Circle Gang are looking for Chinese Bolsheviks, but surely they wouldn't balk at ridding Shanghai of a stray Russian Red. What he needs is work, a job that takes him far from the world of politics. Maybe he can find employment as a bodyguard (surely he's big enough and once again strong enough) for a rich Chinese businessman. Pacing near the banks on the Bund, he notices that the guards riding in the front seats of limousines are all Sikhs, wearing their turbans. He thinks of applying at the Central Station for a policeman's job – there are many foreigners in the Municipal Police. But what language can he use? Not Russian if he carries a German passport. Not German because he doesn't speak the language well enough.

Why can't he be Russian? he asks himself, strolling down the Bund. He is Russian, so why not admit he's Russian? Because Russians in Shanghai are all Czarists. How can he identify with the enemy? Better starve on the waterfront than pretend he is a White.

Kovalik decides to make woodcarvings for a living, if he can. A day of wandering through the jumbled city and asking questions in his primitive Chinese brings him finally to a tin-roofed shed with many kinds of wood for sale. He buys – clearly the merchant is cheating him – a few pieces of seasoned cherry and pear, avoiding the soft pines and cedars. He still has his old clasp knife. Sitting in a noisy lane alongside some ragged food vendors, Kovalik starts to whittle. The work, absorbing him, is heartening and he hums a few songs. Some people gather to watch him carve diagonally across the grain of the wood, giving both control and smoothness to the cuts. Some little boys squat and watch for a long time until a dancing bear emerges from the chunk of cherry. Kovalik works all day, stimulated by the danger of overworking the piece, of taking its life away by giving it too smooth a surface. He turns it critically; the shape is in tune with the rhythms of the grain. With a little of the wax he bought, Kovalik gives the bear a tawny finish and holds it up in the fading light. Curious yellow faces bend, stare, and move away. He eats a bowl of noodles that night, then huddles in a doorway to sleep. He awakens often, hearing people nearby cough in their slumber, rustle and move in their doorways or against wheelbarrows under which they curl. At dawn he sleepily watches them, a streetful of people, rise stiffly and trudge away into the cool morning.

By noon it's almost hot where Kovalik sits cross-legged in the alley, carving a buxom Russian girl with a scarf on her head, carrying a scythe. That day, alternating images, he does three bears and three girls. Exhausted and hungry, he gobbles down two bowlfuls of noodles and sleeps in the same doorway. Nobody quarrels over his right to it, although he watches two young men squabble in the opposite doorway, the stronger taking it and the weaker crawling off to use a mud wall for his pillow. Next morning, when Kovalik is finishing another bear, someone speaks to him in Russian. Startled, he looks up into the grinning face of a thin, elderly Chinese.

'I thought you were Russian,' the man says approvingly. 'Are you carving those to sell?'

'Yes. Is there somewhere I can take them?'

The man nods thoughtfully and points down the lane. 'They sell carvings on a street not far from here. But you won't sell these.'

'Why?' Kovalik glances at the carvings, which he has laid out in a row near his left knee. 'Aren't they good enough?'

'I wouldn't know about that,' the man says with a shrug. 'But it's what they are that won't sell. You've got dancing bears and farm girls in scarves. That's Russian. How will you sell them in Shanghai?' The man grins in self-acknowledgment of his sound logic.

Sheepishly Kovalik pulls his ear and folds his knife. He had carved Chinese subjects in the past, but that had been when he felt his future was here, these people were his – before Mao proved otherwise. 'I used all that wood for nothing,' he mutters, staring at the line of carvings.

'Don't worry. You can do more.' The elderly man is squatting beside him out of the stream of traffic in the busy lane: the carts, the barrows, the coolies.

'Where did you learn Russian?' Kovalik asks curiously.

'Irkutsk.'

That explains it. For decades the Chinese had settled around Irkutsk in Siberia. The Russians, fearful of their commerical skill and their thrift, had frequently persecuted them. This fellow had probably come to China after a time of such abuse.

'What you must carve is something very Chinese,' the man explains in a friendly voice. He has large glittering eyes, a stubble of sparse gray beard, a deep cough. 'Carve a dragon. He's king of animals and bringer of good harvests. Farmers coming to town will buy him. Put a pear in his mouth – that's the sun. You could make the tiger too. He's power. And a turtle – he's wisdom. And a crane – he's long life. You might sell Buddhas too. You could surely sell Buddhas.' The man grimaces and coughs. 'But no dancing bears, no Russian girls in babushkas.'

'I thank you,' Kovalik says with a smile.

'My name's Ku. I just got over being sick. I bet you can tell that, right? Up in the cold around Irkutsk I never got sick. Here I'm always sick. For the last five years, since I came back here, I've been sick.'

Irkutsk was already Red five years ago. Communism hadn't made the people of Siberia more tolerant of the thrifty Chinese. Studying the pale, thin face, Kovalik realizes suddenly that the man is asking for food. He isn't a beggar, but in a way he's been asking for something to eat. 'I'm having a bowl of noddles,' Kovalik tells him. 'Will you join me?'

The man strokes his chin whiskers, as if considering a difficult problem. 'I'm not busy right now. Actually, I'm waiting for my daughter. Yes, I'll join you.'

In a crowded steamy noodle shop the old man wolfs down his bowl before Kovalik is half done. The man belches, coughs, rubs his scrawny gut contentedly. 'Russia,' he says. 'I miss it.'

'Did they throw you out?'

'Yes. But I miss it. Do you know Lake Baikal?'

'Not well.'

'Let me tell you about it. I lived there for twenty-three years.' Waving his hands about, he describes for Kovalik what the Russian has also seen – the *nerpy*, a fresh-water seal noted for its silver-gray color – and has never seen – the *golomyanka*, a translucent fish so fat that when taken from the lake it melts right in the hand, leaving nothing but skin. Ku smacks his lips while praising the excellent taste of lake strugeon, whitefish, carp, grayling, and fresh-water shrimp found in the blue mud. It occurs to Kovalik that old Ku speaks of food like someone who's never sure of getting it.

'Where do you sleep?' Ku asks when they leave the shop.

'On the street.'

Laughing, Ku says, 'I'm not proud either.' He insists that Kovalik meet his daughter. They wait outside a silk filature until, at the blowing of a loud whistle, a stream of little girls begins to pour out of the low gray building. They drag like old women across the dirty courtyard.

'Here she comes,' chuckles Ku. 'Here's my Hsien-e.'

A very thin little girl is coming toward them. She has braided hair, a long, exhausted face of a strange color – almost blue – and eyes like her father's, bright, glittering. When Kovalik is introduced to her as a 'Russian merchant,' the girl stares at him wordlessly.

It is twilight, the time when Kovalik should go to his doorway and establish dominion over it, so he tells father and daughter that he's going back to his street.

'So are we,' Ku declares gaily. 'We live in the next one. That's how I knew about you. Someone said a big foreign gentleman was there making things, so I came for a look.'

At Ku's insistence, Kovalik goes with them. They live in the back of a tobacco shop – in a shed, actually, strewn with old straw. 'I'll talk to the owner,' Ku whispers. 'I can get you in here.' It costs a few *cash* a night, virtually nothing, but as Ku explains solemnly, it is better to stay off the streets at any cost; thieves and bullies are everywhere. Kovalik isn't afraid, yet in the shed it's warmer – at least a dozen bodies packed in there – so he allows Ku to arrange matters with the tobacco-shop owner who rents the shed. Soon Kovalik and his two companions are stretched out in the straw, looking at the black roof. Someone nearby is giggling; Kovalik wonders if a couple are having sex. Nothing stops that, yet for himself it has been a long time. Hunger is worse, though. His daily bowl of noodles simply takes an edge off the incessant yearning for a full stomach. He can go on this way, he can live, but the keen desire for more food won't let him enjoy living.

'She hasn't eaten,' he says abruptly. Glancing at Ku's daughter, he's surprised to see that she is already asleep.

'They feed them rice gruel at the silk factory. That's most of her pay, you see. Don't worry about her.'

Kovalik stares in the dim light at the haggard girl. He notices that the glands in her neck are swollen.

Next day he buys more wood, although he has little money left. Compelled by necessity he works hard, carving a tortoise and a crane. Later, when Ku comes along, the old man whistles approvingly. 'That will sell,' he declares.

After their bowls of noddles – Kovalik pays – they go to meet Hsien-e at the silk factory. The girls come out of the gray building from whose double chimneys pour immense clouds of steam. Some of the girls, smaller than Hsien-e, manage a smile of relief, but none walk with sprightliness. Hsien-e greets her father with a weary nod, coughs, then bends over to spit.

Kovalik stares at the thick green sputum streaked with blood.

That night, next to him in the straw, Hsien-e has a coughing fit, yet never comes fully out of her sleep of exhaustion. Putting his hand on her forehead, Kovalik finds it hot, drenched with a cold sweat.

'She's sick,' he tells Ku.

'Yes, I know. Don't worry.' He adds after a while, 'She'll get better when she leaves the factory.'

Others in the shed are snoring and snuffling. 'Tell me about that factory,' Kovalik whispers.

Ku does. He imparts information in a monotone, as if describing items in a shop. Hsien-e works twelve hours a day in the spinning room. All the children do, because their agile hands are suited for such work. Women sit opposite them on benches, facing the children, who stand and whose nimble fingers soften and unravel the silk cocoons in basins of nearly boiling water. Once their small fingers find the end of the thread, they hand the cocoons to the women across the hot basins, and the women twist six threads together, then pass them onto a reel worked by their feet. Each child serves two women. 'It's hard work,' Ku says thoughtfully. 'No windows open, you see, because it's the steam that softens the cocoons. And then the overseers can be nasty. They slap the children for flagging. They use clubs on the women. But it's not all bad. When there's an opening in the packing room, the factory owner says I can have the job. So daughter and I will soon be working together,' he says with a triumphant chuckle.

Kovalik says nothing. After his father died, his mother had gone to work in a train-track factory. When he was old enough, he worked there too. He spent his youth in that cold grimy building, finding a film of black soot on his daily bread, even as Hsien-e must find spindle dust on her rice gruel. He worked hard at his job too. They made fishplates, iron spikes, and flat-bottomed rails thirty meters long. His mother had been an inspector. Every day she came through the shop to measure the rails. She always winked at him. One morning she never got out of bed to go to work. She was cold when he tried to rouse her.

'Your daughter's too young for work like that,' Kovalik declares suddenly.

'She's not too young. Plenty are younger. They're seven, eight, nine.'

'Isn't Hsien-e that young?' Kovalik asks in surprise.

'Hsien-e?' Ku laughs faintly and turns toward the Russian, crackling the straw. 'She's thirteen.'

'Thirteen,' Kovalik repeats in wonder.

Ku turns away. 'What did you think?' he demands irritably. 'That she's my granddaughter? How old do you think I am anyway?'

Kovalik thinks sixty. 'I don't know,' he says. 'Fifty?'

'Thirty-seven. Not a year more. And we Chinese are a year old when we're born.' Ku gathers a handful of straw to his thin chest and closes his eyes.

Next day, in Ku's company, Kovalik goes to the street where carvings are sold, but to their mutual dismay, none of the merchants accept the work, although they all admire the carvings. They have their own suppliers: a group of old men, living in a few huts behind this street, who have been carving lohans and mythic creatures since childhood, until their hands are gnarled enough to have come from the wood they carve.

'Let's go,' Kovalik says and shuffles away. He and Ku walk for a long time through the teeming streets, pausing only for the thin little Chinese to catch his breath. 'Where are we going?' he pants, but Kovalik puts his head down and strides forward, looking neither to the left at the austere rank of Western banks on the Bund nor to the right at the raucous waterfront on the Whangpoo.

'Where are we going?' Ku asks breathlessly.

'I'm going on alone. We'll part here,' Kovalik says. 'You've been a friend.'

Ku begins coughing, and he coughs until he spits up green mucus like his daughter. There's no blood yet, though.

Kovalik takes his arm and guides him forward. 'You can come with me – until I have to leave.'

They cross the Garden Bridge. Below them Soochow Creek is greenish too, streaked with garbage. They halt at the square facing the Soviet Consulate.

'This is where I go on alone,' Kovalik explains and to himself says, I will do it, I will give myself up. He starts across the cobblestone with Ku trailing behind him.

Halfway across the square, Kovalik halts and stares at the consulate door – X'd by huge planks; and at the windows – boarded up.

Turning, he looks at Ku. 'What's happened here?'

'I don't know, friend, but let me find out.' Anxious to please, Ku leads the way into a nearby food market. For the next hour he questions vendors and passersby. Kovalik waits beside a fruit cart from which a farmer is selling carb apples.

At last Ku joins him and explains that the Soviet Consulate has been closed by order of Chiang Kai-shek. 'I don't understand all of it. Nobody seems to. But they took Canton last week.'

'Who took it?'

'The Bolsheviks. Then the Nationalists came in and retook the city and murdered the Reds.' Ku frowns, as if for Kovalik's benefit. 'They killed people in the Soviet Consulate there too.'

'Russians?' Kovalik asks in disbelief.

'No, I think they were Chinese working there. But they sent the Russians away – out of the country. And now Chiang Kai-shek has broken off with Moscow. He's closed the consulate here. Is there still one in Peking?'

Kovalik shakes his head. 'Chang Tso-lin took care of that months ago. How does Chiang Kai-shek get into this?'

'Everyone I talked to says he's the government.'

'Officially?'

Ku shrugs. 'That doesn't matter.'

'I guess it doesn't.'

Kovalik walks over to a fence alongside Soochow Creek. He looks down disconsolately at the sampans, junks. He was going to surrender himself to Soviet justice – anything to get out of here – but now there's no Soviet justice anywhere in China. In the distance he hears gongs and firecrackers; on the river some boatmen are screaming at one another, for the joy of it, apparently. How noisy these people are, he thinks. Glancing at his sick companion, Kovalik is deeply depressed. The year 1927 began with the *sovetniki*, under Borodin's leadership, in full control of a large part of China; they harbored a dream of bringing this huge, unwieldly land into the Marxist fold. Now the year 1927 is ending with the Soviet government ousted from China. It is finished, the international dream. And he, an agent of that government, must waste his days whittling pieces of wood into Chinese images for sale to merchants who won't buy them.

Yet he continues to carve. Instead of trying to sell them to Chinese shopkeepers, he ties the carvings in an old rag and peddles them in front of the fashionable hotels where tourists stay. To sell one for a pittance he endures the humiliation of being chased by a Sikh policeman, doubtless paid by the hotel to keep the entrance clear of hawkers and beggars. Still, a sale means Kovalik and his friend will eat tonight. He hurries back to the shed with the cheerful anticipation of bringing good news that has resulted from hard work. Entering it, Kovalik is surprised to find not only Ku but the girl as well. Hsien-e is lying in the straw, her father beside her.

'Sick,' Ku mutters.

Kovalik can see that. The girl's literally fighting for breath, her thin breastless chest moving like a bellows gone wild. Her forehead is extremely hot when he touches it. Her eyes have lost their glitter and stare dully, half shut, red from the exertion of coughing. The blue tinge of her skin has deepened; flecks of blood speckle her chin.

Ku explains that she came home from the factory without the daily meal, and without her money, although this is payday. 'But don't worry,' he says with a tight smile. 'She's a strong girl. That's from living in Russia.'

Kovalik buys soup for the girl and watches Ku try to feed her. After a few sips Hsien-e begins to cough; the fit ends with her spitting up more sputum with large bright gouts of coagulated blood.

'We must get her fever down.' Kovalik goes for a pan of water; use of the pan costs him a few *cash* at a nearby food shop. 'You sonofabitch,' he says in Russian to the grinning vendor.

That night, taking turns, Kovalik and Ku apply moistened cloth to the girl's burning head, body.

Next day, returning to the hotels, Kovalik has no luck and this time is run off by a pistol-waving Sikh who is nearly as tall as himself. 'You bastard! You sonofabitch!' Kovalik shouts at him in Russian, but the dark man in the turban merely levels the gun at him, ready to shoot.

In the shed that evening, Kovalik kneels beside the girl and says, 'She looks worse.'

'Don't worry,' Ku says. 'Hsien-e is very strong.'

Studying the girl, Kovalik shakes his head decisively. 'It's his fault. It's Chiang Kai-shek's fault.'

'Don't say it,' Ku urges, looking around, although no one else is in the shed yet. 'Don't say it even in Russian. He's in command now. His agents are everywhere.'

'It's his fault! The ally of imperialistic bandits!' Kovalik has on his tongue the jargon learned in Moscow at foreign service school. It's the fault of that imperialist puppet,' he mutters angrily.

'Don't say another word. They'll come here. They know everything.'

Kovalik has seen them in the streets today: special police in black gowns, getting out of vans with their pistols, truncheons, and whistles. Injustice, he thinks. It is all appallingly unjust. During the Northern Expedition, when Chiang Kai-shek was losing the battle for Nanchang, Red Chinese units, sent by order of Borodin, came to his rescue. And when Chiang Kai-shek took Shanghai, he didn't actually take it; it was handed over to him by revolutionary workers who were then hunted down in the streets, shot and garroted, their heads nailed to telegraph poles. Unfair, unjust. And now, in the long complicated chain of events that stretch from leaders to people, Chiang Kai-shek is responsible for the lousy way this girl is going to die. She is coughing again. Turning to one side, with a weak groan of terror as much as pain, Hsien-e vomits a quantity of blood into the straw. Although Kovalik has seen many people die, this is almost too much for him to bear. How can she lose so much blood and still live? he wonders in horror, as he bends her over so she won't strangle.

Later, while the girl sleeps a little, Ku touches his arm shyly. 'I thank you.' Then he adds, 'But you mustn't worry. This is a strong girl. She'll be all right.'

'Are you religious?'

'As much as any man,' Ku declares proudly.

'Keep your voices down,' someone calls out angrily from the other side of the shed.

Ku whispers, 'I've burned incense in many temples.'

'Do you believe God will take care of your daughter?'

After a pause Ku replies, 'Well, I do. I really do. Yes. Why not? Anyway, the gods can't be angry with her. She hasn't done anything.' After a long silence, during which someone begins to snore, Ku says, 'I will go back to work tomorrow.'

Kovalik is surprised that the scrawny fellow has ever worked Ku has given the impression that living off his daughter is his work. Kovalik has liked him in spite of it.

'What kind of work do you do?'

'I'm a rickshaw puller.'

Kovalik finds it hard to believe – Ku out there trotting along at six miles an hour twelve or fourteen hours a day? Kovalik ha never watched pullers without marveling at their strength and endurance.

'I'll go back tomorrow. Only I haven't the coppers to rent rickshaw. I used to work for a good contractor. There were thre

642

of us using this rickshaw in shifts, day and night. Then I had some trouble. A policeman stopped me and took the cushion seat out and unscrewed the license plate. He would give them back when I gave him money – it's not that unusual – but I didn't have as much as he wanted. When I returned to the depot, the contractor got angry and had some men beat me.' Ku chuckles mirthlessly. 'Truth is, I got scared by that beating and so I didn't go back and then the cough got worse and she was doing all right at the factory and so – and so, you see . . .' After a long pause he says, his voice loud enough to unsettle a few sleepers, 'I am going back there tomorrow and ask for a rickshaw!'

But toward dawn his daughter gets worse, and her racking cough awakens everyone in the shed. Their grumbling ceases when Kovalik turns and glares at them. He doesn't leave today with his ragful of carvings, but remains in the shed with Ku, who doesn't mention the rickshaw again. Toward noon the girl begins gasping for breath, whimpering, 'It hurts, it hurts,' in little gusts that come more quickly but with less strength as the minutes pass.

'What's going on here!'

Kovalik, turning, looks up at the angry face of the tobacconist who rents the shed.

'People are complaining she spits blood all over the place. It ruins the straw. She coughs so much they can't sleep. Get her out of here.'

'What's he saying?' Kovalik asks his friend.

In a low, breaking voice Ku explains.

Kovalik gets to his feet. 'Tell him sorry, but we can't move the girl. She's very sick.'

Ku tells the shopkeeper, who begins waving his arms angrily and telling them all to get out.

'I don't need a translation of that,' Kovalik says. Smiling at the tobacconist, he says in Russian, 'You are a sweet sonofabitch, aren't you.'

'Where can we take her? What are we going to do?' Ku is dabbing a moistened rag at the girl's brow.

'We're not taking her anywhere,' Kovalik maintains quietly. 'Tell him.'

'I'd better not.'

'Tell him.'

While Ku translates, the Russian moves slowly toward the tobacconist.

'Have you told him?' Kovalik asks.

'Yes.'

'What did he say? He just said something.'

'He said we don't have to leave now. We can wait until the police come.'

'Tell him I'll pay if he lets us stay here. I'll pay him double what he asks for a night in the damn shed.'

'But you don't have any money.'

'Tell him.'

After their exchange, Kovalik says, 'Does he accept?'

'No.' Ku hesitates. 'He says it's not a matter of money. He doesn't want her dying here, it's bad for the shop. People notice such things and won't buy tobacco from him.' Again the little rickshaw puller hesitates.

'Come on. What else did he say?'

'He said we have to pay for the straw.'

'Pay for it?' ·

'He said –' Ku grimaces from the effort of getting the words out. 'Don't worry, all right? He said she ruined straw that was good for another week. Now he'll have to change it and it's our fault. We owe him for the straw.'

Kovalik has been studying the tobacconist during this explanation. The man wears a plain blue gown, a little skullcap, a padded vest. He has a small wart on his chin, a few smallpox scars on one cheek. Altogether he's not unpleasant-looking, but his mouth, set righteously, is a signal he won't yield.

It is unfair, unjust; it is imperialist oppression, Kovalik thinks. It is Chiang Kai-shek's fault. Well, it's more than his fault, it's the fault of the world. This girl should be left to die in peace. This is what the Revolution had been for; this is what countless men, some of them his own comrades, had suffered and died for – the right to live in dignity, the right as well to die in dignity. Hsien-e has the right to die in dignity, even in the straw-filled shed of a Shanghai hutung. In a wrenching moment of perception, it occurs to Kovalik that no revolution ever stemmed the tide of human evil. No amount of sacrifice ever prevented girls like Hsien-e from dying shabbily.

Utterly absorbed in these strange and terrible thoughts, moved by her dying and the injustice of its manner, Kovalik doesn't respond for a long time to the tobacconist, who has begun to pace and gesture furiously and yell. Kovalik has knelt again beside the girl, but finally turns to watch the tobacconist kick at Ku with a sandaled foot. The kicks are ineffectual, feeble enough, but Ku has covered his head to receive a bad beating. Kovalik rises. The tobacconist is sputtering out words so rapidly that the spit flies through the stale cool air. Kovalik in a few steps is at the shopkeeper's side. The man is too intent on kicking the curled-up Ku to notice. Kovalik takes him by the throat with both hands. The tactile reality of his action galvanizes Kovalik. It's as if everything that has happened to him in China is flowing through his body to his hands – the pent-up anger and frustration is streaming into each finger of his huge hands, enabling them to grip with tremendous force the neck of the tobacconist, who struggles briefly, then goes limp. A swollen tongue extrudes from his mouth.

Kovalik, letting him fall, backs away.

There's a scream from the entrance to the shed. Hearing a commotion, the tobacconist's wife has come from the store. Standing in the doorway, she continues screaming, then turns and rushes back into the store, where she can be heard yelling for help.

'Run,' Ku mutters, uncurling himself, looking up at Kovalik. 'Get out of here! Run!'

Kovalik doesn't want to run. Why should he? The man deserved what he got. Justice has finally been done.

'Run or they'll kill you!' Ku cocks his head, listening. 'I hear them shouting about you from the next street. "A foreign devil!" '

So Kovalik runs, he runs for his life.

Now he is deperate for money. Recalling that Ku once told him a 'little Russia' is developing along Avenue Joffre in Frenchtown, Kovalik drifts that way, although aware that any countrymen he finds there will be the Czarist enemy.

For a whole day he hunkers down in a lane and watches what goes on. He overhears Russians, lounging around, discuss ways of living in Shanghai. Standing near the doorways of bars he listens to them say there are Russian girls on the waterfront – the men claim to be disgraced by their female compatriots and yet giggle while they discuss it – who lift their skirts for coolies in dock-front sheds and receive for their ten minutes' work what it took the stupid Chinese stevedores a whole day to earn. He hears of the little street of Chao Pao San and goes there. He sees electric signs like stiff vertical banners above the narrow thoroughfare. Drunken foreign sailors are trailed by child beggars. Chinese hawkers are fighting over their possession of street corners. Music streams from dance halls where girls of all nations grip their dance tickets. He learns the names of the expensive 'knocking shops': the Victoria, the Holiday, and some with Russian names – the Stenka Rasin, the Tkatshenko, the Tchorine Glasa. He locates the Turkish baths, the brothels, the sleazy hotels. And everywhere he hears the enemy talking their hateful White politics: the Legitimists, the anti-Cyrillian monarchists, the Mensheviks, the Socialists, the Cossack Fascists. On Joffre Avenue his third day there (he has managed to sell a dancing bear to a White Guard in the Volunteer Corps of the Shanghai Municipal Council), he watches a regiment of white mercenaries march smartly along. They wear Czarist Lifeguard Lancer uniforms with blue jackets and gray trousers and they are shouting in military unison: '*Doloj Bolshevikov! Doloj Bolshevikov!*'

'Down with the Bolsheviks!' People on the sidewalk clap their hands and whistle shrilly in approval. Watching this scene, Kovalik is unaware of how deeply he scowls until his eyes meet those of another man. He smiles, the man smiles tentatively too and moves away.

Later Kovalik scoops up a discarded newspaper – it's in Russian – and reads fervently. But there's little in it except advertisements:

Come for Turkish Bath and Russian Massage – Merry House!

Venereal Diseases and Maladies of all Kinds cured by Doctor A. Glebov, Surgeon-General in the Imperial Army.

Dance partners wanted for new cabaret. Must have good figure. Bring own evening dress.

When his money runs out, Kovalik tries for two more days to sell another carving, but fails. He'll be too weak for any work if he doesn't get something soon. Going to a Chinese barber, he gets a shave and a haircut and a splash of perfume on his face for the last few coppers in his pocket. Then he goes searching for anything. Back in the Joffre Avenue neighborhood, he notices a sign in Russian – *The Sweetest, Cleanest Girls in Town* – and apparently in English and French as well. Pinned on the door is a piece of paper: *Doorman, Apply Within. No Chinese.* In the three languages.

It is midafternoon and the street is drowsy, almost bereft of the usual blare of China. Inside the cabaret he blinks rapidly, getting used to the darkness. He smells alcohol, smoke, the pungent odor of disinfectant. Small tables are crowded together in front of a tiny dance floor with an orchestra dais against one wall. Naked bulbs, now unlit, hang on cords around the room like a string of Christmas lights. Near the bandstand someone is sitting – Kovalik can see the glow of a cigar.

'What do you want?' a voice booms in Russian.

'That notice for a doorman –'

'Come here.'

Kovalik steps forward. A fat, bearded man is at a table, cigar in hand, a bottle in front of him, and a full glass.

'Well, you're big enough,' the man observes. 'Can you fight?'

'I can fight.'

'What were you, army?'

Kovalik doesn't answer – can't get out either yes or no.

But the man follows his own train of thought. 'We got a Filipino band here. Who doesn't, I guess. They're good, but stay clear of those boys. They're crazy with knives. We got rooms upstairs for the girls. Eight rooms. A dozen girls, maybe fourteen, depending. So a lot of times they stand in line with their customers, right?' He chuckles briefly, then puffs the cigar. 'You won't fuck our girls.'

'No.'

'Do you drink?'

'Not much.'

'If I catch you drunk, you go. Not the second time, but the first time. Turn around.' He studies Kovalik's broad shoulders, long arms. 'You're a real big one, all right. Infantry?'

'No, cavalry.'

The man smiles his approval. 'But you're no Cossack.'

'No.'

'You'll wear a Cossack uniform, though. I never did think the Cossacks are as good as they claim. Know what most of them are? Cocksuckers. Who did you fight with?'

It's a question he can evade no longer. He must lie, he must call himself a White, he must falsify his entire life. 'With Koltchak.'

'What? Speak up? You're mumbling.'

'I said with Koltchak.' He had fought six months against the troops of General Koltchak, pushing them slowly across the frozen wastes of Siberia until they dwindled from a great river to a trickle – a few thousand survivors staggering through the forest into Manchuria, into China, into Shanghai.

The man shoves the bottle forward. 'Here, have a drink.'

Kovalik steps forward and takes the bottle.

'Use my glass. It's all right.'

Kovalik pours and drinks. It is bitter, biting, and he sputters.

'Well, you told the truth – you're no drunkard,' the man says. 'That's Chinese vodka.'

'It's not ours.'

The man takes the glass and pours one for himself. He turns the glass in the dim light – someone has just turned on a light in a back room with the door ajar. The light catches the man's lower jaw, heavy lips, full nose. 'I had a friend who was with Koltchak. He was in the Irkutsk prison when the Reds brought Koltchak in. Through the bars of his cell he saw Koltchak executed. The firing squad got Koltchak out there, but when their commander gave the order to shoot, they wouldn't do it. It was because of Koltchak, my friend says. He says Koltchak was too powerful, he scared the shit out of those Reds. They might have stood there all day, but Koltchak raised his own arm and gave the order – fire!' The man shakes his head, as if by telling this story he can recall something seen by himself. 'That same day, my friend says, Pepeliev was shot too, only he died a coward.'

Kovalik nods without comment. Nothing more than a soldier's tale. He once knew a Red infantryman who bragged of selling Koltchak's cigarette case, handed to him by the general before the execution. Kovalik hadn't believed that either.

'Well,' the man says after drinking the vodka, 'we'll give you a try. All you got to learn in half a dozen languages are the words for taxi, rickshaw, welcome, sir. You keep the tips.' He laughs. 'You better because I sure don't pay you.'

'You don't?'

'Do you think I'm St. Nicholas? I supply the uniform, you supply the charm, big fellow. Charm gets you the tips. Come back this evening.'

Kovalik thanks the man and turns to leave.

'One more thing,' the man says. 'Don't run off with the uniform.'

'No.'

'I'm telling you.'

'If I did, which I won't, would you break my legs?' Kovalik can't help asking with a smile.

648

The man smiles back 'That's unnecessary. The only place in Shanghai someone like you can get a job that'll keep you alive is in the Volunteer Corps or around Joffre Avenue. You take my uniform, you won't get into the Corps because I know people there. And you won't get work in this neighborhood either. Know what that leaves you? The docks. Competing with coolies who can work a big Russian fellow like you into the ground and still have energy for a mahjong game. Or you can beg. Now that's a prospect. Have you seen them begging in Shanghai? You'd be better off if I did have your legs broken. At least it'd be quicker.'

'Do you own this place?'

'No.' The man pours another vodka. 'A Chinese sonofabitch does. I just run it for him. You think you have a problem? Try having a Chinese for your boss.'

That evening Kovalik stands at the cabaret entrance in the regimental uniform of a Lifeguard Cossack. He wears high leather boots, blue trousers, a red demikaftan, a red *chekmen*, gold *praportchik* shoulder straps, a broad swordbelt, a curved saber, a *kolpak* of black lambskin. On his sleeve is the blue coat of arms of General Kornilov. One of his own officers once called Kornilov 'a man with a lion's heart and the brains of a sheep.' Kovalik remembers him as a butcher of captured Reds.

So Kovalik is wearing a uniform of the Tekintsi, the personal bodyguards of a Czarist general – in this case a vicious, deeply hated general. He takes off the *kolpak* and stares at the lambskin. He can take this furhat and throw it as far as possible and walk away. He can do it.

Coming to the doorway, the cabaret manager appraises Kovalik's tall figure. 'You look good. Don't look so fucking sad. Because you're a doorman?' The manager shifts a cigar in his mouth. 'Who are you to be so proud? I got waiters in here serving beer and lemonade who wear the St. George Cross.'

Each night, from dusk almost to dawn, Valdimir Kovalik helps patrons from rickshaws, opens the door, hails cabs. At his back, inside the cabaret, the Filipino band plays American jazz with the zest and freedom of musicians who have heard it only on scratchy Victrola records. When the band is resting, Kovalik hears from nearby houses the clatter of mahjong tiles, the click of abacus beads, and from across the street, where cheaply bejeweled taxi dancers sweat off their mascara trying to earn dance tickets, sometimes a badly played fox-trot or tango. Chinese gentlemen often pull up in cars and wait, staring at Kovalik while taking their snuff (a habit most fashionable in Shanghai), until their chauffeurs return with a girl – usually European or maybe a Burmese, but never one of the three Chinese girls who work for the cabaret. From the rooms upstairs Kovalik sometimes hears the groans and cries of ecstasy, but comforts himself in the knowledge that the girls usually fake it. They have told him. At dawn he goes down the street for noodles. He passes Lungku Street, where each store sells dragon bones (actually fossils) which have been dug up in Honan gullies. After his breakfast, Kovalik returns to the cabaret and sits inside at a table. One by one the girls' customers shuffle down the stairway. It becomes quiet, a time of rare silence. when sunlight has crept into the hallway, illuminating the dirty tablecloths filled with glasses and ashtrays, Kovalik rises. Usually he greets the old cleaning women who come in about this time with their pails- and bamboo brooms. Trudging upstairs, Kovalik knocks at each door, asking girls if they want anything from a nearby restaurant. For this service he gets a few extra coppers. In this way he comes to know each girl, and he yearns to talk, at least to the Russians – about half are his compatriots – but usually he restricts himself to the same dull questions: What will you have? Is there anything else?

When he brings them their orders, Kovalik glances at their sleepy faces and their soft bodies, often not covered by the rumpled sheets, and he covets them. Sometimes he thinks of buying them with his own money in plain disregard of the rule. But even if they cared nothing for the rule, they wouldn't let him. He's only a lowly servant to them, whereas even the fattest Italin businessman or the meanest American drunk is an official customer. Kovalik also knows that even if a girl made an overture, he'd refuse her. He knows he would. It would frighten him to have one of these girls smile invitingly and pat the bed and tell him she has noticed him in his fine uniform. Because what, after all, does he know about women? His adult life has been sacrificed to the Revolution. He has had slim opportunity to know women, really know them. All he knows is a swift encounter in a dark alley or behind a bush on the march or simply his turn in a long line (he'd done that once near Kazan when his unit had come upon three Moscovite whores out to make money on the Civil War). But sitting down on the bed and talking to a girl awhile? And afterward having to see her again, greet her, find something to say? Kovalik tells himself he knows less about these girls and their dreams and their pain than even the Czarist bitch in Qufu could know.

One night when Kovalik is on duty, richshaw pulls up and a tall blond gentleman gets out. Smiling, he says, 'Are you Russian?' in a heavy accent.

'Yes, sir. Welcome, sir. Please step inside.'

'No, I've been inside. Cigarette?' The man pulls out a silver case and offers it to Kovalik.

'Thank you, sir, but no, sir. I can't smoke on duty.' From the man's accent Kovalik guesses he is German. Kovalik had met many of them during the Civil War – cringing, beaten fellows who had been dragged the length of Russia by their White captors. He remembers them. Given their freedom by the Reds, who had no interest in the Great War in Europe, many of the Germans just sat there, too weary to go farther. Without their prison guards to feed them, they starved to death like neglected children. But this tall blond has a strong, alert look.

'I know this place well,' the man says. 'They are nice girls, but I'm too familiar with them. You understand?'

Kovalik nods.

The man takes out a rather large bill. 'I suppose you know the street.'

'Yes, sir. I'm out here every night.'

'When you hear of a new girl on the street, let me know.' The German writes his address on a piece of paper. Kovalik takes the proffered money. 'I can't spend my time going all over Shanghai,' the man explains. 'So you can help me. I especially like Russian girls.'

'Yes, sir.'

The German lights a cigarette and puffs on it hard. 'I had a Russian girl, but I had to throw her out.'

'Sorry, sir.'

'Well, your countrywomen aren't all like her. Remember, there's something in it for you if you let me know.'

Kovalik watches the tall German move down the street into the crowd.

Two nights later a new girl comes to the cabaret. After a long talk with the manager, she takes her place at the bar with the other girls. The manager, going to the entrance, beckons to Kovalik with a crooked finger. 'See that girl there? She's Russian. She's going to be here now.'

The next morning, as usual, Kovalik climbs the stairs and knocks at each door. Getting to the new girl's room, he hesitates, then knocks.

'Who is it?' calls a sleepy voice.

'The doorman. I collect orders for breakfast.'

'Then come in.'

Opening the door, Kovalik sees her lying naked on the bed, a sheet half flung over it. Her large breasts with dark aureoles wobble slightly when, shifting weight, she looks at him from the pillow. 'What can you get?'

'Vendors around here have good chicken wings.'

'I'll take half a dozen. And a sweet cake. Almond.' The blonde moves forward, as if ready to get off the bed. Her heavy breasts swing. 'Do you want the money now?'

He always takes the money before buying anything, but today, with this girl, Kovalik says to pay when he returns.

'All right.' The girl gives him a faint smile.

He looks away quickly, aware that he has been staring at her breasts and the light patch of hair at her crotch.

On the street he heads for the distinctive sound of food vendors in the distance – the tock-tock of bamboo tubes struck together. While he's placing the orders, Kovalik can think only of the new girl, the wonderful pink of her soft body, the way her flesh seemed to slide in little sections, gently, one against another – breast, belly, thigh, buttock – until he forgets to pay and the vendor shouts angrily at him. When he gets back to the cabaret, Kovalik is swallowing hard in anticipation of seeing her again.

When he knocks and enters the room, to his disappointment the blond girl has put on a robe. Yet it is flimsy and so carelessly buttoned that he can still see a ripe curve, a wonderful shift of bone and flesh.

'How much?' she asks.

While she's counting out the money, Kovalik looks intensely at her full lips puckered in concentration, at the flattening out of one fleshy thigh against the bed she sits on. He leans slightly forward, as if by this new position he can have a glimpse, just one more, of the soft little patch of light hair between her legs. He feels himself swelling.

'What's your name?' she asks, holding out the money.

'Vladimir.'

'Mine's Olga. I was at the Red Dragon in Chapai, but they let every type in. Not Chinese, of course,' she adds quickly. 'But Japs, and they let in Filipinos.'

'My name's Vladimir Kovalik. I'm from Petrograd.'

'Well, I'll be seeing you,' Olga says, opening the newspaper containing the chicken wings.

Kovalik doesn't move to leave, but watches her bite into the meat with gusto. The *hoisin* sauce, which covers the chicken, smears across her lips, giving her the look of a hungry child. Sensing him, Olga looks up. 'I'll be seeing you,' she repeats. 'Goodbye, Vladimir.'

'I would –' He wets his lips. 'Could we talk awhile?'

Staring meaningfully at his trousers, Olga says through her chewing, 'I think you want more than talk. I don't do that with people I work with. Goodbye, Vladimir.'

'I mean it. Just a little talk. Maybe we can talk about Russia.'

'Russia?' She squints at him, plainly annoyed, and puts the half-eaten chicken wing on the paper. 'What's there to talk about? I told you I stay clear of people I work with. No offense, Vladimir, but damn it, I had a mean guy in here last night who nearly broke my back. You saw him, didn't you? A big Swede?'

Kovalik doesn't remember. 'Yes,' he says.

'He was on this ship nearly six months without a woman. Can you imagine what it was like – for me?' The pleading note in her voice has an effect on Kovalik. He nods and half turns to go, looking back once more expectantly. 'Thanks for going, Vladimir,' she says with a sigh. 'I need sleep. Last night was my first here, you know. A new place can take it out of you. Then a couple of girls were out somewhere. It's why I have this room all to myself so I can get a good rest. But now they're coming back and I'll have to share it with someone and maybe we won't get along. You get me, Vladimir? I'm tired. I'll see you around the cabaret. Goodbye now.'

Kovalik leaves.

That afternoon he writes a note to the German called Luckner. He writes it in the tiny room shared with two cabaret waiters, one of them Russian, the other Indian. He hates them both: the Indian

653

for talking too much and the Russian for being a Czarist with a St. George Cross.

He has disgraced himself without hope of redemption by putting on the Cossack uniform, but at least his shame doesn't include a loss of contempt for the enemy. He hates the Czarist waiter, he hates the manager, he hates the women.

He mails the letter at a nearby Post Service and takes a long walk before going to work. On a side street he notices a rickshaw puller sitting beside his vehicle. For a moment the man looks like Ku, but when Kovalik draws closer it is obvious to him the puller isn't his friend. It is also obvious the man is dead. Probably a heart attack. Kovalik bends closer for a long look at the dead man, slumped against the poles of the rickshaw. It won't be long before others on the street realize he's dead; then they'll take the rickshaw.

Kovalik straightens up. He hates this place, he hates it, and the job, the cabaret, the women there too, the new woman especially. Nothing has gone right. He's not old, he's no older than father had been when he was born, and yet unlike father he no longer has anything to live for. He has nothing, not a woman, not a country, not even an ideal to live for. He has no future.

Strolling along, he notices that he's near the Great World Fair, so he goes there and stands in front of it. There are six stories of amusement inside the 'palace.' There are acrobatic displays, gambling tables, shooting galleries, distorting mirrors, melon-seed stalls, curio shops. He has heard all about them. He has also heard that opium dealers hang around, and sure enough, he spots a telltale haggard face, someone leaning against a lamppost near the palace. The tall thin Chinese has watery eyes, a runny nose.

'How much will you give for this uniform?' Kovalik asks. When the man stares at him, Kovalik realizes he has spoken in Russian. '*Ta-yen*,' he says. '*Duo shao?*' Removing his fur hat, he holds it toward the man.

Minutes later, hatless, gripping the little paper-wrapped pellets, Kovalik is hurrying down a lane. A man on the corner directs him down another street when he whispers, '*Ta-yen*.' In a recessed hutung he finds what he's looking for: a place that rents lamp, pipe, and space on a bench. After three quick pipes – he sucks in the smoke in a single inhalation – Kovalik lies contentedly in the semidarkness. He has the rest of the uniform to sell. For a while that will pay the rent to landlord *Ta-yen*. And he can return to his room, this evening or maybe tomorrow, and steal whatever the garrulous Indian and the St. George Cross holder have left lying around. Maybe he will do some carving, find wood somewhere, and peddle his art on the Bund. Why not? Anything is possible now that *Ta-yen* has taken him back in. It's wrong to call the old landlord a demon; *Ta-yen* has the sweet disposition of Kuan Yin. And as for food, he needn't waste much money on that. Moreover, a man his size won't have trouble robbing a traveler on the docks, if it comes to rent money or none. He'll get along fine without that job, that uniform, in a cabaret harboring Czarist whores. He has two more pipes, which give him special pleasure because they come from the sale of a Cossack hat. Sitting up with a sigh, Kovalik hands the paper-wrapped pellets to the attendant. *Ta-yen*'s cheap in Shanghai; that's a blessing. He can last, well, infinitely – like a possibility. Ku would say, 'Don't worry,' and he won't. But he watches, when the man prepares a new pipe, to see there's no cheating.

Later, stretched out on the bench, his head on the worn wooden pillow that smells to its core of burnt cinnamon, Kovalik lets himself drift. For some people *Ta-yen* merely clarifies the mind, but for others the old landlord provides a world of visions. Kovalik considers himself lucky to be one of the latter. His vision is now of Russia. He is in a forest, in a grove of trembling larches, and overhead a few eagles are circling in broad-winged silent grace. Like huge cobwebs the lichens trail from tree to tree in the vast Siberian woods. It is summer. He is ankle deep in black-green moss, in a sea of fungus. He breathes in the muggy vegetable air under the countless firs. It is summer in the beautiful forests of Siberia.

27

It is eight in the morning on December 15 when train number 30 approaches the outskirts of Sian in Central China. Many years have passed since General Tang last saw the ancient capital of eleven dynasties. Shortly after dawn he began looking from the compartment window at the winter fields, the frozen ponds, the flocks of birds overhead – wild geese, swallows, and others he can't identify – flapping across the cold brown landscape.

Yesterday on the way from Qufu he had passed through the city of Kaifeng. In his youth he had been stationed there some months as subaltern to a fiercely mustachioed colonel of infantry. The colonel had emulated his appearance by revolting against the Manchu government with his entire garrison, Tang included. Yesterday from the train window Kaifeng had looked exactly as he remembered it from his youth: rutted dusty streets, beggars squatting at the East Gate, a noisy throng milling about the marketplace. Nothing more than a big casual village. Yet for a time during the Sung Dynasty this grimly dilapidated Kaifeng had been a brilliant center of Buddhist culture. The General tried, a hopeless task, to re-create an image of the China that might have been: the ancient music, the polished red-and-gold columns of the palaces, the splendor of bejeweled women, the rock gardens and pavilions subtly placed in the scented compounds where scholar and courtier strolled. Today most Chinese cities look only too much like Kaifeng. It saddened him on the trip yesterday: the same crumbling walls, the same tiled houses jammed together, the same narrow streets, the same monotonous low-slung skyline broken intermittently by the thrust of pagoda or temple. Yet this colorless mélange has at its core the immense energy of people; they possess the power of a harmless-looking snubnosed bullet. Such people could build a new skyline with the visual impact of those European cities he has seen in photographs – intricate arrangements of steel and glass. He will order the renovation of decaying monasteries while shacktowns come down and in their place rise tall apartment buildings with electricity and plumbing. He harbors this dream with the same intensity he gives to his dream of a garden where, as an old man, he can sit on a stone bench beside Black Jade.

If all goes well. In recent days the prospects for the future have looked brighter. Each day the morale of his troops has been improved by the return of wounded comrades to their ranks and by a shift in battlefield memories from horror to pride for having survived that horror. There is also a relaxation of fear of an impending attack from Sun Ch'uan-fang from the south. A spy in Sun's headquarters has relayed the news that the Kiangsu general is sick and can't possibly launch an attack. In that event, Black Jade is probably safer in Qufu than in Peking, where the Old Marshal is in control. Notwithstanding the old man's propensity for reckless acts (Chang Tso-lin is both brave and reckless, a dangerous combination), he has shown good faith lately by sending General Tang the monthly appropriation for the Southern Shantung Army. And he has got Dog Meat to do the same. Even so, before leaving for Sian, Tang decided to get Black Jade out of his reach. He wired Captain Fan to bring her home.

Also before leaving Qufu, he ordered the diviner to cast the Yarrow Stalks again. To their mutual surprise the oracle predicted that a young man would figure strongly in the General's future – exactly the same prediction the oracle had made before the Thousand Buddha Mountain conference. Either of two young men might have been meant in that prophecy: Yang who tried to kill him, the American who saved him. Or perhaps both had been meant?

Before the General left for Sian, another young man entered his life in an effort to influence it: his nephew, Ping-ti, who came all the way from Tsingtao. Wearing a business suit, with a key chain stretched across his vest, Ping-ti spoke plainly over tea. He came with a familiar proposition: If the General cooperates with the Japanese, they will supply his army with whatever the needs for it.

'My army needs nothing,' the General declares.

'After Hengshui, uncle?'

Tang ignores the impertinence. 'Nothing that the Japanese might provide. Unless they can send me five thousand able-bodied Chinese troops.'

Ignoring that sally, Pint-ti says, 'They want nothing more than permission to build a road through your territory.'

'That's all?' When his nephew nods, the General recalls an old saying: A clever man understands a nod. His nephew's nod really means that's not all the Japanese want; they want to invade his land like so many grass-hoppers, the kind that often in China have swept out of nowhere to gobble up entire crops. 'I believe there must be more,' the General says.

After a moment of hesitation, Ping-ti says, 'A little more, yes. They want gangs of coolie labor. If you supply the gangs, believe me, uncle, the Japanese will be appreciative.'

'Meaning they will give me whatever I need.'

'That is correct.'

'Except for the loyal, able-bodied Chinese troops.'

Ping-ti chooses this time to smile, as if in appreciation of the sarcasm. 'Let me just say, uncle, they can be very generous.'

'Who is supplying the construction equipment for the roads they want built? Your father?'

Ping-ti looks steadily at him. 'Yes.'

How confident he is, Tang thinks, to drop every trace of guile or

caution. 'You represent the Japanese, you represent your father
Do you also represent Dog Meat? Marshal Chang Tso-lin?'

'Yes, them too.' Ping-ti lights a cigarette and puffs with
lazy arrogance. 'The Marshal's especially interested in your
cooperation.'

'I'm especially interested in why.'

'As a measure of your loyalty. To him, to his policies.'

'You speak like someone authorized to say so.'

'I am.'

The General is watching his newphew's cigarette; it dangle
from the young mouth with a carefree crudity that surely mus
have been nurtured in America. Yet the American cavalryman ha
never once behaved with such slack grossness. The General i
deeply ashamed for his clan, even while Ping-ti lectures him on th
wonders of Japanese industry in Tsing-tao, especially the Fujigas
and the Naigai Wata Kaisha cotton mills. The ash on the cigarett
grows, until it falls gracelessly at feet wearing Western leather.

Abruptly Ping-ti says, with a broad smile, as if anticipating th
General's favorable reception of his words, 'Father sends his bes
wishes, uncle.'

'Thank him. Send him mine.'

'It would please him if you accepted the Japanese offer. H
believes there's a future for our clan in this.'

'I will not let the Japanese put even a footpath in my territory.
any of you think otherwise, you are, as the saying goes, like a blin
man carrying a looking glass.'

Ping-ti stayed that night at the Residence and left for Jinan th
next morning. He seemed happy with his failure. He would repo
his uncle's intransigence and leave others to solve the problem
Extending the familial courtesy of accompanying him to the trai
the General watched him step into its interior, a young man
Western dress who would return to his Jinan mansion and pro
ably to his Victrola on which, for the delectation of his concubin
and his Japanese cronies, he'd play the wild racket called music
America. Mencius said: The root of empire is in the state; the ro
of the state is in the family; the root of the family is in the indi
dual. Where would that leave China, if individuals like Ping
came to power someday?

Watching the train leave, Tang hoped his nephew would not
the young man prophesied by the oracle to influence his futu
That day he received a letter which predicted a somewhat old

man would surely figure in it. Chu Jui's letter announced that Chiang Kai-shek had married Mei-ling of the Soong family on December first in a Christian ceremony at the Soong mansion in Frenchtown. 'It was followed by a Buddhist ceremony in the ballroom of the Majestic Hotel,' Chu Jui wrote. He added drolly, 'So the marriage is blessed by the gods of two religions whose followers make up the bulk of the world – a good start. A good political move for Chiang Kai-shek too. One brother-in-law is Minister of Finance for the Nationalists. Another is heir to a Shansi family's stores and pawnshops. A problem, of course, is his sister-in-law, the widow of Sun Yat-sen. It is rumored that she fled to Moscow with her stepson in defiance of Chiang Kai-shek, who urged her, obviously in vain, to deny her Communist sympathies. With the Soong power behind him – with the American religious and financial connections too – I expect Chiang will soon reorganize the Nationalist Party. Wang Ching-wei, who has been much in evidence lately, will lose his bid to keep the party in civilian hands. Chiang and the military are in power. Now that Wuhan has collapsed and the Red coup in Canton has been foiled, the Nationalists have only to take Peking and the country will be theirs. Anyone who wishes to survive in China politically must learn to cooperate with Chiang Kai-shek. Of this I am convinced.' After his appraisal of Shanghai politics, Chu Jui wrote of the monastery in Chekiang where he and General Tang had last met, 'I wish to be back there among the pines, in silence, waiting for the prayer gong. Retiring from military life was my first wise decision in years. I think it is surely something the Great Sage would have approved. Now perhaps I can make yet another sensible decision and return to that monastery for the rest of my life. You, my friend, will you join me?'

Gentle mockery in that last question – typical of Chu Jui. Yet seriously meant too, for Tang finds in the question a distinct warning: Don't even consider an alliance with Chiang Kai-shek; get out of the situation at once.

But the General hasn't time or inclination for hungering after retirement, for the pines of contemplation and the deep gongs sounding their eternal rhythm. He'll leave that to Chu Jui. What does interest him is the letter's analysis of Chiang Kai-shek's power; it makes sense that temporarily, at least, Chiang is the second most powerful man in China – next to Chang Tso-lin. His strength is an alliance of southern military might with the business

659

world of Shanghai, augmented now by family ties with an exceptionally gifted clan who have access to foreign resources. The General is therefore confirmed in his decision to seek partnership with Feng Yu-hsiang, who, like himself, is now caught between Chiang Kai-shek and Chang Tso-lin. Tang reasons that he has in common with Feng a northern heritage, an abiding hatred of the Japanese, a long-standing estrangement from Peking politics, and a reputation for superior generalship. Nor is Tang deterred from alliance with someone who has tried to kill him. The bombing at Thousand Buddha Mountain was a matter of strategy, at the time probably justified in Feng's mind as a way of eliminating one of Chang Tso-lin's most important adjuncts. Moreover, the General is impressed by Feng's subtle daring in sending Yang to the Peking meeting. 'Once I paid this man to kill you. Now I send him to make peace between us.' Tang is flattered to think that Feng expects him to understand the message. It is a fine start for their relationship. Or rather to renew a relationship that had a tenuous start six years ago.

In the intervening years Feng Yu-hsiang has by intrigue and warfare contributed often to the chaos of China. He has fought two long wars, flirted with Christianity, fled to Moscow, returned to denounce communism, made alliances and broken them, and finally, today, he stands on the threshold of success – he has only two major foes, Chiang Kai-shek and Chang Tso-lin.

On the basis of a single meeting six years ago, Tang formed a good opinion of the man, in spite of Feng's demonstrable gift for deceit. They met in southern Honan at Hsinyang, where Feng's brigade was stationed. Tang was a colonel then, sent by the Peking Central Government. Entering camp, he noticed troops wearing scarlet armbands printed with the words: *Without hurting the people, die for them*. The camp was bustling with the sort of rigorous training that had fashioned Feng's army into the toughest in China. Headquarters, on the other hand, was no more than a mud hut. General Feng sat in it smoking a long clay pipe, his huge feet crossed on a table. His domelike head was closely shaven, but he also wore a drooping Mongolian mustache – perhaps a vestige of his years in far-flung northern outposts. He fed Tang a soldier's meal of millet gruel and hard bread, while pacing the earthern floor and often halting to pound on a white-plaster wall as he railed at furious length against the state of the nation. Corruption he fairly yelled, had turned the noble promise of a young republic into the pathetic reality of warring provinces, each managed by selfish militarists who used the chaos to their own advantage. Feng's reputation for wild eloquence was proven that day. Tang had come with the unpleasant task of informing him that the Central Government could not (or would not) pay the monthly stipend for his troops – the same thing that would happen six years later to Tang himself. The big man in the shabby uniform, shoeless in the damp hut, hadn't flinched. 'Fuck the Central Government,' he said. 'I'll do what I must to keep going. Tell them that. I'll take care of myself.' And he did.

A week later his troops attacked a train carrying government bullion and confiscated it. After which he informed Peking that he had just received his appropriation – and thanked them.

Today, Tang reasons, this unprincipled man of principle will continue to do what's necessary to survive. At the moment that should be to cooperate with someone against Chiang Kai-shek and Marshal Chang Tso-lin. Feng has always had territorial problems – he is far from the sea, burdened with poor communication lines and bad roads. Tang is better situated, capable of getting to the sea and with access to some good roads, especially those running north and south. Moreover, rumor has the Honan crop this season nearly destroyed by inclement weather. Tang's troops have more than enough grain to share. There is also a strictly military reason for an alliance; it is traditional Chinese strategy to ally with people holding land not contiguous with your own. Tang and Feng, through an alliance, could put their adversaries in the position of facing two fronts. Together they would offer a third force of formidable proportions to confront Chiang in the South and the Marshal in the North.

Given such factors militating for cooperation, Tang isn't afraid of Feng's propensity for faithlessness. As long as both find in the alliance some mutual benefit, it is unlikely that Feng will commit an act of treachery.

Sitting in the compartment, watching the train slow in its approach to the Sian depot, the General coolly assesses the three chief powers, who as yet may not realize he will be the fourth: Feng seems more intelligent but perhaps less tenacious than Chiang Kai-shek, if equally proud. Both men have sufficient wealth, but neither has the wealth and power of the Old Marshal, who in Tang's opinion is the most intelligent, the most tenacious, the proudest of them all.

But it is now Feng Yu-hsiang along whom he must face. Rising, the General adjusts his uniform. He is formally dressed this morning in gray with a Waffenfarbe collar patch of yellow for 'cavalry,' his old arm of service. He wears the three gold stripes of a field general on his sleeves. His hat, billed, has a red pompon on top, with three black stripes around the band; centered is a gold disc bearing a dragon device and within it a red dot to indicate general officer. He bears no resemblance to citizen Po Ming of Shanghai. Even so, he wears no decorations; they are an ostentation he abhors, especially because many officers dishonor themselves by wearing medals purchased in Hong Kong. He has a gold cord looped around his right shoulder, and on his gun belt the holster with his .455 Webley-Fosbery semiautomatic.

As the train comes alongside the depot, he has a quick look at the skyline of Sian. For a moment, thinking of his youth when he was stationed here, General Tang stares at a pagoda rising from the solid phalanx of roofs and trees. He knows that beyond the pagoda – it is the Big Wild Goose – lies the broad, sluggish Wei River and beyond it the great tombs of the Han. He hopes there will be time for him to revisit the Forest of Steles, hundreds of ancient upright stones from the Tang, Sung, and Ming dynasties. He used to stroll among the steles incised with poems, essays, and proclamations; suffused thereafter with the gentle melancholy that develops in the presence of so much history, he often walked under willow trees, alongside delicate pavilions half crumbled from neglect, and recited passages from the poetry of Li Po in this city of Sian, once called Chang An, Everlasting Peace. For an instant more he stands there, letting the rampant images in: tall flagons of hammered brass in the market stalls, fur pelts heaped in the streets, and overlooking the entire dizzying scene of Sian those purple mountains where great emperors rest deep within the bowels of the earth.

His adjutant knocks on the compartment door. Once more straightening his uniform, Tang looks from the window at the platform and sees waiting there, grim-visaged, his erstwhile aide Yang, the man who plotted his death at Thousand Buddha Mountain – waiting to greet him.

They meet with icy formality, and it occurs to Tang, like a bland afterthought, that someday he must kill this young man. When Yang gestures politely at the three waiting limousines, the General tells him to wait. Walking alongside the train, with a half-dozen staff officers in his wake, the General halts at a baggage car near the rear. It is opened, a ramp is set down, and out into the sunlight tramp a squad of cavalrymen leading their horses. At the next car another squad descends. Soon a platoon of mounted cavalry has moved into a column of twos beside the train. They are from the Big Sword Company – what's left of it – and wear Waffenfarbe collar patches of yellow, red pompons, and long curved swords at their belts. Tang looks at them with pride. The accompaniment of an armed guard had been ruled against during the discussions in Peking that laid down the rules for this conference. Trust is a peculiar thing, as Tang has learned through experience: it isn't always created from strict adherence to rules, but is often built precariously. By breaking a rule of two, sometimes a tension is created that leads to more respect. In his opinion, at least one rule for a meeting must be broken. Perfect accommodation might well arouse a suspicion that no amount of good will can overcome.

Turning, the General notices an understanding smile on Yang's face. For a moment he wishes this particular young man hadn't betrayed him. He never had a better aide; it's a loss. As they walk to the waiting cars, Tang tells the young man exactly that: 'I regret losing you. Why did you do it?'

'Excellency, believe me, I didn't want to do it. What you never knew – what I kept secret on orders – is this: I am the second son of General Feng's eldest brother.' In evidence he holds out an old, worn photograph. There, discernibly, is Yang as a boy of fourteen or fifteen, standing alongside a tall thin man resembling him in features; on the other side of Yang, just as discernibly, stands big shambling Feng with his puffy cheeks and drooping mustache. The boy Yang is holding up a wrapped package with a card written in letters large enough to read in the picture: 'Happy Birthday to My Dear Nephew from Uncle Yu.'

Not money or prestige or other gain had determined Yang's perfidy – it had been a family obligation. The General, feeling better, will not kill this young man. In similar circumstances surely he would have done the same.

When they reach the automobiles, Yang with a little bow gestures toward the middle one, but the General chooses to ride in the last of the three.

'I beg you not to worry, Excellency,' Yang says with a questioning look.

663

'I'm not worried.' Tang can't say why he wants to ride in the last car; it's a feeling, and when such a rare feeling comes, he pays attention to it.

After they're seated in the back seat of the third car, Yang says, 'My uncle will do you honor, Excellency.'

'I have more respect for him than you realize.'

'I will be frank,' Yang says gravely. 'It is something I owe you. The fact is, my uncle needs this alliance perhaps more than you do. The Honan harvest has been terrible.'

'I've heard.'

'But do you know the extent of its failure? Uncle faces the problem of feeding his troops all winter on enough food to last no more than a month. Men will starve. On the other hand, your Shantung harvest had a good yield.'

'That's true.'

'Permit me, General – but your casualties at Hengshui were substantial.'

'A battle your uncle encouraged.'

Yang's silence in response to this blunt claim implies it is the truth. And suddenly the General understands why Feng Yu-hsiang wanted that battle to be fought: not to help old Jen (no aid was ever sent) but to encourage Tang to negotiate in the aftermath of a costly battle. For the prestige of an alliance that might deter other warlords from attacking his depleted forces, General Tang would be willing to share foodstuffs from Shantung Province. Therefore, from the viewpoint of Feng Yu-hsiang, the battle of Hengshui was fought so he could feed his troops.

The General smiles as he considers the circumspection of this strategy, and apparently young Yang takes the smile to mean approval. He too smiles. 'Apart from what happened at Thousand Buddha Mountain, my uncle admires and respects you, Excellency.'

'I am honored beyond my merit.'

The slow caravan of limousines, flanked by Big Sword cavalry, moves down the only paved thoroughfare in Sian.

'I have committed an offense by speaking so frankly,' Yang says after a long silence. 'My impertinence is unforgivable.'

The General raises one hand slightly to deny the need for an apology.

'My frankness has been a measure of regret for my own part in Thousand Buddha Mountain.'

The General turns to look directly at the firmly set mouth, the furrowed brow, the bushy eyebrows that make Yang appear somewhat older than he is. 'In times of crisis,' the General says, 'men are forced to do strange things. Do you read *The Water Margin?*'

'At least once a year, Excellency.'

'When I read that book and *The Three Kingdoms* as well, I'm always surprised that they describe worlds much like our own. Change the clothes, change the means of transportation, change the weapons, but the issues of loyalty and honor remain the same.'

Again they ride in silence. A gust of wind carries a fine yellow dust through the open window of the car. The General had forgotten the dust of Sian. So much of youth is forgotten, he thinks, sitting next to a young man who will doubtless forget this difficult interview, this moment of courage.

'Excellency.'

Tang turns to the young man.

'During the entire conference I'll remain with your delegation. I'll eat and sleep in the same quarters. Uncle wants me to stay by your side.'

'I understand.'

'He's sincere in wanting this conference to succeed.'

'I believe you.' And Tang does. Not only because of his own analysis of the situation, but also because Yang has been designated to act as a hostage. Feng is exposing his own nephew to kidnaping or murder if anything goes wrong. The Chairman of the Honan Provincial Government's Commission – a typically grandiose and ambiguous title bestowed on Feng by the Central Government – would never put a member of his family in such jeopardy unless he meant to act in good faith. Tang is assured: This meeting should end in alliance.

The column of three cars and the accompanying horsemen has been proceeding down a boulevard. Now it turns into a narrower street that will lead to the Bell Tower, still a mile away. Pressing themselves against the shop walls, curious pedestrians gawk at the passing caravan. Coolies edge their laden carts out of the way and into tiny lanes, into doorways, so the cars and horses can go through. The column approaches a dusty old truck that is stalled in the middle of the street. Tang from the third car hears violent honking; for an instant he remembers another vehicle blocking the way – that black car athwart the rickshaw's path in Canton.

'They'll have to get that truck out of there,' Yang declares, sticking his head out the window and staring with annoyance beyond the other cars toward the stalled truck with its high side slats and a tarpaulin cover. The words are hardly out of his mouth before it is blown away – lips, teeth, jaw – by the initial blast of fire from the rear of the truck, as the canvas flap is thrust aside and two .30-caliber machine guns shoot a stuttering volley into the caravan. The lead car, an open Tourer, takes the brunt of the initial fire; within seconds everyone in it is dead. The second is a closed sedan and better protected, and so is Tang's car. They sit in the middle of the street, windshields shattered, bullets ricocheting off their fenders, while the Big Swords, beginning to control their panicky mounts, take the truck under fire. Tang's driver, hit, slumps over the wheel and the aide beside him is shot. Crouching on the floor behind the front seat, revolver in hand, Tang tries to get a sense of what's happening, but there isn't time, because from the lanes ahead there suddenly appears a group of horsemen waving pistols and swords. In the few seconds Tang has to look at them their mustaches, fur hats, and ponies tell him they're Mongolians. The narrow corridor of the street is swept by motion and sound: the churning hooves, the shooting riders, the civilians running for cover, the machine gun (one has been silenced) rattling away. Tang can remain in the car or get into the street; he has cover in the car but in the street he's less likely to be trapped. Fire from the machine gun and the milling horsemen have now silenced the middle car, where Tang was supposed to have been. His Big Swords, though fighting hard, are outnumbered as the Mongolians keep coming out of the lanes, some mounted, some on foot. One of them, before he is shot, tosses a potato masher into the second car, blowing pieces of body out of the window. Another grenade, thrown from a distance, bursts on the hood. The second car is obviously the goal.

Opening the door of the third car, Tang slips into the street, looking straight into the frightened eyes of a child who is flattened against a wall. A riderless horse is jittering nearby, the foot of a dead Big Sword caught in the stirrup. The animal's rump backs against the wall, near the little boy, while the faceless Big Sword, like a big flung doll, flails around in the dust at each nervous lunge of the horse. Tang, crouching, moves toward the animal, hammers with the revolver butt on the caught foot and frees it from the stirrup. He feels a little tug at the gold shoulder cord on the left; a bullet has either passed through the cord or hit him. He tries to mount the skittish horse, swings up on it, glancing again at the terrified boy. Hunched low on the withers, he yells at his men to follow and kicks the horse into a gallop. At the first lane three men run out – he can see more coming behind them. Reining in the horse, he coolly shoots each of the three, although the man in the lead has shot him in the left thigh. Now, at either side of him, Big Swords are rallying. They ride through the narrow street until they reach the boulevard, where the General has them turn to face the pursuing Mongolians. Seven, eight, ten of the Big Swords have gathered in a line when Tang gives the order to fire. This salvo disrupts the Mongolian charge – ponies buckle, men hurtle through the air. When the smoke has cleared, other pursuers, reining in their mounts, hang back. The General urges his men into a gallop. The depot isn't far, luckily for the General, who is weak from his wound: left thigh to ankle is drenched in blood. When the station comes into view, waiting passengers scatter at the approach of a dozen riders.

Dismounting, the General looks around for an officer. He calls to an old cavalry sergeant. 'The engine! The engine!'

When the man stares at him, puzzled, Tang tries to walk toward him, but nearly falls. A Big Sword grabs him, holds him up.

'Get me to the engine,' Tang demands. 'Get the men on board. Forget the horses. Get me to the engine.'

Two men half carry him forward to the locomotive, which is gently breathing steam. 'In the cab,' Tang orders his cavalrymen. They lift and push him up the stairwell into the locomotive cab, where two engineers gawk at him. Yanking his gun from its holster, he tells them to pull out of the station. 'Now!' he says, waving the gun. In another minute, while both cavalrymen help an engineer shovel coal from tender into firebox, an outcry from the depot signals the arrival of the pursuers; having regrouped after the charge, they are ready to renew the attack.

Tang slumps down against the side of the cab, watching the men feed coal into the firebox. 'Get us out of here,' he mutters and turns to one of the soldiers, a capless young corporal with a few brave tufts of mustache on his upper lip. 'That's an order. *You*, get us out of here.'

'Excellency?' The young man's eyes widen.

'Pass the word back when we're clear – all the way to Qufu,' the General says with difficulty; he feels himself slipping out of consciousness.

The train shudders, heaves forward, as the churning pistons slowly force the wheels into motion. Alongside the cab rides a Mongolian, attempting to level his rifle before the young corporal shoots him. There is now a steady chug-chug-chug as the wheels get purchase on the track. The throttle engineer reaches up and dutifully pulls the whistle cord, sending a jaunty burst of sound into the morning air, heralding departure.

'You,' the General whispers, motioning slightly with one hand. The young corporal bends down to the General's mouth to catch the faint words. 'When you get clear, that old sergeant will take command. His orders –' Tang swallows hard, attempting to hold on. Both hands bright red, grip his left thigh above the bubbling hole. 'Get us back to Qufu.'

'His orders are to get us back to Qufu, Excellency,' the young corporal repeats.

The whistle sounds again, high above the steady surge of pistons and the intermittent crackle of gunfire beside the moving train, but the General hears none of it. Falling to one side when the train gathers momentum, he has fainted.

Of that long hectic escape through the yellow loess countryside, the track winding around precipitous ravines into wintry valleys, past villages and towns, his men urging the engineers on, General Tang remembered little. Now and then he opened his eyes, but he slept most of the time while the old sergeant, a veteran of campaigns since the Manchu days, managed effectively. The soldiers occupied two cars, the regular passengers four others. Conductors and engineers were so thoroughly controlled that when the train came into stations along the way, they did exactly as they were told, and so General Tang's commandeering of the train was never even suspected until it entered Kaifeng. The word had traveled there from Sian by telegraph. Officials halfheartedly waited on the platform to request the train's return – halfheartedly because they wanted to avoid a confrontation with desperate troops (they had no idea how many occupied the train) or a general who, a few hundred kilometers northward, had recently fought and won the terrible battle of Hengshui. The old sergeant merely ordered the engineer to steam past the depot platform, where three railroad officials, a Kaifeng police chief, and a small detachment of local militia waited listlessly, pro forma.

Arriving in Qufu, conscious now, his leg bandaged with shreds of curtain from a first-class compartment, General Tang ordered the sergeant to pay the train staff. Then the train changed direction in the roundhouse and chugged back toward Sian, none the worse for wear and bearing a dozen lucky passengers from Qufu who wouldn't need to change trains for their journey westward.

Lucky, too, is the General; the bullet grazing the thigh bone didn't fracture it. He has lost considerable blood and strength, however, and lies in his bed, tolerating old Yao's ministrations and listening drowsily to the songbirds warbling in their cages. The words of a poem by Tu Fu often come to mind: 'In these awful times I have gone everywhere. Returning home alive has been an accident.'

Indeed an accident. Or perhaps he must allow himself a measure both of shrewdness and intuition. If he had followed the conference rules and not taken his cavalry escort, the ambush would have overwhelmed the caravan of cars. If he had failed to follow his intuition and had taken the second car instead of the third, not even the Big Swords could have saved him. The Mongolian ambushers had left the middle car a smoking, blasted wreck. Such thoughts are interrupted by old Yao, who scolds him for moving too much or not drinking his soup or forgetting to sleep.

Lying in bed, he asks himself again and again: Who ordered the ambush? The attackers hadn't worn uniforms; that they were Mongolians meant little. Feng's troops, although predominantly men of Honan, contain Mongolian units from Kansu, but so do the armies of most northern generals, his own included – an entire company of the Third Cavalry Battalion consists of Mongolians who defected from Yen Hsi-shan's Shansi army when that general cut their pay.

On the third morning of his return, General Tang is well enough to sit up and give orders. His first is to a subaltern: Send a telegram to Peking demanding that Captain Fan return immediately with Madam Rogacheva. Where are they? They should have arrived in Qufu at least two or three days ago.

Another wireless goes to Major Chia in Peking: See the Feng delegates there and demand an explanation of the ambush.

Not that he believes Feng had anything to do with it. Nephew Yang had been killed instantly. Moreover, if Feng had wanted to murder him, poison or a single assassin would have proved effective at the conference. Tang believes the nephew: an alliance had been Feng's aim.

Clearly, then, the attempt was made to prevent such an alliance. Both Chang Tso-lin and Chiang Kai-shek would benefit if it failed, but how could they know so much about the conference? Its date, let alone the General's arrival time in Sian, had been a closely guarded secret. Could his own staff at Qufu have leaked the information? Only a few had knowledge of his plans, and every one of them had accompanied him to Sian; now they are all dead.

Because of the secrecy, he's inclined to rule out Chiang Kai-shek, who hasn't many agents in the North – not yet, at least. But the Old Marshal was in Peking when the delegates, Major Chia among them, were there. The Major or a subaltern might have informed Chang Tso-lin, who in turn could easily have sent a unit of his best Mongolian horse to Sian, along with a truck equipped with machine guns. If the ambush failed, suspicion would fall on the potential ally Feng, no stranger to perfidy. And Tang might well have suspected Feng if the young nephew hadn't provided strong evidence – including his death – for believing otherwise.

Major Chia an informer?

The General fires off another wireless ordering Chia and the delegation back to Qufu immediately.

Chang Tso-lin arranged the ambush; it makes sense. That's why Ping-ti came here with his Japanese proposal. If the General had chosen to cooperate, Chang Tso-lin might have dropped the whole thing. Ping-ti's negative report must have encouraged the Old Marshal to rid himself permanently of a rebellious commander.

Next day Major Chia stands at attention beside the General's bed. Studying him for signs of guilty nervousness, Tang sees only the stern, competent young man who is the best officer in his army. Chia brings news from Feng's delegation. They profess innocence of the ambush and have given him a wireless from General Feng to submit at Qufu.

The long message is filled with rhetorical protestations of good faith, of bewilderment at the murder attempt, of relief that it failed. Tang looks up from the message and asks Chia bluntly if he or any of his men had given the information to Chang Tso-lin.

'Yes, Excellency,' the Major says without hesitation. 'One of our delegation did.'

'I see,' the General replies quietly. 'How did you find out?'

'Yesterday he left Peking.'

'Who is it, Major?'

'The American.'

'The American,' Tang repeats. It will take time for him to absorb the magnitude of his own error in keeping that fellow in camp – time to understand the need in himself to have under his control a foreigner whom he could treat as a curiosity, as a pet, like the caged birds now cheeping softly behind Chia's back.

'The American,' he repeats again.

Later, when alone, he recalls the Yarrow Stalk Oracle – a young man has indeed profoundly affected his life. But there is something else to consider. An identical prediction from the yarrow stalks led earlier to *two* young men – the American and Yang – influencing his destiny at Thousand Buddha Mountain. Now this second prediction has led to one young man, the American. Is there also another young man to be implicated? Ping-ti? Surely his nephew has tried and will continue to try to influence his life.

Or what about Captain Fan? Another young man, he was in Peking at the time of the betrayal. He had nothing to do with the delegation, no contact with it that the General knows of. And yet –

The General calls in Major Chia. 'In Peking did you see Captain Fan?'

'Yes, Excellency.'

'How did that happen?'

'He learned of my being there from a member of my family.'

'How many times did you see him?'

'Once. He came to our residence.'

'How many times did the American see him?'

'Once. That same time. And then they had dinner that evening.'

'But they saw each other again?'

'I told the American not to see him again.'

'What did the American do in Peking?'

'In his free time he went out for meals and sightseeing. He kept to himself.'

'But he could have met the Captain?'

'He could have.' Chia hesitates, grimacing in the struggle to face the truth. 'I told him not to do it. But he could have.'

'Thank you, Major. That's all.'

Next morning, capable of limping around the room and cooing at the bamboo slats of the bird cages, General Tang Shan-teh halts suddenly. It is true. He has known it ever since returning to Qufu: She will never return. In Peking, though Captain Fan, she met the young American and has gone off with him.

Within minutes a subaltern comes to report that another shipment of weapons has arrived from Shanghai: three cases of Mauser 7.9-millimeter rifles, Gewehr 98 model.

Searching the pinched face of the young officer, Tang asks quietly, 'But what is wrong?'

'Breach mechanisms, Excellency. They are missing, Excellency.'

Luckner's vicious little joke.

That afternoon the General sits down to write a letter that will unfortunately put him under deep obligation to the Green Circle Gang. Each time one of Luckner's defective shipments has arrived he has thought of writing such a letter, but until now he has always balanced his desire for revenge with his fear of contracting a hard debt to pay. Dou Yu-seng is famous for doing favors without hesitation and infamous for demanding excessive payment later on: compensation ranging from currency in foreign exchange to acts of political treachery or worse. Even so, the General makes the decision, leaving the extent of his liability to the future. He works hard on the letter, which is composed in traditional style with repetitious self-deprecation, high compliments, and flourishes of rhetoric. He writes it three times, striving for an elegant calligraphy in which to cast ornate respect for the Grand High Dragon of the Greens. He recalls in it their conversation in Shanghai when they discussed, in passing, the German arms dearler, Erich Luckner. Luckner has broken a contract after receiving full payment for weapons. Since the General has pressing business in Qufu, he humbly requests of the Illustrious High Dragon that something be done to salvage Chinese honor. He asks the Green Circle Society to handle this matter of honor for him in any way its distinguished members see fit.

Contemplating the forceful strokes of his characters, the General ascribes much of his present trouble to the arms deal with Luckner. By inviting Luckner to Qufu, he met the Russian woman, Vera Rogacheva. Had he not taken her away from Luckner in Shanghai, the arms dealer might have kept his word and delivered the weapons – his reputation for honest transactions suggests it. Without the weapons at Hengshui, the General lacked important firepower and substituted for it the lives of many troops, leaving his army hurt, still recovering morale and effectiveness.

Tossing sleeplessly that night, the General grips his hands to his sides in fury and frustration, hating her for the betrayal. Yet more than once during the long dark hours he whispers her name – as if, awakened from a nightmare, he has turned to her for solace.

28

In summer, when wooden coffins crack from the heat, Shanghai undertakers believe the noise is a signal they'll soon sell their wares. Luckner is familiar with the supersitition; like so many things Chinese, it is damn illogical. After all, more deaths occur in the winter, for then people die from exposure as well as disease and starvation. But in Shanghai many of them never get a coffin anyway; they are lugged by cart to the Whangpoo and tossed into the muddy water to be drawn slowly to the sea. And yet, as he strolls down this December street in Frenchtown, Luckner wonders if the superstition isn't well founded after all: The beggars he sees are huddled comfortably around little fires; people who can pay for coffins are more likely to collapse in summer because they have the money for over-indulgence in the sort of food and drink that bring on hot-weather apoplexy. It could be one of the few Chinese beliefs that have validity in the real world. He smiles at the oddity of the thoughts that have accompanied him on this walk.

Luckner stops to read an autobiography written in chalk on the packed earth of a tiny lane. There's an entire block of these messages which are painstakingly composed, doleful incident by doleful incident, each in its own square. Passersby have placed a few coppers in the squares which have aroused their sympathy. Luckner reads: 'My parents sold me to a village landlord when I was eight. For ten years I worked without pay, almost without food.' And so on, through sufficient bad luck in each square to suffice for many lifetimes. Strolling farther, he reads another chalked story of misfortune. 'But when I came to Shanghai, the gods finally looked at me with favor. A good man married me. This year when the army from the South came, some fellows got him in the street and held him still. I watched from the corner. They cut off his head.' The next square continued: 'After that I had no money. They won't give me work in the silk and cotton mills because of my bad health. I tell them they take young girls in bad health, so why not me? But they won't listen and I am starving.' Luckner studies the emaciated woman sitting listlessly beside the woeful tale set out in half a dozen squares. Leaning over, he drops a few coppers in the square describing the death of her husband. Perhaps he gives money to this tubercular woman – it's a practice he usually avoids in a city of desperate beggars – because her spare description of a man's death reminds him of last April 12, when a siren blast from a harbor gunboat heralded the planned massacre of countless Reds. Commies and their sympathizers, many of them disgruntled factory workers, were killed by the Green Gang in full view of coolies at work and foreigners out shopping. Luckner himself had seen one such execution. Three ordinary but very confident young men led another by the arms into the middle of the street, where people gathered curiously around. One of the captors made a brisk announcement. 'This is a traitor to our country, a vicious betraying dog who deserves no mercy.' Without further explanation of the betrayal that made the fellow a vicious betraying dog, they pushed him to his knees and roughly shoved his head forward. Luckner couldn't see his face; his eyes were lowered nearly to the ground, as if fixed upon the movement of a tiny insect. One of the Green Gang captors slipped a thin wire around the man's neck and secured the ends of it to a small block of wood. By turning the wood block, he tightened the wire. Slowly the thin strand cut into the man's neck and his head lifted, while two men held him firmly. His eyes widened, his mouth popped open, the veins of his throat stood out like small ropes. Luckner hated the gleeful expression of the man twisting the wire. Weapons are fine: You shoot a man and bust him up. Torture and needless application of pain, Luckner feels, is the work of barbarians.

Walking farther, he reads another tale of misery. This one, however, ends with an aphorism at once cynical and optimistic: 'Poverty in time of trouble is something riches can't buy.' Chuckling at this peasant wit, Luckner tosses some coppers in the last square. A wrinkled little man, quick as a bird, reaches out with a gnarled hand to scoop them up. Unlike the other writers along the block, he doesn't leave money on the squares to encourage generosity from passersby. He'd rather make sure his coppers aren't stolen. A practical realist. Good. Luckner tosses another copper on the square.

Money is everything in Shanghai, he thinks. It's a mystery he hasn't yet accumulated enough of it for the return to Karlsruhe. Surely he earns enough, now that the Japanese are his clients. Luckner admires the Japanese, who haul good over from Honshu and sell them to the Shanghai Chinese cheaper than anything the Chinese can make in the factories of their own cities – and the Japanese use the raw materials of China to do it. There are thirty Japanese cotton mills in Shanghai. Thirty. A fleet of two dozen trawlers and packet boats ply the China waters, snatching fish and trade from the natives. They have ironworks, paper mills, and own the utilities in most of the large Chinese cities. He is well connected with these clever businessmen, yet Luckner still finds himself almost empty-handed. Of course, he can guess why. The gambling. The women. What the hell, he has never been a man who can work all day, then spend a quiet evening at home. Gambling and women are the rewards for daily labor: a maxim he adheres to faithfully. What he needs right now, in fact, as the daylight wanes over the Shanghai rooftops, is a nice pleasant woman. After that, physically relaxed, he'll go to one of the casinos in Chinese City. It has been a regular routine of his ever since Vera left. But he won't go looking for Japanese girls; God, no. He has had his fill of them in the company of his clients: geishas tirelessly pouring whisky and telling dirty stories – translated for him into exerable Chinese – and playing those whiny samisens well into the morning. What he needs is a robust European woman who knows that a tired businessman wants a slow, satisfying fuck before he can appreciate little scrolls and faces painted white and those drinking games that seem unendingly fascinating to his Japanese companions.

Just today he received a note from a Russian whom he met recently along Chao Pao San; the big fellow is a doorman for one of those cabarets cum knocking shops that have sprung up near the Avenue Joffre in Frenchtown. The message says there's a new Russian girl at the place. It was written in Russian, and for a German who has given his days and nights to the Chinese language now for nearly a decade, it wasn't easy to decipher.

He's on the way there now and glad of it, looking forward to appraising another of those damn Russian girls. Luckner buys a newspaper at a kiosk, then slips into a little restaurant for a quick meal before going to Chao Pao San.

Ordering a dish of stir-fried meat and vegetables, he unfolds the paper and looks at the headline: WARLORD TURNS BANDIT!

Below it is an account, rather muddled and long-winded – typical Chinese journalism, in his opinion – of General Tang Shan-teh's appropriation of a Mikado-type locomotive and passenger train in Sian. Shocked, fascinated, Luckner tries to make sense of it, but in large part the news report reads like a deliberate obfuscation of facts in a detective story: something about gunfire and casualties and a delegation of railroad officials in the city of Kaifeng. Clearer is the reaction of the Nationalist Government; it calls for an end to the criminal activities of lawless warlords. Even clearer is the statement by the reappointed Commander in Chief of the Kuomintang Army, Generalissimo Chiang Kai-shek: 'For the good of the people, I will make it my business to root out the sources of such calamitous and despicable events. I promise never to rest until I have exterminated every bandit in our land.'

Throwing his head back, Luckner bursts out laughing. A number of Chinese gentlemen at other tables regard him with the contempt reserved for undisciplined foreigners. Reading the account again, yet again, Luckner finally sighs and drinks his hot tea, cooling it with his lips in the loud manner of a Chinese. The men at nearby tables, seeing his practiced way with a cup of tea, stop glaring at him.

He has never trusted a pronouncement from Chiang Kai-shek. For that matter, he has little faith in the southerner's future. Between the Westerners who back Chiang Kai-shek and the Japanese who back Marshal Chang Tso-lin, he believes the Japanese have made the better choice. It's only a matter of time before the Japanese bestride the corridor between Shanghai and Peking, denying the upstart southerner access to the capital. Yet reading Chiang's vow to 'eliminate' bandits like General Tang, he only hopes that this time the leader of the Nationalists will make good on a promise.

Luckner had a difficult time discovering who seduced Vera away from him. First he was told that Tang had been with her at the greyhound races. The account was suspicious because his informant claimed the General was wearing a Western suit. Tang's That antiforeigner in clothes of the enemy? Luckner found it hard

676

to believe, unless the General was so enamored of Vera that he'd do anything to impress her. That was possible. Checking the hotels a second time, he finally got evidence from a desk clerk that the woman in the photograph had visited the General.

Luckner rattles the newspaper and reads the account once more. He has heard, as everyone in Shanghai has, of the terrible Hengshui battle; he still wonders if his own refusal to send arms in working condition had a significant effect. Apparently the General won, yet reports trickling into Shanghai indicate the victory was won at great cost. Luckner choose to believe his practice of sending only parts of weapons must have infuriated the General; he *fervently hopes so*. The thought of it causes him to clench his fists as if remembering a physical encounter. By now, surely, Vera must be regretting her recklessness. What had she expected to gain? The Dragon Throne beside Emperor Tang? Was she really so gullible as to believe a Chinaman's tale of oriental splendor, all of which would be hers if she joined his concubines? Luckner feels he knows Vera better than he has ever known anyone. He's convinced that her years of wandering, terror, and incessant insecurity have prepared her to succumb to the witless plans for safety and comfort presented by anyone – including himself. Because he had promised her Karlsruhe, Gateway to the Black Forest, a town house there with carved timbers, a view of snowy mountains from the Turmberg, summers in a cottage among the spruce trees with a glimpse of the sparkling Rhine. His promise to whisk her out of China had been as worthless, as false, as irresponsible as General Tang's claim to an imperial power that would allow her to live like a queen. Luckner tells himself (he does every day) that losing Vera has been his own fault. What he despises in the General is an image of similar ineptitude – his own inability to keep a boastful lover's promise.

Finishing his meal, Luckner pays and leaves. It is dark outside, with lanterns swinging beside neon signs, all urging customers into restaurants, variety shops, cabarets. He turns on Chao Pao San and walks to No. 94 – The House of Romance – where a chunky, bearded doorman in a Cossack uniform gives him a perfunctory salute. 'Where's the big guy?' Luckner asks in Russian.

'What big guy?'

Luckner has wanted to reward the big doorman for sending him notice of a new girl. With a shrug, he brushes past the surly new doorman. Inside the ballroom, with its little jungle of cramped tables, its strings of Christmas lights, Luckner halts and looks around in the light cast by lowpower colored bulbs. The band hasn't arrived yet. Good. Luckner hasn't much use for loud music. A few sailors are morosely drinking beer at a table, getting up their nerve to approach the half-dozen girls clustered at one end of the bar.

Luckner approaches the girls, smiling. 'Where's Olga?' he asks. That was the name in the note.

A sloppily-built woman in heavy makeup says, 'She isn't here. Want to buy me a drink?' They are speaking Russian.

He glances at each of the other girls, halting at one to say in Chinese, 'Go get Olga.'

The girl, probably Burmese, nods dutifully and walks across the dance floor to the stairway.

'What are you drinking, girls?' Luckner asks expansively. With one voice they chorus, 'Champagne.' Reaching into his pocket, he comes up with a fistful of shoe-shaped taels, worth about two-thirds of a Mex dollar each, and tosses them ringing on the bar. The girls crowd around him, waiting for their expensive glasses of colored water.

'Have I seen you here before?' asks the slatternly Russian, but he doesn't answer. For himself he wants a glass of Russian vodka. When the Chinese bartender puts it on the bar, Luckner tastes the liquor cautiously, then shoves the glass away. 'I said Russian.' Smiling, the bartender pours from another bottle. This time, after sipping it, Luckner keeps the vodka. To the girls in general he says, 'That bartender thinks I don't know Russian vodka because I speak Russian with an accent. If it weren't for you ladies here, I'd kick his ass.' He says it carefully in Russian, then carefully in Chinese. The girls smile, but the bartender, a big fellow, glowers at him. Luckner knows it is foolish, but he can't help showing off in front of women. Three customers wander into the cabaret, foreigners in business suits, all wearing scarves against the chill of the December night. After finishing his vodka, Luckner orders another and this time puts banknotes on the bar. 'Give the girls another sip of that wonderful champagne,' he says and goes to a table along the wall, far from the bar and the entrance. In a few minutes he sees the Burmese girl coming down the stairs with a buxom blonde. He has a chance to assess the blonde as she crosses the dance floor: She is wearing a tight cheongsam, slit to midthigh, a dress made for narrow-hipped Chinese girls and quite unsuitable

678

for someone of her ample proportions. But Luckner is delighted and slowly judges the erotic potential of her strong thighs, pneumatic breasts.

'So you are Olga, hello, Olga,' he calls out as she approaches.

His greeting, so light and airy, encourages her to move with self-conscious sensuality. 'I am pleased to meet you,' Olga purrs, sitting down without another glance at the Burmese girl, who waits a moment to see if she will be invited too, before going back to the bar.

In the gloomy light Luckner can see that Olga has the broad cheekbones, the limpid eyes, the frank expression of a Russian peasant. He had seen many of them on his endless trek as a prisoner of war. How often then, numb from the cold, half starved, giddy with fever, he had kept himself going with the vow that if he survived the march he would have such women someday, that he would glory in their pink warmth, in their smell of milk and barnyards.

A limping Chinese waiter takes her order – champagne – after which, propping her chin in her hand with practiced coyness, Olga studies him. 'Don't I know you?'

'I thought you just came here. That's what I was told.'

'Who told you?' She looks puzzled.

'The doorman.'

'Doorman?'

'Not this one, another one. Anyway, he said you were new here.'

'I am. I was at the Red Dragon in Chapai.'

'Ah, Chapai. The Red Dragon.' He thinks he remembers it.

'Only they let in every type, and I hated the fights. The girls fought. It's better here.'

'More Russian.'

'That's it,' she agrees brightly. Olga has a lush, wet smile that dizzies him with desire.

'I came here just to see you. As I said, I was told about you,' Luckner tells her in a low voice.

Olga nods briskly. 'That's wonderful. Do you want to go somewhere now or can we just sit awhile and talk? I wouldn't mind talking with a gentleman – especially one who speaks Russian so good.'

Luckner wants his time with this girl to be interesting, so he decides to humor her. In fact, her desire to talk before they make love is more than he hoped for – he likes her sensitivity. Was Vera such a girl when she worked in these places? Quickly he puts Vera out of his mind – by reaching out and taking the girl's hand. The flesh is soft, a warm padding; he can hardly feel the bones within it. And there are softer hidden places, a whole world of pink and milky warmth. Luckner is surprised by his desire; he has actually to control his excitement.

'I mean it. You speak good Russian, sir,' the girl tells him, squeezing his hand. 'Where did you learn it?'

'I was a prisoner of war in Russia.'

'Ah, that's terrible. You're German?'

'Yes, I got into China with the Whites in 1919.'

The girl frowns in sympathy. He wonders if it's felt or faked. Russian women! Is this what he likes about them, their impenetrable motives – self-serving or wonderfully selfless? 'It was bad then,' Olga remarks. 'I was only a kid, but I still remember a little of it. I was at Novonikolajevsk. Were you there?'

'Yes.' It's all he says, the memory as always rendering him inarticulate. Can this woman, who had been at Novonikolajevsk, ever forget *any* of it? He remembers all of Novonikolajevsk. Nothing to eat, pilfered stores, nothing there by the time a million exhausted refugees, running from the Bolsheviks, entered the city. Thousands dying of spotted typhus in the streets. Those who froze to death before the disease killed them were lucky. This woman remembers only a little of it? She must be made of hard Russian granite. He remembers every moment of Novonikolajevsk, and every moment of Petropavlovsk, Omsk, Krasnojarsk, and the wolves edging closer at Irkutsk, and that acrossing of frozen Lake Bajkal at Goloustnoje.

'My hair was eaten away by scurvy,' Olga says, tossing her blond hair coquettishly.

'What?' Luckner has to force himself out of memory.

'I said my hair was eaten away. Isn't that terrible?' She holds a sheaf of long blond hair in both hands, as if milking it.

'Yes, that's terrible.'

'But it grew back just fine. Didn't it?'

'Let's go upstairs now.' Luckner rises, waiting impatiently.

Olga smiles, getting up too. 'I'm glad we had a talk, sir. It was nice.'

'Me too. Let's go up.' Luckner, taking her hand, draws Olga

along with rapid strides. Maybe it's a gesture of Russian women, but Vera once took her long black hair – she was wearing it long then – with both hands and milked it like a cow's teat. He had never seen anything so erotic. Tonight, momentarily, the sight of Olga doing the same thing has angered him.

On the stairway landing, before the turn to the second floor, Olga bends down and waves gaily at the girls around the bar, but they don't pay attention – the sailors, having drunk their courage up, have crowded there, along with newcomers.

In a shabby but clean little room upstairs, Luckner sits on the bed and watches the girl remove her clothes in a leisurely fashion. Off comes the clinging cheongsam, with difficulty. Luckner might have seen the struggle as humorous – a stout country girl divesting herself of a nymph's garment – but his desire, renewed by the climb, is consuming. Underneath the dress are a cotton brassiere and panties. Standing in them, ruffling her blond hair, Olga is happily conscious of her effect.

Abruptly he says, 'Yes, I know you.'

Shaking her hair, fingering the brassiere, Olga says, 'I thought we'd met. It must have been at the Red Dragon, honey.' Alone with him, she was changed from 'sir' to 'honey.'

'I think I had a Japanese with me.'

'Yes?' Olga says indifferently, placing her hands behind her back at the bra clasp.

'I was also with a Russian woman.'

Undoing the bra, Olga lets it fall to the floor. She smiles, looking down to admire her large pink-nippled breasts.

'I was with Vera. Do you remember Vera?'

Disconcerted by his lack of passion, the girl sits beside him on the bed, determined to give him her attention if that's what he wants. 'Vera? Sure I remember Vera. I know Vera, a nice person. Has anything happened to her? I haven't seen her around.'

'No. Nothing.' Luckner stares at his hands, both resting on his knees.

'Sure, honey, I remember that night. That was when I met Nakamura. You still know him?'

'He went back to Japan.' Luckner is looking at his hands rather than at the glowing, half-naked girl he had wanted so much a few minutes ago.

'So that's why I haven't seen him: he went back. We got along in way. Michio wasn't really mean, he just looked mean with his big neck and shoulders and all. But he sure had imagination, if you get what I mean.' Olga blows out her breath at the recollection. 'Kept telling me he was going to take me to Japan, but I didn't want to go there. Anyway, he didn't mean it. I'd lik to see Vera again, though.'

'Why?' Luckner looks curiously at the girl.

'Because she's nice. Vera is quality, but she never pushed it on me. She wasn't one of these White bitches you see around Shanghai. My father was nothing but a common soldier. He used to say, 'Olga, you and me and your mother are common as pig tracks.' He used to say, 'Olga, if it weren't for their need of luxury and rank and privileges, the Whites could have set up a republic in Siberia. We'd have a country of our own now. There would be a White Russia next to the Red. Only those filthy aristocrats couldn't get along, they fought among themselves like dogs, and lost everything for themselves and for us too, goddamn them!' That's what my father used to say,' Olga concludes solemnly, naked to the waist beside a man who led her eagerly upstairs but now looks down at his hands like a trembling, inexperienced boy. 'Well,' she says after a long silence, putting one hand on his shoulder in a gesture of sisterly concern, her eyes filled with shy puzzlement, 'shall we get started?'

Later, having performed to mechanical completion, Luckner lies beside her in the darkness. From the street below comes the sound of Shanghai night life: the cry of vendors, the neigh of horses, the drunken laughter of men seeking pleasure, the clang of distant gongs, the eruption of firecrackers in celebration of a god or a rich man or a bride.

A scrap of Goethe comes to him out of his youth at a Karlsruhe Gymnasium. It had applied then to a girl he has long forgotten. Softly he recites a stanza:

'O Mädchen, Mädchen,
Wie lieb' ich dich!
Wie blinkt dein Augel!
Wie liebst du mich!'

In a sleepy voice the girl moves beside him, murmuring, 'Wha does that mean?'

Luckner is surprised. He hadn't meant to say the words out loud. 'It's just a poem.'

'Tell me what it says.'

He translates the Goethe song into Russian for her:

'O girl, O girl,
How I love you!
How you eye gleams!
How you love me!'

'You must be educated,' Olga remarks, sitting up.

'No, I'm not. It's a simple little song.'

'I like it, it's pretty. Who do you mean it for?'

He laughs, reaching for the girls's pack of cigarettes placed conveniently on the beside table; she has a professional's eye for details. 'I don't mean it for anyone but you.'

'Sure. I believe you.' she lies back, crossing her arms behind her head. 'Where's Vera?'

'I haven't the slightest idea. Why do you care?'

'I don't. But I think you said the poetry for her.'

Luckner snorts disdainfully and lights a cigarette. Handing it to her for a puff, he says, 'Why in hell do you say something like that?'

'I don't know,' Olga replies defensively. 'Except when I met you that night with Michio, she was with you.'

Luckner refuses to comment, but smokes steadily in the darkness. To hell with them, with every woman he has known, he tells himself. Especially to hell with Vera. Can't a man feel a little wayward sentiment and recite a poem out of his youth without one of these women questioning him about it? He turns to study Olga, whose face is indistinct on the pillow beside him. What does she know about love? She's a wretched creature. Yet he has the need to reach out again, not physically, but again in talk, to find her – a lonely man in search of a lonely woman. So in the offhand manner of a man long married who has just come home, Luckner says, 'Do you know what I saw today? On the street, one of those hardluck stories written in chalk. Know what I mean?'

'Sure. There's lots of them around.'

'Well, this one said, "Poverty in time of trouble is something riches can't buy." '

'That's stupid,' Olga comments lazily. 'There's nothing money can't buy.'

683

'Think about it. Sometimes you're better off as a coolie than a landlord.'

'Tell me when *that* is, I'd like to know.'

'When there's no law, when there's fighting and no constabulary. When there's looting. At times like that, if you want to get out of it with your skin, you'd better not have anything else.'

'I wouldn't care if they got me after I'd enjoyed the riches. Know what I do sometimes? I tell them I was the daughter of a count.'

'But you didn't tell me that.'

'Because I liked your looks.' Olga giggles. 'And you wouldn't have believed me; I saw that in your face. But I like to think of being someone like a countess, one of those White bitches. Wine, clothes, chandeliers. A count's daughter from Kiev. Where's Vera from?'

'Petrograd.'

'But I can't carry it off too well. I'm born honest. If a man ever asked me to marry him, you know what I'd do?' She waits for Luckner's response.

'What?'

'I'd tell him what I am. "How can you marry a whore?" I'd tell him.'

'You wouldn't.'

'I would. It's stupid to be honest, but I'm stuck with it.'

Luckner thinks the girl is hopeless – like the Russian character. Yet he likes her, genuinely, now that they've talked some more. 'I prefer you Russian girls,' he tells her.

'Why is that?' Olga leans on one elbow, looking at him with momentary affection. 'Why us when you can have all these Oriental girls?'

'Because of what you've gone through.'

'I don't get it.'

'The Revolution, the Civil War. Leaving Russia the way you did.'

Olga laughs briefly, still not understanding.

'You have life. The terrible march across all that land put it there in you. Every day you almost died, so you learned how to live.' He feels himself getting vaguely philosophical, out of his depth, so with a sigh Luckner sits up. They have benefited from their conversation; it has made them temporary lovers. Looking at her closely, trying to see the large Russian eyes, the limpid soulful eyes that at the outset reminded him achingly of Vera, he decides to leave her a handsome tip.

Next morning he walks from his shabby hotel to the office. Since Vera left him, Luckner has lived in a run-down hotel to save money – without success, of course. He appreciates the irony of having *really* tried, *only* when she was gone, to accumulate enough money to get them both to Karlsruhe. Walking across the Garden Bridge, enjoying the crisp morning air, he gives a perfunctory glance at the barred and deserted Russian Consulate. Minutes later, having climbed to his second-floor office above the warehouse, Luckner finds not only his secretary waiting for him, but a foreign gentleman as well.

'I am Mister Faure,' the man says in French, rising from the chair with a smile.

They shake hands and with an air of importance Luckner excuses himself to read his mail in the inner office. On his desk is almost nothing: a request for a half-dozen Stuttgart electric fans from a local bank; a letter from an Italian arms client complaining about the bolt action of a hunting rifle he'd purchased; an electric bill. At noon he has an appointment with a Japanese cotton-mill executive who wishes to arm his employees and train them into fighting squads so they can protect the plant from Chinese rioters; the man shares Luckner's dubious opinion of Chiang Kai-shek's ability to bring order.

Luckner calls the visitor into the inner office. Swiveling in his chair, he glances at the Whangpoo as it recedes into bluish-pink distance on its way to the Yangtze and the China Sea.

In polite German Mister Faure reveals his identity – he is a police officer from the General Station in Frenchtown. He has come to request Erich Luckner to leave China as soon as possible; Mister Faure will gladly supply the necessary departure papers within a day.

Luckner smiles at him. Mister Faure is rather elegant, with a white flower in the buttonhole of his black business suit. 'You have me at a disadvantage, sir. I haven't the slightest notion what you're talking about.'

Mister Faure, nodding, repeats the request, only this time with bite in his voice. 'We ask that you consider our request to be something of an order.'

'We? Who is we?'

'The foreign community of Shanghai. I am merely, you might say, the courier. They sent me because of my German,' he adds with a smile.

'Why should I leave? And on such short notice?' Luckner leans forward. 'I've done nothing wrong.'

'As to that claim, there's difference of opinion. We know about the guns.' Faure raises his hand to silence an outburst. 'To be perfectly candid, your arms dealing isn't the issue. Or it will be the issue only if you force us to bring charges.'

'Then what in hell *is* the issue?'

'Chiang Kai-shek. He wants you out of China.'

'But why?' Luckner is bewildered.

'That's none of your business, Mister Luckner. You should consider yourself lucky. In such matters a year ago, say, you'd have been murdered quietly and thrown into the river.'

'Just like that.'

'Yes, I'm afraid just like that. Only Chiang Kai-shek doesn't want, shall we say, an incident of that kind right now. Not when he's courting the foreign community.'

'Someone else must want me out of here. Chiang's doing it for someone – as a favor.'

'Logical,' the Frenchman says blandly. 'So when can we begin? Tomorrow morning? Arrangements won't take long, I guarantee it.'

A favor for someone or for an organization. He has dealt with so many people in Shanghai, it's hard to imagine who wants to get even. What has he done? This French policeman and the rest of them are moving fast, meaning that Chiang Kai-shek is giving the deportation a high priority. Who has that much influence on Chiang? An idea comes with terrific impact: the Green Gang! Is it possible? Perhaps they don't want to use their customary violence. That would be a courtesy to Chiang – not to have an incident: *German national found floating with a stake up his ass in the Whangpoo.* So the dirty bastards are doing one another favors, and who loses? Erich Luckner. What have I done, though, to bring in the Green Gang? A gun deal? It must be a gun deal. Unknowingly I stepped into their territory. But which deal? Which one?

'Are you following me, Mister Luckner?'

'Oh, excuse me. I was – thinking.'

'I thought you weren't following because of my poor German.'

Faure's German is accented but superb. 'Let me say it again: In my company, tomorrow, you'll go to the American Consulate and get a visa for the Philippines. Don't worry, it will go smoothly.'

'Philippines?' Luckner jerks forward, his chin thrust out. 'American Consulate? What in hell are Americans doing in this?'

With a patient sigh – designed to convince Luckner that patience does have an end – Mister Faure explains that, as part of the foreign community in Shanghai, the Americns have kindly agreed to expedite the matter of his departure. 'You are fortunate in having a place to go,' Mister Faure adds, drawing a silver cigarette case from his pocket.

From the expensive look of it, Luckner assumes this is one policeman who has done very well for himself in the graft-ridden city of Shanghai.

Offering a cigarette (Luckner refuses), the Frenchman explains that they really must resolve the 'difficulty' without delay – before the Kuomintang government changes its mind. He lights up and blows a lazy smoke ring into the cramped office. 'The government is willing to cooperate.'

'The Nationalists? What does "cooperate" mean?'

'You keep whatever assets you have when you leave.'

'This is true?'

'Mister Luckner, no one wishes to blow this affair into something big. *Everyone* is willing to cooperate. They simply want you out of here, quick. In return, there's no objection to your taking your profits.'

Luckner nods with a measure of relief. But the Philippines! It's the last place in the world he would go: the jungles, the heat. 'I will accept your proposition if I'm sent to Germany.'

'We've already talked to the German Consulate.' Faure puffs lightly on the cigarette, staring at Luckner from cold blue eyes. 'They aren't prepared to accept you right now. You see, Mister Luckner, your reputation has unfortunately preceded you. As I'm sure you understand, the German government is somewhat touchy about its nationals selling arms abroad. It's hardly a good image in light of the Great War and reparations to pay. In time – ' He shrugs. 'They might gain permission from Berlin to let you in, but at the moment it's impossible. In fact, on short notice the Philippines is the only place arrangeable for someone like yourself, who has created a certain impression here, as I've said.'

'The Philippines,' Luckner murmurs.

After the Frenchtown policeman has left, Luckner dashes out of his office to make a desperate attempt to stop the deportation. Taking a rickshaw, he realizes in sudden panic that he wants to remain in Shanghai – until eventually he returns to Karlsruhe – more than he hates to depart for Manila. Because in spite of himself Luckner has become a 'China hand.' This frenetic city is, after all, one of the richest on earth. Passing the Stock Exchange, he notices the Chinese pouring in and out of the colonnaded entrance. Because of the unsettled political situation, landlords have flocked from the country to become speculators in gold and bonds; stock jobbers have fleeced these newcomers on the exchange. There's all sorts of money in Shanghai, he thinks with manic gaiety. This is the seat of power and money, where a man like himself can feel truly alive! Leave Shanghai for Manila, for anywhere except Karlsruhe? Impossible for Erich Luckner!

Throughout the day he scurries here and there, determined to use contacts created by selling illegal arms to whatever organization or individual needed them: men of diverse nations, paramilitary groups, compradores, agents of warlords, they have all dealt with him. Yet when he calls at their offices, few even consent to see him. Three good friends at the Japanese Consulate are 'regrettably unavailable.'

He waits longest and with greatest hope at the Rue Molißere office of Chen Chi-mei. Luckner had armed and personally trained the guards on Chen's estate; in the process he'd met the famous financier and since he was German the old man had talked at great length to him about Wagner. Chen knew a great deal about Wagnerian musical dramas, especially the *Ring*; Luckner had to fake his own knowledge of it. Through a ship's captain, bringing arms to Shanghai, Luckner bought Victrola records – Freda Leider and Lauritz Melchior singing '*Liebesnacht*' from *Tristan*; Kirsten Flagstad singing '*Liebestod*' from the same opera; and Richard Crooks singing '*In fernem Land*' from *Lohengrin*; all done by the Berlin State Opera under the direction of Felix Weingartner – and persented them as a gift to old man Chen, goddamnit, to the man who years ago had sponsored and then bailed out Chiang Kai-shek, when the young stockbroker lost heavily on the Gold Bar Exchange. Chen is a past chairman of the Chinese Chamber of Commerce, goddamnit, and a present a close adviser ᵗᵒ Finance Minister T. V. Soong. It' a Shanghai rumor that Chen and T. V. Soong are negotiating huge loan from city bankers to support the Nationalist Army in another push northward. So this wily old man, Chen Chi-mei, is now the best contact anyone can have in Shanghai. And Luckner had given him, goddamnit, at personal expense the most thoughtful of gifts, dearly prized by a Wagnerite who would never have the chance of attending the annual festival at Bayreuth. The old man *can't* refuse, Luckner tells himself, while cooling his heels in the anteroom of the Chen mansion.

But Chen, closer to Chiang Kai-shek and the top officials of the government than any other single individual in China, does in fact refuse to see him. After four hours of suffering the polite excuses of underlings, Luckner stamps out in a fury. They can't do this to him. As a young man he had belonged to Leib-Grenadier Regiment Number 8 and wore a spiked tin-plate helmet and a uniform with cuff-slash piping in crimson and was the scourge of Europe goddamnit; a wizened old opium addict like Chen can't treat him this way!

Next morning, however, having given considerable thought to his dilemma, Luckner docilely welcomes Mister Faure, who comes to escort him through the deportation formalities. In the dark but clarifying hours before dawn, Luckner has reasoned that somehow General Tang arranged for this to happen. The Chinese may knife one another in a midnight alley, but during the day they stick together against foreigners. And when the Chinese unite on an issue, the Powers give in to their demands. So be it. Tang will have his revenge, Luckner thinks, but I've had mine as well. Take my woman, will he? I swore whoever did it would pay!

Within twenty-four hours of getting his visa from courteous Americans (one of them tried out awful German on him), Luckner is heading, with two suitcases and his savings drawn from the Bank of China (T. V. Soong's bank), for a ship waiting in Whangpoo Harbor. In undisguised good spirits Mister Faure comments on the fine weather. Glancing at the impeccably dressed Frenchman, Luckner wonders if the fellow learned his German the hard way – in a prisoner-of-war camp during the Great War. It would account for his obvious glee at my ill fortune. Luckner decides. In the front seat of the official Citroën, two Kuomintang agents are sitting. They wear civilian dress, black skullcaps.

'They were come just for the sightseeing,' Faure explains cheerily.

But when the car stops at the wharf, both agents jump out and take hold of Luckner's arms when he emerges from the back seat.

'Do they think I'll disappear among the coolies?' Luckner asks in annoyance.

Faure smiles.

A launch is waiting at the dock, and the two agents march him briskly toward it, while a coolie follows Mister Faure with the two suitcases.

'Wait.' Luckner pulls loose from the plainclothesmen. 'Let me have a last look at Shanghai, will you. It's been home for eight years.'

'Very well,' Faure says. 'Look.'

Luckner does. His eyes sweep the skyline of the Bund, those sturdy façades brilliant in the winter sunlight. They symbolize the wealth and power of a city he has been forced to leave without the compensation of departing for Karlsruhe. Is it possible? The Philippines!

'You've had your look,' Faure says.

'Wait. One moment.' Luckner turns to the north, staring along the boulevard toward the Shanghai Club, the great hotels, the imposing commercial banks; then to the south where other boats and lighters are loading on the turbulent Whangpoo.

Something catches his eye.

A man and a woman are climbing the gangplank of a little steamer at the next pier south of his own.

The man, a blond foreigner, is well built, scarfaced, young.

The woman wears an unmolded sheath with her slender waist-line dropped to the hips by a wide belt.

'You've had your look, Mister Luckner.'

She wears a bell-shaped felt hat with a single perky feather, black gloves. She carries a black jacket on her arm – it is warm in the December sunshine. And the bitch is also wearing a string of pearls – a gift from him last year.

'Come on.' Faure has taken his arm in a firm grip. The two agents take a step toward him.

'Wait.'

They have reached the top of the gangway. The young man – what is he? a Britisher? – is taking her arm solicitiously, the bastard.

'Come on. Now.' Faure shoves him toward the waiting launch, and the two KMT men grab his arms roughly.

'Wait – ' Glancing past the head of an agent, he says, 'Vera.' In

690

louder voice, 'Vera!' as the three men guide him firmly down into the launch and onto one of the thwarts. 'Wait! Vera!' he shouts, attempting to rise, but the men hold him.

'Sit down. Be quiet. No one can hear you in this noise,' Faure tells him impatiently.

The launch shoves off.

'Goddamnit, wait! Vera!' He is still trying to get to his feet.

'That's enough. Now calm down.' Faure opens his coat and draws out a snubnosed pistol.

The launch, rowed by coolies at bow and stern, moves into the muddy channel, gliding alongside sampan and junk and packet boat, while Faure, facing Luckner, holds the pistol on him and the KMT men keep a grip on his arms.

Aware that his outburst must be strange in Faure's view, feeling somewhat calm now that they are on the water, Luckner explains with an apologetic smile, 'That's a woman I used to know.'

Faure stares coldly at him.

He glances past the Frenchman's shoulder at the steamer into whose cabin deck Vera has disappeared with the sonofabitch Britisher.

'You'll be aboard soon,' Faure says.

'Of course. I agree. I'm sorry to bother you, really, but I'd like to contact her somehow.'

'I'd like to remind you, Luckner, a diplomat's aboard the American ship you're sailing on. He has marine detachment with him. They know about you.'

'Don't worry, friend. I have no intention – '

'They have orders to treat you as their prisoner until you arrive the Philippines.'

'I understand. That's perfectly fine. Only – I wonder: Can I signal that boat tied up over there?' He points beyond Faure's shoulder, but the man doesn't turn to follow the gesture. 'That one?'

'No,' Faure says. 'Sit back and be quiet. In a few days you'll be Manila.'

'I'm afraid you don't understand.' Leaning forward, Luckner feels the pressure tighten on both arms. He sits back; the pressure loosens. 'Here's the thing, you see. I know that woman. *C'etait e affaire de coeur*,' he says in careful French to placate the man. 'just want to signal her, that's all.'

This time it is Faure who leans forward, the muscles tense along jaw line. In a voice low, but scarcely in control, he says, 'I don't care what you want, Luckner. It's the last thing on my mind. I just want you on that ship out of here. I warn you, don't press your luck. Frankly, I wouldn't mind the chance to shoot you, *sale boche*. So keep your dirty fucking mouth shut.'

Yes, old Faure here was certainly in the Great War. But Luckner's isn't looking at the Frenchman. 'Vera,' Luckner says quietly, as he looks past Faure at the docked steamer. A ground swell caused by a big ocean liner's wake begins to rock the launch they all sway a little, causing the agents to grip him tightly again.

'Vera!' he calls out, wondering if by now she might have left her cabin for topside. Damn the vengeful Frenchman! 'Vera!' he calls out, ignoring the gun, the pressure on his arms. 'Vera!' She might be standing at the rail, gazing at the Whangpoo as it snakes eastward toward the open ocean that will take the steamer and her and the sonofabitch Britisher – where? *Where is she going?* 'Vera!' he yells. 'Vera! Vera!' His voice is drowned in the harbor noise. He's shouting now with rising agitation. 'Vera!' She's there somewhere, she must hear him! Is this the last chance? What's she doing with a Britisher? 'Vera!' Convulsed by frustration, he attempts to throw off the restraining hands.

Faure, leaning forward, holds the pistol with one hand and with the other slaps Luckner hard across the face.

Stunned by the stinging blow, Luckner stops calling her name. But as the launch comes alongside an accommodation ladder, he calls again, a loud and lusty yell: 'Vera!'

'Get up there,' Faure orders, waving the pistol.

The agents lift and move him to the first rungs of the lowered ladder. 'Vera,' he mutters. She's over there, past the junks and the harbor craft and the gunboats and the cargo ships, goddamni idly gazing across the water to the ocean that will take her forever out of his life. 'Vera!' His voice rises again in fury and despair. An agent is prodding him in the buttocks from a lower rung. With each rung he climbs, Luckner cries her name in a paroxysm of rage and loss. 'Vera! Vera! Vera!'

Each syllable that he screams across the disquieted water is that of a man ripped from death on the Siberian tundra, a man denied what he feels is his by right of love, of suffering.

'Vera!' he shouts; the word lengthens through the sunlit air until it has the sonority and duration of an animal howl.

'Veeera! Veeera! Veeera!'

Slowly he goes up, howling like a dog.

29

esterday they came down from Peking by train. As usual when
iding in a train, Vera recalled the early days of her family's
ttempted escape from Russia – before they took to wagon, then
oot – and the crude railway ties that separated them farther each
our from their beloved Petrograd. Straw, night soil, disinfectant
a the airless boxcars. It came to that. And worse. Later, when
ey waded through snow, the girl Vera would stare wistfully at a
ain carrying Czech legionnaires; she would watch the white
moke trailing behind the caboose, drifting into threads that
anished on the horizon like the dreams left behind in Petrograd.

Today, standing at the rail of the steamer, there's no hint of
ussia around her at the departure. The chanting of the stevedores
n the Whangpoo dock is enough to dispel a fragile memory:
Ley-la, hui-la' ('I'm coming, step aside') and 'Hui-la, hang-la'
Step aside, let me by') drill at her with the insistency of a
emembered nursery rhyme. She will miss China. That realization
artles her into wondering if it's true she's leaving. Looking at the
miliar Whangpoo with its seagulls and floating garbage and
l-streaked water, with its buoyed clumps of ocean vessels and
oisy channel traffic, Vera can hardly believed she's here in
anghai, much less leaving both it and all of China. Leaving
ufu, the moon gates and courtyards and pavilions. Leaving
an-teh when the smell and feel of him are still vivid. Leaving the
an she loves, leaving him for a blond boy who is now belowdecks
lking comfortably in English with one of the Australian mates.

If her departure is a dream, what's happening inside her is only
o real. Vera passes both hands gently over her flat belly, flat
ough, at least, for her to wear a low-slung belt with the sheath
ess. But it won't be flat for long. That inevitability both amazes
d frightens her. And delights her. Something is there, growing
ently, while the noisy world never suspects. Will she have a girl
e Bright Lotus? She hopes it won't be a boy, who would carry in
veins the blood of a warrior. Most of her life has been spent in
rs or near them. None of them seem to make the world better.
t one. And if she had a son and he grew up to fight and die in a
r, could there be anything worse for a woman? But there are
tters to deal with long before such a question might have

relevance. For example, where will she and the child live – with
Embree? Surely they are linked to him; that is hard to believe, even
harder than believing she's in Shanghai rather than in Qufu.

What's easy to believe, now that she has time to think, i
Embree's part in the strange turn of events. She always knew he
attraction for him. That's to be expected of most men. Vera isn'
modest. In Peking, with time on her hands, she had welcomed th
attention of the strange young American who carried an ax every
where (it was under his suit jacket, he told her proudly), bore a
ugly facial scar, could sleep on a horse, served in a Chinese cavalr
unit, fought in the terrible battle of Hengshui, and possessed th
shy, formal manner of an adolescent.

She liked going to the places discovered for them by Captain Fai
who rarely accompanied them after a while. She will always remem
ber the Restaurant of Ten Thousand Flaming Lotus Flowers, i
maze of latticed courts and hidden rooms from which emanated th
shrieking notes of the *so-na*, the private dining room with a *kan*
arranged as a cushioned divan on which she and Embree reclined
while they snacked on watermelon seeds before the main courses o
meat nd prawns. He bought her a whirligig from a toy seller. The
gawked together at a long caravan of camels, loaded with brick te
for Mongolia, that held up traffic at a main thoroughfare. The
went to the opera at a small theater inside the Tung-an Bazaar; s
on a rickety bench and drank tea while ushers sent wrung-out he
towels sailing over the heads of the audience. Once they stood on th
sidewalk in the Legation and watched a detachment of British ta
come marching by, swinging hands and singing lustily. She begg
him to translate the English, which was too fast for her. Embr
didn't get it all, but with a quick memory had managed to rememb
this much of the sailors' marching song:

> She'd a dark and rolling eye,
> A nice girl, a . . . girl,
> But built on a rakish line.
> I handled her, I dandled her,
> I . . . her, I fondled her,
> I . . . her, I tumbled her.
> . . . found to my surprise
> She was nothing but a fireship
> Dressed in a disguise.

*　　*　　*

694

He had explained, at her urging, that 'tumbled her' meant 'enjoying her' and 'fireship' meant she carried a venereal disease; at least that was his understanding of the British terms. Then he tried to change the subject: What was the navy doing here in Peking? Maybe they were gumboat sailors bound for the inland rivers.

Vera didn't let him divert her from the song. She demanded that he repeat the song again and again – just to see him blush. At that moment she thought of her younger brother Alex who at fourteen joined General Kornilov's army in the west. He'd be about the same age as the American. Did she regard Embree in a sisterly way? She got him to repeat the naughty song not only to make him blush like a young brother but also to skirt the boundary of sexual talk, seductively, as she might do with a man. It was true, true. For against her better judgment, almost against her will, Vera allowed herself to indulge her gift for coquetry. Angry with herself for it, she went at flirtation anyway, aware that she couldn't be around a man long without employing her skill. A growing familiarity with Philip Embree encouraged an outpouring of old tricks: the inappropriate but winsome smile, as if she'd been thinking beyond this moment into a deep and timeless passion for him; a girlish laugh high and pleasant in her throat; the many deliberately carefree gestures calculated to emphasize her variety of mood, her gusto for life, her irrepressible spirit; the profile set in a manner to promote her left jaw line, the better one; the studied look of rapt attention when, in fact, her attention was not on him but on her look of attention – these bewitchments and more all had their source in childhood, when she'd been father's little darling, and were then honed to a keen aesthetic edge by the adversities of womanhood. Vera scorned her talent for charming men, yet practiced it with such effect that the young American was soon hopelessly inflamed: an exercise of her power out of mere habit, not unlike a hunter who stalks game for the fun of it.

She just hoped he wouldn't spoil things by a fumbling declaration of love. What Embree did do, in retrospect, was far more subtle than Vera would have expected from someone so young and inexperienced: He bypassed his feelings for her and instead went straight to her deep-seated fears. At first he hinted of her precarious situation in Qufu, a town that might well be attacked by warlords aware of the General's empty victory at Hengshui and the present deplorable state of his army.

That sort of talk reminded her of Hengshui's aftermath: the

return of wounded to Qufu in the wintry cold. She began to see in Embree the quality of persistence that had enabled him to learn how to sleep on a horse. He bored in – the instability of China, the treachery of warlords, the sad predicament of General Tang, a great man surrounded by enemies. And seeing the effect on her whenever he mentioned the Hengshui wounded, he returned to them again and again, describing his own heartbreaking encounters with them on the march. Vera, unable to divert him from the topic, listened and in listening became tormented and in her torment freely mingled her recollections of the Hengshui wounded and the White refugees during the Siberian march. The old nightmare visited with cruel regularity, drove her to vodka in the hotel room and to sleeples nights, followed by morning nausea – a sure sign of her pregnancy. It was certain now: pregnancy, a possible child. Little episodic panics seized her during the day, whenever she imagined herself with a baby in war-torn China. Aware that Embree, in love, was trying to make her cling to him for an interpretation of her trouble, cling to him she did. The shy, remorseless young man became transformed in Vera's mind into a towering prophet, who spoke aloud the secret anxieties that had pursued her, even at the best of times, since Siberia. Words of her own making rushed into her mouth to remain there unspoken, while Embree talked of 'warlords' and 'treachery' and 'casualties': She translated his words into her own, into 'escape' and 'hunger' and 'snow,' mingled together from a desperate time, until they combined with the old nightmare into a single cohesive expression of fear so compelling that she was ready to bolt.

Then one morning, having endured another terrible night, she was startled to find Captain Fan and Philip Embree at her hotel door. They came with news of the General's ambush in Sian. It was the final blow to whatever peace of mind she had left. Vera scarcely heard Captain Fan's explanation of the politics leading to the ambush. Shan-teh was alive, but sought now by the Central Government in Peking and by the Nationalists in Shanghai and Nanking. Sought for banditry.

'We have a saying in Chinese,' the Captain says coolly. 'Tall trees are cut down.'

She asked them to leave her along awhile, to return later. Sitting on the edge of the bed, she conjured Shan-teh in her mind – or tried to; fear shook her memory. But then she told herself a story

Returning to Qufu after the ambush, Shan-teh gathered his assets, just as she had gathered her treasure to leave Shanghai: a bundle of Mex dollars, some old jewelry he hadn't told her about, a few priceless scrolls, the songbirds in their cages. He hastened to Peking, where to her amazement and relief he burst into the hotel room, urging her to get ready, for they would have immediately. Traveling in some sort of disguise – she didn't halt the story for such details – they went by train to Wuhan and thence south, all the way to the fog-enshrouded mountains near Kweilin. Here, combining their funds, they bought a modest cottage overlooking the river that flows beneath steep limestone canyons eroded by time into fantastic shapes once described – she forgot by which poet – as blue jade hairpins. They had their treasures to contemplate and before the baby's birth they got married in both Christian and Buddhist ceremonies (she'd read Chiang Kai-shek did that), and when the baby came, Shan-teh wept for joy.

The story, she told herself, was beautiful, it was false, it was stupid. Seized by a fit of crying, Vera had scarcely repaired her face before the two men returned. Their behavior, restrained but solicitous, reminded her of men giving solace to a widow, and she became more alarmed than ever. They took her for a long stroll in the western, less populated district of Tartar City.

Once, halting, she told them that the General had promised to take her to Tai Shan, the sacred mountain. 'I would like to see it someday,' she added sadly.

A funeral passed; the trio watched as the white-clad mourners and the chanting priests went by. Beggars in ceremonial robes, borrowed for the occasion, carried lanterns and life-sized paper mummies to be burned. The coffin and catagalque were borne by at least twenty coolies. This must have been a rich man, Vera thought. Blue-hooded Peking carts, expensive ones of carved polished wood and iron-studded wheels, held the family. Costumed attendants tossed spirit money into the air to appease demons. As they walked along, Captain Fan explained that when the coffin lid was finally closed at the temple, mourners would draw back, for people believe a man's health can be impaired if his shadow gets enclosed in the box. To avoid having their shadows fall into the grave, coffin bearers and gravediggers often fastened their shadows to themselves by trying a strip of cloth around their waists.

Halting, Vera said, 'Captain Fan, I'm not interested in funerals and superstitions. I'm interested in the General. Haven't you heard from him? Hasn't he sent a wireless? Why don't we have instructions? What will happen now?'

'That's hard to predict,' Fan replied judiciously. 'Forgive my impertinence, Madam, but if I were you, I'd think of myself.'

'The General will think of me too. You haven't heard from him?'

The Captain shook his head.

'Have you wired him?'

'It's for him to contact us when he's ready, Madam. Those are our orders. To return to my impertinent observation; if I were you, Madam, I'd think first of my safety.'

'Safety,' she repeated. 'I'm thinking of the fastest train back to Qufu.'

'You must not do that,' the Captain said with surprising bluntness.

'I want to. I will.'

'Madam – ' the Captain began.

'Today, now, this minute. I want to get the ticket now!' She learned forward, as if quite prepared to run.

'Listen to him,' Embree urged. 'Please do.'

Turning to the Captain, she nodded impatiently. 'Say what you have to say.'

'It's difficult to explain – '

'Oh *say* it!' she commanded, near tears in her frustration.

'I regret it as a citizen of China, but you must know that all of us, including the General himself, consider you a foreigner. We think of you as a foreigner, we never forget it.'

The words, their truth, stunned her into docile silence.

'Look at it from the General's point of view, Madam. He's just been attacked – ambushed. He has enemies in Peking who might have planned it. And you've been in Peking.'

'Both of us,' Embree added.

'It would surely occur to him that you might have cooperated in some way, might have given some assistance – '

'Wait. Don't say any more.' Looking around, Vera noticed a little tea shop and pointed to it. 'Let's go there.'

When they were seated at a table, the Captain asked if she wanted anything with her tea.

'I don't want tea. I don't want anything.'

The Captain waved off the approaching waiter.

'Now,' said Vera, her lips trembling, 'I want you to repeat what you said.'

'Madam.' He hesitated.

Fan's lack of ease, such a departure from his usual confidence, heightened her own anxiety. 'Did you say I might have cooperated? Given assistance? Is that what you said?'

'Madam, I said it would occur to the General that you've been in Peking where his enemies are.'

'And I cooperated with them?' She glanced wildly at Embree as if to get assurance that she understood. She turned back to Fan. 'Do I follow you? The General would accuse me of some kind of betrayal?'

The Captain nodded.

'Without evidence? Just like that? Just because I was in Peking?'

'Madam.' Again he hesitated. 'I haven't been altogether candid. You see, he did send a wireless.'

'I thought so!' Vera, turning, gave Embree a triumphant smile. 'See? I knew it.' Then she demanded to know from the Captain what the message said.

'For you, for both of us, to return at once to Qufu. "At once" was repeated.'

Relief swept through her. 'I knew it. I knew he'd want me to come home.' She stared at the late sunlight falling across the old table, warped through the years by spilled tea. 'I knew it,' she repeated and glared at Captain Fan. 'When did you get the wireless?'

'Madam, I'm afraid that's the problem. Apparently it was sent before he went to Sian.'

'But that's days ago! What do you mean by "apparently"?'

'I never received it until this morning. Chinese communications, Madam – the delays. I didn't have the wireless, so we didn't act on it. There, it's out.'

Vera looked down at the bare warped table where thousands of cups had sat. 'I want tea. No, I don't want it.'

'I regret the lie,' Fan continued, hesitantly. 'But I was too embarrassed today. I hated to upset you needlessly. My apologies, Madam. I – '

'Needlessly?' After a glance at him, she looked at the street, at people bustling home in the dusk of Peking, in the yellow dust-filled haze. She tries to steady her mind. She was supposed to return at once to Qufu. Instead she remained in Peking without sending Shan-teh a word. Then he was attacked. How would that look to him? Having betrayed him to his Peking enemies, she was afraid to return to Qufu.

'Take me to the hotel,' she said to Embree, who leaped to his feet.

'Madam – ' began the Captain.

'Don't say any more. Say *nothing*.' Vera rose unsteadily, feeling weakness pervade her body. 'It's all needless now. Absolutely needless.'

They walked back to the hotel in silence. Vera refused to take a Peking cart or a taxi. As she walked, her legs felt stronger and with determination she straightened her back. Surely it was needless to let herself go. Nothing was irrevocable except death, her father used to say. She must think of what had occurred as a terrible problem which might yet have a solution. And if no solution could be found, she mustn't think of it at all. Toward the end of the walk, she moved resolutely and caught Embree staring at her. What was in his look? Curiosity or bewilderment? Or hope?

In the hotel lobby, aware that further apologies or discussions of the matter were unacceptable, the Captain said a curt goodbye and left.

Vera regarded the young American closely. His face showed a number of fleeting emotions, none of which she could identify. This was no time for her to be alone with her thoughts, and although she feared his intrusion into them, Vera decided to ask him to have dinner with her. 'We might as well go to the dining room,' she said and watched his face suffuse with surprise and pleasure.

I must eat and stay healthy, she told herself. In spite of everything she must do that. There was a child. Wasn't there? Its existence still baffled her.

During dinner, seeing her cut the noodles with her soup spoon, Embree exclaimed, 'You mustn't cut them!'

Amused, she looked at his passionate American face. 'Why not?'

'Noodles represent life to the Chinese. Cut them, you shorten yours.'

Vera brought the soup spoon down into the bowl of noodles. 'I don't care about long life.'

Reaching across the table, he touched her hand. Vera, not

wanting his touch, let his hand remain over hers anyway.

'It's rotten luck for the General,' he said. 'I've learned to admire him.'

'You had to learn it?' Vera asked with a frown.

'It's a long story, but when I first heard of him, I imagined a cold-blooded murderer. And he did kill – or his men did – some people I cared about.'

'Bandits.'

'Then you know the story.'

Vera smiled. 'I happened to be in Qufu when he set out to get his revenge. That's what it was – revenge. Isn't that what men fight and die for?' Studying Embree's features, she wondered if less experience could show in an adult face. He seemed unused by life, yet much had already happened to him. She could imagine him in old age with boyish features that would betray nothing of the tumult he might have witnessed and endured.

Now Embree was speaking of the General, praising his intelligence, his ideals, his courage – but in the manner of a man who wished to impress a woman by his own generosity in giving a rival a just hearing. She made sure that her hand lay inert under his.

Withdrawing his hand in sudden embarrassment, Embree picked up his chopsticks. 'You mustn't worry.'

'Of course not. I won't worry.'

'I'm serious. I'll see to it you don't have to worry.'

Words she had heard so often from men – they brought a smile to her lips. Yet she realized this young man meant them or thought he meant them. His earnestness possessed a certain eloquence which began almost imperceptibly to take command of their conversation. He was telling her about the American university, called Yale, where he had studied. Once again he was starting to brag in an obvious attempt to impress his lady love; it was amusing in its directness and reminded her of young sailors off navy gunboats who presented themselves at the brothel door, money in hand, like children buying cakes in a bakery. 'There's so much I want to see and do,' he said eagerly.

'What are you trained to do?' she asked with interest; it occurred to her that in spite of all his talk he had never told her that.

'It's not what I'm trained to do that counts,' he said evasively. 'it's what I can make myself do. For example, when I came to China, I didn't know how to ride a horse.'

Poor fellow, she thought, so in love. Infatuation in other people

701

has always appealed to Vera. Easily infatuated herself, she has understood the vulnerability, coupled with a wild desire to please, that the emotion can bring. 'Now you can not only ride a horse,' she said, 'but sleep on one as well.'

Putting his chopsticks down, Embree said, 'Are you making fun of me?'

'Of course not.' Poor vulnerable fellow, she thought. 'Actually I'm impressed.' And Vera meant it, there in the lambent candlelight of the hotel dining room. Not many young men could have done what this one had done – prospered as well as survived in a war-torn land. She thought of the ax shoved under his belt beneath the jacket; he had learned to swing that too and split a man's head open: for him, at least, an accomplishment.

It was her turn to reach out and touch his hand – a sisterly gesture perhaps – but misinterpreting it, Embree gripped hers hard.

'I don't want to see you hurt, Vera.'

'I won't be hurt. You told me not to worry, remember?'

'Believe me, the General is going down.'

'Can you be sure of that?' she asked coolly.

'They all agree – Fan, Chia, the others: Hengshui was a victory that defeated him.' Learning forward, his square young face tense and passionate, he explained once again the General's dilemma. His army sat astride the corridor between Shanghai and Peking; who commanded it commanded the approach to both cities, so Chang Tso-lin and Chiang Kai-shek viewed the occupation of Shantung Province, including Tang's portion of it, a matter of vital strategic importance. Yet the General had behaved too independently to foster in either major warlord any confidence in him as an ally. Added to these threats were Feng on the west, old Dog Meat on the east, and General Sun Ch'uan-fang on the south.

The wide face with the sturdy, prominent chin and the steady blue eyes and the American's persistent eagerness all had their effect on Vera. Typically, she cared little for the labyrinthine politics that centered on personal animosities, treachery, and opportunism. But she took her emotional cue from this passionate young American, who had risen again in her estimation from lovesick adolescent to prophet of doom. Through his spoken words she heard the unsaid words of a secret language known to her inner-most being: snow, hunger, cold, escape.

At last, with a sigh, Embree leaned back and said, 'Do you see, Vera?'

After a pause, she nodded. 'Yes,' she replied quietly.

'Fan told us: Tall trees are struck down.'

'Yes, I believe it.' And she did. They would hound Shan-teh, scheme against him, until finally one of them or a combination of them would get him. Not because of territory or anything like that, but because he was a good man, because they recognized in him aspirations that no one, not even himself, could fulfill, because they saw in him someone who had a vision beyond their time, a vision turning backward into the ancient world of simple but noble goals, because ultimately he was wrong for modern China, because he represented what never was or will be.

'You're no longer safe with the General. Do you understand that, Vera? It's important to me you understand.'

'Yes, I do, I understand.'

'Do you also understand I mean to protect you?'

She looked at him; perhaps he was not so young after all. He had taught himself to ride and sleep on a horse, to use an ax.

'Do you understand that, Vera?'

'Yes. I understand that too.'

'I'm glad, I really am. Because it's the truth. I will protect you.'

'Yes,' Vera said. He had told her such things before, and each time she had put them aside as the dire predictions of a moment, their solemnity passing when the moment did. A gypsy fortune-teller used to come to the Petrograd house and frighten everyone with tales of doom; for an hour the house would be solemn and brooding, but soon afterward, as if windows had been opened in a stale room, everyone would laugh and play harder than before. It had been like that with Embree; now it was different. His pessimistic analysis, born of love, was no longer like the gypsy's gloomy divinations over tea leaves; he had really convinced Vera. Without a child in her womb, she told herself, she might find the courage to go back to Qufu, but her fear has been doubled by the double life of her body. 'Yes, I understand,' she said again, this time without prodding. 'I see it. You are right, I believe you.'

Later, with the bill paid, they walked into the hotel lobby. A stairway led two flights to her room, and they both halted to look at the curving banister. Turning to look steadily at him, Vera said, 'Will you come up for a few minutes?'

He nodded wordlessly.

As they ascended the staircase, Vera asked herself why she was doing this. She didn't want him, although it was plain he wanted her desperately. After a while, when she would allow him to kiss, then 'tumble' her – to use that quaint English word – she would defend her decision by pointing to the truth: Shan-teh could no longer protect her, at least not for long, assuming he would accept her back anyway. On the second flight of stairs, Vera wondered if she might send a letter explaining everything. But he would never trust her again, never, a foreign woman. The point to remember was the child. She must think of the child now that she could no longer count on Shan-teh.

Coming to her room, Vera fumbled in her handbag for the key. She handed it to Embree, whose fingers trembled when he bent down to the lock. His face was cloudy and solemn. She pitied him his anxiety.

Later she would contemplate a baleful truth: Before dropping one lover, she has always tried to transfer herself to a new one.

Lo, Love once more, the limb-dissolving Monarch,
The bitter-sweet impracticable thing,
The wild beast that tears me fiecely.

She thought it was strange to remember those lines from Sapph after so many years. She blinked in the morning light streaming through the gauze curtains, giving the room a soft glow. He was gone. She had sent him packing at dawn with a kiss, telling him she needed sleep. Actually, she had dreaded breakfast with her ecstatic young lover, who would be predictably immoderate in his compliments, energetic in his attentions. That was the sort of man he was: more delightful in remembrance than in presence.

Turning on her stomach, Vera stared across the rumpled bed at her clothes neatly folded and placed on a chair. 'The limb-dissolving Monarch' – she and her younger sister had stolen the book from their aunt, the racy one from Kiev, who often came to stay with the family after broken love affairs. Vera and her sister had pored over the strange lines, wondering what many of them meant but convinced they were all heavy with forbidden pleasure. The girls had memorized three or four poems and could hardly declaim the passages under the bending arbor in the garden for their giggling. 'The wild beast that tears me fiercely' had sent them into gales of laughter.

This morning, shaking her dark hair lazily and rolling over on her back, clutching the warm sheet to her bruised shoulders – sore from nipping bites – Vera had to admit with mild surprise that the Monarch of Love had indeed managed to dissolve her limbs last night. She had found Embree's boyish joy momentarily exciting. Surely there were moments when his passion engendered in her body more than the counterfeit of pleasure. He was, of course, sexually ignorant. But his inept ways were endurable because they lacked the component of brutality that usually accompanied ineptitude. In sum, Philip Embree was a better lover than most of the men she had known.

Vera moved the flat of her palm around and around on her belly, as if the gesture might stimulate a little cry of recognition from the life within. She could kill it. She has done so before; yes, and may have lost someone as precious as a Bright Lotus. She won't have an abortion again.

What would Shan-teh think of the child? He would be happy, but under no circumstances could he acknowledge it as his own. Not in his precarious situation. 'What is that you say? General Tang's concubine giving birth to foreign bastards?' Yet another nail driven into his coffin. But she wouldn't think such things. She loved him, that was true, even after a night of energetic lovemaking with another man. Vera sat up, allowing the sheet to fall from her rosy breasts. She could get a train today, risk his fury, plead to be taken back, regain his trust. It would be worth everything, yet mean nothing if hostile armies swooped down on Qufu, threatening the life of her child. Was she honest? Was she thinking of the child or herself? Both, yes, both. She was afraid. Slumping down on the bed again, Vera put her face into the pillow, overcome by the inertia of fear. And then she felt it, the nightmare coming. She could feel it on the way, like the distant tread of an army, its relentless and ordered sequence of images preparing to march like soldiers through her mind. Breathing deeply, she waited, but the moment passed, the tread growing faint.

So many men. Now a new one, an athletic young American who carried an ax and made love with the mindless physicality which he must bring to riding horses and running foot races. Yet she could manage him, at least for a while, as she had always managed her lovers. Then someday, his ardor slaked, her hold on him loosened, he'd leave her, a free and satisfied man.

Why, she asked herself gloomily, had she ever lost Yu-ying?

Before rising from bed, she indulged in a fantasy. She had had the baby and had lifted it high – a little girl, like Bright Lotus – for Yu-ying to see, and Yu-ying, rushing through the crowded Shanghai lane, stretched out her arms to take the child.

Vera didn't get dressed that morning, but merely prepared herself for a new onslaught, knowing it would come. And she was right – a frantic knock on the door about ten. When she opened it he barged in, his kisses feverish and insistent. Aware that he wouldn't be denied, laughingly she pulled him to the bed. Later, as they lay side by side, he told her the news: Captain Fan had booked passage for them from Peking to Shanghai to Hong Kong.

Propped on her elbows, Vera stared curiously at him. Were all Americans as energetic, impulsive? He meant to get her out of China – now. Perhaps it was a measure of his fear that she'd return to the General. He should fear that. Even while she lay naked and sweaty beside this man, her mind returned to Qufu and the bedroom there, to the older, equally ardent, but gentler man she loved.

And yet Embree seemed to know her secret language. When he told her of the unexpected booking, of the 'good news' as he called it, Vera heard 'escape.'

But even if she wished to leave, there was the question of money. She wouldn't tell Embree about her treasure. If this man wanted to get her out of China, he'd do it on his own. As if she had voiced her thoughts, Embree volunteered the information happily: He had the money.

'Where did you get it?' she asked with a bluntness she was learning from him.

'I have it.' Hesitating a moment, he added, 'I sent home to America and got it. We have what we need.'

'Hong Kong,' she mused. She wanted to think about that, but the infatuated young man covered her mouth with his. Once again she let him have her.

Pushing the wet hair back from her forehead, Vera turned to Embree, whose young face was blank with satisfaction. 'Very well,' she said. 'Take me to Hong Kong.'

Standing at the steamer's rail, overlooking the wild Whangpoo river traffic on this crisp December forenoon, Vera has the time and inclination to review the events of the past few days. Fan has stayed in Peking – a new member of Marshal Chang Tso-lin's staff. This confirms her suspicion that the Captain had been connected with the Sian ambush. Surely he'd kept Shan-teh's wireless from her in order to create the distrust that ruined her chances of returning to Qufu. Embree too – he must have been involved somehow; that's clear from his close relationship with Fan. She can despise Embree (as she despises Fan) or judge him by the loose standards the world applies to a lover. Of one thing Vera is now convinced: the failed ambush is only one in an inevitable string of attempts to murder Shan-teh. There's nothing to be done about it. Can she be so practical? She'd better be. Unlike that girl Eugenia whom she met in the Shanghai park with a loathsome little dog, Vera has no wealthy Britisher to protect her. For the moment, at least, she has an adventurous young American who got money somewhere – where is none of her business. She hopes Embree never tells her either; she never believed that story about getting it from America.

There's plenty to worry her without Embree's conscience coming between them – for example, her pregnancy. What will he think when it begins to show in a month or two? She will watch her diet, so the weight doesn't come on too quickly. At least she can count on one irrevocable fact: They went to bed soon enough for her to justify calling the child his. But if it has Chinese features? Perhaps by then he'll like the idea of a little family and accept the General's child as his own. Perhaps, perhaps not. What can she do about it now? Nothing but continue on to Hong Kong. There's also another possibility, which she has considered more than once. She can get off the steamer and go to see Erich Luckner, who might pull out one of his beloved guns and shoot her head off. Or he just might fall to his knees, like a Russianized German, and beg her forgiveness. She has read her Dostoevski! The thought of Erich begging forgiveness is a heady one; Vera smiles as she pulls the jacket collar around her throat. The sun, passing beyond the cabin deck, has left it chilly, but she doesn't want to go inside. This may be her last look at a city where she has lived most of her adult life.

Luckner.

Even if she could, would she go back to him? Who, really, does she prefer, the innocent American or the disillusioned German? She prefers the noble Chinese, but can't have him. Such is life, so no more wondering and quibbling. In Russian she whispers aloud,

707

'Vera Rogacheva, you are going to Hong Kong with an American.'
Then she taps the ship's railing three times in a remembered girl-hood act of decision.

'Take your last look at Shanghai!'

She turns at the sound of his voice. Embree, carrying a full-length marmot coat over his arm, is hastening toward her. He's bringing the coat for her – how thoughtful. Will he remain so, once the novelty has worn off in the time-honored way of men with women? Vera asks herself, while giving him a bright smile when he wraps the coat around her shoulders.

'The Australian mate swears the trip to Hong Kong is almost always smooth. You won't get seasick. He and I guarantee it!'

So boyishly solicitous – how lovely. Yet again the sad question intervenes between Vera and her pleasure in his attentiveness: Solicitous for how long? She has already detected in him moments of restlessness, and in her own moodier moments Vera wonders if perhaps he isn't one of the most disquieted men she has ever known. Is it possible? Vera thinks she recognizes it in his sudden far-flung gaze, his turning away toward the distance, his abrupt removal into a dream perhaps not even he understands. She can't compare him to anyone else. Erich Luckner had been forced into a life of wandering, into adventures he didn't want. What Erich truly is is a German brugher strolling toward his favorite tavern at sunset. As for Shan-teh, given the chance he would be content with a stand of trees, a pond at the foot of some hills, a cup of tea, a scroll to contemplate. Embree may well be driven by a demon only recently known to him. Or is she romanticizing the fellow as she used to do the guardsmen met at Petrograd balls? Better for her if she's wrong about Embree. Searching his young face, Vera sees nothing but happiness and health.

'Look at the shipping,' he exclaims, leaning over the rail. 'See that steamer? It's American.'

'Yes, I saw the flag.'

'The mate says she's bound for the Philippines.' Turning with a smile, he says, 'Would you like to go there?'

'Certainly not,' Vera replies, laughing. 'I don't care for jungles.'

'I'd go anywhere.' Embree adds, 'With you.'

'Or just anywhere?'

'We'll be happy in Hong Kong.'

'Will me?' she asks doubtfully, putting her hand on his shoulder.

'I promise you.'

'I know you promise me, and I'm pleased, only you can't promise a thing like happiness.'

'I promise we'll be happy in Hong Kong,' he declares.

'Let's start more simply. For example –' Vera hesitates. This test has come suddenly to mind. Will she go through with it? 'For example, the ax.'

In the gray light – a cloud bank has obscured the sun – Embree looks curiously at her. 'What about it?'

'Throw it overboard.'

'The ax? Why?'

'As a test of your promise we'll be happy.'

Embree laughs uneasily. 'How can that be a test of happiness?'

Vera isn't sure herself what she means. After a thoughtful pause, she explains. 'The ax means violence. Where we're going, we don't want violence any more. Do we? Isn't that true?'

'Of course it is,' he agrees. 'And I'll get rid of the ax.'

'Good.' She looks at his waist, knowing the ax is there under his coat. 'Throw it overboard.'

'Well, let's wait until we get to Hong Kong.'

'Why not throw it now?'

'Because – well, there are pirates in the South China Sea. I'd feel better if we waited.'

The image of Embree protecting her against a horde of pirates clambering aboard is oddly comforting, although Vera knows a boarding party of cutthroats wouldn't be deterred by one man with an old ax. It means, nevertheless, this man is prepared to give up his life for her. She has no doubt of it whatsoever. He'd give up his life for her, but Vera understands that he'll never give up the ax. Leaning forward, she kisses him on the cheek. 'Then wait.'

In a few minutes he goes below again to check on the mess schedule. Vera watches him disappear down the hatchway: strong back, light blond hair, the energetic step of someone embarking on an adventure. She is swept momentarily by fear of him; in truth she knows less about Embree than about any man to whom she has attached herself. He never speaks of his past. Not like Erich Luckner, for example, who like herself lives as much in the past as the present. Embree never explains himself through his family, as Yen-teh inevitably does in describing thought and action. Embree gives her the strange feeling sometimes of having appeared on earth full-blown – Who did that? A Greek god or goddess? Anyway, this young man seems to have bypassed family and chilhood. A few times, asking him about his early life, Vera has received only a shrug, a halfhearted grin, a vague reply. He went to a university called Yale and studied languages; this is all she knows. Does he believe in God? Such questions come naturally in bed, after lovemaking, when there has been intensity of feeling. But Embree, so ardent in other ways, never wants such conversation. He neither asks for her beliefs nor offers his own.

Yet she can live with him. She thinks it was Dostoevski who wrote, 'Man is a pliable animal, a being who gets used to anything.' That applies to woman as well! This American boy is strong, intelligent, unafraid. Indeed, she may be happy with him, so that on drowsy mornings she can open her eyes and stretch her arms and feel content, secure. Until (she knows this too) a stirring of vague depression reminds her that with him she's merely playing at love.

He's returning from below decks, holding a bottle of beer toward her. They pass it back and forth, enjoying the bitter taste in air made crisp by winter clouds obscuring the sun and shutting off its warmth.

Vera is thinking that the treasure is below in their cabin. She is picturing the suitcase containing her life, even while they are chatting about the weather, the ships at anchor, the big liners heading for sea. He doesn't know about the treasure, about the valuables accumulated in a decade of more degradation than the poor fellow could ever imagine. She must trust him to provide for her in Hong Kong, yet she hasn't faith, can't have it in someone who won't even tell her what he's trained to do. Yet she admire his native ability and his courage. Does she? The Chinese say, 'A discontented mind is like a serpent trying to swallow an elephant.' The boy is yours now, Vera tells herself, so believe in him. And she will. She has not survived until this moment without discovering in herself immense strength. Vera will summon it again. I will, she tells herself, while tilting up the bottle for another taste of the good beer.

'Hong Kong,' Embree mutters, lost in a private image of his adventure. It's as if, for the moment, he has forgotten her.

Handing him the bottle, Vera watches him finish and toss it into the water. A sampan coolie poles over quickly and scoops the bobbing bottle out.

A glance sideways at the blond young man propels Vera into strange vision of the future. She can imagine him accepting the child, once he gets over his masculine disappointment at its features. He's not the sort of man to walk out in a huff. A sense of duty would keep him functioning until – until, perhaps, from the Hong Kong wharfs he watched the ships go out. She can think of him staring for hours at the batwing sails of junks spread to the wind. That might be what would take him from her: just the look of ships on the horizon, lugging their cargo to the far ends of the world. That might be enough to make him pack his bag and stick the ax in his belt and leave. Because like Shan-teh he's a warrior seeking a war. Shan-teh may do it for some deep-rooted foolish sense of honor. Embree does it for adventure. She can imagine him sending her cards with postmarks from all the trouble spots of the world. And always the self-absolving words appended to the end of each one: *I'm sorry*.

Vera feels the purse in her hand; inside is the ink stone that Shan-teh brought from Canton. It is always with her, the white jade which, when contemplated, dispels evil thoughts. The plain white oblong of fine grain. For some reason she thinks of it now, passionately. The purse seems heavier, as if the little ink stone, expanding, has taken up the whole inside.

'Take your last look at Shanghai,' Embree says again. He points at the assembly of ships and junks. 'We'll be sailing any minute.'

Smiling, Vera allows him to press his hand against her thigh. He will want her again before they clear the Whangpoo. Any minute now they will move away from the dock and he'll take her hand and lead her to the cabin. The sequence is inevitable. But she isn't thinking of that. She's thinking of Shan-teh, embattled in the ancient town of Qufu.

She has a strong urge to open the handbag, take out the ink stone, and hold it in her hand. But she can't do that in front of Embree.

'Look,' he says. 'The sun's coming out again. We'll have a beautiful day for sailing.'

'Yes, beautiful.'

In Peking she had visited the shop with songbirds for sale: the old canary, the gray thrush, the cinnamon lark. She had promised to return there and select one.

Vera tells herself, I will never buy him a songbird now.

30

Each morning the General rides out to camp, inspects his troops, and oversees work on the new winter barracks. Last year nearly all the men remained in tents, and many suffered from exposure. With the monthly appropriations still coming from Peking and Jinan (Chang Tso-lin's assassination attempt has not affected the financial arrangement) Tang has been able to continue work on barracks that should be completed before the heavy snows arrive. He no longer has to worry about standard weaponry, having captured tons of munitions and stacks of rifles during the Hengshui campaign. In fact, he now has a surplus of light cannon and trench mortars. It's ironic that if he were to fight the battle now, he wouldn't need the arms shipment from the German bastard who contributed so effectively to his losses at Hengshui. The General goes among his men every day, attempting to rally their spirit. It's difficult to do in the cold gray weather. Daily the wounded return to their duties, but many of them are crippled in some way, a reminder that a battle of inexplicable ferocity has robbed them all of something, something they can't name, something beyond an arm or leg; perhaps it is a belief that war can be fought without such appalling casualties. They have fought a twentieth-century battle.

Fortunately the army is not now threatened, partly because General Sun Ch'uan-fang is lying ill to the south; and partly because other warlords, including Chang Tso-lin and Chiang Kai-shek, are facing morale problems similar to his own during the harsh winter season. General Tang still maintains a busy schedule. He has made a trip to Yi Nan, where a division is quartered, and to Lin Yi, where the entire Second Corps is billeted. Many of the troops at Lin Yi have to be quartered in villages, local farms, and temples. To make these arrangements is time-consuming and costly; over the mild i insistent objections of his Lin Yi staff, the General insists on reimbursing the peasants for boarding his soldiers and at a fair rate.

The news accounts of his 'banditry' amuse him; he views as quite harmless the righteous declarations of Chiang Kai-shek among others, promising to stamp out such 'public depredations. Tomorrow his seizure of the train may well be mythologized into an episode of daring. He has only to offer something of value to the other warlords.

In solitude at night, his hands fisted at his back as he paces, the General poses questions of a philosophical nature. For example, how can a Chinese militarist effectively command a large army? Traditionally, it has been a question without an answer, for history has shown time and again that a Chinese general who begins successfully with a small force nearly always comes to grief in command of a large body of troops. The thesis applies to himself, for that matter. As a division commander he made a reputation for battlefield tactics. Yet as demonstrated to his melancholy satisfaction during certain moments at Hengshui, he lacked confidence (secretly) to command in direct ratio to the size of the force at his disposal. It was a subtle feeling, and at Hengshui must have had little or no bearing on the conduct or outcome of the battle. Yet it was there. Pacing in his quarters near of bird cages, he tries to make sense of this perception. After deep thought, he concludes that the Chinese family is actually the source of a military problem. From infancy the Chinese learns to count on personal relationships; as he moves beyond such intimate bonds, his loyalty and concomitantly his effectiveness begin to weaken. He is like the falcon that goes wild when it transgresses the limit of its master's control. Tang reasons that when an army becomes too big for personal control, the commander must rely on abstract authority, yet his officers and men have been taught to follow a man, not a principle, Glancing back over history, he perceives it has always been so. China has counted on intimate ties in the army and government similar to those existing in the family. His people have developed a system of political and military organization suitable for small countries, like the medieval city-states in Europe he once read about in a world history.

Pacing – he still limps – back and forth in his room, the General wonders if it will be necessary to change the social system of China in order to build an effective army, much less an effective government. It is an awesome thought, yet this sort of philosophical questioning helps him retain his sense of importance in the scheme of things.

For he has been deeply shaken by the Sian ambush. Not by the act itself – not rare in China – but by the manner of betrayal that led to it. The plot itself was doubtless hatched by Chang Tso-lin and implemented by Captain Fan, who saw a means of rising in the military hierarchy. The American's ready cooperation is obvious now, and the General is amazed at his own failure to suspect a healthy young man might try to seduce an attractive woman. Of couse, no Chinese officer would have contemplated an act of seduction as being worthy of the betrayal of his commander. Herein lies a clue to the General's poor judgment: he has been regarding the American the way he would a Chinese. A Chinese officer – witness Captain Fan – would betray him for gain, in either money or position, but certainly not for a woman.

And yet there are few women like Black Jade.

Tang chooses to regard her betrayal as something inexplicable, beyond his understanding; it is fate at its most mysterious. Often in his nightly pacing, he recites aloud an old saying: ' "A woman's heart is like a needle at the bottom of the sea. You may look hard and for a long time, but you won't find it." '

They were doomed by the differences in their people. Black Jade went far in bridging the gap – the effort had been hers; he had done little on his own – but ultimately Vera Rogacheva must have been weighed down by the load of memories she carried from Russia, by her language, by everything in fact that was outside of the love she felt for him. Hopeless from the start. And he knew it. And perhaps she had known it too, making her attempt to hold back the inevitable failure all the more admirable. He ends by loving her.

Every day he brings in the old diviner for a talk. Although he no longer wants the yarrow stalks cast – indeed, they have proved too consistently right for comfort – the General gives the old man opium money just for a short talk about aything: the weather, the state of the army, food supplies in the district, the price of beans. Tang lets the diviner choose the topic, not asking even for stories about the old days when the diviner, then a cavalryman, served under his father. He derives from these pleasant but aimless conversations a kind of special contact with someone from the past. Continuity is what the old fellow means to him. This beggar who shuffles through the courtyards of the Residence is befuddled by opium, saddened by memories of friends now dead, yet once he warred and loved on this selfsame ground, just as millenniums ago the Great Sage strolled under the pines of Qufu, envisioning a nobler world.

Another old man enters the General's world with special vividness – his servant Yao. Although Yao does nothing more or less than he has done for years, there's no female around now with whom he must share the General's attention. Tang is amused by the old man's newfound gaiety in a household bereft of women. Humming folk tunes, Yao patters in and out with bamboo whisks and tea trays and extra clothing, quite prepared to scold his master for not dressing warmly enough against the biting wind that seeps through the masonry cracks.

Sometimes, after morning Tai Chi, the General returns to his quarters and watches old Yao take care of the songbirds. All these years the General never realized how much attention the birds get from Yao, who not only cleans their cages but carefully inspects their droppings – they must be firm, he explains, and not of a greenish color. He gives the birds their grit and cuttlebone, studying them for puffed-up wings and runny noses – signs of illness too. He is partial to the young cock, a frosted-opal bronze, who sings, Yao claims, like a god come down to earth. He often shakes his finger angrily at a broken-capped gold female, whom he has labeled surly. But then he's not altogether happy with the other female either, who happens to be sweet-natured, a joy to her cinnamon mate. Tang stands by quietly when the old man gives them their grooming and clips their nails with a sharp knife. Even with trembling hands he's an expert at missing the little vein near the nail; if he nicked it, the bird would bleed to death. In a thin proud voice he declares that he has never killed a bird, and he has been clipping their nails since the age of twelve.

To relax after a long day, the General strolls through the courtyards to the garden, which it has been his privilege to do ever since Black Jade befriended the child of the Kongs. He goes at times of moonlight, remembering her intense relationship to the moon, her passionate hatred of it, her growing love for it. Under the silvery glow (frost shimmering on the rocks), he often sits by one of the ponds, with its edges iced, and listens to the wind make bare branches tick together. He looks at the shape of a pavilion or at a towering arrangement of Tai Hu stones. He breathes deeply, mimicking the rhythm of his breath while playing Tai Chi Chuan. Chinese mystics have said that a man in harmony with his breath can reach the utmost sympathy for the universe, because its breath has become his own. Such a man can feel in a tree that's flowering the same flowering in his veins; his feet take hold in the earth like the roots of the tree; and in his ears he listens to the energy of leaves. In boyhood, having read such things, Tang used to sit in front of a tree and try to breathe so as to enter its branches. Now, his nightly visits to the garden, he draws again into himself, like a thirsty man who has discovered water. He breathes deeply in the silence and concentrates upon the Tai Hu stones. He feels their beauty with complete faith in his feeling: The netlike texture of worn mineral, the tortuous contours, the labyrinthine holes of a stone untouched by human hand; its artistry has been the work of water rushing across its surface, of hard pebbles rubbing against its soft limestone – the modeling effect of nature. He breathes deeply, steadily, as his eyes translate the moonlit stone into the *Tao*, into the changing forms of the universe, the sum of which never changes. Frozen in motion by its adamantine substance, the stone at which he looks is nevertheless changing. The weather changes it, although deep within its hollows is the dark core of eternal energy. An uncaptured airy thing resides within the packed vigor of stone: This is the *Tao* of the *Tao*. Has he read or heard this or come to the idea himself? The moonlit rockery in the garden brings him to thoughts of death, but without melancholy. He begins to understand the sages who speak of death the way other men chatter of daily tasks – with benign indifference – for them the subject has no harm in it. But when his time comes, will he emulate them? Walking back to his quarters from the garden, Tang often thinks of the dragon: It comes to go. The Taoists call in the *Tao*, the life-force, the undivided essence. For the Buddhist during contemplation it is a vision of the Buddha nature coming out of the clouds. He read somewhere (how much of his reading comes back to him now, alone, on the moonlit walks and at the garden) that dragons must always rise and fall in turbulence, in ecstasy, fearless among the mysteries, beyond smoke or depths, out of time, a creature of our deepest dream. And that is true: The dragon lies asleep, coiled at the bottom of the Chinese dream, ready upon wakening to breathe fire and hurl itself across the world. The idea of the dragon begins to heat his imagination, to pull him back to art.

He hurries home one evening and takes out the albums of paintings that he and Black Jade used to look at together. He goes first to the *Nine Dragons* of Ch'en Jung, a painter of the Southern Sung. Soon he is looking at the work of others, especially that of Hsu Tao-ning. He fixes upon *Fishing in a Mountain Stream*, sits with it on the desk, a cup of cold tea at his elbow. He lets the painting work in him. Going from the whole design, his eyes concentrate on tiny areas, making a world of the ink strokes in a square inch. In this painting the human figures count only insofar as they contribute to the scheme of bleak mountains and wintry marshes shrouded by cold mists. He recalls his youth when he wanted to become a scholar, before filial piety drew him toward the profession of his father. He remembers his desire for the self-effacement admired by scholars. He relives certain moments of his struggle as a young military cadet to act against the doctrine of passive humility.

Slowly, during the solitary nights, General Tang regains his youthful admiration for the genius of his people. He reads deeply in Chinese poetry, turning often to Lu Yu and Yang Wan-li, both masters of the Southern Sung. Yang Wan-li once wrote that a poem has the taste of cold crab marinated in wine. He practiced Buddhist meditation and wrote a rough, honest poetry. Lu Yu came from Chekiang, like Tang's friend Chu Jui. Lu Yu endured a tragic love affair, a turbulent political life, yet wrote ten thousand poems. At his death he wrote a patriotic poem in which he commanded his sons to report to his spirit each year – at the time of family sacrifices – exactly what the state of the nation had become. He loved his country and wished for a united China eight hundred years ago.

Resurrecting in himself his boyhood reverence for solitary contemplation, immersing himself in the deep tides of a philosophy and art that have survived the world's fashions, the General feels he has located the well-spring of a faith that has led him forward all these years to this time and place, to this duty, to his goal.

The snows of January begin to descend in earnest, and with them come two messages that call for the sort of action General Tang has put aside for a while. One is a letter from Feng Yu-hsiang which again argues for his ignorance of the ambush. He offers to set up another meeting, this time of *Qufu* if General Tang wishes. He gives proof once more that he's sincere; otherwise he would not put himself at Tang's mercy by coming to Qufu.

So hope rise again, confirming Tang's expectations of a bright future to come. In harmony with his revived faith in Chinese genius is a renewed belief in his manifest destiny as a leader of the country. He and Feng will establish an alliance that can turn Chiang Kai-shek back and threaten the Old Marshal in Peking. So he writes Feng, but waits to send the letter until an auspicious date for the meeting can be arranged. In this regard he intends to consult the Yarrow Stalk Oracle, establishing again his contact with traditional Chinese ways.

First, however, he must attend to the second message, which is a request from the Kongs that he visit them on Tai Shan. Although the General has suggested a couple of weeks ago that it is safe for the family to return to Qufu, the Patriarch has kept them there for religious observances. Each week the General has sent an aide to see to their needs and report back. This time, however, Tang will go himself, for the Patriarch has honored him with a request to share in a ceremony at the Temple of Confucius near the summit.

As usual, he leaves Colonel Pi in charge, a procedure that no longer causes him anxiety. In recent weeks the little Colonel has shown himself to be a competent administrator without the military skills that might rally the junior staff around him during the General's absence. Apparently sensing the nature of his situation, the Colonel seems less nervous, often even philosophical about his gifts or lack of them, and this time when General Tang tells him to take command for a few days, he shows no eagerness, merely acceptance. Before leaving, however, the General calls in Major Chia for a talk. The young major seems deeply embarrassed by the events at Peking which led to the Sian ambush. Since his return to Qufu he has hovered around headquarters as if expecting – or perhaps even wanting – punishment. Tang has wondered about it himself, but under no circumstances does he wish to discourage or hinder this fine officer. In those flashes of a future in which he assumes his destined place as head of state, the General envisions the brilliant young tactician by his side, fully capable under his direction of dismantling insurrections led by any warlords still running loose in China. Instead of the anticipated reprimand, the General gives him a military project to work on. Chia will draw up to tactical plan for infantry assault teams. The Major seems disappointed that he has been left with an intellectual challenge rather than a scolding. Tang, aware of his mistake with the stern young man, decides to find an excuse to castigate Chia on his return from Tai Shan.

Next morning, scheduled to take the early train, Tang rides to the station with two aides who will accompang him. There's light dusting of snow on the ground that reminds him of scrolls depicting travelers setting out for distant temples in winter. China hasn't changed much since the scrolls were painted centuries ago except that the pilgrims in them went by foot rather than train.

It is a short northward trip to the town of Taian at the base of the central massif of Shantung. Tai Shan rises high above the other mountains, most of them barren, shorn of timber long ago by peasants needing fuel. Seeing Tai Shan in the distance with its little crown of snow, the General remembers his promise to take Black Jade there. He has long carried a vision of doing it: the two of them slowly mounting the famous brick-paved road toward the temples at the summit; at dawn, from that vantage point, they would have viewed the emerging world, pristine gold in the first light.

The sky is overcast when at noon the train pulls into Taian station. The General and his aides stroll from it through the bazaar. Geared for the many pilgrims who come to the sacred mountain, the bazaar has stalls with yellow mud tigers, brass-work, and Kuan Yin figures for sale. They don't have time to stop at Tai Miao Temple for a look at its lovely frescoes and inner shrine, but continue through town to the North Gate, where beggars come forward with outstretched hands. Seeing the General dig into his coat pocket for *cash*, his aides quickly do likewise. Ahead is the long, winding six-mile Pan Lu Road, the Broad Way to Heaven, leading to the summit. Along the way are inscriptions incised into rocks – pious messages paid for by devout pilgrims. Bending down, Tang picks up two palm-sized rocks and hands them to each of his aides. 'Do you know the practice? If you ever build a house for yourself, have your Tai Shan stone inserted in a corner. Get a carver to cut these words into the stone: "A stone from Tai Shan. Let none dare harm the house that has it." '

Bowing in gratitude, each young officer puts his rock in his coat, and they all proceed to the base of the Pan Lu Road. The General waves off a group of palanquin bearers. He stares upward at the steep bulky mountain. Men worshiped here fifteen centuries *before* the birth of Confucius. He tells his aides that. Emperors, calling it the haunt of the gods, paid it the respect due to a god, for Tai Shan keeps the ground from moving and gathers the clouds to its bosom. He tells them that too. Again the young men bow, and he wonders if history and legend mean much to them; sometimes the young frighten him with their empty faces.

Leading the way, he passes under the stone triumphal arch

where a dozen temples stand – Taoist, Confucian, Buddhist –
and begins the long ascent. To the right, as the small party climbs,
is an old temple dedicated to Lao Tzu, the patron saint of Taoism.
Inside the courtyard, Tang remembers, are two ancient steles with
inscriptions more than a thousand years old and still legible in
spite of time and weather. He leads the way into the courtyard for
a look at them. While standing there, he hears rapid movement
behind him and turns to regard a dozen soldiers.

Their rifles are pointed at him.

A short heavyset man wearing an officer's cap hurries forward,
his pistol drawn. 'You are under arrest,' he announces in a high,
nervous voice – as if unaccustomed to speaking to senior officers,
let along arresting them. 'Give us your weapons, please.'

At a signal from Tang, who removes his gun from its holster, the
aides do the same.

While a soldier takes the weapons, the officer plants himself
directly in front of the General. 'You will go with us, Excellency.'
The man's eyes waver, their gaze moves past the General when he
speaks these words.

'By whose order am I arrested?'

'By order of the Governor General of Shantung Province.'

Old Dog Meat.

'On what charge?'

Flustered by the question, the arresting officer replies in a voice
more strident than ever. 'I can't give you that information
General.'

'Where are you taking us?'

'I can't give you that information, General.'

Leaving the temple, they return to the bottom of the Pan Lu
Road, where two hooded mule-drawn carts are standing. Tang is
put into one, his aides into the other, and soon they are off. The
General is worried by the separation. It's just possible their
captors, having no use for the young officers, will take them off
somewhere and shoot them. And indeed, a few hours later when
the rattling cart halts and the canvas hood is rolled back, Tang sees
that the other cart is gone. Ordered by the squat officer to get out
the General asks where his aides are, but the man doesn't answer

They have come to the outskirts of a little village; ahead of
them, where Tang is led, is a wattle-and-plaster hut with wooden
shutters at the windows. To the right of the entrance is a small
woodpile and a little stall strewn with twigs and straw.

'Go inside, General,' the officer tells him, gesturing with a drawn pistol.

Tang notices that the man hasn't touched him, hasn't dared. 'I want to know on what charge I'm being held.'

The officer's eyes shift beyond the General's. 'All I know, Excellency, is you're being held for banditry.'

'By the Governor General.'

'Yes, Excellency.'

Turning, the General enters the hut, which is lit only by a little daylight edging through cracks between the poorly aligned shutters. Even so, there's enough light for him to see what's in the room: Two chairs, a stool, a table, an old bedstead, a *kang* along one wall, an ancient stove.

'We brought in the bed for you, Excellency,' the officer says in an apologetic tone. Because the arrest went well, apparently he feels justified in relaxing his harsh manner.

A cradle of thick basket weave sits in a stout wooden frame in one corner. There's a small cotton gin here too, with two wooden rollers, a treadle connected to a spade-shaped balance wheel, an iron drum, a and crank. Next to the gin stands a rude loom, and a cotton bow to separate fiber from seed.

They have imprisoned him in the house of a village spinner. Why here in an outlying village rather than in the provincial jail in Jinan? Dog Meat obviously wants to hold him in secret. Perhaps he's been taken into custody without his captors having a clear sense of what to do with him. Tang sits at the table in the gloomy room smelling of wood and fiber dust. They have ambushed him this time by using the Kong family. The idea appalls him; it is tantamount to spitting on the image of the Great Sage. Did the Kongs betray him knowingly? Perhaps. If they were forced. After all, they are a family of scholars, whose way of life has been bred into them over centuries. Their loyalty is to books, art, tradition, not to a warlord temporarily protecting them. It is of course possible that they had nothing to do with it. Dog Meat may have had a seal maker fashion a counterfeit of the Kong chop and put it on the letter written by a Jinan forger. One thing is certain: Dog Meat wouldn't have undertaken this adventure on his own; the arrest order must have come from Chang Tso-lin. Having failed at Sian, he is now employing his henchman Chang Tsung-ch'ang to try again. But that's not altogether true. Had they wanted to murder him, they could have done it along any stretch of road between Taian and this village.

Clearly they want to bargain. During negotiations they'll kee[p] him imprisoned secretly.

Rising, the General strides to the door and bangs hard on it unt[il] a soldier answers from the other side. 'Tell your officer,' Tan[g] shouts through it, 'I want food and a fire in here!'

At nightfall the General has a bowl of corn soup, a hard slab [of] heavy bread, and a little fire in the stove. He stretches out o[n] the old bedstead, draws his greatcoat around him, and becaus[e] there's nothing more he must do or can do, the General surrende[rs] reasonably to fatigue and sleeps the night through.

His early-morning visitor surprises him. But upon reflection h[e] feels it isn't surprising to find his nephew, Ping-ti, coming into t[he] spinner's hut with an officer.

Ping-ti is startlingly dressed for such a place. He wears h[is] tortoiserimmed glasses, a comprador's business suit, a jad[e] stickpin in his striped Western tie, as if ready to enter the Shangh[ai] Gold Exchange. He doesn't waste time on traditional ameniti[es] but comes directly to the point: Still at issue is the General's refus[al] to give Japanese contractors access to land where they want to la[y] railway track, among other things.

The General asks what 'other things' means.

Ping-ti shrugs. It is a gesture characteristic of Tang's brother, he remembers Yen-chang. 'They may want to build a mill or [a] plant here and there,' Ping-ti admits. 'Timber concessions. A[s] explained, they are willing to compensate you extremely well.'

'Tell your man' – Tang nods to the officer, who is sitting ne[xt] to Ping-ti at the table – 'I want more firewood. The Gov[er]nor General won't look kindly on anyone who gives me po[or] treatment.'

The officer, worried by this threat even if it comes from [a] prisoner, gets up and leaves immediately.

'Did you stay overnight in Taian?' the General asks his nephe[w.] 'I assume you've been waiting for me.'

Ping-ti doesn't flinch at the sarcasm. 'Uncle, I regret having [to] say this, but unless you give assurances of your willingness –'

'Assurances?'

'Of your willingness to cooperate with the Japanese, I can't [be] responsible for the consequences.'

'Assurances, consequences.' The General smiles.

Adjusting his glasses, Ping-ti looks ill at ease, as if he knows how out of place he is in this dark little hut.

'A matter of curiosity, nephew. Who wrote the letter inviting me to Tai Shan?' Receiving no answer, the General asks, 'Was it the Kong Patriarch?'

'I don't think that's the point, uncle.'

'It's a point that interests me.' He adds, 'That means something to me.'

'The point is, uncle, we need you in this province.' Ping-ti accompanies his little smile with a nod, as if reassuring a child. 'We don't want Chiang Kai-shek to move in here in the spring.'

'Between the Japanese and Chiang Kai-shek, I'd take Chiang if I were you, nephew.'

'Between you and the Japanese, uncle, I'm afraid we must take the Japanese.'

Tang stares at the young man. Why has fate arranged for only three of the Tang clan to survive – and two of them willing to betray their country? He places both square hands flat on the table and stares at them. He wants to shut Ping-ti from his sight, his mind.

The officer, returning, looks curiously at the two silent men, then steps aside for soldiers to bring in a pot of soup, a round loaf of bread, a big load of firewood.

'Thank you,' the General says, then the silence resumes.

Rising at last, Ping-ti clears his throat. 'I have meant what I said, uncle.'

'I know you have.'

'Unless you agree to a plan of mutual benefit, I can't help you any longer.'

'You never spoke of mutual benefit. A plan involving the Japanese never deals with mutual benefit. As for helping me, don't give it a thought.'

'But I do. You are my father's younger brother.'

Tang wonders, looking at the well-dressed comprador, if there is still something Confucian left in him. If so, it is a testament to the strength of tradition. Ping-ti is self-consciously adjusting his glasses again. Perhaps the poor fellow's mind is a terrible battleground, Tang thinks. Neither East nor West governs him, but he's blown about by greed and the old idea of filial duty as well; his nights must be filled with doubt, with bewilderment, with guilt. Or so the General wishes to believe. It would be easier then to believe this is his nephew, a Tang.

'I must be going, uncle,' Ping-ti says crisply.

'My filial respects to your father.'

'I will convey them.' Ping-ti hesitates, as if something holds him here, perhaps a confession unmade, a sentiment unexpressed, but then with a little sigh, perhaps of irritation, he says, 'Please take seriously what I've said.'

'I do.'

'If you change your mind, uncle, let this officer know. I am finished here.' Without another word, with a rudeness almost beyond the General's imagining, Ping-ti whirls around and stamps out of the hut.

My nephew, Tang says under his breath in the growing silence. Fate has a strange sense of humor.

He ladles from the pot a steaming bowl of corn soup, but before he can finish it, the door is flung wide open and someone – obviously shoved with great force – hurtles through the air and crumples on the dirt floor. The door closes, leaving the room dark again.

Tang, sitting at the table, waits.

Rising on one elbow after a while, the man calls out incredulously, 'Is that *soup*? Have you got soup here? Am I smelling soup?'

'On the stove,' Tang tells him.

Staggering to his feet, the man gropes toward the stove. The way he shuffles, he looks as though they've hurt him. In a few moments Tang hears the noise of violent slurping from a ladle as the man eats out of the pot.

'Anything else?' the man asks.

'Yes, some bread here.'

Carrying the pot to the table, the man tears off a fistful of bread, which he stuffs into his mouth. 'How'd you get food out of them anyway?' he exclaims through his chewing. 'First I've had in three days, the bastards.' In the dim light, Tang sees that the newcomer is husky, probably middle-aged, dressed in peasant cotton. There's a dark line on his square face – dried blood running from ear to chin. 'Kicked the shit out me,' he mumbles through the bread. Lustily drawing in more soup, he pauses to study Tang. 'You a soldier?'

'Yes.' Tang is wearing a plain uniform without an indication of rank.

'They beat you?'

'No.'

'What have they got you for?'

Tang decides not to reveal his identity. 'Only an infraction.'

'That's why they didn't beat you. They got me for organizing.'

'What do you mean?'

'I was in this village not far from here, organizing them. I'm a Communist,' he says proudly, scraping the bottom of the pot with the ladle.

'What are you doing in villages around here?' Tang nearly adds, 'in villages under my jurisdiction.'

'Well, that's a story, but I guess we've got time.' Although born and raised in this province, he claims that for many years he lived much farther south. He's done a lot of farm work, but in recent years he served in the army under Chu Teh. 'I left Chu Teh before he defected from the Nationalists. I knew he'd do it someday. He's a good Bolshevik.'

'I hear he's a good general.'

'None better,' the man says. 'As good as General Tang of this province.'

'That good?' Tang asks wryly.

Leaning across the table, satiated on bread and soup, the man speaks earnestly. 'Listen to me, soldier. Chu Teh once had a lot of concubines, smoked opium, had plenty of money, but he gave up everything for the cause. I've seen him on a march walk as far and fast as any man.'

'For what cause?'

'You know,' the man says, leaning back and stretching. 'The red cause.'

'You were arrested for preaching it?' Tang would have had him arrested for preaching it.

'That's right. You see, I'm no longer young, I'm getting old, and even if I'm not really old, the life I've lived makes me feel damn old. So I gave up marching around in the army to come up here and organize. It's closer to home. A man should get close to home in his old age.' He guffaws. 'Looks like I got home just in time to die. Call me Wen-yun.'

The General hesitates. 'Call me Shan-teh.'

The man belches loudly. 'That's good soup. Nothing better than Shantung food in all of China.'

'I don't understand. You were organizing, but there's no Red organization around here.'

'I just took it on myself to preach the cause.'

Tang regards the man steadily. A streak of light falls across the table, revealing the man's rough-hewn features. It's the face of so many of his soldiers. He has always given orders to men with faces like this. Now he says with a smile, 'Tell me how you do it.'

'Sure, why not,' Wen-yun says good-naturedly. 'What I do, I go into a village and look around for peasants – not coolies, you understand; they don't know anything and they're afraid to talk to you – but for some men who work hard, have little, and want a lot more. Not too hard to find, yes? I ask if I can help in the fields, just for some millet gruel and bread. They don't have to give me anything more. We get to talking. I learn the names of the big landlords in the district and the village *ts'un chang*. I listen to the men talk about their troubles – and they've got plenty. I start talking then, only I don't say much they don't already know. I tell them it doesn't matter who the headman is or the district administrator or the military governor or the civil judge or any of the bastards, because whoever comes along, we still have to pay them the damn taxes. They already know it, I just remind them. It's from a stranger, a new voice, so they listen.'

'You stir them up.'

'That's what I do,' Wen-yun acknowledges proudly. 'I get them plenty mad, but I don't leave it at that. I get them to organize. You know, elect someone leader and someone to collect dues and pretty soon they have an organization that's for them and against the assholes in authority. I tell them, look, you don't have to be dirt any more, not if you get together. You can give the assholes trouble even now. And think of later, when there are groups like yours all over China. That's what I tell them.' Wen-yun pauses, shaking his head in memory. 'They look at me like I came from heaven.'

'Is it that simple?' Tang asks with a smile.

'Sure it is. They want liberation.'

'It's simple enough to be liberated from something. For example, we were liberated from the Manchus in 1912. Then what? We formed a republic that hasn't worked. So we were liberated from oppression without being liberated from disorder.'

'You're no fool, Shan-teh,' the Red says with a chuckle. 'Few people ever say anything like that to me when I tell them they can be liberated. All they know is the landlord has got them, and they want to get rid of him.'

'Revolution means people stop obeying the old laws. You must have new ones to replace them, quickly.'

Wen-yun laughs again. 'It's a good thing I don't have to talk to people like you.'

'But you believe in what you tell them?'

'I do,' the man says.

'You believe in taking a foreign idea, *a Russian idea*, and applying it to your own people?'

'I don't know anything about Russians.' Wen-yun sweeps his hand across the table as if to rid it of Russians.

Later that day – the sun has swung around, giving a sliver of light to the *kang* where the General sits – Wen-yun, who has been pacing for exercise, turns suddenly and says, 'You don't like Bolsheviks.'

'I don't like foreign ideas.'

'Then what would you do?'

'Establish a strong government before going into the villages and preaching violence to peasants.'

'Are you a Nationalist? Chiang Kai-shek says he can make a strong government.'

'Chiang's not the right man. But the idea's right. We can't let the peasants loose the way they are: selfish, ignorant, rash.'

Wen-yun sits down at the table. 'Yes, I know. But there's a difference between you and me. You talk like a man who hasn't lived like a peasant, so you don't know what a peasant can do. You can't trust someone you don't know, right? I know the peasants. I have faith in them.'

Still later, after a long silence, Wen-yun gets up and paces again. Tang watches him curiously. Faith in the peasant? Not the way he is, but the way centuries have left him: ingenious in doing complicated work without proper materials, yet undisciplined and lazy; filled with a genius for detail, none for innovation; patient without the confidence to analyze a problem. It will take years of strong government and education before faith in the peasant is justified. Yet Tang can't help admiring Wen-yun for preaching a doctrine of faith held so deeply that he's willing to die for it.

'I have a question,' Tang says after a while. Waiting until the man is down, he says, 'What gives you faith in this cause of yours?'

'I can tell you're an educated man, Shan-teh, yet you listen to me. I'm glad we met.'

'So am I.'

'But you ask a strange question. What's given me faith? I said I

727

had faith in peasants, but maybe I don't know what faith is. I sure don't have any faith in the gods. I just live, nothing more.' He sits awhile with his head in his hands, before looking up. 'No, it's a good question. What's given me faith? I don't have any *faith*, I have *anger* – terrible anger. You see, I used to live not far from here, not three or four hours' walk. I was a young farmer with a wife and three children. Everything went fine until a drought left me without money. So I went into debt, right? The old story. I borrowed from the local temple society. Since it was controlled by a landlord, that meant I was in debt to him. I couldn't pay, but he wouldn't give me more time. He said it was bad for peasants to think they could get away with such things. It was pay up or give him the land, even though he'd known my father and knew I could read and write. I had a field planted in millet. If it could mature I'd have the money, but the sonofabitch wouldn't wait. He took the land.' Wen-yun shakes his head slightly, reexperiencing the frustration. 'We were living on boiled water and weeds. A lot of people were like us, so when we begged, they only smiled and said no. No, no. My wife's milk dried up, so the baby girl died. The millet shoots came up, but they'd be choked by weeds if they weren't hoed, so I asked him permission to hoe them. He said no. He said if they rotted, it would teach us all a lesson in this village. He said if I put one foot on that land, he'd have the local militia shoot me for trespass. From the edge of the village, standing in the road, we watched the weeds kill the young shoots of millet. My youngest son died of dysentery. Then my eldest son got sick. Worms came out of him when he took a shit, and then they came out of him all the time, a whole fucking army of worms. He cried when he saw them. They terrified him, coming out of him that way. "Father! Father!" he'd yell. "Look at them!" He got weaker and said he could feel them crawling down his legs. They were. He whimpered all the time. He said he was more afraid of the worms than of death, so one day I just smothered him. And after he was dead, the worms still poured out. Can you believe it? Then my wife, her belly swollen on weeds, went out to beg and came back beaten. People were afraid then of everyone, even of a helpless woman, so someone beat her. Next day she went out again and never came back. I was too weak to go searching for her. Then a small landowner took pity and gave me some millet. I worked for him a year for nothing but gruel. When I was strong enough, I left my village and went south. I did some laboring and then one day about five years ago I heard someone speaking and I listened and I felt inside of me all of the anger pouring out, just like my child's terrible worms, and instead of the anger I'd felt every day since leaving home, I was filled with something else, with words, with an idea. I begin to think of getting something better out of life.'

'And this idea was communism. You think that's the answer?' Tang asks gently.

'I don't know, my friend. But there's been nothing else, so I give everything to it. Do you understand?'

'Yes.'

Light is fading from the cracks. Before it does, Tang builds a fire. Suddenly the little hut is transformed into his quarters at the Residence, and he sits before the fire with Black Jade, who is showing him her latest calligraphy. From the bedroom one of the songbirds is raising its voice. He can tell it's the cinnamon male –

A soldier comes in with another pot of soup and tosses another loaf of bread on the table. Taking away the empty pot, he pauses at the half-open door, so his face is visible in the waning light. 'You,' he says, nodding at Wen-yun. 'Tomorrow's your last day.'

'You're going to shoot me?'

'That's right. In the morning,' the soldier tells him with a smile. 'Bang, bang. All done.'

'Thank you for telling me,' Wen-yun says.

The soldier closes the door, pushes the bolt.

After a long silence, Tang says, 'I'm sorry.'

'Yes, so am I.' Wen-yun rattles the ladle in the pot. 'Shall we eat now or later?'

'That's your decision.'

'Yes, I think it should be too. Thank you, Shan-teh. We'll eat later.' He sighs deeply. 'Too bad it's so dark. We could play cards, if we had cards.'

'Do you smoke?'

'Sure.'

Tang searches in his pocket. Handing the Bolshevik a cigarette, he says, 'Is there anyone I can notify?'

'No one. Do you have anyone who should be notified about you?'

'Do you think I'm next?' Tang smiles.

'With these assholes – of course. But there's a saying my father taught me: Heaven is the lid of the coffin; earth is the bottom of the coffin; men may rush around, but they're in the coffin all the same.'

Mention of Wen-yun's father causes Tang to think of his own, of the spirit tablet with the red dot that signified one of his father's souls; another was in the ground, buried with the corpse; a third was in Heaven with the Jade Emperor – so his mother had believed. What does *he* believe? In the long evening, when darkness falls and after corn soup and bread, Tang tries to remember some words his father, who wrote well and yet lacked affection for literature, had jotted down in a little notebook he kept near the hearth. Considerable effort calls the phrases to mind again: 'Whoever or whatever it is that gives such things gives us our essence at birth. The design of this essence starts to unfold. To watch it unfold is to live. To watch it with confidence and good humor is to follow the Way.'

How Chinese those words are, Tang thinks. The elder Tang had been a gentleman and a warrior, and those words, penned idly in a notebook, had been in a sense his own epitaph. Now his son mouths the words lovingly in the darkness of a village prison.

When they come for Wen-yun in the morning, Tang rises and bows low to him.

'I am honored,' Wen-yun says, bowing too. 'I've been privileged to spend my last hours with you.'

Tang offers him a cigarette.

'Let's go,' a soldier urges harshly, shoving Wen-yun.

'Let him have the smoke,' Tang says. Lighting the cigarette for him, the General notices that Wen-yun holds it in a steady hand. They exchange goodbyes and the guard of four marches the Reorganizer from the hut.

Minutes later, waiting for them, Tang hears the rifle reports. They sound close, so the firing squad must have shot Wen-yun nearby, perhaps against the neighboring wall.

All that day the General sits at the table or lies on the bed staring at cracks from which the sunlight knifes into the room. Time in this dark place is oceanic, and he floats upon it through the day, allowing images to surface and disappear and resurface, bob awhile, then go away. He remembers Black Jade, lovingly. This is, after all, wartime in a chaotic land. How else could matters have ended between a man and a woman here? He remembers the lines of Li Po:

No one can tell me where you are,
So I lean sadly against the pine.

True words, moving across the centuries to this time and place. He thinks often of Wen-yun too. The man, admirable though he was, was wrong about communism. Had there been time, the General believes, he might have turned Wen-yun to a Chinese solution, to the way of Confucius. Like communism it avoids the otherworldly faith of religions; it too promises justice without spiritual consequences. For the Confucian, as well as the Bolshevik, it is possible to achieve happiness in this world. This he believes. But unlike communism, the ideas of the Great Sage are flexible. There must be a way of rejuvenating them! Lying on the bed, staring into the dark cold room, the General lets his thoughts soar into a Confucian future. A great nation would be created gradually by the consolidation of small political units into larger ones; this had happened in America – he had read about it and considered it the one good thing about that country. A correct interpretation of Confucius would provide for equality, for expanding education, for the sort of independent thought that someday would lead to democracy. Meanwhile, as regent, he would preside in Peking, working for the time when people learned to govern themselves.

It is a lovely vision, dispelled abruptly when the door swings open and a soldier enters with a pot of soup and some bread.

The same soldier who told Wen-yun he would die in the morning.

'Well?' Tang says, as the soldier opens the door to leave. 'Is it pang-bang tomorrow?'

'I don't know anything,' the soldier mutters with sullen reserve. It will be tomorrow.

Tang awakens to the sound of firing. Rising on one elbow he listens for a few moments before realizing that what he hears is the sound of firecrackers. Of course. It is the Lunar New Year, January 20. In the village people must be celebrating.

The door opens and the soldier brings in a new pot of soup. He stumbles, he is grinning, he is so drunk that he nearly falls. 'The Kitchen God comes home today,' he slurs and slams the door behind him.

It's unlikely they will shoot anyone on a festival day, Tang thinks; so he eats with good appetite, while firecrackers in the distance sputter and thunder. The Kitchen God is now returning, he thinks. He smiles at the idea; it is a custom he has enjoyed since childhood – the Report of the Kitchen God to the Jade Emperor in Heaven. Each December Tsao-wang leaves every home in China to report on the family's conduct. At this time his paper image, which has been sitting all year on a kitchen shelf, is burned, preferably in a pine fire, so he can ride up on the smoke to Heaven. Firecrackers are lit to celebrate his journey. Sweetmeats are laid on the shelf, so he'll relate sweet things to the Jade Emperor about the family. Now, on the New Year, he is returning to each house in the land. More firecrackers will guide him to each kitchen where he'll spend the next year. Today in every house that can afford them, red candles and incense will be burned.

The door opens, the drunken soldier peers in. 'Get ready,' he mumbles.

Tang puts down a piece of bread. 'So it's this morning?'

'Get ready.' The door slams shut.

So it will be now, he thinks.

It is now, the first day of the new year. Rising, he straightens his uniform, buttons his tunic. First day of the Year of the Dragon, 1928. Twelve years ago, in the previous Year of the Dragon, his entire clan had been murdered by order of President Yuan Shih-k'ai – 132 members of the Tang. Three remain: one a scheming financier in Hong Kong, another the parasitic servant of the Japanese. And the third? A man without an heir to honor his ancestors. To stem a sudden tide of anguish, the General recites again the words of his father: 'Whoever or whatever it is that gives such things gives us our essence at birth. The design of this essence starts to unfold. To watch it unfold is to live. To watch it with confidence and good humor is to follow the Way.'

So now it is unfolding to the end. In the process, if he would be true to his father and his clan, he must watch it with confidence and good humor. The General sits bolt upright, hands out flat and placid on the table. He takes the deep, even breaths of Tai Chi, the chi of union with the cold air, with the fiber dust, with the half-finished soup and the blackened iron pot, with the entire hut and the spaces beyond it to the far reaches of the world.

He is sitting calmly when the door opens and the officer who had arrested him at the base of Tai Shan comes into the room.

With a curt bow, he announces that the General can leave.

'Then,' the General rises slowly, 'that is all?'

'As far as I'm concerned, Excellency. The charge of banditry no longer stands. You need only deal with your creditors now.'

This is a wry reference to the New Year's custom of paying off old debts. One of Tang's vivid childhood memories is of men going around on New Year's Eve; they carried lanterns that would remain lit until they had either collected their debts or made arrangements with their debtors for payment during the ensuing twelve months.

'It appears I am now in debt to the Governor General,' Tang says dryly.

Instead of replying, the stout little officer gestures toward the door.

Outside, it is snowing lightly. Without a trace of wind the flakes are falling straight down in slow, feathery paths. For a moment Tang remembers her hatred of snow and moonlight – white things that reminded her of death. Black Jade, where are you?

'You may go,' the officer says in a low voice behind him.

Tang whirls around and faces the little man. 'I'm not sure of my whereabouts.'

'You're east of Qufu. There.' He points down a path leading between two huts to a winding rutted road. 'Not half a day by foot, Excellency. Transportation here is all tied up. New Year,' he says with a shrug. 'You can get to Qufu for the festivities this evening.'

The General begins walking. In front of the first hut he comes to, he stops. In the doorway – opened for the purpose – a wrinkled old woman is tossing kernels of corn at a few chickens. Beyond the woman he can see an infant sitting on the cold eathern floor, sucking its thumb. A whiff of baby urine and chicken dung drifts from the house, along with the acrid smoke of a charcoal fire. A little boy comes to the door, munching a boiled dumpling, coughing hard. He runs one dirty hand across his rheumy eyes. And beyond him Tang has a glimpse of the smoke-blackened walls, at the broken jars on the floor strewn with rags and pieces of wrecked farm tools. That night, if he knows China, the household patriarch will welcome the Kitchen God, read a complimentary scroll – or pretend to if he can't read – then burn the paper and thereby send the words to Heaven. Before they go to sleep, everyone in the family will place the soles of his shoes upward, so the Demon of Disease can't plant evil germs in them. Such a custom he understands, yet, striding down the lane to the main road, he wonders how much he has really understood about his people. Wen-yun would argue that no one but a peasant can know anything about China, yet that's a shortsighted view. Even so, the poor peasantry is the sorrow of China, its problem, and maybe someday its hope. Father had told him to look at the poor, and he had and had felt compassion for them. Rarely, however, had he smelled them as he'd just done at the doorway of the hut. Stood close and smelled them. Contemplated the smell. Sight is one thing, smell another: It's his own insight, not father's. You can easily see people at a distance, but to smell them you must get close, close enough to feel their pain. Have I known the people? he wonders. Did the Great Sage, millenniums ago, ask himself the same question? I must learn more, the General vows. To lead my people, I must first smell them.

Without wind the overcast day is not cold, and the snowflakes continue their soft, magical fall through the gray air. Smoke curls from the distant mud chimney of a farmhouse. Up, straight up the thread of whitish smoke leads into the sky, vanishes finally like a ground mist. In front of the house is a horse-chestnut tree and to the side of it a wooden shed, where grain is probably hulled. From along the road comes the thunderous crash of iron wheels against the frozen ruts, a boom that echoes across the wintry fields to some blue hills beyond. The General walks for a while before the carter himself appears, a grizzled old man sitting on the bench of a hooded wagon. Lazily he strokes a swaybacked mule with a long switch.

'Good day, sir,' the carter says with a smile. He doffs his battered felt hat – a Western hat, probably bought years ago on his rare visit to a large city and kept as an object of venerable worth.

The General moves down the road, feeling the sting of a rising wind. Soon his eyes are tearing in a rough gust from the Asian plains. The snow is now slanting at him, momentarily blinding him as it swirls about. But after an hour or less of the little storm, abates suddenly and for a few lovely moments the clouds part and sunlight dazzles down on the fallen snow. This break in the clouds lasts only moments, however, because a great sullen blanket of them again covers the sky, bringing fresh snow in a steady downfall. He has been walking for almost two hours now, seeing no one but a solitary carter now and then. He halts a moment to reach inside his greatcoat and tunic to extract a louse that has been nipping his underarm. He squeezes it between his thumbnails as boys are taught to do. The blood on his nails is encouraging – of course he hasn't lost touch with his people!

He passes through a tiny village. Behind some threshed straw, where in summertime the gourds and cucumbers are planted, a few firecrackers go off, followed by childish laughter. Pigs are eating noisily somewhere. Leaving the village, he notices the low round graves of the dead amid bean patches and millet fields. The dead are here, waiting out the cold winter along with the living. Generations below and above the ground participate in the seasons, and the earth is alive with their spirit. This is China, his land. The long journey on foot has filled the General with a sense of union: man, earth, sky. The back of each hand, going forward as he walks, meets a breath of cold air.

Man is a small heaven. Where had he read that? Or is it a saying learned perhaps from someone old in the family?

The road ends abruptly at a stream that is not yet frozen solid enough to cross by foot. A tiny wooden sign points to the bridge that must be located a little way southward, so Tang heads across a field. The stubble crackles under his feet. A freshening wind comes across the shorn wheat, blowing the thin cover of snow into the air. Clouds, lowering, let drop a new flurry that slants obliquely into his face. Raising his hand to ward off the flakes so he can see better, Tang stops the motion in mid-swing. Ahead is not the end of the field but a group of men coming out of a border pine. They are coming with rifles level and at a fast walk.

So it will be done here, in secret. Tang halts. On the first day of the Year of the Dragon.

Then he feels the impulse to run – it is said 'the hunted tiger leaps the wall' – but there's no place to run.

It is truly ended now.

Yet he can make them work for it. Probably there isn't a sharpshooter among the entire dozen coming now at a brisk walk, almost a run. They'll have to get close before shooting, and that means another hundred yards at least. But to lead them a chase means he must turn away from them and run and finally receive their bullets in his back. He can't do that, not Tang Shan-teh, son of his father.

Halting, he waits for them, arms at his side, his face composed.

735

With 'confidence' and 'good humor' he must watch the *Ta* unfold rapidly now to the end.

Watching him, the soldiers halt too, then come on cautiously Tang looks up at the roiling clouds. He tries to feel keenly the bit of the wind blowing across the wheat stubble, to feel it as deeply a possible. Snow is coming down harder. It won't last, but for th moment enormous flakes of snow fill the air, exciting it, making tremble with life.

It is a wonder –

They are near enough now for him to see snowflakes on th eyelashes of a young soldier. They are near enough for accuracy but to make sure, they all kneel and aim as if forming a firin squad. Good discipline.

Tang waits, looking above them at the cloudy sky, his sky, th sky of China.

A wonder –